THE OXFORD HISTORY OF THE NOVEL IN ENGLISH

The American Novel to 1870

The Oxford History of the Novel in English

GENERAL EDITOR: PATRICK PARRINDER

ADVISORY EDITOR (US VOLUMES): JONATHAN ARAC

Volumes Published and in Preparation

1. *Prose Fiction in English from the Origins of Print to 1750*, edited by Thomas Keymer
2. *English and British Fiction 1750–1820*, edited by Peter Garside and Karen O'Brien
3. *The Nineteenth-Century Novel 1820–1880*, edited by John Kucich and Jenny Bourne Taylor
4. *The Reinvention of the British and Irish Novel 1880–1940*, edited by Patrick Parrinder and Andrzej Gąsiorek.
5. *The American Novel to 1870*, edited by J. Gerald Kennedy and Leland S. Person
6. *The American Novel 1870–1940*, edited by Priscilla Wald and Michael A. Elliott
7. *British and Irish Fiction since 1940*, edited by Peter Boxall and Bryan Cheyette
8. *American Fiction since 1940*, edited by Cyrus R. K. Patell and Deborah Lindsay Williams
9. *World Fiction in English to 1950*, edited by Ralph Crane, Jane Stafford, and Mark Williams
10. *The Novel in English in Asia since 1945*
11. *The Novel in Africa and the Atlantic World since 1950*, edited by Simon Gikandi
12. *The Novel in Australia, Canada, New Zealand, and the South Pacific since 1950*, edited by Coral Ann Howells, Paul Sharrad, and Gerry Turcotte

THE OXFORD HISTORY OF THE NOVEL IN ENGLISH

Volume Five

The American Novel to 1870

EDITED BY

J. Gerald Kennedy and Leland S. Person

OXFORD
UNIVERSITY PRESS

Oxford University Press is a department of the University of Oxford.
It furthers the University's objective of excellence in research, scholarship, and education by publishing worldwide.

Oxford New York
Auckland Cape Town Dar es Salaam Hong Kong Karachi
Kuala Lumpur Madrid Melbourne Mexico City Nairobi
New Delhi Shanghai Taipei Toronto

With offices in
Argentina Austria Brazil Chile Czech Republic France Greece
Guatemala Hungary Italy Japan Poland Portugal Singapore
South Korea Switzerland Thailand Turkey Ukraine Vietnam

Published in the United States of America by
Oxford University Press
198 Madison Avenue, New York, NY 10016

Library of Congress Cataloging-in-Publication Data
The American novel from its beginnings to 1870 / edited by J. Gerald Kennedy and Leland S. Person.
p. cm. — (The Oxford history of the novel in English ; volume five)
"General editor: Patrick Parrinder; Consulting editor (US volumes): Jonathan Arac" — Title page verso.
Includes bibliographical references and index.
ISBN 978–0–19–538535–9
1. American fiction—18th century—History and criticism. 2. American fiction—19th century—History and criticism. 3. Literature and society—United States—History—18th century. 4. Literature and society—United States—History—19th century. 5. American literature—Colonial period, ca. 1600–1775. 6. American literature—European influences. 7. Social conflict in literature. 8. National characteristics, American, in literature. I. Kennedy, J. Gerald, editor of compilation. II. Person, Leland S., editor of compilation. III. Parrinder, Patrick, editor. IV. Arac, Jonathan, 1945– editor.
PS375.A44 2014
813'.209—dc23

2013033712

1 3 5 7 9 8 6 4 2

Printed in the United States of America on acid-free paper

Contents

Part VI: Cultural Influences on the American Novel, 1820–1870

Part VII: Fictional Subgenres

ACKNOWLEDGMENTS

The co-editors wish to thank our esteemed contributors for skillfully delivering excellent essays on time and on topic; we lament the sudden passing of the distinguished scholar George Dekker before he could complete his chapter and appreciate the readiness and ability of Fiona Robertson to fill that significant void. Patrick Parrinder and Jonathan Arac have at several junctures provided insightful suggestions for improving the volume. Brendan O'Neill at OUP has likewise offered valuable advice and encouragement. At Louisiana State University, a superb team of editorial assistants performed historical fact checks and verified the accuracy of all quotations. They also checked scholarly references, constructed the bibliography, and put all essays in correct OUP format. That team consisted of Charles M. "Mitch" Frye, Michael Von Cannon, and James W. Long. Mitch and Michael, modernists laboring slightly afield, showed dedicated reliability. James deserves special thanks for his astute contributions as an antebellum scholar and especially for his extended professional commitment, which began long before he completed his award-winning dissertation in 2011 and continued through his internship at LSU Press in 2013.

CONTRIBUTORS

Jonathan Arac, University of Pittsburgh
Renée Bergland, Simmons College
Anna Brickhouse, University of Virginia
Lara Langer Cohen, Swarthmore College
Monika Elbert, Montclair State University
Betsy Erkkila, Northwestern University
John Ernest, University of Delaware
Wayne Franklin, University of Connecticut
Paul Giles, University of Sydney
Paul Christian Jones, Ohio University
J. Gerald Kennedy, Louisiana State University
Joseph J. Letter, University of Tampa
Caroline Levander, Rice University
David Leverenz, University of Florida
John Lowe, University of Georgia
James L. Machor, Kansas State University
Meredith L. McGill, Rutgers, State University of New Jersey
Gretchen Murphy, University of Texas at Austin
Dana D. Nelson, Vanderbilt University
Patricia Okker, University of Missouri
Scott Peeples, College of Charleston
Leland S. Person, University of Cincinnati
David S. Reynolds, The Graduate Center, City University of New York
Larry J. Reynolds, Texas A&M University
Fiona Robertson, St Mary's University College
Debra J. Rosenthal, John Carroll University

Marion Rust, University of Kentucky
John Carlos Rowe, University of Southern California
Shelley Streeby, University of California, San Diego
Timothy Sweet, West Virginia University
Leonard Tennenhouse, Duke University
Karen A. Weyler, University of North Carolina, Greensboro
Ed White, Tulane University
Ivy G. Wilson, Northwestern University
Michael Winship, University of Texas at Austin

GENERAL EDITOR'S PREFACE

Unlike poetry and drama, the novel belongs entirely within the sphere of recorded history. Novels, like historical records, are written texts superseding the worlds of myth, of epic poetry, and oral storytelling. Typically they are commercial products taking advantage of the technology of printing, the availability of leisure time among potential readers, and the circulation of books. The growth of the novel as an art form would have been unthinkable without the habit of silent, private reading, a habit that we now take for granted although its origins are much disputed among scholars. While novels are not always read silently and in private, they are felt to belong in the domestic sphere rather than in the public arenas associated with music, drama, and the other performance arts. The need for separate histories of the novel form has long been recognized, since the distinctiveness of fictional prose narrative is quickly lost sight of in more general accounts of literary history.

The *Oxford History of the Novel in English* is a multivolume series that offers a comprehensive, worldwide history of English-language prose fiction and draws on the knowledge of a large, international team of scholars. Our history spans more than six centuries, firmly rejecting the simplified view that the novel in English began with Daniel Defoe's *Robinson Crusoe* in 1719. Fifteenth- and sixteenth-century prose fiction has, in fact, been surveyed by many earlier historians, including Ernest A. Baker whose *History of the English Novel* appeared in ten volumes between 1924 and 1939. Unlike Baker's strictly chronological account, the *Oxford History* broadens as it approaches the present, recognizing the spread of the English language across the globe from the seventeenth century onward. The "English" (or British) novel becomes the novel in English. While we aim to offer a comprehensive account of the anglophone novel, our coverage cannot, of course, be exhaustive; that is a task for the bibliographer rather than the literary historian. All history has a commemorative function, but cultural memory is unavoidably selective. Selection, in the case of books, is the task of literary criticism, and criticism enters literary history the moment that we speak of the novel rather than, simply, of the multitude of individual novels. Nevertheless, this *Oxford History* adopts a broader definition of the novel than has been customary in earlier histories. Thus we neither focus exclusively on the so-called literary novel nor on the published texts of fiction at the expense of the processes of production, distribution, and reception. Every volume in this series contains sections on relevant aspects of book history and the history of criticism, together with sections on popular fiction and the fictional subgenres, in addition to the sequence of chapters outlining the work of major novelists, movements, traditions, and tendencies. Novellas and short stories are regarded for our purposes (we stress "for our purposes") both as subgenres of the novel and as aspects of its material history.

Our aim throughout these volumes is to present the detailed history of the novel in a way that is both useful to students and specialists, and accessible to a wide and varied readership. We hope to have conveyed our understanding of the distinctiveness, the continuity, and the social and cultural resonance of prose fiction at different times and places. The novel, moreover, is still changing. Reports of its death—and there have been quite a few—are, as Mark Twain might have said, an exaggeration. At a time when new technologies are challenging the dominance of the printed book and when the novel's "great tradition" is sometimes said to have foundered, we believe that the *Oxford History* will stand out as a record of the extraordinary adaptability and resilience of the novel in English, its protean character, and its constant ability to surprise.

Patrick Parrinder

INTRODUCTION: THE AMERICAN NOVEL TO 1870

J. GERALD KENNEDY AND LELAND S. PERSON

This volume reconstructs in thirty-four chapters the emergence and early cultivation of the novel in the United States of America. Although Margaret Anne Doody and Steven Moore have variously traced this modern literary genre to a host of global narrative forms, the American novel derived most immediately from the prose fiction popular in Great Britain. There the novel achieved cultural influence and prestige during the middle decades of the 1700s, a century fraught with social and political transformation. In the Anglo-American world, this change included the burgeoning of a middle class, the emergence through newspapers and magazines of a mass audience of common readers, and (as Michael McKeon has argued) the destabilization of an aristocratic order that had long controlled political power and national wealth as well as the production of literature and art. A related development, crucial to this volume, saw a deepening political rift between the United Kingdom and the American colonies. Along the Atlantic seaboard from Massachusetts to Georgia, geographic mobility as well as economic independence accelerated the formation of a relatively classless social order, at a time when many novels presented themselves as personal "histories" asserting the significance of the ordinary individual and of middle-class life. As ancestral notions of social hierarchy and patronage gave way in North America to an idea of self-making—a process epitomized in *The Autobiography of Benjamin Franklin* (1791)—novels of personal struggle and survival, especially Atlantic narratives such as Daniel Defoe's *The Life and Strange Surprizing Adventures of Robinson Crusoe* (1719) or *The Fortunes and Misfortunes of the Famous Moll Flanders* (1722), resonated with colonial readers. The novel's recurrent fascination with common people caught in the trammels of power or circumstance, whether as strangers in a strange land or as victims of domestic cruelty or injustice, unmistakably aroused sympathy for plain folk and fostered an incipient democratic ethos.

As the American colonies quadrupled in population between 1700 and 1750 to more than one million inhabitants, booksellers exploited a growing market.

Even when certain novels generated profits, however, provincial printers shrank from direct competition with London publishers; as Melissa Homestead has noted, Franklin's unsuccessful 1742–43 edition of Samuel Richardson's *Pamela; or, Virtue Rewarded* (1740) was the only unabridged English novel issued from an American press until the late 1760s. A handful of novels arguably identifiable as colonial in provenance appeared, however, as early as the middle of the century, beginning with *The Life of Harriot Stuart* (1750). The author of this London publication, the New York–born Charlotte Ramsay Lennox, returned to England at the age of fifteen but located the action of her first novel partly in the colonies. Another London imprint, recently republished in a modern edition, attests to the transatlantic influence of Defoe's *Robinson Crusoe*: Unca Eliza Winkfield's *The Female American; or, The Adventures of Unca Eliza Winkfield* (1767). As contributors to our opening section suggest, the principal precursors of the US novels that circulated after the American Revolution included colonial histories, autobiographies, and diaries, as well as narratives of Indian captivity, religious conversion, and slavery. Despite efforts to categorize certain Revolutionary-era works as quasi-fictional narratives, scholars still regard William Hill Brown's *The Power of Sympathy* (1789) as the first US novel, heralding an era of literary productivity and national consciousness. Cathy Davidson has observed of this post-Revolutionary period: "The American novel first appeared during the time when the domestic publishing industry enjoyed a new sense of vigor, nationalism, and professional pride (but not much capital) and when every printer faced the renewed (and debilitating) competition from foreign imports, especially British imports" (1986, 16). This industry mostly consisted, she adds, of small, local presses.

Although Boston, New York, and Philadelphia eventually developed into publishing centers—as, to a lesser extent, did Cincinnati, Baltimore, and Charleston—the uneven distribution of print materials across the country inhibited the formation of a coherent national culture. Instead, it created provincial enclaves, each projecting a version of regional history and experience as ostensibly "national." James Russell Lowell exposed this oddity, still prevalent in the 1840s, when he noted that American literature "has no centre. . . . It is divided into many systems, each revolving round its several suns." Lowell added that "Our capital city [Washington], unlike London or Paris, is not a great central heart, from which life and vigor radiate to the extremities, but resembles more an isolated umbilicus, stuck down as near as may be to the centre of the land, and seeming rather to tell a legend of former usefulness than to serve any present need" (1845, 49). The early cultural irrelevance of the nation's capital underscores the decentered nature of US literature. What Lowell describes here as the fragmented structure of national literary production moreover helps to explain certain formal peculiarities of the early American novel. The absence of a dominant publishing hub, with influential journals and demanding literary critics, arguably contributed to the haphazard, experimental forms, fictional and quasi fictional, that appeared before and after the founding of the republic. As our contributors demonstrate in part I, local impulses sometimes inspired eccentrically conceived narratives, whimsical in their inattention to novelistic conventions, but these same volumes often provided revealing glimpses of an emerging American culture.

This provincialism paradoxically existed alongside a pervasive consciousness of transatlantic cultural currents and revolutionary events unfolding in Europe as well as elsewhere in the Americas. As Leonora Sansay's *Secret History; or, The Horrors of St. Domingo* (1808) illustrates, hemispheric struggles for liberty engaged the attention of US novelists. Americans closely followed the rise of new literary fashions from abroad, and writers worried about a postcolonial subservience to foreign criticism. To be sure, the prestige of British models and the weight of European tradition long generated a fair amount of frankly imitative American literature. The Revolutionary War had created a conundrum: how could the former colonies develop a national culture and literature of their own when their cultural inheritance, literary traditions, and even their common language derived from the nation against whom the federated states most urgently needed to differentiate themselves? The proliferation of *Clarissa*-inspired novels of seduction, often told through letters, best illustrates this residual attachment to English conventions, although one suspects that the lecherous rake, eager to ravish a virtuous maiden, occasionally projected a symbolic American scorn for an erstwhile tyrant. One exception to that pattern may be the profoundly Anglo-American *Charlotte Temple* (1791), the best known of these moralized narratives and a work set both in England and America. The novel had been written (and first published) in England by Susanna Rowson, a British-born actress who spent her childhood in colonial Massachusetts, returned to England for eighteen years, and lived the last three decades of her life in the United States; these vacillations aptly illustrate the vexed, entangled literary relations between the mother country and the defiant infant republic.

Especially after the burning of Washington during the War of 1812, however, the project of constructing an American cultural identity separate from that of Britain became a US national obsession. In Boston, the prestigious *North American Review* openly campaigned for the nationalizing of American literature. Playing the peacemaker, Washington Irving reasserted Anglo-American kinship in *The Sketch Book* (1819–20) and celebrated his country's English heritage; yet despite the book's popularity, Irving, the longtime expatriate, found his own national loyalty questioned. Ralph Waldo Emerson famously urged American authors in 1837 to stop listening to "the courtly muses of Europe" (1983, 70), and Edgar Allan Poe in 1845 went even further, urging a "Declaration of War" (1984a, 1078) to dismantle British cultural authority. Across the Atlantic states, cultural attachment to England varied significantly: in New York and Charleston residual Anglophilia prompted reviewers to invoke tradition and to inveigh against literary radicalism; elsewhere editors, authors, and critics clamored for a national culture and a literature that reflected life in what Francis Scott Key rhapsodized in 1814 as "the land of the free, and the home of the brave" ("The Defence of Fort McHenry," ln. 8).

Part II examines the crucial role of the novel in the construction of a distinctive national literature. From the eighteenth century forward, nation building varied idiosyncratically from country to country, yet the "invention of tradition" (in Eric Hobsbawm's wry phrase) formed an integral phase in the construction of national culture. Producing the myths, symbols, and images that give particularity to national identity comprises a process as crucial to the nation-state as its articulation of law and polity. The entire project depends, as Benedict Anderson has suggested, on the establishment of a shared vernacular language and on a print culture able to disseminate newspapers, magazines, and books to far-flung readers. And, to a great extent, the work of inventing national traditions has relied upon narrative—especially the novel. Patrick Parrinder observes that "with the rise of the novel came a shift in the literary idea of nationhood." Prose fiction emanated from the "cultural nation," the grassroots citizenry, as opposed to the apparatus of government, the "political nation" (2006, 17). The novel, with its fables of individual and collective endeavor, quite literally enabled a diverse, dispersed population to imagine itself as a nation. The novel also became a locus for contesting the nation's character, for gauging its historical accomplishments, and for critiquing its failures or evasions. As our contributors suggest in part II, the historical novel popularized by Walter Scott provided an attractive model for US authors keen to reconstruct national myths and memories. The Puritan past, the Indian wars, the American Revolution, and the exploration of the West all inspired fictions of American struggle and self-discovery.

These works entered a literary marketplace still dominated well into the nineteenth century by books imported from Europe. The irregular contours of the American publishing world form the focus of part III, which broadly treats the evolution of print culture and the place of the novel in the US book trade from about 1780 to 1870. Competition with British publishers produced an incongruous situation in which American publishing houses, under pressure to promote literary nationalism and homegrown talent, nevertheless depended economically on the reprinting of foreign books. In this context, pirated (that is, unsanctioned) editions of British novels proved hugely profitable in an era when international copyright laws did not yet exist. Publishers could thus profit from European authorial reputations without the expense of royalty fees—a circumstance that placed American authors at some disadvantage in negotiating payments for original manuscripts. The practical realities of this messy publishing scene, as contributors to part III attest, reveal both the obstacles that complicated the production of American novels and the developments in print technology, book manufacturing, transportation, and commercial distribution that spurred domestic novelists. The economic boom of the 1820s and early 1830s encouraged the publication of both books and magazines, and periodicals played a key role in popularizing American novels through serialization—Harriet Beecher Stowe's *Uncle Tom's Cabin; or, Life Among the Lowly* (1852) offers a spectacular example—as well as through the advertising, excerpting, and reviewing of contemporary works of fiction. Journals such as *Brother Jonathan* regularly published pirated European novels in serial form, and the unregulated periodical reprinting of fiction and poetry complicated the very concept of literary property. Innovative printing methods, cheap paper, cloth binding, and reduced postal rates eventually encouraged sensational, hastily written "dime novels," which remained popular for decades and left a lasting imprint on the literary culture in the United States.

The growth of urban populations, the spread of literary magazines, and the rise of publishing houses such as Ticknor and Fields in Boston, Harper and Brothers in New York, and Carey and Lea in Philadelphia all combined to create, during the Jacksonian era, a relatively robust, albeit still regionalized, culture of letters and a bustling trade in US novels. Irving and James Fenimore Cooper had provided early models of successful professional authorship, and especially as the nation recovered from the depression following the Panic of 1837, publishers of the 1840s and early 1850s promoted the careers of novelists such as Herman Melville and Nathaniel Hawthorne. During the 1830s and 1840s Catharine Maria Sedgwick figured as the most eminent female novelist in the United States, a position not jeopardized until Stowe's best-selling novel brought unprecedented international fame. By 1850 New York boasted a population of almost 700,000 and emerged as the undisputed center of American literary culture; Harper Brothers launched a still-influential monthly magazine; and the publication, within a span of two years, of Hawthorne's *The Scarlet Letter: A Romance* (1850), *The House of the Seven Gables: A Romance* (1851), and *The Blithedale Romance* (1852), Melville's *Moby-Dick; or, The Whale* (1851), and Stowe's *Uncle Tom's Cabin* seemed to signal a Belle Epoque of national letters. Parts IV and V present profiles of the leading novelists of the antebellum period and discuss their most enduring fictional works.

As a careful reading suggests, however, the novels ostensibly most "American" in character manifest a patriotism quite at odds with uncritical nationalism—a candor that acknowledges distinct failures of the early nation while recalling its democratic promise. The landmark narratives examined in part V variously expose the gap between US founding ideals and sociohistorical realities. Many other American novels of the same era confronted this dilemma. Attempting to depict the distinctive conditions of US experience, they expose the inhumane practices upon which the promise of "life, liberty, and the pursuit of happiness" had been made to depend: African chattel slavery and the displacement of Native tribes whose presence impeded US empire. Both atrocities contradicted the high-minded principles by which slaveholders George Washington, Thomas Jefferson, and even Benjamin Franklin (who held domestic slaves) justified their improbable yet finally successful struggle to repel colonial rule. Both national sins quite literally colored the novels produced during this turbulent epoch.

As several chapters in this volume suggest, the Native American posed a peculiar symbolic problem for myth makers as well as a threat to white settlers. For a nation desperate to differentiate itself from Britain and those other European cultures that contributed to what J. Hector St. John de Crèvecoeur called this "new race" of "Americans" (*Letters from an American Farmer* 1782, ltr. 3), the Indian represented a beguiling half-romantic, half-repulsive Other, alternately demonized as "savage" and idealized as noble. From the early seventeenth century, when colonists in Virginia confronted the Powhatan tribes and New England Puritans incinerated the Pequot village at Mystic, hostilities between Native tribes and white men bent on erecting a New Jerusalem—or at least a profitable outpost in the American wilderness—settled into a saga of mistrust and violence. The Indian practice of taking prisoners to replace lost tribal members inspired the earliest of North American narrative forms: the captivity narrative. Introduced by Mary Rowlandson in 1682, this genre gained enormous popularity and influenced frontier novels by Charles Brockden Brown, Cooper, Sedgwick, and William Gilmore Simms. Although some novelists occasionally portrayed white atrocities (Sedgwick's *Hope Leslie* [1827] is a notable example) or conceded the failure of Christian love to curb border violence, the typical narrative in this age of nation building—like the nationalist painting and sculpture aggregated in the US Capitol rotunda at the same time—underscored the cultural superiority of Euro-Americans, the hostility or subservience of the doomed Indian, and the triumph of Anglo-Saxon civilization. Robert Montgomery Bird's notorious novel *Nick of the Woods* (1837) luridly illustrates the racist terrorism practiced in defense of US national aspirations. The 1830 policy of Indian removal divided US citizens: novelists took sides, explicitly or implicitly, as they spun narratives of frontier hostility, while Native versions of the clash mostly emerged in memoirs.

The problem of slavery likewise affected the production of US novels, although the subject emerged in fiction mostly after the rise of the abolitionist movement in 1831. John Pendleton Kennedy's *Swallow Barn* (1832) ironically marked the onset of the literary battle to frame slavery as either integral or dehumanizing to life in the South. Kennedy had sought to reconcile sectional differences on slavery by romanticizing plantation life while discreetly advocating liberal modifications to the "peculiar institution." Yet his narrative heralded a surge of controversial, slavery-inspired writings, fictional and nonfictional. While writers like Nathaniel Beverley Tucker and Simms disseminated proslavery novels idealizing plantation life, abolitionists, such as Richard Hildreth, devised fictional narratives exposing the horrors of the system. The proliferation of actual slave narratives intensified the reciprocal bitterness felt by opponents and defenders of bondage. This volatile controversy drove Poe to disguise, masking his fears of slave revolt as a horrific native uprising in the deepest South he could imagine, the Antarctic, and thus bringing his 1838 adventure novel, *The Narrative of Arthur Gordon Pym*, to an apocalyptic conclusion. The vexed Compromise of 1850, which attempted to defuse the slavery crisis, only succeeded in sharpening differences and exacerbating tensions. Inspired by the new law governing fugitive slaves, Stowe's *Uncle Tom's Cabin* pushed the nation toward Civil War by exploding the myth of national unity. The shocking profusion of anti-Uncle Tom novels in the 1850s, together with sympathetic imitations, exposed an irreparable divide. The rise of the African American novel, as represented by William Wells Brown's *Clotel; or, The President's Daughter* (1853); Harriet Wilson's *Our Nig; or, Sketches from the Life of a Free Black* (1859); and Martin Delany's serialized, unfinished *Blake*; *or, The Huts of America* (1859, 1861–62), introduced into American fiction the radically alienated perspective of an exploited yet increasingly defiant minority.

During the four decades between the Missouri Compromise of 1820—which first confronted sectional differences over slavery—and the advent of civil war, US culture witnessed many unsettling changes reflected in contemporary novels. The contributors to part IV address some of these developments, which range from the controversy over slavery and the influx of foreign immigrants to the rise of a women's movement advocating equal rights, challenging the notion of separate, gendered "spheres," and questioning self-serving ideas of American manhood. The various reform movements of the early nineteenth century (of which abolitionism and female rights afford conspicuous examples) drew heavily upon Christian scripture and precept; yet despite the Second Great Awakening, American religion was also undergoing a crisis, as new sects challenged mainstream denominations and (as we see in the works of many novelists) secular skepticism undermined established beliefs. Meanwhile the relentless extension of Anglo-Saxon settlement into a mostly primitive wilderness produced environmental destruction, as vast expanses of tree stumps marked the progress of civilization. Likewise, efforts to extend American interests into the wider world beyond the nation's borders, and especially into contiguous portions of the Western Hemisphere, gave rise to novels projecting imperial aspirations. Yet contact with southern neighbors also evoked anxiety about the violent rebellions in Central and South America, which simultaneously confirmed the influence of the American Revolution and exposed the threat of radical democracy. Part VI explores these diverse influences on the antebellum novel, investigating both the kind of narratives they provoked and the broader transformations of consciousness they exemplified.

Part VII locates a handful of specific fictional subgenres that also capture the cultural changes of this period. For example, the just-mentioned expansion of global mercantile interests, which coincided with increasing US tourism abroad, produced an astonishing number of novels and quasi-fictional narratives depicting international travel. As William Spengemann observed in *The Adventurous Muse* (1977), movement through space has always been one of the defining modalities of US fiction, and the many novels of travel or exploration promulgated during this period bear witness to a chronic national restlessness. But of course not all Americans were sailing off to foreign places or emigrating to the frontier.

During this period, American cities also experienced dramatic growth. While New York increased from 200,000 residents in 1830 to more than 800,000 in 1860, Philadelphia saw proportionately greater expansion from 80,000 to 565,000 inhabitants. Huge throngs, crowded housing, urban poverty, and red-light districts produced the underworld depicted in the sensational "city mysteries" novels of the 1840s and 1850s by George Lippard, Ned Buntline, and others. Inspired by novels such as Charles Dickens's *Oliver Twist* (1838) and Eugène Sue's *Les Mystères de Paris* (1842–43), these cheaply published volumes purveyed sex and violence as they exposed the dark side of American cities. A related subgenre emerged from the temperance movement, which elicited a plethora of novels graphically portraying the evils of drink; mostly set in the city, such narratives tended to be formulaic, hyperbolic, and pietistic. Temperance ideology permeated many of the best-known novels of the age, including of course Mrs. Stowe's antislavery bombshell. A somewhat more historical theme provides the focus for a concluding chapter on the novels of the 1860s—a set of narratives linked by the grim cultural fixation of the decade: the sectional conflict that destroyed the Union and collapsed the illusions of nationhood promoted by US novels for more than a half century. In these seven parts, we have attempted to provide an authoritative account of this popular fictional genre and its role in the articulation of American cultural identity.

The habit of categorizing literary genres in relation to national cultures—to insist on entities like "the English novel," "the American novel," and the like—now seems to many critics and theorists, and perhaps to general readers as well, a perpetuation of nationalism itself. Surely the twentieth century witnessed enough holocausts driven by nationalistic delusions to inspire a yearning to see the age of nations recede into history. With the inception of the World Wide Web, communications satellites, and international cable television has come what Frederick Buell has called the "new global system," a consciousness of human connections across geographical and political frontiers. The current emphasis on global or transnational perspectives and the practice of reading beyond or across borders has provided a powerful interpretive model that seems to challenge the rationale of this volume, which presumes the critical usefulness and historical cogency of examining together the novels published in the United States between the American Revolution and the decade of the Civil War. As illuminating as it may be to regard US fiction in terms of hemispheric and oceanic cultural flows (and several chapters in this volume do precisely that), the idea of the nation remains, in this new millennium, a potent source of human identity and cultural logic, and that was manifestly the case during the first century of the novel's history in the United States. From the 1780s to the 1870s, this popular genre took root in the new Atlantic republic and with sometimes astonishing insight mirrored its early vicissitudes.

The cultural renewal that followed the Civil War entailed the re-formation of US nationhood and the reconstruction of "American literature" as a coherent idea. Designating a representative literary canon presented an immediate challenge, one that has persisted over time amid dynamic demographic change. "Each age, it is found, must write its own books; or rather, each generation for the next succeeding," Emerson wrote in "The American Scholar" (1837), and the same is true of canons (1983, 56–7). For all practical purposes, the pre-1870 canon of US fiction has always been an evolving concept. Authors and works once "lost" are suddenly found. Even well-known writers and works move into the foreground or recede depending on contemporary critical preoccupations. Pre-1870 authors and works contribute significantly to our understanding of the modern nation, as reinterpreted from emerging critical and cultural perspectives. Most scholarly studies work, subtly or explicitly, to define the canon. At some moments—the 1950s and 1960s come to mind—widespread critical rethinking produces paradigmatic change.

In *The First Century of American Literature* (1935), Fred Lewis Pattee recalls Charles Francis Richardson, who published one of the first scholarly surveys of the field, *A Primer of American literature* (1878). As Winkley Chair of English at Dartmouth College in 1883, Richardson added a course in American literature to the curriculum. "The radical nature of this step it is hard today to realize," Pattee observes (v), but many of us who have taught in the academy for thirty to forty years have often felt—even recently—as if we had to fight the American (literary) Revolution again and again. The oft-quoted question by Sydney Smith hung in the American air for a long time: "In the four quarters of the globe, who reads an American book?" (qtd. in Pattee 1935, 269).

Indeed, University of London lecturer Ernest A. Baker's single-authored, 10-volume *History of the English Novel* (1924–39), the precursor of the present *Oxford History of the Novel in English*, includes few references to American writing. The only pre-1870 American novelists meriting extended attention were Brockden Brown and Cooper. "Rude though Brown's achievements were," Baker condescendingly notes, "he was the precursor of those American novelists, Poe, Hawthorne, Oliver Wendell Holmes, Herman Melville, Henry James, who were to explore strange mental cases with a more scientific or at least a surer understanding" (5: 213). Baker considers Cooper the "earliest disciple of Scott of any standing" (7: 78). His appeal, like Brown's, involves his novels of "wild life"—"the romance of nature, instinct, simple manliness" (7: 79)—and Baker considers the Leather-Stocking series, "taken as a single whole," to be the "most considerable American work of fiction, and the finest embodiment of national characteristics" (7: 81). Otherwise, American writers receive only passing mention. Richard Henry Dana and Melville, for example, are identified as "successors" to Tobias Smollett as authors of sea novels (4: 206). Baker does note *The Scarlet Letter*, comparing its story of a Calvinist minister's adultery and public confession to James Gibson Lockhart's *Some Passages in the Life of Mr. Adam Blair* (1822), and giving Hawthorne more credit than his precursor for "lofty poetic symbolism" (4: 250–51).

If Baker had been more interested in American novels, he could have found a number of significant studies already in print—for example, Lillie Loshe's *The Early American Novel* (1907), John Erskine's *Leading American Novelists* (1910), Carl Van Doren's *The American Novel* (1921), Arthur Hobson Quinn's *American Fiction: An Historical and Critical Survey* (1936), as well as Pattee's *The First Century of American Literature*. These early studies, furthermore, include a broad range of authors and works—much broader than we find in D. H. Lawrence's *Studies in Classic American Literature* (1923), which begins with Franklin and Crèvecoeur and then devotes chapters to Cooper, Poe, Hawthorne, Dana, Melville, and Walt Whitman.

In her short survey of American novels from 1790 to 1830, Loshe focuses on Brockden Brown and Cooper as the only two early novelists of "real importance" (*v*), but she discusses many other writers and works—eighteenth-century novels by Hugh Henry Brackenridge (*Modern Chivalry* [1792–1815]), Rowson (*Charlotte Temple*), Hannah Foster (*The Coquette* [1797]), Royall Tyler (*The Algerine Captive* [1797]), and Tabitha Tenney (*Female Quixotism* [1801]), and many nineteenth-century frontier novels by women as well as men. Although Erskine limits himself to a half dozen "leading" novelists, the six he chooses may surprise many readers: Brown, Cooper, Hawthorne, Simms, Stowe, and Bret Harte. Van Doren's *The American Novel* gives Cooper, Hawthorne, and Melville separate billing, but the chapters and sections he devotes to other pre-1870 writers are much more inclusive than exclusive. Besides the early novels Loshe mentions, Van Doren notes works by John Davis, Isaac Mitchell, and Samuel Woodworth. He devotes half of the chapter on "Romances of Adventure" to Melville, but in the other half he cites John Neal, Sylvester Judd, Daniel Thompson, James Kirke Paulding, Caroline Kirkland, James Hall, Kennedy, Bird, Tucker, and even William Ware (*Zenobia* [1837]) and William Starbuck Mayo (*Kaloolah* [1849]). He devotes slightly more attention to Simms, whom he considers "Cooper's closest rival among the romancers" (60). Finally, in a chapter entitled "Blood and Tears," he surveys popular adventure and sentimental fiction writers, including E. D. E. N. Southworth, Mary Jane Holmes, Augusta Evans, Susan Warner, Maria Cummins, Donald Grant Mitchell, George William Curtis, T. S. Arthur, and Josiah Holland. He devotes the most attention to Stowe, the "most effective of all these sentimentalists" (117).

Examining virtually the same period covered in this volume (1770–1870), Pattee goes further than Van Doren in establishing a broad and varied canon of American writing, including an impressive collection of novels. Notoriously, he relegates much women's fiction to a single chapter—"The Feminine Fifties"—although he does label *Uncle Tom's Cabin* one of five "revolutionary documents" (565), the others being *Moby-Dick*, Henry David Thoreau's *Walden; or, Life in the Woods* (1854), John Greenleaf Whittier's *Poems* (1849), and Whitman's *Leaves of Grass* (1855–92). A chapter entitled "The Fight for the Novel" includes treatments of *The Power of Sympathy*, *Charlotte Temple*, *The Coquette*, and *Female Quixotism*. When he turns to Western literature, he begins with Gilbert Imlay's *The Emigrants* (1793) and also discusses Brackenridge's *Modern Chivalry*, judged essential reading for understanding "the America of the two decades before Jefferson" (165). Among frontier novels, Pattee lists thirty-four works published over a twenty-five-year period (1817–41). Besides Cooper's five Leather-Stocking Tales, he cites Neal's *Logan* (1822), James McHenry's *The Spectre of the Forest* (1823), Lydia Maria Child's *Hobomok* (1824), and Sedgwick's *Hope Leslie*, as well as Paulding's *The Dutchman's Fireside* (1831), Bird's *Nick of the Woods*, and Timothy Flint's *The Shoshonee Valley* (1830). He includes a chapter on southern novels as well, emphasizing Kennedy, whose *Horse-Shoe Robinson* (1835) is "the best historical romance created in America before the Civil War" (426), and Simms, whose Revolutionary War novels (e.g., *The Partisan* [1835]; *Mellichampe* [1836]) "unquestionably" surpass Cooper's (431).

In *American Fiction*, Quinn surveys the field from the beginnings to the early 1930s. He devotes a chapter to eighteenth-century novels, with emphasis on Rowson's *Charlotte Temple* as well as *Reuben and Rachel* (1798), which he calls "extraordinary" for its "use of American materials" (16). He accords separate chapters to Brown, Irving, Cooper, Poe, Hawthorne, and Melville before taking stock of early realistic fiction, notably Stowe's novels *Uncle Tom's Cabin, Dred* (1856), *The Minister's Wooing* (1859), *The Pearl of Orr's Island* (1862), and *Oldtown Folks* (1869). He notes familiar works by Oliver Wendell Holmes (*Elsie Venner* [1861]) and John William De Forest (*Miss Ravenel's Conversion from Secession to Loyalty* [1867]), but he also discusses Theodore Winthrop's *John Brent* (1862), arguably the first western novel, and Bayard Taylor's *Joseph and His Friend* (1870), which some critics consider the first gay novel published by a US author. Given their "rediscovery" and republication many years later, his treatment of Rebecca Harding Davis's *Life in the Iron Mills* (1861) and *Margret Howth* (1862), Elizabeth Stuart Phelps's *The Silent Partner* (1871), and Elizabeth Stoddard's *The Morgesons* (1862) seems progressive. And even by contemporary standards of expansiveness the pages he devotes to John Townsend Trowbridge's *Neighbor Jackwood* (1857), a "powerful anti-slavery novel" (163), will open many readers' eyes to an unfamiliar work. Even more intriguing, Quinn devotes a chapter to "The Fiction of Fantasy," with discussions of Donald Grant Mitchell's *Reveries of a Bachelor* (1850) and *Dream Life* (1851), which "represent the border line between fiction and essay" (207). He also cites Curtis's *Prue and I* (1856) and *Trumps* (1861), a "penetrating satire" of New York society and politics (208) and Harriet Spofford's *Sir Rohan's Ghost* (1860).

Most scholarly surveys before 1940 seem designed to identify and classify a broad canon of authors and works. Pattee and Quinn in particular seem determined to be as inclusive as possible, as if attempting to do for American fiction what Baker was doing for the English novel. The American canon would contract in subsequent decades, at least as represented by the most influential critical works, which were thesis driven and often motivated by a desire to promote distinctively American works. No single scholarly work had more influence in defining a limited canon than F. O. Matthiessen's *American Renaissance* (1941). Focusing on a single half-decade, 1850–55, Matthiessen highlighted five male writers (Emerson, Thoreau, Hawthorne, Melville, and Whitman) who published major books during that period: *Representative Men* (1850), *Walden*, *The Scarlet Letter* and *The House of the Seven Gables*, *Moby-Dick* and *Pierre; or, The Ambiguities* (1852), and *Leaves of Grass*. This concentration of excellence justifies itself, but Matthiessen's other criterion involved common thematic ground—one grand, overarching idea: a "devotion to the possibilities of democracy" (ix). Today, it is hard to think of a work more dedicated to democratic possibilities than *Uncle Tom's Cabin*, but Matthiessen mentions Stowe only three times in passing, and he mentions *Uncle Tom's Cabin* only once. Acknowledging that his choice of authors may be "arbitrary" (x), he mentions others he could have included: Whittier, Henry Wadsworth Longfellow, Lowell, Holmes, Simms, T. S. Arthur, Warner, Fanny Fern, Cummins, and Southworth. He devotes a lengthy footnote to his exclusion of Poe, who wrote mostly, he says, in an earlier period (1835–45) and was bitterly hostile to democracy.

Otherwise, Matthiessen's all-male hall of fame created a foundation for the American canon that persisted for three decades. For example, *Eight American Authors: A Review of Research and Criticism*, edited by Floyd Stovall for the Modern Language Association in 1956, included bibliographic essays on Poe, Emerson, Hawthorne, Thoreau, Melville, Whitman, Mark Twain, and James. Stovall updated and republished the volume in 1963 and James Woodress edited another update in 1971, with no changes in the authors covered. *Fifteen American Authors before 1900*, edited by Robert Rees and Earl Harbert (1971, 1984), took up where Stovall and Woodress left off by creating a secondary, supplemental gallery of authors, only six of whom (Henry Adams, Cooper, Stephen Crane, Holmes, Longfellow, and Frank Norris) wrote novels. Despite prominence in earlier surveys, Brockden Brown figures nowhere, nor do female novelists or African American writers. Stowe is absent, and so is Frederick Douglass. Citing both bibliographical studies in a 1972 review, Lewis Leary could judge that the twenty-three writers "may be fairly looked upon as the native writers of the past century who in present judgment are considered by people in the academic literary establishment as being most important" (235). Ironically, in retrospect, 1972 marks a watershed moment in American literary canon formation, as the decade of the 1970s featured a revolutionary explosion of the canon.

We can track this expansion by examining the forty-six years of *American Literary Scholarship*, the annual review first published in 1963. Woodress acknowledged in his inaugural foreword that *Eight American Authors* "was the model for this work" (v), and for its first ten years (1963–72), *American Literary Scholarship* devoted six separate chapters to individual nineteenth-century authors—all of them members of Stovall's original eight. Thoreau joined Emerson in a chapter entitled "Emerson, Thoreau, and Transcendentalism," and Poe got no individual billing at all until 1967, when he was given a section in the newly entitled chapter, "Poe and Nineteenth-Century Poetry." The persistence of Hawthorne and Melville chapters and the relatively slight changes in the list of authors named in chapter titles preserve a core canon that belies the canonical expansion of pre-1870 fiction over the past several decades. That change is reflected, however, in the chapters devoted to nineteenth-century literature. Individual writers pop in and out of these section titles from year to year, as critical interest waxes and wanes. Each of the following novelists has been mentioned in a section title since 1994: Louisa May Alcott, Bird, Child, Cooper, Fanny Fern, Harriet Jacobs, Longfellow, John Rollin Ridge, Sedgwick, Simms, Stoddard, Stowe, and Warner. Altogether, this collection of writers approximates the more expansive canon that has come into being over the past four decades. It also reflects the writers discussed by contributors to this volume.

The work performed by these bibliographical projects reflects the efforts after World War II to establish a canon of US authors and works that might compete with English literature. That canon came together in critical studies of the 1950s and 1960s but did so by excluding authors and works that vied for attention earlier in the century and have been "rediscovered" during the past forty years. By the time Joel Porte published *The Romance in America: Studies in Cooper, Poe, Hawthorne, Melville, and James* (1969), he felt confident in stipulating that "thanks to a series of major critical studies that have appeared in the past decade and a half, it no longer seems necessary to argue for the importance of romance as a nineteenth-century American genre" (ix). The studies he identifies are Charles Feidelson's *Symbolism and American Literature* (1953), R. W. B. Lewis's *The American Adam* (1955), Richard Chase's *The American Novel and Its Tradition* (1957), Harry Levin's *The Power of Blackness* (1958), Leslie Fiedler's *Love and Death in the American Novel* (1960, 1966), and Daniel Hoffman's *Form and Fable in American Fiction* (1961)—all of them required reading for those schooled in American myth criticism during the 1960s and 1970s, and all featuring similar lists of authors and works from the pre-1870 period. Literary nationalism went hand-in-hand with political nationalism, both fueled by notions of American exceptionalism.

Lewis begins *The American Adam*, for example, by explaining his interest in the "outlines of a native American mythology," a paradigm that crystallizes around the "authentic American as a figure of heroic innocence and vast potentialities." He draws this "representative imagery" from literary culture of a "century ago" (1), but the impulses that inspire his work derive as much from the enthusiastic spirit of the post–World War II era as from the early nineteenth century. The "American myth," he says, "described the world as starting up again under fresh initiative, in a divinely granted second chance for the human race, after the first chance had been so disastrously fumbled in the darkening Old World" (5). Chase's *The American Novel and Its Tradition* includes separate chapters on Brockden Brown, Cooper, Hawthorne, and Melville and seems sponsored by a similar desire to define a "native tradition" of the American novel in exceptional terms. English novels are novels; American novels are romances—characterized, in a famous formulation, by

> an assumed freedom from the ordinary novelistic requirements of verisimilitude, development, and continuity; a tendency towards melodrama and idyl; a more or less formal abstractness and, on the other hand, a tendency to plunge into the underside of consciousness; a willingness to abandon moral questions or to ignore the spectacle of man in society, or to consider these things only indirectly or abstractly. (ix)

Feidelson's *Symbolism and American Literature* features Hawthorne, Whitman, Melville, and Poe, with Melville exemplifying the symbolist movement, and his Ishmael—an American Adam by another name—is the "archetypal figure" of "Man Seeing, the mind engaged in a crucial act of knowledge" (5). Feidelson means "seeing" as if for the first time, ahistorically or transhistorically, as the word "archetype" implies. He too captures the optimism of the postwar era even as he focuses on the earlier American Renaissance.

Directed by his "desire to define what is peculiarly American in our books" (1966, 11), Fiedler's iconoclastic *Love and Death in the American Novel* features a more expansive canon of authors and works, but Fiedler also emphasizes Brockden Brown, Cooper, Poe, Hawthorne, and Melville, among pre-1870 novelists, even though he devotes space to William Hill Brown, Rowson, and Foster, among eighteenth-century writers, and to Stowe and Lippard (*The Quaker City* [1844]). Best known for his "theory" about "the relationship between sentimental life in America and the archetypal image, found in our favorite books, in which a white and a colored American male flee from civilization into each other's arms" (12), Fiedler's self-styled "vulgar" study (8) opened a critical space for gay and queer criticism even if, ironically, his main point was the "failure of the American fictionist to deal with adult heterosexual love and his consequent obsession with death, incest and innocent homosexuality" (12). In its emphasis on interracial relationships in a state of co-dependency, *Love and Death* also resonated with its age—the 1950s and 1960s—as blacks and whites increasingly found themselves joined in "each other's arms," struggling for and against civil rights.

As Paul Lauter remarked twenty years ago, "Changing the canon has over the past fifteen years become a major objective of literary practitioners of women's studies, black studies, and other 'ethnic' studies—the academic wings of the social movements of the 1960s and 1970s" (1991, 23). Antiestablishment and antiauthoritarian energies of this era translated into anticanonical revolutions, initially targeting traditional authors and works as a kind of enemies list, but then evolving into recovery projects that created alternative or parallel canons or a larger canon that seemed, in practice, no canon at all. Probably no publishing project did more to express this canonical explosion than *The Heath Anthology of American Literature*, which first appeared under Lauter's editorship in 1989. American literature anthologies, regardless of the publisher, would never be the same again, as all moved in the direction of inclusivity and an expanded canon.

But there have always been countercurrents. We think of Lewis, Chase, and others as cementing a canon in place, formed around wild romances featuring Adamic males and the power of blackness, but as late as 1948, in his remarkably comprehensive survey of early American fiction, *The Rise of the American Novel*, Alexander Cowie covered a very ambitious and eclectic group of male and female writers. Cooper, Hawthorne, and Melville all receive full-chapter treatment, but Cowie marks out some innovative fictional categories in order to include other authors. His first chapter, "At the Beginning," divides what most would consider a sparse field into three categories: Domestic, Sentimental, Didactic Fiction; Gothic Romance; and Historical Novels, especially those featuring "the Indian." Cowie includes Hill Brown, Rowson, Foster, Tenney, and Ann Eliza Bleecker, but also Enos Hitchcock (*Memoirs of the Bloomsgrove Family* [1790]), Caroline Matilda Warren (*The Gamesters* [1805]), Sally Wood (*Julia and the Illuminated Baron* [1800]), and John Davis (*The First Settlers of Virginia* [1805]). Although Cooper gets top billing as author of historical romances, in two following chapters Cowie includes Child and Sedgwick, Simms, Bird, and Kennedy, as well as Paulding, Flint, Neal, and Daniel Pierce Thompson (*The Green Mountain Boys* [1839]). Cowie also devotes a lengthy chapter to "The Domestic Sentimentalists and Other Popular Writers"—mostly, but not exclusively, women. Included are Warner, Southworth, Cummins, Fern, as well as Caroline Lee Hentz (*Ernest Linwood* [1856]), Marion Harland (*Alone* [1854]), Ann Sophia Stephens (*Fashion and Famine* [1854]), Mary Jane Holmes (*Lena Rivers* [1856]), Augusta Jane Evans (*St. Elmo* [1866]), and Mrs. H. B. Goodwin (*Sherbrooke* [1866])—but also three male writers: Arthur (*The Withered Heart* [1857]), Josiah Holland (*Arthur Bonnicastle* [1873]), and E. P. Roe (*Barriers Burned Away* [1872]).

Efforts such as Cowie's to honor the variety of American fiction were supported by several publishing ventures aimed at printing authors and works out of the mainstream. Beginning in 1967, for example, Gregg Press published an Americans in Fiction Series edited by Clarence Gohdes. Gohdes deliberately chose books—seventy in all—by noncanonical writers, including Stowe. Most of the works in this series were originally published after 1870, but the few exceptions include a healthy sampling of early southern novels, such as William A. Caruthers's *The Kentuckian in New-York* (1834) and *The Cavaliers of Virginia* (1834); John Esten Cooke's *The Virginia Comedians* (1854), *Surry of Eagle's-Nest* (1866), and *Mohun* (1869); and four of Simms's novels, including *The Partisan*, *The Scout* (1854), and *Woodcraft* (1854). At the same time, Gregg Press launched a series of American muckraking novels, and the pre-1870 titles stage an intriguing debate, among others, between anti- and pro-slavery novels, as well as novels "blasting" Northern prejudice. Gohdes includes Hildreth's *The Slave; or, Memoirs of Archy Moore* (1836), Stowe's *Dred*, Mary Eastman's rejoinder to Stowe, *Aunt Phillis's Cabin* (1852), as well as Sarah Hale's *Liberia; or, Mr. Peyton's Experiments* (1853), Trowbridge's *Neighbor Jackwood*, and Davis's *Waiting for the Verdict* (1868). In addition to the novels dealing with slavery,

Gohdes chose Tucker's *The Partisan Leader* (1836), Sylvester Judd's *Margaret* (1845), Cooper's final novel, *The Ways of the Hour* (1850), and Taylor's *Hannah Thurston* (1863)—the latter two novels about struggles for women's rights.

No scholarly work did more to open the nineteenth-century canon to novels by women than Nina Baym's *Woman's Fiction: A Guide to Novels by and about Women in America, 1820–1870* (1978). Baym's guide highlighted recovery work initiated some years earlier and created a new canon of women authors and titles. Among her featured writers were Sedgwick, Southworth, Hentz, Susan and Anna Warner, Cummins, Maria McIntosh, Ann Stephens, Mary Jane Holmes, Harland, Caroline Chesebro', and Evans. Scholarship drives pedagogy, which in turn drives publishing. For teachers, the canon for practical purposes includes texts available in relatively inexpensive paperback or online editions or in anthologies. Not surprisingly, series of nineteenth-century women's fiction began appearing in the 1970s. The newly founded Feminist Press published an edition of *Life in the Iron Mills* in 1972 and, later, an edition of *Margret Howth*. The press would also publish Phelps's *The Silent Partner* (1983). Rutgers University Press inaugurated its American Women Writers series in 1986. Titles include *Hobomok*, *Hope Leslie*, Kirkland's *A New Home, Who'll Follow?* (1839), Cummins's *The Lamplighter* (1854), Fern's *Ruth Hall* (1855), Southworth's *The Hidden Hand* (1859), and Alcott's *Moods* (1864). In 1985 two important anthologies of women's writing appeared: *Provisions*, edited by Judith Fetterley, and *Hidden Hands*, edited by Lucy Freibert and Barbara White. The latter includes nothing but excerpts from novels or quasi-fictional long narratives—a total of twenty works, from *Charlotte Temple* to *Ruth Hall* and including still little-known works, such as Wood's *Dorval* (1801), Hale's *Northwood* (1827), Metta Fuller Victor's *The Senator's Son* (1853), Chesebro's *Isa, A Pilgrimage* (1852), Hentz's *The Planter's Northern Bride* (1854), Frances Miriam Berry Whitcher's *The Widow Bedott Papers* (1856), Evans's *St. Elmo*, and Martha Finley's *Elsie Dinsmore* (1867). By the end of the 1980s, it is fair to say, a robust canon of women's writing had taken shape and was readily available for scholarly and pedagogical purposes.

With the obvious exception of Jacobs's *Incidents in the Life of a Slave Girl* (1861), African American women's writing was slower to be published during this explosive period, but then, in 1988, the Schomburg Library of Nineteenth-Century Black Women Writers, edited by Henry Louis Gates, Jr., brought thirty titles into print and has since published additional important texts. Only a few are narratives from the pre-1870 period—for example, *Narrative of Sojourner Truth* (1850), Mary Seacole's *Wonderful Adventures of Mrs. Seacole in Many Lands* (1857), Eliza Potter's *A Hairdresser's Experience in High Life* (1859), and Elizabeth Keckley's *Behind the Scenes; or, Thirty Years a Slave, and Four Years in the White House* (1868). Gates added to this canon by publishing Wilson's *Our Nig* and Hannah Crafts's *The Bondwoman's Narrative* in 1982 and 2002, respectively. African American male narratives have had no such dedicated publisher. Many slave narratives have been available for some time, either as separate texts or as part of collections. Frederick Douglass's important writings, including "The Heroic Slave" (1853), have been available in multiple editions for years. Brown's *Clotel* and its revised versions have been in print for at least twenty years. Frank J. Webb's *The Garies and Their Friends* (1857) is now available in a paperback edition. Delany's *Blake* appeared in paperback in 1969 and has been recently republished.

Cultural Studies approaches to American literature have further opened the canon toward popular literary works. David S. Reynolds's *Beneath the American Renaissance* (1988), for example, examined popular genres (dark adventure fiction, subversive fiction, reform fiction, crime fiction, city mysteries fiction) and works comprising a fertile underground that percolated upward to influence better-known authors and works. Dark adventure fiction, such as Maturin Murray Ballou's *Fanny Campbell; or, The Female Pirate Captain* (1845) and Harry Halyard's *Wharton the Whale-Killer!* (1848) "gave such primacy to violence and irrationalism that the forces of darkness shattered those of moral rectitude" (Reynolds 1988, 188). Neal gets credit for being the "first American writer [in *Errata*, 1823] to recognize woman's strong sexual drives" (212), and Laughton Osborn's *Confessions of a Poet* (1835) becomes "perhaps the most important American novel of the 1830s, because it combined a violent, gloomy plot with striking accounts of illicit love and woman's sexuality" (213–14). George Thompson thus looms large for insinuating "every type of illicit sex" (219) in novels such as *Venus in Boston* (1849) and *City Crimes* (1849), both recently reprinted. Although Reynolds emphasizes the ways that writers such as Poe, Hawthorne, and Melville assimilated such subversive work into their own writings, in the process he uncovers a rich vein of popular and sensationalistic novels that expand the pre-1870 canon remarkably.

In designing this volume, we considered a final chapter to be titled "Novels Nobody Knows," partly to honor the ever-evolving configuration of the early American canon. That chapter did not materialize, but the principle behind it still holds true. The Harvard Longfellow Institute and Johns Hopkins University Press have launched a series devoted to non-English works published in America. One of the first two titles, Baron Ludwig von Reizenstein's *Die Geheimnisse von New Orleans* (*The Mysteries of New Orleans*), originally appeared in 1854–55 and figures in one of our chapters. Our concept of American literature continues to expand, crossing national boundaries to become "Transamerican" or "Hemispheric." *The Norton Anthology of Latino Literature* (2011) includes antebellum narratives by Juan Nepomuceno Seguín, José Policarpo Rodríguez, and Andrew García. Finally, of course, the increasing availability of electronic books through internet search engines ensures that, fifty years from now, the canon of pre-1870 American novels and other prose narratives will have expanded to a point where the concept of *a* "canon" may have little relevance. The chapters in this volume capture much of the diversity of early US fiction as they delineate principal lines of development and influence. Aside from brief sections on "leading novelists" and "major novels," they mostly avoid questions of canonicity, focusing instead on the integral relation between the novel—in all its multiplicity—and American cultural history.

Part I

THE BEGINNINGS OF THE NOVEL IN THE UNITED STATES

1

BEFORE THE AMERICAN NOVEL

BETSY ERKKILA

America was a place in the imagination before it was a place on the map. In discovering America, explorers and writers did not discover a New World that was "out there" in any unmediated sense of the term: America became a new terrain onto which Europeans projected their desires and fears, their utopian longing for a new beginning and a better world, as well as their fears of unleashed nature, both beyond the self and within. The American Dream—and its abject other, the American Nightmare—began in Europe before any European actually set foot on the continent that would be named after the early sixteenth-century Italian explorer, Amerigo Vespucci, who first discovered that America was not an appendage of Asia but a fourth continent. In a late sixteenth-century engraving of Vespucci "discovering" America by Theodor Galle (ca. 1580), the American continent is represented as a voluptuous and inviting Indian woman, who evokes the sexual desire, fears, and fantasies of conquest that marked the European gaze on first contact (figure 1.1).

But as Terrence Malick's lyrical retelling of the story of Pocahontas and John Smith in his 2005 film *The New World* reminds us, the gaze worked both ways: first contact initiated the discovery of a European world that was as "new" to the indigenous inhabitants as America was to the Europeans. It also inaugurated a New World of cross-cultural negotiation, exchange, and conflict. The clash of Native and European values and the ensuing struggle over the land, identity, and rule of America is evident in the stories of origin told by Native inhabitants and some of the earliest accounts of first contact. These stories of origin, which sought to explain the location of the person and the culture within a meaningful cosmos, are part of the prehistory of the novel, the multiple forms of oral and written nonfiction narrative—history, travel writing, captivity narrative, execution sermon, criminal narrative, confession, and slave narrative—that constitute the history of the American novel.

Fig 1.1 A sixteenth-century engraving of Amerigo Vespucci discovering "America" by Theodor Galle, based on a 1575 drawing by Jan van der Straet, in which the continent is represented by a seductive, inviting, and potentially threatening Indian woman.

Myth as History

"You don't have anything / if you don't have the stories," wrote Leslie Marmon Silko at the outset of her novel *Ceremony* (1977) in a poem that emphasizes the sacred role of Native storytellers in communicating the history and values of the ancient people through myth, story, song, dance, and performance. David Cusick's Iroquois creation story, "A Tale of the Foundation of the Great Island, Now North America—the Two Infants Born, and the Creation of the Universe," published in his *Sketches of Ancient History of the Six Nations* (1827), is the first translation and transcription of the Iroquois cosmogony and the first retelling by a Native American of the history of his people. Cusick's story reveals certain differences between Native American vision, values, and life-worlds and Christian notions of the person, the body, gender, nature, story, and world in early American works such as John Smith's story of the founding of the Virginia colony and William Bradford's history of Plymouth plantation.

Unlike the book of Genesis, in which the world is made out of nothing by a patriarchal God who creates man in his own image to subdue and rule over the natural world, Cusick's story begins with Sky Woman, who is pregnant with twins, in two preexisting worlds—one dark and possessed by "the great monsters," and another "inhabited by mankind." When Sky Woman falls toward the dark world, the earth is created not singularly by an all-powerful God but collectively by "all the species" of animals, including a turtle "varnished" with "a small quantity of earth" on which "[t]he woman alights" and "receives a satisfaction." As in other versions of the tale, Cusick's language suggests the possibility of supernatural intercourse between woman and turtle that magically transforms the turtle into "a considerable island of earth, and apparently covered with small bushes." Sky Woman dies in childbirth after giving birth to one gentle twin, "the good mind," and one insolent twin, "the bad mind." The turtle increases "to a great Island," and the good mind "commences the work of creation"—not out of nothing as in Genesis—but out of the dead body of the mother (pt. 1).

Written and published while the US government was debating the policy of Indian removal beyond the Mississippi, Cusick's story of the founding of North America is a hybrid narrative, a product of contact that appears to be shaped by elements of Christian cosmogony. But as a woman-centered, matrilineal story that identifies a mother with the sun as the generative power of the universe, nature and soul as one rather than two, and the earth as the site of a harmonious exchange among people, plants, animals, forest, fishes, and waters, Cusick's story of American origins reveals a set of values and a life-world very different from Christian cosmogony. The ease with which Sky Woman falls from the upper world of "mankind" into the "lower world" of darkness suggests that the boundaries between dark world and "new world" are more fluid than in Christian religion, and "all the species" of "the great water" who rescue Sky Woman as she descends "to the lower world" affirm values of cooperation, hospitality, and compassion (pt. 1). Human identity is not fixed and separate from the natural world but part of an animate universe in which turtles become the foundation of the "Great Island" of North America, the mother's corpse becomes the foundation of the universe, and the dead continue to exert power in the real world as "Evil Spirits" or ghosts.

Although Europeans regarded Native American stories as myths, or fictions, and signs of their heathen, savage, and uncivilized nature, Native Americans regarded stories, especially stories of origin like Cusick's, as a means of passing on the history, traditions, and truths of the Iroquois League. Precisely these differences in Native American notions of personhood, body, nature, spirit, myth, and history—as well as their communication of traditions and values through storytelling, dance, performance, and song—made Native American people figures of terror to early English settlers of North America. Moreover, the slippage between myth and history, storytelling and truth that shapes Cusick's "Tale" would continue to destabilize not only the "true relations" of Native American and English contact told by the first settlers but also the history of the American novel and what counts as the "true" history of America.

History as Fiction: Pocahontas and John Smith

The generic instability between history and fiction in seventeenth-century English writing is particularly evident in Smith's *The Generall Historie of Virginia, New-England, and the Summer Isles* (1624). This text is at once a history of the first settlements in Jamestown and New England; an economic and commercial tract to draw interest and investment in the English colonies; and an early version of the genres of captivity narrative, adventure story, western, and mystery that would shape the development of the American novel from Charles Brockden Brown's *Edgar Huntly; or, Memoirs of a Sleep-Walker* (1799), to James Fenimore Cooper's Leather-Stocking Tales, to the dime novels that featured such frontier heroes and outlaws as Wyatt Earp and Billy the Kid in the 1860s and 1870s. It also includes the original story of Pocahontas and Smith, a romance of cross-race love—or its fantasy—that inaugurates the American fascination with interracial couples, evident from Susanna Rowson's *Reuben and Rachel; or, Tales of Old Times* (1798), to Cooper's Natty Bumppo and Chingachgook, to Herman Melville's Ishmael and Queequeg, and even to Disney's animated version of *Pocahontas* (1995). While Smith describes his narrative as history, it is presented from a third-person point of view, with Smith as the hero, who seeks to defend the "untoward" colonials from "the fury of the Salvages" and their own improvidence (ch. 2).

The only part of Smith's history to survive in the American imaginary is the story of Pocahontas, a myth or history to which later writers, artists, musicians, and filmmakers would continue to return as a story that embodies the miracle, tragedy, or missed possibility of Native and white contact, the founding of Jamestown in 1607, and the origins of America itself. The story originates in one long sentence about Smith's captivity and possible death by the order of Powhatan, the chief of the Powhatan Confederacy and the father of Pocahontas:

> [H]aving feasted him [Smith] after their best barbarous manner they could, a long consultation was held, but the conclusion was, two great stones were brought before Powhatan: then as many as could layd hands on him, dragged him to them, and thereon laid his head, and being ready with their clubs, to beate out his braines, Pocahontas the Kings dearest daughter, when no intreaty could prevaile, got his head in her armes, and laid her owne upon his to save him from death: whereat the Emperour was contented he should live to make him hatchets, and her bells, beads, and copper. (ch. 2)

Smith's narrative has been popularized as a rescue story in which an Indian woman risks herself to save a white man, an act that preserved the first English settlement in America and later enabled distinguished Southern families to claim royal lineage. One of the earliest literary uses of the story occurs in *The Female American* (1767), an adventure story modeled on the New World island fantasy of Daniel

Defoe's *Robinson Crusoe* (1719) in which the mixed race, multilingual, and transnational narrator, Unca Eliza Winkfield, claims she is the daughter of Pocahontas and evokes the memory of both Smith and John Rolfe.

With the publication of William Wirt's *The Letters of the British Spy* in 1803, the story of the dark woman sacrificing herself for the survival of the white man entered the national imaginary, where it would be popularized by Cooper's *The Last of the Mohicans: A Narrative of 1757* (1826) and other frontier romances featuring the "good" versus "bad" Indian, the difference of "white" from "red" blood, the fantasy or fear of mixture, the myth of the vanishing Indian, the inevitable triumph of white civilization, and in later more primitivist readings, an increasing eroticization of Pocahontas—or the Indian woman—as an incarnation of the American continent. This more sensual and carnal version of Pocahontas, who was finally rejected by Smith, links her with the dark, passionate, and boundary-breaking heroines—from Hannah Foster's "volatile" Eliza Wharton to Cooper's mixed-blooded Cora Munro—who die sacrificial deaths to enable the survival of virtuous republican mothers and (white) American virtue.

From the beginning, Smith's account of his adventures with the "savages" was doubted, especially by historians. In 1662, Thomas Fuller wrote that Smith's actions "seem to most men above belief, [and] to some beyond truth" (1952, 75), suggesting the unstable boundary between history and fiction that would continue to underwrite the development of the British and the American novel. But even if the story is true, as Leo Lemay and others have convincingly argued, the entire narrative is so shaped by Smith's European gaze that meaningful Native ceremonies, songs, dances, and costumes are consistently misread as scenes of devil worship in which "savage" male and "naked" female bodies dance, whoop, and howl in preparation to seduce or consume him. Smith narrates events leading to his "rescue" as a series of wild feastings in which he is being fattened to be killed and cannibalized. As anthropologist Frederic W. Gleach has observed, what Smith witnessed was more likely an elaborate adoption ceremony in which relations between the Powhatan Confederacy and the English colony were being ritualistically renewed.

Although standard accounts have continued to locate the origins of American cultural and literary history in New England, the founding of Jamestown and even the importation of the first African slaves (1619) preceded the settlement of Plymouth in 1620. As Smith's history of Jamestown's founding suggests, it represents a more racially mixed and tragic Southern counter-genealogy, one that Mark Twain would later satirize in *Pudd'nhead Wilson* (1894) when the illiterate slave Roxana imagines herself the descendant of "Ole Cap'n John Smith" and "Pocahontas de Injun Queen," whose "husbun' was a nigger king outen Africa" (ch. 14). These "tangled skeins" of racial genealogies (Jacobs 1861, ch. 14) would shape the Southern gothic from the works of Edgar Allan Poe to William Faulkner's *Absalom, Absalom!* (1936).

Myth, Allegory, and the Providential Plot

While Smith's *Generall Historie of Virginia* is framed by an English imperial perspective and a providential plot that consistently attributes acts of Native generosity, provision, and gift exchange to "almightie God (by his divine providence)" (ch. 2), it has a specificity that locates it closer to history in what Michael McKeon has called the continuum that moves from myth to romance to history and the emergence of the English novel as a major form. *Of Plymouth Plantation* (written ca. 1630, 1646–50; published 1856), William Bradford's history of the founding of the first New England colony in 1620, is not so much a "history" as an "unfould[ing]" of God's will, "[t]he which I shall endevor to manefest in a plaine stile, with singuler regard unto ye simple trueth in all things" (pref.). The problem of truth and interpretation is raised at the outset as Bradford seeks to read the particularities of everyday life as signs of God's truth, revealed in the Bible, Christian typology, and the "spetiall worke of Gods providence" on behalf of the pilgrims in the New World (ch. 9). Closer to myth and allegory than Smith's history, Bradford's moving account of the Separatists' arrival in America after a passage over perilous seas contains some of the formative tropes not only of the American novel but also of American history:

> But here I cannot but stay and make a pause, and stand half amased at this poore peoples presente condition; and so I thinke will the reader too, when he well considers ye same. Being thus passed ye vast ocean, and a sea of troubles before in their preparation . . . they had now no friends to wellcome them, nor inns to entertaine or refresh their weatherbeaten bodys, no houses or much less townes to repaire too, to seeke for succoure. It is recorded in scripture as a mercie to ye apostle & his shipwraked company, [that] the barbarians shewed them no small kindnes in refreshing them, but these savage barbarians, when they mette with them (as after will appear) were readier to fill their sid[e]s full of arrows then otherwise. (ch. 9)

Unlike the cyclical and interdependent relation between humans and the earth in Native American stories of origin, or the fantasy of intercourse between white and Native in Smith's story of first contact, Bradford's story of Puritan origins begins as a separation and a negation. His account empties the land of real time, space, and inhabitants and rhetorically substitutes God's plan for the pilgrims as originally figured in biblical story and revealed in Puritan history as a series of "remarkable providences."

Like John Winthrop's sense of the world historical significance of the Puritan story in "A Model of Christian Charity" (1630)—"we shall be made a story and a by-word through the world"—Bradford dramatizes his story of "this poor people" for the eyes of a future reader not by factual narration but by biblical relation, by comparing their "presente condition" to the biblical story of the apostle Paul, whose similarly "shipwraked company" was treated kindly by the "barbarians." Seen through the lens of biblical symbology as antitypes "of Moyses & ye Isralit[e]s when they went out of Egipte" (ch. 3), Bradford and the pilgrims view the land and the Natives as "a hideous & desolate wildernes, full of wild beasts & wild men" (ch. 9), where they will be held captive and tried as the chosen people of God, just as the Israelites suffered the Egyptian captivity before being led by Moses toward the Promised Land. Unlike Moses, however, Bradford's pilgrims have no Pisgah, no vision of the Promised Land, and no assurance of their errand's success. Alienated from the land, the Natives, and their own bodies, the pilgrims inhabit a world in which "outward objects" provide "little solace or content" except as signs of God's providential design (ch. 9).

Bradford's story of arrival adumbrates three main subjects of the American novel: the Puritan errand, the wilderness, and the colonial struggle. His desire to write in a "plaine stile" as the vehicle of "simple truth" also makes him one of the first in a long line of writers who sought to capture the dialect and rhythms of ordinary American speech. Bradford's symbolic mode of narration—his insistence on linking the particularities of everyday colonial life with some higher biblical or providential meaning—would continue to shape character and scene in early American novels such as Foster's *The Coquette* (1797), where the allegorically inflected characters Lucy Freeman and Mrs. Richman try to preserve the virtue of Eliza Wharton, the "coquette," who is eventually "undone" (ltr. 48) by a "clandestine intercourse" in "the garden" with the devilish rake Peter Sanford (ltr. 41). In its allegorical overtones, the scene anticipates the meeting of Hester Prynne and Arthur Dimmesdale in the "Forest" in Hawthorne's *The Scarlet Letter: A Romance* (1850).

Like Melville in works such as *Mardi: And a Voyage Thither* (1849) and *Moby-Dick; or, The Whale* (1851), Hawthorne subtly critiqued Puritan allegory and symbolism while using these stylistic modes to probe human psychology, the problems of good and evil, knowledge and interpretation, and the ambiguities of American identity underlying the entire democratic project. It was this more symbolic mode of narration that led Hawthorne to define his own works, in the preface to *The House of the Seven Gables* (1851), as "Romances," a term later critics would embrace as the distinctive difference between British realism and the more allegorical, mythic, and metaphysical concerns of the American novel.

Like later novels about colonial history by Hawthorne, Lydia Maria Child, and Catharine Maria Sedgwick, Bradford's *Of Plymouth Plantation* chronicles a declension signaled by a narrative break. By the second part of the narrative, as the pilgrim community began to disperse in pursuit of economic self-interest, the providential plot breaks down, and the story fractures into a seemingly random series of chronological annals underwritten by an elegiac tone of melancholy and loss.

Novel History: The Captivity of Mary Rowlandson

The providential plot is in fact closest to both the novel and history—and most interesting—when it begins to break down. This is particularly evident in *Narrative of the Captivity and Restoration of Mrs. Mary Rowlandson* (1682), which is split between its public doctrinal emphasis on God's providence at a time of increasing uncertainty about the Puritan "errand" and its more personal, individualized, novel, and affecting account of a woman who by sheer instinct, wit, and will to live survived three months of captivity among the Wampanoag and Narragansett Indians during King Philip's War in 1675. Initially advertised on the last page of the first American edition of John Bunyan's *The Pilgrim's Progress* (1678), Rowlandson's narrative (told as a series of "removes") was published at a time when the conventions of literary allegory, Christian typology, and the providential plot were beginning to give way to the historical particularity, individuation, novelty, and adventure—the sensation plus morality—that would mark such eighteenth-century English novels as Defoe's *Robinson Crusoe* and Samuel Richardson's *Pamela; or, Virtue Rewarded* (1740).

While it is commonly assumed that the American novel began in England, Rowlandson's story of survival in the New World "wilderness" and the implicit threat of rape that underwrites her story of being enslaved and held captive by "a company of barbarous Heathen" (13th rmv.), "sleeping all sorts together" (20th rmv.), suggest the New World's influence on seventeenth-century English fiction.

As its full title suggests, *The Sovereignty & Goodness of GOD, Together with the Faithfulness of His Promises Displayed; Being a Narrative of the Captivity and Restauration of Mrs. Mary Rowlandson. Commended by Her, to All that Desires to Know the Lord's Doings To, and Dealings with Her* was intended to explain the "afflictions" of King Philip's War as God's punishment of his chosen people for their backsliding and a call to renewed faith in God's absolute power and justice. As such, Rowlandson's narrative has been interpreted by Sacvan Bercovitch and others as a classic American jeremiad, a typological tale of captivity and deliverance in which Rowlandson as an exemplar of individual piety (like Job, Daniel, or David) and communal faith (like that of Israel) affirms God's "wonderful Power in carrying us along, preserving us in the Wilderness" (8th rmv.).

But even the anonymous "Preface to the READER," signed in Latin PER AMICUM ("by a friend"), and likely written by Increase Mather, evinces a cultural dissonance that pulls away from Puritan typology toward a more novelistic focus, sensibility, and appeal. Like the title page, which reads, *Written by her own hand for her private use, and now made publick at the earnest desire of some friends, and for the benefit of the afflicted*, the preface seeks to increase the appeal of the narrative by emphasizing its essentially private nature. Rowlandson's piety deserves "commendation and imitation," and some friends were "so much affected by the many passages of working providence" that they deemed it "worthy of publick View" by "present and future Generations" (pref.).

But while this friend frames Rowlandson's story Biblically and typologically, its subject, a "Hand maid" and woman "Servant" of God, is new and potentially subversive. Published only a few years before women and servants would become the perpetrators and primary subjects of the Salem witch trials, Rowlandson's story marks an historical and cultural turning point when writers male and female began to focus with increased interest and fascination on the bodies, sentiments, and interiorities of women as exemplars of the values of the home, family, marriage, motherhood, children, and even the health of society and the state. As the first and most powerful of these stories, Rowlandson's *Narrative* opens the drama of female affliction and possible subversion that would be played and replayed in the American novel, from Eliza Wharton and Charlotte Temple in the early period, to Sedgwick's Hope Leslie and Hawthorne's Hester Prynne in the antebellum years, to Kate Chopin's Edna Pontellier and Theodore Dreiser's Carrie Meeber at the turn of the twentieth century.

In emphasizing the particularity and emotional power of Rowlandson's narrative, the preface also defines the aesthetics of imaginative identification, sentimental affect, and sympathy that would become the foundation of the sentimental and domestic novel in England and America. It is "not the general but particular knowledge of things [that] makes deepest impression upon the affections," Amicum avers. Since "none can imagine what it is to be captivated, and enslaved to such . . . diabolical creatures," by producing a "[n]arrative particularizing the several passages of [God's] providence" in her personal experience of "difficulties, hardships, hazards, sorrows, anxieties, and perplexities," Rowlandson augments its "heart-affecting" power "to enlarge pious hearts in the praises of God" (pref.).

Anticipating Adam Smith's theory of imaginative identification and sympathy with "the misery of others, when we either see it, or are made to conceive it in a very lively manner" (1984, 9), Amicum invites readers to experience "the Sovereignty of God" through sympathetic identification with Rowlandson's affliction and deliverance: "Read, therefore, Peruse, Ponder, and from hence lay up something from the experience of another, against thine own turn comes." But the very popularity of the tale, so popular that not a single copy of the first edition survived, suggests that what readers may have found in Rowlandson's "experience" was not "an instance of the faith and patience of the Saints, under the most heart-sinking tryals" (pref.), but the story of a more psychologically fractured and experientially dissonant female subject whose individual agency, bodily instincts, and will to survive continually contest and subvert God's sovereignty, Puritan patriarchy, providential history, and British imperial design in the New World.

From the outset of her story, when she "chose rather to go along with those . . . ravenous Beasts, than that moment to end my days," Rowlandson reveals an instinct for survival in the wilderness that locates her at the origins of both the American western genre and the island fantasy of Defoe's *Robinson Crusoe*. While Rowlandson represents her physical captivity as a type of spiritual captivity, Biblical allegory and the providential plot are undermined by the sheer force of physical desire—especially hunger—that drives the narrative. The power of this hunger in trumping genteel Puritan womanhood, God's providence, and the Bible is most memorably exhibited when Rowlandson snatches a piece of boiled horse's foot from a captive English child's mouth and engorges herself: "and savory it was to my taste," she remembers, citing Job as a precedent. "Thus the Lord made that pleasant refreshing, which another time would have been an abomination," she writes, with absolutely no reference—even in retrospect—to the "abomination" of stealing food from a child (18th rmv.).

Here as elsewhere in her narrative, the most palpable sustenance Rowlandson receives is not from God but from the Natives, especially Native women, with whom and through whom she learns to negotiate social and affective exchange across (and despite) cultural difference. Recollecting the pangs of starvation she shared with the Natives—"after I was thoroughly hungry, I was never again satisfied" (15th rmv.)—Rowlandson seems less an exemplar of "the sovereignty and goodness of God" and more an embodiment of the terrors of survival suffered by Native tribes at the hands of both the Puritan colonists and the British Empire. As early as the fourth remove, the savage/civilized binary breaks down as Rowlandson begins to identify herself not against but with "our poor Indian cheer." By the close of her narrative, after the Native council consents to let her return home, she stops to record "a few remarkable passages of providence, which I took special notice of in my afflicted time." In these passages, Rowlandson, like her narrative, falls from providential into worldly time, raging first against "the slowness, and dullness of the English army" and then against "the strange providence of God" who appears to identify with the "heathens" against the English (20th rmv.).

When Rowlandson writes of going home—"So I took my leave of them, and in coming along my heart melted into tears"—it is not clear whether she weeps *inside* or *outside* the providential plot, out of sorrow or joy that she has left her captors. In fact, it is not completely clear who her captors are: "I was not before so much hemmed in with the merciless and cruel heathen, but now as much with pitiful, tender-hearted and compassionate Christians." While "others are sleeping," Rowlandson's "eyes are weeping": she seems less a regenerate soul than a melancholic victim of the "night season," who cannot bring herself to say, "as David did, 'It is good for me that I have been afflicted'" (20th rmv.).

Published in four editions in 1682 alone, Rowlandson's narrative became early America's first bestseller, and its popularity continued into the early nineteenth century. It is the first American prose narrative published by a woman, and it is one of the best works in a new genre, the captivity narrative, which dominated eighteenth-century American popular culture from the account of Hannah Duston in Cotton Mather's *Magnalia Christi Americana; or, The Ecclesiastical History of*

New England (1702) to Ann Eliza Bleecker's *The History of Maria Kittle* (1797). Brockden Brown was the first to make novelistic use of the Indian captivity narrative as a form of Native American gothic in *Edgar Huntly*. From Huntly's descent into the "savage" in self and world amid Indian warfare and imperial rivalries in Ireland, India, and the American "wilderness," to Cooper's *The Last of the Mohicans*, which imagines the eventual triumph of the Americans as Native tribes yield to

A

NARRATIVE

OF THE

CAPTIVITY, SUFFERINGS AND REMOVES

OF

Mrs. *Mary Rowlandſon*,

Who was taken Priſoner by the INDIANS with ſeveral others, and treated in the moſt barbarous and cruel Manner by thoſe vile Savages: With many other remarkable Events during her TRAVELS.

Written by her own Hand, for her private Uſe, and now made public at the earneſt Deſire of ſome Friends, and for the Benefit of the afflicted.

BOSTON:

Printed and Sold at JOHN BOYLE's Printing-Office, next Door to the *Three Doves* in Marlborough Street. 1773

1773

Fig 1.2 Engraving on the title page of an edition of Mary Rowlandson's *Narrative* published in Boston in 1773.

inevitable defeat in the wake of the French and Indian War, to Melville's *Typee: A Peep at Polynesian Life* (1846), a semi-autobiographical novel and scathing critique of American and European imperial presence in the South Pacific, the captivity narrative would continue as a popular and flexible novelistic genre through which American writers explored the unknown and the "savage," both within human nature and an increasingly terroristic world.

Rowlandson's *Narrative* also anticipates later American novels in placing a white woman at the center of a sensational, gothic adventure story that plays out the culture's simultaneous terror of and fascination with racial encounter, captivity, rape, violence, race mixing, and cultural crossing. This more secular significance is evident in the edition of Rowlandson's *Narrative* reprinted immediately following the Boston Massacre in 1770. Published under the title *A Narrative of the Captivity, Sufferings, and Removes of Mrs. Mary Rowlandson* at a time of rising tensions between the American colonists and the British Empire, as Greg Sieminski argues, Rowlandson's captivity narrative was read as a story about American innocence and freedom held captive by treacherous British savages. In a woodcut that appears on the title page of the 1773 edition of the *Narrative*, Rowlandson points a musket at four British-looking savages who threaten to invade her home (figure 1.2). No longer the antitype of the saintly patience of David, Rowlandson looks more like a prototype of Daniel Boone, Natty Bumppo, or Annie Oakley. As instanced by John Filson's "The Adventures of Col. Daniel Boon" (1784), the meaning of the American wilderness had been secularized and transformed by the late eighteenth century. No longer a spiritual signifier of sin, corruption, and the temptations of the devil, the wilderness and its inhabitants became part of a broader cultural landscape, a mythic off-space where individuals discovered and tested their virtue and essence as Americans and, as in John Neal's *Logan: A Family History* (1822), white men.

Literary Hybrids and the Transatlantic Imaginary

In the eighteenth century, Bunyan's ur-story of the good Christian life in his 1678 allegory *Pilgrim's Progress* was individualized and secularized in life-writings that included captivity narratives, conversion stories, adventure stories, travel writings, journals, memoirs, biographies, and slave narratives. Criminal confessions, execution sermons, and other forms of religious writing focused increasingly on spectacular accounts of seduction, rape, infanticide, and murder, such as the story of the celebrity killer, Hannah Duston, whose tale of escape from captivity by killing and scalping ten of her Indian captors was rescripted by Cotton Mather within the providential frame of *Magnalia Christi Americana*.

In one of the earliest criminal conversion narratives, Esther Rodgers, a white woman servant, tells of her fall into "Carnal Pollution with the *Negro* man belonging to that House" and her secret murder of two babies born of this union (1701, 124). Appended to three sermons by the minister John Rogers (no relation) and written after she had been condemned to execution for infanticide, "The Declaration and Confession of Esther Rodgers" (1701) focuses on her internal struggle with lust and sin and her final miraculous conversion as an instance of God's free grace. This taste for sensational stories of sin and crime, anchored in "true" history, and framed by didactic and moralistic sermons, would structure early American novels such as William Hill Brown's *The Power of Sympathy* (1789), where the initial crime of incest is contained and framed by a surplice of sermonizing letters that stand in for the minister.

The secular and urban counterpart of *Pilgrim's Progress* and early forms of religious life-writing is Benjamin Franklin's story of his arrival and survival in the sink or swim world of eighteenth-century Philadelphia, where capital ruled, identities were fragile, and appearance seemed all. As an urban version of the wilderness myth and new beginnings, this story became a mainstay of the American novel from Brockden Brown's *Arthur Mervyn; or, Memoirs of the Year 1793* (1799–1800) to Walt Whitman's *Franklin Evans; or, The Inebriate* (1842) to James Leo Herlihy's *Midnight Cowboy* (1965). Although usually treated and indeed drawn on by biographers and historians as a "true" story of his life, Franklin's narrative reveals a shrewd social and novelistic intelligence that is arguably more complex, realistic, and "fictive" in the development of character, dialogue, and action than *The Power of Sympathy*, commonly regarded as the first American novel. If the eighteenth-century epistolary novel originated from private letters turned outward toward the world, as Jürgen Habermas has argued, then Franklin's "recollection," which began in 1771 as a "private" letter to his illegitimate son, William Franklin, might be a candidate for the first American novel. Against the Poor Richard caricature of Franklin, it is important to recognize that his narrative, like his narrator, is split between the early Benjamin, who embodies the homespun American republican values of virtue, industry, and frugality, and the later cosmopolitan Franklin, who sported a coon-skin cap and winked, as he was wined, dined, and toasted by kings, philosophers, and aristocratic French women.

Although usually read as a unified and quintessentially American work called *The Autobiography*, this title—added in 1868—has tended to shift attention away from the different historical and national contexts in which it was written: in England in 1771, in France in 1784, and in Philadelphia between 1788 and 1790. These different frames split the narrative from itself, giving it a discontinuous and disjunctive quality that refuses to cohere around any single self, history, or nation. Ironically, the best-selling life of America's most popular hero was written primarily in Europe rather than America; and it was first published in French in Paris in 1791. Until well into the nineteenth century, later editions of Franklin's life continued to be retranslations from French into English or retranslations into French of the English retranslation.

While we have come in recent years to recognize the circuits of literary exchange between America and England, the exchanges between America and France are less well known. And yet, it was a Frenchman, a naturalized British subject, and an immigrant farmer in New York, Michel-Guillaume Jean de Crèvecoeur, who first mythologized the American land as the source of a distinct New World identity in *Letters from an American Farmer*, which was published in England under his new English-sounding name, J. Hector St. John, in 1782. "What, then, is the American, this new man?" the American farmer asked: "Here individuals of all nations are melted into a new race of men, whose labours and posterity will one day cause great changes in the world. Americans are the western pilgrims who are carrying along with them that great mass of arts, sciences, vigour, and industry which began long since in the East: they will finish the great circle" (ltr. 3).

But who speaks in this letter that has been widely anthologized as the origin of a distinctly American voice, identity, and vision? And to whom is it addressed? The author of *Letters*, like its subject, straddles three different and potentially conflicting national identities: the enlightened Frenchman (Crèvecoeur); the naturalized British subject (Hector St. John); and the American persona Farmer James, the Pennsylvania farmer who, as the title page indicates, addresses a series of letters about the "interior circumstances of the British Colonies in North America" to "a friend in England." Critics have tended to collapse the multiple and transnational authorship and fictive construction of *Letters*—widely regarded in eighteenth-century Europe as the best source of information on America—into a nonfiction account of conditions in America, told from the viewpoint of Crèvecoeur, who speaks through the voice of Farmer James as a thinly disguised mask for himself. While recent critics have argued that James is "the protagonist of an emerging literary form wholly compatible with the fledgling nation . . . the novel" (Rice 1993, 105), *Letters from an American Farmer* might best be understood as a hybrid that skirts the fluid boundary between fact and fiction, floating between rather than being contained within any single nationality.

These classics of American national and literary self-definition were shaped by the French and, specifically, *philosophe* imaginary at the same time that they contributed to the grammar of equality, justice, and popular retribution that fueled the French and Haitian Revolutions. Narrated by unreliable narrators, who break down under the pressure of the contradiction between dream and reality—especially the contradictions of African slavery and genocidal violence against Native peoples—their fractured narratives reveal the nightmare of darkness, blood violence, and apocalypse that would continue to haunt the American story. Inhabiting the unstable ground between novel and history, the myth of the Garden and the American gothic, Crèvecoeur's *Letters* (like Thomas Jefferson's *Notes on the State of Virginia* [1784]) also probed the relation between social contradiction, violence, and psychic breakdown. Thus, they prepared readers for the madness and other forms of psychic distress and trauma that would continue at the center of the American novel from Brockden Brown and Foster in the Revolutionary years to Poe's homicidal narrators, Hawthorne's monomaniacs, and Melville's Captain Ahab, Pierre, and the confidence man.

The Creole Atlantic and the Origins of the American Novel

Skirting the boundaries between identities and genres, *The Interesting Narrative of the Life of Olaudah Equiano, or Gustavus Vassa, the African* (1789) is also a transatlantic narrative that straddles three continents (Africa, Europe, and the Americas). Although canonized as a prototype of the African American slave narrative, foundational to the African and African American literary tradition, and among African scholars, as the earliest historical account of Igbo identity and values, it does not fit easily into any single genre or national tradition, or into any simple distinction between history, autobiography, and novel. Rather, like the ship that is the primal scene of Equiano's enslavement, liberation, and movement across the spaces of Africa, Britain, the Caribbean, the Americas, Europe, Turkey, and the North Pole, Equiano's intermixed, fractal, and ultimately Creole Atlantic narrative defies many of the field boundaries and terms that have come to define the history and prehistory of the novel, American, British, or otherwise.

Shaped by multiple genres—including the pastoral romance, captivity narrative, slave narrative, travel narrative, spiritual autobiography, adventure story, and story of "wonder" or the "exotic"—and drawing on the conventions of the sentimental, gothic, and picaresque novel, Equiano's *Interesting Narrative*, which was published the same year as *The Power of Sympathy*, is arguably one of the most historically illuminating, novelistically complex, psychologically fascinating, and politically powerful prose narratives published in the eighteenth century. While it has not usually been identified as a novel, or as a precursor of the American novel, the national origin and identity of its author and the "truth" of his story have been contested from its first publication. On April 25, 1792, *The Oracle* claimed "that *Gustavus Vasa* [*sic*], who has publicly asserted that he was kidnapped in Africa, never was upon that Continent, but was born and bred up in the Danish Island of Santa Cruz, in the West Indies" (qtd. in Equiano 2003, 237). More recently, Vincent Carretta has found evidence suggesting that Vassa was born in South Carolina and thus "may have invented rather than reclaimed an African identity" (2005, xiv).

At a time when blacks were legally forbidden to testify against whites throughout the British Empire, the multiple voices and multigeneric forms of Equiano's narrative may have been precisely the right narrative strategy for reaching multiple readers on a range of levels. The narrative is split between the older, wiser, and more critical voice of Gustavus Vassa, who sees himself as "a *particular favourite of Heaven*" (ch. 1), a black Moses leading his "countrymen" from captivity to freedom, and the voice of the younger, credulous boy of feeling, Olaudah Equiano, whose affecting story of being torn away from his Eboe family and community seeks to inspire sympathetic identification in the reader. But the narrative is also authored by "*the African*," a diasporic figure with whom Equiano came to identify only *after* he left Africa, and this figure does not necessarily align with either Vassa, the name the author assumed in real life, or Equiano, a name Vassa used only in his book. Moreover, while the story is told from the first-person point of view of Equiano, Vassa, and the African—or some combination of the three—it is narrated with the imaginative and symbolic resonance and detail of a more sophisticated "author." This confusion and profusion of voices allows for a complexly masked and canny narration with multiple levels of picaresque irony and satire elicited not only by the terrified and wonder-struck boy, Equiano, or the seemingly knowing and now "civilized" Vassa, but also, and most forcefully, by an entire Atlantic world enriching itself on the sale, enslavement, and oppression of human beings who happen to have black complexions.

On the day the eleven-year-old Equiano and his sister were kidnapped, the author writes:

> [T]wo men and a woman got over our walls, and in a moment seized us both; and, without giving us time to cry out, or make resistance, they stopped our mouths . . . and then they put me into a sack. . . . The next day proved a day of greater sorrow than I had yet experienced; for my sister and I were then separated, while we lay clasped in each other's arms. . . . I was left in a state of distraction not to be described. I cried and grieved continually. (ch. 2)

In simple sentences uttered from the aggrieved perspective of a black child, the terror and inhumanity of slavery are both narrated and critiqued: slavery originates in an act of kidnap, theft, and piracy; it stops the mouths of black people as a means of silencing their cries and foiling their resistance to being put "into a sack" and transformed into cargo; it violates the most sacred bonds of family and community; it inflicts physical and psychic wounds and sorrow beyond description; and it underlines the importance of the unstopped mouth, the black subject, who thinks, speaks, writes, and creates *back* as a means of resisting the black person's material and symbolic status as "cargo," slave, and other in the white imperial imaginary.

Equiano's youthful inexperience is the source of sympathetic *affect*, sly irony, and satiric critique. Against eighteenth-century representations of Africa as a dark continent of heathens and cannibals, his imaginative reconstruction of Eboeland appears to mirror Jefferson's ideal American republic of virtuous and hard-working farmers, and the New World resembles a New Hell of commerce in human flesh. This reversal of Western and "enlightened" codes of white and black, civilized and savage crystallizes in Equiano's first terror-struck vision of the slave ship, where "white men with horrible looks, red faces, and long hair" appear to be cannibals preparing to eat him: "I was now persuaded that I had gotten into a world of bad spirits, and that they were going to kill me. Their complexions too differing so much from ours, their long hair, and the language they spoke, which was very different from any I had ever heard, united to confirm me in this belief" (ch. 2). Here, as elsewhere, Equiano reverses the gaze, representing the "horror and anguish" of the transatlantic slave trade from the point of view of its terrified black victims.

But Vassa's narrative not only relates the horrors of slavery: as the author notes on the first page, it is also a "memoir," a "history of neither a saint, a hero, nor a tyrant" (ch. 1), but a poor black man, who rose from being "one who was ignorant, a stranger, of a different complexion, and a slave!" (ch. 3) to being one of the most "[i]nteresting," well-known, and successful black men of his time. After his first master imposes the seemingly ironic but in fact providential name of "*Gustavus Vasa*," the Swedish liberator of his people (ch. 3), Equiano expresses his alienation from white regimes of literacy and knowledge through the culturally resonant figure of a book that speaks only to his white masters but not to him. Borrowed from James Albert Ukawsaw Gronniosaw and other black Atlantic writers, and theorized by Henry Louis Gates as "the trope of the talking book" through which Africans symbolize their marginalization from Western culture (1988, 127–69), the trope also suggests the movement from oral to written culture (and back again) that was crucial to the history of the novel. On another occasion, Equiano suggests the brute and colonizing power of skin color, as he tries "oftentimes" by washing his face to make it the same rosy color as his white playmate, Mary: "but it was all in vain," he laments, "and I now began to be mortified at the difference in our complexions" (ch. 3).

"[M]y surprise began to diminish, as my knowledge increased" (ch. 3), Equiano observes, but after three or four years "at sea," where he is in effect acculturated to European ways by participating in several bloody sea fights between the English and the French during the Seven Years' War, the knowledge he gains—and the reliability of Equiano and Vassa as narrator(s)—is open to question. "From the various scenes I had beheld on ship-board," Equiano notes, "I soon grew a stranger to terror of every kind, and was, in that respect at least, almost an Englishman" (ch. 4). This passage, like the entire narrative, is multivoiced: it might be read simply from the point of view of the African boy, who has overcome his terror "at the first sight of Europeans" in his journey from ignorance to knowledge; from the perspective of Vassa, who congratulates himself on now being "almost an Englishman"; or from the more nuanced reverse gaze of the author, who slyly rewrites Englishness as an insensibility "to terror of every kind," including the terrors of the slave trade and slavery that underwrite both Englishness and Equiano's story.

"I now not only felt myself quite easy with these new countrymen, but," Equiano continues, "relished their society and manners. I no longer looked upon them as spirits, but as men superior to us; and therefore I had the stronger desire to resemble them; to imbibe their spirit, and imitate their manners" (ch. 4). The passage anticipates Frantz Fanon's reflection on the colonizing power of whiteness in *Black Skin, White Masks* (1952), but here the distinction between the voices of Equiano and Vassa and the potential irony are more ambiguous. The frontispiece engraving of Vassa reveals a thoroughly acculturated English gentleman in everything but skin color (figure 1.3). But is this acculturation or mask, imitation or repetition with a difference? This problem of interpretation continues throughout: it is part of the complexity of the narration and a potentially radical critique that extends beyond

Fig 1.3 Frontispiece painted by the miniaturist William Denton, depicting Olaudah Equiano dressed as an English gentleman and reversing the gaze as he hands a Bible opened to a passage from Acts 12:4 on salvation by Christ to his readers.

Fig 1.4 Frontispiece engraving of *Bahama Banks* shipwreck in volume two of the first edition of *The Interesting Narrative*. Vassa described himself as "chieftain" and "principal instrument in effecting our deliverance" in this 1767 shipwreck.

the immediate political cause of ending the slave trade and slavery to an attack on Western hypocrisy, sin, and degeneration and a prophecy of final apocalypse signified by the engraving of the *Bahama Banks* shipwreck on the frontispiece of the second volume (figure 1.4). This specter of apocalypse underwrites the formal organization of the narrative's second part around a series of shipwrecks featuring Equiano as an antitype of Job, indeed "the principal instrument in effecting our deliverance" (ch. 8).

By the end of *The Interesting Narrative*, Equiano, the African, has proven himself—and by implication his African "countrymen"—to be a better laborer, soldier, Christian, captain, parson, Englishman, gentleman, reader, and human being than whites. An ironic frontispiece suggests this by showing him dressed as an English gentleman and handing a Bible opened to a passage on salvation through the Gospel of Jesus Christ to his mostly white—and possibly damned—readers (figure 1.3). But when at the close of his narrative Equiano proposes an economic alternative to African slavery by offering the "[p]opulation, the bowels and surface of Africa" as "an endless field of commerce to the British manufacturers and merchant adventurers" (ch. 12), has he also become a better capitalist and imperialist than his white oppressors? We do not know. Like the multiple voices, masks, symbols, and genres through which the author, or Equiano, or Vassa, or the African, or some combination of these narrates his story, the *Interesting Narrative* raises questions about the definition and boundaries of identity, nation, novel, history, and genre that underwrite the prehistory and history of the American novel.

As this chapter has sought to elucidate, Native and early American writings reveal a slippage between myth and history, between storytelling and truth, that destabilizes any clear line of development from early nonfictional writings such as Cusick's "Tale" of American origins, Smith's *History*, or Rowlandson's *Narrative*, to hybrid and quasi-fictional narratives such as Crèvecoeur's *Letters*, to the publication of *The Power of Sympathy* in 1789 as the "first" American novel. The course of the American novel was far more circuitous, intermixed, and transnational. Captivity narratives, adventure stories, westerns, and mysteries shaped early American histories before they developed into distinct genres of the American novel; and histories created the fundamental myths, symbols, and images that would structure the American novel. The most influential definition of the "American" as a distinctive New World identity was written by a Frenchman, and the most complex and novelistic portrayals of American character, psychology, locale, and speech appeared in works such as Crèvecoeur's *Letters* and Franklin's *Autobiography,* which refuse any easy definition as history, fiction, or novel.

What this chapter suggests finally is that the field boundaries and terms that have come to define the history of the American novel are less settled and more unsettling than they seemed to an earlier generation of scholars who pioneered in defining American literature as a distinctively national field of study. If, as some scholars have argued, the publication of Rowlandson's American captivity narrative marked an epoch in the emergence of the modern British novel, then the American novel may have begun in 1789, not with *The Power of Sympathy* in Boston, but in London with Equiano's Creole Atlantic narrative about the interesting life of a former slave, born in Africa or South Carolina, an origin that (re)locates the American novel within a transatlantic commerce of culture, capital, and African slaves.

2

THE SENTIMENTAL NOVEL AND THE SEDUCTIONS OF POSTCOLONIAL IMITATION

KAREN A. WEYLER

Long before novels were written *by* Americans, novels were being written *about* Americans and the Americas. It's clear that the prospects entailed by the New World—the dangers of the transatlantic voyage; the disruption of the family, traditions, and authority that such a voyage necessitated; the Native inhabitants of the New World; and the potential economic opportunity offered by new lands—captured the imagination of Europeans. Such textual preoccupations prompted critic William Spengemann to argue in *A New World of Words* that it is neither the national identity of the author nor the place of publication that identifies a work as American but rather the language of a text and its concerns. While this provocative definition is probably broader than most scholars would accept, it helpfully accentuates the crucial influence of "American" novels well before colonists would have identified themselves as such. The earliest novels authored by self-described Americans represent not a break from this tradition but an adaptation, as they draw upon the cultural traditions, philosophy, and stylistic and aesthetic features of European fiction (especially of Britain) and meld them with New World settings and social and economic dilemmas. Courtship in particular provided a fertile field for the sentimental novel to explore how American social structures developed. While new social and economic opportunities were opening to young men, American women continued to be largely dependent on parents or marriage to secure their social status; this dependence and the unequal power relationships that accompanied it help explain the sentimental novel's fascination with family, courtship, seduction, and marriage.

Particularly influential in the formation of American-themed fiction were English novelists Aphra Behn's *Oroonoko* (1688) and Daniel Defoe's *Robinson Crusoe* (1719). *Robinson Crusoe* in turn inspired dozens of imitators, the so-called Robinsonades; one of the most notable such novels is *The Female American* (1767), which has a decidedly colonial British flavor and models the alchemy that would produce fiction we can more definitively label as American. Interweaving a revisionary history of the Virginia colony with the family history of the narrative's pseudonymous author and heroine, Unca Eliza Winkfield, *The Female American* invokes many of the thematic elements of *Robinson Crusoe*, including the isolated setting on an island, the Christianity of the castaway, and the colonizing relationship of the castaway to native peoples. But unlike the very English Crusoe, the intrepid heroine of *The Female American* blends the faith of her English father with the language and survival skills of her Native American mother—along with the wealth of the Americas. Unca is truly the heiress of the New World; this wealth prompts her stranding on a deserted island when she refuses to marry the son of the ship's captain on a transatlantic voyage. Aided by the diary of a hermit who inhabited the island for decades prior to her arrival, Unca learns to survive on her own and puts an end to the pagan worship of nearby native peoples, converting them to Christianity by using the relics of the earlier pagan practices. Published in the wake of the French and Indian War, this new imperial fantasy is a peaceable one, facilitated by Unca's linguistic skills and the receptivity of the native peoples to Christianity; there's none of the violence that complicated the earlier colonization of Virginia by Unca's father and grandfather. Although the novel was first published in London, followed by American reprints in 1800 and 1814, the pseudonymous author's name, Unca Eliza Winkfield, underlines the author's familiarity with the history of colonial Virginia, rewriting that history, however, to make her the granddaughter of the colony's first leader, Edward Maria Wingfield, who actually died without descendents. This familiarity makes it entirely possible that a British colonial authored *The Female American*, which predates by more than two decades any novel printed in the United States that we can authoritatively identify as written by a US writer.

European novels such as the Crusoe-inspired fiction were important not only for early depictions of the Americas but also for how they shaped the taste of colonial readers. It's important to acknowledge the extent to which British taste influenced the market for novel reading in the decades before and after the Revolution. Throughout the eighteenth century, most of the novels Americans read had been written and printed in Britain and then imported for sale in the colonies by booksellers. Although there were differences, the same novels that were popular in Britain tended to be popular in the English colonies. Among the most popular works in Anglo-America were Daniel Defoe's aforementioned *Robinson Crusoe* and the novels of Samuel Richardson, particularly *Pamela; or, Virtue Rewarded* (1740) and *Clarissa; or, The History of a Young Lady* (1748), as well as *The History of Sir Charles Grandison* (1753) to a lesser degree. Also popular were Oliver Goldsmith's *The Vicar of Wakefield* (1766), Laurence Sterne's *Sentimental Journey* (1768), and Henry Fielding's *Joseph Andrews* (1742) and *Tom Jones* (1749), although Fielding's novels seem to have exercised relatively less influence on American novelists than some of these other books. Most of these works grew in popularity over a period of decades after their initial publication. By contrast, German writer Johann Wolfgang von Goethe's *The Sorrows of Young Werther* (1774) quickly became popular and influential among both readers and writers.

Although American booksellers imported, usually from London or Dublin, the vast majority of novels read in eighteenth-century Anglo-America, American printers began issuing their own editions of popular British works in 1742 with Benjamin Franklin's edition of *Pamela*, which took him two years to complete. Franklin's *Pamela* was only the beginning. In *The Popular Book*, James D. Hart notes that there were at least fifty-six reprints of foreign fiction between 1744 and 1789, with an untold number of imported editions. Printers increased in number and sophistication as the century progressed, with "local publishers alone turn[ing] out over 350 different foreign novels and 37 American ones, several in many editions" between 1789 and 1800 (1950, 52). *Robinson Crusoe,* for example, appeared in forty editions between 1757 and 1800; at least four of those editions were in German, suggesting that even non-English speakers living in early America had succumbed to the lure of the novel.

The American editions of these European novels often differed substantially from the versions that circulated most widely in their countries of origin. Because of the high costs of printing and the tastes of American readers, many texts were produced in heavily abridged editions, which helped make novels affordable and accessible to individuals with limited literacy skills. For example, virtually all the American editions of *Robinson Crusoe* that appeared in the eighteenth century were abridged. About a third of them contained fewer than thirty pages, with several editions coming in at sixteen pages; another popular abridged version of *Robinson Crusoe* was 138 pages. As Leonard Tennenhouse has demonstrated, these abridged editions resulted in quite different texts. In surveying the various editions of *Pamela* and *Clarissa*, which surged in popularity after the Revolution, Tennenhouse points out that the editions of *Pamela* that circulated in England contained about 250,000 words, while *Clarissa* ran about one million words. "In striking contrast," he explains, "the *Pamela* that appeared in Philadelphia in 1792 totaled only about 27,000 words in length, and the *Clarissa* that appeared in 1795 ran to somewhere around just 41,000 words, or about the same length as Susanna Rowson's *Charlotte Temple* (1791). Furthermore, every edition of Richardson published in the United States from the late 1780s through the first two decades of the nineteenth century observed pretty much the same model of abridgement" (2007, 54–55). The net effect of these abridgements of *Pamela* and *Clarissa*, Tennenhouse concludes, shifts the emphasis from their production of writing and interiority to the plots surrounding their heroines' physical bodies. In that sense, it is possible to see continuity between the British texts that were popular with American readers and the seduction novels produced by Americans at the turn of the nineteenth century, which place tremendous emphasis on the risks of sexuality to the bodies and minds of their heroines.

Why, if Anglo-American readers were so fond of novels, whether imported from Europe or printed in abridged form in the colonies, was there a delay of several decades before US printers began printing novels written by people who identified themselves as Americans? The answer to this question is complex. As many critics have argued, reading British books helped maintain a continuing sense of cultural affiliation between colonials and Great Britain. But the delay in the production of novels by American authors also reflects the ways in which the technological and cultural situation of the colonies differed from Britain, particularly London. Printing in early America was very much locally or regionally based; even in the decades after the Revolution, there were no national publishers or book distribution networks. Books cost a great deal to produce; most one- or two-volume novels cost around a dollar, and multivolume novels cost more. Fine paper products and printing types had to be imported from Great Britain or Europe. The typesetting necessary to produce any kind of book—especially novels, which usually ran to two or more volumes—required skilled typesetters and was laborious and time consuming. Many printers made their money either through printing small jobs, such as broadsides, the most simple of which required only basic typesetting skills, or government contracts; they simply could not afford to tie up their presses by printing lengthy novels whose sales were not guaranteed. The significant capital necessary for book-printing projects also explains why subscription publishing flourished in the early United States long after it had faded from popularity in England. Many early novels were printed by subscription, among them Judith Sargent Murray's *Story of Margaretta*, which appeared embedded in her compendium *The Gleaner* (1798); Sally Sayward Barrell Keating Wood's *Dorval; or the Speculator* (1801); and Sukey Vickery's *Emily Hamilton* (1803).

Even after a novel had been successfully printed, the relatively low population density of the colonies limited local sales. Printers were often booksellers as well, and to expand their sales opportunities, printers arranged exchanges with or sales to other booksellers, whether in the same town or the region. Transporting books to other areas was difficult and costly. While it was relatively easy to arrange for the transportation of books along the Atlantic coastline via packet ships, getting books to the interior of colonies or the backcountry presented significant challenges. Printers and booksellers found it easier and more economical to import novels with strong sales from London, Dublin, Edinburgh, and the continent than to tie up labor and capital in the work of an unproven author.

Stand-alone books were not the only source of novels for American readers, however; sentimental fiction of all kinds—short stories, sketches, novellas, and even full-length novels—provided much of the content of literary magazines, particularly in the post-Revolutionary era, and there was considerable overlap between periodical and book publication. Indeed, one of the more popular seduction stories of the day, *Amelia; or, The Faithless Briton*, first appeared in the *Columbian Magazine* in 1787. Closer to a novella than a full-length novel, it was serialized in at least five other periodicals serving the regional markets of Philadelphia, New York, and Boston between 1789 and 1810. This story of Amelia Blyfield, a virtuous American girl tricked into a sham marriage by Doliscus, a wounded British soldier whom the Blyfield family had taken into their home to nurse back to health, clearly spoke to patriotic sympathies; like most subsequent American seduction stories, it results in an illegitimate pregnancy and the utter destruction of both families. After printers had ample time to assess the work's popularity with readers, *Amelia; or, The Faithless Briton* was also included in three anthologies of poetry and fiction in 1798.

By the 1780s, however, incipient American nationalism, as well as desire on the part of authors and readers to capture American experience via fiction, led to the production of book-length native works. These early novels represent not so much a break with the dominant themes and narrative modes of European fiction as an adaptation; certainly the kinds of American books that authors produced and readers embraced were shaped by their previous reading experiences, not only of European novels but also of poetry, history, biographies, sermons, devotionals, conduct literature, and steady sellers such as almanacs, schoolbooks, home medical manuals, and the Bible. The influence of these other kinds of reading is readily apparent in the strong Protestant orientation of many American novels emphasizing self-examination of conduct, as well as a republican emphasis on the importance of educating citizens of the new nation. This variety of reading material exerted a shaping influence on William Hill Brown's *The Power of Sympathy* (1789), the work most widely recognized as the first American novel—that is, the first novel that was published in the United States by a person who claimed American identity and that was marketed as such by its shrewd and prolific publisher, the Massachusetts-based Isaiah Thomas. The characters of *The Power of Sympathy* quote poetry to one another, engage in extended discussions of the merits of reading fiction, and agree that a broad-based education will best prepare women to safeguard their own interests.

Although not all early American fiction is sentimental, *The Power of Sympathy* powerfully influenced the stylistic and thematic concerns of subsequent sentimental and seduction fiction through its four interpolated stories of seduction. The novel announces its intent on the dedication page of the first edition, which reads: "To the Young Ladies of United Columbia, These Volumes, Intended to represent the specious Causes, and to Expose the fatal Consequences, of Seduction; To inspire the Female Mind with a Principle of Self Complacency, and to Promote the Economy of Human Life, are inscribed with Esteem and Sincerity, by their Friend and Humble Servant, The Author." Lest readers overlook this dedication, the preface reminds them that in this novel "the dangerous Consequences of Seduction are exposed, and the Advantages of Female Education [are] set forth and recommended." To fulfill these goals, the novel traces via letters the love affairs of the children of the Harrington family, Myra and her brother, simply called Harrington. Myra is engaged to the admirable Jack Worthy, friend and correspondent of her brother. Over the course of the novel, the younger Harrington meets and falls in love with Harriot Fawcet, an orphan who is serving as a companion to the wealthy Mrs. Francis. Harrington at first contemplates Harriot's seduction, because she is dependent and friendless and hence vulnerable. When his friend Worthy urges him to marry her instead, Harrington replies:

> But *who* shall I marry? That is the question. *Harriot* has no father—no mother—neither is there aunt, cousin, or kindred of any degree who claim any kind of relationship to her. She is companion to Mrs. *Francis*, and, as I understand, totally dependent on that lady. Now, Mr. *Worthy*, I must take the liberty to acquaint you, that I am not so much a republican as formally to wed any person of this class. How laughable would my conduct appear . . . to be heard openly acknowledging for my bosom companion, any daughter of the democratic empire of virtue! (ltr. 3)

Harrington's initial assessment privileges social class and family, rather than Harriot's character and sensibility, and with that privileging gestures toward Anglo-European values. Harriot, alas, belongs to no one, and her only value is her virtue, which is common enough to be labeled "democratic." Over the course of their short relationship, however, Harriot illustrates her perfect understanding of Harrington and his motives; she confronts him by asking, "Is the crime of dependence to be expiated by the sacrifice of virtue?" (ltr. 6). Her sincerity changes Harrington's mind: they find themselves to be sympathetic, kindred spirits, and they fall in love, only to learn later that they are kindred indeed—half-brother and sister—and thus unable to marry. While seduction is not the dynamic of their relationship, readers soon learn that a familial history of seduction pays dividends of misery forward.

How, then, does *The Power of Sympathy* qualify as a seduction tale if Harriot's virtue and like-mindedness persuade Harrington to desire her not as a mistress but as a republican wife? It's here that the four interpolated seduction tales become important. The first of these inset stories is that of the historical Elizabeth Whitman, a single woman who died after bearing a child in a tavern (and whose widely reported experiences also inspired Hannah Foster's *The Coquette; or, The History of Eliza Wharton* [1797]). Referred to only briefly by the characters as an example of a young woman who read badly—that is, who came to believe the romantic fantasies of books, Whitman's story is elaborated in an authorial footnote, in which reading novels explains her downfall: "She [Elizabeth Whitman] was a great reader of novels and romances, and having imbibed her ideas of *the characters of men*, from those fallacious sources, became vain and coquettish, and rejected several offers of marriages. . . . Disappointed in her *Fairy* hope . . . she was the more easily persuaded to relinquish that *stability* which is the honour and happiness of the sex" (ltr. 11). The narrative form of this particular interpolated story, in which an authorial footnote conveys much information, exposes Brown's desire to control readers' understanding of a tragedy well known in New England; the responsibility for the pregnancy, in his interpretation, is all Whitman's. The second interpolated seduction story is that of Ophelia, who was a cousin of Mrs. Francis, the employer of Harriot. Ophelia was seduced by her brother-in-law and bore "at once the son and nephew of *Martin*" (ltr. 21). Rejected by Martin and rebuked by her father, Ophelia poisoned herself from shame and grief. Ophelia's story, too, was based on actual events; as Carla Mulford explains, "Frances Theodora Apthorp bore a child whose father, Perez Morton, was married to her sister, the poet Sarah Morton. Charles Apthorp, father of the two women, tried to force a settlement from Perez Morton, and Fanny Apthorp ended her life (in suicide) as a result" (1996, xxxviii). The third interpolated tale, that of Fidelia, who was perhaps not so faithful after all, follows in quick succession. Stolen away shortly before she was to marry her childhood sweetheart, Fidelia was either seduced or raped. She was eventually recovered, only to find that her fiancé, Henry, had killed himself; her mother dies not long after. Fidelia survives the loss of her virtue, but grief and despair leave her "distracted" and "deprived of her reason" (ltr. 28). None of these three stories has any real bearing on the plot of *The Power of Sympathy*. However, as Mulford has remarked, "By providing subplots that acted as varying reflections on the themes of the novel, novelists created dramatic intensity while offering additional examples of the problems their novels were interrogating" (1996, xxix).

These interpolated stories thus function primarily to set the stage for the final and most important interpolated story, the seduction of Maria Fawcet by the elder Harrington, which provides an integral back story to the plot of *The Power of Sympathy*. We learn, at the same time as the Harrington children, that their married father had seduced Maria shortly after her father died, leaving her family impoverished. Directly refuting the fantasy of *Pamela* and the reformed hopes of the younger Harrington—that a gentleman can be so overcome by the charms and virtues of a poor woman that he marries her—Maria forewarns, "A young woman in no eligible circumstances, has much to apprehend from the solicitations of a man of affluence" (ltr. 39). After Maria bears a child, the older Harrington suffers an attack of conscience and breaks off their relationship. Abandoned by her lover and taken in by strangers, Maria dies, leaving her daughter, Harriot, to the care of her benefactor, who educates her and finds employment for her as a companion to Mrs. Francis. The revelation of Harriot's parentage and the elder Harrington's perfidy serves as the crux of the novel. Their marriage plans disrupted by learning that they are half-brother and sister, Harriot dies of grief, after which the younger Harrington kills himself.

While readers of antebellum fiction generally find sympathy to be positive (if hierarchical and not always efficacious), demonstrating, as in *Uncle Tom's Cabin*, the capacity of characters to feel for others and urging readers to positive action, sympathy in the novels of the early period operates rather differently. Often linked with sensibility, sympathy tends to be based on similitude or equality; that is, characters (and their authors) tend to extend sympathetic relations toward those who are most like themselves, white, middling sorts of men and women, while the poor or those in reduced circumstances are more likely to be the recipients of hierarchical benevolence. Displays of sensibility, the capacity to exhibit finer feelings, such as pleasure, joy, grief, and pain, through bodily expression, are one way that characters demonstrate their sympathy. However, the sympathy that exists between Harrington and Harriot is based on excessive likeness. Rather than being simply like-minded—that is, rather than Harrington simply being able to imagine himself in Harriot's position and feel the way that she would feel, in the sense that Adam Smith discusses in *The Theory of Moral Sentiments* (1759)—they are alike in status and body, as well as mind.

Noting that the threat of brother-sister incest is a repeated trope in early American fiction, not only in *The Power of Sympathy* and Rowson's *Charlotte's Daughter; or, The Three Orphans* (1828) but also in Sally Sayward Barrell Keating Wood's *Julia, and the Illuminated Baron* (1800) and others, Anne Dalke has argued that incest speaks to the social disruptions caused by the Revolution and subsequent concerns about the responsibilities of fathers, particularly in determining the social status of their children. Elizabeth Barnes has also commented on the recurrence of incest as a trope, arguing in *States of Sympathy* that there is a peculiarly political bent to these stories of incest, in that "sociopolitical issues are cast as family dramas . . . where *family* stands as the model for social and political affiliations" (1997, 2). Characters tend to feel for those who are powerfully like them, but there is a cost for imaginatively aligning the family and the state; the result, as Barnes argues, is "that the conflation of familial and social ties results in an eroticization of familial feeling of which incest is the 'natural result'" (19). "Put in this context," she continues, "incest denotes more than the power of filial feeling; it becomes a metaphor for a particular way of relating to others, one that relies on likeness and familiarity as a precondition for sympathy" (20). Excessive likeness may also signal ongoing discomfort on the part of novelists with an American culture still in thrall to a dominant imperial culture.

And yet, demonstrations of likeness, often through expressions of sensibility, offered a way to establish social bonds during a time of social disruption. Expressions of sentiment, especially tears of sympathy, purportedly revealed a feeling heart and an individual's inner nature, delving beneath polite exteriors to reveal something authentic and "natural." Expressions of sentiment and sensibility extended beyond purely social interactions, as Stephen Shapiro has convincingly argued, into the regulation of commercial behavior to enable trust and credit among the bourgeoisie. Even so, as Paul Goring has demonstrated with regard to eighteenth-century Britain, there was an entire industry, including stage practices, oratory, and fiction, devoted to what he calls "elocutionary discourse," with the express goal of producing eloquent bodies that would communicate the feelings (2005, 6). These uses of sentiment and sensibility beg the question of their naturalness and authenticity;

dramatizing such performances of feeling and examining the relationships thereby created represent some of the central aims of American sentimental fiction.

A drama of likeness similar to that of *The Power of Sympathy* was enacted four decades later in Rowson's *Charlotte's Daughter*, the sequel to the extraordinarily popular *Charlotte Temple*. Ironically the "Americanness" of *Charlotte Temple* is debatable. Its author was born in England but as a child and young teen lived in the colonies with her father, who was a retired British army officer, until they were repatriated to England after the American Revolution. *Charlotte Temple* enjoyed relatively modest success when it was first published in London in 1791, but Rowson had much better fortune with the 1794 reprinting of the novel after she returned to the United States, where she wrote, acted, and taught school. *Charlotte Temple* quickly grew in popularity to become the most successful novel from the early republic era, with at least 200 editions appearing before 1900.

Unlike *The Power of Sympathy*, seduction determines the plot of *Charlotte Temple*, which traces the relationship of Charlotte, a virtuous British girl of moderate means, as she is pursued by Montraville, a British army officer. Her seduction is facilitated by the evil intent of Montraville's friend, Belcour, and Charlotte's teacher, the depraved Mademoiselle La Rue. The seduction itself receives little attention. Rather, the narrator portrays Charlotte as a victim of the machinations of others and her own tender sensibilities. She never consents to seduction, and if she is guilty of anything, it is concealing her correspondence with Montraville from her parents. At a crucial moment in the novel, when Montraville presses her to elope from her parents and accompany him to America, Charlotte's sensibilities overcome her, as Montraville rebukes her for supposed cruelty in dashing his hopes. Charlotte cries out, "Alas! My torn heart!" and wonders "How shall I act?" (ch. 12). At that point, words literally fail Charlotte, and she faints, only to be carried off by Montraville. Isolated on the transatlantic voyage from her family and friends and ensconced in a small cottage in New York, Charlotte must depend on Montraville. Victimized once again by Belcour's machinations, when he persuades Montraville she has been unfaithful, the pregnant Charlotte is abandoned by Montraville and depends on the kindness of strangers. Her family never gives up on her, however, for her father arrives just in time for his dying, delirious, and repentant daughter to bequeath to his care her daughter, Lucy.

Thirty-seven years later, *Charlotte's Daughter*, popularly known as *Lucy Temple*, picked up the narrative. Here, as in *The Power of Sympathy*, the price of seduction continues to be paid forward when Lucy Temple falls in love with Lt. Franklin, who is revealed to be the son of Montraville and Julia Franklin, the woman for whom Montraville had discarded Charlotte. Unlike most fictionalized illegitimate progeny, who die as babies due not only to the deaths of their mothers but also to the failure of their fathers to care for them, Lucy represents redemption for the Temple family: she's educated, wise, benevolent, and rich, and she would be a good match for Lt. Franklin—were she not his illegitimate half-sister. Both families suffer the consequences of seduction: her father, Montraville (who took his wife's name to inherit her family's fortune), dies maddened from years of guilt over his treatment of Charlotte, while Lucy's would-be lover and half-brother, Lt. Franklin, sacrifices himself fighting Napoleon. Dedicating herself to good works, Lucy never marries, and so the ultimate result of Charlotte's seduction is the ending of the Temple, Montraville, and Franklin familial lines.

While many sentimental novels from the early republic rely on letters, the narrative style of *Charlotte Temple* differs markedly. The omniscient narrator herself becomes a character in the novel as her warm, motherly persona controls our interpretation. Words may fail Charlotte, but they never fail the narrator, who intervenes in the narrative to describe how readers should be feeling. Such a narrator is typical of the didactic novels that would predominate in the early nineteenth century; as Susan K. Harris notes about *Charlotte Temple*, "the narrator always makes her presence felt, addressing a female consciousness she perceives as extremely susceptible to whatever error her tale is designed to prevent. In these novels, the narratee is representative, standing in for a class of readers susceptible to similar error" (1995, 45). Shortly after introducing Montraville, the narrator directly addresses the reader, ridiculing the ease with which girls are impressed by a military uniform and advising them, "Oh my dear girls—for to such only am I writing—listen not to the voice of love, unless sanctioned by paternal approbation: be assured, it is now past the days of romance" (ch. 6).

Although Foster's *The Coquette*, the second-most frequently reprinted novel from that era, similarly features a heroine susceptible to romance, that novel differs markedly from *Charlotte Temple.* Absent a narrator, its epistolary format enables each character to develop a distinctive voice, and characters gain or lose the sympathy of readers based on those voices. Like *Amelia*'s Doliscus and *Charlotte Temple*'s Montraville, the seducer figure of *The Coquette* is a military man, an American officer, Major Peter Sanford. A man of leisure in the postwar era who refuses to get a job, Sanford "cannot bear the idea of confinement to business" because "it appears . . . inconsistent with the character of a gentleman" (ltr. 32); even after he has wasted his fortune, he dismisses the idea of productive labor for fear of becoming "a downright plodding money-catcher, for a subsistence" (ltr. 54). Instead, Sanford lives off his reputation, disdaining marriage until it becomes a "dire necessity . . . [a] dernier resort" (ltr. 54). His leisure, financial profligacy, and amoral relationships with women signal his libertinism, as he uses his letters to his friend, Charles Deighton, to mock the self-discipline and self-sacrifice that were lionized as the basis of republican manhood. As Julia Stern has suggested, oppositional libertine figures such as Sanford were crucial in delineating middle-class republican values, which helps explain the frequent appearance of libertines in popular literature. After his marriage to Nancy, an heiress, Sanford depends on the common law doctrine of coverture to control his wife's fortune of £5,000, a sum that temporarily staves off bankruptcy and further enables his profligacy. Although Sanford's initial response to Eliza implies malice—he labels her a coquette and vows that he "shall avenge my sex, by retaliating the mischiefs, she meditates against us" (ltr. 8), he later comes to love Eliza and recognize her worth as well as his wife's, but he's trapped in an outdated mode of libertine manhood. He exclaims to his friend about Eliza, "Love her, I certainly do. Would to heaven I could marry her! Would to heaven I had preserved my fortune; or she had one to supply its place!" (ltr. 37), but Sanford literally cannot imagine earning a living. His representation of libertine manhood stands in stark contrast to the stultifying middle-class ethics of the Rev. Boyer, for whom work literally shapes every aspect of his character.

While Sanford is the obvious villain of the novel, Foster also uses him to expose the shallowness of middling and elite American society and the problems surrounding marriage itself. Sanford cannot converse about books and ideas in the same fashion as most of Eliza's circle; Eliza confesses to her friend Lucy that when the conversation turned to "literary subjects . . . I cannot say that the Major bore a very distinguished part" (ltr. 19). He nonetheless gains social entrée due to his appearance of wealth and polished politeness. Supremely conscious of the importance of property and material goods in shaping his image—what he labels "show and equipage" (ltr. 17)—he proves less able to negotiate interior qualities such as virtue, learnedness, sincerity, and seriousness, qualities that the novel tries to convince us are assuming increasing importance. Notwithstanding their suspicions about Sanford's character, Eliza's friends and family socialize with him; he's even invited to Lucy Freeman's wedding to Charles Sumner, despite Lucy's outrage over his treatment of Eliza. Sanford gloats over "bear[ing] off the palm of respect" despite his neighbors' dislike (ltr. 54). While Brown attributed the seduction of the real Elizabeth Whitman to unregulated novel reading, Foster imagines Eliza's problems as both social and financial: How can an impoverished but genteel young woman navigate a social world that requires her to demonstrate politeness to all the elite, regardless of their characters? Eliza's cousin, Ann Richman, concedes that "even the false maxims of the world must be complied with in a degree" (ltr. 9). This *Clarissa*-like dilemma, as Ann later acknowledges, warns Eliza that Sanford "is a second Lovelace" (ltr. 19). Much more engaged with the economic structure of the early United States than either *The Power of Sympathy* or *Charlotte Temple*, *The Coquette* indicts the American social scene as a whole; had elite American society not tacitly encouraged Sanford by tolerating him, he would have been unable to pursue Eliza for so many years. Foster's novel thus acknowledges the uneasy, complicated, and incomplete American social transition from a landed elite who inherited their wealth and practiced politeness to a productive middle class that valued individuals based on intrinsic qualities such as virtue or liveliness of mind. Eliza's crucial flaw, in Foster's retelling of the Elizabeth Whitman story, is that she overestimates the value of these intrinsic qualities in the marriage market.

Foster has Eliza struggle with the notion that marriage is the only choice for young women. She imagines alternative social relationships based on friendship and sisterhood, labeling marriage "the tomb of friendship" (ltr. 12), but her dependent status means that remaining unmarried is not a viable option; at the same time, her lack of an inheritance limits the pool of eligible men vying for her attention. The novel implicitly indicts the absence of opportunities for young women like Eliza, who is educated, intelligent, beautiful, and charming. Her friends, styled the "republican chorus" in a label popularized by Julia Stern (1997, 72), love her for precisely these qualities but reprove her lack of moral seriousness. As a woman whose father and former fiancé were both highly respected clergymen, Eliza has solid middle-class social credentials but no way to maintain them except through marriage. If the United States was the land of opportunity for the new American man that J. Hector St. John de Crèvecoeur and Benjamin Franklin extol in *Letters from an American Farmer* (1782) and *Autobiography* (1791), for American women it was simply more of the same. Common law forced young women into dependence on parents or a husband, while social etiquette compelled them to wait passively for a proposal. Cathy Davidson famously describes this dilemma by arguing that early sentimental fiction is about "silence, subservience, and stasis (the accepted attributes of women as traditionally defined) in contradistinction to conflicting impulses toward independence, action, and self-expression (the ideals of the new American nation)" (1986, 147). Most women's first legal act of consent was to the marriage contract, which then deprived them of the future right of consent to manage their own property, earnings, or inheritance. These unequal power relations between men and women and the utter dependency of American women on parents and spouses illuminate the preoccupation of the early novel with the marriage plot.

Where a Franklin has the chance to make mistakes, improve himself, and reinvent himself, sentimental novels anxiously circle around marriage, the one opportunity that most women had to secure their social and economic positions. Even a "good" marriage is no panacea for the women of *The Coquette*. The marriage of General Richman and his wife, Ann, is held up as the beau ideal of republican marriage, a model of companionate happiness, but even Ann Richman loses her child, and there are no available men of General Richman's caliber. Eliza's only choices seem to be the libertine Sanford or the tedious Rev. Boyer. Boyer may very well represent the virtuous rising middle class, but his sanctimony repels. While Eliza's wealthy friend Lucy may also have found a good man, Sanford's heiress bride by contrast loses her money, child, and her dignity during their marriage, forcing her return home to her parents.

The unequal playing field between men and women and the lack of social and economic opportunities for women suggest that seduction novels are less about sex than about the exercise of unequal social and legal power. The absence of a parent usually exacerbates this inequality in power relationships. Without a father, mother, or siblings, young women such as the orphaned heiresses Clemenza Lodi in Charles Brockden Brown's *Arthur Mervyn* (1799) and Frances Wellwood in

Murray's *Story of Margaretta* were rendered extraordinarily vulnerable to their seducers, who also steal their inheritances. That's not to say that coercion is absent in seductions in early American fiction, because certainly there are varying degrees of coercion, ranging from the out-and-out rape of Lucinda, the protagonist of *Lucinda; or, The Mountain Mourner* (1807), the kidnapping of Fidelia in *The Power of Sympathy*, and even the carrying off of Charlotte Temple. But most seduction novels rely less on physical coercion than the potential for power with which the seducer tantalizes his victim. That is to say, it is neither the physical strength nor the sexuality of the seducer but more often the illusion of power the seducer grants that prompts women to consent. Montraville, in begging Charlotte to see him again before his ship sails for New York, whips up her anxiety on his behalf, invoking "the perils of the oceans—the dangers of war." Montraville beseeches her to visit him again, saying, "'tis my last request. I shall never trouble you again, Charlotte." Here, Charlotte's words begin to fail in the face of his skillful rhetoric: "'I know not what to say,' cried Charlotte, struggling to draw her hands from him" (ch. 9). Montraville, however, tells her that his life is literally in her hands: "'Cruel Charlotte,' said he, 'if you disappoint my ardent hopes, by all that is sacred, this hand shall put a period to my existence. I cannot live without you" (ch. 12).

The relationship between Peter Sanford and Eliza Wharton of *The Coquette* also illustrates this dynamic. As a single, supposedly wealthy man with a military title, Sanford holds a position of power over Eliza, a woman without a father or an inheritance. And yet he repeatedly tells her that she has the power to make him happy; on one occasion, when he accosts her in the Richmans' garden, he "bowed submissively [and] begged pardon for his intrusion." He implores that he "be admitted to enjoy [her] society, to visit [her] as an acquaintance" (ltr. 19). When Selby, the friend of his rival, Rev. Boyer, visits the Richmans, Sanford watches her "with an attention, which seemed to border on anxiety" (ltr. 26). And when Eliza is on the verge of accepting Boyer's proposal, Sanford writes a desperate letter to her, telling her that he came to "plead [his] cause . . . but was cruelly denied the privilege of seeing [her]!" He warns her, "To what lengths my despair may carry me, I know not! You are the arbitress of my fate!" (ltr. 41). Eliza is both coerced and tempted into meeting Sanford, only to be discovered by Boyer, who angrily rejects her. After destroying Eliza's relationship with Boyer and marrying another woman, Sanford weeps while begging her forgiveness and asking for her friendship with his wife. These overwrought, emotional scenes illustrate Sanford's slow seduction of Eliza; although Eliza lacks social power, Sanford lures her with the promise of directing his sentiments. Bryce Traister has argued persuasively that the greatest threat posed by the libertine in sentimental fiction is his "ability to counterfeit genuine sentiment," an ability which "posed a significant threat not only to young females but also to a young nation besieged, according to former president John Adams, by smooth-talking libertine males" (2000, 2). The most successful villains of early American sentimental fiction are those who, like Sanford or the eponymous villain of Sally Wood's *Dorval*, can feign shared feelings with their victims, whether targets of seduction or financial fraud. In such a schema, it is easy to see how fictional women come to stand in for the body politic and cultural sovereignty, always threatened by forces both external and internal.

If novels such as *The Power of Sympathy*, *Charlotte Temple*, and *The Coquette* show the consequences of seduction, other sentimental novels offer antidotes to seduction: wise parents, friends who stand in as mentors, and a sensible education that encourages reading widely beyond the novel. Family makeup was beyond the control of young women, but wisely chosen friends and a proper education were seen as within their control. Foster's *The Boarding School; or, Lessons of a Preceptress to Her Pupils* (1798), published a year after *The Coquette*, serves as a sort of coda or metacommentary on that novel through its advocacy of a particular kind of mentorship and education. Sarah Emily Newton aptly describes it as a "conduct novel," a hybrid of the novel and the conduct literature popular at the time (1994, 140). In *The Boarding School*, Mrs. Williams runs a small finishing school that the female students affectionately name Harmony Grove. As preceptress, she emphasizes conduct and self-regulating virtue among her students, encouraging them to form mutually supportive social networks. These corrective friendships stand in for what Frank Shuffelton calls "the brotherly watch" (1986, 222), a remnant of the Puritan idea of a covenanted community, where individuals act as their brothers' and sisters' keepers, morally obligated to correct those in error. In the Lockean pedagogy that predominated in early America, individuals would ideally develop sufficient self-discipline to monitor themselves, but parents and "friends," designating not merely peers but others interested in an individual's welfare, facilitated this monitoring. *The Coquette*'s Eliza finds this monitoring oppressive; when Ann Richman encourages her to be receptive to Rev. Boyer's courtship, Eliza tells her that she "hope[s] my friends will never again interpose in my concerns of that nature." Recalling this conversation in a letter to Lucy, Eliza rejects Ann's advice, commenting that although "Mrs. Richman has ever been a beloved friend of mine; yet I always thought her rather prudish" (ltr. 5). Other sentimental protagonists, such as the eponymous heroine of *Emily Hamilton* and the graduates of *The Boarding School*'s Harmony Grove, thank their friends for their interest and rely on their advice, a situation facilitated especially by the epistolary novel.

The profoundly antisentimental countertext to these novels—the exception that proves the rules—is Tabitha Tenney's *Female Quixotism* (1801). Inspired by *Don Quixote* (1605; 1615) and its subsequent derivations, such as Charlotte Lenox's *The Female Quixote* (1752), *Female Quixotism* skewers sentiment, sensibility, a poor education, indulgent parents and friends, and excessive novel reading through its protagonist, Dorcas Sheldon. The only child of wealthy parents, Dorcas loses her mother at an early age and rules her indulgent father's heart. Infatuated by sentiment and exquisite sensibility, she renames herself Dorcasina and rejects an honorable marriage proposal (albeit from a slave owner) in search of a storybook romance. Over the succeeding decades, her indulgent servants become her closest companions as she becomes the dupe of her own illusions, building romantic fantasies out of dust and noble lovers out of servants, humiliating herself and only narrowly escaping seduction or rape—dangers that never seem quite real to her. While satirizing romance and excessive sensibility, *Female Quixotism* manages to foreground social class and race in ways that other early sentimental and seduction novels tend to obscure. Awakened at last from her fantasy life and chastened by realizing that she has lost her chance for a satisfying marriage, Dorcas sinks into deep depression. When her maid, Betty, tries to raise her spirits "by talking of the times that were passed," Dorcas replies, "My own conduct will not bear reflecting upon; I cannot look back without blushing for my follies" (bk. 2, ch. 18). Like Lucy Temple, Dorcas devotes herself to a life of benevolence, but where Lucy was without fault in her courtship, Dorcas acknowledges in a letter to her friend Harriot Stanly Barry, "I have passed my life in a dream, or rather a delirium; and have grown grey in chasing a shadow, which has always been fleeing from me, in pursuit of imaginary happiness, which, in this life, can never be realized" (bk. 2, ch. 18).

Although Dorcas Sheldon pursued a different route, *Female Quixotism* ultimately arrives at a conclusion similar to many sentimental novels, and that is the elusive nature of marital happiness for American women, caught among the rhetoric of the companionate marriage, the legal realities of coverture, and the near impossibility of securing their social status by any means other than marriage. Although decidedly a satire of sentimental and seduction fiction, *Female Quixotism* ultimately affirms—through their absence—many of the same ideals propagated by sentimental and seduction fiction: the importance of self-examination, a good education, and friends who are not afraid to participate in the "brotherly watch."

The metanarrative of the American sentimental novel suggests, then, two intertwined lines of cultural critique, one regarding gendered behavior and the other national identity. The American Revolution changed virtually nothing with regard to the inferior, dependent social and legal status of women. Nominally British prior to the Revolution and nominally American afterward, women continued to be sentimental subjects, rather than citizens, in every sense of the word. Still subject to the legal doctrine of coverture, women were also subject to the sexual double standard. Women were not the sole focus of this cultural critique, however, for it also targets libertine pretenders to aristocratic values, who failed to regulate their sexuality and to adapt to new American modes of manhood. The American Revolution, the sentimental novel suggests, was not revolutionary enough—at least with regard to the personal and economic lives of the middling and elite sorts of people who garner the attention of the earliest novelists.

3

COMPLEMENTARY STRANGERS

Charles Brockden Brown, Susanna Rowson, and the Early American Sentimental Gothic

MARION RUST

In the quixotic search for the author of the "first American novel," Susanna Haswell Rowson and Charles Brockden Brown remain leading candidates, and as the best-known Anglo-American novelists of the early national period the two had much in common. Both lived in Philadelphia for most of the 1790s, when it was the nation's capital as well as its cultural center. Both wrote quickly, with little taste for revision. Neither was afraid to try something new; while they are best known for their novels, between them the two produced political pamphlets, musical melodramas, textbooks, poetry, periodical pieces, and more. Perhaps not coincidentally, given their hasty and wide-ranging authorial tendencies, both have been taken to task as exemplars of that aesthetic deficiency seen to plague the American literary canon until Washington Irving and James Fenimore Cooper came on the scene. Concerning William Dunlap's 1815 biography of Brown, the first such study of the author, an anonymous review claims that Brown "never seems to have laboured with a view to do justice to his powers," whereas Rowson, a female author writing mass-market fiction, was assumed not to have many powers in the first place (Rosenthal 1981, 27). Generally, we are told, Brown's and Rowson's works matter more for what they can tell us about the worlds the authors inhabited than those they depicted imaginatively. Unified plots, credible characters, and pleasing turns of phrase are said to elude them. This chapter aims to challenge such claims. Reading lesser-known works by these two major public figures, one indeed encounters the emerging American city in all its fear and fascination. But another thrill accompanies this almost sensory historical illumination—discovering the early national literary aesthetic shaped and shared by these two authors. This aesthetic was characterized by an uneasy synthesis of high and low culture, conformity and rebellion, nationalist fervor and transatlantic sophistication, craft and carelessness. The best work of both authors captures a particular cultural moment with timeless innovation.

Both these pleasures—the historical and the literary—only increase when we read Brown and Rowson in tandem. And yet surprisingly, given their many commonalities, critics tend to pit them against each other, rather than exploring their mutual constitution of a cosmopolitan US literary culture. There is no denying their dissimilarities. Rowson was a schoolteacher; Brown, a law practice dropout. Rowson wrote tearjerkers; Brown, horror stories. Rowson published the first bestseller in the United States and catered to popular taste throughout her career; Brown, while never achieving the wide readership he desired, helped foster a vibrant intellectual elite in a nation widely assumed not to have produced a single good book. As Bryan Waterman suggests, "Brown or his friends systematically distributed copies of his novels with the express purpose of belonging to high-minded [patrons'] collections," while "more popular books like Rowson's were . . . deemed only retrospectively to have historical significance" (2009, 240).

Brown and Rowson also felt quite differently about their work. According to their own prefaces, Brown's novels aimed to study social and ethical mores; Rowson's, to instill them. Thus, when Brown called himself a "moral painter" in the brief preface to *Edgar Huntly; or, Memoirs of a Sleep-Walker* (1799), he had in mind "wonderful diseases . . . of the human frame." Authorship, for him, represented notions of good, not its inevitable decay. But Rowson, a "moral painter" herself, would have meant something quite different by the term. According to her most famous preface (to *Charlotte Temple* [1791]), an author was a painter who *was* moral, whose "purity of . . . intentions" ensured virtuous, if not "elegant," literature. Thus, a skeptic might accuse Rowson of tending toward platitudes, Brown toward riddles. Nevertheless, to take either author at face value regarding their intentions is misleading. Like other novels of the day, Rowson's provided many of the illicit pleasures they claimed to inoculate readers against, while Brown consistently articulated a set of prescriptive norms meant to influence readerly behavior.

Literary scholars have been quick to accept and even exaggerate the authors' seeming antinomy, lining up behind one to slight the merits of the other. Rowsonians tend to think that sentimental literature, with its emphasis on what R. F. Brissenden called "virtue in distress" (1974, 127), is the single most fascinating genre of the long nineteenth century, given that it employed female authors to depict the problems of women in language that revealed their deep influence on the culture at large. Brown, one might politely opine, while fascinating in his way, wasn't that widely read, and who could understand him? Most Brownians might not be as extreme as, say, Leslie Fiedler, who claimed that Rowson and her female cronies singlehandedly ruined American literature by forcing it indoors. But they hold little truck with all that crying and fainting; they might even believe, with Steven Watts in *The Romance of Real Life* (1994), that "sentimental strategies" obscure, rather than reveal, "cultural content" (138). Whether modern scholars consider Brown primarily a psychological gothicist, precursor to Nathaniel Hawthorne and Edgar Allan Poe, or a social commentator worthy of substantial discussion (as in a special

2010 issue of the *Journal of the Early Republic* devoted to "Political Writing"), they find his influence on American culture all the more profound for not having been sufficiently noted in its time.

This chapter aims to make peace between these camps in order to introduce an approach that emphasizes mutuality over binary opposition. In it, I hope to show how much we learn by juxtaposing these authors rather than by projecting them as adversaries to expose the deficiencies of one or the other. In part, this approach seems necessary because each author's body of work already contains its own dialectic of progressive and conservative elements. As Paul Downes writes, Brown's work should "be used to question persistent polarizations and to help construct a new vocabulary for assessing postrevolutionary political culture" (1996, 414). My own book *Prodigal Daughters* (2008) argues that Rowson too proves most revealing when we examine her attempts to reconcile personal autonomy with female deference and prescribed hierarchies with voluntaristic formations. Reading Rowson and Brown together encourages us to reject "polarization" in favor of more multifaceted and hence realistic models of early national culture.

Complementarity begins with their biographies. Myriad coincidences link the two lives; these links, in turn, highlight significant cultural events of the period. To begin with the most obvious example, consider their ties to the Revolutionary War: while Rowson was born in Portsmouth, England in 1762 and Brown in Philadelphia nine years later, both lived a significant part of their childhoods in Revolutionary America. Both, moreover, had fathers who refused to join the American cause. Rowson's father, William Haswell, was a British naval officer. Born in London, she had joined him and his new wife in Massachusetts, four years after her birth and the consequent death of her mother. But when William refused to take an oath of loyalty to the Revolutionary cause in 1775, the family was put under house arrest and eventually sent back to England. Brown's father, Elijah Brown, supported the goals of the Revolution, but as a Quaker pacifist, he also refused to take the oath of loyalty. As a consequence, he was exiled to Virginia for eight months and, like Rowson's family, lost his property.

Exile, both literal and figurative, is unsurprisingly a prominent trope for both writers. Their authorial personae manifest a certain alienation from character, text, and reader alike, as documented by scholars as diverse as Norman S. Grabo, Julia A. Stern, and Paul Witherington. These remote narrative sensibilities are different in kind. In Brown's novels *Wieland; or, The Transformation* (1798), *Arthur Mervyn; or, Memoirs of the Year 1793* (1799–1800), and *Edgar Huntly*, a first-person protagonist "alienates personal affections" to the extent that the authorial persona's own perspective is hard to discern. (Witherington uses this phrase in reference to Clithero's impenetrable box in *Edgar Huntly*, which he sees as potentially representative of "art itself" [1981, 180].) Rowson, on the other hand, is notorious for narratorial interventions telling her readers exactly what to think and feel. In *Charlotte Temple*, Mademoiselle La Rue is to be despised, at least until she meets her own just deserts; in its posthumous sequel, *Lucy Temple* (1828), the foolish Mary Lumly is to be pitied following her seduction and inevitable abandonment. By contrast, even when Brown uses a predominantly third-person narrator, as in *Ormond; or, The Secret Witness* (1799), he tends to pose rhetorical questions (as Witherington also points out in his discussion of *Edgar Huntly*) rather than offering interpretive guidance.

Witherington divides these methods into the "aesthetic" and the "moralistic" (1981, 175). These terms, in turn, can stand in for the two most discussed types of novelistic discourse in early American studies: the gothic, in which outsider status is a representative state, and the sentimental, which operates to reconcile estranged parties. Discussing Brown and Rowson in tandem provides an ideal opportunity to consider the potentially symbiotic relationship of these long-estranged forms. As one who favors the gothic aesthetic over the sentimental moral, Brown, in *Ormond,* tells how a seemingly sane man commits a sequence of murders that ends only with the attempted rape of his once-intended. Rowson tends to chart the opposite course, from foolishness or even criminality to wisdom. One versified dramatic dialogue in *A Present for Young Ladies* (1811), for instance—a collection of dramatic recitations—has recalcitrant schoolgirls finally agreeing that studying beats shopping. In a darker tracing of the same narrative arc, the novel *Trials of the Human Heart* (1795) shows how a seemingly defamed young woman endures financial hardship, sexual catastrophe, and the sneers of spoiled cousins to achieve marital satisfaction and social respectability. And yet tracing these disparate impulses necessitates the invention of a third term: the "sentimental gothic." For while Ormond may indeed have become immoral—or more precisely, amoral—the book bearing his name capitalizes on readers' condemnation of his crimes, intensified by the vulnerability of his victims, which would not be possible in a completely "nonmoralistic" novel. Meanwhile, in *Trials of the Human Heart,* despite the fact that the good are finally rewarded and the bad punished (as is conventional in sentimental novels), a story arc as convoluted and disaster strewn as any Brown might have contrived fosters a disoriented anxiety that undermines the sanguine plot resolution.

If these authors experimented with the potentially complementary aesthetics of the gothic and the sentimental, they also both recognized the novel's potential for social commentary and critique. Thus, despite Rowson's seeming obsession with wedging her threatened protagonists into the familial fold that Shirley Samuels revealed, in *Romances of the Republic* (1996), to be both site and symbol of patriarchal nationalism, she also challenged the narrowing of opportunities for women in post-Revolutionary US culture as well as the shortsightedness of US nationalist perspectives on global affairs. To do so, she often capitalized on her own unusual subject position as neither native-born American nor domesticated maternal figure. In the epilogue to her play *Slaves in Algiers; or, A Struggle for Freedom* (1794), for instance, she rushed onstage to trumpet her female literary ambition as both humorous and appealing. In *Sarah; or, The Exemplary Wife* (1813), she made it clear that she knew what it was to be stuck in an unhappy marriage. And in a nation that both imitated and resented British class hierarchy, she fomented populist national self-regard while capitalizing on her status as a member of the British gentry. Her celebrations of US imperialist expansion on and beyond the North American continent were among the most fervent by any author (consider her play *Slaves in Algiers*, her patriotic drinking song "America, Commerce and Freedom" [1794], or the "Ode on the Birthday of *John Adams*, Esquire, President of the United States of America, 1799," as well as many other works written for an American audience). And yet, in her preface to *Trials of the Human Heart*, she articulated a transnational perspective that conferred unique wisdom regarding ongoing conflicts between England and the United States, even as it prevented her from taking a definitive stand.

If Rowson capitalized on not quite belonging to the nation she loved—if she possessed a surprising solitariness for an author known for promoting reconciliation—Brown's isolationist tendencies were much more widely recognized during his lifetime. The same anonymous review cited earlier finds him "alone in the fields . . . acquiring a love of solitude and habits of abstraction" (Rosenthal 1981, 27) much like his eponymous character Theodore Wieland in his self-made temple, "unaccompanied by any human being" (ch. 1). And yet, like Rowson, Brown labored throughout his career to reconcile warring factions at both the social and the familial level, while at the same time registering the potential futility of righting entrenched power imbalances or communicating across cultural chasms. In *Wieland*, Theodore makes North American Indians "the first objects for . . . benevolence," while remaining perfectly willing to exploit "the service of African slaves" in order to enhance the resources that make such "benevolence" possible (ch. 1). *Edgar Huntly* paints a compelling portrait of the Native American upheaval wrought by white westward expansion, without eliding the protagonist's own aggressive impulses toward these forbidding strangers. In its account of the yellow fever epidemic, *Arthur Mervyn* perpetuates the urban legend of free African American Philadelphians callously abusing the victims they attended in makeshift hospitals, a job they assumed erroneously supposing themselves immune to the disease. As an editor of the *Monthly Magazine and American Review*, however, Brown in 1800 published a piece (by one "H. L.") entitled "Thoughts on the Probable Termination of Negro Slavery in the United States of America," which predicted that "every moral cause tending to annihilate servitude, will increase in force" (84). And in 1803, Brown agreed to write (but never finished) a history of slavery and manumission.

Although Brown and Rowson shared a mutual fascination with conflict and resolution—with ostracism as a personal, social, and political phenomenon—they also inhabited a nation whose recent history and expansionist ambitions made such fascination inevitable. For this reason, it would be simplistic to attribute their common interests to having both been forcibly expelled from familiar surroundings as children by a remote, inscrutable political entity. But it bears remembering that these authors were, in their own way, participants in a form of that second-generation deterioration depicted by Perry Miller in "Declension in a Bible Commonwealth" (1967) and Andrew Delbanco in *The Puritan Ordeal* (1991). Declension involves both a sense of having missed out and a doubt about the truth supposedly disregarded. And as Ed White writes, during the second Jefferson administration in 1804, as dissenting Federalist alliances with Britain rendered "the U.S. revolutionary tradition a seemingly marginal oddity," there was plenty of room for skepticism (2010, 198). Practices such as the establishment of the War Department in 1789, which militarized the "Indian Problem," and the passing of laws like the Alien and Sedition Acts of 1798, which made it a crime to criticize the government, foreclosed on a prior era's declarations of independence. Born too late to parents who chose the wrong side and shaped by conflicts they were too young to understand, both authors write with a degree of remoteness that, while it has often been attributed to faulty craft, can equally well be seen to reflect their alienation from the past. Brown and Rowson were far more than allegorists of the sociopolitical maelstrom they survived; rather, one might say that the maelstrom itself allegorized their authorial modes.

Turning Professional

Rowson and Brown were among the first professional novelists of the day, and in fact professionalism was a new and mutable concept in the early republic. In its most basic sense as we now understand it, to be professional is to support oneself through the practice of a particular set of skills. Neither Brown nor Rowson managed to support themselves as authors: hence their respective moves to the periodical desk and schoolhouse. But the term had many other crucial meanings as well. Most important in the case of these two figures, to become a "professional" author meant rejecting anonymity in favor of building a personal reputation. As Waterman notes in *Republic of Intellect* (2007), Brown and his cohorts in both Philadelphia's "Belles Lettres Club" and New York's "Friendly Club" believed "that reputation served as a counterweight to republican injunctions toward anonymous participation in public discourse" (6). What these men emphasized, Rowson embodied, as the public came to "know" her through her career as an actress, her widely read novels, and her establishment of a school for young women from socially prominent families.

As Rowson's self-consciously groomed public image makes clear, more was involved in cultivating one's professional reputation than the mere publication of texts. Various modes of sociability were also crucial, whether enacted on stage, behind the scenes, or through the informed conversation that characterized

Brown's clubs. Often, one type of self-promotion would feed another. Rowson, for instance, used her acting career to promote sales of her fiction by noting it on the frontispiece of an American edition of *Charlotte Temple.* Three years later, enrollment in her school grew because that novel made her a household name. Thus, we remember both authors today not only because they wrote important books, but also because they benefited from a relatively new admiration for authors as public personalities. These personalities both shaped their works and emerged from them.

If professionalism depended on the art of reputation, it equally concerned the nature of that acclaim. One could not, that is, be known for just anything. Today, professionalism implies a degree of status partly on the basis of certification, as exemplified by a college diploma or medical license. During the period under discussion, the earliest professional fields, such as law, medicine, and preaching, began to be subject to new forms of accreditation. Print culture, however, was less subject to regulation, as the weakness of early American copyright laws makes clear. Brown's rejection of legal practice in favor of the writer's life, after six years in a Philadelphia law office, may in part suggest the greater perceived freedom of the author's life. And since for women, the advent of professional specialization in many ways narrowed their horizons, institutionalizing their exclusion from the ranks of law, medicine, and clergy, Rowson clearly also benefited from a more open and accessible print culture. At the same time, one reason Brown and Rowson were so successful is that they anticipated new refinements in the field, including the demand for "native" authors in response to improved US print technologies. The word "publisher" did not exist when Rowson was a child, because the publisher's job was distributed among writers, printers, editors, and booksellers. By the time Brown and Rowson were ready to publish their works, however, they proved themselves adept at knowing whom to approach and how. A short time after her second arrival in the United States in 1793, Rowson established a relationship with the nation's most prominent publisher, Mathew Carey. And as Donald A. Ringe notes, Brown successfully bargained with Hocquet Caritat, the publisher of *Wieland*, to publish *Ormond* before it was even completed.

One effect of their self-conscious immersion in the print market scene could not have been anticipated: the distinction that would be drawn between their novels and their other writings in posthumous discussions of their work. In part, this distinction has to do with the much vaunted "rise of the novel" in eighteenth-century England and the Americas. Despite widespread assumptions to the contrary, early national readers were not ashamed to read novels. These books were indeed pilloried in the popular press as causes of everything from seduction to bankruptcy to poor parenting. But the strident outcry against them only attests to the fact that they were being purchased, borrowed, circulated, bestowed, displayed, and, most importantly, read, in direct proportion to the frequency of these tirades. Moreover, many periodical authors, Brown and Rowson included, wrote in defense of them. We emphasize Brown's and Rowson's novels, then, because we recognize the increasing importance of the genre during their lifetimes. In addition, we tend, without even noticing, to think of novels as the most important kind of prose literature, a result of the very "rise" noted earlier.

Another cause for the disproportionate attention paid to Brown's and Rowson's novelistic careers (over their other publications) has to do with the physical qualities of the texts in question. Many of their non-novelistic publications took the form of less durable media: the periodical (such as the *Weekly Magazine,* the *Monthly Magazine,* and the *Literary Magazine and American Register*, all of which Brown was significantly involved with, as well as the *Boston Weekly Magazine*, which Rowson may have edited); the musical score (such as the surviving libretto to Rowson's play *The Volunteers* [1795]); and the textbook (such as Rowson's *An Abridgment of Universal Geography* [1805]). Other forms may have seemed either too "experimental" (as in Brown's feminist dramatic dialogue, *Alcuin* [1798]) or too conventional (as in Rowson's later biblical writings for youths) to merit widespread consideration.

Whatever the reasons, today Rowson and Brown are best known for a small number of novels written at a feverish pace within a brief span of time. Critics from Jay Fliegelman in 1991 to Philip Barnard and Stephen Shapiro in 2009 identify Brown's four major novels as those published within two years of one another, from 1798 to 1800: *Wieland*, *Ormond*, *Arthur Mervyn*, and *Edgar Huntly*. All these books remain in publication. His final two novels, *Clara Howard* and *Jane Talbot*, published in 1801, await the deserved scrutiny that the final pages of this chapter hope to encourage.

Rowson published at her fastest pace between 1791 and 1798. Among the surviving novels printed then are *Charlotte Temple*, *Mentoria; or, The Young Lady's Friend* (1791 London; 1794 Philadelphia), *The Fille de Chambre* (1792 London; 1794 Philadelphia; second American edition titled *Rebecca; or, The Fille de Chambre*, 1814), *Trials of the Human Heart*, and *Reuben and Rachel; or, Tales of Old Times* (1798). The play *Slaves in Algiers* was also published during this period, as were other plays no longer extant. But her career began as early as 1778 with songs written for the London theaters of Drury Lane and Covent Garden, and extended past her death, with the belated publication of *Lucy Temple* in 1828. Clearly, in addition to sustained, intense bursts of authorial output, both authors wrote a great deal more over near-lifetime careers in publishing. In addition, they played important roles in other arenas of knowledge production, from Mrs. Rowson's Young Ladies' Academy to the several periodicals where Brown worked as an editor and contributor.

Urban Legends

Brown and Rowson are synonymous with the urban Mecca of late eighteenth-century Philadelphia, the nation's capital from 1790 to 1800. At the beginning of the decade, it was the nation's third most populous city; by the end, it was the second. (Brown also lived in New York, the nation's largest city, and Rowson lived in Boston, which declined from second to fourth during the 1790s.) This birthplace of revolution was famed for its international, multiethnic population, as well as its building booms, scientific discoveries, libraries, and theaters. It was also a city where prostitution thrived, plagues struck, and fortunes came to ruin. However crowded, dangerous, and dirty it may have been, Philadelphia nevertheless played a primary role in shaping both these authors and their works. Their passion for urban culture began early: at the age of sixteen, both authors made it their mission to partake of whatever their respective urban centers had to offer. Still in England, Rowson began frequenting London's Drury Lane and Covent Garden theaters, occasionally writing songs for the stage. At the same age, Brown formed his first salon, the Belles Lettres Club, with eight Philadelphia friends. In 1796, after moving to New York, he joined the Friendly Club. By his early twenties at the latest, he also frequented the theaters in which Rowson was by then performing. In fact, the novel *Ormond* alludes to Rowson's theater company's return to Philadelphia as a sign of cultural renewal after the cessation of the 1793 yellow fever epidemic.

Brown and Rowson were significantly influenced by this event, a particularly horrific installment of the late-summer yellow fever epidemics that frequently broke out in North American cities in the wake of the African slave trade (whose ships probably introduced the mosquito-borne virus). Approximately 5,000 Philadelphians died during the 1793 epidemic, and about 17,000 out of 55,000 left the city, making the catastrophe one of social and economic, as well as medical, proportions. Rowson emigrated from London that year as a member of the New Theatre Company, which quickly relocated to Annapolis to play out its first season. Brown, however, remained at home, and a significant part of his work reflects the widespread horror and intimate devastation he witnessed: devastation not of bodies alone but also of buildings, streets, psyches, and an entire spatial, social, and financial infrastructure. Rowson's cities are almost never as specifically located or meticulously detailed as Brown's (with the possible exception of *Trials of the Human Heart*, set in London). For both authors, however, the city served as a shaping force, by turns malevolent and redemptive.

Early in *Arthur Mervyn*, Arthur begins his optimistic journey to Philadelphia: "I rose at the dawn, and without asking or bestowing a blessing, sallied forth into the high road to the city which passed near the house. I left nothing behind, the loss of which I regretted" (ch. 3). This young man travels to the city to make his fortune, but his physical journey is also a quest for knowledge premised on frequent and intimate "converse" with new acquaintances, who seem constantly to appear out of nowhere. As in many a Brown novel, in which matter and mind, physical and psychic state intertwine, Arthur equates movement through space with mental development, and the accumulation of capital with intellectual attainment. Hence his initial excitement on leaving his rural home, where his father's crass new wife has made him feel unwelcome. Young Arthur associates cities with truth and beauty, so his perambulations throughout Philadelphia and its environs become a form of spiritual quest.

The outbreak of the "pestilential disease" of yellow fever about a third of the way through the novel puts an end to Arthur's sunny complacency (ch. 13). As with the prior equation of material comfort and wisdom, here the excruciating bodily symptoms of yellow fever correspond to an epistemological crisis. Its "sleepless panics . . . for which no opiates could be found" typify the discomforts attendant upon Arthur's once-optimistic thirst for wisdom, since with the knowledge he seeks comes awareness of human iniquity (ch. 14). The extent of human perfidy becomes especially clear to Arthur in what Barnard and Shapiro, in their edition of the novel, call "the cosmopolitan world of commerce and finance capital," to which Arthur's country upbringing makes him a stranger (2009, 44n.1). As a consequence of his "limited and rustic education" (ch. 5), he has been "prone, from [his] inexperience, to rely upon professions and confide in appearances" (ch. 7). As innkeepers overcharge him, counterfeit bills tempt him, and banknotes jump out of Italian manuscripts, Arthur begins through both fever and economic uncertainty to come to terms with the perils as well as pleasures of urban sociability.

If there is one area in which Arthur maintains his security regarding the happy coincidence of material and mental well-being, it is that of marriage. Indeed, Brown's treatment of gender seems inseparable from his consideration of urban and rural spaces and their relationship to both financial and spiritual development. Arthur's conviction that only wealth allows for the highest wisdom—his "equal avidity, after the reputation of literature and opulence"—serves him well when he meets Achsa Fielding (ch. 11). She embodies Arthur's belief that "[r]iches may be rendered eminently instrumental," aiding "the accumulation of knowledge, and the diffusion of happiness" (ch. 13). Her well-employed wealth more than makes up for her personal deficits, in the eighteenth-century sense of physical appearance, and may atone as well for her religious nonconformity (Achsa is Jewish; strangely, given her nonconformity in most matters, she comments at one point, "I suppose there is some justice in the obloquy that follows [Jews] so closely" [ch. 23]). It also seems to allow Arthur the freedom to forget about his earlier love interest, Bess, whose rustic upbringing and limited resources more closely approximate his own.

This forgetfulness will be addressed—indeed, it will become the fulcrum—of Brown's subsequent novel, *Clara Howard*, in which the esteemed but unloved Mary Wilmot presents an almost insuperable obstacle to the sophisticated Clara and her intended, Edward Hartley. Edward meets Clara after he is already engaged to Mary. In this case, only Mary's belated receipt of a misplaced inheritance and her love match with another man allow Edward and Clara to fulfill their long-declared passion. In both novels, however, the male protagonist unashamedly prefers one woman over another on the basis of both wealth and character, acknowledging outright that her mental attainments would not be possible without her social, economic, and geographic privilege. Indeed, where Rowson represents marrying for money in the worst possible terms (consider how Mademoiselle La Rue, in *Charlotte Temple*, seduces foolish Colonel Crayton into an engagement aboard the ship carrying them to New York), Brown, here and elsewhere, openly embraces it. Money, after all, purchases the refinement that makes love possible. Brown may have tempered his assessment of urban cosmopolitanism, but he never lost a taste for it, as symbolized by the intelligent, urbane female sensibility with which he rewards his happier male protagonists.

Rowson tended to associate cities and women quite differently: urban centers, rather than gently molding her characters into Pygmalions of politesse, tended to finish them off. Alone, pregnant, and in little more than her nightgown, Charlotte Temple stumbles into New York on a rainy night only to find herself rebuffed by those she once trusted. Meriel Howard, the heroine of *Trials of the Human Heart*, finds London a wretched cesspool that almost drives her to prostitution in her attempts to save her dying mother. And in the historical novel *Reuben and Rachel*, the appealing young Rachel Dudley exhibits her only questionable behavior while alone and temporarily friendless in the same city. When she tells a nosy neighbor that "whilst my own heart acquits me of any breach of my duties either moral or religious, I am perfectly indifferent as to what opinion the world in general may form concerning me," her disregard for censure demonstrates her spotless character, surely; but it also shows her to be a fool, as the narrator makes clear by remarking that "her ideas were erroneous" (v. 2, ch. 10). Insofar as Rowson traveled more widely than Brown, crossing the Atlantic three times and making her adult homes in London, Philadelphia, and Boston, she was perhaps even more of a cosmopolite than he. And she did acknowledge her pleasure in urban surroundings: even those novels that made London look frightening represented it in great and appreciative detail. But no city ever became in a Rowson novel a literal or symbolic force akin to Brown's Philadelphia. Instead, cities often served as a punishing wilderness for her young, almost exclusively female, protagonists.

Brown's often homely yet intelligent objects of romantic fascination—to say nothing of the progressive ideas about women that loop through the revolutionary *Alcuin*—set him apart from nearly every other male author of his time, and also from Rowson and many female colleagues. Rowson, after all, used her poem from the 1790s, "The Rights of Woman" (collected in *Miscellaneous Poems* [1804]), to argue for women's duty to take care of their menfolk. Despite Brown's association with what his brother James called the "gloom" of his first four novels, then, he remained optimistic about gender equity in an urban context: an optimism that Rowson ground underfoot in novelistic tales of disaster befalling those who naively assumed such equity. As we will see, however, other genres allowed her more room to share in Brown's theoretical musings on the role of women, musings that can help us read her novels in new ways.

Testing Limits

Here we focus on works that challenge each author's stereotypical reputation—Rowson's popular songs and Brown's last two novels, *Jane Talbot* and *Clara Howard*—in order to suggest a more porous literary culture than their so-called representative texts would indicate. Brown's late novels have been dismissed for "seek[ing] out the bosoms of conservative matrons" and as such meriting no further consideration (Witherington 1981, 166). In them, it is commonly assumed, radical gothicism gives way to sentimental convention. Rowson's songs, meanwhile, have been merely ignored. In contrast to the conservatism (consistent or late blooming) associated with each author, these ignored texts celebrate bodily pleasure and defy, even mock, social convention. By emphasizing some of Rowson's lesser-known compositions, I hope to complicate her reputation as a benign and compliant sentimentalist while also suggesting that Brown's turn to sentimentalism in no way lessened his capacity for social critique, gothic terror, or epistemological skepticism.

By the end of his novelistic career, it is widely assumed, Brown was no better than a "bourgeois moralist," to quote from the title of Watts's chapter on the late novels in *The Romance of Real Life* (1994, 131). Having abandoned his early political and social radicalism to pursue respectability and profit, the story goes, Brown now wrote tales of romance under siege, where his protagonists emerge older, wiser, and most importantly, married. *Clara Howard* and *Jane Talbot* focus on new subject matter for Brown, and the romantic and economic concerns they delineate mesh with other novels of the time better than the author's earlier phantasmic inventions. But because Brown takes a new route in these last novels, readers should not assume that his destination has changed. Like his other novels, sometimes here evoked thematically, *Clara Howard* and *Jane Talbot* investigate the basis of knowledge, trust, and tolerance. Moreover, where a dismissive categorizing of these novels as conventional implies that they are indistinguishable, in fact they diverge significantly, with *Jane Talbot* representing one of Brown's greatest literary successes and most important social commentaries.

Jane Talbot is the perfect book to upset tidy categories. This domestic novel focuses on the households to be established (or lost) as young, vulnerable protagonists choose their spouses. And yet its hero, Henry Colden, is almost always on the road (hence the necessity of the letters that make this an epistolary novel). This is also a sentimental novel, insofar as it focuses on the fragile emotional state of characters under extreme duress: and yet one of its primary claims is that reason and love are inextricable. As Jane Talbot writes to her adoptive mother Mrs. Fielder, who opposes her intended marriage to a man she adores: "as a rational creature, I *cannot* change my resolution" to marry for love (ltr. 14). Women, in particular, must learn the importance of having "reasoned for themselves," lest "habit or childish fear or parental authority" lead them astray (ltr. 34). Jane's battle with her mother revolves around Jane's "propensity to reason," which her mother considers a fault; her happy outcome validates this propensity (ltr. 35). Thus, like all Brown's work, *Jane Talbot* is primarily a novel about how we know what we know, exploring the murky distinction between belief or faith and knowledge or truth, and the hidden wellsprings that direct our actions as we desperately attempt to reason our way out of uncertainty. If Jane is more successful than most Brown protagonists at following reason, perhaps this is because, from the outset, she treats it as akin to emotion, rather than its mismatched opponent.

Jane's embrace of reason accordingly transforms female discourse. As *Jane Talbot* opens, the reader may recall another initially chatty early national protagonist, Eliza Wharton of Hannah Foster's *The Coquette* (1797). Like Eliza, Jane pens her first letters flirtatiously, caught up in the opportunity that writing affords her to celebrate other freedoms as well. For Eliza, freedom means release from the shackles of imposed engagement. For Jane, it means getting to tell her whole story to someone who really wants to hear it: a newly acquired beloved who craves acquaintance with "all the incidents of [her] life, be they momentous or trivial" (ltr. 2). In such a context, Jane can "prate" unceasingly without fear of the term's harsher gendered associations. Indeed, she mocks her own ebullience by using exactly that word to describe her endeavors: "When present, my prate is incessant; when absent, I can prate to you with as little intermission; for the pen, used as carelessly and thoughtlessly as I use it, does *but* prate" (ltr. 2).

Meaning something like "female chatter," "prate" or "prattle" refers exclusively to women throughout the novel, especially to describe Jane's malicious acquaintance, Polly Jessup, whom Jane finds "not entirely without design in her prattle" (ltr. 9). Miss Jessup almost ruins Jane by forged additions to an unfinished letter implying that Jane has had unmarried sex. As such, Polly exemplifies the anxieties regarding female language that lurk behind the seeming levity of the term "prattle." Her words are excessive, unreliable, and ultimately destructive to the social compact.

Like Eliza, Jane will soon reflect on her former lightheartedness from a position of sorrowful wisdom regarding the inequities of gender. As her brother runs through the family fortune unrestrained either by their ineffectual father or by a decorum that would make such behavior unthinkable, Jane comes to see language as her only weapon. Finding herself unable to persuade her brother, she realizes that the world sees women as doing nothing but "[p]rate away." Jane responds by claiming the term for her own, remarking with savage irony, "I never shall bring myself to part with the liberty of *prating* on every subject that pleases me" (Brown's emphasis, ltr. 3). Clearly, Jane's "prate" is no meaningless chatter, but rather the voice of righteous reason, which sympathetic readers ignore at their own peril. Brown's ability over the course of a novel to transform the power and meaning of this term from lighthearted sexual innuendo into a scathing critique of patriarchal commercial practices in the new nation exemplifies his underappreciated craft. Perhaps, here and elsewhere, he did in fact "labor . . . to do justice" to powers far from insignificant.

If there is one bodily fluid that epitomizes the sentimental genre associated with Rowson, it is the tear. In late eighteenth-century England, male sensibility mattered: the narrator of Laurence Sterne's *A Sentimental Journey Through France and Italy* (1768) has no trouble confessing to shedding tears at the grave of his old friend. The United States likewise began to feminize sensibility by the turn of the nineteenth century, but as tears became women's work, they were increasingly undervalued. Rowson's reception, past and present, emblematizes both the feminization of sensibility and its concomitant devaluation. Thus it is hugely important to attend to texts in which kisses, liquor, and laughter predominate, while lamentations are nowhere to be found. This is not to say that those who condescend to female sorrow are right to direct women away from that register of emotion, but merely to show that female authors, like their male counterparts, required a variety of literary modes to express the complexity of their experience.

Rowson's songs best represent the fun-loving aspect of her literary personality. Some were written to stand on their own, others as musical interludes for the plays she wrote and performed in. For years, Rowson engaged intermittently in a highly successful partnership with Alexander Reinagle, a prominent composer of her day. As a general practice, she wrote lyrics, and he (as well as others) set them to music. One of her earliest extant songs, printed anonymously in London after her departure for the United States, is called "I'm in Haste" (1794). It features a country lass who encounters a squire on the hunt for more than game. Catching her by the waist, he asks for a kiss, which she agrees to as long as he's quick about it. In the third and final stanza, the reason for her haste becomes clear: her fiancé approaches, ring in hand, to accompany her to church. "I'm in haste," the last three words of each stanza declare, implying illicit sexual attraction, but the song ends with a couple safely on their way to church. In this way, the song brilliantly captures the bawdy desire that Rowson, in her early years, loved to evoke.

Rowson's songs are important, then, not only on their own terms but also for the new insights they provide into her novels. In a word, they remind us to attend to the playful and even joyous sexuality that the novels provide as a counterpoint to ruined heroines. The difference, as suggested by the clever wordplay of "I'm in Haste," has to do with whether a specific type of sexuality comports with contemporary decorum. In *Charlotte Temple*, Mrs. Beauchamp may blush at the compliments of her husband even as she rushes to assist the pregnant and abandoned Charlotte. In *Reuben and Rachel*, Rachel, whose only fault is "too great openness of disposition," such that she is "easily led into scenes of dissipation, in which . . . she took but little satisfaction," nevertheless marries Hamden Auberry with no permanent ill consequences (v. 2, ch. 14). And in *Lucy Temple*, Lucy's disastrous near union with her half-brother and her subsequent vow of celibacy as the founder of a school for young girls is complemented by her adopted stepsister Aura's delightfully romantic, peaceful, and virtually trouble-free courtship and marriage.

Rowson's songs also point to another aspect of her work that often remains shrouded under its didactic sentimentalism: namely, its deep investment in US transnational commerce. The same year that "I'm in Haste" appeared, she produced another song, which interwove the earlier piece's emphasis on omnivorous youthful flirtation with another of her signature moods, exuberant imperialism. First published as a broadside under the title "New Song, Sung by Mr. Darley, Jun. in the Pantomimical Dance, called The Sailor's Landlady" (1794), with music by Reinagle, this song soon became known, for reasons which will become obvious, as "America, Commerce and Freedom"—in which guise it became one of the most popular drinking songs of the day. Singers whose own lives offered little variety could imagine themselves sharing in the fabled excitement of a sailor's life, which in these verses, at least, mixed endless adventure ("The scene delights by changing") with pleasing nostalgia for "[t]he friends we left behind us" (lines 4, 8). In the first chorus, brave men raise a glass to the "pale" landsmen they've left behind, while toasting "America, commerce, and freedom" (lines 10, 12). As with the refrain "I'm in haste," the latter phrase changes meaning each time it closes the chorus. Here, the sailors clearly value their own intrepid if undervalued role in international trade over the more sedentary labors of the merchants and tradesmen they leave behind. Their endeavors, it is implied, are the real backbone of "American freedom," and their "freedom" is first and foremost the freedom to take whatever they like from whomever they can get it from. Thus, when they arrive on shore, they merely begin the cycle anew: "Our prizes sold, the chink we share. . . . And when 'tis gone, to sea for more;/ We earn it, but to spend it" (lines 25, 31–32).

What does "freedom" mean in this song, especially in the context of the transnational, personal, political, and institutional frameworks addressed in Rowson's novels? *Reuben and Rachel*, the historical novel that Rowson declared her last as she dedicated herself to her school, is particularly relevant here. (Rowson's last novel, *Lucy Temple*, was published posthumously.) In both the song and the novel, freedom inevitably gets mixed up with sexual innuendo. Thus, the second time the signature phrase figures in the song, it bursts from female lips: "And each bonny lass will drink off her glass,/ To America, commerce, and freedom" (lines 23–24). Lighthearted, sexualized liberty here provides a mirror and a stimulus to the sailors' own wide-ranging and frequently extralegal activities (as in the "prizes" or "chink" they find where they can). Far from being opposed to sexual "license" (as it so often was in this period), liberty—in the sense of personal and political self-determination—reenergizes itself in a playful romp on the beach. One might say the same of Rachel's frequently noted laxity regarding the company she kept, which as remarked previously, the novel treats quite sympathetically. More importantly, perhaps, it is through a complex genealogy of sexual union, marriage, and reproduction that the novel manages to span four centuries, countless ethnicities, and several continents, from the castle in Wales where it begins with the widowed Spanish daughter of a Native American queen, to the banks of the Pennsylvania Schuylkill, where it concludes with the suicide of Reuben's spurned Native American love interest, following his marriage to a longtime sweetheart, the English Jessy Oliver.

Many have claimed that this progression, particularly the break from historical to domestic romance represented by the novel's two volumes, means that "the novel's early radical visions of a hybrid and hemispheric American history are ultimately marginalized by the dominant, circumscribed narratives available in the making of the U.S. national identity" (Carrere 2013, 184). And there is certainly no doubt that even Rowson's most original and outspoken works, such as this novel, the drinking song, or the play *Slaves in Algiers*, finally employ female independence in the service of imperialist expansion and nationalist white racial consolidation. (*Slaves* was modeled on the United States' "Algerian Crisis" of the late eighteenth century, in which North Africans captured British and American ships and held their inhabitants hostage for ransom. In that play, the Moors not only release their English and American captives but willingly convert to Christianity, while the Anglo-Americans marry to end the play on a seemingly joyous note.) But the rebellious female sexuality of these works, whether on the part of bonny lasses, innocent and curious maidens of mixed racial descent, or the memorably flirtatious captured Jewish Englishwoman Fetnah, remains allied throughout the bulk of the narrative with the support of "transnational, interreligious, and interracial encounters" as the foundation of US identity (Carrere 2013, 183).

At the same time, it would be wrong to deny the cavalier, if highly informed, attitude Rowson's novels took to the consequences of US imperial expansion. "America, Commerce and Freedom" embodies this callousness in its very title, where the ability to profit from exchanges abroad is equated with US savoir faire. *Slaves in Algiers* intensifies it by suggesting that national political self-determination presumes the right to prescribe the convictions of other nations subdued through a complex alchemy of military, political, and commercial means. (The ultimate irony here, of course, was that Algeria and its Muslim neighbors fared relatively well in the ensuing Tripolitan War with the United States, the Jefferson administration paying ransom for the remaining Algerian captives.) And Eumea's suicide in *Reuben and Rachel*, while representative of the extinction of an entire complex of Native American peoples, is also that of a woman dedicated to modeling herself on European ways. Pragmatic to the end, Rowson's novels maintained a cautious stance toward altering entrenched power imbalances of all kinds. *Lucy Temple*, whose primary register of value was not sexual capital but financial know-how, provided the following lesson in charity: give only to the industrious, and never give too much.

As a deeply informed consumer of the political affairs of her day, Rowson lambasted Jefferson's Embargo Act of 1807 in favor of maintaining an international trade that could bring higher quality goods to the United States and with it an appreciation for the finer things in life, including the arts. The embargo, as Rowson saw it, was impractical; the extinction of most Native American tribes was inevitable; and while one must certainly lament the fallen, progress ultimately trumped sentiment. Every novel, every song, every letter Rowson wrote emanated from and reinforced this resolute, informed, and intelligent pragmatism. Hence, to see her as a doe-eyed sentimentalist akin to her most vulnerable heroines is not only to misread her work in the worst of ways but also to deny that cosmopolitan urbanity more generally associated with Brown and his circle.

At the same time, as his last novels indicate, Brown had a heart to rival that of any female contemporary. And yet like Rowson, he was a pragmatist above all, as expressed in his novels' support of marriages based on financial incentives. Neither author accepted Jefferson's famous opposition, laid forth in his satiric 1786 letter to Maria Cosway, between the "head" and the "heart." Both argued for romance as a form of intellectual companionship, as expressed by their novels' focus on the sexual desirability of brilliant, conventionally unattractive women. Both wrote novels in which love and finance, national pride and international appreciation, and other unlikely pairings interwove comfortably within loosely knit stories whose ultimate stakes were discerning truth from falsity by means of fiction. If, as some might argue, the ultimate goal of any novel is maintaining prestige culture, I would argue that the work of these two novelists complicates that endeavor. Their novels challenge the idea of prestige itself in a place and a time where competing and often incompatible definitions abounded.

The works discussed above show Brown, known for terrors that drive men and women alike to the brink of insanity, arguing for the cozy contentment afforded by a truly companionate marriage, while Rowson, romance adviser to a generation of young women, sought freedom from unhappy unions in female adventure and financial independence. Surprises such as these suggest not only that "polarization" poorly explains the relation between these two novelists, but also that their so-called lesser works subvert such characterizations. One hopes that subsequent challenges to the supposed Brown/Rowson dichotomy will more fully elucidate their mutual contributions to literary, cultural, political, and commercial stirrings in the early republic.

4

TRENDS AND PATTERNS IN THE US NOVEL, 1800–1820

ED WHITE

For a generation, critics have stressed the revolutionary social dimensions of the early US novel. Cathy Davidson's influential *Revolution and the Word* (1986) formulated this argument most forcefully in a Bakhtinian vein, arguing that the early American "dialogic text" was able "to challenge, frustrate, and finally deny the interpretive propensities and ideological premises of the individual, especially of the individual committed to a rationalist model of mind, a rigid ideal of a static hierarchical social order, and a concept of fiction as some mechanical rehearsal of the pieties of the time" (2004, 355). Whatever the truth of this assessment, it is also worth remembering that the US novel of the 1790s was largely an outlet of conservative values. William Hill Brown, author of *The Power of Sympathy* (1789), also penned the satirical "Shays to Shattuck," depicting a seditious, demagogic Daniel Shays, and was eulogized by arch-Federalist Robert Treat Paine, Jr. Jeremy Belknap (*The Foresters,* 1792) stressed the need for a strong central government—again, against the Shaysites—in both fiction and historiography. Samuel Relf, author of *Infidelity* (1797), edited a Federalist gazette. In 1798, the anonymous "Young Lady of the State of New-York" published the Tory novel *The Fortunate Discovery,* referencing the notorious civil conflicts of Revolutionary New York before concluding with all the major characters ennobled and resettled in England. Royall Tyler, who served in the military suppression of the Shays Rebellion, collaborated with arch-Federalist Joseph Dennie as he composed *The Algerine Captive; or, The Life and Adventures of Doctor Updike Underhill* (1797). Tabitha Gilman Tenney (*Female Quixotism,* 1801) emerged from the Federalist stronghold of Exeter, New Hampshire, where her husband served as a Federalist congressman. The didactic authors Enos Hitchcock (*Memoirs of the Bloomsgrove Family,* 1790; *The Farmer's Friend,* 1793) and Henry Sherburne (*The Oriental Philanthropist,* 1800) were members of New England's Federalist clergy. The prolific Susanna Rowson and Charles Brockden Brown are harder to situate, but Rowson's *Trials of the Human Heart* (1795) was written under the patronage of the Federalist Binghams of Philadelphia, while Brown's last novel, *Jane Talbot* (1801), redeemed its male protagonist from the dangers of Godwinite atheism; Brown later produced harsh polemics against Jeffersonian policy, drawing on the standard Federalist caricatures.

We must be cautious about assuming what "conservative" means in the early republican context, and critics such as Joseph Fichtelberg and Karen Weyler have demonstrated the challenges of politically situating many of the aforementioned writers. Tenney's novel challenged the extremism of the Connecticut Wits; Rowson famously sparred with Peter Porcupine; and many of these writers were abolitionists of some variety. Nonetheless, the first US novelists were typically part of an informal Federalist intellectual establishment ranging across newspapers, churches, courtrooms, and academies. The frequently cited—and exaggerated—antinovel sentiment has implied that novelists squared off against Federalists, but these occasional critics were members of the same Federalist intellectual movement, committed to hierarchical culture. Distaste for the plebs, alarmist references to "mobs," disgust with class leveling and the nouveau riche, praise for those who know their place—all these are basic elements of the novels of the 1790s. One can best appreciate the Federalist hegemony by considering the most notable exception, Hugh Henry Brackenridge's *Modern Chivalry* (1792–1815). Brackenridge was also of the Revolutionary-era intelligentsia, serving as a military chaplain, propagandist, journalistic booster, and constitutionalist during the Pennsylvania ratification debate. But his relocation to Pittsburgh put him within the sphere of Democratic-Republican politics and service to the nascent party. He sparred with the Connecticut Wits, and his proximity to the Whiskey Rebellion resulted in his interrogation by Alexander Hamilton: one can scarcely imagine other writers of the period in a like situation. Of course, *Modern Chivalry* hardly displayed an unambiguous commitment to democracy: its plebeian Irish character Teague is the butt of jokes and violence, and popular social pretensions are mocked throughout. Nonetheless, the cautious approval of the French Revolution, mockery of high society, ridicule of quasi-aristocratic Federalism, and skepticism toward systematic religion remind us what early US fiction *could* have looked like in different circumstances. Even the novel's scatological humor, ethnic-racial dialect, and sexual innuendo demonstrate contact with, if not endorsement of, a more democratic civil society absent in contemporaries.

Accordingly, we may better appreciate the tremendous change marked by the election of 1800. If it seems categorically inappropriate to tie literary history with certain historical events, especially those of institutional politics, the rise of the Democratic-Republicans may be an exception. Federalist electoral success was virtually confined to New England, and in 1804, Jefferson swept all but two states. The Seventh Congress found Federalists losing twenty-two House seats, the Ninth another eleven, and even after the gains of 1808, Federalists barely held more than a third of the seats. In the Senate, Federalists dominated twenty-two to ten in the Sixth Congress; by the Tenth Congress, Federalists held but six of thirty-four seats.

If Federalists enjoyed a long tradition of authority, from the mobilization against Shays, the suppression of the Democratic-Republican Societies, and through the Alien and Sedition Acts, they now belonged to a fading oppositional party that flirted with secession and helplessly witnessed a war they opposed, never regaining the presidency. Such shifts signaled a dramatic reconstitution of the intelligentsia with the further growth of the press, a restaffing of governmental positions, and the extension of Democratic-Republican institutions as the Federalists struggled to regroup.

Such changes were far from "progressive" in any unambiguous sense: slavery was tremendously fortified; militarization and expansionism became the norm; and many advances for women were arrested or reversed. Nor did Federalists yield the novel to more democratic authors: one could list Martha Meredith Read, George Watterston, William Jenks, Samuel Lorenzo Knapp, and Thomas Pettengill, Federalists all. But in the generational shift that occurred—most of the 1790s authors were born between 1741 and 1765; most of the post-1800 writers were born between the late 1770s and 1793—hegemonic affiliation and authority could no longer be assumed. The result was an intensification of class warfare that in its extreme form produced the anti-Jefferson satires of the 1810s, but in its more common form necessitated a retooling and recombination of the novel's basic components—character, plot, narration, setting—to revivify literary conservatism.

Modern Chivalry again provides some index of these changes. In 1800, Brackenridge had helped launch a Democratic-Republican newspaper in Pittsburgh, had supported Jefferson over Burr in the election, and had been rewarded with a seat on Pennsylvania's Supreme Court. But the democratization of the state party resulted in an assault on the judiciary, perceived as the Federalists' last governmental stronghold, and by the time he published *Modern Chivalry*'s next installments, in 1805, he had just survived an attempt to remove him from the court. The novel's new volumes register these changes. The first four volumes featured an itinerant Captain Farrago traveling through society with an Irish (or Scottish) sidekick; this narrative frame allowed for a series of critiques of new social institutions, popular and elite. The new volumes, however, found Farrago first returning to his hometown to face the contradictions of community politics, then leading a host of rowdies (O'Fin, Will Watlin, Harum Scarum, Tom the Tinker) to become "governor" of a new settlement, along the way encountering communities characterizing populist foibles (the "mad-caps," the "Lack-learnings," the "democrats"). Roaming satire of emergent institutions yielded to community critique focused on problems of integration. If the early volumes targeted elite professionals as much as presumptuous weavers, the later volumes defend the professions as a bulwark against democratic excesses, depicting the democratic mania as so threatening as to challenge the very distinction between humans and animals. Humor increasingly gave way to sober meditations on the law as a means to moderate the self-destructive leveling tendencies of the "multitude"; the latter term, which had appeared a dozen times in the

1790s volumes, appears fifty-eight in the nineteenth-century volumes. In sum, one of the novels most attuned to democratic culture under Federalism reemerged as a text of the centrist elite trying to manage the new democratic politics.

Two recurrent figures—the Irish and the Methodist—may help us approach the broader shift signaled by Brackenridge. *Modern Chivalry* could initially present the Irishman as a comic, violent, oversexualized buffoon, and the 1797 volume sent the animalized Irishman to France. But the 1804–1805 installments brought Teague back from exile, apparently in response to the Irish figure's great popularity. The narrator several times interrupts his critique of democratic populism against the legal profession to insist he is not mocking the Irish through Teague—indeed, another Irish character complains about the stereotyping:

> [I]s it a genteel ting, to trow a ridicule upon de whole Irish nation, by carrying about wid you, a bog-trotter, just as you would an allegator; or some wild cratur dat you had catched upon de mountains, to make your game of paple dat have de same brogue upon deir speech; and de same dialect upon deir tongues, as he has? By de holy faders, it is too much in a free country, not to be suffered—(pt. 2, v. 2, ch. 8)

As equivocal as these remarks are—shifting the joke from the social-climbing, bestial Teague to plebeian resentment—these volumes nonetheless acknowledged the rising anti-Irish sentiment in a brief treatment of "paddie-burning," the ritual destruction of Irish effigies. A similarly ambiguous treatment appeared in *Moreland Vale* (1801), the second novel of the "Lady of the State of New-York." The plebeian O'Needys play a brief role in the novel, moving from complicity in the heroine's betrayal to redemptive subordination and service; but the most notable Irish figure is Patrick Kilkenny—still a clown close to the bottom rung of British-imperial hierarchy, but nonetheless a figure of bombastically good-natured loyalty. Watterston's *Glencarn* (1810) likewise presented a crowd of ethnic rowdies, including an Irishman crying "By the holy St. Patrick! . . . Jefferson must be our next President; he's the only man who can save us from these bloody pirates, the English." But shortly thereafter, the title character, now a victimized fugitive, is rescued solely through the hospitality of "this warm hearted Hibernian," Patrick O'Dougherty (v. 2, ch. 11).

A less ambiguous consideration of the Irish was also visible. Samuel Woodworth's experimental account of the War of 1812, *The Champions of Freedom* (1816), gave an Irish immigrant family a central role. The novel stages the marriage of the Anglo-American with the Irish in the relationship between its hero, George Willoughby, and Catharine Fleming, granddaughter of an Irish harper, whose songs nostalgically commemorate Erin and stress US-Irish parallels of British oppression. One of Catharine's uncles dies in the British navy, a victim of impressment, while another embraces the patriot cause in 1812; he functions in much of the novel to chronicle US naval heroism. The anonymous *The Irish Emigrant* (1817), "by an

Hibernian," made the US-Irish parallel even more explicit in the central character of Owen McDermott, "an Irishman of the purest cast," and survivor of the failed United Irishmen's mobilization of 1798 (v. 1, 7). Where Woodworth largely evaded the problem of Catholicism, the "Hibernian" presented his central character as a Roman Catholic, but "liberal in the extreme" toward "the different denominations of Christians" (v. 1, 8). While the novel focused entirely on events in Ireland, it concluded with the hero and heroine "meeting each other in a country wherein they could speak their sentiments without dread, where all things had now come to a proper level, and man was found as he ought to be" (v. 2, 199). The growing appearance of the Irish was in part a Democratic recoding of the early French-English split so central to the 1790s. The bloody, atheistic, tyrannical, decadent, saltatory French could now be reimagined as the playful, devout, victimized, folkish, musical Irish, with a correspondent recoding of the English—no longer bulwarks of freedom against continental predations, but now occupiers of a colonized people struggling to reenact the American Revolution. More fundamental, however, was the very significance of the Irish as immigrant or emigrant. *The Champions of Freedom* presented its Irish family quietly settled in a remote village minding its own business, and in this depiction of the unobtrusive "Irish neighbors" we see a crucial departure from both the ethnic (and generally masculine) caricature *and* the older assumption of the homogeneous village. The Irish is an emigrant attached to Irish republicanism but also to US freedoms—"American" by choice and affinity, not by accident of birth—and an immigrant in the sense of quietly settling down to fit in. The connotations of Irishness—quick temper, rough learning, musical gifts, nostalgic sensibilities—become, for a time, inflections of an American type rather than marks of alterity.

We see a similar trend in the growing presence of the Methodist. Susanna Rowson cast the Methodist as a byword for sentimentality in *Trials of the Human Heart*, and Methodists appear as types of piety—often false—for decades thereafter. The anonymously authored *The Soldier's Orphan* (1812), for example, describes a figure as "meek and godly like a methodist" (ch. 8), while Read's *Margaretta* (1807) presented a "waiting-woman . . . suddenly turned methodist" though "both a cheat and a liar" (337). Thomas Pettengill's *The Yankee Traveller* (1817) presented a still more negative depiction with a Jeffersonian Jacobin who "travelled the circuit of the States in company with a Methodist preacher, for the sole purpose of revolutionizing the politics of the people, and to bring them back to first principles." "I am bold to say," the character continues, "that I have made thousands of democrats, all good men and true, who when called upon to turn out and do their duty, will stand fire to a man" (ch. 2). Other references were more neutral. Most notable, perhaps, was *The Life and Adventures of Obadiah Benjamin Franklin Bloomfield, M.D.* (1818), which combined Franklinian autobiography with Sternean metafiction in a comic *Bildungsroman*. Obadiah, over the course of his narration, rises from being the son of a mechanic (a carpenter who labored from poverty to an estate of "SEVENTY THOUSAND POUNDS STERLING!!" [ch. 1]) to his third and final marriage to the daughter of a haughty patrician merchant. Obadiah opts for a career in medicine, but to fulfill his father's wish to hear his son preach before he dies, follows the guidance of a local preacher, "Mr. Method," and becomes a "humble methodist circuit-rider" (ch. 10). While his father wishes him to remain a good Presbyterian and exacts a promise to quit the Methodist convention, Obadiah insists, "Forms and ceremonies have no manner of weight with me. A sincere christian must be a sincere christian all the world over, whether he be a presbyterian, episcopalian, baptist, methodist, or Roman catholic. . . . Heaven is the haven to which they all direct their steps" (ch. 6). Obadiah's adventures with the Methodists are hardly flattering—he is repeatedly recognized as being a better sort, and as a charismatic preacher has his first sexual encounter, with a seventeen-year-old girl willing to "do any thing in the world to oblige a minister" (ch. 9).

Prior to these new references, Protestant affiliation in this era was a given; its definition practically unnecessary because it was assumed and unimportant. The major exceptions—the Papist, the Quaker, and the Jew—signaled hereditary and quasi-national histories and oddities rather than choice. "Methodist" thus signaled a new kind of creature with the very idea of the denomination: one opted to become, to name one's self, a Methodist as a sign of a self-fashioning program—"methodizing" one's spirituality. At issue, then, was less a corresponding political affiliation, Pettengill's assertions aside, because Methodists were hardly associated with one party, and in their apostolic structure were far from being the most democratic of the emerging denominations. Their significance is more a matter of the reformulation of moral and personal identity, in which one did not automatically adhere to the traditions of the family or community, and even took one's self as a field of reforming practice under the guidance of an institutionalized movement. In that respect, Obadiah's use of the Methodists—he preaches before his parents, then leaves the convention—is consistent with the idea of the denomination itself, something one can leave as well as join. And his marriage across class lines occurs only because his love interest's patrician father experiences a conversion—"you have shown me how much greater, how much nobler, the *true christian* is, than the *man*" (ch. 28)—as denomination trumps status.

This larger reorientation of the novel's moral program is evident in the changing didactic novel. Hitchcock's *The Farmer's Friend* could confidently express hegemonic authority in the tale of Charles Worthy's integration into a New England community. Even as we look for tensions and resistance in the epistolary novels of the 1790s, this hegemony likewise determines the parameters: the Bourn women, nouveaux riches appearing in *The Power of Sympathy*, are integrated into Mrs. Holmes's Belleview, taking instruction from the patriarchal Reverend Holmes. By 1800, Sherburne's *The Oriental Philanthropist* (perhaps influenced by the booming East Asian trade) revealingly recast didactic fiction as orientalist fantasy, its republican hero a Chinese prince aided by genies and flying carpets. Programmatic works that spelled out moral types and scenarios, like *The Art of Courting* (1795) and *The Boarding-School* (1798), increasingly gave way to works like *The Life and Reflections of Charles Observator* (1816) by Elijah Sabin a prominent Methodist itinerant in New England. This foray into fiction sought to negotiate, and in some ways transcend, class distinctions, as in this account of manners:

> When a right education and amiable qualities of mind are wanting, such are prone to be imperious, proud and extravagant, and rarely fit for wives or mothers. These defects can never be supplied by a *mimic politeness* and a round of *empty ceremony*. . . . A gentle spirit, a sensible, easy manner of address, a graceful, modest behaviour, at an equal distance from ceremony and rudeness, adorned and sanctified by rational piety; are traits of the real polite. . . . But among the rich, one cannot always be sure of such accomplishments as these, as unsubstantial as they are. Their daughters, sometimes, shew a Gothic rudeness, joined with an intolerable insolence, occasioned by the supposed merit of riches; which make them of all creatures in the world, the most to be dreaded. (ch. 8)

Here the search for that elusively "unsubstantial" middle path of behavior—more sincere than the "empty" forms of the rich—speaks to a reformulation of morality consistent with the denominational realities of the broader society, in which the intrinsic "worth" of the self yields to the more embedded, differentiating role of "observator." We see a similar formulation in Sarah Savage's *The Factory Girl* (1814), in which the factory is less the definitive setting of subjectivity shaped by labor than a very different social context for morality. Mary is not defined by work in the factory but encounters the factory as a venue of interchangeability in which to distinguish herself as a moral role model. Thus she ventures to reform William Raymond, at one point a potential spouse, until he transfers his attentions to a woman who "took [Mary's] place in the factory" (ch. 4). William's sister Nancy chooses a different moral path, as if their familial connection is nullified by the systematization of the workplace. Mary herself finds marriage as the second wife of the minister Mr. Danforth, her final status as stepmother reinforcing the elective nature of religious affections.

The Irish and the Methodists are thus two different indices of a changing sociopolitical landscape in which some relation of adjacency—like "neighbor" or "meeting"—supplanted a more organic fiction of community belonging. This reformulation is not, however, a phenomenon of urbanization. To be sure, the city does loom larger in the nineteenth century, most notably in Robert Waln's quasi-novelistic *The Hermit in America* (1819), which included illustrations of urban dandies promenading before rows of townhouses. But it seems more accurate to say that the idea of the variegated states, regions, populations, and lifestyles of US residents was definitive for a rurally inflected modernity. In such a vein, we might note the didactic fictions of George Fowler, *The Wandering Philanthropist* (1810) and *A Flight to the Moon* (1813). Where the former, like Peter Markoe's *The Algerine Spy in*

Pennsylvania (1787), used the familiar figure of the Oriental outsider to describe US institutions, the latter formulated a radically different vantage point: Randalthus, the voyager to the Lunarians, is not interested in learning about a new society, but rather he lectures the nearsighted natives about the amazing planet they see in the sky. While Fowler's preface disavows any attempt at "systematic discussion" in a work of "fancy," it nonetheless stresses systems in their astronomical, geographical, biological, political, and cultural dimensions—using "system" or related terms throughout the text. As Randalthus at one point states, "The difficulty, Oh Lunarians, which my native race have to encounter is . . . not to adapt a system suitable to their nature, but to adopt their nature to a suitable system!" This revealing formulation, seeing the United States as a global region, immediately prompts a microcosmic inference about the self: "Now of all governments that of self is to them the most difficult; and, while they often find it easy to overcome external obstacles to subdue those which are internal imposes a task in which an anxious life may be spent in vain" (47).

The early US novels discussed above suggest how the designations of Irish and Methodist offer two complementary designations of social proximity: one denoting an objective subjectivity of sorts (one is born Irish, has Irish characteristics), the other a subjective objectivity (one chooses to become a Methodist, to methodize oneself). One need simply imagine Irish or Methodist figures playing a significant role in the Federalist novels of the 1790s—as significant characters, not as caricatures or objects—to appreciate the change. Amélie Oksenberg Rorty's distinction between "figures" and "persons" is helpful here (1976, 302–11). "Figures" are exemplary idealizations, whether cautionary or heroic, as in the early US readings of Plutarch's *Lives*. They differ from the earlier "characters" in having an interiorized sense of themselves: they discover what they are (because of ancestry or tradition) and act accordingly. Conversely, in the novels of the 1790s, "figures" discover their affinity to Young Werther and put bullets in their heads, or they turn their experiences of persecution into circumstances for a life of Christian suffering. "Persons" appear as this sense of one's role becomes increasingly a matter of differentiated *choice*: the person chooses roles and is judged by those choices. A reader encountering a literary person considers her a moral, legal actor with responsibilities and liabilities; intention and self-understanding displace social role and habit as foci for judgment. The "figure" does not have identity crises; the "person" does. The figure is, as one character is described in Isaac Mitchell's *The Asylum* (1811), "an heterogeneous compound of right and wrong, honour and dishonesty, candour and hypocrisy" (v. 1, ch. 5). In Rorty's account, "persons" appear alongside legal thinking, and we might note the proliferation of legal frameworks at this moment (1976, 309). The later volumes of *Modern Chivalry*, with their fixation on common law and juridical liberality; Caroline Matilda Warren Thayer's *The Gamesters; or, Ruins of Innocence* (1805), which introduces a moral problem, gambling, as originating with economic inheritance and the problem of lifestyle choices; or Watterston's *The*

Lawyer; or, Man as He Ought Not to Be (1808), which uses the figure of the lawyer to accentuate the institutional catalysts of one's immoral choices—all register the growing significance of legal discourses and practices, central to the battles between Democratic-Republicans and Federalists. But the increasing politicization of cultural institutions suggests not simply a *legal* but, more widely, a *civic* sensibility in which citizens were liable for broader national developments. It was this new sensibility that most profoundly marks the departure from confident Federalist hegemony, as political and cultural conflicts are increasingly matters of management.

In fact, the transition to the person had been prepared by political discourse through the late 1790s, when a standard mode of political argumentation became the characterological portrait—accounts of the founding fathers as persons of certain tendencies. The supreme examples were the four big founders—Washington, Franklin, Jefferson, and Hamilton—each drawn in detail in the popular press every election season in the form of biographical sketches, intercepted letters, and satirical caricatures. The notorious controversy between Jefferson and Aaron Burr unfolded in this vein as well, with a series of pamphlet portraits beginning with John Wood's *The History of the Administration of John Adams* (1802) and continuing with a series of sketches by editor James Cheetham as well as by Washington and Peter Irving. Political impact aside, this popular form of writing plays a significant role in US literary history and partially explains the return of the satirical novel in the late 1810s, mostly penned by extreme Federalists and anticipated by Irving's 1809 *History of New York*, which presented its "history" as conflicts among colorfully eccentric Dutch administrators, modeled on US politicos. This hypothetical history of "persons" found more overtly Federalist counterparts after the War of 1812, with the appearance of *The Adventures of Uncle Sam* (1816) by F. A. Fidfaddy, Pettengill's *Yankee Traveller*, and *Fragments of the History of Bawlfredonia* (1819) by "Jonas Clopper," depicting a land whose inhabitants constantly cried freedom. The goal in each was to articulate, or perhaps map, political-cultural personality types and tendencies at work in the United States. Thus Pettengill's narrator sets out with his flighty uncle and associates to meet their archetype, Thomas Conundrum. To modify Rorty's argument, the issue was *political* liability—attributing responsibility for the state of the nation—rather than a narrower legal liability.

This combination of systems and persons, then, verged on the presentation of historicity that emerged in the novels of the 1820s, though the historical formulation was still difficult to conceive. On the eve of the War of 1812, *The Soldier's Orphan* illustrated the problem allegorically. The titular soldier, whose fall at Quebec in 1775 unites North American Whiggery from the 1750s into the 1780s, appears only in the introductory chapters' backstory, leaving the orphan, Emily, to fare in a world of commerce disconnected from historical patterns. Tellingly, her guardian "uncle" is a privateer deemed more prosperous than he actually is, and much of the novel is devoted to the mercantile ventures whereby he and Emily's beau are captured by Algerines. In a basic sense, the orphanhood signals a shift from the clearly progressive history of North American politics to the vagaries of Atlantic commerce and concludes not with Emily's marriage but rather with the community erecting a monument to Emily's parents, dead since 1776—"persons" commemorating the heroic "characters" of the past. Woodworth's later novel of the War of 1812, *The Champions of Freedom*, made similar attempts to enact historicity, putting characters within notorious contexts to create narrative verisimilitude, convey factual information, and promote patriotism. That the novel relied so heavily on direct reproduction of newspaper accounts and magazine sketches of military figures again indicates some challenges of this shift. The most imaginative treatment of historicity appears early in the novel, in the backstory of the Revolutionary father and the depiction of the Native American ghost; the war reportage reads more like a chronicle of events than formative context.

These texts lend themselves to a clarification of the older economistic narrative whereby something like "liberalism" supplanted "republicanism." Commercial values did not simply percolate into the novel form with the growth of the capitalist economy. In his 1808 counterfactual novel, *Memoir of the Northern Kingdom*, William Jenks posited not a clash between republicans and their liberal successors, but an admission that "republicanism" was so vague a concept as to accommodate any number of conflicting identities—Francophile plantocracy and Yankee federalism, but also Anglo-Canadian and Latin American varieties. The resulting dystopian vision—the collapse of the United States into Anglophilic northern and Francophilic southern kingdoms, with Illinois fanatics to the west—clarified the problem as one of association and organization, rather than ideology. It would be more helpful, then, to see the novel in these decades as a sphere of class conflict in the shadows of a massive political shift. The constellation of "republicanism" could no longer appear, even in fiction by Federalists, as a unifying moral and social rubric. The literary components making up the novel—characters, didacticism, satire, historicity—increasingly came under pressure, only to be relatively stabilized with the historical novel of the 1820s. As some aforementioned examples suggest, the War of 1812, with its formulation of militaristic (specifically naval) nationalism relative to other global states, played a tremendous role, in part by strengthening the Democratic Party, in part by minimizing the values and mythology of what Margaret Botsford's *Adelaide* (1816) called "waistcoats embroidered, and three cornered hats" (ltr. 11). Thus the novels of these decades are less literary derelicts than enactments of this reformulation, as should become clear with a concluding consideration of a cluster of novels published about 1810: Mitchell's *The Asylum*, Jesse Holman's *The Prisoners of Niagara* (1810), Rebecca Rush's *Kelroy* (1812), Leonora Sansay's *The Secret History; or, The Horrors of St. Domingue* (1808), Watterston's *Glencarn*, and the anonymous *Rosa; or, American Genius and Education* (1810).

Mitchell was among the oldest of the period's novelists, and he had published versions of *The Asylum* in the Democratic newspapers he managed. That he viewed himself as a republican of the Revolutionary generation is apparent throughout the novel: the love plot between Alonzo Haventon and Melissa Bloomfield is a story of the struggle for independence from tyranny. The long subplot of the Berghers, who flee monarchical Europe, face colonial hardship, enjoy American prosperity, and finally patriotically affiliate with the United States, dominates the first volume. The second features Melissa's incarceration in a feudal, Gothic castle; Alonzo's naval service in the war; and an encounter with Ben Franklin—again reinforcing the revolutionary narrative. More revealing, however, are the repeated indices that such a narrative can barely accommodate established generic conventions. In the terms outlined earlier, *The Asylum* is a republican novel splintering into republicanism's conflicted components.

One sign of this is the novel's doubling of forematter—an introduction and a preface "Comprising a Short Dissertation on Novel." The introduction discusses and defends the novel form, depicting a writer describing for a skeptical friend the lonely enterprise of literature in a society of few readers and feeble critics. Singled out for special attention is Goldsmith's comic, conservative *The Vicar of Wakefield* (1766), a novel that never finds its US counterpart. The preface then shifts perspectives to provide a politicized overview and defense of the "novel" from a critical perspective, as if oscillating between subjective, romantic engagement and objective, clinical abstraction. This oscillation defines the novel, for example, in the long natural tableaux that are interrupted by footnotes on birch beer, sugar maples, and lightning bugs. The masculine protagonist is now Alonzo, now Haventon, depending on his intersubjective location. When he encounters Franklin in Paris, having succumbed to despair over Melissa's presumed death, he receives an equally conflicted lecture. First Franklin corrects Alonzo's philosophical errors, telling him his romanticism is childish, that love can never satisfy, and that family and country need service rather than moping. But once Alonzo has decided to return home, Franklin becomes a practical businessman, explaining the machinations behind Alonzo's father's bankruptcy, resolving the financial crisis, and finding Alonzo a passage home. The subsequent shipwreck accentuates the split further: the event is at once an act of God and a commercial catastrophe; when locals learn of the wreck, they go both to bury the dead and to collect valuables; and Alonzo, as the ship is sinking, saves both the miniature of Melissa and the financial papers clearing his father's accounts. When Alonzo, seeing his parents in poverty, declares "Alas! . . . I now perceive the value of wealth in this life" (ch. 9), this is less a lament that commercialism has infested republicanism than an admission that they cannot remain antithetical. Accordingly, the concluding reunion with Melissa attempts a resolution of these modes. Alonzo, during his captivity in a British prison, heard the tale of Malcomb, who, subject to the prank staged by his sister, shot his fiancée in the head while stabbing his sister to death. Having returned to Charleston, Alonzo encounters Melissa through a similarly elaborate drama, complete with false backstory and disguise, but his emotional reunion lacks the excessive passion of her death and segues into banal details, shared over breakfast, of family history, press errors, and a counterfeiting ring. One might say that the novel thus concludes with a kind of secularization of republicanism itself, whereby it learns its proper place and limitations. The titular concept thus has many resonances—the homestead to which Alonzo and Melissa retreat, the United States itself as a global asylum in a world of European corruption, and even republicanism itself as a limited sphere within a complex world of commerce and politics.

Chronologically earlier but arguably more post-Revolutionary in sentiment was Sansay's *Secret History*, a novel that has received deserved critical attention for its engagement with the Haitian Revolution in Saint-Domingue, not to mention depictions of Cuba and Jamaica, all locales implicitly or explicitly compared with the United States. These settings clearly reveal the transnational dimensions of US fiction more generally, most obviously signaled in such other works as Read's *Margaretta*, which juxtaposes Haiti, Britain, and the United States; Botsford's *Adelaide*, which juxtaposes Barbados, Britain, and the United States; and immigrant Gotthilf Lutyens's *The Life and Adventures of Moses Nathan Israel* (1815), which offers an artisan's Jeffersonian travel narrative through German and Italian landscapes before concluding with treatments of Canada, Britain, and the United States. The power of the Haitian context, however, is that it establishes something of a formula for analysis, with its constantly changing sexual, class, and racial relationships, so that the island's Cape François can be a scene of social delights and of dramatic sexual violence within the same chapter. The result is a kaleidoscopic sense of the mutability of the person in different contexts. Far from having a fixed national, sexual, or ethno-racial identity, one can be an odd aggregate of these histories, like Don Carlos, an Irishman moving between Peru, Spain, and Jamaica, or more constant in character yet differently inflected by one's environment, like Clara, who is far more than a simple heroine. As her sister describes her at the novel's end, Clara

> seizes intuitively on what is true, and by a sort of mental magic, arrives instantaneously at the point where, even very good heads, only meet her after a tedious process of reasoning and reflection. . . . She accumulates knowledge while she laughs and plays: she steals from her friends the fruits of their application, and thus becoming possessed of their intellectual treasure, without the fatigue of study, she surprises them with ingenious combinations of their own materials, and with results of which they did not dream. (ltr. 32)

The echoes of Madame de Staël's *Influence of the Passions* (1796), with its dream of a mathematically precise political science, are strong, and suggest the great analytical significance and force of women as the best gauges of their political milieu. Thus one might read Sansay's romantic novel of a year later, *Laura* (1809), as a more domestically focused narrative of a similar process, its romanticism less a marker of character than an index of setting.

Rosa; or, American Genius and Education, published anonymously in New York, could be considered a "southern" novel—its plot focuses on Maryland's western shore—and some index of southern Democratic sensibilities, with gibes at Boston Yankees terrified of French naval invasion. Its dominant modes are sentimental narrative—the main marriage plot—and farcical satire, the two combining in a theory of education. Most interesting is the novel's focus on two older characters—Mrs. Dorinda Charmion, aged forty, and Mr. Derwent, fifty—each single after disastrous marriages. Derwent's wife abandoned him for a Frenchman in Barbados, while Charmion, due to her poor education, botches her marriage before seeing her husband murdered by British troops. Each of these characters ultimately discovers a long-lost surviving child—married to one another, no less—but they are figures of ridicule, the Longpees, one a simpering fool to the other's domineering selfishness. Although "English education" has ruined their natural children, even reversing the gendered order, Charmion and Derwent nonetheless find redemption through their adopted wards: the lady starting over with ten-year-old Rosa, a mysterious poor girl from nearby; while the gentleman patronizes Richard, a fifteen-year-old literary protégé. These children become exemplars of their respective sexes and are united in marriage in the final chapter.

At a basic level, the novel confirms a common argument about education, especially for women—Mrs. Charmion's disastrous marriage results from her combination of natural genius with inadequate guidance, so that she becomes, in one depiction, a lonely woman reflecting sadly on the past and the loss of her family. At the same time, however, Mrs. Charmion is one of the novel's most appealing persons—urbane, generous, witty, beautiful, fashionable, and aloof. What would have been cast as the signs of a flawed character in the 1790s now appear as the very basis for a new subjectivity. So it is that four years' "tuition" of Rosa is focused not simply on the usual skills ("the needle" and "domestic economy"), nor even observation of the foibles of others (Mrs. Bagatelle, Miss Seemly), but on a privacy that borders on secrecy:

> She likewise invariably inculcated to her protégée the necessity of being extremely cautious not to confide to strangers, nor even to common acquaintances, her sentiments or her opinions; and with respect to all her views of life, previously to certain fruition, to make her own bosom the sole depository of them. (ch. 6)

This privacy is understood in terms of gossip, the subject of two satirical interludes, and as the overview of Rosa's education continues, we're told "Mrs. Charmion also taught her never to repeat in one company what she had heard in another; nor to give the least currency to scandal or calumny by the sanction of her name: to beware of overstrained courtesies, of panegyric, and of sudden and enormous professions of friendship" (ch. 6). Education, then, is less about giving positive content to a subject than to giving a strictly formal and well-armored coherence to that subjectivity. What emerges, then, is a dialectic between genius (one's potential merit) and education (one's sociality) that illustrates some of the contradictions of the Democratic Party. On the one hand, the novel celebrates the Incan descendent

Sol and his progressive views on education, delivered to ignorant Eurocentrists in England; the great surprise, at the novel's end, is that Rosa is Sol's daughter, deliberately planted in Mrs. Charmion's household to prove his pedagogic theory. This assertion of a kind of abstract equality is countered, though, by an unrelentingly condescending and negative view of most ordinary citizens, including many members of urban high society, newsmongers, local law and court officials, clergymen, young people, litigants and lawyers, and partisans and orators. These people must be ignored and left to act in their lowly spheres—one should not engage—which may explain why Mrs. Charmion's loyal black slaves are less the butt of jokes than most whites, and how the Incan Sol can pursue a career as a Virginia overseer on "villa lands" to the south. If Sol and his daughter are the equals of some whites, it may reflect the heritage of the Incas, who civilized "those whom they conquered" (ch. 6). In this account, democracy is a formal matter, its actual content determining whether others are compatible souls or farcical animals.

Holman's *Prisoners of Niagara* may be considered a "western" novel; its author read law in Henry Clay's Kentucky offices before relocating to the Indiana Territory to serve as prosecutor, legislator, and judge. The novel's imaginative geography reflects this range as well, Richmond and Baltimore serving as corrupting urban social spaces, western Pennsylvania as a practical space of militant masculinity, and western Virginia as a site of domestic compromise. At first glance, the novel suggests great anxiety about social identity, so much so that its protagonist William Evermont assumes multiple names and costumes even as he accumulates a perplexingly long list of potential parents. Likewise, by novel's end, his love interest Zerelda is layered in disguises, having shifted from her mysterious veils to a double cross-dressing disguise of a Revolutionary patriot masquerading as a loyalist. The concomitant confusion is such that through much of the novel Evermont wonders if he has killed his father and slept with his sister. Though he has not committed incest, the crime's taint is removed not by discovering the lover's identity but through the absolution of his fiancée, who tells him that it is only a crime with incestuous intentions. The thrust of this hyper-romantic novel, then, is not toward a return to stable identity, lineage, and social order, but toward a form of identity grounded in masculine independence and enterprise, somewhat demonstrated by Evermont's concluding decision to free his inherited slaves. The best illustration, however, is the militarized culture of war. This is not the institutional militarism that would appear after 1812; here most characters come and go from the military as emotions and situations dictate, typically fighting in impromptu groups, dressed as Indians. The career of the one historical cameo—the Marquis de Lafayette—reflects a choice of calling rather than an obligation. Military activity is more of an existential calling than a matter of patriotism, and masculine identity is highly individualized and determined by extreme behavior rather than social ties.

In some ways, Rush's *Kelroy* might be read as an inversion of Holman's novel. Often read as the most polished and modern of early US fictions, this novel of manners sketches its characters with nuance and irony surpassing most contemporaries. Yet it does so to devastating, almost self-defeating effect—its thwarted lovers, Emily Hammond and the vaguely romantic Kelroy, are both dead at the conclusion. The prime mover of events seems at first to be Mrs. Hammond, whose malice embodies an avarice surpassing her resources. But her scheme is ultimately furthered by both well-intentioned friends and accidental social acquaintances: that is, the plot unfolds not solely via intentional scheming but also through the complex dynamics of a society so class riven that it takes a full community to foil and kill two lovers. Indeed, the novel's intensive characterizations lead to the tragic stalemate of the narrative, as if individuation itself is the problem. In this light, one of the most revealing figures is Dr. Blake, a man whose socially inappropriate strangeness—"you are really—a very—strange person," he is told at one point (ch. 7)—speaks to a sense of social opacity beyond the class interlopings of Marney and the Gurnets, local vulgarians. Where the novels of the 1790s might have cast "manners" as a guide to social clarity, manners here index misleading social appearances or intentional deceptions.

Watterston's *Glencarn* is often misleadingly compared to Brockden Brown's novels but reads more like pastiche, as its titular protagonist articulates himself in diverse generic modes (romantic, sentimental, and pastoral). This confusion illustrates the novel's decidedly modern thesis, which the preface presents as the belief that "happiness is the result of a certain physical organization of the nerves, modified by habits of virtue"—that is, the genres that cycle through the text are reflections of different cultural habits laid upon the organic material (the cairn in the glen) of the main character. This problematic is itself an overt attempt to transcend Revolutionary republicanism. Glencarn's surrogate father, Mr. Richardson, is an ideal republican whose positive moral and educational influences on Glencarn are counterbalanced by his family: for all his insights, his second wife, "sly" and vindictive, murders her husband and tries repeatedly to undermine Glencarn's social status (ch. 1). Richardson's daughter Amelia, Glencarn's love, is sent to a boarding school to escape Mrs. Richardson's influence, while his son, Rodolpho, becomes a dandy and is later killed trying to murder Glencarn. Glencarn's actual father, Montjoy, is an erratic, republican paranoid driven to insane jealousy. Notably, Glencarn experiences almost identical manipulations, weathering them more productively. A number of other episodes serve to negate republican orthodoxy: Glencarn's attempt at writing didactic essays fails—no one responds—while he wastes his formal education as "an automaton" (ch. 10). In sum, the republican legacy is less an inheritance or a program than a nervous condition to overcome. As for society at large, Glencarn meets a series of scoundrels with few exceptions. After his adopted father is killed, a contingent of barely motivated adversaries gathers around Mrs. Richardson and Rodolpho. His college friend Gray tries to steal Amelia and becomes a lifelong adversary. In a world of gratuitous social villainy, the "good" and virtuous characters not only fail to inspire but are also defined by basic flaws. Phebe's virtues are offset by her "negro" superstition and verbosity; Mary Baldwin, who stands by Glencarn when he is wrongly imprisoned, attempts suicide because she cannot resolve her love for her seducer. Her father, who helps Glencarn restore his reputation, cannot transcend his grief over his daughter's death. Sophia, the child of nature, goes mad from misdirected love. And so on. In fact, the solidly virtuous characters appear briefly and become background figures in a reversal of the older novel's conventions. One might even read the Wilson subplot, in which banditti prey on river traffic, as a "secret history" of sorts—a parallax representation of US society, in which group behavior, transforming individuals' nerves, reveals the degraded free-for-all of Jeffersonian America. Of course, since Wilson divided Glencarn's parents, these pirates of the interior are also revealed as the mysterious history behind Glencarn himself. We might also see the serial structure of the novel as a marker of a patchwork of rural and (increasingly) urban spaces, in which individuals circulate fruitlessly in repetitive attempts to stabilize themselves.

In the end, Glencarn's discovery of his parentage does not situate him within a meaningful history. He is rather fixing the muddled relationship between his parents, placing it beyond his own history, by putting it together after the fact. In a larger sense, this is the story of the early nineteenth-century novel itself, naturalizing and muting republicanism as progenitors are created anew. Each of the novels just surveyed placed established republican conventions under mutative pressure, producing narratives of familiar elements but in unexpected combinations. The dynamics of capitalism and the shift in class power were less new intrusions than a different center of gravity, reorienting, compressing, displacing, or amplifying older republicanisms, until the historical novel of the 1820s emerged as the hegemonic means to manage the past.

5

UNSETTLING NOVELS OF THE EARLY REPUBLIC

LEONARD TENNENHOUSE

Regardless of the critical school, most accounts of the American novel show it pulling together a cohesive national readership to form what Benedict Anderson has called an "imagined community." The tendency among scholars is consequently to scour early American fiction for self-conscious signs of national aspiration, to analyze plots for what they might say about a national politics, to study landscapes for their uniquely American topography, and to explain the sheer number of gothic and sentimental texts in terms of how they might have united quite different segments of the readership around those aspirations, ideals, and political goals. All this critical ingenuity is expended in an effort to locate signs of a coherent American character that can be declared an early version of the ideal citizen subject. While a few novels do indeed reward the stalwart critic with evidence to justify one or more of these procedures, most do not. This is especially true of those novels written before the 1820s. Hence, histories of the American novel tend to skip over most earlier novels in order to settle on James Fenimore Cooper's frontier fiction—particularly *The Pioneers; or, The Sources of the Susquehanna* (1823), *The Last of the Mohicans: A Narrative of 1757* (1826), and *The Prairie* (1827)—as the first to offer a uniquely American hero who can mediate diasporic French, British, and American cultures and so give shape to the new nation. Current research on novels written for an American readership between the 1780s and 1820s finds no such unified cultural ethnos.

Despite a plenitude of fiction written and read in the North American colonies, few if any of these novels use narratives of individual development to signify an emerging genre, an American readership, and ultimately a nation. Like the surplus of British fiction both imported and reprinted in America, few of the novels written in America during the period in question confine their plots solely to a US geography or make an effort to represent a unified American identity. While various writers and intellectuals such as Charles Brockden Brown, Edward Tyrrell Channing, and Isaac Appleton Jewett felt the need for something like an American novel or more generally an American literature, their calls for this kind of novel indicate that there was in actuality no such thing. This raises the question of whether a history of the American novel that includes the early period can identify what is distinctly and originally American about the United States in the same way Ian Watt's *The Rise of the Novel* (1957) gives us to understand what is English about the British novel. Indeed, the novels themselves suggest that a very different narrative form appealed to the early American readership.

In combination, Franco Moretti's nonlinear "geography" of the novel's spread (in *Atlas of the European Novel*) and Paul Gilroy's description of cultural circulation during early oceanic exploration (in *The Black Atlantic*) suggest that a circum-Atlantic flow of people and information made the early American novel a cosmopolitan form. A novel like William Hill Brown's *The Power of Sympathy* (1789) or Royall Tyler's *The Algerine Captive; or, The Life and Adventures of Doctor Updike Underhill* (1797) envisioned a world as distinctive and coherent as any imagined by British domestic fiction. Novelists from Jane Austen to George Eliot encouraged the new mass readership to measure the health and well-being of the state in terms of who was inside and who had to be kept out, what kinship rules held them together, and whether they could reproduce that same community in other places and climes. By formulating a coherent character and showing how it developed over time—as when, say, Cooper's Pathfinder gives way to the English colonist who establishes a household in the wilderness—the nineteenth-century American novel also naturalized the liberal fantasy of a nation that expands one household at a time. In marked contrast to this model, the early American novel choreographed the available cultural materials to imagine a cosmopolitan world that was neither territorially bounded nor centrally organized.

The Network Novel

To understand the formal principles organizing this imaginary world, we begin by recalling that during the period from 1790 to 1802, Congress passed four different naturalization acts. This was also a decade when at least 100,000 immigrants entered the United States. The Naturalization Act of 1790 enabled an immigrant who was both free and white to become a citizen after just two years of residency. Worried about the number of potential citizens entering the country from revolutionary France and the increase in immigrants fleeing troubles in Ireland, Congress passed the Naturalization Act of 1795 extending minimum residency to five years. Those who were naturalized were required to swear allegiance to the United States, renounce loyalty to their former sovereigns, and give up any and all claims to noble ranks and titles. This act was in turn revised by the Naturalization Act of 1798, which required immigrants to register with a proper agent within forty-eight hours of arriving in the United States, stretched the waiting period for citizenship from five to fourteen years, and prohibited anyone from obtaining citizenship who was a citizen of a state with which the United States was at war. The Naturalization Law of 1802 repealed the Act of 1798. With a national debate on immigration running for the entire decade, it is not surprising that novels seeking to imagine a cosmopolitan but still American nation would have so much popular appeal.

Michael Hardt and Antonio Negri's *Multitude: War and Democracy in the Age of Empire* (2004) can help us understand how a novel made sense of a nation of immigrants and imagined a national culture formed by the dispersion, collision, assimilation, and adaptation of various practices and beliefs. Rather than "a people," such a population, in their view, is composed of "singularities," or groups whose difference cannot be reduced to sameness. Where "the component parts of the people . . . become an identity by negating or setting aside their differences," the many "singularities" that make up a multitude "stand in contrast to the undifferentiated unity of the people." But while a population "remains multiple," this does not make it "anarchical, or incoherent" (Hardt and Negri 2004, 99). To understand the principle of population as a genuine alternative to the fantasy of a unified nation, Hardt and Negri urge us to see it as "an active social subject, which acts on the basis of what the singularities share in common" (100). This model of community does not require a fixed character of the kind ascribed to the French or British and is usually based on the style of its elite members or prevailing ethos. In speaking about a population, we should think less in terms of what it is and more in terms of what it can become, for it can become any number of things, depending on one's vantage point within it and the interaction among its constituent parts. In this respect, the character of a population is rather like Herman Melville's *The Confidence-Man: His Masquerade* (1857), that is, able to actualize many different characters but steadfastly resistant to unification around any single one.

In place of the opposition between identity and difference (which compels us to determine if person X is the same as or different from us), the new nation serves as the connective tissue, or commonality, between groups of people who are simply thrown in together and subjected to the same environment. In seventeenth-, eighteenth-, and early nineteenth-century America, such commonality was a conspicuous fact of life; various elements of the population came up against the same limits of food, shelter, language, weather, and a host of other challenges exacerbated by successive waves of immigration. Many of the writers of the new republic, Hugh Henry Brackenridge and Susanna Rowson for example, were either born outside of the colonies or, like Washington Irving and Philip Freneau, lived and wrote abroad for many years. Then again, some emigrated from the United States, as Hanna Webster Foster did when she chose to live out her remaining years in Canada. Rather than understand community as a matter of inclusion as opposed to exclusion, most of the novels written in America before Cooper's locate themselves imaginatively in a community of dispersed groups whose linkages form a network. A dynamic network provides not only a figure of community but also the means of producing a coherent system of relationships in narrative form. Each such relationship overturns some hierarchy, crosses a boundary, and bundles together bodies that would otherwise belong to different groups. In contrast to the household, the network as a model for the nation establishes points of commonality among different singularities, while leaving their heterogeneity intact.

(Un)settlement Narratives

Picaresque novels of the early republic imagine the community in precisely these terms. They begin by presenting a form of cultural unity that excludes ethnic differences, which they later identify with either Old Europe or the Ottoman Empire. The traveler nevertheless carries this opposition with him from the beginning as the lens that enables him to see the new United States as a diverse citizenry and a territory that can be easily infiltrated. Peter Markoe's *The Algerine Spy in Pennsylvania* (1787), an epistolary novel consisting of letters largely by Mehemet, an Algerian official, provides a good example. The notorious Osman, Dey of Algiers, has dispatched Mehemet to the United States to learn of the new nation's political ambitions. Disguised as a Frenchman, he travels to Gibraltar where he formulates the model he will carry with him across the Atlantic. Mehemet observes that Spain's tendency to cast out groups such as the Moors "weakened Spain at least as much, as the banishment of the protestants reduced the internal resources of France in the reign of Lewis [*sic*] the XIVth" (ltr. 2). The self-defeating practice of intolerance characterizes Mehemet's homeland as well. Rumored to have become a Christian, he receives a harsh edict: "By order of the Dey, thy lands, house, furniture and slaves (two excepted) are confiscated to the state" (ltr. 21). Should he "be found within the territories of Algiers," his correspondent warns, "thy life will be forfeited" (ltr. 21). No more tolerant than Spain or France, Algiers sustains its identity as a nation by casting out Christians. Pennsylvania, by contrast, provides both Mehemet and his estranged wife with farmlands on which to start separate households. Pennsylvania, he writes, "hast promised to succor and protect the unhappy, that fly to thee for refuge" (ltr. 24). Mehemet may seem to compromise his praise of American openness when he proclaims himself "formerly a Mahometan." But he makes it clear that to become part of the Pennsylvanian community, he has freely chosen to renounce his Algerian citizenship along with his religion. Although he forsakes the very basis of his difference from the rest of the American community to facilitate his integration into it, Mehemet insists that in doing so he is rejecting Oriental absolutism for the privilege of enjoying "in the evening of his days, the united blessings of FREEDOM and CHRISTIANITY" (ltr. 24). Because absolute freedom of religion enables commonality, even the most tolerant community must preserve its identity as such by excluding the intolerant.

The Algerine Spy in Pennsylvania starts as a rather traditional picaresque narrative. Once it begins to unfold in a North American context, however, this novel takes on the distinctively American form of a settlement novel, as the narrator looks for a country that will not only accept but also protect him. If we read the picaresque narratives set in the United States as relatively aimless, providing little besides a slice of very heterogeneous social life, we are bound to be disappointed. For there is clearly an undercurrent of instrumental desire at work beneath the story's desultory surface—a sense that the narrator is actually looking to find out where he fits in and to meet the conditions for doing so. If, on the other hand, we read the American picaresque as a settlement narrative in keeping with Markoe's novel, we are bound to be disappointed again: the ethnographic exploration that aims at identifying satisfactory conditions for settlement usually fails to arrive at its destination. Indeed, many, if not most, picaresque narratives of the New World proceed as if they had settlement in mind, only to defer and finally reject that possibility in favor of continuing circulation.

Narrated by a Frenchman, Samuel Lorenzo Knapp's *Extracts from the Journal of Marshal Soult* (1817) finds much to praise in the United States. The novel concludes when he is about to leave New England for the South. Although he does admire what he sees in New England, he expects to find the American South even more congenial to his habits and sensibility. At that point, Knapp dropped the narrative of the French traveler and more or less rewrote the entire account—which he then published the following year as *Extracts from a Journal of Travels in North America* (1818). Rather than record the encounters of a French marshal with various groups of Americans, Knapp's second narrative presents the new nation from the perspective of the caustic Ali Bey, who has come to America to advise his master the Dey on the possibility of converting its people to Islam. This mission obliges Bey to report to his superiors on the foibles of the Americans, ranging from the practices of certain religious sects to the fashions of Boston Brahmins and their ladies. Even on visiting a political caucus, Bey is "surprised to find all the speakers coincide in their opinions" (ch. 4). While such unanimity may be the case within local groups, it does not hold true for relations between them.

By the conclusion of the travels, Bey has completely revised his opinion. As the appendix reveals, he comes to understand that religious divisions among the Christians

> extend through the country. Scarcely a week passes but the belligerent parties assail each other from the press or pulpit. . . . The state of irritation produced by this warfare can be easly [*sic*] imagined. And a change that will restore harmony is doubtless considered a desideratum by all.

To the Muslim protagonist, it seems as if religious differences among the many Christian sects flourishing in America foreclose the possibility of coherence at a national level. Knapp's narrative makes it clear that just the opposite happens to be true: "the press or pulpit" acts as something like a public sphere, providing a framework for even the most heated arguments. The capacity of such a framework to contain so many different religious groups, along with the conspicuous lack of a state religion, is precisely what sets the new nation apart not only from Europe but from the Ottoman East as well. The fact that "harmony" is simultaneously "considered a desideratum by all" makes American diversity superior to the Islamic absolutism that Ali Bey considers the only way of dealing with the squabbling among Christian sects. Bey's inability to recognize the virtues of a public sphere capable of mediating such contentious religious diversity would certainly have struck an early nineteenth-century American reader as ironic.

If we can call *The Algerine Spy in Pennsylvania* a settlement novel, then Ali Bey's account of his travels in North America unsettles that model by refusing to oppose diversity to commonality. Put another way, the lack of unity that characterizes the new United States is not formless so much as an advanced form of government. Where a novel like *The Algerine Spy in Pennsylvania* comes to see multiplicity as greatly superior to unity, what might be called the unsettlement novel comes to the same conclusion by negating the proposition that a community must unify a people. In so doing, the unsettlement novel distinguishes the United States as a heterogeneous community in which the purpose of government is to mediate differences rather than to end them by draconian measures.

The work of fiction perhaps most characteristic of this form is Brackenridge's *Modern Chivalry*, published in parts from 1792 to 1815. Brackenridge's protagonist wishes to find a place to settle but instead finds himself unable to do so for reasons peculiar to the new nation. In the first sections of the book, "the people" select Captain Farrago's Irish servant, Teague O'Regan, for positions he is unqualified to fill. In this respect, we might consider Teague the very figure of "the people" as Brackenridge pejoratively conceives them. The question that his narrative raises—one that perplexed Federalists and anti-Federalists alike—is the question of commonality: What indeed do all members of the new national community share? Are we to understand national character in terms of the lowest common denominator, or average man, in which case, according to Brackenridge, national history will tell the story of how public opinion came to dominate over government by qualified representatives, as Alexis de Tocqueville was soon to predict? Or should the man best qualified to represent the interests of his particular group rule the nation? In this case, national history might trace the rise of a ruling elite that Rousseau condemned in his *Discourse on the Origin of Inequality* (1755). Caught between two forms of potential tyranny, Brackenridge's narrative seeks a way out of this double bind. Proposed for positions in the state legislature, the Philosophical Society, and the clergy, Teague is just as unfit for these posts as he is for tasks he later undertakes as editor, auctioneer, orator, and judge. He even contemplates posing as an Indian chief in order to negotiate a treaty. By virtue of the fact that he has absolutely nothing to recommend him save for his stereotypical Irish features, the people rightly feel Teague is one of them. On this basis, they put him forward for state representative. In response to Captain Farrago's objections, the people contend, "He [Teague] may not be yet skilled in the matter, but there is a good day a-coming. We will empower him; and it is better to trust a plain man like him, than one of your high flyers, that will make laws to their own purposes" (pt. 1, v. 1, ch. 3). In that "'We the people,' admits of no exclusion" (pt. 2, v. 4, ch. 1), "the people," from Brackenridge's satiric perspective, represent something more like a mob than a governable political body.

Brackenridge argues that in order to understand itself as such, any community must draw a boundary to distinguish those who are qualified as members from those who are not. This constitutive exclusion implies a hierarchy internal to the community based on those who better meet the standard for admission than others. To Farrago's consternation, this is precisely what "the people" seem unable to do for themselves. In puzzling out who should enjoy suffrage, the people (in what must be a scornful allusion to the three-fifths rule by which slave property gave the South greater voting power) decide not to stop with just those who own property but to extend the vote to the property itself: "From the light thrown upon the subject, the right of suffrage to grown cattle had become so popular, that there was no resisting it" (pt. 2, v. 4, ch. 4). For lack of a reasonable standard of citizenship, Brackenridge's narrative more or less stalls. Teague never develops the skills and sensibility that would allow him to fill one of the many roles he assumes. Farrago, on the other hand, becomes a governor. To assume a political role for which his rationality qualifies him, however, he sets himself outside and above the people to be governed and so fails to develop the qualities required to woo a woman and head a household. As a composite character, then, Farrago and Teague possess many of the qualities required to bring resolution to a settlement novel: a man who is both of the people and above the people, thus defining a community capable of self-government. But because these types exist in tension with each other, neither can settle down. After writing and rewriting the pieces of this novel over a period of twenty some years, Brackenridge could not figure out how to imagine a community that would accommodate either protagonist without raising the hackles of the other.

In order to demonstrate the form of national community that does emerge from the story of unsettlement, let us turn briefly to Tyler's *The Algerine Captive.* To introduce his protagonist, Updike Underhill, Tyler endows him with a genealogy—both British and American—and then demonstrates that this amalgam of Old and New Worlds cannot grow into the farmer his father wants him to be. Like the protagonists of Daniel Defoe, Underhill travels to prove that he does not belong anywhere. So long as he wanders from region to region within the United States, Underhill is hospitably received everywhere, but nowhere is he allowed to enter into the kind of relationship that would establish commonality. In every region, the people regard him as different, preserving the regional character that makes it impossible for him to settle down. When a schoolteacher, he finds his students mock rather than learn from him. When a physician, he discovers his patients prefer the nostrums of frauds and quacks. Because he is a New Englander, southern women steadfastly refuse his advances. Why create an American protagonist who cannot find a home in the new United States?

If the first volume of *The Algerine Captive* fails to produce a protagonist who can establish a fixed character through a process of identification and difference, the second volume uses that protagonist to imagine distinct regional and national types as part of a single population. Underhill is a citizen of the United States, a Christian, a doctor, and a man well read in classical letters. Once taken captive by Algerine pirates and thrown in with segments of the world population, his vision of the human community expands exponentially while losing none of its diversity. Although he keeps all the features that distinguish him as an American after he is thrown in first with one group and then another, these features do change function and importance. His literacy and skill as a doctor are used to care at times for other slaves so that they might retain their value as laborers. His Christianity marks him as someone a Muslim might seek out to convert or with whom a Jew might negotiate a business transaction. His status as a man of some education allows him to stroll about the city and observe the multinational character of Algiers. True to the principle of the unsettlement narrative, these experiences do not add up to a narrative of growth. To the contrary, those thrown in together retain their national characteristics, social position, skills, and cultural predilections. As part of so many different groups, however, Underhill comes to understand the bare humanity he shares with others in his situation. Nowhere is this commonality clearer than in Underhill's account of his stint at hard labor. Of his "fellow slaves," he claims, "the wretched are all of one family; and ever regard each other as brethren" (v. 2, ch. 3). It is noteworthy that he does not use the first-person plural to describe the abject condition of the group, for he does not consider them actually his brethren. The menial slave is illiterate, while Underhill is a man of letters, and there is nary a whiff between them of the moral sympathy extolled by Adam Smith. The fellow feeling Underhill professes depends not on identification but on his recognition that his humanity extends to those at the lowest level of the social hierarchy. It is the hunger they feel, the couch of straw on which they sleep, the labor they endure, and their willingness to lighten the load of someone unaccustomed to these privations that prompt him to acknowledge this shared humanity.

The Seduction Novel

Where the American picaresque features men who cannot settle down, another form of fiction, at least as popular in the United States if not more so, features a seduced woman. Like the picaresque, the seduction novel unsettles the settlement narrative. The American seduction novel takes a European genre—in this case, domestic fiction—and spells out by extravagant narrative means why it cannot produce a stable household in the new United States. If there is an American prototype for domestic fiction, it has to be the colonial form of the captivity narrative famously exemplified by Mary Rowlandson's *The Sovereignty and Goodness of God* (1682). Rowlandson's narrative testifies to her ability to remain both English and Protestant under the harsh conditions of Indian captivity. As Nancy Armstrong has argued, the narrative—which was picked up and reproduced in numerous variations, fictional as well as autobiographical—defined the English woman as the culture bearer whose purity guaranteed that an English Protestant home would remain English and Protestant even when transported and reproduced in the North American colonies. Published four times in 1682, then essentially ignored for decades, this narrative was reprinted nearly twenty times in the 1790s. When, in that same decade, novels of seduced and abandoned women start to appear in significant numbers, we have to sit up and take notice. This coincidence suggests that the features of the woman as bearer of English culture were undergoing an important revision.

The plots and subplots of most sentimental fiction in America—more than half the novels of the early national period alone—were stories of seduction. Seduction provides the main plot of novels as different as Hill Brown's *The Power of Sympathy*; Rowson's *Charlotte Temple* (1791 England; 1794 United States); *Amelia; or, The Faithless Briton* (1798); *Ira and Isabella* (1807), attributed to Hill Brown; and Mrs. P. D. Manvill's *Lucinda; or, the Mountain Mourner* (1807). Moreover, seduction plots driven by libertines provide the narrative spine holding together a complex snarl of subplots as different as Brockden Brown's *Ormond; or, The Secret Witness* (1799) and his *Arthur Mervyn; or, Memoirs of the Year 1793* (1799–1800), Leonora Sansay's *Laura* (1809), and *Rosalvo Delmonmort* (1818) by "Guy Mannering." In Foster's *The Coquette; or, The History of Eliza Wharton* (1797), the coquette finds the tables reversed when she is ensnared by the libertine, Sanford, and becomes one more seduced woman.

In the seduction novel, the libertine serves as the agent to unsettle the narrative of settlement. Speaking of Charlotte Temple, Montraville tells Belcour, "It was I seduced her, Belcour. Had it not been for me, she had still been virtuous and happy in the affection and protection of her family" (ch. 24). Ah, but they never are. In *The Power of Sympathy*, the libertine's work extends into the next generation. Young Harrington cannot marry his beloved Harriot once he learns that his father is hers as well by a secret liaison. In the sequel to *Charlotte Temple*, *Charlotte's Daughter; or, The Three Orphans* (1828), Lucy Temple is similarly prevented from marrying the man she loves when he turns out to be the son of her biological father, Montraville. The libertine's assault on the family destroys the woman's rootedness and condemns her to wander in the world, so that homelessness becomes more her state of being than something that happens to her. Although *The Coquette*'s Major

Sanford provides a home for the woman he has seduced and her unborn child, she describes herself as nonetheless homeless. She complains in a letter to her mother, "This night I become a wretched wanderer from thy paternal roof!" (ltr. 68). By disrupting the form of desire that results in future generations of an established family, the libertine renders the woman a stranger to a respectable home and her proper kin group, a rupture that would no doubt have seemed especially poignant to a North American readership. In all cases, the marriageable woman loses her special status as culture bearer and merges with the elements of the population vulnerable to hunger, disease, and poverty. In so dispatching the domestic heroines, the seduction plot dismantles English domesticity and renders it useless as a model for the nation.

What, then, are we to make of those American heroines who either successfully fight off the libertine or replace the seduced woman in her parents' affection? Surprisingly, we find that their purity does not make them capable of reproducing a household, at least not in the United States. Lucy Temple returns to England with her grandfather as a replacement for his daughter, Charlotte, a casualty of seduction. In *Charlotte's Daughter*, though the product of seduction, the heroine retains her purity. Lucy is so pure indeed that she falls in love with a man who happens to be Montraville's son and her half-brother, the one man whom she can never marry. Brockden Brown's *Wieland; or, The Transformation* (1798) ends on a similar note with Clara Wieland leaving the United States to join her uncle in France. It remains but a possibility that Clara might marry a man, now a widower, she has long loved platonically. That Brockden Brown finds it all but impossible to marry off a heroine in the United States is underscored by the end of his novel *Ormond*. Constantia Dudley leaves America for Britain to join her female confidant after killing the eponymous libertine for attempting to rape her. Where Mary Rowlandson could, having maintained her purity, return to the English colony in 1675 and resume her domestic life, American-born heroines cannot. The seduction novel renders marriage all but impossible by making hybridity an omnipresent threat: If there is as yet no reliable definition of American manhood or womanhood, how, after all, can a novel imagine an American household that is not born of improper couplings?

The early American novel indeed regularly personifies lineage and inherited property in the unflattering figure of the libertine. This is no simple democratic slap in the face of aristocratic pretensions, but rather the novel's means of tailoring marriage and the family for a nation of immigrants. There is perhaps no clearer sign that blood relations get in the way of forming a national community than the frequency with which the threat of inadvertent incest forecloses the possibility of marriage, mandating marriage outside of one's immediate kin group. But far more troublesome even than incest are marriages of convenience, for this is where the libertine inserts himself in the American household. In *The Coquette*, for example, the libertine Major Sanford explains in a letter to his friend, "Necessity, dire necessity" forced him to marry so that he could maintain his "show, equipage, and pleasure" (ltr. 54). While there is strictly speaking nothing illegal in this, the novel makes it clear that the marriage of convenience, necessary and even desirable though it may be, nevertheless fails to provide a solid basis of community.

Given that the preponderance of seduction novels aim at invalidating traditional forms of community, we should find it instructive to discover how a few novels of the new republic manage to bring individuals together to fulfill the fantasy of settlement. The new household is made of compatible subjectivities who hold each other in high esteem rather than the English model, which requires people to be of comparable rank and lineage before this meeting of minds can come to pass. As a substitute for the Grand Tour that ensured the well-born English gentleman would have knowledge of the world, the literacy of the educated American enabled him to acquire the equivalent through wide reading that gave him multiple perspectives. The American demonstrated his literacy in written self-expression, especially letter writing. Thus, for example, in *The Power of Sympathy*, Myra Harrington marries Mr. Worthy only after he has demonstrated a rich and refined sensibility by reporting his views on art and literature to her in personal letters. By the same token, in Brockden Brown's *Clara Howard: In a Series of Letters* (1801), Edward Hartley's extensive reading of literature in the library of Clara's British stepfather proves to be the essential precondition to winning her hand.

These novels make it a given that someone who has acquired this kind of literacy will remain faithful even when separated from his beloved for long periods of time. His fidelity is demonstrated by the very act of writing letters. A protagonist who carries on a faithful relationship via pen and paper will also respect the terms of a contract that can bind individuals when separated geographically. Indeed, successful relationships in novels of the early republic are invariably tested by geographical dislocation and long periods of physical separation. This is certainly true of the lovers in Isaac Mitchell's *The Asylum; or, Alonzo and Melissa* (1811). Initially permitted to woo Melissa because theirs would be an economically advantageous marriage, her father's permission evaporates along with Alonzo's inheritance. Finding Alonzo no longer a suitable match once his father's investments fail, Melissa's father relocates and renames her and even fabricates an account of her death. To reclaim his beloved from the dead, Alonzo has to cross the Atlantic, escape from a prison ship in England, and track down none other than Benjamin Franklin in Paris, so that his father's former business partner can restore the family's wealth. We might again turn to Rowlandson's Indian captivity for purposes of understanding the narrative logic of Melissa's separation from Alonzo simply by substituting Melissa's secular love for Alonzo for the Puritan's devotion to God. Either heroine will lose her cultural value should her devotion fail, and inconvenient devotion consequently replaces material "convenience" as the basis for imagining community.

The male protagonist proves his fitness to found a new community in another way. Brockden Brown's Hartley undergoes an odyssey similar to Alonzo's. Although considered suitable husband material by Clara's British stepfather, a reformed libertine, Clara takes over the father's prerogative and determines how Hartley must prove himself before she marries him. Using the language of the contract to undo the curse of the seduction novel, she insists that Hartley fulfill the promise he made to wed another woman many years before. His fidelity to the agreement, though long expired, puts Hartley in a double bind where he cannot marry Clara unless he fulfills his promise to the other woman. In fact, however, the contract operates as the only form of magic that can resolve the conflict between the value of purity and the need to court danger and enter into marriage with a stranger. After months of searching, Hartley tracks down the woman whom he promised to wed in return for economic support for his sisters, only to find that she is in love with another, miraculously freeing him to marry Clara. To be sure, marriages are problematic if they overstress purity, as this invites the threat of incest. But in leaning in the other direction and overvaluing marriage to a stranger simply because it seems advantageous in material terms, one risks the danger of marrying an imposter who just might turn out to be a libertine. Going by the example of Major Sanford in *The Coquette*, the libertine marries only for money and will hold to a contract only so long as it serves his interests. The marriage contract miraculously resolves the problem of distinguishing between a suitable stranger and an imposter or a libertine by transforming two people unrelated by blood or place of birth into kin on the basis of their compatible sensibilities and capacity to keep a promise—especially when doing so proves enormously inconvenient.

Gothic Realism

During the period when tales of seduction were being widely consumed by the reading public, American readers also developed a voracious appetite for gothic fiction. These novels were imported in substantial quantities from England and often reprinted in the United States. The gothic flourished in both England and America at precisely the moment Sir Walter Scott was proclaiming Jane Austen's *Emma* (1816) evidence par excellence that the British novel had achieved its mature form. Austen's *Northanger Abbey*, published in 1818 but written in the 1790s, makes it clear that she saw domestic realism as an antidote to the gothic possibility of unsettling the boundary between kin and strangers, thus between the traditional household and a rapidly modernizing world. In terms of the geography within the novel as well as the geographic dissemination of the novels themselves, gothic fiction is a contrastingly cosmopolitan form. Strangers enter the scene from another country, heroines are locked away in country estates far from home, alien customs and rituals bring their magic with them, and the dead return to life from regions distant and obscure. Once these foreign influences are removed, as they invariably are by English novelists such as Anne Radcliffe, Mary Shelley, Wilkie Collins, and

Bram Stoker, British customs reassume control and realism returns. But gothic fiction understandably found other work to do in the United States, where radical forms of unsettlement had very different implications than in Britain. In the gothic novels that flourished during the early republic, neither stranger nor host remains the same by virtue of their contact. More often than not, the agency of such a transformation cannot be dismissed as supernatural, as the occult was especially fraught with meaning in a nation composed of a large number of immigrants.

In his famous treatise on cosmopolitanism, "Toward Perpetual Peace: A Philosophical Sketch" (1795), Immanuel Kant argues that a stranger should be allowed to pass freely through other countries and never required to change his beliefs, practices, or customs as a condition of doing so. The British gothic invariably tests its heroine, much like the American captivity narrative, to make sure she can resist the temptation to succumb to the pressures of another place and foreign customs. The successful heroine returns to her community unchanged. But it certainly does not work out this way in such novels by Brockden Brown as *Wieland*, *Edgar Huntly; or, Memoirs of a Sleep-Walker* (1799), *Ormond*, and *Arthur Mervyn*; Sarah Wood's *Dorval; or, The Speculator* (1801); the anonymous *Adventures in a Castle* (1806); or Mitchell's *The Asylum*. In these and other gothic novels written during the period of the early republic, whenever a host takes in a stranger, neither remains the same. The guest incorporates certain characteristics of his new environment, and by incorporating the stranger, the character of the host community changes reciprocally.

Perhaps the most extreme example of the protagonist so transformed by his environment is Edgar Huntly. Finding himself in a cave surrounded by "savages" (beasts as well as Indians) and desperately thirsty and hungry, Huntly kills a panther, drinks its blood, and consumes its flesh. His body suffers acutely from ingesting the uncooked meat, but Huntly also finds himself curiously invigorated by the experience of going native. And no wonder, for he has domesticated the wilderness by turning it into a source of nourishment. Arthur Mervyn, on the other hand, is absorbed by the new cultural geography. He starts out, as a "stranger, friendless, and moneyless" (pt. 1, ch. 3), only to be taken in by the charlatan Welbeck, who dresses him in the clothes of a dead man and treats him as the late Clavering brought back to life. Later in the novel, Mervyn reappears as a sentimental protagonist who courts the daughter of the utterly traditional Hadwin family. Once yellow fever decimates the little community, Mervyn shifts shape again. He loses his sentimental features, abandons Eliza Hadwin, and to the consternation of many readers, takes up with the arch stranger Achsa Fielding. He is both feminized and Europeanized by this association with a Portuguese Jewess. Because none of Brockden Brown's protagonists develops a stable character or consolidates a community around himself, even the most ingenious reader will have trouble construing any one of them as a coherent individual who fulfills a narrative of progress paralleling that of the new nation.

Indeed, they so resemble Brackenridge's Teague that these gothic protagonists seem hardly to be protagonists at all, mediocre and lacking in self-definition as they are. This problem is compounded by Huntley's and Mervyn's resemblances to charlatans such as Carwin, Welbeck, Craig, or Clithero, as they, too, opportunistically acquire the personal attributes of the position available in the communities they happen to enter. If there is an empty suit of clothes, Mervyn will fill it. If there is a woman to be wooed, he will woo her. But none of these positions can fix his character for very long. For instance, Mervyn carries on as if he were a sentimental suitor to Eliza until the prospect of marrying her causes him to lose interest, and he finds himself attracted by Achsa's foreign features. But although such behavior sets Brockden Brown's heroes at odds with the contrastingly faithful Hartley, Worthy, or Alonzo, the gothic protagonist is not a fraud. Where the charlatan surveys each situation from a distance as an opportunity to serve his personal interests, the true gothic protagonist simply fits in where there is an opening and performs the required role. Thus where the charlatan is consistently a charlatan, the only remarkable feature of the gothic protagonist is the fluidity of character enabling him to make narrative connections between otherwise disconnected regions and forms of community. It may be as mundane as the connection between Philadelphia and the Hadwin farm, or something as primal as the connection between the American wilderness and European culture that Huntly establishes. By virtue of his mutability, the gothic protagonist is simply the most pronounced version of the unsettling heroes of the unsettlement novel.

But this is only half the story. American gothic novels also violate the other premise of Kant's cosmopolitan model of hospitality by having the stranger transform the community into which he is received. Mervyn's journey began when his father took in a bondservant and married her. As Mervyn puts it, "The house in which I lived was no longer my own, nor even my father's" (ch. 2). Indeed, Brockden Brown's novels are littered with households that take in a stranger only to have their members dispersed. But, we might well ask, is this not true of most eighteenth-century American novels? *The Coquette, Charlotte Temple,* and *The Power of Sympathy* are just the tip of the iceberg. Show me a sentimental household in an American novel that could find a home in one of Austen's novels, and I will show you a household about to be dismantled. The Hadwin household in *Arthur Mervyn* lends itself to a conceptual analysis of this trend. This version of the sentimental household is neither closed in the manner of the village of Highbury in Austen's *Emma* nor able to discern the congenial outsider by his genteel name, trustworthy acquaintances, and polite demeanor. By virtue of its openness to commerce with a cosmopolitan population, the domestic idyll in *Arthur Mervyn* quickly succumbs to a yellow fever epidemic in Philadelphia. What may seem a pointless attack on the sentimental household destroys the British model of community in order to offer a new way of imagining community. Domestic relationships that might yield a traditional domestic model are indeed held together only by significantly elastic and perplexed contracts. These households—if they can be called such—are thus able to travel, suffer dispersal, and have many of their components replaced. This trend explains Mervyn's flagging interest in Eliza in favor of her exotic replacement, the European Achsa.

Novels by Brackenridge, Sansay, Markoe, Brockden Brown, Tyler, Mitchell, Rowson, and Foster, as well as the other writers of the early republic mentioned in this chapter, offered what they considered a coherent model of America, though one that seems markedly different from both its British counterpart and the novels that now define the mainstream of an American tradition. The early novel indeed pulls off the rather amazing feat of detailing both the peculiar practices and idiosyncratic kinship rules defining local communities, while also situating those characters and their practices within a circum-Atlantic network of people, goods, services, and information. In these early novels, the aleatory interaction of large groups of people deliberately violates every boundary that would eventually define the United States. Thus, whenever we assume that a modern nation must take the form of a unified character, or people, in order to be a nation, we effectively push the unsettling behavior on the part of the population of the new United States into the background. As Nancy Armstrong and I have shown elsewhere, Harriet Beecher Stowe was among those major nineteenth-century American novelists who clearly understood the dynamic, international character of a population—a deracinated population at that. All those novelists worked with the peregrinations of the unsettlement narrative, the seduced woman and her libertine companion, and the gothic protagonist haunted by some charlatan. This same tradition provided Nathaniel Hawthorne with the material for dense and highly improbable psychodramas that take place at the conjunctions of a network.

The Scarlet Letter: A Romance (1850) can be read as a virtuoso performance of this kind. As the condition for shipping off to the New World, Hester Prynne and Roger Chillingworth must be separated soon after their marriage, never to reunite and produce a household in America. The novel begins, moreover, with the appearance in a Puritan community of the seduced woman and her illegitimate daughter as the two are freed from prison to become the iconic limit figures of a community that has cast them out. In England, Chillingworth may have been Hester's legal husband, just as she once was his dutiful wife, but he enters this colonial setting as if he had just stepped out of a captivity narrative. It is obvious that he, like Hester, has gone native. Chillingworth has taken on the character, knowledge, and power of his captors, signaled by the clothes in which they dressed him, "a strange disarray of civilized and savage costume" (ch. 3). Rather than assume his place by Hester's side, he proclaims himself to be "a stranger" and "a wanderer, sorely against my will. I have met with grievous mishaps by sea and land, and have been long held in bonds among the heathen-folk, to the southward; and am now brought hither by this Indian, to be redeemed out of my captivity" (ch. 3). As soon as he sets eyes on Dimmesdale, Chillingworth drops his role as the protagonist of some captivity narrative. He becomes a gothic charlatan and uses occult knowledge to manipulate his rival. Never much of a libertine, Dimmesdale consequently usurps Hester's feminine position as victim and suffers privately for her public shame. Resembling nothing so much as the tension between Welbeck and Mervyn or Clithero Edny and Huntly, the Chillingworth-Dimmesdale relationship reproduces precisely the parasitic bond that broke up and dispersed so many households in the gothic fiction of the new republic. The two men, different though they seem, constitute a single body rather than two different individuals. As testimony to their singularity, we learn that at Dimmesdale's death, "All [Chillingworth's] strength and energy—all his vital and intellectual force—seemed at once to desert him," and "he positively withered up" (ch. 24). As for Pearl, she is closer to nature than "the wild Indian" who recognizes in her "a nature wilder than his own" (ch. 22). Upon kissing the dying Dimmesdale, on the other hand, she instantly becomes a domestic woman who will no longer have to "do battle with the world, but be a woman in it" (ch. 23). Like Constantia Dudley, Clara Wieland, and so many other American heroines, Pearl will have to cross the Atlantic in order to create a traditional household, while Hester remains at the edge of the Puritan community to collect and repair the bits and pieces of that model. Thus, if we read *The Scarlet Letter* in relation to novels based on a network rather than a household, it is entirely reasonable to say that the cosmopolitan novels of the early republic, perhaps more so than the culture of Puritan New England, provided Hawthorne with the material out of which he crafted what is unquestionably a great American novel.

Part II

THE NOVEL AND AMERICAN NATION BUILDING

6

WALTER SCOTT AND THE AMERICAN HISTORICAL NOVEL

FIONA ROBERTSON

In 1835, Catharine Maria Sedgwick published *The Linwoods; or, "Sixty Years Since" in America*, a patriotic tale combining public facts with domestic fictions of the War of Independence but also implicitly acknowledging the possibility of a gradual national forgetting. As Sedgwick declares in her preface, the young must learn about their country's past in order "to deepen their gratitude to their patriot-fathers; a sentiment that will tend to increase their fidelity to the free institutions transmitted to them." History, here, protects the interests of the present and the future. The subtitle of *The Linwoods* seems to guarantee the fiction's historicity by association with Walter Scott's first novel, *Waverley; or, 'Tis Sixty Years Since* (1814), a tale of the failed 1745 Jacobite uprising in Britain. In 1835, three years after his death, Scott continued to command prestige and unsurpassed authority in historical fiction. Having invoked Scott, however, Sedgwick evades him, declaring herself innocent of "a charge of such insane vanity" as likening her project to that of "the great Master." In claiming to have selected her subtitle "simply to mark the period of the story," she essentially dismisses him as anything more than a marketable ploy. In fact, characters and situations in *The Linwoods* repeatedly echo Scott. "The pythoness Effie" (ch. 1) recalls both Meg Merrilies in *Guy Mannering* (1815) and Norna of the Fitful-head in *The Pirate* (1822)—via, disconcertingly, Scott's most sexualized heroine, Effie Deans from *The Heart of Mid-Lothian* (1818). Like Norna, Sedgwick's Effie is fortune teller to two contrasting heroines, Bessie Lee and Isabella Linwood, each with her own imaginary genealogy of Scott heroines, from Lucy Ashton (*The Bride of Lammermoor*, 1819) to Alice Lee (*Woodstock*, 1826). Yet *"Sixty Years Since" in America* also hints at the possible superiority of the American past, inviting readers to imagine that rebellion had brought national unity and a new beginning, rather than exile, exclusion, or ideological compromise. Sedgwick's deceptively simple homage exposes the problem that this chapter explores: the complications of Scott's role in the fictionalization of America's past.

Scott has always loomed as an important figure in American literary history. As George Dekker emphasizes in the most detailed full-length study of US historical fiction: "Inspired by Scott's affectionate, indeed patriotic, evocations of the scenes and manners of old Scotland, American historical romancers turned to the histories of their own states and regions for the matter of their fictions" (1987, 62). His example shaped an entire style of thought. Scott's importance for American writers derived in part from a shared inheritance in Scottish Enlightenment culture—in Scottish "Common Sense" philosophy, in stadial models of social development, and in Enlightenment historiography. But Americans also responded to specific aspects of his subject matter and artistry. Tales of religious and political division such as *The Tale of Old Mortality* (1816), *The Heart of Mid-Lothian*, and *Peveril of the Peak* (1822) were directly interpretable in terms of life in the British American colonies. Scott also returned repeatedly to the subject of revolution, potent in the new contexts of the early United States and of the increasingly disunited states of the nineteenth century. Just as importantly, Scott explicitly wrote histories of Scotland in the context of its constitutional union with England, creating a national identity precisely because such identity must now function imaginatively and emotionally, rather than politically. However, entangled in what Washington Irving called Scott's "benign" influence on American literary culture lie some sharper questions about authority, cultural authenticity, and the ideological freight of literary genre.

For acknowledgments of Scott's importance have also, traditionally, contained seeds of discontent. Dekker's emphasis on the "readily adaptable model"—for example, the interweaving of fictional plots with historical events—available in *Waverley* and its successors inevitably positions American literature as secondary, as deriving from Old World narrative and representational structures (1987, 8); while Leslie A. Fiedler's castigation of the impact Scott's "middlebrow imagination" and nostalgic conservatism had on an American national literature written "for boys" (1966, 164, 181) continues to influence perceptions. Even if Mark Twain had never indicted Scott as the cause of the American Civil War or associated him (in *Adventures of Huckleberry Finn*, 1884) with a wrecked Mississippi river boat, the decline in his literary reputation by 1900 would have tainted the perceived achievement of his successors. Scott's influence came to be seen as having impeded American originality, and this has led to a defensive rhetoric of American "counterparts," "equivalents," and "translation." Some accounts of American fiction thus dissociate it from the formal and social conservatisms Scott represented by aligning it instead with older forms of allegory, romance, and fantasy. The border between "novel" and "romance" became a recurring preoccupation of American novelists (prominent in commentaries by William Gilmore Simms, Nathaniel Hawthorne, Herman Melville, and most influentially in Henry James's 1907 preface to the New York Edition of *The American*) and of critics from F. O. Matthiessen and Richard Chase to those who have disputed their readings, including Nina Baym, Elissa Greenwald, Michael Davitt Bell, G. R. Thompson, and Eric Carl Link. One might say that the difficulty posed by Scott's centrality has redirected the entire flow of subsequent interpretations of American fiction.

This special literary relationship now requires reinterpretation. Scott was central, but he was also far more various and experimental than critics' reflections on "the *Waverley* model" as a paradigm for works of historical fiction have suggested. Also, models change. In 1960 Fiedler's *Love and Death in the American Novel* represented the accepted view of Scott: "As an artist, Scott is deficient in moral intelligence, clumsy in style, inadequate in characterization . . . untidy in form; as a maker of legends, however, he possesses authenticity and greatness" (1966, 174). Today, scholarship has transformed that view. The *Edinburgh Edition of the Waverley Novels* (1993–2012) has established his texts in ways truer to his original intentions, restoring in the process his careful artistry and commitment to literary aesthetics. His works command new readerships and a revised cultural significance, not least in the United States. Critically, it is easier now to look beyond "the *Waverley* model," always somewhat misaligned with American tradition, and to consider traditionally less venerated works by Scott that resonated in America. *A Legend of the Wars of Montrose*, for example, from the Third Series of *Tales of My Landlord* (1819), deals succinctly with a complex series of allegiances and hostilities, entwining with the conflict between Montrose and Argyll in 1644–45 the fate of an "outlaw" group of Highlanders called the Children of the Mist. Like the better-known works of the four series of *Tales of My Landlord* (including *The Tale of Old Mortality*, *The Heart of Mid-Lothian*, and *The Bride of Lammermoor*), *A Legend of the Wars of Montrose* has a frame narrative set in the early nineteenth century: in this case, describing a veteran of the peninsular campaign against Napoleon and his allies, Sergeant More MacAlpin, who has settled in the Borders after finding the Highland glen of his childhood deserted as a result of forced displacement. *A Legend of the Wars of Montrose* quietly confounds many ingrained assumptions about Scott: notably that he avoided the controversial Clearances, or that he imposed on historical conflict a romanticizing perspective governed by the rules of the picturesque. The outlaws of the Mist (a "wild tribe" of "children" [ch. 19], an "unhappy race" [ch. 20]) increasingly dominate the latter half of the novel; their rhetoric is conspicuously modeled on the "last of the race" discourse which, by 1819, linked representations of Scottish Highlanders and American Indians and had already been used by Scott in his 1818 *Rob Roy*. The long dying speech of Ranald MacEagh to his "young savage" grandson is indebted to at least half a century of Scottish-American representational practice, from Ossian in the 1760s to Thomas Campbell's *Gertrude of Wyoming* in 1809; but it could stand independently as an influence on subsequent American writing: "We are now a straggling handful, driven from every vale by the sword of every clan, who rule in the possessions where their forefathers hewed the wood, and drew the water to ours. But in the thicket of the wilderness, and in the mist of the mountain, Kenneth, son of Eracht, keep thou unsoil'd the freedom which I leave thee as a birth-right" (ch. 22). Typically of Scott, the narrative turns from this ending to linger on others which it treats as more legitimate (the marriage/inheritance plot and the subsequent histories of its "main" characters). American writers proved especially sensitive to this disjunctive way of suggesting historical continuity, so that Scott's influence continues to register technically and structurally even when writers might seem to have moved far beyond his historical subject matter of clans, loyalties, and ideologies in conflict.

Just as Scott's acquaintance with traditional representations of American Indians lay behind his account of the Children of the Mist (and Highland clans elsewhere), America itself influenced his career and imaginative development. Scott's earliest political memories were associated with the reports he heard of the Revolutionary War in America; and in the frame narrative of his last publication, the two novels in the Fourth Series of *Tales of My Landlord* (1831), the supposed author's brother absconds to America to publish the unrevised manuscripts there. This fiction reflects a fact of Scott's publishing career. Several American publishing houses (including M. Carey and Son and Edwin T. Scott in Philadelphia, S. G. Goodrich in Hartford, and J. Seymour, J. & J. Harper, and E. Duyckinck in New York) assembled parts of Scott's novels from uncorrected second-stage proofs, expediting publication in the United States and preserving a stage in the editorial process that would otherwise now be invisible. Many novels from the early 1820s onward were published in the United States in significantly different form, these pirated editions preserving many readings corrected or revised by Scott and his compositors at the last stage of prepublication in Britain. In the late 1830s, anger at the way in which Scott had been deprived of earnings from his novels in the United States fueled the drive for copyright legislation in Britain.

Scott was also well read and well connected as an interpreter of American history. His library at Abbotsford contained about 200 works relating to North America. He had a succession of American guests at Abbotsford and corresponded with some of the new scholarly custodians of US culture, including George Ticknor, through whose offices Scott, like Robert Southey, became an honorary member of the Massachusetts Historical Society. When American writers of historical fiction cited Scott, it was not only because he had acquired a unique cultural status as an external model, but also because Scott's intellectual inclusiveness had always been alert to American history—to its continuities with British history and also to its differences. In 1821 Scott's publisher, Archibald Constable, urged him to write a historical novel on the subject of Pocahontas. Scott declined, arguing that such a tale could only be written by someone who "understood" American Indian customs and manners. He nominated Irving, with whom he maintained a close transatlantic friendship. Irving's *Abbotsford and Newstead Abbey* (1835) describes his four-night visit in August–September 1817, part of the tour which led to *The Sketch Book* (1819–20). Scott first read Irving in 1813 in *A History of New York from the Beginning of the World to the End of the Dutch Dynasty* by "Diedrich Knickerbocker" (1809). Scott and Irving rivaled each other as inventors of authorial and pseudo-editorial personae, and Irving's gratitude for Scott's role in securing John Murray as the publisher of *The Sketch Book* is recorded in his 1848 preface to the revised edition. Irving's account of his 1817 visit presents Scott as both attentive and indifferent to social rank, as rooted in the traditions of the Scottish Borders, but fascinated by other cultures and histories, and excited to think of being "in the midst of one of [America's] grand wild original forests" amid trees which would shame "the pigmy monuments of Europe." Irving's feeling that "it seemed as if a little realm of romance was suddenly opened before me" ostensibly validates the view of Scott (traditional by 1835) as the guardian of legend and folklore, the living proof as well as the purveyor of "real history." Irving emphasizes his role as guest in the house, though he is also, as narrator, the controller of Scott's "little" realm. Even to this most Anglophilic and traditionalist American observer, Scott's energies seem caught up in what Irving regards as "inferior" things: his dogs, his favorite employees and dependents, leisure rather than work. By 1835, too, the old farmhouse Irving had visited in 1817 had disappeared, in its place the baronial mansion completed in 1825, just as the Scott with whom Irving prudently never discussed the (anonymous) authorship of *Waverley* and its successors had long since become public property, internationally. Irving's essay memorializes and honors Scott and a traditional milieu which, because of him, remains alive; but it also silently contains and contextualizes these things in a broader, freer play of imagination and cultural connection—something imaginably American.

In the traditional trajectory of literary history, that is, Scott appears as the honored precursor of an eventually freer American style. His second novel, *Guy Mannering*, however, suggests a more intriguing possibility. *Guy Mannering* pivots on moments of uncanny recognition. It shows memory to be simultaneously superficial, pragmatic, and assured, as well as magical, inexplicable, and spellbound. *Guy Mannering*'s literary debts seem clear: to Shakespeare's *Othello* and late romance-plays, and the fictions of Tobias Smollett and Maria Edgeworth. In his introduction to the Magnum Opus edition, Scott anchored the novel in local and personal memory, quoting his sources on the Galloway gypsies and recalling his childhood memories of particular gypsy figures. More recently, critics have emphasized the significance of the (Asian) Indian subtext; however, the chapter relating the Derncleuch displacement quotes a passage from John Leyden's poem *Scenes of Infancy* (1803) beginning "So the red Indian, by Ontario's side" (ch. 8), and a later chapter describes Meg Merrilies as a defiant defender of her tribe, "the wild chieftainess of the lawless people amongst whom she was born" (ch. 55). The action of *Guy Mannering* is ringed by Britain's colonial difficulties in North America, from Mannering's initial Scottish tour of 1760 to late 1782, and the disruptions—especially the financial disruptions—caused by the American war complicate its plot.

Scholarship thickens the making of this plot. Born in Philadelphia a few months before Scott, Charles Brockden Brown shared his contemporary's experience of childhood illness and lasting infirmity; was trained for the law but was privately absorbed in reading; and explicitly set out to build a distinctive national literature, most clearly in his address "To the Public," which prefaced *Edgar Huntly; or, Memoirs of a Sleep-Walker* (1799). Brown wrote and published *Edgar Huntly* between Parts One and Two of *Arthur Mervyn* (1799 and 1800); and the name "Arthur Mervyn" reappears in Scott's *Guy Mannering* as Mannering's old friend, responsible for looking after Mannering's daughter Julia but notably unsuccessful in protecting her from the romancing of a young man called Brown.

Although *Guy Mannering* contains some first-person epistolary narrative, its literary style is entirely distinct from that of *Edgar Huntly*, and any similarities of plot are broadly generic. The whole of *Edgar Huntly* is narrated in the first person, and at least two principal narrators are on the edge of mania and delusion. Set in 1787 in Pennsylvania, *Edgar Huntly* combines the stories of two sleepwalkers—the American, Huntly, who is haunted by the unsolved murder of his friend Henry Waldegrave; and the Irish emigrant, Clithero—who pursue each other through the wilderness of the Norwalk. As a result of his sleepwalking, Huntly lies injured in an underground maze; is tracked by, and eventually kills, four American Indians; and visits and revisits an isolated hut in which, hidden from view, he witnesses scenes of violence. The hut, he eventually realizes, is the retreat of a Delaware Indian called Old Deb. Although she is not mentioned until the final third of the novel, Old Deb holds the key to all its mysteries. Thirty years before the action of the novel, the Delawares have been driven from their ancient lands by the "perpetual encroachments of the English colonists." Edgar's uncle's farmstead now occupies the land on which the village of the "clan," as he calls them, once stood. Wielding special authority, "zeal and eloquence," however, Deb opposes the Delawares' exile and is determined to "maintain possession of the land." Despite being savagely opposed to what he regards as the "savage," Huntly has formed a childhood bond with Deb and has nicknamed her Queen Mab because of what he calls "her pretensions to royalty, the wildness of her aspect and garb, her shrivelled and diminutive form, a constitution that seemed to defy the ravages of time and the influence of the elements" (ch. 20).

On several different levels, then, *Edgar Huntly* traces the consequences, public and psychological, of an enforced dispossession and removal. In terms of the Philadelphia in which Brown was writing in the late 1790s, this fiction of the recent past swivels guiltily on the half-acknowledged savagery of the white displacer and the potentially schizophrenic new country he represents. *Edgar Huntly* suggests the cultural and psychological elisions of modern nationhood in a way no other fiction had done before it. In some respects, *Guy Mannering* puts right what Brown had left unresolved in *Edgar Huntly*, not only restoring its hero to his rightful inheritance and name but also giving him, in Mannering, a benevolent father-figure (unlike Brown's sinister and ambiguous Sarsefield). In other ways, it revisits Brown's fictive territory, and the romance terrain of the dark, winding, secretive landscape—forked pathways, hollows, caves, subterranean passageways.

Scott found in *Edgar Huntly* a way of spatializing scientific and moral analyses of states of mental distortion and breakdown. The most intriguing connections are those between Old Deb and Meg Merrilies. Deb is diminutive, Meg tall; Deb permanently displaced and silenced in the narrative, Meg brought to its center and sentimentalized as the loyal protector of the novel's hero. Scott gives Meg an idiosyncratic, persuasive, voice, as well as language that recalls Chief Logan's speech to Lord Dunmore, recorded in Thomas Jefferson's *Notes on the State of Virginia* (1785), and that reinforces the American Indian share in her imaginative heritage.

Brown reviewed Scott's poetry in the *Literary Magazine* in 1805, but Scott does not discuss Brown in his letters or *Journal*, nor in any of his novels, introductions, or notes, although when he put together *Ballantyne's Novelist's Library* in the early 1820s, he planned to include novels by Brown. Only one other thread of evidence connects them. Samuel Griswold Goodrich describes in his 1856 autobiography, *Recollections of a Lifetime*, a dinner at the Lockharts' on June 2, 1824, after which Sophia Lockhart (Scott's elder daughter) politely initiated a conversation on American topics. Cooper is discussed first, though Scott is unable to join in the assessment of *The Pioneers*, not having read it. John Gibson Lockhart then declares that, good as Cooper is, in his opinion Brown was "the most remarkable writer of fiction that America has produced," especially in his depictions of the "darker passions." Scott replies, "Brown had wonderful powers, as many of his descriptions show; but I think he was led astray by falling under the influence of bad examples, prevalent at his time. Had he written his own thoughts, he would have been, perhaps, immortal: in writing those of others, his fame was of course ephemeral" (ltr. 42). The flow of influence seems clear: Brown, like American literature in general, was regarded as essentially imitative. Nor do Scott's views on Brown sound at all promising. However, the evidence of his library at Abbotsford suggests a different story. Scott owned early 1820s editions of four of Brown's novels, the first published versions of which date from 1798 to 1800. He also owned the London (1822) edition of William Dunlap's 1815 *Memoirs of Charles Brockden Brown*. Three of Brown's novels in the Abbotsford library, however, are earlier London editions: Brown's last novel, *Jane Talbot* (1801; London, 1804), *Philip Stanley* (London, 1807; published in America as *Clara Howard*, 1801), and *Edgar Huntly*, which Scott owned in the Minerva Press edition of 1803. Whatever Scott thought after dinner in 1824, in 1803 he must have felt himself to be in the vanguard of discovering a new literature; and he was sufficiently interested to read more. Fourteen years after Brown's death, he could assess Brown's fame as "of course ephemeral," though in fact Brown's reputation in Britain revived throughout the 1820s, and in 1831 *Edgar Huntly* was reintroduced to a general British readership as volume 10 of Bentley's Standard Novels series. The resonance of *Edgar Huntly* in *Guy Mannering* reveals that works generally accepted as precursors of American romance could also be creative recollections *of* American romance.

The dominance of historical fiction in the American market throughout the 1820s reflects far more than the adaptability or transferability of "the *Waverley* model." American writers conversed with Scott and competed with him throughout his years of established fame. Scott's best-known "follower," Cooper, is more accurately seen as his interlocutor. The full title of Cooper's *The Pioneers; or, The Sources of the Susquehanna* (1823) revealingly counterpoints pioneering with multiple "sources." As its final sentence proclaims, the novel projects the Leather-Stocking, and the United States, westward, "opening the way for the march of the nation across the continent" (ch. 41) while developing a plot predicated on "sourcing" the outcast hero and true heir, Oliver Edwards/Effingham. *The Pioneers* pioneers in its particular depictions of American life "thirty years since" (1793–94), in its range of character types within this historical setting, and in its independence, or wryly suggested evasions, of established narrative practice. Chapter 17, for example, Cooper's celebrated account of a turkey shoot, takes on all the conventions of semi-allegorical representations of male rivalry and female prowess, while noting both the abundance of American nature and the wastefulness of its new possessors. This single chapter manages to be both routine and troublingly compelling. Its epigraph quotes Scott's poem *The Lady of the Lake* (1810) and announces its topic as "sports." Once again, the citation seems to validate, but actually marks difference, uncertainty, and aggression. *The Pioneers* references Scott in many details; on the other hand, it reflects explicitly on "American genealogy," on the social mixtures of the new world, and on democracy and republicanism in social practice (see especially ch. 18, in which the "demi-savage" Oliver is taken into Judge Temple's household). In novelistic history Cooper innovates, most of all, in his depiction of a broad range of American characters and social groups, a particularity which was criticized by some contemporaries and which he depicted, in his 1832 introduction to *The Pioneers*, as a "rigid adhesion to truth, an indispensable requisite in history and travels" that restricted the wider arts of fiction.

"Let the American reader imagine one of our mildest October mornings," Cooper writes while setting the scene in the final chapter of *The Pioneers*. The remark validates a new group of implied readers, but it also indicates the multiple readerships for which the Leather-Stocking series was designed. These tales, and Cooper's other historical fictions, have important formal and technical continuities with Scott that prepared the ground for their international success. But more extensive critical attention has been devoted to shared motifs and plot lines such as the contrasted fair (domestic) and dark-haired (tragic) heroines, the hero torn between competing ideologies representing the "past" and the "future," characters who connect past and present, and the exile or destruction of characters and causes "ardent" and/or "enthusiastic" to excess. Cooper is faithful to Scott's narratorial style and tone, keeping direct commentary and moral direction to a minimum. He continues Scott's preference for dialogue over description, though like Scott he carefully specifies historical and geographical setting. He emphasizes, as in his

1850 "Preface to the Leather-Stocking Tales," his "very desultory and inartificial manner" of composition, maintaining Scott's declared distance from the pretensions of high art and the lure of the marketplace alike. He continues the practice of chapter epigraphs, and, like Scott, he appends historical notes that extend the descriptive and analytical reach of his fictions. Both of these latter practices implicitly defend the artistic and intellectual status of prose fiction, even as Scott and Cooper slight their own claims as artists. The implied reader in both Scott and Cooper, meanwhile, is informed, rational, but not yet familiar with the wilder locales to which the narrator acts as guide. Scott's many addresses to his "fair" readers fix assumed gender differences in response and reading preferences, though without the hostility with which Cooper advises "all young ladies, whose ideas are usually limited by the four walls of a comfortable drawing room" not to read *The Last of the Mohicans* (1826, pref.).

At the same time, Cooper consciously deviates from Scott in one particular, especially important to the history of the novel in America. This swerve, which is in fact in Harold Bloom's terms a classic misprision or willed misunderstanding of the precursor text, concerns the relationship between the authority of written and oral narrative, and the cultural status of books. All Scott's writings, in all the literary forms he practiced, highlight the tensions between received versions of "history," and the differences between hearing and reading stories. *The Antiquary* (1816), for example, apparently the most "bookish" of novels, consistently ironizes the claims of the educated antiquarian and collector. Orality, however, is necessarily transmuted to Scott's readers in the shape of printed words, and the "Author of *Waverley*" never loses his delight in books as physical objects. The book as a mark of civilized culture retains its status in nineteenth-century British fiction, but is an object of a more fundamental unease in the most self-consciously American writings of the same period. Rooted in rebellion against "written" law, American fiction's valorizations of the truth and immediacy of oral testimony gather force in Cooper. In *The Last of the Mohicans*, set in 1757 during the French and Indian War (1756–63), Hawk-eye's distrust of books as opposed to "experience" is dramatized in his exchanges with the singing-master David Gamut in chapter 12 and with Duncan Heyward in chapters 18 and 21. Gamut himself, presented explicitly as an emasculated relic of Old World minstrelsy, irritates and puzzles modern readers, but would have struck Cooper's contemporaries as almost too crude a satirical amalgam of characters in Scott. Gamut's debts to the physique and deportment of *Guy Mannering*'s Dominie Sampson, in particular, would have underlined the ways in which he represents an Old World dedication to the authority of books and convention, even as Cooper's first account of him, as a body out of all proportion to itself, tall yet diminutive, suggests untellable anxieties of influence. Although Cooper's novels, like Scott's, necessarily contain orality and "experience" in the form of a printed text, they set up a more resistant relationship with printed authority, a sense of a literary tradition which knows itself to be on the wrong track.

One other break with Scott and the tradition he represented is Cooper's artistic decision to substantiate in a series of fictions an imagined, lived actuality for Leather-Stocking. Although telling different parts of Hawk-eye's story involved different settings, historically and geographically, the decision to return to a single connecting character was essentially an act of centripetal and accumulative, rather than historical and expansive, imagination. More important than the often-repeated claim that Hawk-eye draws together different "American" traditions is the formal fact of this novelistic series, in which Cooper creates a single narrative structure for an "American" history. Scott imagined creating a series of novels depicting different periods in Scottish history, while Cooper created a single character around whom an American history could be written. In terms of literary history, this is a significant innovation, but it is especially telling in an American context, reflecting the novelist's desire to center and ground the nation.

The Prairie (1827), set in the Great Plains in 1804–05, ends with Hawk-eye's death and explicitly revisits characters and episodes in the first two fictions. In effect Cooper creates a fictive history *of* his own fictive histories, while also mapping the future of the American West. The novel remains subtly intertextual with Scott, however, with a heroine called Ellen (the most romantic of all Scott's heroines, from *The Lady of the Lake*) and an aged Sioux warrior nicknamed Le Balafré ("scar-face"), who attempts to claim the Pawnee Hard-Heart as his son. The French nickname, as Cooper notes, is traditional, but for readers of 1827 it would immediately call to mind Ludovic Lesly, "Le Balafré," an Archer of Louis XI's Scottish Guard in *Quentin Durward* (1823), a novel that introduces through the Bohemian or gypsy Hayraddin the ways of a nomadic people untamed by law or religion. As in *Guy Mannering*, Scott's depictions of gypsy dispossession were an imaginative resource for Cooper's Indians. After seven years in Europe and several historical novels about the European past (*The Bravo*, 1831; *The Heidenmauer; or, The Benedictines*, 1832; *The Headsman; or, The Abbaye des Vignerons*, 1833), Cooper reconstructed the earlier years of Leather-Stocking in *The Pathfinder; or, The Inland Sea* (1840) and *The Deerslayer; or, The First War-Path* (1841). When he ventured into the more distant American past, as he did in *The Wept of Wish-ton-Wish* (1829), set in the time of King Philip's, or Metacom's, War (1675–76), he was refashioning for a different kind of subject matter and a different readership models of cultural conflict found in long-familiar Scott novels—most importantly *The Tale of Old Mortality* from 1816—and simultaneously engaging in a far more immediate novelistic conversation. One of Scott's best later novels, *The Fair Maid of Perth* (1828), published in the United States as *St. Valentine's Day*, challenges the heroic conventions of earlier *Waverley*-style representation, pressing hard on paradigms of masculinity, and so produces one of Scott's most memorable male characters, Conachar, just as Cooper was working on his own conflicted masculine hero-substitute, Philip's Narragansett ally, Conanchet. Both are adopted into other households; both die when reintroduced to their "true" cultures. Cooper's Conanchet marries cross-racially his white counterpart, Ruth Heathcote or Narra-mattah, taken captive as a child. The confluence of ideas in *The Fair Maid of Perth* and *The Wept of Wish-ton-Wish*, published a year apart, is a reminder that throughout Cooper's writing career Scott was less a "model" or precursor than an interlocutor.

The older view of American historical fiction as dominated by Cooper has now been replaced by scholarship attentive to the different models of fiction developed by others and especially to the consciously feminized styles of Lydia Maria Child and Catharine Maria Sedgwick. From her first novel, *Hobomok* (1824), set in seventeenth-century New England, to her last, *A Romance of the Republic* (1867), Child highlighted women's experiences of historical events and aligned race with gender in (failed) opposition to social convention. In works like *The Rebels* (1825), this was relatively uncontroversial, and Child was astute in working within accepted sentimental conventions and contexts. In *Hobomok*, too, the interracial marriage between Hobomok and Mary Conant is eventually superseded by a marriage that ensures a "white" family line. Even so, as Carolyn L. Karcher points out, the novel essentially allows Mary to take both her rival lovers, only-just-acceptably negotiating questions of race and of female desire. The problem of race in emerging American society pressed the conventions developed in Scott's fiction to their limits; though even as late as *A Romance of the Republic*, written and published during Reconstruction, the names of Child's mixed-race sisters, Rosa and Flora Royal, recall those of the two heroines of *Waverley*. In terms of technique, Child writes limber tales that she nevertheless traces to older "authorities," including Scott. The brief frame narrative of *Hobomok*, and the move away from the "uncouth spelling" of an old manuscript in chapter 2, are pared-down versions of characteristic Scott-inflected conventions, and Scott is cited in the frame narrative as someone at once all-conquering and inimitable, "a high and solitary shrine" (pref.). Although their explicit references to Scott are few, Child and Sedgwick seem to feel his influence differently—Child unabashed by his "proud, elastic tread" (*Hobomok*, pref.), Sedgwick more self-consciously entangled.

All Sedgwick's historical novels—*A New-England Tale* (1822), *Redwood* (1824), *Hope Leslie* (1827), and *The Linwoods*—alternately invoke and revoke Scott's authority. *Redwood* adapts the techniques and some of the motifs of Scott's first two novels (*Waverley* and *Guy Mannering*). But revolt is clear in the preface, which repeats claims made in the first chapter of *Waverley* about constant "principles of human nature" only to emphasize that these manifest themselves differently in different times and different countries; lauds "the Unknown" and his new category of "what is called historical romance," but adds that we also need accounts of the present; and describes the United States as intrinsically more exciting in its "expanding energy and rapid improvement" even than models of perfection: "The future lives in the present." Sedgwick's most successful novel, *Hope Leslie*, incorporates elements of Scott's earlier fictions and also suggests the influence of his most recent, *Woodstock*. The courtship rivalry of the first-generation characters repeats elements of Scott's novel, while the second generation (the generation of the novel's heroine, Hope) represents a self-consciously "American" new beginning both fictionally and historically. Again, individual characters echo Scott's (Nelema, eventually tried for witchcraft, refashions Old Alice from *The Bride of Lammermoor*), chapter epigraphs continue Scott's practice and cite American authors, and discursive notes support details of depiction (most concern the depiction of Indian characters, especially the heroic Magawisca). At the same time, Sedgwick's deferral to Cooper makes clear his perceived preeminence on Native American subjects. As in *The Linwoods*, there are signs of struggle in Sedgwick's relationship with the historicity of her materials. When William Hubbard unsuccessfully seeks Hope's hand in marriage, for example, the narrator notes caustically that in refusing she "lost at least the golden opportunity of illustrating herself by a union with the future historian of New-England" (ch. 11); then, ironically, Sedgwick intersperses unattributed quotations from Hubbard's account of the Indian Wars with her own narrative, while expressly championing the version of the Pequot wars which Everell Fletcher hears from Magawisca. Everell is familiar with the colonists' accounts of Indian atrocities:

> [B]ut he had heard them in the language of the enemies and conquerors of the Pequods; and from Magawisca's lips they took a new form and hue; she seemed, to him, to embody nature's best gifts, and her feelings to be the inspiration of heaven. This new version of an old story reminded him of the man and the lion in [Aesop's] fable. But here it was not merely changing sculptors to give the advantage to one or the other of the artist's sculptures; but it was putting the chisel into the hands of truth, and giving it to whom it belonged. (ch. 4)

Magawisca's (female) account transcends rivaling claims and is (or at least "seems" to Everell to be) "truth." In the larger narrative of *Hope Leslie*, as narratorial comments throughout the final chapter reveal, there is an anxiety about the danger of modern "forgetting," an amnesia and disconnectedness which devalue the sufferings and idealisms of the past. Most importantly, Scott's nuanced appreciations of the culture of his own times bifurcate then solidify in fictions like *Hope Leslie*. The implicit narratorial validation of Magawisca's account, for example, is difficult to reconcile with the historical perspective offered in the final chapter of *Hope Leslie*, in which the Puritan founders are represented as visionaries who see multitudes replace the "solitary savage," cities replace forests, and highways replace "the tangled foot-path," while (in a supremely ironic phrase) "the consecrated church" rises "on the rock of heathen sacrifice" (ch. 27).

All Sedgwick's novels were published near simultaneously in the United States and in Britain, emphasizing the extent to which the market for American fiction remained transatlantic. For other writers of American historical fiction, London and Edinburgh were the primary places of publication. Cooper is a prominent example of this, but a more intricately transatlantic publishing career is that of John

Neal. Neal co-wrote a history of the American Revolution and planned a history of American literature, while being closely involved in literary circles in London and Edinburgh throughout the 1820s. His most interesting novels are *Brother Jonathan* (1825), written in Britain and published in London and Edinburgh, and the Salem witchcraft tale *Rachel Dyer* (1828). An important and extensive authorial reflection at the opening of volume 2 of *Brother Jonathan* anatomizes conventional terms for, and representations of, "the Original North American:—the native, and legitimate Proprietor of the Western World" (ch. 14), asserting his cultural uniqueness and the failure of previous literature to give anything other than generalized accounts of him. Neal's own representations of Indian characters unravel linguistically, however, revealing the breach in conventional representation between supposedly realistic renditions of the hero's speech ("You no fight?—you fight?—Ole oomans—wite hart—you speak 'um lie—bad lie") and supposed translations from "the beautiful Seneca speech" that produces speeches like "Farewell; farewell, for aye. She told me that I should sing my death song, yet, in the ears of my own white brother" (v. 2, ch. 17). *Brother Jonathan* represents a recurrent strain in transposing Scott's interests to American subject matter in that it is more eloquently elegiac in its treatment of the survivors of "older" forms of society than Scott ever allowed himself to be; while, at the same time, the very prominence and directness of the elegiac mode reveals a stronger commitment to social "progress" than Scott ever endorsed. In the case of *Brother Jonathan*, in particular, the action and its implications repeatedly echo the situations of *The Tale of Old Mortality* and *Rob Roy*, Neal's superimposition of those novels serving to reveal their very different approaches to historical material but also responding to the retreats from historical representation that Scott's endings enforce on his readers.

Scott's influence in the US South has always commanded special interest. *Anne of Geierstein* (1829), which features the Germanic Vehme-gericht, influenced the formation of the Ku Klux Klan, and the Klan drew elements of its rituals from the poem *The Lady of the Lake*. Scott's influence on historical fiction in the South, however, as distinct from his popularity among readers, is concentrated in the postbellum period, and at its strongest in the historical writings of the late nineteenth and early twentieth centuries. In this later period, Scott's novels proved especially useful in negotiating narratives of defeat and spiritual, artistic, or quasi-national survival—that is, in preserving identity in emotional and spiritual rather than in political or institutional terms. However, a very different use of Scott, and a conspicuous stylistic departure from "the *Waverley* model," can be found in the prolific antebellum writings of the Charleston-based novelist and editor William Gilmore Simms. In a largely positive essay, "Cooper, His Genius and Writings," (later reprinted as "The Writings of James Fenimore Cooper"), Simms cites Scott's novels as examples of "the harmonious achievement" of a fictional world (*Views and Reviews* 1962, 265). The phrase is striking, the tone untroubled. Simms's novels silently adopt some of Scott's conventions but are essentially forward looking, treating the matter of history as something to get right rather than to complicate, and focusing instead on action, pace, and immediacy of impression. In his best-known work, *The Yemassee* (1835), the structure of contrasting ideologies has been traced to Scott, chapters are given (unattributed) poetical epigraphs, and two chapters (11 and 25) include passages of "Indian" poetry and prophecy. The relative spareness of Simms's characterizations and contextualizations serve an ethically (and ethnically) clear-cut America. The purpose of evoking the past has, simply, changed, as is evident in many technical details and shifts such as the change to the present tense in the account of Harrison's rescue of Bess Matthews at the end of chapter 49.

After *The Yemassee*, the Revolutionary War became Simms's main focus, dominating eight of his novels, but Simms also emphasized the distinct locales of the southern states and marketed his novels by location (*Guy Rivers: A Tale of Georgia*, 1834; *Richard Hurdis; or, The Avenger of Blood: A Tale of Alabama*, 1838, and comparable tales of Mississippi, Kentucky, Florida, and Texas). The expansiveness of his fictional topics in itself proclaims the variety available in American history and the new glamour of regional difference. Just as forays into the more distant American past (such as *The Lily and the Totem; or, The Huguenots in Florida*, 1850) emphasized the master narrative of American freedom, secession and civil war came to dominate Simms's present. Although they owe their appeal to the "romance" of "history," Simms's fictions of frontier struggles, American Indian warfare, and Revolutionary patriotism have an unexpected relationship to temporal change. The influence of Cooper's practice can be seen in the relationship between *The Partisan* (1835), *Mellichampe* (1836), and *Katharine Walton* (1851), in that *Mellichampe* and *Katharine Walton* develop episodes and characters in *The Partisan* rather than moving forward in time. Simms's theorizations, notably the claim in "The Epochs and Events of American History, as Suited to the Purposes of Art in Fiction" (1845) that "the poet and romancer are only strong where the historian is weak" (*Views and Reviews* 1962, 76), typically raise more questions than they answer. In his advertisement to *Mellichampe* he states that the "entire materials" and "the leading events—every general action—and the main characteristics, have been taken from the unquestionable records of history, and—in the regard of the novelist—the scarcely less credible testimonies of that venerable and moss-mantled Druid, Tradition." Technically, Simms's novels respond primarily to the new terrains and epochs made available by Scott, and they reflect an emerging punchiness and concentration on dramatic contrast and event, something marked in the striking chapter titles adopted in his later novels ("The Half-Breed and the Tory," "Picture of Lynch-Law," "Swamp Strategics," "Cow-Chasing"—all from *Mellichampe*). Despite Simms's technical and tonal shift toward a more direct, less bookish style, reflections of Scott are still evident in the late novel *The Forayers* (1855), which features Scottish Highlanders exiled after the 1745 Jacobite rebellion but loyal to George III during the Revolutionary War, and bardic interludes that take readers back to the "authenticity" of re-creations like Canto 6 of Scott's poem *The Lay of the Last Minstrel* (1805). In the "Introduction: Historical Summary" of this late novel, Simms reprises the terms of chapter 1 of *Waverley*, stating that, as in previous fictions, he has sought to subordinate history to "other events" that "illustrate the social condition of the country, under the influence of those strifes and trials which give vivacity to ordinary circumstances, and mark with deeper hues, and stronger colors, and sterner tones, the otherwise common progress of human hopes and fears, passions and necessities."

The complications of "bookish" textuality and oral tradition are especially important in Hawthorne's historical fictions. Hawthorne's links with Scott are obvious on the level of subject matter, and his Puritans, in particular, are shaped in part by Scott's. *Fanshawe* (1828), Hawthorne's "negligible" and anonymous first novel regarded as "an imitation of Scott" (Dekker 1987, 131), shares character names with Scott and is set "about eighty years since" (ch. 1)—that is, "about" the same time as *Waverley*. To a heroine who reads as many romances as Lucy Ashton, a legend-haunted fountain indebted to the Mermaiden's Well from the same novel (*The Bride of Lammermoor*), and inn and hovel scenes that recall *The Antiquary* and *Kenilworth* (1821), Hawthorne adds a "blighted" scholar-hero who has spent his youth "in solitary study, in conversation with the dead" (ch. 2). This hostility toward moribund textuality, constant throughout Hawthorne's fiction, is in direct, though undeclared, conflict with Scott's antiquarianism. Of the inscription on the rock that marks the grave of the novel's villain, Butler, Hawthorne writes, "Traces of letters are still discernible; but the writer's many efforts could never discover a connected meaning" (ch. 9). In this detail lies the heart of Hawthorne's mode of historical fiction, and in it, too, a fascination with the found object that recurs in many of his stories and frame narratives (see, for example, the poignant revivification conjured by the chance discovery of an old arrow-head in "The Old Manse," 1846), and which echoes iconic moments in Scott (see Aiken Drum's Lang Ladle in chapter 4 of *The Antiquary*). In Hawthorne's preface to his last completed novel, *The Marble Faun; or, The Romance of Monte Beni* (1860; published in Britain as *Transformation* prior to its US printing), it is the ideal reader who is imagined as "under some mossy gravestone, inscribed with a half-obliterated name which I shall never recognize." Although, notoriously, this preface declares that "no shadow, no antiquity, no mystery" is available to writers "in the annals of our stalwart republic," the act of interpretation is as fragile and haunted here as in any of Hawthorne's writings. In many ways, *The Marble Faun* is an antihistorical novel. Insistently, its Rome lies "like a long decaying corpse" (ch. 36). The "massiveness of the Roman Past" voids the present of substance and reality (ch. 1): it "will crowd everything else out of my heart," fears the American copyist, Hilda (ch. 12), who has sacrificed her originality to "the immortal pencils of old" (ch. 6). The materiality of the novel's account of Rome and its artifacts, however, has distracted attention from its questioning of novelistic tradition and its still-close relationship with Scott. True to the fascination with *The Bride of Lammermoor* notable in *Fanshawe*, Hawthorne refashions Wolf's Crag as Donatello's tower at Monte Beni and extends the legend of the fountain nymph. Blood seeps from a corpse in the presence of its murderer, a tradition crucial to chapter 11 of *The Fair Maid of Perth*. Miriam's identity and secrets generate competing narratives, something that Hawthorne admits in his original final chapter characterizes any story, "whether we call it history or romance" (ch. 50). The terms reverberate from Scott, as does the tension between the artist's need for secrets and his readers' demands for "further elucidations respecting the mysteries of the story" (conclusion).

In his greatest historical fiction, *The Scarlet Letter: A Romance* (1850), Hawthorne sets out not to explain the past or to make it legible but, again, to emphasize its fragile survival as an incomplete set of signs and implications. As Hester stands on the scaffold at the start of the novel, the narrator states that "her mind, and especially her memory, was preternaturally active," at a critical *present* moment assembling aspects of her past so that they take temporary shape not quite as a story but as a set of interrelated images (ch. 2). Here, Hester is a private historian, prefiguring the glimpses the novel itself will offer. Everyone in *The Scarlet Letter* is a seeker and would-be interpreter, except, in the end, Hester's daughter Pearl, the sender of letters marked with armorial seals, who has become something to be read, but also something reabsorbed into European aristocratic tradition. The clearest indication of the relationship between *The Scarlet Letter* and Scott is not thematic or topical but technical, and it is a return to the imagined power of the found object and the fantasy of origin and transmission. Hawthorne's deceptively indulgent, circumstantial, introduction to *The Scarlet Letter*, "The Custom-House," was originally intended to introduce a volume called *Old-Time Legends*. Its larger architecture, that is, always loomed over the novel it eventually came to serve, like an inflated return to Scott's complicated series of paratextual tales. (Hawthorne's soldier-collector, General Miller, is recognizably in the mold of Sergeant More MacAlpin in the frame of *A Legend of the Wars of Montrose*.) The haunted house of custom (as is developed at greater length in *The House of the Seven Gables: A Romance*, 1851), is a regressive, restrictive presence, inimical to "fancy and sensibility" and to artistry. While he works there, the characters Hawthorne attempts to write into life "retained all the rigidity of dead corpses." In order to write the American past as he wishes, he has to eject himself from American and literary "custom." What most distinguishes Hawthorne's historicity from Cooper's, in this respect, is an insistence on the inescapability of the written, even as the written eludes explication and containment. In the abandoned space of the attic in the Custom House, Hawthorne discovers a bundle of papers described in visceral terms that unnervingly echo those of the exhumation of their author, Mr. Surveyor Pue. *The Scarlet Letter* repeatedly presents the search for historical information as a form of grave robbing, a transgressive and potentially dangerous act. As Scott's Maxwell of Summertrees comments in chapter 11 of *Redgauntlet*

(1824), "[T]here are some auld stories that cannot be ripped up again with entire safety to all concerned."

With the symbolic intensity of *The Scarlet Letter*, American historical fiction seemed to have moved decisively beyond Scott and his fuller depictions of historical scenes and contexts. The historical experimentations of Melville, Poe, and, later, Twain and Faulkner, seemed to distance Scott still further from what had come to be accepted as a sparer and more concentrated "American" style. Yet *The Scarlet Letter* also anticipates these later experiments in being intricately and profoundly responsive to Scott's self-conscious textuality, linguistic and social inclusiveness, and sophisticated historical irony. As this chapter has argued, the American historical novelists reputed to have followed Scott most closely—Cooper, Child, Sedgwick, and Simms—constantly questioned and reconfigured his approach and style. Their writings show repeatedly that "the *Waverley* model" did not fit the American past or the new national present; and that expanding historical writing into the new territory of their own land also meant concentrating and, formally, curtailing it, whether through what I have called the centripetal impulse in Cooper or through Simms's pruned-back narrative style. Scott's most lasting contribution to American literature was the awareness of historical disjuncture itself—of the material, textual, presence but also the unreconstructability of the past. "But the past was not dead," Hawthorne realizes on discovering Hester's densely worked letter *A* in the Custom House: nor was it ever, quite, alive.

7

REVOLUTIONARY NOVELS AND THE PROBLEM OF LITERARY NATIONALISM

JOSEPH J. LETTER

In 1855, when Herman Melville dedicated his only Revolutionary novel, *Israel Potter: His Fifty Years of Exile*, to "His Highness the Bunker-Hill Monument," he was acknowledging the symbolic ascendance of a monolithic national history over the myriad local landmarks and individual stories of the Revolution. The narrative, which sketches the travails of a forgotten Revolutionary soldier, fades into obscurity when juxtaposed against the soaring granite monument. And that is the point, for despite its sarcasm and bitter comic irony, *Israel Potter* mourns the last remnants of Revolutionary reality, and it also marks the end of the Revolutionary novel as an antebellum literary genre. The genre's defining feature had been its direct connection to local memories of the Revolution, but as these faded into the past, so too did the cultural work of a literary form that transcribed and translated the often disturbing oral accounts and legends of Revolutionary history. Without their vital link to the past, Revolutionary novels became as fanciful and temporally distant as any other historical romance, but from 1820 to 1850, during three decades of US myth-making, the genre disrupted the national narrative of progress with local stories that served as present reminders of the nation's fragmented and conflicted Revolutionary past.

Revolutionary narratives were situated between historical fact and popular legend, a space of particular importance in early national culture because it signified the ambivalent status of a nation that had not yet settled upon a coherent narrative of its own history. They were "novels," rather than "romances," because they reinforced a "revolutionary" break with the past that ultimately subverted rational historiography and Old World romance archetypes, even as they drew upon the narrative conventions of both modes. Revolutionary novels were contemporary expressions of America's postcolonial ambivalence. They used the Revolution to represent the complex and various historical legacies of the individual states, and they also gave literary form to the oral histories and folkloric traditions that appeared after the Revolution. Whereas official Revolutionary histories documented the war's events in order to consolidate the new nation, Revolutionary novels memorialized the war's various local legacies.

As the "heroic" founding generation gave way to its partisan successors, the location of national origins shifted from living memory to historical record. Invariably, the shift created conflicts over how a national history would be imagined and who would control that imagining. As Michael Kammen has put it, "By the second decade of the nineteenth century, we can trace the very human lapses of memory by which history is transmuted into something else—call it tradition, aberrant legend, or national mythology" (1978, 19). Revolutionary novels narrated this "transmutation," but where Kammen suggests a stable "history" that was corrupted by failures of "memory," Revolutionary novelists interrogated both terms equally. Their novels reinscribed oral histories, legends, myths, *and* historical events. Like the Revolutionary events they narrated, the novels represented a break or breach. They told stories of a divided country filled with political and domestic strife, and they therefore rejected the present as much as the past. In their fictional narratives, historical source material, and local settings, Revolutionary novels repeatedly opened the very wounds of history that literary nationalists (and in a broader sense the American nation) attempted to deny or ignore as sectional conflicts gradually led the country toward the Civil War.

The dominant sentiment of Revolutionary novels was mourning and loss, and in this sense they contradicted the optimism of national progress. These narratives treated history as a site for moral instruction in the present. Quite the opposite of historical fulfillment or Manifest Destiny, the Revolution provided a reminder of the disparity between the original heroic ideal of liberty and democracy and a politically divided antebellum nation. Revolutionary veterans, a dwindling band, offered physical proof of decline and historical decay; thus, Walter Benjamin's discussion of a "saturnine vision" of history is helpful for understanding the complexities of Revolutionary novels. In *The Origin of German Tragic Drama* Benjamin writes:

> In nature they saw eternal transience, and here alone did the saturnine vision of this generation recognize history. . . . In the process of decay, and in it alone, the events of history shrivel up and become absorbed in the setting. The quintessence of these decaying objects [the ruin] is the polar opposite to the idea of transfigured nature. (1998, 179)

In early Revolutionary novels like James Fenimore Cooper's *The Spy: A Tale of the Neutral Ground* (1821) and John Neal's *Seventy-Six* (1823), Revolutionary veterans personified historical ruin. More commonly, local landmarks functioned as Revolutionary ruins, for example "Major André's tree" in Washington Irving's "The Legend of Sleepy Hollow" (1820), or the overgrown graveyard at Dorchester, South

Carolina, in William Gilmore Simms's *The Partisan* (1835), or the Province House in Boston that inspired Nathaniel Hawthorne's four "Legends" (1838–39), or the Quaker meeting house and graveyard in George Lippard's *Blanche of Brandywine* (1846). Such ruins *located* the historical ambivalence that characterized the novels. The ruin was indeed "the polar opposite to the idea of transfigured nature." It starkly contrasted with the symbolic logic that characterized nationalist discourse, as, for example, when Daniel Webster called upon the whole nation to "become a vast and splendid monument" at the original Bunker Hill Monument dedication in 1825.

Despite the optimistic rhetoric of nationalists, the Revolution never gently assimilated into a monumental whole; instead, its ubiquitous remnants disturbed assumptions about the future of the nation. The war's geography was well known by Americans; not only were battles fought near all the major cities (Boston, New York, Philadelphia, Charleston), but also local Revolutionary landmarks abounded and inspired countless myths and legends of the war. Equally important, Revolutionary war veterans were a living presence in the young nation, and their decrepit and often destitute condition raised difficult questions about everything from war pensions to governmental regard for elderly citizens. Furthermore, war veterans comprised an unsettling vestige of rebellion against social and political authority. They were disconcerting, ambiguous figures who split the nation, part of the modern national "self" but also signifiers of a violent revolt against an established government.

The Revolution's many historical paradoxes have always posed problems for critics seeking a unified or coherent theory of national literature. In *The Rites of Assent*, Sacvan Bercovitch argues that Revolutionary novels were dismissed by critics because "those [classic] writers through whom the American imagination has been defined remained silent on the subject, or at most ambivalent" (1993, 169). Bercovitch contends that the most famous American writers sublimated the problem of the Revolution. They converted the reality of a rebellious break with the past into a myth of progress that extended back to the original Puritans and ultimately to the Israelites. What he calls a theory of "continuing revolution" represents the nation's steady rise and progress; it explains how canonical American writers displaced the Revolutionary War's concrete historical reality. But the very ubiquity of Revolutionary novels contradicts such a theory of American culture. In the first half of the nineteenth century America was anything but "silent" on the subject of the Revolution, and popular writers shared the ambivalence of canonical authors. In early American culture the Revolution was never elided for the purposes of historical continuity; it was a juncture, a defining historical moment debated in Congress, celebrated in countless orations, and rhetorically manipulated in poems, plays, short stories, and novels.

Revolutionary novels enjoyed popularity precisely because they represented a familiar and local alternative to broadly national Revolutionary histories. They also tapped into anxieties about democratic representation in the young nation. On a fundamental level they concerned inclusion or exclusion from a national narrative. Because they typically subverted the generic conventions of time and space associated with historical romance, the cultural impact of Revolutionary novels came closer to what Homi Bhabha (writing of more recent postcolonial texts) describes as an intervening "performative" discourse, one that "introduces a temporality of the 'in-between'" (1990, 299). In their narrative details Revolutionary novels evoked an "intermittent time, and interstitial space, that emerges as a structure of undecidability" (312). They had a "supplemental" relation both to the American historical romance and, more broadly, to literary nationalism.

The "performative" function of Revolutionary novels stands out more starkly when juxtaposed against the "pedagogical" function of literary nationalism. In Bhabha's terms, "pedagogical" discourse represents a "will to nationhood . . . that unifies historical memory and secures present-day consent" (310). This national will is "itself the site of a strange forgetting of the history of the nation's past: the violence involved in establishing the nation's writ. It is this forgetting—a minus in the origin—that constitutes the *beginning* of the nation's narrative" (310). On the contrary, Revolutionary ruins memorialized originary violence, as when Neal writes in *Seventy-Six*, "political convulsion chisels out the head and face of her chosen ones. Look at the men of our revolution—their very countenances are the history of the time" (v. 1, ch. 8). Revolutionary novels recalled a local and immanent vision that defied assimilation with a modern national and transcendent one.

Early literary critics recognized the ambivalence in historical novels but missed their significance as complex representations of the Revolution. For example, in a review of Lydia Maria Child's Revolutionary novel, *The Rebels* (1825), the *North American Review* noted:

> The narrative is greatly deficient in simplicity and unity, and is not so much one story as a number of separate stories, not interwoven, but loosely tied together. . . . We think it the more necessary to comment on this fault, because no point has been so much neglected, by the writers of historical romances, from the author of Waverly downwards, as the management of their narrative. (Gray 1826, 402)

The aesthetic objections suggest the larger issues at stake in narrating the nation. Where critics looked for narrative "simplicity and unity," Revolutionary novels gave them densely plotted and serialized narrative structures. Ironically, today most historians would argue that the novels were accurate reflections of Revolutionary history. As Gary B. Nash put it in *The Unknown American Revolution* (2005), "What is the lasting value of a 'coherent' history if coherence is obtained by eliminating the jagged edges, where much of the vitality of the people is to be found?" (xxix). Revolutionary novels were a people's history of the war, a concatenation of local stories "not interwoven, but loosely tied together."

Revolutionary novelists embraced the historiographic problems that later national historians, like George Bancroft in his influential *History of the United States* (1834–74), either elided or mythologized in establishing a national narrative. Bercovitch sees Bancroft's *History* as the key text in the myth of "continuing Revolution" and argues that "Bancroft's outlook has direct precedents in the patriot historians of the preceding generation" (1993, 174). Undoubtedly, Bercovitch is correct in noting Bancroft's powerful role in shaping the myth of American essentialism, but that genealogy leaves out the role of the Revolutionary novel, which emerged precisely in-between the "patriot historians" and the first volume of Bancroft's magnum opus. Bancroft's work represents the historiographic component of literary nationalism, the way that historians synthesized various provincial histories into an epic "narrative of 'America' as the United States" (Bercovitch 1993, 177). By contrast, Revolutionary novels interrupted the historiographic process of nation building, and their American genealogy extends back to early experimenters in historical narrative like Charles Brockden Brown, the early Knickerbocker writer Samuel Woodworth, and Neal, who was not only a novelist but an important coauthor of Paul Allen's *A History of the American Revolution* (1819).

Although he is rarely considered in connection with Revolutionary novelists, Washington Irving was also critically important for understanding the local sensibility that would later characterize the genre. The two most famous stories from *The Sketch Book* (1819–20), "Rip Van Winkle" and "The Legend of Sleepy Hollow," depend on Revolutionary history without ever directly representing it. Irving's reticence involved more than polite consideration for English readers; "Rip" and "Sleepy Hollow" rejected national versions of history by favoring local legend and popular myth. Irving repeatedly notes that the tales are vernacular histories recorded by the fictional Dutch historian, Diedrich Knickerbocker; moreover, he questions historiography through Knickerbocker. No story better exemplifies Irving's ambivalence toward national history than "The Legend of Sleepy Hollow."

"Sleepy Hollow" is deeply rooted in local Revolutionary history. The famous encounter between Ichabod Crane and the Headless Horseman takes place exactly where the "unfortunate Major André" was caught carrying plans for the fortress at West Point, given to him by Benedict Arnold. André was captured by three yeomen and later hanged on Washington's orders. The incident fascinated Americans, many of whom saw André as a tragic hero, an accomplished English gentleman who died for Arnold's treachery. André became the subject of poems, plays, and, as will be shown, numerous popular stories of the Revolution. By staging Ichabod's confrontation at the very spot where the three men had hidden, Irving unmistakably links these common democratic heroes of the Revolution with a ghostly figure who prevents Ichabod from marrying Katrina Van Tassel, selling off her family's farmlands, and moving to the West. By intervening, the three patriots had saved New York from the imperial tyranny of British rule, just as Brom Bones, ironically masquerading as a Hessian soldier, prevents the destruction of local Dutch culture by sparing it from Ichabod's (and the nation's) western speculation.

For Irving, what began in *A History of New York* (1809) as a burlesque of provincial histories had by 1819 become a sharper edged satire of American national identity. Irving's local approach set a precedent for the whole genre of Revolutionary novels, which are best understood as resisting the synthesizing movement of literary nationalism. In 1821, Cooper returned to the same location, the "Neutral Ground" in Westchester, New York, for his enormously successful Revolutionary novel, *The Spy*. Like Irving, Cooper used the legend of Major André to stress the ironic ambivalence of Revolutionary history. *The Spy* was a landmark work; it established the American Revolutionary novel and inspired numerous other literary works. Typically, the narrative is described as the story of the Whartons, an aristocratic family whose mansion is located between battle lines. Cooper's narrative foregrounds New York's divided identity in the Revolutionary era and uses the local setting to complicate myths of the Revolution as a purely ideological conflict.

The Spy established the convention of representing the Revolution as a familial conflict: the Whartons' mother is dead, the father is an ineffectual Tory, and the children are torn in their allegiances. The elder daughter, Sarah, is a Loyalist, engaged to a British colonel, Wellmere; the younger, Frances, is a spirited patriot in love with her Virginia cousin, Peyton Dunwoodie, a major in the Continental army. In the end, Sarah loses her mind after Wellmere betrays her, Frances marries Peyton, and the Whartons move to the Dunwoodie plantation in Virginia. Such plot dichotomies neatly fit the model of romance narratives, or what Shirley Samuels calls "romances of the republic," where family stands for nation and narrative events allegorize a myth of national unity and historical progress.

But Cooper also includes a son, Henry Wharton, who significantly complicates the binary oppositions of romance. Henry's story ironically mirrors Major André's: a British captain, he is captured and accused of espionage after innocently visiting his family. The capture takes place in the fall of 1780, just months after André's hanging, further reinforcing the theme of "divided loyalties." Even more significant, the novel's actual hero is Harvey Birch, the titular spy, a mysterious and scorned figure who personifies Revolutionary ambivalence. Neighbors believe that Birch is a Yankee peddler who roves the Neutral Ground selling military secrets, but in the course of the narrative Birch rescues the Whartons from their burning home, reveals Wellmere's bigamy, saves Henry from execution, and facilitates the marriage between Frances and Peyton. He is irrefutably the key to plot resolution in *The Spy*, and if there is an allegorical relation between family and national narrative, then he is the figure who makes the present nation possible. Yet Cooper emphatically stresses Birch's anonymity and misrepresentation throughout the narrative. Childless, Birch loses all his possessions and his last living relative, his father. Only George Washington and Frances Wharton know of Birch's heroic service, and neither ever reveals the secret.

Through Birch, Cooper created an iconic figure of forgotten democratic heroism, not as an affirmation of the Revolution but as a criticism of its present history. Birch is a cipher at the very core of the American historical novel's first iteration. His anonymity represents the ideological skewing of official history, which had largely ignored the sacrifices made by common Revolutionary heroes. By 1821, Washington had ascended to become the symbolic national father, but Birch, his democratic obverse in the narrative, descends into oblivion. Birch personifies what Bhabha calls a "minus in the origin" of the nation that Revolutionary novelists converted into the critical signifying space of their narratives. *The Spy* asked readers to *remember*, even as it told a story about what had been forgotten, and in that sense it established the Revolutionary novel's function as a mnemonic device, a way of memorializing the Revolution for morally instructive purposes.

Like the Westchester Neutral Ground, the area around Saratoga, New York, also became an important site for Revolutionary novels. Eliza Lanesford Cushing's novel, *Saratoga* (1824), an interesting proto-feminist work, not only reinterpreted the meaning of the Revolution but also addressed problems of national exclusion and marginalization. In *Saratoga*, Cushing portrays the Revolution as a sustained effort of resistance, rather than a neatly divided ideological conflict. When the heroine, Catherine Courtland, gets caught between devotion to her Loyalist father and her patriot lover, she submits to neither but rather endures until she brings about a resolution between the two opposing parties. Catherine suggests a neutral alternative, a "third" possibility for understanding the Revolutionary contest, and the novel's historical settings, first at Saratoga and then at Valley Forge, reinforce Cushing's model of patient but firm resistance.

Saratoga is also notable for reviving the legend of Jane McCrea, a young woman who was killed and scalped by Indians employed in Burgoyne's army. As Margaret Reid explains in *Cultural Secrets as Narrative Form* (2004), the exact details of McCrea's death were never clear, but apparently she stayed behind when local residents evacuated. She was waiting for her lover, a New Jersey man serving with Burgoyne's forces. Newspapers on both sides of the Atlantic seized upon the lurid details of McCrea's murder; they portrayed her as a helpless victim, an example of how the war had become a conflict involving Indians and civilians. Much like the story of André, McCrea's legend invoked conflicted loyalties. She, too, inspired plays, poems, and paintings, but in the hands of Revolutionary novelists the ambiguities surrounding her death signified the open space between historical truth and fictional romance. For example, in *Saratoga*, Cushing inverts Jane's story yet retains its echoes through repeated allusions that make her a foil for Catherine. Jane waited behind, hoping to be escorted to a Loyalist lover in the British camp; Catherine ventures into the forest searching for her father, a wounded prisoner in the American camp. Where Jane was a figure of resignation and apathetic submission, Catherine has clear agency as a healer nursing the wounded and as a mediator involved in the novel's political discussions.

Another interesting work set in the area near Saratoga is Delia Salter Bacon's *The Bride of Fort Edward* (1839). Written in the form of dialogues, Bacon claims that these "embod[y]" the "abstract truth" in the historical record (pref.), but if there is such an abstract truth, her fictional embellishments, which combine the legends of Jane McCrea and Major André, undermine its certainty. Helen Grey, the Jane McCrea character, recalls both Helen of Troy and the British General Charles "No Flint" Grey. Her death is portrayed as the epicenter of Revolutionary history; just as Burgoyne is about to clinch victory for the British, news of Helen's death becomes a rallying point for demoralized American soldiers who had been deserting in droves and contemplating surrender. The name "Grey" ironically links Helen to André, who served under Grey in the Philadelphia campaign but was never at Saratoga. Grey gave the infamous order to use a bayonet charge on sleeping Americans at the Paoli Massacre. Bacon's André is the perfect English gentleman, a poet, a painter, a musician, and a friend of Helen's British lover, Everard Maitland. Moreover, Benedict Arnold, who actually fought at Saratoga, also appears, and Bacon represents him as an inspired leader who seizes the opportunity of announcing Helen's death, rousing the American soldiers who, in the novel's last line, shout, "To the death! Freedom for ever!" (pt. 6, dialogue 2). The disturbing historical contradictions of André's presence and the speech from Arnold (which echoes Mark Antony's speech for Caesar) are typical of Revolutionary novels in that they deliberately complicate historical knowledge to represent a deeper conflict at the core of the Revolution.

While the legends of Jane McCrea and Major André emerged from New York's strong Loyalist sympathies during the Revolution, they continued to flourish as historical motifs in Revolutionary novels because they suggested a deference toward English culture that Elisa Tamarkin has termed "Anglophilia" (2007). In *The Linwoods* (1835), Catharine Maria Sedgwick inverts this typical motif; instead of a patriotic narrative complicated by latent Tory sympathies, Sedgwick foregrounds Tory characters within British-occupied New York City and reinscribes the patriot legend of Nathan Hale, an American spy captured and executed in 1776. Hale's story of heroic loyalty to the American cause, made famous by his legendary final words, "I only regret that I have but one life to lose for my country," binds Sedgwick's novel, which in all its plotlines concerns loyalty.

The main character, Isabella Linwood, begins as a strict Tory but gradually shifts her political allegiance as the narrative progresses. Her conversion parallels her romantic interests. At first she loves Jasper Meredith, a handsome but obsessively self-interested suitor. Meredith becomes a British officer only when he realizes that it will help him rise socially. His foil, Eliot Lee, with whom Isabella eventually falls in love, represents rational devotion to the Revolutionary cause. Eliot, a New Englander, also contrasts with the immoderately passionate Herbert Linwood, his friend and Isabella's brother. Herbert defies his staunch Tory father by running off to join the Continental army but later is captured while trying to visit the family and imprisoned in New York's infamous Rhinelander Sugar House. The Sugar

House was run by William Cunningham, the corrupt provost marshal of New York, who also oversaw New York's prison ships. Cunningham executed hundreds of American prisoners, including Hale, and also starved thousands to death in the overcrowded jails.

In a rather bizarre historical irony, Sedgwick distorts the legends surrounding Hale and Cunningham. For example, the hero Eliot Lee combines the exploits of Hale and his close friend, William Hull. Hull originally publicized Hale's last words but later became infamous (and was court-martialed) for surrendering Fort Detroit to the British in the War of 1812. Furthermore, instead of having Lee captured and sentenced to hang like Hale, Sedgwick substitutes his simple-minded servant Kisel who is wrongly accused of involvement with a band of "Skinners." Before Kisel can be executed by Cunningham, he starves to death in the Sugar House. Cunningham also ironically figures in Herbert Linwood's escape, when a former slave, Rose, switches places with Herbert during a visit. Rose, another model of loyalty (she remains with the Linwood family after being freed), physically beats Cunningham and ties a noose around his neck, threatening to hang him if he cries out. Too embarrassed to reveal the truth, Cunningham later claims that he was spared by the gentlemanly Herbert Linwood. Even while Sedgwick appears to tell a story of the nation's rise and progress, she includes disturbing echoes of Revolutionary atrocities, especially those suffered by common people who bore the brunt of the war's horrors.

Like the New York novels, the Revolutionary novels of New England addressed unresolved issues from the war, but they also focused on questions of national origins. For example, Cooper's *Lionel Lincoln; or, The Leaguer of Boston* (1825), which was timed to coincide with the nation's fiftieth anniversary celebrations, addresses Revolutionary violence and ideological conflict in Boston. Cooper traveled to the city and did extensive research on the historical, architectural, and geographic details of the area, but the narrative devolves into gothic convolutions when he tries to superimpose Lionel's family history on the factual events of the war. Ironically, Cooper's faith in historical detail—he went so far as to research the weather and moon cycles—only produced deeper ambivalence about the war's origins. The fine distinctions between mob violence and democratic heroism, loyalty to the king and objections to Parliament, aristocracy and republicanism never become clear. Lionel personifies the confusion: born in Boston but raised in England; a British soldier but involved with American rebels; an aristocrat but sympathetic to the republican cause. As the narrative unfolds, Lionel discovers that Ralph, a mysterious and insane figure who has inspired Boston's mob revolt, is his father, but Cooper juxtaposes Ralph's insanity and mob incitement against the rational arguments of Samuel Adams and the heroic yeomen who volunteer at Dorchester. Finally, disenchanted and disturbed, Lionel marries and returns to England, effectively ending his family's aberrant relation with America.

The novel failed, and Cooper blamed the failure on its historicity. In the 1832 preface for a new edition, he claimed that the Revolution was too recent and well known for "imagination to embellish" and that readers were not interested in complex truths about Revolutionary history. "There is no blunder more sure to be visited by punishment, than that which tempts a writer to instruct his readers when they wish only to be amused . . . in no instance more obviously than in the difficulties he encountered in writing this his only historical tale." *Lionel Lincoln* was to be the first in a series of "Legends of the Thirteen Republics," but Cooper abandoned the project, no doubt in part because it offered little hope for amusing an audience. Yet *Lionel Lincoln*'s failings were not the fault of naive readers. The narrative had exposed the limitations of history in Revolutionary novels: its events were recent enough to conflict with living memories, and factual, historical details simply did not add up to a coherent national story.

Domestic Revolutionary novels from women writers generally offered better solutions to the genre's problems. Unlike Cooper's adventurous narratives, which were retrofitted into actual battlefield histories, domestic narratives, by necessity, had a parallel relation to the war's events. Child's *The Rebels* offers a fascinating alternative to Cooper's unsuccessful version of Revolutionary origins. Like Cooper's novel, Child's appeared during the nation's fiftieth anniversary, and the narrative addresses mob violence, Loyalist/Whig political allegiances, and class conflict, but through the personal choices of a female character, Lucretia Fitzherbert.

Narrative events in *The Rebels* are situated between the Stamp Act riots of 1765 and the Boston Massacre in 1770, suggesting a political resistance to colonial authority that parallels Lucretia's own resistance to parental authority. A rich heiress, Lucretia lives under the guardianship of Lieutenant Governor Thomas Hutchinson, who severely censures her when she refuses marriage with an unprincipled British suitor, Frederic Somerville. Lucretia chooses Henry Osborne instead, the patriot son of a Boston minister. Well before Hawthorne's "Legends of the Province House," Child created fictional representations of Hutchinson and the Loyalist minister/poet Mather Byles. Through Lucretia's spirited resistance, Child rejects the established colonial order that Hutchinson and Byles supported, but what seems like a simple narrative choice in favor of historical progress—the story of America's break from the colonial past through an assertion of its own will—becomes much more compelling as it digresses to reveal Lucretia's family history. On the day of the Boston Massacre, Lucretia discovers that she was switched at birth, that she was not the daughter of a wealthy East India trader but instead that of a local witch, Molly Bradstreet. Nevertheless, Bradstreet is a powerful Revolutionary (and feminist) figure who incites and then is killed during the Massacre.

Child's story, like so many other Revolutionary novels, unravels its own myth of historical progress. Lucretia's identity change makes the novel a kind of antiromance. The actual Lucretia, Gertrude Wilson, an archetypal heroine, is peripheral to the narrative, and is Canadian, not American. In the end, she inherits the

Fitzherbert fortune, marries her lover, and moves to the family estate in England. Lucretia, on the other hand, accepts her true identity as Gertrude Osborne, displacing the conventional romantic ending with an ideal, republican one. Rather than a wealthy aristocrat, she becomes a simple wife and mother. The Lucretia/Gertrude dichotomy suggests the very Old World/New World boundary in romance narratives that Revolutionary novelists deconstructed. If in *Lionel Lincoln* Cooper had identified a historiographic limitation for Revolutionary novels, then Child's work reflects upon the limits of conventional Old World romance structures for telling the story of Revolutionary origins.

In the "Legends of the Province House," Hawthorne recasts the problem of narrating the Revolution by suggesting that the modern nation, not the Revolution, has destroyed the continuity between past and present. The four stories comprising the "Legends" were first published in John L. O'Sullivan's *United States Magazine and Democratic Review*, a platform for literary nationalism and Jacksonian democracy, but the tales hardly mark a straightforward endorsement of the contemporary nation. The present-day narrator, who refers to himself as a "thorough-going democrat," never fully grasps the ironies implied by the "legends." Unlike Cooper, who was frustrated by the attempt to narrate Revolutionary origins with historical accuracy, Hawthorne's narrator blithely admits that "despairing of literal and absolute truth, I have not scrupled to make such further changes [to the stories] as seemed conducive to the reader's profit and delight." And he further notes, "It is desperately hard work, when we attempt to throw the spell of hoar antiquity over localities with which the living world, and the day that is passing over us, have aught to do."

The Province House mansion, much more than the narrator or even the publication format, indicates Hawthorne's critique: it has become a tavern among a nondescript row of stores and warehouses in Boston, a place where the narrator elicits tales from the elderly patrons and then embellishes them for "profit and delight." The mansion exemplifies the paradox of the ruin in American culture; instead of suggesting "hoar antiquity," it represents what Bhabha (critiquing Ernest Renan) has called "the site of a strange forgetting of the history of the nation's past" (1990, 310). Yet from "Howe's Masquerade," which occurs on the last night of the British occupation of Boston, to the last story, "Old Esther Dudley," which explains the transfer of the Province House over to the new governor of Massachusetts, John Hancock, the legends comprise a series of lessons in prideful ignorance, ultimately the same kind of ignorance that the contemporary narrator expresses.

While Hawthorne's "Legends" exploit the temporal distance between the present and the Revolutionary past to develop a critique of the modern nation, the earliest Revolutionary novels about the South, even those penned by northern authors, used geographic distance from northern publishing centers and readers as a space for the fanciful embellishment of history. Cushing's *Yorktown* (1826) and the anonymously authored *Frederick de Algeroy* (1825) treat the South as a site for romance narratives that eulogize America's pre-Revolutionary colonial aristocracy.

They associate the region with an early colonial idyll, a time before British imperial domination became oppressive. In each, the Revolution signifies a violent end to a corrupt era that began with the Seven Years' War, not a heroic intervention that created a new republican social order.

In *Yorktown* the struggle for control over a Virginia plantation allegorizes America's colonial history. Colonel Walstein, a villainous German interloper, insinuates himself and then usurps the plantation from its rightful French and English heirs. The narrative culminates at the Battle of Yorktown, where Walstein's plans are foiled by the American victory, and the plantation is restored to its true heirs. *Frederick de Algeroy* (read anagrammatically, "allegory") praises the heroism of titled aristocrats while representing commoners as rustic clowns. Like *Yorktown*, the novel was dedicated to the Marquis de Lafayette who had recently completed a hugely popular tour of the United States. Despite his egalitarian politics and strong opposition to slavery, Lafayette is figured as the "Marquis," a chivalric European nobleman who championed America's fight for liberty. Historical events in *Frederick de Algeroy* are based on the Battle of Camden Plains, but the narrative's gothic twists occur in the ruin of an old plantation house. Instead of an actual historical landmark, the plantation serves as a mournful signifier for the decay and corruption of the colonial aristocracy. *Yorktown* and *Frederick de Algeroy* represent a fascinating alternative to other Revolutionary novels; they both lament the decline of a southern plantation aristocracy and deny the Revolution as historical progress. The heroine of *Yorktown* ultimately moves to France with her new husband, and *Frederick de Algeroy* ends with the hero dying and his love entering a convent.

Notwithstanding the achievement of John Pendleton Kennedy, whose *Horse-Shoe Robinson* (1835) dramatized partisan strife in the Carolina backcountry, William Gilmore Simms was the most important Revolutionary novelist of the South. Simms wrote eight Revolutionary novels, which, as Sean Busick notes, "together constitute the most extensive treatment of the Revolutionary War in nineteenth-century American literature" (2005, 68). His novels provided a local specificity that was absent in the representative southern characters and settings from earlier northern novelists, as for example in Cushing's *Yorktown*, which lacks geographic specificity, or Cooper's *The Pilot* (1824), whose heroines have both fled to England from a Carolina plantation. In the 1856 introduction to a new edition of *The Partisan*, Simms claimed that his Revolutionary novels were inspired by the ruins of an old graveyard at Dorchester, South Carolina. Overgrown and forgotten, the site evoked numerous Revolutionary legends that Simms had heard as a child, but its historical distance also allowed space for new embellishments: "It was with the revival of old memories, and the awakening of new impulses and sentiments, that I rambled through the solemn tabernacles of decay . . . as I went among the mouldering tombstones, I found food for sad thoughts and a busy fancy at every step I took."

The Partisan, much like Simms's other novels about the Revolution in South Carolina, was "mostly historical" (intro.). Even in its romantic subplots of daring rescues and military skirmishes he relied upon "local chronicles" (intro.). Simms worked very closely with authoritative accounts and was in his own right a highly respected historian. For Simms, the ambiguous middle ground between history and legend was expressed in the very geography of South Carolina, in the swamps and rivers that hid the small bands of guerrilla fighters who resisted British military might and Tory militia groups. *The Partisan* describes a style of guerrilla warfare that captured the complexities of the war in the South. Of the title, he noted, "the work, indeed, must teach the reader to look rather for a true description of that mode of warfare, than for any consecutive story comprising the fortunes of a single personage" (intro.). One hears in Simms's explanation an apology for the loose and fragmentary narrative but also an assertion of its fundamental truth as Revolutionary history.

The ruins of Dorchester were the point of origin for a trilogy of novels: *The Partisan*, *Mellichampe* (1836), and *Katharine Walton* (1851). Unlike Cooper, who after *Lionel Lincoln* abandoned what he saw as the didacticism of Revolutionary history, Simms maintained a desire to write "the unwritten, the unconsidered, but veracious history" (*Partisan*, intro.) of the war in South Carolina; moreover, he saw in the ruin a way of representing the instructive power of history. As he put it in "The Epochs and Events of American History, As Suited to the Purposes of Art in Fiction" (1845), "Ruins speak for themselves, and, to this extent, are their own historians. They equally denote the existence and the overthrow;—the was and the is not" (*Views and Reviews* 1962, 35). Simms locates the link between his historiographic and philosophical objectives in the fragmentary ruin. Dorchester's remnants were present-day markers of local Revolutionary history, but they also comprised a sad statement on the contemporary nation's "decay of moral purpose, and, accordingly, of moral power" (*Partisan*, ch. 32). Thus, the lessons of the ruin capture the ambivalence of the Revolutionary novel. In their very form, Revolutionary novels gave voice to the forgotten or "unconsidered" remnants of history ("the was") and served as mournful reminders of what the nation was losing in the march of progress ("the is not").

In the historiographic sense, Simms's Revolutionary novels were "performative" interventions in nationalist discourse, but his critical association with the Young America movement caught him in the bind of writing the nation as "pedagogical object." In the late 1830s Simms had befriended the founding members of Young America, the New Yorkers Evert Duyckinck and Cornelius Mathews, and became in his own right an important figure in the literary movement; furthermore, his *Views and Reviews in American Literature, History and Fiction* (1845) was "a virtual manifesto" (Holman 1962, ix) for the group. Yet, politically he remained loyal to the South and the institution of slavery, even as sectional debates pulled the nation apart. The growing gap between nation and section exemplified the differences that literary nationalists had attempted to resolve through abstractions like the "American mind" or "American spirit." In *Views and Reviews* Simms tried to articulate a theory of writing local history as national literature by defining a "genius of place" (1962, 126), but he is never clear on how the *genius loci* translates to a national identity. As a reviewer from the *Boston Morning Post* aptly noted:

> If we understand Mr. Simms and his colleagues, ("Puffer-Hopkins"-Mathews and the rest,) it is necessary that our writers should choose American subjects, in order that their productions, however good, should constitute a real "American literature;" and that they should fill their books with a certain mysterious "American spirit," very difficult to describe and exceedingly hard to imagine. . . . It is a pity that some one of these gentlemen should not *produce a work* which would serve to show what this singular "American literature" really is. One look at such a *model* would be more convincing than the perusal of scores of essays. (qtd. in *Knickerbocker* Dec. 1847, 556)

Unfortunately, Simms, Duyckinck, and other literary nationalists gradually divided along with the nation in the 1850s, and assertions of local southern identity became increasingly associated with the logic of secession rather than national genius.

Revolutionary novels about Pennsylvania offer another interesting geographic concatenation within the genre. The earliest examples, *The Betrothed of Wyoming* (1830) and *Meredith; or, The Mystery of the Meschianza* (1831), were written by James McHenry, an Irish immigrant to Philadelphia. *The Betrothed* retells the story of the Wyoming massacre described by Crèvecoeur in *Letters from an American Farmer* (1782) and later made famous in Thomas Campbell's poem *Gertrude of Wyoming* (1809). Like Robert Montgomery Bird's Revolutionary novel *The Hawks of Hawk-Hollow* (1835), *The Betrothed* addresses the complex history of colonial settlement on the Pennsylvania frontier, which during the Revolution became another "Neutral Ground," subject to lawless raids from Tory "refugees" and Patriot "skinners" alike. *Meredith*, despite its absurd narrative, is the more original work. It describes the "Meschianza" celebration during the British occupation of Philadelphia in May of 1778, an elaborate fete held in honor of General William Howe that was organized by Major André. Instead of representing Philadelphia as the heroic origin of the Continental Congress and the Declaration of Independence, McHenry's narrative exposes the profound ambivalence that characterized the city and its environs during the Revolution. André appears in McHenry's version as a perfect gentleman who twice saves the life of the patriot Edward Meredith. He even provides a special pass from General Howe that allows Meredith to escape through the British lines, deliberately inverting the story of André's own capture, which involved a pass supplied by Benedict Arnold.

In the Revolutionary novels of Pennsylvania, Quaker history suggests another kind of "minus in the origin" of the nation, an indeterminate center that implied ambivalence toward military and political conflict and dramatically differed from the Puritan national narrative of "continuing revolution." While McHenry's Pennsylvania Quakers are benign Tories who counsel peace, in the later Revolutionary novels of George Lippard, Quaker origins connect much more emphatically to the birth of democracy in the New World. Throughout the 1840s Lippard produced an extraordinary number of Revolutionary novels and "legends," especially about Pennsylvania, that functioned as a counter-mythology to the Puritan progress narrative. As he states in *Blanche of Brandywine*:

> God grant the time may come, when our battle-fields will find a chronicler . . . when this eternal cant about Pilgrim fathers, and Plymouth rock, will be succeeded by a healthy admiration of our own Apostle, William Penn. For while flowing from Plymouth Rock, the bitter waters of Persecution and intolerance, deluged New England; William Penn, under the Elm of Shackamaxon, founded a nation, without a priest, without an oath, without a blow. (ch. 16)

Quakerism literally intervenes in Lippard's Revolutionary tales, as, for example, in *Herbert Tracy* (1844). When the patriot title character encounters his father, a British major, during the Battle of Germantown, a herculean Quaker suddenly appears, takes the father's sword, and breaks it over his knee. Yet, as if to preserve narrative ambivalence, Tracy's father is later killed by a sniper who fires from a nearby Quaker graveyard. And the same neutral representation reoccurs in *Blanche of Brandywine*, a narrative involving a series of fratricidal conflicts during the Revolution. In *Blanche*, Lippard embellished the Revolutionary legend that local Quakers held services at the Birmingham Meeting House while the Battle of Brandywine raged outside. Lippard situates the meeting house and its adjoining graveyard at the ironic core of the narrative, which culminates, after a dizzying array of plotlines spanning two generations and myriad trans-Atlantic complications, in hand-to-hand combat within the "Quaker Temple" and graveyard. Additionally, the novel's darkest villain is a murderous Quaker bent upon revenge for his own father's execution during the Seven Years' War.

Lippard never tired of the irony that Philadelphia, the Quaker "city of brotherly love," had not lived up to the patriotic ideals of the Revolution. His short Revolutionary "legends," which he read as popular lectures and collected in *Washington and His Generals* (1847) and *Washington and His Men* (1849), developed an elaborate mythology of the democratic nation that ironically resonates with Bercovitch's Puritan thesis. That is, Lippard went so far as to invent a typology of the nation whereby the Revolution was the fulfillment of a radically democratic world history. He contrived elaborate historical legends of Washington as a Christ figure of humble origins, a democratic savior who, through the Revolution, redeemed the New World from the corruption of the Old one. Like other Revolutionary novelists, Lippard mourned the present decay of Revolutionary ideals, but not to eulogize. His typological fictions prophesy a return of revolution; they predict that a new savior will wash the fallen nation clean and restore the democratic principles that the Revolution's heroes had fought for.

Undoubtedly, Lippard's prophetic legends responded to the present civil unrest in Philadelphia and other American cities (for example, the nativist riots that were commonplace in the 1840s), but they were equally influenced by a radical mysticism that he connected to Quaker origins. In *The Rose of Wissahikon; or, The Fourth of July 1776* (1847) and *Paul Ardenheim: The Monk of Wissahikon* (1848), Lippard interwove rituals and symbology (the kind typically associated with secret societies like the Illuminati and Freemasons) and tied them to local histories of radical Quaker and Pietist sects that had settled along the Wissahickon Creek near Germantown. Lippard grew up in the area, hearing stories about Johannes Kelpius, Jacob Boehme, and other German mystics. The ruins of Kelpius's "temple" near the juncture of the Wissahickon and the Schuylkill in Philadelphia—the same ruins encrypted in Charles Brockden Brown's *Wieland; or, The Transformation* (1798)—often figure in Lippard's Revolutionary tales, linking the radical religious desire for worldwide "reformation" and the political one symbolized by the American Revolution. In 1849 Lippard formed the Brotherhood of the Union, a secret organization that advocated labor and land reform (and also supported racial and gender equality). Lippard connected his contemporary democratic agenda to a genealogy of reformation that extended all the way back to ancient Egypt; thus, for him the Revolution represented the secular manifestation of a sacred will to fight oppression that was as old as history. Lippard saw his work as a novelist as a means of broadcasting a social reform agenda and had no patience for "paper wars" like the Young America debates. As he put it:

> We need unity among our authors; the age pulsates with a great Idea, and that Idea is the right of Labor to its fruits, coupled with the re-organization of the social system. Let our authors write of this, speak of it, sing of it, and then we will have something like a National literature. . . . [A] literature which does not work practically, for the advancement of social reform . . . is just good for nothing at all. (qtd. in Reynolds 1986, 280–81)

Lippard's fanciful reinscriptions of the American Revolution depended on temporal distance from the war's events; his Revolutionary novels exploited the possibility that secret histories had been suppressed in order to preserve a corrupt power structure in the nation. Lippard's radical embellishments of history marked the beginning of the end for Revolutionary novels because they displaced the tension between local memory and national history. By 1855, when Melville published *Israel Potter*, the tension had disappeared almost entirely.

Israel Potter began as a simple rewrite of an obscure memoir first published in 1824. The actual Israel Potter fought at Bunker Hill, became a prisoner of war, and was sent to England. He escaped, but then spent nearly fifty years in destitute anonymity before finally returning to New England. Decrepit and without means (his pension was denied on a technicality), he told his story to a writer, Henry Trumbull, who converted the account into the *Life and Remarkable Adventures of Israel R. Potter* (1824). Although in the novel's dedication Melville claimed that he was preserving "almost as in a reprint, Israel Potter's autobiographical story," his novel takes tremendous liberties with Trumbull's version, which, of necessity, had taken liberties in converting an oral history into an autobiographical narrative. Not only did Melville shift the *Life* from first to third person, but he also amplified, invented, and interwove other historical events and persons into the novel, among them John Paul Jones and Ethan Allen, neither of whom Potter had ever met.

Whereas Lippard manipulated the gap between past and present to counter the hegemonic Puritan version of national origins, Melville used temporal distance to express a bitter sense of loss. *Israel Potter* is an ironic monody; it does not attempt to recover history so much as mock a national failure of memory. During a visit to a London book shop, Melville found the obscure Revolutionary memoir, "a tattered copy, rescued by the merest chance from the rag-pickers" (dedication). Long out of print, the book itself had become a literary remnant, another kind of Revolutionary ruin. Within his lifetime Melville had witnessed the Revolution's transition from living memory to historical record, from primary accounts to secondary and tertiary ones, and in his novelized version of the memoirs he explores the digression from lived experience to historical record. *Israel Potter* intervenes in the "literary" space between second and third removes from the Revolutionary era.

Melville treats Israel Potter as a rhetorical figure rather than a biographical or historical subject. The novel is an extended pun that begins with the dedication: "To His Highness the Bunker-Hill Monument," an obvious play on the height of the monument, which stands over two hundred feet high, but it extends beyond that. The references to "your Highness" also assert ambivalence, a monarchic ideology encoded in a national monument to the Revolution. Even more deeply sarcastic, Melville juxtaposes the public monument against the "privacy" of Potter's anonymous grave: "Israel Potter well merits the present tribute—a private of Bunker Hill, who for his faithful services was years ago promoted to a still deeper privacy under the ground, with a posthumous pension, in default of any during life, annually paid him by the spring in ever-new mosses and sward."

The novel's punning technique goes beyond comic wordplay; it signifies *Israel Potter*'s performative intervention. In other words, Melville's rhetorical art opposed the Bunker Hill Monument's solid granite by destabilizing its monolithic representation of the nation. The novel's original signifier was the actual Israel Potter, a forgotten common soldier, but by 1855 his life had been reduced to a name, an obscure title. And Melville took it from there, using the ironic juxtaposition of "Israel-Potter" to spin a deeply allusive historical yarn. Israel's story echoes that of the biblical Israelites but only to refute the implied typology. The New England Puritans had constructed a narrative of typological fulfillment, a story of salvation and release from captivity to an American promised land. Israel Potter, another

New Englander, never truly escapes from bondage and remains unredeemed. His life inverts the transcendent Puritan story of fulfillment and progress; thus, the novel—the only one that Melville wrote in serial form—digressed as the installments unfolded. Chapters move through a symbolic geography from "The Birthplace of Israel" in the Berkshire Mountains of New England (ch. 1); to "Israel in the Lion's Den" where he meets George III in London (ch. 5); to "Israel in Egypt" where, destitute, he is forced to dig clay for bricks in "a sort of earthy dungeon, or gravedigger's hole" (ch. 23); to "In the City of Dis," the Dantean hell of London's lower orders (ch. 24); finally to "Requiescat in Pace," the last chapter, where Israel returns to Boston during the jubilee celebration and views the "incipient monument" at Bunker Hill from the graveyard on Copp's Hill, a "true 'Potters' Field'" (ch. 26).

Israel Potter certainly did not end the production of Revolutionary romances, but it did suggest the end of Revolutionary novels as a distinct genre. Having lost their living connection with the past, Revolutionary narratives became indistinguishable from other fanciful historical romances. In fact, Melville's novel was quickly overshadowed by Charles J. Peterson's Revolutionary romance, *Kate Aylesford: A Story of the Refugees* (1855), which was praised for its archetypal structure. As a critic from the Philadelphia *Dollar Newspaper* put it: "Morality, patriotism, and all the virtues, are prominently held forth—the good are made to prosper, while the evil are punished" (*Kate Aylesford*, advertisement). Just as the Bunker Hill monument had absorbed Israel Potter's individual history into a monolithic symbol of the nation, so too the Revolutionary novel was absorbed into the detemporalized form of the American historical romance. The genre's connection to local history disappeared along with the Revolutionary ruins that were memorialized in its individual texts, and by 1865, when the nation finally emerged from another devastating fratricidal conflict, the Revolution had become what it remains today, a popular symbol, a "spirit of '76" used to represent everything from conservative Tea Party ideology to liberal democratic reform.

8

FRONTIER NOVELS, BORDER WARS, AND INDIAN REMOVAL

DANA D. NELSON

America began, the story goes, as frontier. There British colonists, like John Smith and John Winthrop, encountered, negotiated with, fought, raided, borrowed, and learned from America's indigenous peoples and nations to carve out from the wilderness what would become, more than a century and half later, the United States. American expansion, figured as the triumphal progress of the frontier across the continent, is one of the United States' most enduring ideologies: treasured *and* bitterly contested. From British colonial efforts to civilize the "savage" lands and peoples, to the Indian-haters of history and myth who battled Indians and pushed the frontier across the Ohio Valley and toward the Mississippi in the early nation, to Indian removal, Texas annexation, the US-Mexico War, the gold rush, and finally the Indian wars that engrossed the United States in the aftermath of the Civil War, American history through the end of the nineteenth century was framed by the inexorable westward movement of the US frontier; the inevitable seizure of Indian lands; and the forcible removal, dispossession, and sequestering of Native peoples. This was, mid-nineteenth-century commentators insisted, the United States' "Manifest Destiny," a term coined by a woman writing for John L. O'Sullivan's *The United States Magazine and Democratic Review* in 1845, though the author had toyed with the general concept since 1839. As Linda S. Hudson details, Jane McManus Storm, under the pen name "Montgomery," meant the phrase to suggest a divinely ordained expansion of the United States from the Atlantic seaboard to the Pacific, over the entire North and Central American landmasses.

Authors, intellectuals, and artists of the colonies and early nation registered their fascination with frontier conflict, Native America, and US Indian policy in poems, paintings, essays, fiction, ethnographies, and histories. From Mary Rowlandson's captivity narrative, first published in 1682, Thomas Jefferson's scientific reporting on Indians in his *Notes on the State of Virginia* in the early 1780s, John Vanderlyn's famous 1804 rendering of *The Death of Jane McCrea,* Cooper's memorable Leather-Stocking series (1823–41), to John Augustus Stone's blockbuster 1829 play *Metamora; or, The Last of the Wampanoags*, William Apess's resonant *Eulogy on King Philip* (1836), Henry Rowe Schoolcraft's mid-century series of ethnographic sketches of Indians, George Catlin's portraits, Henry Wadsworth Longfellow's epic 1855 *Song of Hiawatha*, Francis Parkman's histories of white-Indian conflict beginning with *The Conspiracy of Pontiac* (1851), John Gast's iconic 1872 painting *American Progress*, and Helen Hunt Jackson's moving plea for Indian policy reform in her 1884 novel *Ramona*, North American intercultural contact and conflict provoked memorable works by leading intellectuals, activists, and artists.

Described in 1893 by historian Frederick Jackson Turner, the "frontier thesis" dominated American history and popular culture well into the twentieth century. Turner's casting of the frontier as the place where civilization meets savagery, his insistence that the fact of the progressing frontier undergirded American culture and success, and his speculations on what its closing meant won him a posthumous Pulitzer Prize in 1933. Its resonant terms captivated generations of scholars and novelists as well as radio, movie, and television producers. In Turner's evocative description, the frontier had dominated American experience from the colonies to the end of the nineteenth century, a "recurrence" of a sociopolitical and economic "process of evolution" as the frontier transitioned westward (2008, 2). For Turner, this "perennial rebirth" had for nearly four centuries funded the characteristic mobility of American character and society: its fluidity, expansiveness, simplicity, and aggressiveness (2). The frontier created and defined American history, culture, economics, politics, and identity, providing the unifying impetus that galvanized the American Revolution and forged a single culture from many different occupational, religious, ethnic, and national immigrant heritages. It birthed US democracy, which was exemplified in the muscular, pragmatic individualism of the Indian-fighting president, Andrew Jackson. And in turn, as Americans advanced, their "lines of civilization"—networks of travel, commerce, and communications—spread, in Turner's words, like "a complex nervous system for the originally simple, inert continent" (14). White Americans, shaped by the frontier, in turn gave meaning, sensibility, and life to the continent.

By mid-century, scholars began challenging this thesis. As intellectual historian Perry Miller posed the problem in his 1956 *Errand into the Wilderness*, if American cultural self-understanding was grounded in an apparently irresolvable opposition between nature and civilization, the problem for scholars was to understand how the simple monolith created by this seemingly factual opposition contains "congeries of inner tensions" (1). For Miller, "wilderness" was better viewed as a metaphor—for not just nature but the unruliness of men's hearts and human impulsiveness—encouraging unity in the face of internal heterogeneity and conflict. Miller's work continued a critical trend that informed Henry Nash Smith's landmark 1950 book, *The Virgin Land: The American West as Symbol and Myth*, where Smith studied ideas about the "empty" West in American history. Absent from his investigation, however, were the American Indians, who in fact had occupied the putatively vacated symbol of the American West. Soon Roy Harvey Pearce's influential 1953 study, *Savagism and Civilization*, described Indians as a myth system. Pearce analyzed what the belief in Indian "savagery" meant for white Americans, particularly their conviction that white civilization had long ago surpassed its own savagery and against which it had constantly to maintain itself. Pearce proposed, in other words, that in its long focus on the "Indian question," white America had not been looking at actually existing Indians but instead fortifying myths about itself.

The Civil Rights movement surging in the 1950s and 1960s accelerated the energy of these "myth and symbol" investigations, while changing political sensibilities converged to pose a more pointed challenge to the Turner hypothesis. If the myth had created what Pearce termed an "impassible gulf" in whites' ability to "know" the Indian, it did not inhibit scholars' ability to assess the impact of white racism, white supremacy, and US domestic and international imperialism on the environment as well as on historical and living native peoples. Beginning in the 1960s and 1970s, scholars began calculating the savagism of *civilization*. Richard Slotkin's trilogy of frontier studies, launched in 1973 with *Regeneration through Violence,* confronted how national expansion was driven by genocide, white supremacy, and environmental destruction. Annette Kolodny's germinal 1975 *The Lay of the Land* married psychoanalysis with cultural history to trace how female personifications of America and its "virgin" lands by male writers, intellectuals, and policymakers had fused male mastery to environmental domination in American history. In 1978, Robert F. Berkhofer readdressed Pearce's subject, turning his study of *The White Man's Indian* to a direct confrontation with the myth's implication in bad science, bad politics, and bad policy, emphasizing how the navel-gazing aspects of the Indian question for whites produced living realities for Native America. These works were part of a political reassessment of tropes of the frontier and westward "progress" that began with historians; cultural theorists; and American Studies scholars like Michael Paul Rogin, Francis Jennings, Richard Drinnon, Carolyn Merchant, William Spengemann, Tzvetan Todorov, and Reginald Horsman; and that has led more recently to studies like Philip Deloria's *Playing Indian* (1998) and Devon Mihesuah's *American Indians: Stereotypes and Realities* (1996).

In 1992, Kolodny proposed that we relinquish the grand narrative of The Frontier by reconceptualizing "frontier" as the many local settings of intercultural encounters, while also recognizing how specific geographies shape their dynamics—for the Spanish and Pueblos in the 1600s Southwest as inevitably as for Dominicans and Hassids in 1990s Brooklyn. Around this time, and with similar impetus, what is known as the New Indian and New Western Histories took hold in a series of important studies by historians like Richard White, Jane Merritt, Daniel Richter, Colin Calloway, Nancy Shoemaker, Daniel Usner, Patricia Nelson Limerick, Jean O'Brien, Jill Lepore, and Neal Salisbury. These studies offered histories that balanced or prioritized the perspectives, knowledge, agency, and strategies of Native American actors and nations. They collectively demonstrated—quite differently from

Turner's grand narrative—that the "frontier" had been, well into the nineteenth century, a fluid sociopolitical milieu of inclusion, bargaining, alliance, mixture, inter- and multi-culturalism, diplomacy, hostility, realignment, and exchange. Importantly, this work establishes that the frontier's dynamic space can no longer be understood as synonymous with "The West" because it also included, for instance, the Caribbean, Quebec, and Florida. This nuanced historiography traces how the complex sociology of what White terms the "middle ground" flourished across the Americas in the eighteenth century but, in the case of the US West, was undermined, attacked, and finally closed by the heavy-handed inexperience of British diplomats in the aftermath of the Seven Years' War, the exigencies of the American Revolution, US nation-formation, growing environmental pressures, and emerging white racism. These forces combined with pan-Indian politics and the growth of a newly racialized and increasingly militant self-awareness among Indians who could no longer ignore the unilateralist aims of United States policy, despite the family metaphors of its treaty rhetoric.

Insights from these more recent historical approaches offer new windows into the so-called frontier novels of the early United States and suggest how powerfully the Turner thesis has limited historical understandings of these works. Quite differently from depicting a stark, westward-moving battle between "savagery and civilization," these novels offer a steady acknowledgment of the legacies of and possibilities for intercultural co-creation, an emphasis that intensified as those possibilities came under heavier assault. This literature tracks how nineteenth-century white racism makes the hard lines of the "frontier" cut through and permanently divide the mutualism and multilateralism possible in the middle ground.

The Nation's First Frontier Novel

The United States' first frontier novel, *Edgar Huntly; or, Memoirs of a Sleep-Walker* (1799), is an odd forerunner of the genre. Charles Brockden Brown's second novel is, as literary historians Philip Barnard and Stephen Shapiro note, set in the backcountry of 1787 Pennsylvania, in an area that the novel's references tie to the infamous Walking Treaty, by which William Penn's sons defrauded the Delaware of roughly 1,200 square miles of tribal lands. In his opening letter "To the Public," Brown promises to avoid "Gothic castles and chimeras," turning instead to specifically American themes and landscapes. But his surreal depictions of "incidents of Indian hostility, and the perils of the westward wilderness" inaugurated a distinctively US gothic mode.

Its setting evokes settler-Indian conflict, but the novel takes more than half its length getting there. Narrated mostly in a long letter from Edgar Huntly to his fiancée, Mary Waldegrave, the first half of the novel details his attempt to find her brother's murderer. His suspicions land on a local Irish servant, Clithero Edny, whom he encounters one night behaving suspiciously at the foot of the elm where Waldegrave was murdered. Edny turns out to be sleepwalking, which Huntly interprets as evidencing Edny's guilt. Huntly confronts Edny, demanding a confession, which he soon gets. But it's not the one he expected: rather, Edny tells a convoluted tale of his childhood in Ireland, where he believes he killed his benefactress. Then he flees into the woods. Now obsessed with relieving Edny's conscience, Huntly searches for him in the ever-more terrifying wilderness, imagining schemes by which he will rescue and redeem him.

Soon, Huntly is sleepwalking too. His first nocturnal adventure leaves him at the bottom of a rock pit, from which he awakens to a nightmarish adventure in a gothic landscape. Overtaken by hunger, he kills a panther and drinks its blood before blundering into a cave encampment of raiding Delaware Indians (whom he remembers as types for the "assassins" who killed his parents, early settlers on the frontier [ch. 16]). After killing one Delaware with his own gun and freeing their white female captive, Huntly takes her to the apparently abandoned home of an old Delaware woman who has refused to leave her ancestral lands. There, Huntly discovers the gun he's taken from the Delaware is actually his own. He concludes that his home has been raided and his remaining family slaughtered. Now desperate, Huntly kills several more Indians, bayoneting one to death in what he describes as an act of "cruel lenity" (ch. 18). Next, he stumbles across a burned cabin, which, he concludes, evidences a massive Indian attack. Afraid of the desolation he'll find at home, Huntly heads for his neighbor's house, where he discovers a former teacher. When Huntly queries Sarsefield about the scope of the attacks, Sarsefield responds with astonishment: there has been no such massive uprising, but only a small raid and retaliation. One of the Delaware involved in planning the failed raid probably murdered Waldegrave before its launch.

From here, the novel returns for its denouement to the plot surrounding Edny, for Sarsefield coincidentally has married the benefactress Edny imagines he has murdered. Freed from his chimerical notions of Delaware uprising, Huntly returns to his obsession with saving Edny by freeing him from his delusions. Edny—either already mad with guilt or driven mad by Huntly's revelation that his benefactress is alive—sets off to kill her. He doesn't succeed, but Huntly's letter to Sarsefield, warning them of impending danger, causes her to miscarry, and the novel ends on this strangely irresolute note.

Critics still debate whether the novel critiques or corroborates the emerging racism of legendary Indian-haters like Tom Quick, who lived in the immediate vicinity of the novel's setting and who on his deathbed in 1795 allegedly begged his family to bring him one more Delaware to murder before he died in order to fulfill his promise to kill one hundred. What is certain is that the novel's setting and themes refract important shifts in indigenous-US relations in the long aftermath of the Seven Years' War, the Revolution, and the formation of the United States. As historian Colin Calloway notes, most of North America was still Indian country in the aftermath of the US Revolution. Throughout the eighteenth century, Indian country, in what is now the eastern seaboard frontier and the Ohio Valley, had been a land of cultural and ethnic mixture, of multicultural village republics where Indians of different nations, squeezed by European colonization, worked out ways to coexist with French trappers, European immigrants, and African Americans. Its precarious intercultural dynamic was under increasingly heavy pressure as waves of European emigrants and white migrants and speculators flooded into Indian country after the Seven Years' War, looking for land, subsistence, or fortune. In the backcountry of the eighteenth century, Indians and whites lived in interconnected communities, as neighbors and not just as enemies. This very neighborliness, as Calloway observes, heightened the sense of betrayal as the American Revolution divided communities. Indeed, Crèvecoeur's Farmer James flees with his family to middle ground as a protection from the battles of the Revolution in his famous letter XII, "Distresses of a Frontier Man." Farmer James's response was by no means fictive: historians note that during the Revolution, the white population west of the Appalachians stood at 50,000 or more.

Writers before Brown had utilized Indian characters but had relegated them to a distant past. Joel Barlow's 1787 epic poem *The Vision of Columbus* seized on Aztecs and Incas as heroic counterparts to Christopher Columbus, simultaneously "noble" and yet irredeemably "savage." Invoking Columbus (an enduring symbol for many peoples throughout the Americas of the savagery of Western "civilization") as the nation's visionary forebear, Barlow accelerated a trend of claiming a non-British but still European origin for America in the aftermath of the Revolutionary war. Novelist and playwright Susanna Rowson's *Reuben and Rachel; or, Tales of Old Times* (1798) similarly claimed Columbus, offering a story that charted ten generations of his descendents, starting with a son who marries a Peruvian princess, Orrabella. Thus Rowson provides a sentimental genealogy for "Columbia." She notably features this American princess as the product of intermarriage across ethnic, national, and religious lines: her Columbia (the granddaughter of Orrabella and Ferdinando) is an intercultural heroine. Rowson uses this interculturalism, as Joseph F. Bartolomeo notes in his fine introduction to a recent edition, to challenge the conventions of the captivity narrative, the quintessential literary form for Indian encounter in British colonial literature, where beating back the threat of interculturalism was the mark of spiritual triumph.

Literary critic Greg Sieminski has described how the popularity of captivity narratives beginning in the late eighteenth century secularized and politicized what had been a spiritual genre. The multiple reprintings of Mary Rowlandson's 1682 and John Williams's 1704 accounts in the 1770s, the public's fascination with John Filson's narrative of Daniel Boone's two captivities, other fictional accounts like the Abraham Panther narrative, and nonfictional accounts like the Pennsylvania Black-Boy ("Scoowa") James Smith helped to organize Revolutionary and patriotic feeling by analogizing Indian captivity to America's colonial "captivity" by the British. They worked to racialize Americans, presenting whiteness as something that had to be protected from Indian threats in the very moment that the United States was envisioning Indian country east of the Mississippi as land that could become part of the United States—without Indians. As Joanna Brooks explains, captivity narratives used the trials of imperiled whites to sidestep larger questions about settlers' complicity with English imperialism, consolidating a pure identity that was innocent of both politics and history. These narratives helped consolidate patriotic identity and usher into being the oppositional frontier that Turner described as an eternal fact.

Thus, in the late eighteenth and early nineteenth century, the "Middle Ground" of the backcountry was recast as frontier, approached only in enmity, never friendship. Soon charismatic figures, like the Seneca religious leader Ganioda'yo (Handsome Lake), would preach the evils of cross-racial contact to the Iroquois, as the internationally famed Mohegan Methodist minister Samson Occom gave up on intercultural Christian community, instead forming the Brothertown Indian Nation in the mid-1780s. It is this reconfigured, racialized frontier that Brown's novel refracts as a gothic nightmare, where the middle ground has become a killing ground, where the white subject calls Indians "savage" and describes his own savagery as *gentle*: "cruel lenity."

Playing Indian, Loving Indians

The next significant wave of frontier novels began in the 1820s, in the wake of then General Jackson's triumphal wresting of massive land cessions following the Creek Wars and the first Seminole War. Jackson ran for president on his image as a military figure and Indian fighter. His popularity among common folk in the early nation fueled the push for universal white manhood suffrage. As citizenship qualifications for men in the early United States transitioned from economic to racial status, so too Native American peoples began rethinking their political organization in terms of a pan-Indian alliance. Political leaders, following the example of predecessors such as the Shawnee Tecumseh, increasingly appealed to people from other tribes to unite against all whites in order to save Indian country, even as some, like Choctaw leader and commissioned US Army Brigadier General Pushmataha, held to the ideals of middle ground, urging his fellows to remember the neighborly ideals that had previously ruled.

In contrast to *Edgar Huntly*, whose narrator emphasizes the distinction between himself and "savage" Indians, the next two frontier novels staked out a possessive relation to Indianness: in them, white men claimed manly "independence" by appropriating Indian behaviors and identity. John Neal's *Logan: A Family History* (1822), invokes the legendary Cayuga chief Logan, whose "lament" Jefferson had memorialized in his *Notes on the State of Virginia*, exciting a controversy over whether the speech recorded by Jefferson had been invented by him. Jefferson famously responded: "[W]herefore forgery? Whether Logan's or mine, it would still have been an American" (1954, 213). Neal takes up this confusion of white manly achievement with tragically imperiled Indian prowess. His convoluted plot invokes the historical Logan only to replace him with an ungovernably ambitious British aristocrat, George Clarence of Salisbury, who takes Logan's name and identity and is the progenitor of the "Indian" hero of the novel, Harold. The white Indians of the novel, noble and foolhardy, all encounter tragic endings similar to that of their symbolic father, repeating his lonely lament: "no friends, no children, no wife, no home" (pref.). Less melodramatically, James Fenimore Cooper's first frontier novel, and the first volume in his famous Leather-Stocking series, *The Pioneers; or, The Sources of the Susquehanna* (1823) is set in a post-Revolutionary upstate New York almost denuded of Indians, except the aging, drunken Indian John (or Chingachgook in the younger, soberer days of later novels) and Oliver Edwards (also known as "Young Eagle"), who hints broadly that he has a claim to the lands of Judge Marmaduke Temple, appealing to the guilt of settler colonialism through his sullen demeanor and his mysterious behaviors throughout the novel (even while winning the heart of Elizabeth Temple). Happily for the young lovers, Oliver reveals at the end that he's not really an Indian except through the Mohegan adoption of his grandfather, Major Effingham. He has been sullen not because he's a dispossessed Indian, but because he is the descendent of dispossessed Loyalists—his father had given his best friend, Judge Temple, his land titles to hold for safekeeping when he entered military service during the Revolution. Thus the "happy" ending of the novel sees the securely white Oliver united in marriage and fortune with Bess Temple. If *Logan* appropriates middle ground for the performance of white manhood, making Indians props that shore up its lonely independence, *The Pioneers* makes the middle ground disappear altogether in a plot device that, while seeming to make Indian-white relations central, finally reveals Indians to be little more than a trick of the imagination.

In a swift rejoinder, the young Lydia Maria Child launched her novelistic career with *Hobomok* (1824). This frontier romance, published anonymously, proffered an early version of an argument she would make more explicitly in the next decade, insisting that racial intermarriage was an antidote to hardening racial policies. *Hobomok* turned to the early Puritan settlement, taking aim at the patriarchal rigidity of Calvinist theocracy. The protagonist's Puritan father separates Mary Conant from the man she loves, the Anglican Charles Brown, whose religious affiliation her father cannot accept. Rebelling, Mary betroths herself instead to a well-admired neighbor, the Indian Hobomok, who, like the Wampanoag historical figure on whom he is based, was considered a friend by the Puritans for his willingness to assist in provisioning and with diplomacy. Living in his wigwam, Mary develops pride in the marriage castigated by her Calvinist community. But shortly after the birth of their child, Brown, said to be dead, reappears. Hobomok, deciding that Mary and their child would be happier with Brown, magnanimously heads west. Brown, as magnanimous, agrees to take Mary and "that swarthy boy" to raise as his own (ch. 20). Thus the novel's happy ending sees the doctrinaire Mr. Conant, as Carolyn Karcher observes, acceding to the second of two marriages that his religious commitments forbade. Mary and Charles and the Cambridge-educated little Hobomok proceed into a happy future, reverencing the memory of the boy's nobly accommodating father.

Soon Catharine Maria Sedgwick would draw on the same historical archive, featuring characters who create middle ground across frontier boundaries. *Hope Leslie; or, Early Times in the Massachusetts* (1827) begins immediately after the Pequot Massacre (or War) in 1637. The Fletcher family, leaving Boston to help settle Springfield, takes as servants two children of the defeated chief Mononotto: Magawisca and Oneco. Magawisca enchants the youthful Everell Fletcher. But their budding friendship is imperiled by Mononotto's plans for rescuing and revenge. Magawisca tries to warn Everell by telling him the story of the Pequot "War" from her own perspective. What the Puritans framed as a righteous response to menacing savages is a genocidal attack in Magawisca's telling, and Everell is "touched by the wand of feeling" (ch. 4).

Such receptiveness to other perspectives, the narrator suggests, might help change the course of contemporary white and Indian relations, for Everell is able to maintain this radical openness even after his mother and his infant brother are slaughtered in front of him and he is taken captive along with an adopted sister, Faith. Magawisca rewards his open heart by interposing—and losing—her arm at the moment of his execution, enabling him (but not Faith) to escape. Some years later, Faith's sister Hope, who has heard the stories of Magawisca from Everell, and who like Everell demonstrates a principled understanding of Indian neighbors and their different beliefs and practices, assists Magawisca in escaping from prison when she is captured along with Faith by the Puritans. Closer to home, Hope struggles with Faith's refusal to be "liberated" from her captivity: Faith has married Oneco and chooses to stay with him.

Unlike Child, who makes Indian removal the Indian's choice, Sedgwick attributes the westward retreat of Magawisca, Oneco, and Faith to Puritan aggression and bad faith. More expansively than Child, Sedgwick insists that women *and* men can cultivate the intercultural sympathy that might counter the ugliness of "Indian hating." Both writers insist on the valuable legacy of "middle ground." But they undercut its contemporary potential by locating its closure two centuries in the past—precisely as the Cherokee nation was designating New Echota as its capital in Georgia in the early 1820s. They created a constitution, crafted a Cherokee syllabary, and launched the first Native American newspaper, *The Cherokee Phoenix* (1828–34), in their aggressively publicized effort to create a basis for intercultural accommodation.

In this moment, Cooper weighed in again with his vision for the middle ground in what is perhaps his best-loved installment of the Leather-Stocking series, *The Last of the Mohicans: A Narrative of 1757* (1826), set during the Seven Years' War. This story brings it closer in time but urges that opportunities for white-Indian cooperation closed before the Revolution because of intertribal enmity. Cooper bifurcates his Indians into "nobles" (Delawares) and "savages" (Mingos), while his whites mourn the passing of the last of the "good" Indians. The novel simultaneously crafts a lesson in sympathy (perhaps aimed at Child), showing how women's principled compassion, like Cora Munro's insistence that men not be judged by their color, leads to trouble (Cora's generosity toward Magua gets her and her sister captured). Soon after, Cora is revealed (quite differently from Natty Bumppo, who brags repeatedly that he is a man "without a cross" in his blood) as the daughter of a cross-racial union. This racial mixture fires the romantic attention of Magua and Uncas, leading to Cora's death at the end of the novel. Natty's moving declaration of friendship to Chingachgook at Uncas's funeral underscores the idea that frontier-savvy white men, and not women, are the proper guardians for interracial sympathy: they know when to stop.

Indian Removal, Indian Hating

President Jackson signaled his impatience with notions of intercultural cooperation by signing the bitterly debated Congressional Act for Removal in 1830 (Tennessee congressman and fabled frontiersman Davy Crockett, among others, fought it). The "Trail of Tears" that ensued—first for the Choctaw, finally for the Cherokees—was not silently observed, as Cooper's funeral for Cora and Uncas projected. Whites, such as Jeremiah Evarts, editorialized, and Native American activists campaigned for a different outcome. In a series of publications and speeches, William Apess, a Pequot intellectual, campaigned against US Indian policy with polemics (like his 1833 "An Indian's Looking-Glass for the White Man"), histories (his 1833 *The Experience of Five Christian Indians of the Pequot Tribe* or his lecture *Eulogy on King Philip* in 1836), and legal/policy analyses (his 1835 *Indian Nullification of the Unconstitutional Laws of Massachusetts Relative to the Marshpee Tribe; or, The Pretended Riot Explained* where he argued for Indian sovereignty) that made, as Andy Doolen has argued, a case for an intercultural democratic movement. Apess encouraged white Americans to see Indians as living the values that the United States professed to treasure and to question their own passive endorsement of savage US policy—he urged, as Lisa Brooks has argued, that whites and Indians create a common community. His democratic optimism was not always shared by fellow Native Americans. For instance, Black Hawk's 1833 autobiography, like Apess's essays, offers pointed critiques of the bad faith in US policy and treaties. But differently from Apess, or Cherokee activists such as Elias Boudinot, who appealed to white Americans for democratic inclusion, Black Hawk wanted, as Mark Rifkin argues, to forestall US policies that aimed to isolate Indian nations by impeding intertribalism.

The vision of Indian co-sovereignty with the United States, shared by Apess and the Cherokee Nation, was effectively sidestepped by a series of rulings in the 1830s by Supreme Court Chief Justice John Marshall. In *Cherokee Nation v. Georgia* (1831), Marshall coined the term "domestic dependent nation," describing a limited sovereignty, like the rights of a ward, for indigenous nations. A year later, in *Worcester v. Georgia*, he would craft a more careful definition. As Nancy Shoemaker notes, rather than imagining Indian nations as children, Marshall turns to European history and redefines the relation as that of a "tributary" nation (2004, 102), a durable concept that connoted inherent equality. The forced relocations of the 1830s facilitated the racially expansionist consolidation of the United States, as western territories were opened for settlement by newly enfranchised white citizens.

And frontier novels and narratives proliferated. Some of these works aimed to accelerate Indian hating, increasingly celebrated as "frontier spirit." Others followed the path of Stone's play *Metamora*, elegizing the nobility of "vanishing" Indians who died with an independence of spirit that evoked the heroism of the white nation's founding. And still others wrote frontier novels that redirected conflict, replacing Indians with the menace of poor, "outlaw" whites, like William Gilmore Simms's 1838 *Richard Hurdis; or, The Avenger of Blood*, which plays up the threat of an underclass counter-nation being consolidated on the frontiers. This "mystic brotherhood" composed of squatters inhabiting Creek Territory rejects US laws privileging the wealthy elite. In its own rules for citizenship, members are committed—among other things—to an absolutely fair division of all spoils. Its danger forms the dramatic backdrop to the story's central tale of a fratricidal struggle between Richard Hurdis and his oldest brother John. The novel's ending—where Richard helps kill his brother and defeat the brotherhood—warns against equalitarian idealism. Somewhat differently, Caroline Kirkland's 1839 *A New Home—Who'll Follow?* highlights the productive exchange of "civilized" representative democracy with the "primitive" equalitarianism of frontier whites. But like Simms, Kirkland whitewashes the Michigan frontier, occluding still-resident Indians entirely as potential members of the "homely fellowship" her narrator celebrates with "our kind" (ch. 46). Such stories offered the frontier as a whites-only space, priming readers to ignore the ongoing political efforts of Native America, for instance in an 1844 petition to the Michigan legislature, where Ottawas pleaded for recognition as American citizens of the state "by the ties of their common humanity."

Indian-hating novels at least granted a strategic relevance to Ottawa efforts, acknowledging the necessity of convincing white readers that Indians could not be part of the polity. These novels sometimes conceded the humanity of Native Americans, but they posed the inevitability of their demise or removal as a necessity to appease whites whose humanity had been warped by Indian "outrages."

In tales like James Hall's popular "The Indian Hater" (1828), which fictionalized the story of a frontier resident who avenged the death of his family by randomly murdering even friendly Indians (to the dismay of neighbors), Indian-haters were depicted as tragically broken outsiders to civilization, themselves a doomed breed.

More classically, Indian-hating plots were ambivalent about white "haters" and entirely unambivalent about their targets. Perhaps the most memorable, Robert Montgomery Bird's 1837 novel *Nick of the Woods; or, The Jibbenainosay*, opens with Kentucky backcountry settlers taunting the hapless Quaker Nathan Slaughter for his refusal to take up weapons against raiding Indians. In a convoluted tale of Shawnee attacks, sieges, and capture, along with a backstory of white familial intrigue that, as in Simms's novel, confirms the dangers of trusting fraternity, the novel eventually reveals Nathan to be the legendary "Jibbenainosay," the name Indians give the spirit who lurks in the Kentucky woods, lethally tomahawking crosses into the chests of Indians. Nathan's motive ups the ante on Hall's Indian-hater: his family had been murdered with the very knife Slaughter handed to the Shawnee chief to prove that he was a "man of peace." Nathan's frontier trauma effectively splits his personality—he maintains a public reputation as a man of peace but secretly hunts the woods to satisfy his blood lust. The novel climaxes when Nathan, covered in the gore of murdered Indians, wears the belt of his family's scalps that he has just seized from the Shawnee chief, Wenonga, the spitting image of the "savage" Indians whose menace he compulsively repudiates.

The novel's Indians have no such redeeming backstory. "*Bo-zhoo*, brudders," may be the most clearly intelligible thing Bird's habitually drunken and degraded Indians say (ch. 14). And worse, they make a habit of eating their so-called brothers. Early on, the frontier leader, Colonel Bruce, describes a Delaware defeat of a Pennsylvania military expedition: "Beaten! . . . cut off the *b*, and say that the savages made a dinner of 'em, and you'll be nearer the true history of the matter" (ch. 2). The novel negates the political possibility of equalitarian democracy among whites as it rules out any chance for Native–Anglo-American alliances.

Despite Bird's efforts to cast Indians beyond the pale, other novelists remained interested in the dilemmas that European and US colonization presented to Native nations and intertribal relations. In his 1835 novel, *The Yemassee,* Simms rendered white-Indian frontier conflict in an historical account of the Yamasee War of the early eighteenth century, a southern counterpart to King Philip's war in the late seventeenth-century New England colonies, that offered as serious a setback to British colonization in the South. His historical depiction of this century-old middle ground conflict could not defang its contemporary relevance. Here, as in *Richard Hurdis*, Simms's plot repudiates claims for democratic equalitarianism. Simms foregrounds the heroism of the South Carolina governor, Charles Craven, who spends most of the novel disguised as the mysteriously cultured Gabriel Harrison, undercutting white frontier equalitarianism and orchestrating the necessary resistance to Indian uprising. Yet a father-son conflict between two

Yemassees provides the drama: the chief Sanutee, who wants to keep trading with the French and Spanish, and to enlist the Spanish for help resisting the new British colonists; and his cowardly son Occonestoga, who leagues with the British and is condemned to death for betraying his people. Though the climax of the novel cultivates sympathy for the whites imperiled by the Yemassee uprising, Simms concedes that there is little to redeem the white historical record: "An abstract standard of justice, independent of appetite or circumstance, has not often marked the progress of Christian (so called) civilization, in its proffer of its great good to the naked savage" (v. 1, ch. 3). His observations about the compromised history of British colonization (he later calls "our European ancestors . . . monstrous great rascals" [v. 2, ch. 7]) reflected critically on emerging US claims for Manifest Destiny.

Perhaps the most turgid but thematically interesting of this decade's frontier novels, Charles Fenno Hoffman's *Greyslaer: A Romance of the Mohawk* (1840), takes the sociopolitical dismantling of the middle ground during the Revolution as its very plot. Deploying actual historical scenes and characters, like Guy and John Johnson (sons of the famed Sir William Johnson, an Irishman who as a youth in the colonies had learned Mohawk and Iroquoian customs, acquiring influence and lands, and who was eventually appointed superintendent of Indian affairs for the northern colonies), the novel is ostensibly about the struggles of Max Greyslaer, an impetuous young revolutionary, first to free Alida de Roos from her Indian and British captors and then to win her heart, allegorizing the patriot's battles for a symbolically female "America." But by setting the novel in Tryon County of upstate New York, in the heart of Iroquoia, Hoffman makes it clear that the Revolution was an anticolonial battle and civil war for Indians as for whites. Indeed, the more convincing hero of the novel is the historical figure Joseph Brant, or Thayendanegea, who witnesses the breakup of the Iroquois confederacy as its nations individually decide to ally with the British or the patriots, or to remain neutral. Hoffman's Brant leads the Mohawks into an alliance with the British out of his fear of "the blighting influence" an independent republic would bring on the Mohawks, but the narrator emphasizes how "his private partialities were from the first at war with the dictates of his ambition and his policy . . . his old friends and neighbors in the valley of the Mohawk were adherents of the popular cause . . . the comrades of his hunts, the companions of his youth, were banded together against the party which he had joined" (bk. 1, ch. 2). Brant fears not just the new enmity between former Indian allies but also the new lines of difference cropping up between Indians and whites.

Hoffman emphasizes Brant's patience with the youthful Greyslaer. He models practices of mutuality and respect that maintained the historical middle ground described by White, even as he rejects Greyslaer's assertions of cultural superiority ("I had rather die by the most severe tortures ever inflicted by the Indian than languish in one of your prisons a single year!" [bk. 1, ch. 12]). But the plot of the novel gradually substitutes the romance between Alida and Max for the relationships of the middle ground, and by its end, readers are relieved that Max is able (with the help of the Indian-hater Balt) to defeat both the Tories and Isaac Brant. The novel ends with Max and Alida's marriage, the romantic architecture of settler colonialism and the white republic replacing the interracial friendships and marriages—like William Johnson's own common law marriage to Mary Brant—that kept alive the practices of the middle ground.

Manifest Destiny

Cooper returns to the theme of middle ground in his final, "first" installment of the Leather-Stocking Tales, *The Deerslayer; or, The First War-Path* (1841). Quite differently from the middle-aged "man without a cross" in *Last of the Mohicans*, the youthful Deerslayer denominates himself "a man with a Delaware heart," professing that "I hope to live and die in their tribe" (ch. 2). This novel reprises *Last of the Mohicans'* look at how human feeling can open avenues for interracial relationships. *Deerslayer* elevates it into an ethical inquiry: the ability to identify interracially becomes the novel's standard for heroism. Natty's Delaware heart makes him as noble an Indian as ever could be imagined and even more so for his "white gifts"—his Christian caution about the taking of life in warfare. His "playing Indian" goes beyond colonialist appropriation by adding responsibility for intercultural community to the posture of personal independence. "I would never bring disgrace on the Delawares," Deerslayer emphasizes (ch. 27).

Cooper appealed for interracial community and responsibility in a time of rapidly hardening racial policy and aggressive territorial expansion. In the 1840s, polygenesis (positing races as separately created species) reigned as scientific "common sense," and politicians used this "science" of white supremacy to justify US territorial expansion into Texas (annexed in 1845) and to buttress the theory of Manifest Destiny as whites' rightful domination of the continent and even hemisphere. The US-Mexico War (1846–48) came as a direct consequence of annexation, and when Mexico conceded defeat in February 1848, it relinquished massive swaths of territory, including Texas, California, Utah, Nevada, and chunks of New Mexico, Colorado, and Arizona. Polk's war, and his bellicose threats to England (which won the US half of Britain's Northwest Territory), established the United States' continental purview.

The simultaneous discovery of gold in California (January 1848) brought waves of white settlers and adventurers from the world over to the new US territory. The California gold rush was, as historian Susan Lee Johnson summarizes it, one of the most multiethnic, multiracial, and multinational events of the nation's history, a place where white US adventurers encountered Mexican, French, Peruvian, Chilean, Australian, Sandwich Island, and Chinese counterparts, in territory populated by Miwok, Nisenan, Yokut, Pomo, Wintun, Shasta, Modoc, and many other tribal peoples, and Californios—residents of Latin-American descent. The influx of fortune-finders and white immigrants' hostility toward Native Americans resulted in genocide for indigenous Californians. Some historians estimate that as many as 100,000 Indians died from 1848 to 1850. White settlers were no less hostile toward Californios and Mexicans, driving them away from mining claims, harassing families, and lynching "outlaws." Some Mexicans formed retaliatory gangs, and soon legends of "the five Joaquíns" were used to explain every incident of cattle rustling, robbery, and murder. California organized its first law-enforcement arm, the Rangers, to break up the supposed band, eventually decapitating someone and displaying his head as the ringleader, Joaquín Murieta.

John Rollin Ridge's 1854 dime novel *The Life and Adventures of Joaquín Murieta, the Celebrated California Bandit* richly memorialized the cause of this mythical outlaw, a Robin Hood figure to Californios, who also served as one inspiration for the legend of Zorro. Himself one of the Forty-Niners, Ridge (Cheesquatalawny, or Yellow Bird) had been born in Cherokee New Echota in 1827. His own freighted history—in the center of the violently disintegrating middle ground that, as is noted in the original publisher's preface, "made the Cherokee nation a place of blood"—endowed his sensationalist and sentimental version of the emerging Joaquín legend with added insights into the social, political, and affective complexity of border conflict. He shows how inspiring ideals of US independence and entrepreneurialism are compromised and contradicted by the racism fueling nationalist expansion. His outlaw hero Joaquín originally idealizes the United States, and stands for values much like those practiced in New Echota's rejected "experiment," hoping for alliances and intercultural bridges as the United States moved into California (Ridge himself had argued in 1848 that the Cherokee Nation be recognized as its own state within the United States). White settlers viciously and repeatedly dispossess Joaquín of these hopes, robbing and beating him publicly, raping his wife, and lynching his brother "without judge or jury," a record that finally provokes a literal change of heart: "the barriers of honor, rocked into atoms by the strong passion which shook his heart like an earthquake, crumbled around him" (12). He forswears his former "admiration of the American character" (8), taking up vengeance and forming a gang of like-minded Mexican men and women to aid him in his cause.

Ridge avoids, however, boiling the plot down to race science. His Mexicans, like his Indians and whites, are a complex lot—an assortment of mindlessly vindictive, cunningly entrepreneurial, and honorable men. As Rifkin argues, Ridge challenges white audiences to consider what happens to peoples whose polities were annexed into the expanding United States' "domestic" space in the prevailing context of racist lynch-mania, where absorbed peoples became "outlaw" suspects merely on the basis of their nonwhite status—targets for extralegal harassment, expropriation, and murder.

The California conflicts Ridge's novel allegorizes were soon sweeping eastward, as the Colorado gold rush in 1858 launched another wave of westward immigration. This enacted a pincer-like pressure on Native peoples in the Plains and Great Basin, creating ruinous environmental and political pressures for the populations residing there. Many of the indigenous nations in the West of the 1850s had turned relatively recently to a nomadic lifestyle enabled by horses in the sparse vegetation of the region. The incursion of thousands of settlers—with their cattle, sheep, and horses—put extraordinary demands on sparse resources (Elliott West calls wagon trains "grass-gobbling machines" [1998, 223]), devastating indigenous peoples' carefully calibrated strategies for sustaining themselves and the horses on which they depended. Cheyennes, Arapahoes, Shoshones, and the many other groups maneuvering—and fighting—for survival in summer ranges and winter camps were castigated by the military and white settlers as "savage" threats to "civilization" and attacked without mercy, just as the nation entered into the Civil War.

Afterword

Citizens mended the civic injuries of Civil War with a renewed celebration of whiteness. Newly freed African Americans saw significant legal gains in the thirteenth, fourteenth, and fifteenth amendments to the US Constitution. But ground-level federal, state, and territorial policies intensified injuries and exclusions for African Americans as well as Chinese immigrants, Mexicans, and Native Americans. As with the Revolution, the conclusion of the Civil War boded badly for Indians, when the US military once again renewed its efforts to subjugate indigenous peoples and conquer lands. The nation's literary output focused on the traumas of war and national healing, with little immediately memorable writing about the accelerating efforts of the US military to subjugate the remaining Native peoples of the West.

Seemingly in response to the vicious Sand Creek Massacre (a sunrise attack by the Colorado Militia on an encampment of Cheyenne and Arapahoe in 1864) a press in Cincinnati resurrected Joseph Doddridge's 1823 play *Logan, the Last of the Race of Shikellemus, Chief of the Cayuga Nation*. The reprint suggests that the celebrated Colonel Chivington, who urged his Colorado troops to kill women and children in Sand Creek by pronouncing that "nits make lice," paraphrased a line from this play while completely mistaking its point, for the character who utters the phrase is the villain. The play resonantly credits Indians with the more genuine fraternal idealism: Logan extracts his revenge for the terrible massacre led by "Captain Furioso," but he counters the whites' fanatical racism with his own interracial tolerance. Far more common in the 1860s and 1870s, as the Indian wars intensified in the Plains, Dakotas, and Great Basin, were the dime novels that celebrated white Indian killers, lawmen, outlaws, and cowboys like Buffalo Bill, Wild Bill Hickock, Calamity Jane, Billie the Kid, and Wyatt Earp.

As William Dodge, the man who saw Doddridge's *Logan* back into print in 1868, seemingly feared, the white citizens of the United States mostly celebrated attacks on Indians and their sequestering to barren reservation lands. As reports of General Custer's "Last Stand" in the Battle of Little Big Horn, on June 25 and 26, 1876, filtered east, the nation's self-appointed bard, Walt Whitman, would memorialize the nation's loss—of Custer and of any lingering hope for the legacies of middle ground—in "From Far Dakota's Cañons." The ethos of intercultural creation that so many had participated in, worked toward, hoped for, and written about becomes, in Whitman's mythically resonant phrasing, a "fatal environment"—fatal, in his handling, not because of the actions of the military or policymakers but because of "Indian . . . craft." As Slotkin notes, the term references not just the Dakota battlefield but the epic terms of Manifest Destiny, what Whitman terms "the old, old legend of our race."

Before the proverbial "closing" of the frontier between civilization and savagery came its creation. The advance of the "grand narrative" of the frontier helped end the complex intercultural diplomacy that had sustained the practices of middle ground. Whitman's racist mythologizing, his "glad triumphal sonnet," would set the stage for the next wave of frontier novels, which launched in 1902 with Owen Wister's *The Virginian*, and, as importantly, for Turner's 1893 celebration of how the frontier fused with US national destiny.

9

AMERICA'S EUROPE: IRVING, POE, AND THE FOREIGN SUBJECT

J. GERALD KENNEDY

Evoking the moment in literary nation building when Americans renounced their "subserviency" to British opinion and "plunged into the opposite extreme" by flouting all criticism from abroad, Edgar Allan Poe wrote in *Graham's Magazine* in 1842:

> The watchword now was, "a national literature!"—as if any true literature *could be* "national"—as if the world at large were not the only proper stage for the literary *histrio*. We became, suddenly, the merest and maddest *partizans* in letters. . . . Our Magazines had habitual passages about that "truly native novelist, Mr. Cooper," or that "staunch American genius, Mr. Paulding." . . . [O]ur reviews urged the propriety—our booksellers the necessity, of strictly "American" themes. A foreign subject, at this epoch, was a weight more than enough to drag down into the very depths of critical damnation the finest writer owning nativity in the States; while, on the reverse, we found ourselves daily in the paradoxical dilemma of liking, or pretending to like, a stupid book the better because (sure enough) its stupidity was of our own growth, and discussed our own affairs. (1984a, 1027–28)

Poe here deplores the nationalistic turn in fiction that had popularized many a "stupid book" purveying American themes. But what prompted his vexation at abuse of the country's "finest writer," merely because that author chose a "foreign subject"? Poe was perhaps thinking of Washington Irving, whose long expatriation and whose fondness for European legends produced a succession of cosmopolitan miscellanies, from *The Sketch Book* (1819–20) to *Tales of the Alhambra* (1832), as well as lively histories of Christopher Columbus and of Spain's recapture of Moorish Granada. During Irving's exile, American pundits indeed criticized his Anglophilia and fondness for Continental culture.

Poe *might* have been defending Irving—but he was not. Having suffered various indignities in his quest to publish *Tales of the Grotesque and Arabesque*

(1840), Poe tacitly designated himself America's "finest" author and protested his "damnation" for supposed German mysticism. While he had sought (and received) Irving's endorsement of his *Tales* and paid him homage in magazine reviews, Poe privately thought him "much overrated" (2008, 1:177). In an "Autography" profile that preceded his "Exordium to Critical Notices" (cited at the outset), Poe opined that Irving had been "so thoroughly satiated with fame as to grow slovenly in the performance of his literary tasks" (*Graham's Magazine*, Nov. 1841, 226). He belittled Irving partly to mask his indebtedness to the author and partly to assuage his envy of Irving's success. After the expatriate's return in 1832, New Yorkers feted Irving with a gala dinner. Then the author toured the Oklahoma territory and recouped his former popularity by producing three narratives on national themes—*A Tour on the Prairies* (1835), *Astoria; or, Enterprise Beyond the Rocky Mountains* (1836), and *The Adventures of Captain Bonneville* (1837). Gotham booksellers finally lionized him at a lavish 1837 banquet attended by the obscure, impoverished Poe.

Rankled by his own invisibility, Poe vied secretly with Irving—first by penning a novel of adventure, *The Narrative of Arthur Gordon Pym* (1838), and then by confecting a serialized western narrative, "The Journal of Julius Rodman" (1840), in both instances plagiarizing heavily from Irving's recent volumes. In "The Devil in the Belfry" (1839), Poe produced a farcical homage to Irving's Knickerbocker drollery, and when he blasted literary nation building in 1845, Poe tacitly invoked Irving in protesting the disloyalty of certain American authors: "We know that in the few instances in which our writers have been treated with common decency in England, these writers have either openly paid homage to English institutions, or have had lurking at the bottom of their hearts a secret principle at war with Democracy" (1984a, 1077). Despite Poe's own quarrel with democracy—(see "Some Words with a Mummy" [Apr. 1845])—he was no Anglophile and mocked Irving as a turncoat who had parlayed seventeen years abroad into international renown. It is tempting to conclude that Irving's return to American soil and his embracing of national themes in the 1830s partly inspired Poe's audacious attempt to claim the "foreign subject" as his fictional domain. While Irving parlayed frontier themes, Poe sought fame by conjuring an imaginary Europe.

In quite different ways, Irving and Poe ultimately influenced American literature and the national novel. The unprecedented achievement of Irving's *Sketch Book* and his international popularity created a model of professional authorship that inspired American writers for decades. Yet, if Irving's visit to Sir Walter Scott in 1817 attracted him to the life of writing, he avoided competition with Scott in the production of historical romances; instead, Irving became (like Scott) a collector of legends and a historian, adopting the latter vocation around 1826, during his sojourn in Spain. Over his career, Irving worked in three distinct yet congruent forms—prose medley, narrative history, and travelogue—which might all be termed quasi-novelistic. With his genial style and graceful storytelling, Irving influenced the US novel by working at its margins.

Poe's impact on novel writing in the United States derived from his fiction—which included one novel (*Pym*) as well as the unfinished "Rodman"—and from his endeavor as a magazinist to impose standards on American fiction and to elucidate principles of narrative construction. His innovations in fiction created new, popular subgenres, and his experiments with unreliable, first-person narrators influenced later novelists. Poe's one-and-a-half novels hardly changed the genre's development in the United States, but his strange foreign tales and sometimes scorching reviews challenged the predilection for "strictly 'American' themes" in fiction evoked by US literary nationalism.

Irving honed his style by reading English satire: he imitated Addison and Steele in launching the collaborative *Salmagundi* papers (1807–08), and he aped Henry Fielding, Jonathan Swift, and Laurence Sterne to produce the mock-epic *History of New York* (1811). In the guise of Diedrich Knickerbocker, Irving presents history as comedy, using occasional bawdy humor to expose the follies of New Netherlands under three governors (one of whom resembles Thomas Jefferson). By reducing the past to parody, Irving fictionalizes history. Although the *History of New York* lacks a central protagonist or connected plot, it stitches together comic episodes to reconstruct the story of a colonial community. While satirizing the Dutch, Irving's history indirectly mocks the supposed Puritan origins of American identity.

When Irving decided to become a professional author, forsaking both law and business, he devised a composite form, a miscellany of short prose sketches interlaced with reflective essays and tales, calling his collection *The Sketch Book*. The volume traces the latter-day pilgrimage of an Anglo-American returning to his roots to record impressions of people, landscape, and culture—aiming to arouse nostalgia for the mother country and to revive Anglo-American friendship after two divisive wars. Between sketches such as "Westminster Abbey" and "Stratford-Upon-Avon," Irving inserted a handful of American pieces—the tales "Rip Van Winkle" and "The Legend of Sleepy Hollow," as well as the essays "Traits of Indian Character" and "Philip of Pokanoket." He thus appealed to two audiences simultaneously, emphasizing cultural commonalities that favored rapprochement while also delineating national differences. "Rip Van Winkle" and "Sleepy Hollow" became classic tales, models of the short story, and the composite volume charmed American and English audiences while introducing a new blend of travelogue, essay, and fiction that produced a virtual narrative of the search for cultural origins.

The sequel, a "medley" called *Bracebridge Hall; or, The Humourists* (1822), was, as Irving explained in a letter, "not like a novel" (1978, 1:661), even though most of the short pieces compose a linked narrative ending with Guy Bracebridge's marriage to "the fair Julia," a ward of Squire Bracebridge. Irving portrays the Hall's inhabitants and celebrates the leisurely existence of the English country gentry. But he also interpolates several tales supposedly related by its residents: "The Stout Gentleman," "The Spanish Student," "Annette Delarbre," and a brace of American stories, "Dolph Heyliger" and "The Spectre-Ship." These tales, three of which conclude with weddings, thus complement the nuptial theme while injecting a cosmopolitanism. If the volume was not exactly a novel, it nevertheless unmistakably inspired John Pendleton Kennedy's *Swallow Barn; or, A Sojourn in the Old Dominion* (1832), often cited as the paradigmatic southern plantation novel.

Less unified, Irving's next volume, *Tales of a Traveller* (1824), presents four clusters of stories, each with a different focus. Reaching back to *Bracebridge Hall* to retrieve the narrator of "The Stout Gentleman," he presents several ghost tales told by guests at an English mansion—narratives set variously in England, France, Belgium, and Italy. The second section, "Buckthorne and His Friends," presents, however, a different kind of suite. Jack Buckthorne gives Crayon a glimpse of the "republic of letters" in England by inviting him first (in "The Poor Devil Author") to a literary banquet and then to a tavern frequented by Grub Street hacks. But in "Buckthorne, or The Young Man of Great Expectations," Irving unfolds the story of a budding poet who leaves home believing that he will inherit the estate of his grumpy uncle (hence his "great expectations"). After a stint with a theatrical troupe and a desultory education at Oxford, however, Buckthorne discovers at his kinsman's death that he has been disinherited—and all because his juvenile poem "Doubting Castle" mocked his uncle's abode. The protagonist's literary accomplishments remain untold, but despite his eventual acquisition of the uncle's property, his story implies a critique of the English class system in its grim differentiation between wealth and poverty. Collectively the "Buckthorne" stories form a narrative cluster, a proto-novel that in the first American edition exceeds 200 pages.

The last two sections of *Tales of a Traveller* shift the reader's gaze to Italy and to colonial America, respectively. Stories of "The Italian Banditti" portray the former land as infested with crime, as Italian, English, and French travelers recount stories about the dangers posed by robbers menacing the road between Terracina and Fondi. Irving's concluding section, "The Money Diggers," resumes the theme of American treasure hunting broached in *Bracebridge Hall.* The sequence melds interconnected tales about pirate booty allegedly buried near Manhattan Island. "Wolfert Webber, or Golden Dreams" limns the growth of New York as it portrays a Dutchman so consumed by dreams of buried wealth that he excavates his cabbage patch, becoming "the destroying angel of his own vegetable world." In "The Adventure of Sam, the Black Fisherman" the title character aids Webber and another gold-seeker in locating a treasure chest protected, in this mock-gothic romp, by the ghost of Captain Kidd.

Amid these tales of old "Manhatta," Irving inserts "The Devil and Tom Walker," a story that shifts the treasure hunting to New England, allowing Irving to indulge his scorn for Puritanism. Both "Tom Walker" and the New York tales uncover the colonial origins of a materialism that seemed to Irving rampant in the early United States in what Charles Sellers calls the "market revolution." The "Money Diggers" cluster finds the author eschewing the miscellany for an integrated sequence, a species of composite novel.

Irving's fondness for the prose medley produced another notable volume of connected stories and sketches: *Tales of the Alhambra*, a work inspired by his residence (May–July 1829) in the grand palace at Granada. But *The Alhambra* incorporates a model fundamentally different from the earlier collections. The pieces all cohere around the romantic history of the Alhambra, giving the book greater cohesiveness than previous composites. The sketches also loosely reconstruct Irving's own journey to Granada, his investigation of the palace, and his accumulation of legends associated with Moorish royalty. Some of the best tales, such as "Legend of Prince Ahmed Al Kamel; or, the Pilgrim of Love" and "Legend of the Three Beautiful Princesses" can stand alone, yet as Andrew Burstein observes, they also "encapsulate the spirit and tone of the 'Spanish Sketch Book'" (2007, 219). *The Alhambra* likewise documents Irving's research into Moorish history and culture. Indeed, his fascination with what critic Edward Said has called "Orientalism" gives this volume new currency as an early Euro-American effort to comprehend the otherness of the Islamic world.

The collection that Jeffrey Rubin-Dorsky has called Irving's "last major work of fiction" (1988, 221) also affords a glimpse of the professional transition then in progress, the making of a historian. Disappointed by criticism of *Tales of a Traveller*, Irving went to Spain in 1826 to pursue a new gambit, having been invited to translate materials pertaining to Columbus and his discovery of the Western Hemisphere. But when Irving plunged into the work, he recognized that the assembled texts lacked narrative coherence. Working from documents arranged by Spanish historian Martín Fernández de Navarrete, the American devoted two years to a multivolume biography, *A History of the Life and Voyages of Christopher Columbus* (1828). William L. Hedges aptly remarks: "*Columbus* is—as much as any American novel—a romance. It makes the career of the discoverer of America a fabulous quasi-allegorical quest" (1965, 250). If Irving uncovered no new information, he nevertheless made Columbus an appealing, vividly human character, driven by what Hedges calls his relentless "quixotism," an almost fatalistic desire to see the Caribbean rim as the long-sought verge of the Asian subcontinent.

The life of Columbus fascinated US readers, for whom Irving produced a proto-American romantic hero empowered by a golden dream and emboldened by faith in divine destiny. In an age of nation building, Columbus provided the example of courage requisite to a myth of origins. Gone are the gibes and hilarities in the *History of New York*; largely missing as well is the close documentation of conventional biography. Instead, Irving creates what Rubin-Dorsky calls a "work of imagination," one that anticipates the hybrid genre of the "nonfiction narrative"

(1988, 221–22); Ilan Stavans has similarly likened the five-volume opus to a "novelistic adventure" (2001, 22). Here, the explorer attains mythic status through sheer indomitability in the face of uncertainty, desperation, and mutinous unrest. Identifying with his subject even to the point of recreating his dreams, Irving gave the first biography of Columbus in English a novelist's attention to internal conflict and external drama. His subject linked the Old World to the New, even as Irving fancied himself an intermediary between Europe and America. Columbus discovered land after two agonizing months at sea and immediately felt a "tumultuous and intense" feeling of accomplishment: "The great mystery of the ocean was revealed; his theory, which had been the scoff of sages, was triumphantly established; he had secured to himself a glory durable as the world itself" (bk. 3, ch. 4). As told by Irving, *Life and Voyages* resembles an epic. And it sold well, becoming (as Burstein notes) the "most commonly owned book" (2007, 196) in the United States by the 1850s, appearing in 175 editions before the century's end.

The author's turn to history soon revealed a new subject of investigation—Moorish domination of Spain from the eighth century. By the fourteenth and fifteenth centuries, although most of Spain had been recaptured, Granada remained the last seat of Moorish power; its overthrow preceded by seven months the first voyage of Columbus, who received his royal commission at the Alhambra. Irving was compiling notes for *The Conquest of Granada* (1829) well before he completed the life of Columbus. Recognizing that he was no Scott, Irving explained his new work as "an attempt, not at an historical romance, but a romantic history" (1978, 2:331). Unlike his Columbus biography, however, this narrative would lack a central character or plot, instead depicting a succession of violent, chivalric clashes that blurred together. To enliven what he described as a potentially "monotonous" chronicle (1978, 2:327), Irving adopted the persona of a Catholic historian, Brother Antonio Agapida, infusing a certain playfulness by flaunting the religious bias of this imaginary scholar and thus exposing the subjectivity of history writing.

Irving sympathized with the Moors, who were hopelessly besieged and fated to lose their paradise in Andalusia. Even so, he portrayed their culture, Hedges notes, as "weak internally," wracked by jealousy, indolence, and "effeminacy." When Ferdinand and Isabella force the last king of Granada, Boabdil el Chico, to surrender the city and withdraw to a distant valley, his departure epitomizes the theme of "mutability" that Hedges calls "the chief significance of the book" (1965, 254–55). The defining moment occurs when Boabdil and his men, leaving the city, take a "farewell gaze" at Granada: "Never had it appeared so lovely in their eyes. . . . The Moorish cavaliers gazed with a silent agony of tenderness and grief upon that delicious abode, the scene of their loves and pleasures" (v. 2, ch. 54). Irving evokes a similar poignancy at the end of *The Alhambra* to dramatize his own departure from Granada in 1829. While completing that collection on English soil, he also produced *Voyages and Discoveries of the Companions of Columbus* (1831).

When he left Europe in 1832, Irving did not abandon history. Indeed, all three western narratives of the 1830s reflect a consciousness of the historical moment—the opening of the trans-Mississippi West for white settlement. *A Tour on the Prairies* represented for Irving a new kind of writing, a firsthand account of history in the making: the exploration of Osage and Pawnee lands in present-day Oklahoma. The author welcomed an opportunity to accompany the commissioner designated to inspect the newly opened Indian territory and determine its suitability for tribal resettlement. Despite Irving's long-standing sympathy for native people (cf. "Traits of Indian Character"), he served—as Burstein notes—as secretary for an expedition implicated in Indian removal. Despite occasional condescension, however, his depiction of Indians encountered along the way and his willingness to let a French-Osage hunter speak for Native people everywhere complicate political judgments about Irving's complicity in Jacksonian policies.

No volume from Irving's pen more closely approaches the novel than this travelogue. *A Tour* savors personal adventure; its narrator plunges into the action and vividly conveys both the visual spectacle and Irving's consequent reflections. With two other traveling companions, he accompanies Henry Ellsworth on an expedition that stretched, by Irving's reckoning, "three hundred miles beyond human habitation," into a region filled with hostile Pawnees as well as fierce bears and wolves (1978, 2:735). The narrative moves forward episodically, assuming a picaresque structure in which successive challenges expose human desires and foibles. Peter Antelyes contends that *A Tour* satirizes the "Indian adventure tale" underpinning the ideology of American territorial expansion (1990, 96). Irving himself downplayed the novelistic qualities of his narrative, professing in the "Author's Introduction" that those who sought a "marvelous or adventurous story" needed to understand that he had "none to tell." But *A Tour* indeed delivers a rousing account, one that anticipates the fictionalized real-life experience of Herman Melville's *Typee: A Peep at Polynesian Life* (1846), *Redburn: His First Voyage* (1849), and *White-Jacket; or, The World in a Man-of-War* (1850).

A Tour takes the form of a journey out and back, an escape from civilization—as Irving understood it—into an uncharted prairie wilderness. The literary celebrity shares the hardships of guides, hunters, and rangers attached to the government party: he faces the nightly threat of a Pawnee attack; the danger of prowling wolves; the risk of becoming lost on a trackless prairie; and the privations of hunger, cold, and exhaustion. Despite passing comparisons to European scenes, his adventure into wild nature is distinctly American, a Cooperesque narrative of pioneering and conquest. The rangers create a show of force to intimidate the Osages, stray Creeks, and Pawnees (who keep their distance); the party captures and tames wild horses; and their hunting forays devolve into gratuitous slaughter. Their invasion presages the incursion of white settlers that culminated in the Oklahoma land rush of 1884. Even though Irving himself succumbs to the hunting frenzy, bringing down a massive buffalo (to his immediate regret), he witnesses with remorse a collective violation of the natural order. He hopes that every captured mustang will escape, and he betrays an emerging environmental conscience when he portrays the group's abandoned encampment:

> The surrounding forest had been in many places trampled into a quagmire. Trees felled and partly hewn in pieces, and scattered in huge fragments; tent-poles stripped of their covering; smouldering fires, with great morsels of roasted venison and buffalo meat, standing in wooden spits before them, hacked and slashed by the knives of hungry hunters; while around were strewed the hides, the horns, the antlers, and bones of buffaloes and deer, with cooked joints and unplucked turkeys, left behind with that reckless improvidence and wastefulness which young hunters are apt to indulge in a neighborhood where game abounds. (ch. 28)

The passage underscores changes in Irving himself since the expedition embarked; now "improvidence and wastefulness" offend him. And when, in chapter 27, he permits Beatte, the mixed-blood hunter, to articulate "the wrongs and insults that the poor Indians suffered in their intercourse with the rough settlers on the frontiers," Irving reveals another facet of his alienation from the operation in which he is engaged. These gestures transform *A Tour* into a novel of education—and chagrin. As Antelyes remarks, "To question the rights of Americans to dispossess Indians of the land was to challenge not only the superiority of American civilization but the sanctity of its mission" (1990, 101). Irving's narrative, calculated to reaffirm his patriotism through its nationalistic theme, thus acquires fascination as a quasi-novel precisely by its ironic portrayal of what Antelyes calls the young nation's "adventurous enterprise."

Irving thereafter published two biographies of western adventurers, both stemming from his employment by John Jacob Astor to write a history of Astor's attempt to establish a fur-trading center on the Pacific Rim. With his nephew Pierre conducting archival research, Irving converted his assistant's notes into *Astoria*, a sweeping chronicle of exploration. On the heels of Lewis and Clark, Astor's men were among the first whites to blaze an overland route to the Pacific; Irving portrays "Mr. Astor" as the orchestrating genius of a bold, romantic effort to extend civilization by spreading capitalism. Focusing initially on Astor's ill-fated trading ship, the *Tonquin*, Irving captures the geographical sweep of this bid to establish a Pacific outpost—a project interrupted by the War of 1812—but he also ignores Astor's indifference to the fatalities entailed in commercial empire building. Irving bases the narrative on documented facts but invests history with drama, depicting with novelistic suspense the trek of Winston Hunt and his men, their encounters with Indian bands, and their hardships en route from the Missouri to the headwaters of the Columbia. Idealized but never fabricated, Irving's *Astoria* indulges in hero worship, likening the financier to Christopher Columbus. The narrative prefigures a succession of American novels about millionaires, stretching from Henry James's *The American* (1877) to F. Scott Fitzgerald's *The Great Gatsby* (1925) and beyond.

At Astor's summer home, Irving also met Captain Benjamin Bonneville, an officer with extensive service in the West. Irving quoted approvingly (in the appendix to *Astoria*) from Bonneville's call for a vigorous US military presence to subjugate "roving hordes" of Osage, Pawnee, and Kansas Indians and to render them "dependent" on government assistance. To Irving, Bonneville epitomized the western man, and books such as Timothy Flint's recent biography of Daniel Boone suggested the commercial value of Bonneville's story. *The Adventures of Captain Bonneville* (1837) forms an explicit sequel to *Astoria*, not only in summarizing Astor's project but also in chronicling the western fur trade since 1810. Despite Irving's attempt to thrust the young officer into an emerging pantheon of frontier heroes, the narrative lacks direction and purpose. Projected (according to Burstein) as a "romance" (2007, 288), the volume falls short in part because Irving never quite discovered in Bonneville's "rambling kind of enterprise" (as he calls it in the "Introductory Notice") anything like heroic achievement. As Antelyes provocatively notes, Bonneville's abortive attempt to construct a base for the western fur trade ironically mirrors Astor's unsuccessful attempt to found a Pacific outpost—and in a volume that exposes Irving's own doubts, during the Panic of 1837, about literary enterprise in the "Jacksonian marketplace" (1990, 196).

In fact, though, *Bonneville* sold well, and during the 1840s and 1850s Irving continued to pursue historical projects, which included a biography of Oliver Goldsmith and a full-length, five-volume life of George Washington. His historical writing also included a study of the origins of Islam entitled *Lives of Mahomet and His Successors* (1850), a volume inspired by his two-year stint as US ambassador to Spain under President Tyler. From 1839 onward, Irving also contributed to the monthly *Knickerbocker Magazine*, eventually gathering these tales and legends into a last miscellany called *Wolfert's Roost* (1855).

If he never produced a bona fide novel, Irving nevertheless exerted a far-reaching influence on the Anglo-American literary world of his time. His 1849 biography of Goldsmith may explain his hold over contemporary readers, for it begins with a eulogium pertinent to Irving himself:

> The artless benevolence that beams throughout his works; the whimsical, yet amiable views of human life and human nature; the unforced humor, blending so happily with good feeling and good sense, and singularly dashed at times with a pleasing melancholy; even the very nature of his mellow, and flowing, and softly-tinted style, all seem to bespeak his moral as well as his intellectual qualities, and make us love the man at the same time that we admire the author.

Irving was the consummate stylist of his time, a citizen of the world (to invoke one of his favorite Goldsmith novels), whose urbanity and cosmopolitanism enabled him to transform commonplace materials—folk tales, legends, travel notes, letters, historical records, and chronicles—into absorbing narratives infused with humor, melancholy, and sympathy. He was, despite Poe's querulous criticisms, the most beloved prose writer in antebellum America.

Poe never was—or wanted to be—a novelist. As a precocious schoolboy in England he read sensational tales in *Blackwood's Magazine* and probably discovered Defoe and Scott near the end of his sojourn abroad. In his adolescence he likely perused gothic novels such as Horace Walpole's *Castle of Otranto* (1764) and William Beckford's *Vathek* (1786). His tale "The Oval Portrait" implies a familiarity with Ann Radcliffe's *Mysteries of Udolpho* (1794). He also seems to have read Miguel de Cervantes' *Don Quixote* (1605–15), Alain-René Lesage's *Gil Blas* (1715–35), and William Godwin's *Caleb Williams* (1794). From childhood, however, *Robinson Crusoe* (1719) captured his imagination, and much later he recalled reading Defoe by firelight, roused by "the spirit of wild adventure" as he "labored out" the meaning of each line and "hung breathless and trembling with eagerness over their absorbing—over their enchaining interest!" In his fiction, Poe sought the Crusoe effect, though ironically he spurned the longer form in which he first discovered "the potent magic of verisimilitude" and the "faculty of *identification*" (Defoe's ability to lose his "individuality" in that of a character) that created an "intensity" of interest (1984a, 201–2).

Poe's earliest aspiration, though, was to become a poet, and between 1827 and 1831 he wrote enough lyric, narrative, and meditative poems to fill three volumes. When poverty compelled him to begin writing for periodicals and newspapers, however, Poe turned to prose fiction and composed a spate of tales, mostly comic imitations of popular magazine subgenres. To publish these pieces as a book, he contrived an Irvingesque framework—a group of bibulous storytellers comprising the "Folio Club," said to be "a mere Junto of *Dunderheadism*" (Poe 1984b, 131). To the oddly named members, the author attributed his first eleven tales, which included several farces.

Crafting short narratives that tested his ingenuity (or so he later explained), Poe had no early inclination to write a novel and regarded the elaboration of an extended plot as tedious work. In a self-profile published anonymously, he much later remarked: "The evident and most prominent aim of Mr. POE is originality, either of idea, or the combination of ideas. . . . Thus it is that he has produced works of the most notable character, and elevated the mere 'tale,' in this country, over the larger 'novel'—conventionally so termed" (1984a, 873).

His early tales reveal his attraction to sensation. "Metzengerstein" (Jan. 1832) ends in a spectacle of fiery destruction, and "MS Found in a Bottle" (Oct. 1833) closes with ship and narrator plunging into a "roaring, and bellowing, and thundering" polar vortex. Another tale with a jolting conclusion, "The Assignation" (Jan. 1834), contains circumstances complex enough to fill a novel, even an Italian *Scarlet Letter*: a beautiful young woman, unhappily married to a revolting old

Marchese, has delivered a child apparently begotten by her paramour, a lionized English poet and aesthete. But Poe's interest lies not in the torment of guilt, nor in the psychological drama of covert relationships. Instead, his tale juxtaposes two stunning scenes: the poet's rescue of the infant from a canal into which the despairing mother has cast it and then—after the narrator glimpses the exotic, "visionary" décor of the hero's apartment—the poet's suicide at dawn to complete a death pact with the Marchesa. During this apprentice period, when Poe was not evoking gothic terror, he composed sepulchral burlesques, such as "Loss of Breath" (Nov. 1832), or spoofs about wagering with the Devil ("The Duc de L'Omelette" [Mar. 1832] and "Bon-Bon" [Dec. 1832]). Everything Poe wrote embodied a poetics of brevity. But when his mentor, John Pendleton Kennedy, sought a publisher for the "Folio Club" tales, the proprietor balked, claiming that readers wanted something "larger and longer" than "short stories" (Thomas and Jackson 1987, 142).

By 1835, Poe was contributing reviews to a new journal, the *Southern Literary Messenger* of Richmond. His May notice of Kennedy's novel *Horse-Shoe Robinson* praised its originality and predicted that the Baltimore lawyer would soon assume a place "in the very first rank of American novelists" (1984a, 648). In June, Poe unveiled an altogether new creation: a long work of experimental fiction called "The Unparalleled Adventure of One Hans Phaall." Conceived as comic science fiction—Poe includes Irvingesque caricatures of the Dutch—the story portrays a flight to the moon by a desperate bellows-mender from Rotterdam. The tale opens with an odd-looking balloon descending close enough to a crowd to permit a tiny figure (ostensibly a moon man) to deliver a letter from Phaall (or "Pfaall" in later versions), relating his adventure to the mayor, Von Underduk, and Professor Rubadub of the Rotterdam "College of Astronomers." The missive recounts how, to escape his creditors, the impoverished Phaall had five years earlier constructed a balloon and launched it on April Fools' Day. But in reconstructing the flight, Poe's comic framework falls away, as the narrator assumes a matter-of-fact, Defoesque style, larding his narrative with plausible-sounding calculations of ballast, altitude, velocity, atmospheric density, and the like. Happily Phaall carries a device to make thin air breathable and ascends confident that decreasing atmospheric pressure will produce no dire consequences.

But problems arise: Phaall draws off some blood to ease the effect of dropping air pressure, and he must activate his breathing apparatus. Later he deploys a "gum-elastic bag" to enclose the gondola, creating a pressurized cabin with windows. The aeronaut provides glimpses of the entire Atlantic coast of Europe as well as North Africa, for at this height "the proudest cities of mankind had utterly faded away from the face of the earth" (1984b, 974). By April 3, he adopts the journal format of *Robinson Crusoe*, noting daily changes in the apparent diameter of the earth, the balloon's course relative to the moon's orbit, and certain odd noises emanating from the balloon. On April 17, Phaall discovers the cause of the creaking—the balloon has traveled so far into space as to reach the edge of the earth's gravitational field and begins to respond to the moon's tug. But only when he observes the lunar surface beneath him does he understand that the balloon and gondola have reversed positions. Fortunately, Poe's imaginary moon possesses oxygen sufficient to permit normal breathing and enough gravity to pull the balloon down. Phaall lands in "the very heart of a fantastical-looking city" amid "a vast crowd of ugly little people" who have no ears (993). Each moon-dweller, Phaall explains, has a specific, living counterpart on the earth.

Heavily indebted to Sir John Herschel's *Treatise on Astronomy* (1833), Poe's narrative stretches to fifty pages, and Phaall's letter finally hints at amazing discoveries about the universe, the moon, and its inhabitants that he proposes to reveal at a price—producing, as Marcy Dinius has suggested, "an allegory of authorship and marketplace reception" (2004, 4). But the conclusion undercuts the claims of this letter delivered by the little man; among the "rumors and speculations" (996) swirling about Rotterdam is the accusation of a hoax. Despite its now-laughable assumptions about space travel and its incongruous mix of silliness and plausibility, "Hans Phaall" marks a provocative experiment, an early effort to sustain a plot through multiple episodes, using precise, often plagiarized details to conjure a precarious verisimilitude.

Over the next eighteen months, Poe's experiences pushed him further toward the novel. An editorial position at the *Messenger* obliged him to review a dozen or more books each month, including volumes of fiction. Poe's criticism sometimes consisted of plot summary and stylistic nit-picking, but he also exposed improbabilities, artificialities, and descriptive excesses. He reviewed two novels of the American Revolution, panning Robert Montgomery Bird's *The Hawks of Hawk-Hollow* (1835) as "a bad imitation of Sir Walter Scott" (1997, 53) and praising Catharine Maria Sedgwick's *The Linwoods* (1835) for its "grace, warmth, and radiance" (63). His occasionally scathing reviews stirred controversy: with inspired sarcasm he "used up" flimsy novels by New York editors Theodore S. Fay and William Leete Stone. Poe praised Charles Dickens's *Watkins Tottle, and Other Sketches* (1836), the American edition of the author's popular *Sketches by Boz*, as a collection of sketches, judging "unity of effect" to be "indispensable in the 'brief article'" but "not so in the common novel" (218). Although Robert D. Jacobs has concluded that Poe the reviewer "never thought deeply about the novel" (1969, 255), he did identify certain attributes of successful long fiction: originality, believability, and intelligence.

Even as his editorial duties compelled him to critique dozens of novels, Poe renewed his bid to publish the "Folio Club" tales. With the help of novelist James Kirke Paulding, he approached Harper & Brothers of New York, but they rejected the project in part because the manuscript consisted of "detached tales and pieces" when the reading public preferred "a single and connected story" of one or two volumes (Thomas and Jackson 1987, 212). Doggedly, Poe offered the collection to a Philadelphia publisher and then to a London firm but drew no interest. By autumn, he concluded that to publish a book of fiction, he must write a novel.

Three titles that he reviewed for the *Messenger* influenced the narrative he began in late 1836. The anonymous *Report of the Committee on Naval Affairs* urged the government to explore and colonize the South Seas; an *Address on . . . a Surveying and Exploring Expedition to the Pacific Ocean and South Seas* by Jeremiah N. Reynolds unfolded a similar argument to Congress; and Irving's *Astoria* depicted overland trailblazing as well as Pacific enterprise. In all three reviews (the last two published in January 1837), Poe celebrated exploration and—despite his hostility to literary nationalism—appealed blatantly to national pride and self-interest. Had Poe succumbed to the lust for empire or was he cunningly preparing the ground for a novel about discoveries in the South Seas?

Despite Poe's termination as *Messenger* editor, its January and February 1837 issues carried the first installments of "The Narrative of Arthur Gordon Pym," the account of a young man from Nantucket who survives shipwreck, a skewered neck, and entombment in the hold of a ship—all in the opening episodes of what promises to be a serialized novel. But readers of the Richmond journal heard no more about Pym after Poe moved to New York, in search of employment during the Panic of 1837. He likely completed most of the manuscript that winter, for in May, *Knickerbocker Magazine* listed the novel as forthcoming from Harper & Brothers. Although the economic crisis postponed publication for one year, Harpers issued the novel, auspiciously, three weeks before the departure of the Wilkes expedition to map the Pacific and South Seas for US commercial exploitation.

The Narrative of Arthur Gordon Pym purports to be the true account of A. G. Pym, who in the preface explains the *Messenger*'s attribution of serialized episodes to "Mr. Poe" as a "*ruse*" intended to protect Pym from attacks upon his "veracity" by publishing his amazing story "*under the garb of fiction*." This sleight of hand, actually devised to conceal Poe's authorship, prefigures a narrative laced with deception from beginning to end, for nowhere else did Poe so relentlessly explore the disparity between appearance and reality. Pym himself practices duplicity from the opening episode, concealing his neck wound and the destruction of his sailboat and then devising a ploy to escape aboard the *Grampus*, a whaling ship commanded by the father of his best friend. Pym also confronts his *own* misreading of the deceptive phenomena he encounters on his long, strange journey: in *Pym*, as scholars have long remarked, nothing is as it seems. A scene in chapter 10 epitomizes this pattern: after a mutiny and countermutiny have convulsed the *Grampus* (killing the captain and most of the crew) and after the ship itself has been reduced to a hulk, Pym and three companions observe an approaching ship. They experience "ecstatic joy" and hail a sailor who appears to encourage them; but moments later an ungodly stench reveals that the "crew" consists of rotting corpses. After their rescue by a British schooner, the *Jane Guy*, Pym and the grotesque half-Indian Dirk Peters (the last survivors of the *Grampus*) reach the South Seas, where the interlopers engage in reciprocal duplicity with a black tribe living on a remote island.

Concealing their weapons, the sailors pose as "friends" to exploit local resources but stand ready to impose their colonizing will with deadly force; the blacks conversely exhibit cheerfulness and hospitality as they prepare the artificially induced rockslide that buries the invaders.

The narrative itself mirrors the treacherous world that Pym explores. Repeatedly his account generates contradictions: in chapter 5, Pym tells us that "many years elapsed" before his friend Augustus apologized for his "weakness and indecision" in failing to rescue Pym from the ship's hold, yet less than two months later, Augustus dies from his wounds. Such inconsistencies may betray Poe's carelessness in preparing the manuscript, yet they also fit a pattern of overturned expectations that culminates in the bizarre conclusion—in which Pym and Peters (with a native named Nu-Nu) seem doomed to destruction in an immense, milky vortex. But in chapter 24 a "shrouded human figure," one of "perfect whiteness" and "very far larger in its proportions than any dweller among men," looms in their "pathway," apparently to rescue them. Because the manuscript terminates here, however, Poe leaves the reader mystified. Is the "figure" a last delusion, or has Pym been saved by God or (as Richard Kopley suggests) the snow-white figure of Christ in the Book of Revelation? Or has an angel saved Pym so that he can publish his account? The narrative's very existence implies the narrator's deliverance, and yet how *did* Pym return to Richmond from the edge of annihilation? A final, puzzling "Note" by an unnamed editor reveals that Pym has subsequently "perished" in an accident, leaving his memoir unfinished. This circumstance prompts the disclosure that Mr. Poe, "the gentleman whose name is mentioned in the preface," has declined to write a conclusion because of "his disbelief in the entire truth of the latter portions of the narration." Like a work of postmodern metafiction, *Pym* finally implodes, casting doubt on its own authenticity.

Forced by popular taste to write a "single and connected story," Poe had spliced together a succession of harrowing episodes packed with authoritative information—most of it plagiarized—about ships, oceanography, and natural science. Burton Pollin's scholarly edition of *Pym* documents Poe's many borrowings, including his heavy reliance in the last half of the novel on Benjamin Morrell's *A Narrative of Four Voyages* (1832). Blatant plagiarism (sometimes from *Astoria*) permitted Poe to give plausibility to fantastic scenes. His nautical digression on "proper stowage" (ch. 6) may thus comment covertly on filling a novel with imported, even purloined, materials.

J. V. Ridgley's essay "The Growth of the Text" suggests that Poe composed the novel in four stages, producing a patchwork narrative. As critics have noted, the adolescent Pym metamorphoses rapidly: once he boards the *Jane Guy* he forgets the savagery in which he has just participated (including cannibalism), discourses like a seasoned explorer, and dispenses what Dana Nelson calls "colonial knowledge"—interpretation driven by self-interest and intended domination that tragically overlooks the taboo of whiteness portending the massacre of the Caucasian crew (1993,

107). In the *Messenger* review of Reynolds, Poe had warned: "The savages in these regions have frequently evinced a murderous hostility—they should be conciliated or intimidated" (1997, 354). If Pym's narrative exemplifies the "hostility" to subjugation that might complicate US imperialism in the Pacific, it also taps anxieties about slave uprisings that pervaded the South after the 1831 Nat Turner rebellion. Whether the narrative warns, as John Carlos Rowe contends, of a threat to "Southern aristocratic life" (1992, 127) or, as Joan Dayan argues, of an "inevitable catastrophe," perhaps divine retribution for "the offense of slavery" (1991, 109), remains a thorny question.

Whatever the novel's coded national meanings, readers soon recognized—and resented—Poe's hoax. Reviews were decidedly mixed; William Burton, Poe's later employer, called it "a mass of ignorance and effrontery" (Thomas and Jackson 1987, 254), and Poe himself called it "a very silly book" (2008, 1:218). Its legacy seems unclear: Melville's preoccupation with whiteness in *Moby-Dick; or, The Whale* (1851) owes a debt to *Pym,* Jules Verne wrote a fabulous sequel, and Henry James alludes to the novel's ending in *The Golden Bowl* (1904). But, despite the appearance of an English edition, *Pym* never achieved commercial success, and this public failure perhaps confirmed Poe's preference for the brief tale.

Still without regular employment, Poe resumed writing magazine tales in 1838, achieving a creative breakthrough in "Ligeia." The following year he composed his masterpiece, "The Fall of the House of Usher," for the periodical he was then helping to edit, *Burton's Gentleman's Magazine.* Poe's irksome stint as Burton's assistant paid a mere ten dollars per week, mostly for book reviews, but the proprietor probably inspired Poe to attempt a second novel by launching a literary contest. Burton reserved the biggest prize ($250) for a set of tales depicting "distinct periods in the history of North America." Ineligible to compete but determined to capitalize (in the form of supplemental pay) on Burton's yen for Americana, Poe must have seen his extended "western" narrative as a potential bonanza.

Like *Pym,* "The Journal of Julius Rodman" represents a hoax—a narrative ostensibly written by the first white man to cross the Rocky Mountains in search of a passage to the Pacific. Pollin has documented that, as in the sea story, Poe depended on passages lifted from published sources—primarily the journals of Lewis and Clark. Details from Irving's *Astoria* and *The Adventures of Captain Bonneville* as well as Alexander MacKenzie's *Voyages from Montreal . . . through the Continent of North America* (1801) also figure in "Rodman," which Poe projected as an epic trek across the Rockies to the Yukon Territory and then back to civilization. Poe tried to trump both the Lewis and Clark expedition and the travels of Winston Hunt in *Astoria.* And he intended to make his account more compelling than any preceding narrative by casting Rodman as a romantic figure, beset by melancholy but alive to the beauty of the western landscape. Indeed, Poe's opening chapter claims that the putative author's "burning love of Nature" has made him "*the man* to journey amid all that solemn desolation."

Through its first six episodes, Rodman's "journal" reconstructs an expedition up the Missouri River toward its headwaters in present-day Montana. The journey involves scrapes with wild animals as well as encounters with Indian bands, friendly and hostile. In one skirmish, the white men use a small cannon to terrify the Sioux; on another occasion, a handful of Assiniboins surprise Rodman's party to satisfy their curiosity about Toby, an African American servant. The first four chapters alternate between dated passages from Rodman's journal and editorial summaries of excluded portions, while five and six present only journal entries. The narrator concedes in chapter 5 that the "intense excitement" he feels about "the wonders and majestic beauties of the wilderness" surpasses any interest in pecuniary objectives. He wishes to gaze "beyond the extreme bounds of civilization" at the "gigantic mountains" that demarcate "*the unknown.*" But Rodman never penetrated that boundary; his account terminates at chapter 6, due to Poe's dismissal by Burton in May. The author never revived the project nor did he undertake further experiments in novel writing.

Indeed, Poe soon proclaimed his theory of "single effect," arguing that the prose tale composed according to a "pre-established design" and short enough to be read in an hour or so constituted, after the poem, the fittest literary test of "high genius." According to this rationale, the "ordinary novel" by virtue of its length lacked "the immense force derivable from *totality*," because interruptions in reading tended to "modify, annul, or counteract . . . the impressions of the book" (Poe 1984a, 572). Poe's theory of narrative privileged his stock in trade, the tale of sensation. In works as diverse as "The Tell-Tale Heart" (Jan. 1843), "The Masque of the Red Death" (May 1842), and "The Facts in the Case of M. Valdemar" (Dec. 1845), he subordinated every detail to a preconceived design.

Yet Poe never restricted his fiction to tales of effect; throughout his career he produced farces, parodies, and hoaxes as well as landscape sketches, prose poems, and dialogues. His experimentation led in 1841 to the tale of ratiocination, the precursor of the modern detective story. The translated *Memoirs of Vidocq* (1828–29), the founder of French criminal investigation, apparently suggested Poe's creation of the eccentric Parisian detective, C. Auguste Dupin, whose analytical powers and lynx-like observation enable him to untangle seemingly insoluble crimes. In three lengthy tales—"The Murders in the Rue Morgue" (Apr. 1841), "The Mystery of Marie Rogêt" (1842–43), and "The Purloined Letter" (1844)—Poe established the basic conventions of the detective story. These narratives lack the riveting unity of the gothic tales and typically juxtapose two accounts of the crime: the narrator's preliminary, always-incomplete description of the case followed by the detective's reconstruction of his secret inquiries and insights.

The detective tales thus involve mystification, for Dupin always conceals crucial discoveries from his narrator-friend, the ever-obtuse Prefect of Police, and of course the reader, before presenting his astounding solution. In "Rue Morgue," Poe anticipated what would become the locked-room mystery, and in "The Purloined

Letter," he imagined a criminal genius as the detective hero's sinister counterpart. In "Marie Rogêt" he transposed an American mystery to Paris, played detective himself, and tried to puzzle out a woman's disappearance by reading newspaper accounts against each other. But after three long installments, which extended the tale to novella length, Poe dissociated the Parisian murder from the recently solved death of New York cigar-girl Mary Rogers, lamely lamenting (as Maurice Lee notes) the failure of probability theory.

In other fictional experiments as well, Poe popularized ideas and techniques that novelists later adopted. Intrigued by William Gilmore Simms's *Martin Faber: The Story of a Criminal* (1833), Poe composed many tales narrated by alienated, obsessive types. "Berenice" (Mar. 1835) features a narrator whose dental fixation leads him to mutilate a corpse; the narrator of "William Wilson" (Oct. 1839) apparently kills his conscience while trying to slay his namesake and nemesis. In both "The Tell-Tale Heart" and "The Black Cat" (Aug. 1843), Poe represents domestic atrocities motivated by delusions, and in "The Cask of Amontillado" (Nov. 1846) Montresor coolly walls up his alter ego, Fortunato. In these tales, Poe merges the detective and criminal, as the narrator unravels his own perverse deeds. This economy avoids the bifurcated ratiocinative plot and enables Poe to achieve an impressively unified effect. But blind to the monstrosity of his deeds, the narrator of the crime tale also betrays a radical unreliability. Later novels exploring the criminal mind—from Fyodor Dostoevsky's *Crime and Punishment* (1866) to John Fowles's *The Collector* (1963)—often reveal a debt to Poe's explorations of aberrant psychology.

Poe's exercises in science fiction also persisted. In 1844, he published "The Balloon Hoax," depicting in plausible detail a three-day flight from England to South Carolina, and also "A Tale of the Ragged Mountains," a narrative revealing the spiritual transmigration of a Virginia man whose medical treatment involves morphine and mesmerism. The following year he composed "The Facts in the Case of M. Valdemar," ostensibly reporting an experiment in which the narrator-mesmerist leaves a dying man in a state of suspended animation for nine months. As John Tresch has reminded us, these tales—along with *Pym* and the intermittently humorous "Hans Pfaall"—helped found a tradition of science-inspired fantasies stretching from Jules Verne to Ray Bradbury and contemporary science fiction.

As a magazinist, Poe continued to discuss contemporary novels and genre conventions. In a review of Edward Bulwer Lytton's *Night and Morning* (1841), he described the perfect plot as "*that in which no part can be displaced without ruin to the whole.*" He recurred to the importance of interdependent plot elements in his 1845 "Chapter of Suggestions," arguing that "in fiction, the *denouement* . . . should be definitely considered and arranged, before writing the first word." He pursued this idea in 1846 in "The Philosophy of Composition," alluding to a note from Charles Dickens (whom he had interviewed) explaining that William Godwin had written *Caleb Williams* "backwards." This enabled Poe to extend his theory of preconceived effect to the novel: "It is only with the *dénouement* constantly in view that we can give a plot its indispensable air of consequence, or causation, by making the incidents, and especially the tone at all points, tend to the development of the intention" (1984a, 148, 1294, 13). Yet he illustrated this principle, famously, by explaining how he constructed his poem "The Raven" backward from the bird's "nevermore," which accentuates the irreversibility of a beautiful woman's death.

Poe arguably exerted his greatest influence on the American novel, however, not by extolling plot management, plausibility, or verisimilitude, but by attacking nationalistic literature as inherently provincial. In challenging the literary jingoism of the 1830s and 1840s, he was virtually alone. That "an American [writer] should confine himself to American themes" seemed nonsensical to Poe, who as late as 1845 argued that "a foreign theme" was "to be preferred." Because "the foreign subject," for the author of "Ligeia," carried no compromising Europhilia (Poe's Old World breeds terror), he felt no compunction in assailing Irving's early "homage" to English culture. Troubled by the talk of "maintaining a proper *nationality* in American Letters," he advocated "self-respect," even a cultural "Declaration of Independence" (1984a, 1076–78). But Poe probably failed to recognize how much Irving's professional success had encouraged literary independence, including that of Poe. To what extent either Poe or Irving affected the production of national narratives cannot be documented definitively. Both writers, as we have seen, mostly avoided the formal challenges of the American novel—Poe resisting nationalism and championing the tale; Irving embracing the national project yet adhering mainly to nonfiction and legend. But both unmistakably influenced the far-flung culture of letters from which antebellum fiction emerged.

Part III

THE AMERICAN PUBLISHING WORLD AND THE NOVEL

10

PUBLISHERS, BOOKSELLERS, AND THE LITERARY MARKET

MICHAEL WINSHIP

In 1742, just two years after Samuel Richardson's *Pamela* first appeared in London, Benjamin Franklin began work on an American edition, which he planned to publish at his own risk and expense. This was an unusual step for a colonial printer, for the few books published in the American colonies were generally issued for individuals or corporate bodies, who paid the cost of publication not with profits in mind, but rather with the aim of disseminating a text that they felt worthy of support. Most books that circulated in the colonies were imported from England, Ireland, or Scotland. Franklin, during his twenty years as sole proprietor of his printing office, published only sixteen bound books on his own account, and these were almost always small, inexpensive reprints of English books that had already proven popular and for which demand was not being met by imports.

Pamela had certainly enjoyed success in Britain, but no other American had reprinted a popular English book so soon after its publication. It was also a substantial text and, with Franklin's presses busy with other work, the second volume, though dated 1743, was not completed before late summer of 1744. By that time, the American market had been filled with imported copies, and Franklin still had copies of his edition, which retailed at six shillings, about half the cost of imported copies, on hand in 1748, when he sold the stock of his bookshop to his new partner, David Hall. If Franklin did not lose money on this venture, his profits must have been small, and he never published another novel.

Indeed, as James N. Green has pointed out (in work I have drawn on extensively for this chapter), Franklin may not have recognized that his was the first publication in the American colonies of a new genre that would subsequently become so important. In his autobiography, Franklin names *Pamela* as a stylistic successor to the *The Pilgrim's Progress* (1678) by John Bunyan, who "was the first that I know of who mix'd Narration & Dialogue, a Method of Writing very engaging to the Reader, who in the most interesting Parts finds himself as it were brought into the Company, & present at the Discourse" (Franklin 1987, 1326). In making this connection, Franklin names not only Daniel Defoe's familiar novels *Robinson Crusoe* (1719) and *Moll Flanders* (1722) but also his conduct manuals *Religious Courtship* (1722) and *Family Instructor* (1715).

For many years following Franklin's pioneering act of publication, American readers had to satisfy themselves with imported editions of novels, which they most certainly did. A quarter century passed before an American printer again ventured to publish another. During the 1760s, a number of British printers and booksellers emigrated to America, many from Scotland and Ireland, where the reprinting of cheap editions of London publications in smaller formats was standard practice. Once they arrived in the colonies, the more enterprising of these immigrants continued the practice of reprinting, and, among other works, a small number of English novels were reprinted in American editions: in Boston, Mein and Fleming published Oliver Goldsmith's *Vicar of Wakefield* (1767) and Laurence Sterne's *Sentimental Journey* (1768); in Philadelphia, Robert Bell published Samuel Johnson's *Rasselas* (1768) and another edition of *Sentimental Journey* (1770). A few others joined in.

With the outbreak of the Revolution in 1775, the reprinting of novels largely stopped, but as peace approached, Bell and others took up where they had left off. Bell, for instance, reprinted several of Henry Mackenzie's sentimental novels, including his popular *Man of Feeling* (1782), Samuel Jackson Pratt's novel of the American Revolution, *Emma Corbett* (1782, and again in 1783), and Johann Wolfgang von Goethe's international blockbuster, *Sorrows of Young Werther* (1784). Others followed, though the severe economic depression that began in 1784 slowed all publishing activity. Altogether, about twenty-five novels were printed in America in the 1780s, but the pace picked up in the following decade, when nearly 200 were issued.

Almost entirely, the novels printed in America during the eighteenth century were of British or European origin. Furthermore, they were invariably of proven popularity—the American reprint editions competing with or replacing imports—and they were short. Only at the very end of the century was anything approaching the length of *Pamela*, the work with which Franklin had pioneered the practice of reprinting novels in America, attempted. For most longer works, such as Richardson's *Clarissa* (8 vols. 1748) or Henry Fielding's *Tom Jones* (4 vols. 1749), American readers had to depend on imported editions of the full text or, more often, American-printed selected or abridged editions like the 16-page abridgment of Defoe's *Robinson Crusoe* printed in Boston as early as about 1760. These last—known as chapbooks, "small books," or "small histories"—were sometimes marketed as children's books, though their actual readership must have been much broader. Many do not today survive in even a single copy, but an indication of their ubiquity is given by the title-page imprint of that early Boston *Robinson Crusoe*, which states that it was "Printed and sold at Fowle & Draper's printing-office in Marlborough-Street; where country traders, shop-keepers and others, may supply themselves with a compleat assortment of small histories, &c. &c. by the gross or dozen, and considerable profits will be allow'd to those who purchase to sell again."

Those printers and booksellers who, in the 1790s, actively participated in the reprint trade began to approximate, in our modern sense, the role of publishers, and some, such as Mathew Carey and Thomas Dobson in Philadelphia, gave up printing and binding on their own, and ceased to import books for retail, in order to concentrate their entrepreneurial energy on the distribution and sale of works reprinted for them in America by others. These fledgling publishers developed a number of strategies for marketing their books beyond their immediate vicinity. One was to employ an agent who traveled from market town to market town or from court session to court session with a supply of books for sale or with samples with which to take orders. Another was to develop a network of affiliated printing shops, post offices, and general stores—often these were combined in a single place of business—where they could place their books for sale on commission. Increasingly, these pioneers began to take control of the new nation's book trade by using a system of exchange that allowed them to diversify their stock, to place their publications in distant markets, and to avoid excessive competition. Under this system, American reprints of the standard works for which there was a steady market replaced imports: each publisher would publish one or two, then all would exchange their editions with one another, with no money changing hands, to build up a varied stock to supply their regional market. Thus, publishers could produce larger editions than were needed for immediate, local sale, reducing the cost per copy, and through exchange arrange that each publisher had a full assortment of standard works.

This emerging American book trade depended largely on works of British origin, and an "American" book usually referred to a book of American manufacture rather than one written by an American citizen or resident. Thus, a pioneering "Catalogue of Books Printed in America" published in Mathew Carey's magazine, the *American Museum*, in 1792, lists seventy-one titles—only fifteen are by Americans, and five of these are pamphlets. Furthermore, novels were not a major part of the output of these early American publishers—only five, at most, works of fiction are included in the *American Museum* list, including what is generally considered today as the first American novel, William Hill Brown's *The Power of Sympathy* (1789). The others were a British novel—Anne (Urtick) Burke's *Ela, or The Delusions of the Heart* (1790)—a 1792 edition of a juvenile entitled *The New Robinson Crusoe*, a selection of *The Beauties of Fielding*, and a pamphlet by an American entitled *Adventures of John Ferrago and Teague ORegan*. This last, presumably the first published installment of Hugh Henry Brackenridge's *Modern Chivalry*, eventually filled six volumes, published from 1792 to 1805.

The 1792 "Catalogue" presents, of course, only a partial record of American publishing of the period, even if it was printed in a magazine issued by one of the major players, but the sense it gives of the place of novels is, if anything, exaggerated.

According to figures compiled by Green, only twenty-five novels of more than 100 pages were published in America in 1798, and ten of these were more than fifteen years old, including standard works of fiction by Defoe, Fielding, Goethe, and Richardson. Of the fifteen new works, six were by American authors. Moreover, twenty-five novels represented just over 1 percent of the total number of imprints published in America that year, and can be compared to ninety-two shorter fictional works (such as chapbooks and juveniles), 134 works of verse, and fifteen plays. Nor was 1798 an exception: in 1804, only nine new novels were published, four by Americans. In all, a total of twenty novels of over 100 pages by Americans were published in the 1790s, and only twenty-five in the following decade.

In 1790, Congress passed the first national copyright law, "An Act for the Encouragement of Learning," which granted authors, for a limited number of years, ownership in the literary property of their works that had not already been published. The right to copyright protection was, however, restricted to citizens and residents of the United States and did not extend to foreign authors. This feature of the new law not only encouraged American authors to enter their works for copyright but also encouraged publishers to pay an American editor to revise or expand standard British works, thus making them eligible for American copyright protection. The advantage in publishing a copyrighted work was considerable, as a publisher could control the market for such works without fear that another publisher would print a competing edition, and America's earliest novelists certainly took advantage of the copyright law. Of the twenty-one American novels listed in a *Catalogue of All the Books, Printed in the United States* that was published by the booksellers in Boston in January 1804, copyright was secured for all but four.

It has often been claimed that American copyright law discouraged the development of American authorship because publishers were free to reprint works by foreign authors without payment. A foreign work, especially one whose appeal had been established from sales and reviews of imported copies, could indeed be reprinted in the United States without payment to its author, though any publisher who did so ran the risk that another printer or publisher would do the same and compete for the American market. On the other hand, an original, copyrighted work, though untested, could not be reprinted without its author's or publisher's permission, a feature that protected a publisher's outlay for paper, composition, and presswork. In this way, payments to American authors for their copyrighted works could be considered an investment rather than an extra expense, especially if additional editions were expected. Of course, any book, whether copyrighted or not, that did not sell was a loss, and no publisher could take on many such works, unless the author or some institution was willing to cover the cost of publication.

As Green has shown, a number of cases prove that at least some early American novels were published at their publisher's, rather than their author's, expense. Brown's *Power of Sympathy*, issued the year before the first national copyright act was passed, was published by Isaiah Thomas's Boston partner, Ebenezer Andrews, who over the following decades almost alone made a specialty of printing or publishing American copyrighted works, including novels such as Enos Hitchcock's *Memoirs of the Bloomsgrove Family* (1790) and *The Farmer's Friend* (1793), and Jeremy Belknap's *The Foresters* (1792). Charles Brockden Brown's first novel, *Alcuin* (1790), was published at the expense of his friend Elihu Hubbard Smith, but thereafter Brown was able to find publishers who were willing to purchase the copyright to his works, including *Wieland* (1798), *Ormond* (1799), *Arthur Mervyn* (1799–1800), and *Edgar Huntly* (1799). Ten years later, Washington Irving's *A History of New York* (1809), a fictionalized history, was published at the sole risk of its publisher, Philadelphia's Bradford & Inskeep, in an edition of 2,000 copies, and earned Irving $2,100.

The publishing history of Susanna Rowson's *Charlotte. A Tale of Truth* (1794), generally considered the first American novel to become a bestseller, is instructive. Born in England in 1762, Rowson spent most of her childhood in Massachusetts, where her father, an officer in the Royal Navy, served as customs collector. In 1778, after the outbreak of hostilities in the colonies, Rowson returned to London, and there, between 1786 and 1792, published six novels. *Charlotte*, the fourth of these, appeared in 1791 over the imprint of William Lane, proprietor of the Minerva Press and its associated network of circulating libraries. Lane's empire was built around the publication of popular fiction and in this company, Rowson's work did not stand out. It was simply one of the many sentimental Minerva novels published and quickly forgotten—only two copies of this London first edition survive today.

In late 1793, however, Rowson returned to America with her husband as part of a touring theater troupe that had been recruited to perform at Philadelphia's "New Theatre," and *Charlotte* fared much better when published in that city by Mathew Carey the following spring. It became a steady seller in America over the next century: a second edition by Carey appeared in 1794, followed by editions bearing the more familiar title *Charlotte Temple* in 1797, 1801, 1802, 1808, 1809, and 1812, as well as a possible, unlocated "sixth edition" sometime between 1802 and 1808. In 1801, new editions also appeared in Hartford, New Haven, and Philadelphia (this last by Peter Stewart), and from that point forward Carey was no longer the primary American publisher of *Charlotte*. In 1825, Silas Andrus of Hartford published the first edition printed from stereotype plates, which were subsequently used for many more printings, and at least fifteen sets of stereotyped plates were used over the next eighty years. R. W. G. Vail, in our best record of the work's publication history, lists 105 American printings or editions of the work before 1870, many of which were issued together with its sequel *Lucy Temple*—first published posthumously in 1828—often with the omnibus title *Love and Romance*.

In a letter of 1812, Carey reported to Rowson that "the sales of Charlotte Temple exceed those of the most celebrated novels that ever appeared in England. I think that the number disposed of must far exceed 50,000 copies; & the sale still continues" (qtd. in Homestead and Hansen 2010, 641). But if it was by far the most successful novel by an American resident during the early national period, its publication history more nearly resembles the long-established pattern for American reprints of popular British works—say, an abridgement of *Robinson Crusoe*—than that for any other American novel. And from the point of view of American publishers, their editions of *Charlotte* were indeed British reprints, because of its prior London publication it was ineligible for American copyright protection. Nevertheless, Carey, the work's first American publisher, did pay Rowson twenty dollars and gave her twenty copies in recognition of her "copy right," and this may explain why other reprinters held off from offering their own editions during the 1790s. Besides being ineligible for copyright, *Charlotte* had other features that appealed to reprinters: it was short and, in volume two, set in America. Once reprinting began, it flourished. Lack of copyright protection may have been a necessary condition for its publishing history in the United States, but it is an insufficient explanation for the work's popularity. Several of Rowson's other pre-1793 works first published in London were also reprinted in America during the 1790s, but only *Charlotte* became a hit.

The era of publishing based on the reprinting and exchange of British works that developed during the first decades of the new nation reached its highest point of organization early in the nineteenth century when American booksellers from major publishing centers came together to form the American Company of Booksellers, which was responsible for managing a series of at least five book fairs between 1802 and 1805. By this point, cheaper American editions had largely replaced imported editions of standard British works, including novels, a process that was furthered when the Acts of Union of 1801 put an end to the Dublin reprint trade. The fairs fostered the exchange system more or less nationally, and they served not only as a way for booksellers to reach a wider market while enriching their own stocks with those of others, but also as a place for social interaction and financial interchange. But they also encouraged overproduction, especially of hastily or cheaply printed works prepared by country printers who wanted to take part in the trade, and eventually the market became saturated. This result brought an end to the fairs and—with the economic hardships of the embargo, War of 1812, and Panic of 1819—the American publishing trade did not recover fully until the 1820s. Green reports that of the sixty-four publishers who attended the fair in 1803, only thirteen were still active in 1815.

The preceding year, in July 1814, an anonymous work entitled *Waverley* appeared in Edinburgh and London, heralding a series of novels by Walter Scott that would have a profound effect on American readers, authors, and publishers. Before *Waverley* the reading of novels, which were widely associated with sentiment, seduction, and even eroticism, was considered suspect, if not immoral, especially for women. Scott's combination of historical fiction with the romance changed this, and his popularity in America quickly grew widespread. *Waverley* itself was reprinted in 1815 by three American firms, and Scott's subsequent novels were also quickly reprinted and eagerly purchased by American readers. With the economic recovery of the 1820s, the reprinting of Scott intensified. *Ivanhoe*, published in Edinburgh on December 20, 1819, was available in a Philadelphia edition on February 17, 1820, and three more American editions appeared that year, as well as four American editions of the next novel in the series, *The Monastery*. The following year, 1821, *Kenilworth* was issued in six American editions, *Rob Roy* in four, and every one of Scott's earlier novels was reprinted, for a total of at least thirty-one editions.

The competition between American publishers to meet the demand for each new novel by Scott became cutthroat: to be first in the market meant success; to be late could be disastrous for those attempting to sell off their editions in an already glutted market. To get a jump, publishers rushed to get the first copy of a new Scott work off the ship from Britain or plotted to get early sheets, either by purchasing them from Scott's publisher or by bribing workmen in the Edinburgh printing office. Copy was then divided among several printers in order to shorten the time of manufacture—an edition of 3,000 could be turned out in one day. In the end, the competition over the American market for Scott proved ruinous, and in 1826 J. & J. Harper of New York agreed to purchase at cost one-half of the edition of *Woodstock* produced for Carey & Lea of Philadelphia and to issue it with its own title page. Cooperation won out, at least as far as Scott was concerned, and when *Chronicles of the Canongate* appeared in 1827, the Harper issues of the Carey edition listed seven co-publishers in New York, four in Philadelphia, and two in Boston.

As Wayne Franklin has chronicled, James Fenimore Cooper was the American novelist who most benefited from American enthusiasm for Scott. His first work, *Precaution* (1820), written in response to a challenge from his wife, was a novel of manners set in England and had small success. His second, *The Spy: A Tale of the Neutral Ground* (1821), was intentionally modeled on Scott and, with the added appeal of an American setting and theme, was a hit—second and third editions were called for within six months. Perhaps inspired by the financial success that Irving was having with his self-published *The Sketch Book* (1819–20), and despite the statement "Published by A. T. Goodrich & Co." on the title page of *Precaution*, Cooper undertook to publish his early works at his own expense, paying Goodrich or, for *The Spy*, Charles Wiley a 5 percent commission on wholesale sales to manage production and distribution. This gave Cooper full control over the wholesale discounts allowed to the trade and, because his goal was to profit as much as possible from his writing, he allowed on the largest orders—one hundred or more copies—a mere 33 percent and six months credit, where 40 or even 50 percent would have been usual. Firms like Carey & Lea, which supplied the southern market, complained, but demand for Cooper's work forced them to accept these terms.

As his popularity grew with *The Pioneers; or, The Sources of the Susquehanna* (1823) and *The Pilot* (1824), Cooper continued to publish under this same arrangement and attempted to push discounts even lower. He originally planned to publish his fifth novel, *Lionel Lincoln; or, The Leaguer of Boston* (1825), in the same manner but later revised his contract with Wiley. Under the new arrangement, Wiley was to pay Cooper $5,000 for the exclusive right to publish and market the work at his own expense, up to a total of 10,000 copies, for one year. Although it sold over 4,500 copies in six months, Wiley's precarious financial position forced him to assign the remaining copies to Cooper as security for the latter's endorsement on three notes. Thus, when the contract for *The Last of the Mohicans: A Narrative of 1757* (1826) was negotiated, the earlier arrangement was agreed to. Serving as Cooper's agent, Wiley was overseeing the production of 5,000 copies of the new work at his death in January 1826. Within days, Cooper completed arrangements with Carey & Lea to take over the edition and to publish it at their own risk for a period of four years, paying Cooper $5,000 for the privilege. Later that year, Carey & Lea purchased the copyrights to Cooper's five earlier works, as well as to his next one, *The Prairie* (1827), for $7,500. The Philadelphia firm and its successors would remain Cooper's primary American publisher for two decades.

Following the example of Irving again, Cooper was one of the first American authors to attend to the publication of his work abroad. Unauthorized British reprints of American fiction had appeared from time to time for many years, and Cooper's first two novels were indeed pirated in London soon after publication. With Cooper's popularity established, John Murray, who was Irving's London publisher, agreed to take on *The Pioneers* at his own expense, dividing the profits, if any, with the author. This "half-profits" arrangement was standard in England, and under these same terms Cooper arranged with John Miller for the publication of his next three novels in London. As Miller pointed out, the publication of these works involved some risk, as none of these early works were protected by copyright in Great Britain. British law, though it offered protection to the work of foreign authors, also required that a work appear first in Great Britain, a condition that Cooper had not met. After his move to Paris in 1826, Cooper addressed this issue, and that November he signed an agreement with Henry Colburn to provide for £200 a set of early sheets of *The Prairie* (1827) for London publication prior to its appearance elsewhere—in this case, both Paris and New York. Similar arrangements were made with Colburn for *The Red Rover* (1827) and subsequent works. In February 1831, *The Pilot* was reprinted as the first volume in Colburn & Bentley's *Standard Novels* series, published without copyright protection, but for *The Spy*, third in the series, and his other early novels that were subsequently included, Cooper, for a fee of £50 each, prepared new introductions and revised the texts, thus allowing a claim for copyright. Colburn, and later his partner Richard Bentley, remained Cooper's London publishers for the remainder of his life.

The examples of Scott and Cooper set the pattern for the publication of serious novels in the United States until mid-century and beyond. Following Scott's *Waverley*, most novels were published in London in three octavo volumes priced at half a guinea each for a total of £1 11s. 6d. (roughly $7.50). In the United States, these same works, printed in smaller type, would be reduced to two duodecimo volumes, typically priced sixty-two and a half cents or seventy-five cents each for a total of $1.25 or $1.50, though, from about 1850, it became more common for novels to appear in a slightly heftier single volume, priced anywhere from fifty cents to a dollar, but most commonly seventy-five cents. Once an American novelist had established a reputation, the author, or more commonly the publisher of the American edition, would arrange for English copyright and publication, sending early sheets to England for a flat sum and holding back American publication to be simultaneous with or to follow its English publication. After the 1854 decision of the House of Lords in the case of Jefferys *v.* Boosey denied copyright protection to the works of non-resident foreign authors, it was not unusual for an American author to travel briefly to Canada or England in order to establish residence in a British territory on the day of publication.

A number of American novelists began writing in the 1820s, at first issuing their works through various publishers, but during the 1830s the successor firms of the two that in 1826 had brought some order to the republication of Scott's novels in the United States came to dominate American novel publishing. These were the Carey firms of Philadelphia, in various manifestations, and Harper & Brothers in New York. During the 1830s, the Philadelphia firms published not only Cooper and Irving, but also Robert Montgomery Bird and John Pendleton Kennedy; the Harper firm, Henry W. Herbert (Frank Forester) and James Kirke Paulding, among others; Edgar Allan Poe, Catharine Maria Sedgwick, and William Gilmore Simms were published by both.

If by the 1830s the publication of novels by Americans was on the rise, it could hardly be said to predominate. George Palmer Putnam, in the initial issue (Jan. 1834) of his early book trade periodical the *Booksellers' Advertiser*, lists nineteen "novels and tales" by Americans for the entire year of 1833, but gives forty-six entries for such works in a list "American Reprints of Foreign Works" from just July 1833—including the "Complete Works" of Jane Austen (6 titles in 12 vols.) and Miss Edgeworth (9 vols.), as well as two editions in progress of the revised Waverley novels (44 vols. and 24 parts, respectively). For 1834, the *Booksellers' Advertiser* lists nineteen original American "novels and tales" only, compared to ninety-five foreign reprints. The Harper firm, which had started in business as reprinters for the trade, was especially dependent on English novels: of the sixty new works issued in 1830 that are listed in the catalog prepared by William H. Demarest in 1878, at least twenty-six were classified as fiction, not one by an American author. Twenty years later, Harper's record was much the same: of eighty-eight works listed as first issued in 1850, at least thirty-one were classified as fiction, but only four, including Herman Melville's *White Jacket; or, The World in a Man-of-War* (1850), by Americans.

By 1850, the Harper firm was one of the country's largest publishers and, while the number and proportion of English novels on its list may have been exceptional, these figures point to the continuing importance of reprints of foreign works, especially novels, to American publishers. American copyright legislation meant that any American publisher could reprint any foreign work that it chose to, but as the experience with Scott's Waverley novels had proved, cut-throat competition could be ruinous. Accordingly, well before mid-century American publishers had, in order to encourage cooperation, firmed up a set of conventions, referred to as "courtesy of the trade," that established a de facto copyright in the publication of a foreign works, at least in book form. According to these conventions, the first American firm to advertise a work as "in press" was entitled to claim a right in that work, as well as to any subsequent work by the same author. Both claims were considered stronger if the American publisher also made a payment to the foreign publisher, usually for an early set of sheets, or author—the Harper archives contain a separate volume (referred to as the "priority list") that from 1846 recorded such payments, as well as memoranda books that collected clippings of "in press" announcements.

The rhetorically charged discussion in the press over the failure of American copyright law to extend protection to the works of foreign authors often argued that this disadvantaged American authors and held back American literature, but the discussion usually failed to take trade courtesy into account. Payments made under the "trade courtesy" system could be substantial, often approaching or equaling the amount that would have been paid to an American author under a standard contract, in which case there was no economic incentive to prefer foreign works. Nor was it usual for the works of American authors, at least in their first edition, to be priced higher than those of foreign authors. British authors often complained that the lack of an international copyright law robbed them of proper remuneration from American editions, but in at least a few cases they did so without understanding that their English publisher might well have received an advance payment from the United States. Such complaints also seem to misunderstand the economic reality of the American book trade, where novels were often priced at one-tenth the price of the British edition, thus reducing substantially the potential profit to author and publisher alike.

The trade courtesy system worked remarkably well through 1870, and surviving publishers' archives document many examples of two firms that, after inadvertently advertising the publication of the same work, reached a compromise that ceded the right to publish to the firm with the strongest claim under courtesy of the trade. So strongly were these conventions viewed by at least some in the trade that in 1865 the New York publisher Sheldon & Co. went to court in an unsuccessful attempt to establish a legal precedent for its claim to property rights in a collected edition of Charles Dickens's novels under trade courtesy. As Ellen B. Ballou's discussion of the case shows, trade courtesy was widely acknowledged to exist, though how widely or forcefully it was followed was a matter of debate—especially when it came to the works of wildly popular authors such as Dickens. Novels seem to have been particularly vulnerable, and the practice did break down over a few popular works such as Edward Bulwer Lytton's *Rienzi* (1836), Charlotte Brontë's *Jane Eyre* (1848), and Wilkie Collins's *No Name* (1863). Periods of economic downturn also seem to have encouraged unauthorized reprinting of works normally covered by trade courtesy conventions.

The Panic of 1837 was, as James J. Barnes has argued, especially important for introducing a number of innovations in publishing, especially of cheap books. The so-called mammoth weeklies *Brother Jonathan* and the *New World* both first appeared in 1839. Following the pattern pioneered in 1832 by *Waldie's Select Circulating Library*, these periodicals offered a selection of prose and poetry, including serialized novels, in a format designed to take advantage of postal laws that subsidized the distribution of newspapers and serials through the mail. These in turn spawned supplements or extras, which contained the complete text of a novel in a single issue at a price of twelve and a half cents, and sometimes less. Much, if not most, of what was published in these periodicals was of British origin, reprinted without authorization, but American authors were also represented, including Walt Whitman, whose *Franklin Evans; or, The Inebriate* appeared as a *New World* extra in 1842.

During the 1840s, further story papers, such as the *Flag of Our Union* published in Boston by Frederick Gleason's Publishing Hall, proliferated, as did series of cheap, sensational fiction by authors such as Emerson Bennett, J. H. Ingraham, E. Z. C. Judson (Ned Buntline), and George Lippard that were mass-produced and issued in paper covers, much like periodicals. Such works became a continuing feature of American publishing. In 1860, Ann S. Stephen's *Malaeska: The Indian Wife of the White Hunter*, which had first been published serially in three issues of Snowden's monthly *Ladies' Companion* in 1839, was reissued as the first number of the Beadle's Dime Novel series, and the same decade saw the publication of a number of thrillers by Louisa May Alcott, over her pseudonym A. M. Barnard, in Elliott, Thomes & Talbot's Ten Cent Novelette series of Standard American Authors. Many trade publishers, such as Harper & Brothers and Stringer & Townsend in New York, also began to include such cheap editions of fiction, priced at roughly one-half the cost of their regular trade publications, in their lists, counting on increased sales to make up for tighter margins. In Philadelphia, T. B. Peterson & Brothers made a specialty of this type of publication, publishing works by T. S. Arthur, Caroline Lee Hentz, E. D. E. N. Southworth, and others.

The publishers of novels in cheap editions were taking advantage of new technologies that were industrializing book manufacturing, and most of their publications would have been printed on power-driven cylinder printing presses, chiefly designed for newspaper and periodical production, using the larger sheets made possible by paper-making machines. More important than these innovations, however, was the increasingly widespread use of printing plates, at first stereotype and later electrotype, by American publishers. However produced, printing plates stored the text in the form that could be put to press whenever additional copies were required. Plates changed the economy of publishing: although the up-front cost of producing plates roughly doubled the cost of composition, they allowed publishers to keep a work in print over time by producing small press runs to match market demand, thus avoiding the considerable expense of the paper required for large editions and the danger of overproduction.

Introduced in the United States in 1813, stereotype plates had been originally used for standard works, including the Bible, with a proven steady sale. Carey and Lea's original edition of Cooper's *The Prairie*, stereotyped in 1827, was likely the first original novel stereotyped in America. The cost of stereotyping that work ($461), on top of the substantial sum Cooper received for his copyright ($5,000), meant that the first edition of 5,000, which sold at wholesale for $1.50, barely broke even. According to Green's calculations, once these investments were paid for, subsequent editions were particularly profitable, earning the publisher about $1.13 per copy. Small wonder then that the Carey firm proceeded to stereotype each of Cooper's works that it published, as did Harpers for nearly all new works published after the late 1820s. This investment in plates, and the flexibility that their use allowed, supported a number of new publishing practices, all of which depended to some extent on making use of what we now think of as the publisher's backlist. In the late 1820s, the Carey firm began issuing Cooper's novels in a uniform binding with the title *Cooper's Novels* on the spine—the first multivolume, collected edition of the works of a living American literary author. The 1830s saw similar sets of the works of Irving, also published by the Carey firm, and of Paulding, by the Harpers.

The Harper firm, in particular, initiated a number of "libraries," or series, in which, as in the collected editions, the issue or sale of one title encouraged or supported the sale of others. The most famous of these was its *Harper's Family Library*, which was started in 1830 and eventually extended to 187 volumes that retailed for forty-five cents each or eighty dollars for the set. The next year the Harper firm launched its *Library of Select Novels*, which was mostly made up of British reprints but also included Paulding's *Dutchman's Fireside* (1831) and *Westward Ho!* (1832), as well as *Tales of Glauber-Spa* (1832), a collection of American stories edited by William Cullen Bryant. The original *Library of Select Novels* was apparently not a success—its publication was suspended in 1834 with number 36—but the Harpers resumed the series in 1842 in a new octavo format with the text in smaller "brevier" type that was set in two columns, priced at twenty-five cents a number. The revived series contained only foreign works, but a second series of *Pocket Editions of Select Novels*—inaugurated in 1843 with Simms's *The Yemassee* (originally published in 1835)—reprinted a few American works, including most from the original *Library of Select Novels*, in smaller format in wrappers, again priced twenty-five cents. Over the following years at least some American novels were reissued as part of a publisher's series or, occasionally, first published in this way.

For trade publishers, another significant change in book manufacture of the period was the adoption from the late 1820s of cloth publishers' bindings. Although books had always been sold to retail customers in some sort of binding, often of plain sheep or calf leather, before that time books had usually been exchanged between wholesaling booksellers in folded gatherings or perhaps stitched and inserted in a paper wrapper or temporary binding of boards. During the 1820s and 1830s, methods were developed to treat linen or cotton muslin with size to turn it into an acceptable binding material. Treated cloth could also be dyed and grained to create a variety of effects, and methods were developed to decorate bindings with a further design and lettering stamped in gold or blind. Finally, these bindings were constructed in a manner, now referred to as casing, that allowed the folded sheets and the decorated cloth covering to be prepared independently, in quantity, and brought together as the final step in preparing the book for distribution and sale. The result was a cloth-covered binding considered durable enough to be treated as permanent.

This was an important development, for now the publisher—not the wholesaler or retailer—was responsible for the appearance, both inside and out, of the book that reached the customer. The binding design became a way of attracting the customer's attention and, the publisher hoped, convincing the customer to purchase a copy of the work in question. Over time, the style of binding design, and even color and grain of the cloth, was subject to fashion, and publishers spent substantial sums to ensure that their bindings appealed to purchasers. In many cases, the cost of binding came close to equaling the cost of paper, and together these expenses typically made up about 80 percent of the cost of manufacture. Furthermore, because most copies were now offered in a uniform binding, it became feasible to attach a fixed retail price to the entire work, whereas earlier that price would have varied depending on the style and quality of binding on individual copies.

A publisher could now use the binding design to signal the subject matter of a book or to identify it with his firm or as part of a particular series. Thus, copies of Harriet Beecher Stowe's *Uncle Tom's Cabin; or, Life Among the Lowly* (1852) were issued with a vignette scene of a slave cabin—apparently depicting the departure of the runaway slave George Harris—on their covers, whereas copies of Melville's *Moby-Dick; or, The Whale* (1851) signaled the novel's nautical subject matter more subtly with a blind-stamped life preserver. On the other hand, Nathaniel Hawthorne's novels issued by Ticknor and Fields during the 1850s all appeared in that firm's characteristic brown ribbed "T" cloth binding with an acanthus design stamped in blind on the covers; the same binding that was standard for that firm's publications, including the works of other New England authors such as Henry David Thoreau's *Walden; or, Life in the Woods* (1854), Ralph Waldo Emerson's *The Conduct of Life* (1860), and several volumes of John Greenleaf Whittier's poetry.

If cloth publishers' bindings determined the outer appearance of nineteenth-century American books, it was the manner of their distribution that defined the national trade book-publishing system that emerged in the United States during the decades preceding the Civil War. The publishers that participated in this system were to be the major purveyors of most new American novels for years to come. Reaching the market had always posed a problem to American publishers, and that problem intensified through the nineteenth century as the trade-publishing industry concentrated itself in only a few of the largest East Coast cities—Boston, Philadelphia, and, increasingly, New York—while Cincinnati, first, and later Chicago served as western outposts. Meanwhile, the market grew ever-more expansive, as the West was settled and new states joined the Union. Given the size of the United States, one might have expected publishers to develop a series of regional markets, as the periodical trade did for most newspapers and many magazines; instead, by mid-century, trade publishers had succeeded in establishing a national market for their books. Regional publishing did persist on a small scale, but such publications were chiefly of local interest or produced for and at the expense of local authors.

In order to function effectively, this national book-distribution system needed to develop means for managing the transportation of books to buyers from the centers of publication, as well as for the efficient exchange of information and transfer of credit. During the decades before the Civil War, infrastructural and organizational changes to the American economy brought about what has been dubbed a market revolution. Between 1840 and 1860, railway mileage expanded tenfold, from 2,818 to 30,626 miles, then nearly doubled again, to 52,922 miles, by 1870. Perhaps more important were the numerous express companies that, following Harnden & Co.'s establishment in 1841, used transportation networks to manage the shipment of packages from producer to consumer. The Panic of 1837 and its aftermath inspired Lewis Tappan in 1841 to found America's first commercial credit-rating agency, the Mercantile Agency (later to become R. G. Dun & Co.), that sold to businessmen information about the creditworthiness of their customers. The following year, Volney B. Palmer founded the American Newspaper Subscription and Advertising Agency, the nation's first advertising agency. In 1844, Samuel F. B. Morse demonstrated the telegraph to the country's leaders, and by the 1850s the firm that would become the Western Union Telegraph Company was already emerging as the nation's largest domestic carrier.

If such innovations changed American business generally, a number of important developments were specific to the book trade. Key to the national trade book system was the rise of dedicated, independent bookstores in cities and towns across the nation. Most carried a variety of goods in addition to books and stationery, including games, fancy goods, and such things as razors or musical instruments, but identified themselves chiefly as bookstores. With the exception of popular or new books, including fiction, laid out on tables, the book stock in bookstores was chiefly inaccessible to customers, and, it seems, usually shelved by publisher rather than subject. Thus, customers must have relied on clerks not only for advice but also for access to most books, though window displays and posted advertising "shewbills" would have drawn attention to new publications. Though chiefly retail outlets, in many cities and larger towns some of these bookstores also served as wholesale booksellers, supplying books not only to their retail customers but also to local schools, libraries, and nearby country general stores, which might stock a few books where the population could not support a dedicated bookstore.

One important source of stock for these bookstores was the trade sale—special auction sales that were restricted to members of the book trade. The first of these was organized by Henry C. Carey, son of Mathew, and held in Philadelphia in August 1824. Trade sales were also held in New York from 1825, in Boston from 1827, and in Cincinnati from 1838. These trade sales—held regularly twice a year, spring and fall, except for Boston, which held a single sale each summer—brought the trade together as had book fairs at the beginning of century, but with the important difference that the price at which books changed hands was established by a system of bidding that reflected true market value. Furthermore, at the trade sales books were sold for negotiable money, unlike the earlier system involving the exchange of books between publishers that was associated with the book fairs. The trade sale auctioneers thus played an important role in managing the movement of credit through the trade, offering advances to publishers when they submitted their invoices and extending credit to purchasers by accepting their promissory notes. Finally, the trade sales were instrumental in supporting the growing distinction between publishers and booksellers: it was no longer necessary for booksellers to have publications of their own to exchange in order to build up their stock.

By the 1850s, trade sales had become very large indeed. The catalog for the sale managed in March 1856 by Leavittt, Delisser & Co. for the newly formed New York Book-Publishers' Association was 384 pages in length and contained the invoices of 112 publishers. The sale itself took ten days, from eight in the morning until ten at night. According to reports in the *American Publishers' Circular*, over 300 buyers attended: 7,500 volumes of Cooper's works were sold, as were 2,400 copies of Henry Wadsworth Longfellow's popular poem *Song of Hiawatha* (1855). At the same sale, according to the business records of Ticknor and Fields, thirty-two sets of the eight volumes of Hawthorne's "Tales and Romances"—including *The Scarlet Letter: A Romance* (1850), *The House of the Seven Gables: A Romance* (1851), and *The Blithedale Romance* (1852)—from the firm's backlist were also sold, as were one hundred copies each of English novelist Charles Reade's more recently published *Peg Woffington* (1855) and *Christie Johnstone* (1855). This was only one of two trade sales held in New York that March, and purchases at the spring sales were usually smaller than those in the fall.

The emergence in the decades before the Civil War of a group of wholesalers and jobbers in the major centers of publication provided bookstores with another source of stock and supported the emerging national trade book system. These firms, many of which began business under the earlier exchange system, provided different services. Some merely acted as agents, gathering together books that a distant bookseller ordered on their own account from local publishers and packing them into a single box for shipment. Other firms acted as regional agents, carrying the entire list of publishing firms from another place and supplying them to regional booksellers, taking a commission on sales. The largest wholesale firms kept a full inventory of in-print or imported trade books on hand, purchased in quantity at deep discounts, and profited from the smaller discounts that they passed on to bookstores. All these wholesalers were also publishers, and this is how we remember them today. D. Appleton & Co., and John Wiley and George Palmer Putnam—first in partnership, and later separately—in New York; J. B. Lippincott & Co. in Philadelphia; Phillips, Sampson & Co. and later Lee & Shepard in Boston; and S. C. Griggs & Co. in Chicago were all active as wholesale distributors as well as publishers of books. Indeed, the Lippincott firm, which supplied the southern market, was claimed by Henry C. Carey in 1854 to be the largest wholesaler in the world.

These wholesale middlemen were also responsible for the beginnings of systematic communication within the book trade by initiating the publication of trade journals and reference tools. As Ezra Greenspan has chronicled, George Palmer Putnam was a pioneer. As clerk at the New York wholesale firm of Leavitt, Lord & Co., he edited the *Booksellers' Advertiser*, one of the earliest book-trade journals, though it only survived for the single year of 1834. In 1836, he prepared the *American Annual Catalogue*, a classified list of all works available in New York, including six full pages of "novels and tales." During the 1840s, Wiley and Putnam and D. Appleton & Co., both important wholesalers and importers, issued monthly newsletters that listed new publications—these were the beginnings of the systematic trade bibliographical record that would eventually be carried on by *Publishers' Weekly*. In 1849, Orville A. Roorbach, then a clerk with Putnam, published the first volume of his *Bibliotheca Americana*, a catalog of American publications, both original and reprint, issued since 1820. Ten years later, Roorbach issued the earliest surviving directory of American bookstores, his *List of Booksellers in the United States and the Canadas* (1859), containing the names of 3,126 sellers of books in some 1,100 towns across the nation.

By the 1850s, the elements of this trade-publishing system were largely in place, and it would prove remarkably resilient—lasting in its general features through the twentieth century and the advent of internet book sales. While many trade publishers developed specialties in specific genres or subjects, almost all included at least a few novels, American or foreign, on their lists. The enormous success of Stowe's *Uncle Tom's Cabin* may have tested it—about 310,000 copies were produced during its first year in print—but the system was certainly sufficient to enable the publication and marketing of Hawthorne's more steady-selling *The Scarlet Letter* and Maria Cummins's best-selling *The Lamplighter* (1854). By mid-century, American trade publishers had established an effective system for reaching a national market for their publications, including novels.

11

THE PERILS OF AUTHORSHIP: LITERARY PROPERTY AND NINETEENTH-CENTURY AMERICAN FICTION

LARA LANGER COHEN AND MEREDITH L. McGILL

We tend to think of the early nineteenth century as marking the establishment of American authorship, ushering in a new era in which writers coaxed recognition, respect, and in some cases, a livelihood from their pens. But while publishing conditions and emerging ideas of authorship opened up new fields of opportunity for writers, they also presented distinct perils. American writers grappled with the vagaries of literary property in a period before standardized author contracts and international copyright; the difficulties of carving out identities as authors in a democracy where little precedent for such a role existed; and the pressures, as well as the possibilities, of writing at a time in which literature assumed an unparalleled cultural importance. Nineteenth-century authorship presents perils for contemporary literary criticism as well, including the risk of organizing our critical inquiries around an emergent category that has come into focus only retrospectively.

The study of the novel presents a case in point. The genre looms large in classes on antebellum literature and has probably done the most to cement our ideas about authorship during the period. Aside from the stalwart James Fenimore Cooper, however, those novelists who enjoyed the most success in their own time are seldom read today. When was the last time a teacher assigned Theodore Sedgwick Fay's *Norman Leslie: A Tale of the Present Times* (1835)? William Gilmore Simms's *The Yemassee: A Romance of Carolina* (1835)? Emerson Bennett's *The League of the Miami* (1851)? Ann S. Stephens's *Malaeska: The Indian Wife of the White Hunter* (1860)? Despite its tendency to dominate our canons of nineteenth-century literature, the American novel hardly dominated antebellum literary culture. Of the sixty-eight authors Rufus Wilmot Griswold profiled in his 1847 *The Prose Writers of America*, only fifteen had ever written a novel (and several of those, including

Henry Wadsworth Longfellow, Edgar Allan Poe, and Charles Fenno Hoffman, were more famous as poets, writers of tales, or editors). In his analysis of the 1840–1841 inventory of Homer Franklin's New York City bookstore, Ronald J. Zboray has shown that "novels on the average accounted for only about 4.3 percent of the total value of all books in the store—far, far less than in modern counterparts." Given the numerous other genres represented, this is certainly "a significant amount," Zboray concedes, but it "lends little support to the idea that there was a 'mania' for novels" (1993, 140). Moreover, of the novels that Franklin did stock, the vast majority were British. Most interesting of all, Zboray finds that the very identity of the novel as a genre was more fluid than we might assume. Analyzing the frequency with which books of any given genre were grouped together (signaling that they shared a common classification), he concludes that novels "probably had the weakest identities as clearly recognizable, specific, and separate" (1993, 153). Indeed, novels as such are not named as one of the major generic categories in the list of works on hand at the time of the disastrous Harper & Brothers fire in December 1853; they are subsumed within the category of "General Literature." Although the number of works published by the Harpers in "General Literature" (690) vastly exceeded titles in "History and Biography" (329), "Educational" (156), "Travel and Adventure" (130), and "Theology and Religion" (120), this is largely due to the vigorous transatlantic reprint trade: "General Literature" is the only category in which reprints outnumber original productions, and by a ratio of 2:1 (Exman 1965, 358). These complexities do not obviate the study of either authorship or the novel; rather, they urge us to approach these topics with new energy and nuance. What does antebellum authorship look like, if not a triumphant success? What do the legal and socioeconomic constraints that shaped it do *for* the American novel?

Intellectual Property and the Culture of Reprinting

American novelists' fictions, their careers, and their understanding of the limits and possibilities of their vocation were profoundly affected by the new nation's disposition of intellectual property rights. Section 8 of the US Constitution granted Congress the power "to promote the Progress of Science and useful Arts, by securing for limited Times to Authors and Inventors the exclusive Right to their respective Writings and Discoveries," justifying this conferral of limited monopoly rights through an enlightenment appeal to usefulness and progress. Defining copyright as a federal right ensured that American authors and publishers could control the distribution of their books across the vast expanse of the republic, removing formidable barriers to interstate trade. Copyrights were a source of national pride and national identity, and many authors and publishers were eager to take advantage of their protection.

And yet historical and structural unevenness in the conferral of these rights limited their effectiveness and helped determine the distinctive character of American publishing. The first copyright statute (Copyright Act of 1790) granted a federal right to American authors and publishers long before the development of a national trade system. The decentralization of American publishing—its dispersal across multiple, regional print centers—meant that, until mid-century, a national market for books was more a fantasy than a reality, making copyright a questionable tool for nation building. Where the distribution of books is a challenge, the right to control circulation by restricting copying is of limited value. Many of the texts that circulated most widely in the new republic, such as newspapers, magazines, tracts, and pamphlets, did so without the protection of copyright. Moreover, the same law that granted copyrights to citizens and residents denied such rights to foreign authors, bestowing on American publishers the right to republish foreign texts without restriction. The new nation's cultural dependency on Europe—its appetite for imported books and for cheap reprints of foreign works—and the profits to be made in an uncertain, expanding market by publishing texts that had already proven popular with readers produced a literary marketplace that was suffused with foreign texts.

The circulation of popular novels often soared when copyright restrictions were removed and print monopolies broken. As William St. Clair has noted, when perpetual common law copyright was overturned in Great Britain in 1774, British editions of Daniel Defoe's *Robinson Crusoe* (1719) greatly expanded from a handful of authorized editions in the "high monopoly period" to numerous competing editions, abridgements, and rewritings after 1774 (2004, 507). In the nineteenth century, this effect was compounded by transatlantic publishers who regularly experimented with reprinting already-established fiction in a variety of inexpensive formats, hoping to reach new readers. The American refusal to award copyrights to foreign authors proved a boon for the circulation of British novels, which, in many cases, first achieved mass-readership outside the boundaries of Great Britain. For instance, Clarence S. Brigham has noted over a hundred editions of *Robinson Crusoe* published in America between 1774 and 1830. Boston, New York, and Philadelphia publishers famously competed to be the first to reprint Sir Walter Scott's *Waverley* novels (1814–28), setting type as soon as packet ships carrying the latest novel arrived on the docks. Reprinting foreign novels was crucial to the growth of the American print trades and for cultivating the habit of novel reading within a broadly literate public. Indeed, the success of the *Waverley* series helped American publishers establish the size of the market for popular novels. The competition to capture market share led publishers such as Carey & Lea of Philadelphia and Harper & Brothers in New York to develop more efficient and ambitious printing and distribution systems, paying Scott and his publisher for advance sheets of the novels and nurturing contacts with booksellers in far-flung southern and western cities.

By the 1840s, American authors and some publishers began to push for the passage of an international copyright law. The literary nationalist movement propelled the cause by insisting that the prevalence of foreign reprints would prevent American writers from ever realizing their powers. In 1843, poet and editor William Cullen Bryant was elected president of the American Copy-Right Club, which convened meetings and published manifestoes in favor of an international agreement. Cornelius Mathews, one of the movement's most fervent proponents, felt so strongly about international copyright that he made the issue a subplot in one of his many attempts to create an "indigenous" American work, the 1845 novella *Big Abel and the Little Manhattan*. The main plot follows the two title characters—the great-grandson of Henry Hudson and the great-grandson of the Native American chief who sold Manhattan to the Dutch—as they travel around the city, dividing up the parts to which they are entitled. Most of the story accordingly consists of a panoramic view of New York and a minutely described account of the streets, people, food, and drink found there. But everywhere Big Abel and the Little Manhattan go, they coincidentally meet the "Poor Scholar," a young author who has recently written a wonderful book but whose publishers keep deferring publication in order to reprint texts from England, France, and Germany for free, leaving the Poor Scholar distraught and unable to marry his sweetheart. While *Big Abel and the Little Manhattan*'s copyright subplot hardly advances the story, it offers a mirror image of the main plot. Both revolve around the protection of original property—whether national literature or Native American land rights—from foreign incursions. The awkward shoehorning of the Poor Scholar subplot into the narrative testifies to Mathews's devotion to the cause of international copyright. Yet it also reveals something of the effort it took to make the case for American literary property at this moment. Conflating literary originality with aboriginality, Mathews's subplot strains at once to naturalize literary originality and to make it a recognizably national cause.

In spite of the efforts of Mathews and his colleagues in favor of international copyright, changes to the law were resisted by tradesmen, chief among them newly unionized typographers, who worried that such a law would give London publishers too much power over the American market. When literary nationalists protested that American authors could not compete with the flood of cheap reprints of popular British novels, members of the print trades responded with a canny analysis of the politics of book distribution, arguing that, with the backing of an international copyright law, heavily capitalized London publishers could potentially print off large American editions from British-made plates, greatly benefiting from economies of scale. Opponents of the law argued that international copyright would enable London publishers to supply books to the American market at high prices without the risk of underselling, maintaining a stranglehold on American reading. Reprint publishers contrasted the democratizing virtues of the frequent resetting of type with the dangers of centralized media, arguing that reprinting allowed for local control over the circulation of print and for a more equitable distribution of profits. In their view, multiple American editions of foreign works were not excessive or inefficient, but proof of the general diffusion of knowledge and the benefits of competition between and among small-entrepreneur publishers. While supporters of an international copyright law chiefly sought to bring order to the transatlantic book trade, opponents defended a system that served the publishers of newspapers, magazines and pamphlets, as well as books. Reprinting occurred across a variety of formats: poetry and tales that were first published in expensively bound gift books reappeared as filler in local newspapers; entire novels were closely printed in double columned pages and sold for as little as twelve and a half cents; and elite British magazines were reprinted in their entirety or mined for essays that were reassembled into regionally published, eclectic magazines.

While American opposition to internal copyright was successful in blocking proposed laws and treaties, it did not prevent the consolidation of publishers' power. Faced with potentially ruinous undercutting, reprint publishers developed a system of de facto copyright known as "courtesy of the trade," in which a newspaper announcement of the intent to publish a foreign work informally carried the weight of a property claim. This kind of gentlemanly agreement enabled reprint publishers to invest considerable sums in stereotyped editions of foreign authors' collected works without the threat of competition. Publishers secured informal rights to foreign texts by advertising their association with a particular author and by voluntarily sending payments to foreign authors (or their publishers) to establish goodwill, to obtain advance sheets of their books, and for the right to produce authorized editions. Such extralegal arrangements, enforced by campaigns of retaliation when printers broke with the custom of voluntary restraint, continued to regulate the reprint trade throughout this period despite the fact that they were unenforceable at law.

Authorized editions, complete with frontispiece portraits and facsimile signatures, became a popular way for reprint publishers to distinguish their editions. Other publishers resorted to economic tactics, attempting to discourage rivals by saturating the market with editions at every conceivable price point. Philadelphia publisher T. B. Peterson & Brothers, for example, advertised thirteen different octavo editions of Charles Dickens's works bound in seven different styles, two different illustrated editions, and a "People's Duodecimo," available in eight different binding styles; prices ranged from nine to seventy-five dollars for a complete set. Reprinting also conferred a new kind of value on illustrations. While type could easily be reset, engravings were more difficult and expensive to reproduce, enabling publishers to secure property in their texts by investing heavily in ornamental plates, a practice that Hugh Amory has called "proprietary illustration" (1993, 137). While this practice distinguished particular editions from one another, it blurred the novel generically, as it came to resemble more closely the heavily illustrated gift books, magazines, and weekly newspapers that were so popular during the period.

The profits to be made through authorized or unauthorized reprinting of British novels were substantial, so long as rivals could be kept at bay. During the depression of 1837–43, weekly newspapers such as *Brother Jonathan* (1842–43) and the *New World* (1840–45) engaged in cutthroat competition, reprinting popular British novels and French novels in translation on enormous folio newspaper sheets and in quarto size as "extra issues," sold to enhance circulation of the periodicals. These newspaper supplement-novels were printed in the tens of thousands, hawked on street corners, and circulated at favorable rates through the mail. While competition from better-capitalized book publishers and changes to the postal code ultimately brought an end to the cheap weeklies, they successfully demonstrated the viability of cheap printing on a massive scale—aiming for narrow profit margins on high-volume sales—in a widely literate and expanding nation.

On his 1842 tour of the United States, Dickens was both thrilled and horrified to discover the extent to which unauthorized reprints of his novels had preceded him. Dickens had included the humble and oppressed in his novels as objects of sympathy, but cheap American reprints of his fiction enabled the poor to be drawn into the orbit of literary culture as actual or potential readers. Dickens was warmly welcomed by his American audience: statesmen and literati organized lavish banquets in his honor, and every stage of his trip was covered obsessively by local newspapers. But the tour became something of a public relations disaster because Dickens's insistence on speaking publicly on behalf of an international copyright law was met with incredulity and suspicion. Dickens seemed unaware that he owed much of his popularity to the system of reprinting he continued publicly to attack, while many Americans interpreted his advocacy of international copyright as mercenary and ungrateful. Dickens's encounter with his American readers left him with an acute sense of vulnerability to the mass public that sought to embrace him. Although in advocating foreign authors' rights, Dickens thought he was championing both his own cause and that of American novelists crowded out of the market by foreign competition, reprinting did not simply hinder the growth of the American novel. Even as reprint publishers, such as Harper & Brothers, built substantial enterprises publishing uncopyrighted texts, they began to make different kinds of investments in the American works that, thanks to copyright, they controlled outright.

Copyright and the American Novel, at Home and Abroad

In weighing the influence of copyright on the American novel, it helps to get beyond simple oppositions between domestic and foreign works, legitimate and pirated texts, and the needs of authors and those of publishers to consider how the uneven distribution and enforcement of intellectual property rights shaped the literary marketplace as a whole. After all, American novelists were affected by the culture of reprinting whether or not their work was itself reprinted. From the perspective of print format, for instance, American authors navigated a literary marketplace characterized by an unusually intimate relationship between novels and periodicals. At times the two were materially indistinguishable, as in the case of newspaper supplement-novels such as Edward Bulwer Lytton's *Zanoni* (1842) and Walt Whitman's *Franklin Evans; or, The Inebriate* (1842). But even novels published by major publishing houses depended for their circulation on the climates of opinion and networks of readers created by periodicals; both Harper & Brothers (*Harper's Monthly Magazine*) and G. P. Putnam's Sons (*Putnam's Monthly Magazine of American Literature, Science, and Art*) started magazines in the early 1850s to build demand for their books through serialization, advertising, and the cultivation of a loyal readership.

Most antebellum American novelists published for a significant part of their careers in newspapers and magazines. Throughout the nineteenth century, periodicals had significantly larger circulations than books, and many managed to pay authors enough to make writing for magazines worthwhile as a prelude, adjunct to, or substitute for book publication. Edgar Allan Poe noted that American authors' poor prospects in the book market created a bonanza for literary periodicals: "The want of an International Copy-Right Law, by rendering it nearly impossible to obtain anything from the booksellers in the way of remuneration for literary labor, has had the effect of forcing many of our very best writers into the service of the Magazines and Reviews" (Feb. 1845, 103). Nathaniel Hawthorne, Herman Melville, Harriet Beecher Stowe, and Fanny Fern all moved (with differing degrees of agility, canniness, and resentment) between book and periodical publishing. Significantly, none of the author-figures who appear in mid-nineteenth-century American novels are themselves novelists: Holgrave in *The House of the Seven Gables: A Romance* (1851) writes sketches and gothic tales for ladies' magazines, while the heroine of *Ruth Hall: A Domestic Tale of the Present Time* (1855) writes, like Fern, for weekly newspapers. The eponymous hero of Melville's *Pierre; or, The Ambiguities* (1852) is a renowned poet who fails to publish his novel manuscript. Yet, even as periodical publishing helped make authorship a viable profession, its conventions ensured that authorial identity was less stable, and less in the control of authors and publishers, than we often assume. Hawthorne's early short stories, most of which were published pseudonymously in gift books and monthly magazines, were easily mistaken for Catharine Maria Sedgwick's, while Poe's "The Fall of the House of Usher" (1839), reprinted without acknowledgment in a London monthly magazine, was later republished in the *Boston Notion* (Sept. 5, 1840) under a heading that suggested British authorship: "From Bentley's Miscellany for August."

The culture of reprinting thus complicates our sense of the novel's role in American literary history, as well as emergent conceptions of authorial identity the novel is often seen to anchor. It also complicates our understanding of what made American novels American. Despite the protests of Mathews and others, British publications did not so much crowd American works out of the market as shift the ways in which they were read, as the reprint history of "The Fall of the House of Usher" attests. Even the staunchest literary nationalist addressed readers whose tastes were whetted by reprinted foreign novels and who were carefully attuned to the opinions of the European literary press. American literary culture took many of its cues from British magazines such as the *Edinburgh Review*, the *Quarterly Review*, *Blackwood's Magazine*, and the *Westminster Review*, which were reprinted both in whole and in part, excerpted and reshuffled by literary miscellanies such as *Littell's Living Age* and the *Eclectic Magazine*. The ready availability to ordinary American readers of essays from these elite British journals created a climate of reception for the novel that was acutely dependent on foreign opinion. In a biographical essay praising Poe's critical acumen, James Russell Lowell fulminated that "before we have an American literature, we must have an American criticism" (Feb. 1845, 49). But American novelists understood that they wrote for a dual audience, and that success with American readers could best be achieved by way of a positive British review, which was certain to be eagerly reprinted in the United States. For this reason, American novelists tended to complain less than their British counterparts about the unauthorized reprinting of their novels abroad.

Although, for much of the nineteenth century, American publishers were caricatured as ruthless pirates, British and European publishers also derived great benefit from the lack of international copyright. French publishers Galignani and Baudry, who specialized in providing British tourists with cheap editions of the latest London books, reprinted numerous novels by James Fenimore Cooper, themselves often copied from British reprints. Beginning in 1841, German publisher Bernhard Tauchnitz published hundreds of volumes of British and American works in a numbered series for circulation throughout the Continent, paying authors nominal sums for the right to advertise such volumes as an "author's edition" or a "copyright edition." Many authors considered having a novel reprinted by Tauchnitz to be a mark of international recognition. The standardized, plain style of Tauchnitz volumes made them easily recognizable across Europe; the series was a hallmark of affordability, portability, and literary quality. The Tauchnitz series, as well as British railway reprint series such as Henry Bohn's "Standard Library," launched in 1846, and George Routledge's "Railway Library" (1848–98), helped modern novels gain acceptance as "standard literature," signaling an inverse relationship between literary value and material value that readers occasionally sought to overcome. For instance, although it was no more than a cheap reprint, the Tauchnitz edition of Hawthorne's *The Marble Faun; or, The Romance of Monte Beni* (1860) was frequently rebound by Italian booksellers as a keepsake, which included numerous photographs of artworks and landmarks mentioned in Hawthorne's Rome, as well as blank pages on which tourists could paste photos they had purchased or taken on their trip.

Perhaps the most telling example of the influence of transatlantic reprinting concerns the American publishing sensation of the century, Stowe's *Uncle Tom's*

Cabin; or, Life Among the Lowly (1852). Stowe's novel was a runaway bestseller in the United States, with over 300,000 copies sold in the first year of publication, but its domestic sales paled next to the novel's success in Great Britain, where over a million copies were reportedly sold within a year of publication. The circulation of *Uncle Tom's Cabin* in Britain far exceeded that of Scott's or Dickens's novels, and its quick translation into numerous European languages was taken as a sign of the persuasiveness and power of the abolitionist cause. In the case of *Uncle Tom's Cabin*, the novel's British success formed one of the foundations of its American reputation. Moreover, it prompted a sea change in the domestic politics of copyright. In the wake of Stowe's wildly successful 1853 tour of Great Britain, the *United States Review*, which had, under its earlier, better-known title, the *Democratic Review*, vigorously opposed international copyright on protectionist grounds, suddenly threw its support behind the measure. From an economic standpoint, the enthusiastic reception of Stowe's novel abroad made it newly plausible that American authors and publishers might profit from access to the British market. But this influential partisan monthly magazine was mostly concerned about how reprinting, and the transatlantic print culture it sustained, might affect the domestic struggle over slavery. In an August 1853 editorial, the *United States Review* argued that the adoption of an international copyright law might help arrest abolitionists' growing influence on American readers. The political threat of transatlantic abolition suddenly seemed more important than the need to support small-entrepreneur printers or to preserve a decentralized literary marketplace. The reception history of *Uncle Tom's Cabin* not only testifies to the international dimensions of national literary celebrity, but it also reminds us that the nineteenth-century push for tighter controls over intellectual property was motivated by concerns beyond authors' rights and national reputation.

Literary Nationalism and Literary Fraudulence

When antebellum writers did attempt to carve out an authentic national tradition, they faced a host of accusations that their efforts were manufacturing a sham American literature. The perils of authorship, in other words, were not confined to the socioeconomic conditions that made it difficult for American authors to establish and maintain an audience; they also lay in the emerging definition of "American authorship" itself. In a review of Lambert Wilmer's satirical poem, *The Quacks of Helicon* (1841), Poe concluded that American literature amounted to nothing less than "one vast perambulating humbug" (1984a, 1006). He scoffed:

> Should the opinions promulgated by our press at large be taken, in their wonderful aggregate, as an evidence of what American literature absolutely is, (and it may be said that, in general, they are really so taken,) we shall find ourselves the

> most enviable set of people upon the face of the earth. Our fine writers are legion. Our very atmosphere is redolent of genius; and we, the nation, are a huge, well-contented chameleon, grown pursy by inhaling it. (1010)

His friend Lowell agreed. "We are farthest from wishing to see what many so ardently pray for—namely, a *National* literature," Lowell observed. "But we do long for a *natural* literature" (1843, 1). His much-quoted 1848 satire, *A Fable for Critics,* skewered the reigning confusion between the two, blaming critics for nationalist puffery:

> With you every year a whole crop is begotten,
> They're as much of a staple as corn is, or cotton;
> Why, there's scarcely a huddle of log-huts and shanties
> That has not brought forth its own Miltons and Dantes;
> I myself know ten Byrons, one Coleridge, three Shelleys,
> Two Raphaels, six Titians, (I think) one Apelles,
> Leonardos and Rubenses plenty as lichens,
> One (but that one is plenty) American Dickens,
> A whole flock of Lambs, any number of Tennysons. (72–73)

Lowell's list of critical darlings lampoons one of the most telling paradoxes of literary nationalists' obsession with originality: the highest compliment paid to American writers was to give them the names of European masters. Thus Cooper became the "American Scott," Lydia Sigourney the "American Hemans," and eternal laughingstock Mathews the self-appointed "American Dickens." (Even Young America, literary nationalism's umbrella movement, borrowed its name from the revolutionary examples of Young Ireland, Young Germany, and Young Italy.) Furthermore, Lowell's pastoral setting, full of "log-huts and shanties" in which these authors and artists grow like "crops" and "lichens," becomes ironized as he juxtaposes it with the artifice of a manufactured literary culture. Nationalism here appears quite literally unnatural, an impossible profusion of American genius. Others took Lowell's concerns one step further, depicting American literature as not just unnatural but horribly supernatural. The anonymous author of an article in the *American Review* titled "Literary Phenomena" pictured American literature as the living dead:

> A newspaper reputation can be made in a day, and by pickling and ordinary care may be made to last like the gravedigger's tanner, "some eight year or nine year," or it may be caught like the mesmerized M. Valdemar *in articulo mortis,* by a special conjuror six months longer, till it falls to pieces, "a nearly liquid mass of loathsome, detestable putrescence." (Oct. 1846, 406)

In memorably grotesque terms, "Literary Phenomena" predicts the inevitable dissolution of a moribund literature artificially animated by the exertions of the press.

Moreover, it demonstrates once again the ease with which texts circulated free of their authors, for the writer borrows his assessment of American literature—without citing his source—from Poe's "The Facts in the Case of M. Valdemar" (1845), which had been published in the *American Review* ten months earlier. In its appropriation of Poe's story, "Literary Phenomena" thus testifies at once to the practical difficulty of establishing an authorial reputation (Poe's name is eclipsed by the sensational demise of one of his characters) and to the perils generated by the unstable nature of American authorship, which subjected those who wished to promote it to charges of fraudulence.

Marginalized Authors and the Problem of Originality

While all American writers faced the obstacles of uncertain markets, unstable identities, and accusations of fraudulence, the perils of authorship nonetheless hounded some writers more than others. Especially as literary culture became increasingly centralized, women writers, writers of color, working-class writers, and those outside the northeastern publishing centers were often portrayed as being incapable of true originality. The categorization of some classes of authors as more fraudulent than others helped to stratify a rapidly expanding literary field. Yet writers who were seen as particularly dubious did not always seek to avoid authorship's perils. At times they embraced them, taking advantage of the uncertain conditions of literary production to carve out new possibilities for themselves. The career of novelist and newspaper columnist Fanny Fern, the pen name of Sara Payson Willis, offers one striking instance of the unexpected potential of literary fraudulence. Fern's detractors dismissed her writing as grossly contrived, but her fans devoured her writings in the *New York Ledger*, where she was the highest paid columnist of her time. Readers made her novel *Ruth Hall* a runaway bestseller; enthusiastically named waltzes, boats, and children after her; and made her true identity the subject of heated debate. Fern periodically found her literary property under attack, and her newspaper columns complain of imitators on the page, in photographs, and even on the lecture circuit. More often, however, she played havoc with the very idea of "true" authorial identity. "I'm a regular 'Will o' the Wisp;' everything by turns, and nothing long. Sometimes I'm an old maid, then a widow, now a Jack, then a Gill, at present a 'Fanny.' If there's anything I abominate it's *sameness*. . . . That's *what* I am, and as to the '*who*,' I'm rather mystified *myself*, on *that* point. Sometimes I think, and then again I don't know!!" she announced (Mar. 1852, n. p.). While many writers used pseudonymy as a means of protecting private selfhood, Fern immersed herself in its fictitiousness: she signed her letters to friends and family "Fanny Fern," her husband called her "Fanny," and when she died, her gravestone at Mt. Auburn Cemetery bore only the inscription "Fanny Fern." Playing with notions of originality throughout her career, Fern confronts us with the prospect of a writer who, when widely condemned for her artifice, responded by enthusiastically exploiting it.

Fern built her reputation writing for newspapers, a publishing format whose antebellum conventions were as likely to destabilize notions of authorship as to strengthen them. But Fern also published *Ruth Hall*, a *Künstlerroman* (artist-hero novel) of equal parts pathos and sarcasm that possessed unmistakable parallels to her own life. We might expect a novel, and particularly one in which the heroine prevails over poverty, sickness, misuse, and the iniquities of the literary marketplace, to promote the ideal of individual authorship. Yet for all its emphatic narrative of self-fulfillment, *Ruth Hall* confounds these expectations. First, it evinces little of the formal unity we tend to associate with the novel. Indeed, it reads much more like a newspaper. Rather than knitting together its parts, the novel ricochets between scenes and narrative perspectives without warning, so that the cumulative effect resembles the newspaper's juxtaposition of multiple stories. Its chapters are extremely short (usually only a page or so in length) and often internally broken up with blank spaces, contributing to the impression that they are a collection of newspaper columns. Moreover, in the book that bears her name, in which she figures as the main character and whose plot revolves around her literary celebrity, Ruth has surprisingly little voice. Instead, Fern unfolds her story through the numerous characters who surround Ruth, from her cruel in-laws to her lecherous fellow boarders to the editors, critics, publishers, and booksellers who thwart her literary efforts. Oddly enough for a book about a writer, we never see Ruth's writing. We only hear others' opinions of it, in numerous reported conversations on the subject and in the stacks of letters that, under the pen-name "Floy," she receives from her readers, which are "reproduced" in full. Against expectations, *Ruth Hall* turns out to look very little like a novel, and it shifts attention away from the novelist-as-originator to the field of reception—the institutions, communities, and individuals through which her writing circulates.

If *Ruth Hall* proves surprisingly resistant to the generic conventions of the novel, as well as to the version of authorship it appears to consolidate, the book's reception tells us something about the stakes of this resistance. Although *Ruth Hall* was enormously popular, reviewers were largely unimpressed. Many reviewers repeated familiar complaints about Fern's derivativeness as an author, accusing the novel of simply piecing together well-worn conventions, making it as false as a "glittering string of inflamed paste." Yet, just as this same *Southern Quarterly Review* critic denounces the book for being wholly "extrinsic," he also maintains that it discloses a (distasteful) interiority: "How much of auto-biography may be found in the work, we know not, inasmuch as we have no inkling of who is meant by the vegetable pseudonym of 'Fanny Fern.' But there must be much self-infusion in the book, or even inspired mediocrity could not have so completely forgotten and merged the woman Ruth in the authoress Floy" (Apr. 1855, 449). Fern's reviewers turned their critical gaze on her person so persistently that it became a running feature of her

New York Ledger columns, where she lamented, "What a pity when editors review a woman's book, that they so often fall into the error of reviewing the woman instead" (May 1868, 8). Fern sees this "error" as a symptom of professional jealousy, but it may be as wishful as it is vengeful, for calling attention to the figure of the author keeps at bay Fern's more unsettling mode of literary production, which played fast and loose with authorial identity.

For the African American novelists who began to publish after mid-century, authorship held its own set of dangers. In many ways, the novel as a genre offered great opportunities to African American writers. By mid-century, novels were becoming increasingly important forces for political change, and the opportunity they offered for the creation of entire fictive worlds also afforded African American writers significantly greater scope than the documentary genres in which their writing was often corralled by abolitionist sponsors and promoters. Yet, in other ways, the novel was a problematic genre for African American writers. Authors of slave narratives, probably the most widely read genre of antebellum African American writing, faced enormous pressure to prove their veracity, as the customary barrage of documentation from white supporters demonstrates. The suspicions that dogged writing by all African Americans, and former slaves in particular, made the concept of an African American novel almost unthinkable, a logical blind alley that helps explain why only four known novels by African Americans had appeared in print by 1860: William Wells Brown's *Clotel; or, The President's Daughter* (1853), Frank J. Webb's *The Garies and Their Friends* (1857), Harriet Wilson's *Our Nig; or, Sketches from the Life of a Free Black* (1859), and the first part of Martin Delany's serialized *Blake; or, The Huts of America* (1859, 1861–62). The climate of reception for African American writing in the United States perhaps also explains why the first two of these novels were published in London, while the third languished in obscurity. Although most nineteenth-century readers could readily envision African Americans lying, this racist assumption, which cast their inventiveness as pathological rather than artistic, seems to have left little room to imagine them crafting a deliberate work of literary fiction.

The challenges the novel presented for African American authors appear nowhere so clearly as in Brown's *Clotel,* the work generally cited as the first novel by an African American author. Despite the book's claim to fame, its classification as a *novel* proves at odds with the literary mode of *Clotel* itself, which defies the originality, unified plot, narrative voice, and self-containment we have come to expect of the form, and traffics instead in quotation, fragmentation, and iteration. Indeed, it makes little sense to speak of Brown's novel as a single text. In the fourteen years following *Clotel*'s first publication, Brown would reproduce it in three different versions—as the serialized *Miralda; or, The Beautiful Quadroon* (1860–61), as *Clotelle: A Tale of the Southern States* (1864), and as *Clotelle; or, The Colored Heroine* (1867). Even if one confines oneself to the 1853 *Clotel,* the novel proves no less various. Eschewing a strong, unifying narrative voice, Brown instead borrows freely from a host of other texts: abolitionist poetry, Lydia Maria Child's short story "The Quadroons" (1842), Grace Greenwood's poem "The Leap from the Long Bridge" (1851), slave laws, Englishman John Relly Beard's biography of Haitian revolutionary Toussaint L'Ouverture, anonymous newspaper articles, and his own previous writings. Furthermore, rather than creating a stand-alone fictive world, Brown interweaves his story with historical facts and figures. *Clotel*'s textual clutter raises a confounding literary historical question: why is this landmark in the history of the African American novel almost unrecognizable as a novel?

Brown's apparent lack of authorial control over *Clotel* often baffles or frustrates modern readers, but we might better understand it as evidence of Brown's predicament: in order to create the fully fledged imaginative world of a novel, he had to forego the role of author and assume a role closer to that of editor. We begin to glimpse this dynamic in *Clotel*'s first chapter, "The Negro Sale," which introduces the main characters, Currer and her daughters Clotel and Althesa, and sets in motion the separation that will propel the plot. Yet this storytelling work is deferred as Brown turns away from fiction toward history, launching into a lengthy disquisition on slavery's destruction of families that assembles quotations from former Secretary of State Henry Clay and Virginia statesman John Randolph, statistical proof of extensive race mixture, and examples of slave laws and rulings from southern Christian organizations. When Currer, Clotel, and Althesa finally appear five pages into the novel, Brown does not introduce them himself but secondhand, through a newspaper advertisement for a slave auction that he quotes in full. In his distinctly un-novelistic aversion to narration, Brown cedes textual authority to other sources, constructing his own argument by drawing out dissonances among them.

Clotel offers yet another example of the instability of antebellum authorship, but its long bibliographic history also documents the eventual consolidation of authorship as a surer organizing principle for literary culture. By the time Brown revised *Clotel* into the 1860–1861 *Miralda*, the novel had largely shed its textual heterogeneity—the snatches of poetry, plagiarized passages, and quotations from legal rulings and recorded history that once peppered it. This revision foregrounds Brown's narrative voice, a transformation that would continue in the 1864 and 1867 revisions. In these versions, for example, the main characters do not enter through the mediation of the auction advertisement but are (promptly) introduced by the narrator himself, without *Clotel*'s lengthy detour through historical facts about slavery. Once again, these changes highlight the importance of print format in the literary history of the novel, for although we tend to use the term "novel" as if it were interchangeable with "book," the changes that make *Clotel* more recognizable as a novel begin with its adaptation for a newspaper, probably under the pressure to maintain focus and narrative momentum that came with weekly serialization. More broadly, the transformation of *Clotel* points us toward larger transformations in the meaning of authorship, as the more prominent authorial role Brown is able to assume in the 1860s indicates both the beginnings of a shift in racialized expectations for literature and the increasing cultural legitimacy of the concept of authorship itself.

Mastering Authorship, Managing Markets

The radical expansion of publishing in the post–Civil War era brought a number of changes to the intersecting histories of literary property and literary nationalism, changes that had consequences for how authors understood their profession. As publishing in the United States grew from a gentlemanly business into an industry, written contracts and the intervention of literary agents between authors and publishers became more common. Popular essayist Gail Hamilton's dispute with James T. Fields over royalty payments, chronicled in excruciating detail in Hamilton's *A Battle of the Books* (1870), serves as one index of this shift. Fields had quietly switched from paying Hamilton royalties as a fixed percentage of her sales to paying a fixed rate per volume sold, a change that insured that, as book prices rose, the author's profits became a smaller percentage of the whole. Hamilton's satirical public account of their dispute broke with the decorum of authorial subservience in matters of business and signaled the eclipse of the informal arrangements that were characteristic of antebellum publishing.

In the late nineteenth century, American authorship became both more professionalized and potentially more profitable. William Cullen Bryant helped to revive authorial interest in pressing for changes in the copyright law, founding the Copyright Association for the Protection and Advancement of Literature and Art in 1868. This time, authors' arguments on behalf of an international copyright agreement found more receptive soil. For most of the nineteenth century, international copyright was governed by a patchwork of bilateral treaties, allowing for considerable experimentation in the interstices of these agreements. But the mounting numbers of international copyright treaties—Great Britain signed reciprocal copyright agreements with a number of German states in 1844; with Prussia in 1846; with France, Belgium, and Spain in 1852; and with a number of Italian states between 1861 and 1870—made the United States' refusal to enter such arrangements begin to seem anomalous. By the 1880s, the tide was turning in favor of an international copyright agreement of some sort. In 1878, the British Copyright Commission tendered a blistering report on the obscurity and inconsistency of British law, strongly recommending that Great Britain accept American protectionist demands that copyrighted foreign works be manufactured in America. Harper & Brothers, a firm that had long been a staunch opponent of international copyright, responded to this report by drafting treaty conditions that became the focal point of the American campaign for changes to the law.

American law lagged behind American culture when it came to acknowledging authorship as a principle of textual regulation. It would take until 1891 for a protectionist international copyright law (the Chace Act) to be passed by Congress, and until 1909 for the discourse of authorship fundamentally to transform the statutory definition of copyright. In the major recodification of copyright passed into law in that year, the 1790 statute's denomination of kinds of works ("maps, charts, and books") and its emphasis on the protection of useful texts was recast to cover "all the writings of an author" (17 U.S.C. § 4). But cultural evidence of the increasing importance of authorship to the circulation of texts can be found as early as 1861 in the card game *Authors*, which enjoyed enormous popularity throughout the second half of the nineteenth century. On the one hand, the publishing history of *Authors* exemplifies the continuing insecurity of intellectual property; although Salem, Massachusetts, game publishers G. M. Whipple and A. A. Smith brought out the original *Authors*, in the absence of a copyright law broad enough to include playing cards, numerous competitors quickly issued their own versions. On the other hand, the game itself serves to consolidate literary property under the purview of authorship, as the object of the game is for players to collect each author's "works," matching titles to the author's card. Later versions often featured engravings or photographs of authors, further solidifying players' mastery of authorial identity. Moreover, the game condensed the field of authorship by equating "Authors" writ large with the particular writers it assembled. The selective elevation of these authors to "Authors" helped reinforce what we have come to know as a national literary canon, while demonstrating how canons can be formed through mass cultural phenomena as well as through more familiar, top-down, critical or institutional fiat.

With American authorship on a surer footing, however, new dangers emerged. As the recognizability promoted by the game of *Authors* suggests, many postbellum authors found their identities somewhat too public. In Louisa May Alcott's *Jo's Boys, And How They Turned Out* (1886), once Jo becomes a famous novelist, "the admiring public took possession of her and all her affairs, past, present, and to come." Besieged by visitors, autograph seekers, photographers, and reporters, Jo complains, "There ought to be a law to protect unfortunate authors. . . . To me it is a more vital subject than international copyright" (49). Henry James's "The Aspern Papers" (1888), published two years later, presents an even more ominous picture of readers' hunger for authors in its depiction of a biographer's zeal for a dead poet's papers, a passion so great that it ultimately leads to the papers' destruction. Once unstable, uncertain, and difficult to establish, authorial identity had become by the late nineteenth century all too perilously knowable.

Many of the connections we have traced in this chapter between literary property, literary nationalism, and literary fraudulence, and the consequences for American authors of the shift to a better organized, more stratified literary marketplace, are epitomized by the No Name Series, a group of thirty-seven contemporary novels issued anonymously by Boston publisher Roberts Brothers between 1876 and 1887. The No Name Series indexes striking changes in the cultural meaning of authorial anonymity, as what had in the antebellum period been an unfortunate predicament, a mark of gentlemanly discretion, a sign of female modesty, or, for many women, a threshold condition for their participation in public literary culture, is transformed by enterprising publishers into a clever marketing device. "Curiosity will naturally stand on tiptoe, eager to discover through the author's style his or her identity," the *Chicago Daily Inter-Ocean* predicted, and Roberts Brothers worked hard to produce precisely this effect. After the publishers launched the series in 1876 with a novel by Helen Hunt Jackson, some subsequent novels included a blank page pasted into the volume headed "GUESSES AT THE AUTHORSHIP of MERCY PHILBRICK'S CHOICE." Roberts Brothers stoked debates over the identities of the authors in magazines, and when they issued the collection *A Masque of Poets* (1878), they asked readers to submit their guesses at the authorship of each poem directly to the publishers. Indeed, the publishers acknowledged in correspondence that the point of anonymity for this series was less to shield authors from the public than to encourage readers to identify them. "People say it will be impossible to keep the secret, for an author's style cannot be hidden," the editor of the series told one prospective author, but "*if it is not admitted*, there will be uncertainty enough to make it exciting, and create a demand—we hope a large one" (qtd. in Stern 1991, 378). In other words, the No Name authors' anonymity was a riddle meant to be solved. Whereas anonymity had once signaled the instability of authorial identity and authors' tenuous hold over their literary property, here it reinforces both, as publisher and reviewer alike trade on the belief that an author's style will confirm his or her distinctiveness and tether the author more closely to the work.

And yet, despite its innovative use of anonymity, many aspects of the marketing campaign for the No Name Series hearken back to the cardinal points of antebellum literary culture: the hope that an authentic American literary tradition might emerge from the practice of a democratic literary criticism; an abiding concern that a mass-produced literature could only be a fraudulent one; and an orientation to British literary culture that is curiously compatible with literary nationalism. Notably, for a series that was initially imagined to promote "Original American Novels and Tales," the publishers justify the project at every level with references to British texts they assume are common knowledge among American readers. The Publishers' Advertisement begins with a throwaway reference to Leigh Hunt; the title of the No Name Series deliberately echoes that of Wilkie Collins's 1862 novel; and the title-page motto is taken from George Eliot's newly published *Daniel Deronda* (1876), a motto that expectantly alludes to the transatlantic success of Sir Walter Scott: "Is the Gentleman anonymous? Is he a Great Unknown?" (qtd. in Stern 1991, 377). In fact, most of the novelists who published in the series were not gentlemen at all, but women authors who already had some success publishing novels, histories, and short fiction. Though their identities were fiercely protected from the public (and even from the publisher's employees) as part of the marketing scheme, the series was also sold to readers as an exercise in democratic criticism, one that was particularly appropriate—even salutary—for American literature. According to the Publishers' Advertisement, authorial anonymity ensured that "[n]o name will help the novel, or the story, to success. Its success will depend solely on the writer's ability to catch and retain the reader's interest" (qtd. in Stern 1991, 377). The scene of reading imagined here recalls antebellum literary nationalists' fervent hopes that a great American novelist might spontaneously arise out of a field of indifferent and indistinguishable writing. If antebellum authors suffered from the lack of authoritative cultural mechanisms for sifting and sorting the literary field, the No Name Series trades on the fantasy that a democratic literature might yet be able to do without them. A reviewer in the *New York Graphic* hoped that the series would short-circuit the interference of the literary-critical elite, helping readers "learn to trust more to their own taste and judgment, and rely less on reputation." Anonymity would make the series an antidote to puffery, according to *Harper's New Monthly Magazine*, which praised it for "absolutely prevent[ing] that trading on reputation which is the greatest vice of American *litterateurs*" (qtd. in Stern 1991, 376). The idea that the No Name Series could eliminate editorial and critical mediation between writer and reader is clearly a fantasy, since the very prominence of these titles is a product of the publisher's intervention in the market. The No Name novels' experiment in democratic criticism was underwritten by the Roberts Brothers, who solicited and selected titles and ensured the coherence and visibility of the series, issuing each volume in uniform bindings. If the author's name was withheld, the publisher's name still appeared prominently in advertising, on the title page, on the cover of each volume, and as the copyright holder.

Marking a decisive shift toward a marketplace in which authorial identity was carefully managed and relentlessly promoted, the No Name Series also demonstrates the surprising half-life of antebellum literary culture and the shaping force of its constructions of authorship on the very idea of the American novel. Although the perils that attended writing fiction for a scattered, diverse, and print-hungry mass public would change with the shifting nature of the literary marketplace, the challenge of a democratic literature—one that not only represented the aspirations of the new nation but that also operated according to democratic principles—would remain an elusive, if generative, ideal.

12

PERIODICALS AND THE NOVEL

PATRICIA OKKER

On August 1, 1850, Harriet Beecher Stowe published "The Freeman's Dream: A Parable" in the antislavery weekly newspaper, the *National Era*. Stowe's first piece in the *Era*, this story reveals her growing dismay over political efforts to create a compromise to resolve the national crisis of slavery. Although these compromise proposals had been debated throughout the year, "The Freeman's Dream" was especially timely, appearing less than one month after the death of President Zachary Taylor and less than two months before the new president, Millard Fillmore, signed the Compromise of 1850 into law. In the months following the compromise, opposition to these new slave laws grew, as did press reports of kidnappings of African Americans living in the North. As Joan D. Hedrick confirms, Stowe was deeply moved by these newspaper accounts, and she was also outraged by the defenses of slavery published in the religious press, which she also read. Increasingly committed to writing about the evils of slavery, Stowe continued to publish occasional pieces in the *Era*, and the editor Gamaliel Bailey urged her to send more. In March 1851, Stowe wrote to Bailey proposing a serial that would become *Uncle Tom's Cabin; or, Life among the Lowly*, which ran in the *Era* from June 5, 1851, through April 1, 1852. Among the many sources Stowe used for this novel were the accounts within the press documenting the effects of the new slave laws. Periodicals indeed figured within the narrative itself: the August 28, 1851, installment shows the slave catcher Mr. Haley reading a newspaper advertisement for a slave auction. Even after the novel was issued in book form in March 1852, these connections between the novel and periodicals continued. Widely reviewed and debated, *Uncle Tom's Cabin* continued to exist in the periodical press in which it was first conceived.

Even this cursory overview of Stowe's novel suggests the rich connections possible between novels and periodicals. In this case, Stowe's contributions to a newspaper established her relationship with an editor and provided a framework for her to imagine publishing a larger work within the same newspaper. During the composition of the novel, recent news and public debates—all documented within the periodical press—served as sources for Stowe's developing narrative, and Stowe included newspapers within the narrative itself. Even before the novel was completed, periodicals also began publishing rich commentary on it, some of which continues today within literary journals. The history of this particular novel, then, is deeply imbedded in periodical culture.

While the details of this story are unique to *Uncle Tom's Cabin*, the interconnection between periodicals and the novel reflects a much larger cultural reality. However much readers still imagine the novel as a bound book, the development of the novel in the United States (and indeed in much of the world) is intimately connected with the rise of periodicals. Whether by announcing recently published novels, directing readers to (and away from) particular novels, shaping readers' expectations about the form, serving as source material for novelists, or publishing novels in serial form, American periodicals have long played a key role in the development of the American novel.

Regardless of how interconnected novels and periodicals may have become over time, most critics have described American magazines as particularly hostile toward the novel form in the late eighteenth and early nineteenth centuries. As numerous critics have noted, magazine editors regularly published attacks on the novel, often describing the form as outright dangerous, particularly to young and/or female readers. A 1791 essayist in the *Massachusetts Magazine*, for instance, denounced novels as "literary opium" that "lead many on the path of vice": "The sorrowful effects of reading novels and romances have been delineated by many, but one need not go far to be an eye witness of the fatal consequences which result from such chimerical works. Every town and village affords some instance of a ruined female, who has fell [*sic*] from the heights of purity to the lowest grade of human misery" (Nov. 1791, 662–63). In 1792, the *Lady's Magazine and Repository* likewise insisted that novels "are a species of writing, which can scarcely be spoken of without being condemned" (Nov. 1792, 296).

But as popular as such denouncements were (and as frequently quoted as they are in histories of the American novel), the role of periodicals in the development of the novel in the 1780s and 1790s is considerably more complex. Editors did, to be sure, condemn novel reading as potentially addictive and dangerous, but they often used these pronouncements as arguments in favor of periodical reading. In his oft-reprinted essay on the "Importance of Female Education," for example, Noah Webster dismisses novels as "the toys of youth" and instead urges young women to focus on periodicals, specifically the British magazine the *Spectator*, which he insists "should fill the first place in every lady's library." As much as he objects in the *American Magazine* to novel reading, Webster does not denounce all novels. Instead he concludes that "some of them are useful—many of them, pernicious—and most of them trifling" (May 1788, 369).

Fairly typical of periodical assessments of the novel form in the 1780s and 1790s, Webster's concession that "some" novels proved "useful" suggests that periodical editors were not nearly so hostile to fiction as some literary histories suggest. Rather than condemn all novel reading, many magazine editors argued that readers (especially impressionable ones such as young women) needed the help of editors to distinguish between what Webster calls "useful" and "pernicious" novels. Such a strategy suggests that the real motivation in these attacks was not to denounce all novels but rather to bolster editorial authority. This strategy must have been especially appealing to late eighteenth-century magazine editors, who faced overwhelming odds against success. As Frank Luther Mott has documented, many American magazines of this period lasted less than a year, and circulations remained quite limited, often numbering in the hundreds. Even the most successful magazines of the period boasted circulations of little more than 2,000, and delinquent subscribers were all too common.

While periodical editors had little chance for success, they were no doubt aware of the growing availability—and popularity—of fiction, especially through circulating libraries. As Robert B. Winans has explained, between 1765 and 1800 fiction jumped from 10 to 50 percent of the stock of circulating libraries. Aware of the ever-increasing number of novels available to readers, magazine editors insisted that, unlike circulating libraries which simply made volumes available to readers, editors alone were capable of distinguishing between the "useful" and the "pernicious" novels. Such a defense of their own cultural authority explains why so many periodical attacks on the novel included recommendations for particular novels the editors *could* recommend. One reviewer in the *Monthly Review and Literary Miscellany*, for example, insisted that "nineteen in twenty" novels "are positively mischievous" but also offered a specific novel worthy of recommendation (Jan. 1805, 5, 14–15). Similarly, the reviewer in the *Lady's Magazine and Repository* who described novels generally as a "species of writing, which can scarcely be spoken of without being condemned" recommended Mary Robinson's *Vancenza: or, the Dangers of Credulity* (1792) as a novel "superior to the general run of those publications" (Nov. 1792, 296). These editors and reviewers, then, sought their cultural authority *through*, rather than *against*, novel reading.

Editors' willingness—even eagerness—to fulfill readers' desires for novels appears even more dramatically in the ways that late eighteenth-century editors promoted the fiction within their own pages as "novels." Although many of these early texts are not long enough to be classified as novels by today's standards—some are as short as 2,000 words—they nevertheless document the efforts magazine editors undertook to capitalize on the growing popularity of novels and demonstrate the early role that periodicals had in promoting the reading of novels. In October 1787, the *Columbian Magazine*, for example, promoted "Amelia: or the Faithless Briton" as "an original novel" that was intended to be the "first of a series of novels," and the magazine encouraged readers to submit other novels (677). Demonstrating the relatively loose use of the term "novel," the *Columbian Magazine* likewise featured six texts identified as novels, only one of which required a second installment.

At the same time that some magazines were promoting relatively short fiction as "novels," they were also featuring long fiction, sometimes described as "tales." As Winans has suggested, the term "novel," rather than indicating a particular length, was generally used synonymously with *story* or *tale*. Thus, at the same time that it published the short "Amelia: or the Faithless Briton" (described as a novel), the *Columbian Magazine* was also serializing Jeremy Belknap's *The Foresters* (1792), a long satirical narrative of the American colonies. Although not called a novel within the magazine itself, *The Foresters* was described as an "American Tale" and a "Historical Romance"—terms often used to identify other early American novels, including Charles Brockden Brown's *Wieland; or The Transformation* (1798) and Susanna Rowson's *Charlotte: A Tale of Truth* (1791). The form of Belknap's narrative, which appeared in nine installments, was likewise similar to other novels of the period. Serial fiction never dominated the periodicals in the early republic, but the *Columbian Magazine* was not the only periodical to experiment with serialization. Other notable examples include Ann Eliza Bleecker's *The History of Maria Kittle* (in the *New-York Magazine* in 1790–91), Judith Sargent Murray's *Story of Margaretta* (in the *Massachusetts Magazine* in 1798), and Rowson's *Sincerity* (in the *Boston Weekly Magazine* in 1803–04).

Brockden Brown's engagement with periodicals likewise points to the close connections between the American novel and American periodicals, particularly the way that writers used periodical publication to experiment with the still unfixed genre of the novel. As Steven Watts has shown, Brown's experimentation was particularly concentrated in 1798 when, in Philadelphia's *Weekly Magazine*, he published a series of texts that reflect his interest in the novel form, including a thirteen-installment series titled "The Man at Home," which combines elements of the novel with an essay on economic subjects; an epistolary exchange between a law student and his sister titled "A Series of Original Letters"; "Alcuin: A Dialogue" (also issued in book form), which consists of a fictionalized conversation between a Philadelphia schoolteacher and a women's rights advocate; an extract from his unpublished (and now lost) novel *Sky-Walk*; and the opening chapters of his novel *Arthur Mervyn*. Like all these publications, *Arthur Mervyn* highlights Brown's interest in publishing novels serially: its run in the *Weekly Magazine* ended only when the paper was forced to suspend publication because of the death of its editor. While Brown ultimately relied on publishing in book rather than serial form—at least in part because the periodical industry was not yet stable enough to support extensive serial publications—this intense year of serial experimentation was nonetheless extremely productive, and he almost immediately published four of his best novels: *Wieland*, *Arthur Mervyn; or, Memoirs of the Year 1793* (1799–1800), *Ormond; or, The Secret Witness* (1799), and *Edgar Huntly; or, Memoirs of a Sleep-Walker* (1799).

Sales of these novels proved unsatisfactory to Brown, and he continued working within periodicals. Perhaps instinctively recognizing that a thriving periodical press was essential for the development of the American novel, he immersed himself in editing literary magazines in New York and then Philadelphia. Here, too, Brown continued his support of the novel form, publishing two of his works serially—*Memoirs of Stephen Calvert* (1799–1800) and *Memoirs of Carwin the Biloquist* (1803–05)—as well as an excerpt from *Edgar Huntly* and an essay defending the novel form. While Brown's efforts to create lasting literary magazines ultimately failed, his understanding of the connection between periodicals and the novel anticipate the interdependence of these two forms in later decades.

In the early nineteenth century, magazines continued to be dominated by essays and sketches, with some of them publishing reprinted serial novels, occasionally in translation. Only a few periodicals, such as the *New York Mirror,* regularly published original serial fiction. Even in this climate, however, magazine editors were attuned to the growing popularity of novels. Reviews of novels frequently quoted lengthy passages from such fiction, and sketches of famous authors (often with portraits) were also increasingly common. One writer who captured the attention of editors and readers alike was James Fenimore Cooper. While the numerous essays and reviews on Cooper benefited the periodical editors, who were able to offer readers news about the nation's most famous and popular author, this same material likewise enhanced Cooper's reputation and assured that the reading public was aware of his latest novel. Such mutually dependent strategies were typical throughout the mid-century, and countless authors benefited, like Cooper, from the popular fascination with authors, as evidenced by the numerous magazine series of biographical sketches of authors and even, sometimes, descriptions of their homes. These authors would likely not have been able to establish a national reputation without a thriving periodical press, but that press benefited from their celebrity as well.

Many other novelists enjoyed a more direct relationship with periodicals, especially after 1830. Suggesting an intense relationship of mutual influence and dependence, this period is marked by dramatic growth—for both the American novel and American periodicals. In contrast to 1800, when there were probably twelve magazines published in the United States, by 1850 that number had grown to 600, and to more than 1,200 by 1870. Such growth was fueled primarily by increased literacy rates, improvements in transportation (which enhanced distribution), and technological developments that created new opportunities for production. Circulations during this same time period likewise increased dramatically. While circulation figures of the early national period were often counted in the hundreds, mid-nineteenth-century literary magazines sometimes reached more than 100,000 readers. When *Harper's Monthly Magazine* was launched in 1850, for instance, 7,500 copies were issued, but sales quickly topped 100,000. *Godey's Lady's Book* and *Peterson's Magazine* likewise boasted more than 100,000 subscribers, and the circulation of the *New York Ledger,* which serialized many of E. D. E. N. Southworth's novels, topped 400,000.

Such growth within the periodical industry would not have been possible without the emergence of new models of authorship. Challenging the eighteenth-century idea of the author as someone who neither needed nor wanted recognition or compensation, some innovative magazine editors actively promoted a more professional image of authors. When Sarah J. Hale began editing the *Ladies' Magazine* in 1828, for example, she rejected the practice of "scissors editors," who compiled their periodicals by literally cutting and pasting from other sources, and instead emphasized original submissions. At the same time, she encouraged attribution, and she supported the idea that authors should be paid for their work, both by paying her contributors and by encouraging her subscribers to buy books rather than borrow them from libraries. She expanded these practices in 1837, when she assumed the editorial position at *Godey's Lady's Book*, a position she held until 1877. Perhaps even more important to the increasing professionalization of authorship was *Graham's Magazine*, founded by George R. Graham in 1841. With rates for prose ranging from four to twelve dollars a page, *Graham's* quickly became one of the most desired periodicals for literary authors, and nationally celebrated writers such as Cooper and Henry Wadsworth Longfellow could command rates unmatched by most periodicals. *Graham's Magazine* reportedly paid Cooper $1,800 for "The Islets of the Gulf; or, Rose Budd," which was later published in book form in 1848 as *Jack Tier*. The number and quality of American novelists who published in the *Lady's Book* and *Graham's*—including Stowe, Nathaniel Hawthorne, Catharine Maria Sedgwick, William Gilmore Simms, and Edgar Allan Poe—suggest the extent to which this support of authorship nurtured the development of American novelists.

In addition to shaping cultural perceptions of authorship, periodicals in the antebellum period also influenced cultural understandings of the novel itself. As Nina Baym has documented, periodicals devoted considerable attention to reviewing novels, and in doing so, they frequently made pronouncements about many different aspects of novels, including plot, characterization, narration, and morality. While such reviews exhibit a full range of opinions and beliefs, the sheer volume of such reviews nevertheless attests to the fact that periodicals were actively involved in shaping public perception of the novel. As Baym puts it, "So closely connected have been the form and the commentary on it—both being products of a print culture—that it does not seem extreme to say that the novel has responded to discourse about it almost as much as reviews have responded to the novels they reviewed" (1984, 270).

The interdependence of the periodical and the American novel took a dramatic turn in the late 1840s and 1850s when serial publication exploded as an international phenomenon. Inspired, at least in part, by the popularity of serial novels by Charles Dickens and Eugène Sue, the dramatic growth of serial novels was made possible by technological advancements that eased publication and distribution issues and by a growing middle class that increasingly had the leisure time, the literacy skills, and the financial resources necessary to indulge in reading for pleasure. This demand for serial fiction in American periodicals spread to virtually every kind of periodical imaginable, including elite literary magazines, middle-class family papers, reform periodicals, women's magazines, cheap weekly papers, penny dailies, children's periodicals, and general and political newspapers. Many periodicals published more than one novel at a time, and some story-papers, like *Brother Jonathan*, relied almost exclusively on serial novels, reportedly publishing as many as eight different serials at a time.

Stowe once again provides a useful example not only of the potential for serial publication but also the more extended way that American novelists of the mid-nineteenth century depended on a thriving periodical press. Like many other nineteenth-century novelists who initially established their careers by contributing to magazines, Stowe had been publishing in periodicals for over fifteen years before the *National Era* began publishing *Uncle Tom's Cabin*. During this long apprenticeship period, Stowe published first in regional papers, such as Cincinnati's *Western Monthly Magazine* and the *Chronicle*, and in religious papers such as the Presbyterian *Evangelist*, but she soon established a reputation in national periodicals, most notably *Godey's Lady's Book*. The increasing opportunity for financial compensation for authors, particularly in periodicals, was especially important to Stowe. As biographer Joan D. Hedrick has recounted, faced with mounting debt and family expenses, Stowe turned to writing as a means of support. As she admitted in 1838, "I *do* it for *the pay*" (1994, 136).

The publication history of *Uncle Tom's Cabin* and Stowe's continued reliance on serial publication throughout her career further demonstrate the strong connections between nineteenth-century American periodicals and the development of the American novel. Published in forty-one installments, Stowe's novel attracted almost immediate attention. As editor Gamaliel Bailey described in an 1853 letter (that was eventually published in the *Atlantic Monthly*): "[T]he story grew,—it seemed to have no end,—everybody talked of it. I thought the mails were never so irregular, for none of my subscribers was willing to lose a single number of the Era while the story was going on. . . . Of the hundreds of letters received weekly, renewing subscriptions or sending new ones, there was scarcely one that did not contain some cordial reference to Uncle Tom." Continuing, Bailey notes: "[M]y large circulation had served as a tremendous advertisement for the work, which was now about to be published separately" (June 1866, 748–49).

While Bailey's reference to *his* "large circulation" conveniently elides the extent to which Stowe's novel helped drive his paper's growth, his comment nevertheless accurately describes the fact that for many nineteenth-century novels, initial serial publication actually increased demand for the novel in book form, thus creating two opportunities for authors (and publishers) to earn money. As Hedrick documents, such was certainly the case for Stowe's publishers. When the novel was first issued in book form in March 1852, it sold 10,000 copies in the first week; by the end of the first year, sales topped 300,000. In Great Britain, the novel sold a million and a half copies in the first year. Stowe continued throughout her career to publish many of her novels first in serial form, including *The Minister's Wooing* (*Atlantic Monthly*, 1858–59), *The Pearl of Orr's Island* (*Independent*, 1861–62), *Agnes of Sorrento* (*Atlantic Monthly*, 1861–62), *My Wife and I* (*Christian Union*, 1870–71), and *Pink and White Tyranny* (*Old and New*, 1870–71).

While the extent of Stowe's success was unusual, she was one of many serial novelists before 1870 who commanded large audiences. Many periodicals contracted with individual novelists (who were sometimes described on a paper's masthead as an editor) to provide regular and often exclusive serials for the magazine, sometimes for decades. While the pressure to produce was often unrelenting—some magazine novelists wrote sixty or even one hundred novels in their careers—this type of arrangement nevertheless provided successful careers for writers such as Southworth, Ann Stephens, Sylvanus Cobb Jr., and Joseph Holt Ingraham. The authors were not the only ones to benefit from these sustained relationships with periodicals and their audiences. Editors and publishers likewise depended on the steady supply of their exclusive novelists to sustain circulation. Even before one novel ended, a new serial was announced, thus insuring reader interest. Stephens, for instance, joined *Peterson's Magazine* in 1843, a year after it was founded, and she published *Lost and Found*, her first yearlong serial in the magazine, in 1848. Only after she died in 1886 did the magazine appear without a novel by Stephens. Indeed, when announcing her death to the magazine's readers in October 1886, publisher Charles J. Peterson promised that Stephens would continue to appear, explaining that she had left behind a novel: "[I]t is already in our hands, and will appear, next year, in these pages. . . . There may be other novels by her in MS.; but of this we have no positive knowledge as yet." This connection between Stephens and *Peterson's Magazine* for more than four decades attests to the interdependence of the American novel and American periodicals. As much as she depended on the magazine, so, too, apparently, did it depend on her steady publication of serial fiction.

The enormous popularity of these novelists is also suggested by the response to Southworth, who published exclusively in the United States for Robert Bonner's *New York Ledger* for more than three decades. Her most popular novel, *The Hidden Hand*, was initially serialized in 1859 and featured an unconventional heroine named Capitola or Cap, who spends her childhood in a New York City slum, where she dresses as a boy to sell newspapers. When a guardian takes her to Virginia, Capitola continues to rebel against expectations for young women. A self-described "damsel-errant in quest of adventures" (ch. 35), she rescues other endangered women, captures criminals, and fights a duel. As Joanne Dobson has suggested, Capitola was beloved by readers, who named boats and racehorses after her and wore the stylish "Capitola" hats. Demand for all things Cap lasted decades, and the novel was reserialized in 1868 and 1883. Unlike most *Ledger* serials that appeared only as serials, *The Hidden Hand* was issued in book form in 1888.

Even those novelists who did not rely heavily on serialization nevertheless frequently turned to periodicals, either as venues for other kinds of publication or even as subject matter for fiction. One noteworthy example is Fanny Fern (Sara Payson Willis Parton), one of the most successful newspaper columnists of the nineteenth century. Her 1855 autobiographical novel *Ruth Hall: A Domestic Tale of the Present Time* traces the protagonist's rise from impoverished mother and widow to periodical celebrity. Embedded in this tale of female self-reliance is a scathing critique of the periodical industry, particularly its patronizing male editors.

Hawthorne's career, like Fern's, depended heavily on periodicals. Although initially inclined toward book publication, Hawthorne moved relatively quickly to periodicals, and throughout the 1830s and 1840s (and well before the publication of *The Scarlet Letter* in 1850) he published tales and sketches, most often in the *New England Magazine* and the *Democratic Review*. As Meredith L. McGill's study of reprinting demonstrates, Hawthorne's periodical publications were also widely reprinted. Although he did not benefit financially from such printing, this practice nevertheless increased his reputation. Hawthorne also edited the monthly *American Magazine of Useful and Entertaining Knowledge* for part of the year 1836. Like Stowe, Hawthorne looked to periodicals for some financial stability, but his editorship of the *American Magazine* proved disastrous: four months into his tenure there, he had received only twenty dollars of his expected five hundred dollars in salary, and before the year ended, the magazine was bankrupt. Despite this setback, Hawthorne continued to look to periodicals as a source of income, especially after he married in 1842. Although he had no difficulty publishing during these years, he was, as Baym has explained, frustrated that the low pay forced him to produce far more quickly than he would have liked. Despite a few attempts at serialization, none of his major novels first appeared serially. For Hawthorne, and no doubt for other writers of his day, book rather than periodical publication provided a kind of creative freedom he preferred.

Despite his eventual shift to publication primarily in books, it is inaccurate to say that periodicals had no effect on Hawthorne's development as a novelist. Besides his decades of publishing mostly short works in literary magazines, Hawthorne was perhaps most indebted to the literary critics of his day who recognized him as a writer whose reputation would extend well beyond his time. Especially important to Hawthorne's growing reputation was the 1840s Young America movement, known for its exuberant political and literary nationalism. Linked closely with several New York literary magazines, most notably the *Literary World* and the *United States Magazine and Democratic Review* (the latter of which published twenty-five Hawthorne stories), Young America promoted authors such as Hawthorne, Herman Melville, Margaret Fuller, and Poe—writers who, as these reviewers insisted, were producing art that was distinctly American. Without the support of these and other reviewers (including Poe, who published several important reviews of Hawthorne in *Graham's*; Melville, who published "Hawthorne and His

Mosses" in the *Literary World* in 1850; or Evert Duyckinck, whose essay "Nathaniel Hawthorne" appeared in the *United States Magazine and Democratic Review* in 1845), it is hard to imagine Hawthorne's reputation and fiction developing as they did.

Unlike Hawthorne, whose career began in periodicals and then shifted primarily to books, Melville started writing books but later turned to periodicals. Still, like Hawthorne, Melville benefited from a long and complex relationship with periodicals, even though he did not obtain the level of popularity (or financial success) in periodicals that some of his peers enjoyed. In addition to his important relationship with the Young America reviewers, Melville's periodical reading proved to be especially important to his development as a writer. Mary K. Bercaw's listing of Melville's sources includes an astonishingly varied group of American and British periodicals, including, for example, *Littell's Living Age, New York Herald, Literary World, Harper's, Knickerbocker, Putnam's, Boston Pearl and Literary Gazette, Nantucket Daily Telegraph, Sailors' Magazine, Democratic Review, Blackwood's Edinburgh Magazine, Albany Evening Journal, Atlantic Monthly, Dollar Magazine, Cosmopolitan Magazine, New York Times,* and *Military and Naval Magazine.* Tom Quirk's extended study of the sources of Melville's 1857 novel, *The Confidence-Man: His Masquerade* (particularly Melville's use of newspaper accounts of the swindler first arrested in 1849) likewise depicts a writer heavily influenced by the newspapers and magazines he read.

Melville's deep engagement with periodical culture is also seen in his keen awareness of the periodical conventions of the day. Critical of the class and racial assumptions of popular magazine tales, Melville used his own periodical fiction to challenge these very conventions. At the same time, however, Melville was more than willing to work within periodical expectations, and he tailored his own fiction to meet the preferences of various editors. As Sheila Post-Lauria has shown, Melville's work published in *Harper's*—including "The Fiddler," "Jimmy Rose," "Cock-a-Doodle-Doo!" and "The Paradise of Bachelors and the Tartarus of Maids"—fits that magazine's preference for sentimental rhetoric and its policy of avoiding controversy. His fiction in *Putnam's*—including "Bartleby, the Scrivener" and "Benito Cereno"—on the other hand, matches that magazine's more liberal and politically engaged perspective. Melville's awareness and manipulation of these different editorial policies may even account for some of the peculiarities of his novel *Israel Potter: His Fifty Years of Exile*, which was serialized in *Putnam's* in 1854–1855. According to Post-Lauria, Melville initially submitted the first sixty pages of the manuscript to *Harper's.* But for unknown reasons *Harper's* did not publish the novel, and Melville continued writing with an eye toward *Putnam's.* Thus, while the first sixty pages conform closely with editorial policies of *Harper's*, the remainder of the novel fits more closely with practices common in *Putnam's.*

As the example of Rebecca Harding Davis likewise suggests, tailoring submissions to a specific magazine's editorial policies meant that writers could publish in very different markets, thus increasing their overall financial compensation. Eager to establish a reputation among the nation's elite writers, Davis sent her first piece, "Life in the Iron-Mills," to the *Atlantic Monthly*, where it was published in April 1861. This magazine was an especially good fit for Davis since, like the author herself, it had an interest in the development of realistic fiction. But Davis did not limit herself to realism or even to the elite literary marketplace, in large part because she wanted the better salaries that came with publication in more popular magazines. Thus, almost immediately after "Life in the Iron-Mills" appeared, Davis began publishing serial novels, including murder mysteries, in more popular venues. According to Sharon M. Harris, Davis earned as much as $1,000 for her popular serials, far more than the *Atlantic* offered.

As tempting as it may be to create a sharp distinction between these two markets, with one providing Davis the creative freedom she desired and the other better financial compensation, in fact, these two markets reveal significant similarities. Davis's more literary editors sometimes pressured her to please the audience—*Atlantic* editor James T. Fields wanted her fiction to be less gloomy—and the more popular family magazines published novels with bleak endings, which Fields would most certainly have objected to, as well as novels on controversial subjects, including alcoholism and the conditions within the nation's insane asylums. For Davis, as for so many writers of the nineteenth century, one periodical (or even one type of periodical) was insufficient for meeting her particular needs. Thus she targeted specific kinds of texts for publication in different periodicals.

The potential for targeting periodical audiences likely to be sympathetic to a particular work is also amply demonstrated by the role of African American periodicals in the development of the African American novel. As Eric Gardner has recently explained, the black periodical press "was *the* central publication outlet for many black writers—and especially for texts that were *not* slave narratives" (2009, 10). Such is certainly the case for the significant number of African American novels before 1870 whose initial publication in the United States was within African American periodicals. These include Frederick Douglass's novella "The Heroic Slave" (1853), Martin Delany's *Blake; or, The Huts of America* (1859, 1861–62), William Wells Brown's *Clotel; or, The President's Daughter* (1853, 1860–61), Frances Harper's *Minnie's Sacrifice* (1869), and Julia C. Collins's recently recovered novel, *The Curse of Caste; or, The Slave Bride* (1865). The complicated publication histories of Delany's and Brown's novels in particular attest to the importance of serialization. With many book publishers unwilling to publish African American fiction, these writers naturally turned to the African American press, which offered a sympathetic audience. As Katy Chiles has recounted, Delany wanted to publish his novel as a book, but he was evidently unable to find a publisher. One of the many unanswered questions about this novel is whether publishers rejected it because of its plot and characterization. One of the most radical antislavery texts of its day, Delany's novel of black nationalism focuses on a man who leads an international slave rebellion and kills those who oppose him. Unable to find a book publisher, Delany published the novel serially: twenty-six chapters appeared in the *Anglo-African Magazine* in 1859, but the serialization was aborted when Delany left for Africa. Upon his return, the novel was serialized again, beginning in November 1861, this time in the *Weekly Anglo-African*. Unfortunately, however, the issues of the *Weekly Anglo-African* containing the final installments of Delany's novel have never been found. Not published in book form until 1970, the novel remains incomplete, with an estimated six chapters still missing.

Wells Brown's *Clotel* is another early African American novel that was published serially in the *Weekly Anglo-African*, and, like Delany's *Blake*, its complex publication history suggests both the challenges African American novelists faced in the mid-nineteenth century and the unique circumstances of serial publication. As Christopher Mulvey has documented, the novel was actually published four different times (with four different titles), and these "versions" are different enough that some scholars prefer describing them as four separate texts rather than revisions. Suggesting the obstacles African American novelists faced at mid-century, the first publication was in London in 1853 in book form, but when Brown published the first US version of the novel in 1860 and 1861, he turned, like Delany, to the African American press. The novel was published under the title *Miralda; or, The Beautiful Quadroon. A Romance of American Slavery, Founded on Fact*, in the *Weekly Anglo-African* in 1860–1861 in sixteen installments (fourteen of which survive). The differences between the 1853 and 1861 versions of the novel are significant: in addition to substantive changes in the text itself (as suggested by the change in title), the novel was directed toward two different audiences. While the 1853 version reached an international audience sympathetic to abolitionism, the 1860–1861 novel was published in a forum for African American readers, an audience far more easily reached through serial rather than book publication.

African Americans were not the only minority group more easily reached by periodical than by book publication. The serial novel was, in fact, widely distributed within minority communities in the United States, and many of these novels and periodicals were published in languages other than English. Regardless of whether these periodicals served communities first established by slavery and its aftermath, immigration, or annexation, these serial novels were popular among readers, and the serial novel in the United States before 1870 is surprisingly multilingual. New Orleans periodicals, for example, were publishing serial novels in French, Spanish, and German as early as the 1840s and 1850s. The vibrancy of this multilingual press can also be seen by the popular translations of Heinrich Bornstein's 1851 *Die Geheimnisse von St. Louis* (*The Mysteries of St. Louis*), which was modeled, of course, after Eugène Sue's *Les Mystères de Paris* (1842–43). According to Steven Rowan, Bornstein's novel was translated from German into English, French, and Czech for St. Louis newspapers. Although much more work must be done, it is likely that literary scholars will find many more serial novels published in the United States in the vibrant nineteenth-century periodical press, which includes periodicals not only in French, German, and Spanish, but also, for example, in Chinese, Yiddish, Swedish, and Norwegian.

However diverse the periodicals that published serial novels were, the overall reading experiences of serial novels are surprisingly similar. Fundamentally different than reading a novel in book form, reading a novel serially in a periodical requires that the experience is both extended over time and interrupted, either in daily, weekly, or monthly installments. Prohibited from the pleasures of reading voraciously, serial readers nevertheless enjoy a different kind of pleasure, one that some nineteenth-century critics compared to the pleasures of an elaborate feast. As one *Harper's* commentator put it, "Readers who complain of serials have not learned the first wish of an epicure—a long, long throat. It is the serial which lengthens the throat so that the feast lasts a year or two years. You taste it all the way down" (Dec. 1855, 128).

Many nineteenth-century novelists enhanced the pleasure of this extended reading experience by manipulating the form of the novel itself. Double-plotted novels, which heightened suspense as the narrative switched from one storyline to another, were especially popular in the antebellum serial novel. Still other novelists carefully attended to the structure of an individual installment, which often included more than one chapter. Although editors did not always break installments where authors intended (often due to space constraints), many nineteenth-century novelists composed with specific installments in mind, and in such cases, serialization influenced not only the reading experience but also the very structure and form of the novel.

One technique that has been frequently associated with the serial novel is the so-called cliff-hanger ending, in which the narrative stops at a moment of crisis. Although some examples of this installment structure do exist in the antebellum period, many other installments are structured to provide the reader with some closure. In *Uncle Tom's Cabin,* for instance, Eliza's dramatic escape across the Ohio River and George and Eliza's action-filled climb over a cliff to escape the slave catchers both occur in the middle rather than at the end of an installment. Suspense remained an important element of serial reading, of course, but novelists frequently imagined the installment as a coherent entity that, like an individual course within a meal, offered both satisfaction and appetite for more.

One of the most significant effects of the forced interruptions required by serial reading is that all readers of a serial novel are inevitably at the same point in the text as other readers. Unlike reading a novel in book form, which can often be an individualistic experience, serial reading necessarily occurs within a social context, as the metaphor of the feast suggests. Much like televised soap operas of the twentieth and twenty-first centuries, nineteenth-century serial novels created a community of readers who read together—and then waited, again as a community, for the narrative's progression in upcoming installments. In addition to allowing readers the pleasure of talking with each other about the narrative's latest developments and speculating about upcoming installments, the extended pacing of serial fiction (as some scholars have suggested) allowed readers to develop more intense relationships with the characters. Suggesting this personal connection, as well as the experience of reading within a community, William Dean Howells recalled reading Stowe's *Uncle Tom's Cabin* "as it came out week after week": "I broke my heart over Uncle Tom's Cabin, as every one else did" (1895, 63).

This communal context for serial reading extended as well to include authorial-reader relations. Readers of serial novels had the luxury of expressing their own ideas about characters and novels, and editors frequently published such reader accounts, which, in turn could be read by the authors, who many times were still composing subsequent installments. As Susan Belasco Smith and Wesley Neil Raabe have noted, for example, the *National Era* received numerous letters from readers during the publication of Stowe's *Uncle Tom's Cabin*. Reinforcing this collaborative exchange between author and reader, the editor published some of these letters, including those that offered detailed instructions to Stowe about their hopes that she would not rush to finish the novel. Unlike readers of a novel in book form who always have the physical object to remind them of how close they are to the narrative's completion, Stowe's serial readers—and even her publishers and herself—were often unaware of exactly how long the novel would continue, making such published suggestions more powerful.

While it is not clear how frequently writers adjusted their novels in response to comments from readers, authors did encourage readers to imagine that the author-reader relationship was quite intimate. Authors frequently addressed readers directly, often as "dear friends" or "dear readers," and they sometimes directed more extended digressions toward the reader. Stowe and Southworth both offered epilogues of their enormously popular novels, addressed directly to their "wide circle of friends" and "dear" readers. Even more dramatically, Stephens interrupted her novel *Palaces in Prisons* in *Peterson's Magazine* in October 1849 to inform readers that she had been writing the novel while attending to own brother's serious illness. Announcing that "between this chapter and the last," her brother had died, Stephens assured readers that the novel would continue: "There is nothing to interrupt me now—no faint moan, no gentle and patient call. . . . [N]othing is here to interrupt thought save the swell of my own heart—the flow of my own tears" (ch. 10). While direct addresses such as these have always been understood in the tradition of sentimental literature, it seems equally important to recognize that this kind of intimate exchange was encouraged within periodical culture.

In addition to this sense of community surrounding serial readers and novelists, the very format on the page also influenced the reading experience of serial novels. Scholars of the American serial novel, including Smith, Raabe, Barbara Hochman, Michael Lund, and the present writer, have noted the importance of other contents—other literary texts, news items, advertisements, and fashion plates—in readers' overall experience with the novels. Thus, for example, the extensive coverage of the Constitutional Convention in Philadelphia's *Columbian Magazine* during the serialization of Belknap's *The Foresters* in 1787 encouraged readers to connect current events with Belknap's novel. Such connections would have been even more likely in novels like *Uncle Tom's Cabin,* which includes direct references to the controversial Fugitive Slave Law and to figures such as Hungarian rebel Louis Kossuth, then in the news. Davis's fictionalized account of the Whiskey Ring scandal, her serial novel *John Andros,* began just days after Tweed's conviction (in 1873); it appeared in the magazine *Hearth and Home,* which had been covering the scandal. Such integration of serial fiction with contemporary events was enabled not only by the contents surrounding the novels but also by the condensed time between composition and publication. Such timely references would become much more easily dated with book publication.

Just as the juxtaposition of news items and serial novels could have affected readers' experiences with the texts, so too did illustration provide an important context for serial novels. One of the innovators regarding illustration was *Godey's Lady's Book,* which promoted its elaborate fashion plates, some of which were actually hand colored, as early as the 1830s. Technological advancements in the 1840s allowed images to be reproduced on a large scale, which led to the rise of the pictorial weeklies, which generally combined illustrations with both sensational fiction and news. But these pictorial weeklies, such as *Frank Leslie's Illustrated Newspaper, Gleason's Pictorial and Drawing-Room Companion,* and *Harper's Weekly,* were not alone in pairing serialized fiction with illustration. General family magazines and children's periodicals also relied heavily on illustrated serial fiction.

As much as serialization offered new opportunities for readers and novelists alike, it also created challenges and obstacles. For readers the biggest threat was missed installments or, even worse, aborted serials, the conclusions of which were never offered. One dramatic example is Poe's "The Journal of Julius Rodman," which was serialized in *Burton's Gentleman's Magazine* in 1840. Poe left the magazine before the narrative was completed, and the last installment (June 1840) leaves the adventurers stranded on the Missouri River. While editors and publishers did occasionally have to apologize to readers (sometimes profusely) for delays or cancellations, the vast majority of antebellum serials continued without any interruptions. Such expectations, of course, created challenges for writers, who faced considerable pressure to produce quickly and regularly. Only those rare authors who began serialization after the novel was completed were completely free from these pressures.

Another common challenge to serial novelists was editorial interference. While such frustrations are possible in any editor-author relationship, the time constraints associated with serialization increased such tensions, and editors sometimes made changes without authorial approval. In 1867, Davis experienced such frustrations during the serialization of her novel *Waiting for the Verdict* in *Galaxy.* Eager to be involved in decisions about the novel's publication, Davis offered suggestions and comments about illustrations, installment breaks, and proofreading. Such collaboration with her publishers was threatened, however, when they asked her to make significant cuts. Outraged, Davis compared the requested cuts to asking an illustrator to cut the heads off figures to fit a particular paper size.

As much as novelists complained about such pressures, editors, too, faced challenges with serialization, including the risk of offending readers. Unlike book readers, who could simply refuse to buy a book they believed offensive, readers of serial fiction often received these novels in the mail, regardless of whether they approved them. Indeed, the premise of periodical subscription assumes that the editor is capable of determining—and controlling—what is and what is not appropriate for the readership. Thus, when readers did object strongly to a specific novel, their likely action was to cancel the subscription to the magazine, something that editors obviously wanted to avoid. John W. De Forest's struggles with his novel *Miss Ravenel's Conversion from Secession to Loyalty* demonstrates the potential conflicts regarding serialization and editorial concerns for propriety. In December 1865, De Forest signed a contract for the novel to be serialized in *Harper's New Monthly Magazine*, but this contract was later withdrawn because the editor, Alfred H. Guernsey, objected to the novel's strong language. Rather than serializing it in *Harper's*, which would not publish anything the editors considered inappropriate for family reading, Guernsey issued it directly in book form.

Guernsey's unwillingness to publish the novel in serial form was not without cause, and the 1860s and 1870s seemed especially difficult years for such editorial interference. Magazine editors were all too aware of the scandals that emerged because of questionable material. The *Atlantic Monthly*, for example, watched its subscribers cancel in protest over the sexual contents of three different selections in the late 1860s: Charles Reade's *Griffith Gaunt*, Oliver Wendell Holmes's *Guardian Angel*, and Stowe's "The True Story of Lady Byron's Life." The public fury over Stowe's account of Lady Byron's story of her husband's incestuous relationship with his half-sister Augusta Leigh demonstrates most clearly the risk of offending readers; the circulation of the *Atlantic Monthly* dropped from 50,000 to 35,000 following the scandal.

As much as such scandals must have terrified nineteenth-century periodical editors, they also suggest the extent to which readers were invested—emotionally, intellectually, and financially—in the periodicals they read. These same readers' contact with novelists was, likewise, mediated by these periodicals. Although stories of the rise of the American novel often seem to ignore periodicals altogether, the American novel and the American periodical (especially the magazine) came of age together, and the growing popularity of one necessarily influenced the other. Like periodicals, then, the American novel before 1870 was created—and consumed—in a complex environment in which authors, editors, publishers, readers, illustrators, and, sometimes, even advertisers all participated in the making of a text.

13

CHEAP SENSATION: PAMPHLET POTBOILERS AND BEADLE'S DIME NOVELS

SHELLEY STREEBY

Although the story of the US novel from the 1830s to the Civil War era has generally centered on the American Renaissance writers and, to a lesser extent, on the sentimental novel, the most popular literature through the 1850s was the cheap sensational fiction written by George Lippard, Ned Buntline, A. J. H. Duganne, and others who wrote for the story-papers that began to flourish in the 1840s. Lippard's *The Quaker City; or, The Monks of Monk Hall* (1844–45) was the most popular novel in the United States before the publication of Harriet Beecher Stowe's *Uncle Tom's Cabin* (1852). Buntline, who invented the legend of Buffalo Bill, also got his start in the story-papers. Published in Boston, New York, and Philadelphia, the first mass-circulation story-papers had patriotic titles such as the *Flag of Our Union*, the *Star Spangled Banner*, and the *Flag of the Free*. Later, during the 1850s, other popular periodicals with larger circulations emerged, such as Robert Bonner's *New York Ledger*, to which sensational novelist E. D. E. N. Southworth, best known as the author of *The Hidden Hand; or, Capitola the Madcap* (1859), often contributed. Finally, beginning in 1860, Beadle and Company began to publish their famous dime novels, and before long a host of imitators emerged, many of whom, like Beadle, also issued story-papers in which many novels appeared either before or after being issued as inexpensive books. These new forms of cheap sensational literature typified the print and transportation revolutions that took place in this period. The transformation of print and paper-making technologies; the invention of the telegraph; the extension of railroads and other transport systems; and the emergence of an increasingly literate, mobile, and urban readership fundamentally changed the field of popular literature.

The Quaker City, a "Romance of Philadelphia Life, Mystery, and Crime," was just one of many cheap, popular "mysteries of the city" novels that proliferated during the 1840s and 1850s. As Michael Denning shows in his ground-breaking study *Mechanic Accents: Dime Novels and Working-Class Culture in America* (1987), the city mystery novel was an international genre. Eugène Sue's *Les Mystères de Paris*, which was serialized in the *Journal des débats* beginning in 1842, and G. W. M. Reynolds's *The Mysteries of London* (1844–56), a serialized penny dreadful, offer two of the most notable examples. In the United States, Lippard's novel marked the first big success in this genre, but many other "mystery" novels soon followed, including several by Buntline (Edward Zane Carroll Judson), the author of dozens of plays and novels, including *The Mysteries and Miseries of New Orleans* (1851), *The Mysteries and Miseries of New York: A Story of Real Life* (1848), *The B'hoys of New York* (1850), and *The G'hals of New York* (1850). Lippard also wrote several other city mystery novels, including *The Killers: A Narrative of Real Life in Philadelphia* (1850), *The Empire City; or, New York by Night and Day. Its Aristocracy and its Dollars* (1850), and its revised and expanded companion novel, *New York: Its Upper Ten and Lower Million* (1853). David S. Reynolds's early work on Lippard, especially *George Lippard, Prophet of Protest: Writings of an American Radical, 1822–1854* (1986) and *Beneath the American Renaissance: The Subversive Imagination in the Age of Emerson and Melville* (1988), helped readers better understand the larger social contexts that shaped this body of popular fiction. These novels respond to emerging US class, ethnic, and racial hierarchies when their authors dwell on contrasts between the callous, immoral rich and the exploited and suffering poor, as well as between the vicious and the virtuous, often by rendering them as spatial contrasts in rapidly expanding US cities. As Peter Brooks and Dana D. Nelson have suggested, novelists such as Lippard and Buntline, like other authors in the melodramatic tradition, make women's bodies privileged symbols of working-class vulnerability and exploitation. Scenes of persecution by villainous rich seducers, as well as those exalting virtue, exposing hidden identities and relationships, or staging different kinds of rescue, often lie at the heart of these novels.

In *The Quaker City*, the outraged body of Mary Arlington, a merchant's daughter, serves as the primary symbol of the corruption and hypocrisy of the rich men who rule the city. The seducer, Gus Lorrimer, a wealthy libertine, is one of the monks of Monk Hall, the fraternal den of iniquity, gambling, and crime presided over by Devil-Bug, a one-eyed, "thickset specimen of flesh and blood" resembling "a huge insect," and his two "Herculean" black henchmen (ch. 7). Without realizing that his new friend Byrnewood is actually Mary's brother, Lorrimer invites Byrnewood to Monk Hall to witness his sham wedding to "an innocent girl, the flower of one of the first families in the city" (ch. 1). To his great horror, Byrnewood discovers that the girl is his sister, whereupon he is transformed into a "young man whose footsteps trembled as he walked, whose face was livid as the face of a corpse, whose long black hair waved wild and tangled, back from his pale forehead," and whose eye "shone as with a gleam from the flames of hell" (ch. 10). Throughout the rest of this densely plotted novel, one primary thread revolves around Byrnewood's recognition of Lorrimer's villainy and Mary's outraged virtue and his own efforts to foil Devil-Bug, escape Monk Hall, and exact a just revenge. By the end, the wealthy brother has learned to feel for seduced and abandoned working girls by compassionating with his ruined sister; he has also broken the rules of upper-class fraternity by exposing and avenging the villainy of one of his rich "brothers." In these ways, Lippard tries to reconfigure class sympathies by appealing to feelings about virtue, victims, villains, gender, and sexuality that had deep roots in antebellum culture.

Lippard's decision to place a rich libertine, a seduced woman, and her avenging brother at the center of *The Quaker City* sprang from a sensational crime story featured in the Philadelphia penny paper, the *Spirit of the Times*, that he was then writing for. In February of 1843, Singleton Mercer was found not guilty by reason of insanity of the murder of Mahlon Hutchinson Heberton, whom Mercer claimed had raped his younger sister a few days earlier. The migration of such a story from the crime news of the penny dailies to the pages of a sensational novel typifies the genre and shows the permeability of the boundary between crime reporting and the sensational novel. Lippard initially published the novel as a series of pamphlets beginning in 1844, and between 1845 and 1850 twenty-nine editions of *The Quaker City* appeared in book form. A theatrical version of the novel was also planned, but the play was never performed because, according to Lippard, the mayor found "the arm of the civil power, too weak to protect the theatre, in a city where churches had been laid in ashes by a Mob" and so suppressed the play "because Riot was threatened." Also in the preface to the 1845 edition of the novel, which he dedicated to Charles Brockden Brown, Lippard crowed that despite such efforts to suppress his story, it had met "with a success, almost without parallel in the annals of our literature," selling "near 40,000 numbers of the book" since its first publication.

The unprecedented success of the novel enabled Lippard to start his own story-paper, the *Quaker City*, which he claimed was "widely circulated and eagerly read in the Homes of the Poor, not only in New York, but in the city which is more directly the scene of our labors" (Jan. 29, 1849). The purpose of the paper, according to Lippard, was to promote the "development of certain views of social reform," especially "the defence of the Laborer against the exactions of the Capitalist," through "the medium of popular literature" (June 30, 1849), since he believed that a "literature which does not work practically, for the advancement of social reform, or which is too dignified or too good to picture the wrongs of the great mass of humanity, is just good for nothing at all" (Feb. 10, 1849).

In order to develop such a popular literature, Lippard experimented with a number of different genres, including early science fiction. He wrote a "time travel" novel entitled *The Entranced; or, The Wanderer of Eighteen Centuries* (1849), which was serialized in his story-paper and then retitled *Adonai: The Pilgrim of Eternity* and incorporated into *The White Banner* (1851), a collection of his writings that he circulated among the membership of the Brotherhood of the Union, a secret benevolent society founded by Lippard that attained considerable popularity. *Adonai* presents a sensational, violent, and apocalyptic historical and religious fantasy that spans the time from Nero and the Roman Empire to the nineteenth-century United States by tracing the intermittent awakenings of Lucius, or Adonai, a Christian martyr who falls into a magnetic trance that lasts for centuries. Combining an alternative history of Protestantism with a dystopian narrative that surveys modern institutions such as a prison, a factory, and a slave mart in Washington, DC, Lippard exposes the contradictions and impasses in republican thought as he critically juxtaposes abstract formulations of liberal-democratic personhood with the "sensational" bodies of slaves, factory workers, prisoners, and the poor of the whole world.

In thus imagining the role of popular literature, Lippard partly followed the example of Sue, who after writing his novels became a socialist and even represented Paris in the Assembly after the revolution of 1848. In the United States such a trajectory was more unusual, and other sensational novelists, such as Buntline, embraced a different kind of politics. Buntline was a nativist who serialized some of his writings in his story-paper, *Ned Buntline's Own*, where advertisements for nativist organizations such as the Order of United Americans and the Order of United American Mechanics also appeared. Buntline spent time in jail for helping foment the nativist Astor Place theater riots and also included nativist plots in novels such as *The Convict; or, The Conspirator's Victim* (1851), which was loosely based on his imprisonment.

Most of the story-papers, however, avoided polarizing politics, since they hoped to appeal to a mass audience that included diverse sectors of working-class people and also cut across multiple classes. Frederick Gleason's Boston-based *Flag of Our Union* enjoyed perhaps the greatest popularity among mass-circulation story-papers in the 1840s. According to Henry Nash Smith, publishers Gleason and Maturin Murray Ballou pioneered "the development of a national system of distribution" and "developed the standard procedures of the popular adventure story" (1950, 95–96). Ballou wrote many popular adventure novels himself, including *Fanny Campbell, the Female Pirate Captain. A Tale of the Revolution* (1845), *The Spanish Musketeer: A Tale of Military Life* (1847), and *The Adventurer; or, The Wreck on the Indian Ocean: A Land and Sea Tale* (1848). The *Flag of Our Union* also published several novels by Buntline, such as *The Black Avenger of the Spanish Main; or, The Fiend of Blood. A Thrilling Story of Buccaneer Times* (1847) and *The Red Revenger; or, The Pirate King of the Floridas: A Romance of the Gulf and its Islands* (1847).

Instead of defending the laborer against the capitalist, as Lippard aspired to do in the pages of the *Quaker City*, Ballou and Buntline wrote patriotic novels about pirates, foreign adventure, war, empire, and international romance for the *Flag of Our Union* and other popular story-papers of the era, such as Justin Jones's *Star Spangled Banner*, where Buntline's serialized novel *The Last Days of Callao; or, The Doomed City of Sin! A Historical Romance of Peru* (1847) first appeared.

These story-papers claimed circulations of up to 40,000 during the years of the US-Mexico War and they tried to avoid partisan politics in their effort to, as Gleason put it in the *Flag of Our Union*, appeal to "the million, and at a cost, and in a shape, that places them within the reach of all" (Oct. 7, 1847). The papers sold for three or four cents per issue, a price that many working-class readers would have been able to afford, but the publishers sought to appeal to a wider audience that included other classes as well. They therefore declared themselves neutral or independent, although they all issued patriotic US-Mexico War stories that imagined, idealized, and promoted a new "Anglo-Saxon race" defined in relation to Mexico and Mexicans (Horsman 1981, 4). They also often featured pairings of elite and nonelite male characters reminiscent of those in Royall Tyler's nationalistic play *The Contrast* (1787) as they struggled to turn representatives of different classes and nations into a band of white brothers united by war and empire building. In *The Rise and Fall of the White Republic* (1990), historian Alexander Saxton named this project "white egalitarianism" (10): a leveling of distinctions among whites at the expense of nonwhites, with "hard" formations of white egalitarianism associated with the proslavery and expansionist politics of the Democrats and "soft," but still severely hierarchical, versions fashioned by the Whigs and Republicans over the course of the nineteenth century.

Lippard also wrote patriotic US-Mexico War novels for his story-paper, but conflicts of class, race, and nation persistently reemerge in his imperial gothic narratives rather than being reconciled in visions of white fraternity and international romance. The meaning of these novels was shaped by the other material within the story-papers: news about the revolutions in Europe, articles about land-reform and working-class politics, and organizations Lippard founded or sponsored, such as the Brotherhood of the Union and a labor cooperative for seamstresses. Because of these contexts, readers of novels that were serialized in his paper would see on the same page juxtapositions of excerpts from the stories and an array of material about political and labor issues, which contributed to the meanings of the novels. Lippard wrote two sensational novels about the US-Mexico War as it was taking place: *Legends of Mexico* (1847) and *'Bel of Prairie Eden: A Romance of Mexico* (1848). Both were serialized in his story-paper, and both expose the violent scenes of empire building that were conjoined to nationalist fantasies of white working-class freedom. While in *Legends*, Lippard tries to heal the wounds of war through a marriage plot between a Mexican woman and a US soldier, in *'Bel* he rejects this solution and morbidly ends the novel with the premature death of the Mexican bride of a Texan soldier in the US-Mexico War. The bride pines for her dead brother, who unbeknownst to her was killed by minions of her husband to avenge the rape of his sister and the murder of his father and brother. In the end, the war and the dueling cycles of passion and revenge that they engender lead only to misery, loss, and death for both sides: a bleak conclusion rather than a celebratory affirmation of national expansion and empire building.

Buntline also wrote two US-Mexico War novels: *The Volunteer; or, The Maid of Monterey, A Tale of the Mexican War* (1847) for Gleason and the *Flag of Our Union*, and *Magdalena, the Beautiful Mexican Maid. A Story of Buena Vista* (1847), which was published as a book by a rival New York City firm, the Williams Brothers, and appeared in their story-paper, the *Flag of the Free.* While Buntline, more than Lippard, celebrates the US citizen-soldier and inter-American friendship between (white) men in *The Volunteer*, in *Magdalena* the romance between a Mexican woman and a US soldier ends tragically when he dies in the battle of Buena Vista. *Magdalena* is also unique among US-Mexico War novels in making a half-Mexican soldier, Charley Brackett, the US hero, but Buntline abruptly kills him off in the final scenes and refuses the closure of the international romance, thereby suggesting a reluctance to make this couple the model for a possible future between the United States and Mexico.

Most of the other dozens of popular sensational novels about the US-Mexico War that were published in the story-papers during these years celebrated the war and the annexation of northern Mexico, though some raised fears of racial contagion and worried about the incorporation of large numbers of Catholics and Indians into the United States. While Newton Curtis's *"The Prairie Guide; or, The Rose" of the Rio Grande* (1847), like many sensational US-Mexico War novels, ends with the marriage of a rich, white Mexican woman to a white man linked to the US army, who thereby shares her "immense estate" and considerable wealth, other novels imagine a union between representatives of different nations to be impossible or undesirable, such as Arthur Armstrong's *The Mariner of the Mines; or, The Maid of the Monastery* (1847), which marries the elite US soldier-hero to a white New Orleans merchant's daughter, demonizes a "native Mexican" woman who falls in love with him, and represents her Mexican brother's desire for a white US-American woman as rapacious and tyrannical. Many of the other sensational US-Mexico War novels of this period similarly reveal anxieties about the boundaries of the nation and of whiteness, such as Harry Halyard's *The Chieftain of Churubusco; or, The Spectre of the Cathedral* (1848) and Charles Averill's *The Mexican Ranchero; or, The Maid of the Chapparal* (1847), which focus on Irish immigrant villains who desert the US army and join the Mexicans in wildly imaginative nativist retellings of the story of the San Patricios, a group of foreign soldiers who fought for Mexico.

More than a decade later, the US-Mexico War also provided the setting for part of Southworth's *The Hidden Hand*, another best-selling novel of the mid-nineteenth century. Southworth was one of the century's most enduringly popular novelists, penning more than sixty novels, first for the antislavery newspaper the *National Era*, where *Uncle Tom's Cabin* first appeared, and then, after 1856, exclusively for Robert Bonner, the editor of the *New York Ledger*. Many book versions of her novels carried the imprint of Philadelphia cheap publishing firm T. B. Peterson, including titles such as *The Deserted Wife* (1849), *Fallen Pride; or, The Mountain Girl's Love* (1868), and *The Fatal Marriage* (1863). *The Hidden Hand,* first serialized in the *New York Ledger*, was then serialized twice more, in 1868–69 and 1883, before it was published as a book for the first time in 1888. Christopher Looby suggests that Bonner, like Gleason and the other story-paper publishers of the 1840s but to a greater degree, tried to maintain an "apolitical neutrality" (although this too, of course, involves a politics) in order to achieve a massive circulation of 500,000 readers by 1859, and that Southworth's *Hidden Hand* was the "fictional correlate of Bonner's determined political non-partisanship and anti-sectionalism" in the years leading up to the Civil War, striving to magically heal sectional differences (2004, 181).

One of the ways Southworth tried to reconcile regions and classes was by incorporating the US-Mexico War novel into the mix of genres she adapted and transformed in *The Hidden Hand*, which also combines the city mystery genre with the plantation romance. The irrepressible heroine Capitola moves from the streets of New York, where she cross-dresses in order to work as a newsboy, to a Virginia plantation, where she has to outmaneuver a villainous uncle whose regiment is sent to Mexico just as he is plotting to have her killed. The city scenes of the opening chapters recall the economically and spatially bifurcated worlds of Lippard's *New York: Its Upper Ten and Lower Million* and Buntline's *The Mysteries and Miseries of New York*, while the final parts incorporate aspects of the plots of the story-paper novelettes of the US-Mexico War era. Capitola's love interest, Herbert Greyson, serves in the war, but although he becomes an officer, his friend Traverse Rocke soon regrets enlisting, partly because he is subjected to antidemocratic military hierarchies but also because he decides that the war is one of invasion and feels that it is wrong to "[invade] another's country" (ch. 45). The villain's plans are foiled in the end, and the US-Mexico War scenes serve as a theater for the exposure of villainy and the recognition of virtue. At a moment of extreme sectional division and impending civil war, these scenes further reconcile North and South by appealing to contemporary nostalgia for an earlier foreign war in which northerners and southerners had joined forces against the Mexicans. Even though Southworth characteristically refuses to take sides and instead represents characters who both endorse and criticize the war, her setting of many final scenes in the Southwest contributes to the remembrance of a time when North and South came together. Perhaps this is also why Bonner ran several US-Mexico War novels in his paper during these years, even though that conflict had ended long ago.

This strategy of reducing sectionalism through war nostalgia became more difficult to achieve after 1860 (the year that the first dime novel appeared), since the Civil War broke out not long after Beadle and Company issued a revised and expanded version of Ann Stephens's *Malaeska, the Indian Wife of the White Hunter*. Perhaps, as Bill Brown suggests, the nation's East-West conflict was a welcome distraction during the years of Civil War, although the Indian wars also proved bloody and divisive. Stephens's novel, which is set in colonial New York and focuses on an Indian woman and the tragic fate of her half-white son, William, had first been serialized in 1839 in the *Ladies' Companion*, a magazine that Stephens edited. William is the child of Malaeska and a white hunter who has "gone native," much to the chagrin of his wealthy parents back home, who take in the boy and his mother after the hunter dies. But the boy's grandfather, John Danforth, full of bitter hatred against the Indians who killed his son, imparts these prejudices to William, who succumbs to self-hatred and kills himself after he discovers that he is Malaeska's son. Is this tragic ending the result of the boy's "passionate nature" or the hateful way he was nurtured by his grandfather?

Stephens does not supply an answer to this question, choosing to focus instead on what Yu-Fang Cho calls "women's shared predicament" across racial lines. This focus "is strengthened in the dime novel," since "added chapters elaborate" on "young William's growing indifference to Malaeska" and the confrontations between Malaeska and Danforth. Cho observes that "Malaeska's self-reliance and heroism are highlighted in several action scenes" and that the dime novel "adds an explicit statement about women's common fate in patriarchy," thereby appropriating "the Indian question" to erase "racial and class differences within the category of the universal 'woman,'" and in the process "displacing racial issues onto gender concerns by constantly conflating white supremacy with patriarchy" (2007, 11). Even though a different formation of white supremacy complicated the Civil War, perhaps the move of erasing racial and class differences by focusing on gender offered diversion in the context of the emergent North-South conflict over slavery.

Stephens was already a well-known author before she started writing for Beadle, as the publishers acknowledged in a notice that appeared in the first edition, which announced that "the novel chosen to begin the list, is a proof of the high standard which the publishers have adapted. It is one of the best stories ever written by a lady universally acknowledged to be the most brilliant authoress of America, and cannot fail to insure the success of the series, and amply sustain the reputation of the writer." Beadle's intention to appeal to a mass audience that cuts across classes, genders, and generations informs the promise that there "shall not be a line or a sentiment in any of these books which may not be placed in the hands of a child, or be uninteresting to the grandmother of a family" (pref.). Indeed, Beadle's dime novels aspired to a respectability that had eluded most earlier story-paper literature, and the company drew on the sentimental as well as the sensational to reach a broad national audience. And although the Civil War disrupted transportation networks and made it harder for dime novels to achieve a national circulation until the conflict had ended, by the late 1860s and in the wake of the war these novels would reach millions of southerners as well as northerners.

Beadle's novels represented a new literary commodity, easily recognizable because of the trademark dime on their bright-orange covers, their standard length of approximately 100 pages, and their small size: they could easily be carried around, concealed behind books and other larger items, obtained from news stands, and read while traveling on new forms of transportation such as railways. By 1861, they also featured a striking illustration on the cover that focused on a significant moment of crisis, confrontation, or revelation in the novel. In addition to the specific literary commodity marketed by Beadle beginning in 1860, however, the term "dime novel" also refers to a variety of cheap novels that were sold for prices ranging from a nickel to a quarter in a wide range of formats, including the story-paper, the pamphlet novel, the cheap library, and the thick book. Dime novels incorporated a variety of genres, although the western has often been treated as the most typical and important one, especially westerns written by, about, and for boys and men. Other important genres include the seduction narrative; city mystery; imperial adventure; historical and international romances; and pirate, war, and detective fiction.

One of the most popular and influential of the early dime novels was *Seth Jones; or, The Captives of the Frontier* (1860), written by Edward Ellis, a New Jersey schoolteacher who, Beadle bragged, was "the best delineator of Border and Indian life now writing for the press." *Seth Jones* eventually sold nearly 600,000 copies, partly because advertising posters raising the question "Who is Seth Jones?" were papered all over various cities before the novel was released, thereby piquing public curiosity. Seth Jones turned out to be the gentleman Eugene Morton, who impersonated the already stock character, the "Green Mountain Boy," in order to hide his true identity, and readers responded most enthusiastically to Ellis's Yankee, whose "Anglo-Saxon" abilities are tested but not defeated by the Mohawks who kidnap a white pioneer's daughter. Ellis wrote many other dime novels, including some that focused on contemporary conflicts such as the US-Dakota War (1862), including *Indian Jim: A Tale of the Minnesota Massacre* (1864) and *The Hunter's Escape: A Tale of the North West in 1862* (1864). Both of these novels itemize many of the Dakotas' grievances, such as broken treaties and poor reservation lands, and include representations of exceptional "good" Indians. But both ultimately suggest that the war revealed the "truth" of the Indian's "fallen nature," and that idealistic boys who romanticize Indians must grow up and become men who, instead of imitating Indians, should master them to protect the white family.

Although we often remember dime novels as a male genre and privilege examples, such as *Seth Jones,* the early years of dime-novel production saw women such as Stephens and Metta Victor also authoring westerns and other kinds of stories. Readers' letters as well as commentary of publishers and editors suggest that women formed an important sector of the audience throughout the 1860s and 1870s and that publishers did not begin to distinguish consciously between male and female readers of dime novels until the early 1880s. And even then, they often did so in superficial ways, such as by changing the author's name from a woman's to a man's or by putting the word "boy" in the subtitle.

Stephens's status as the author of the first of Beadle's dime novels offers one prominent sign of women's significant participation in this new culture industry, illustrating as well the permeable boundary between sentimental and sensational literature. Like other Beadle's authors, such as Mary Denison, Stephens wrote for periodicals that were a part of the culture of sentiment, such as *Godey's Lady's Book*, the *Olive Branch*, and the *Ladies' Companion*. Her books reached a diverse audience that included women of multiple generations as well as men and boys. Her novels encompass a range of genres—from stories of the American Revolution and colonial times to city mysteries, captivity narratives, and imperial adventures. She went on to write several more dime novels for Beadle and Company, including *Myra, the Child of Adoption* (1860), *Ahmo's Plot; or, The Governor's Indian Child* (1863), *Mahaska: The Indian Princess* (1863), *The Indian Queen* (1864), *Sybil Chase; or, The Valley Ranche* (1861), and *Esther: A Story of the Oregon Trail* (1862). She composed a famous letter to Victor Hugo defending the execution of John Brown on grounds that the rule of law must be sustained. In novels such as *Myra*, which, as the third Beadle novel, concerns a New Orleans heiress, slaves figure as degraded beings who aid the villains. Although her work generally suggests a northern Republican worldview, like most other Beadle's authors of this era, she tries to reconcile North and South imaginatively and adapts and defends racial hierarchies and white egalitarianism even when she criticizes the institution of slavery.

This was true of most of the Beadle's dime novels that focused on slavery, including Victor's *Maum Guinea, and Her Plantation "Children"; or, Holiday-Week on a Louisiana Estate* (1861) and *The Unionist's Daughter: A Tale of the Rebellion in Tennessee* (1862). Victor, who married Beadle's editor Orville Victor, also wrote several dime-novel westerns, including *Alice Wilde, the Raftsman's Daughter* (1860), *The Backwoods' Bride: A Romance of Squatter Life* (1860), and *The Two Hunters; or, The Canon Camp: A Romance of the Santa Fe Trail* (1865). *Maum Guinea*, a special double number that sold over 100,000 copies, unfolds on a Louisiana plantation and relies heavily on romantic racialist humor and descriptions of, in Victor's words, "barbecues, negro-weddings, night-dances, hunts, alligator-adventures" and "slave-sales" that she claimed were "simple reproductions of what is familiar to every Southerner." Thus during the war she purveyed nostalgic scenes of antebellum plantation life in the South to a national audience. In the introduction, Victor also advises readers that she has sought "in the guise of a romance, to reproduce the slave, in all his varied relations, with historical truthfulness" and that the novel was not meant "to subserve any special social or political purpose." While black characters and typical southern scenes form the main focus in *Maum Guinea*, in *The Unionist's Daughter*, which was written in the middle of the war, white people replace slaves as objects of sympathy as Victor imagines villainous southerners persecuting white border-dwellers who are loyal to the Union. But although this novel exposes the divisions the war created within the white nation, by 1865 Victor welcomed the South back to a more expansive national family in her novel *The Two Hunters*, as she marries her northern hero to the daughter of "Spanish" southerners with investments in plantation slavery and Mexican gold mines.

As Saxton suggests, by the 1850s, when the crisis over slavery intensified, white egalitarian heroes in story-paper fiction had moved "decisively in an anti-slavery direction" as northern writers increasingly tried to imagine a future based on "free labor" and "free soil," in opposition to chattel slavery and the southern plantation (1990, 196). And yet, this northern version of white egalitarianism could easily coexist with contempt for slaves and free black people or the opinion that black people were naturally subordinate to white people. Dozens of Beadle's novels published between 1860 and 1865 respond to the crisis from such a white egalitarian, northern Republican perspective, although some push the boundaries of this world view, such as N. C. Iron's *The Two Guards* (1863), which is full of romantic racialism but also shows much more sympathy for the escaped slave at the center of the novel than is usually the case in dime novels. Dime novels enjoyed popularity among northern soldiers during the Civil War, and several cheap novels about the war appealed to those who wanted to read war stories loosely based on topical events, such as Charles Anderson's *Pauline of the Potomac; or, General McClellan's Spy* (1862) and Buntline's *The Rattlesnake; or, The Rebel Privateer: A Tale of the Present Time* (1862). According to historian Alice Fahs, dime novels about "women spies, scouts, and cross-dressing soldiers" imagined "a more active—and transgressive—women's role in the war" and also sometimes "allowed for expressions of autoeroticism and homoeroticism not socially acceptable within the confines of heterosexual society" (2001, 231, 240). Like the US-Mexico War romances of the 1840s, these novels often tried to reconcile the two warring sides by imagining a romance between a northern male soldier and a cross-dressed woman from the South, and most featured scenes of intense friendship and rivalry among men of different classes, races, and regions.

Like Beadle's dime novels about the Civil War, their early westerns and other cheap novels of imperial adventure also reveal northern Republican, free-soil, and white egalitarian sympathies. The crisis over slavery haunts dime novels of imperial adventure and international romance such as Mary Andrews Denison's *The Prisoner of La Vintresse; or, The Fortunes of a Cuban Heiress* (1860). Like Stephens, Denison had already made a reputation as a contributor to story-papers and women's magazines before she began contributing novels to Beadle, including *Chip, the Cave Child* (1860), *The Mad Hunter; or, The Downfall of the LeForests* (1863), and *Ruth Margerie: A Romance of the Revolt of 1689* (1862). Denison had connections to the antislavery movement because her husband, Charles, edited the New York antislavery journal the *Emancipator*, and she had written an antislavery novel, *Old Hepsy* (1858), before becoming a Beadle's contributor. Even so, in *The Prisoner of La Vintresse*, Denison presents a half-English, white Cuban heiress as the heroine of her international romance; depicts black people in Cuba as abject, malevolent slaves; and identifies the Spanish with the Black Legend and tyranny in ways that resonate with nativist anti-imperialism that opposed the addition of large numbers of nonwhites and foreigners to the nation. Although the novel culminates in marriage and the incorporation of the Cuban heroine into the white American family, scenes of the hero, who is accused of being a spy for the Yankees, being starved and mistreated on a remote Cuban slave plantation suggest that US expansion threatens to not only add undesirable people to the nation but also to fatally weaken white US manhood.

Land reformer and poet A. J. H. Duganne, who in 1850 served a term as a representative of the nativist Know-Nothing Party in the New York state assembly, articulated some of these anxieties in his two dime novels about Mexico, *The Peon Prince; or, The Yankee Knight-Errant. A Tale of Modern Mexico* (1861) and the sequel *Putnam Pomfret's Ward; or, A Vermonter's Adventures in Mexico* (1861). Duganne also wrote two other dime novels for Beadle, *The King's Man: A Tale of South Carolina in Revolutionary Times* (1860) and *Massasoit's Daughter; or, The French Captives* (1861). During the 1840s, Duganne authored city mystery novels such as *The Knights of the Seal; or, The Mysteries of the Three Cities* (1845) and *The Daguerreotype Miniature; or, Life in the Empire City* (1846). During these years he became very involved in George Henry Evans's project of national land reform and contributed poetry about it to reform newspapers such as the *Voice of Industry* and Evans's *Young America*. Duganne's two dime novels about Mexico, which both take place more than a decade earlier, also address some of these ideas and thereby reveal many of the contradictions of anti-imperialism, white egalitarianism, and changing ideas about land and labor at this time. In both novels, Duganne suggests that Mexico is best ruled by Mexicans, partly because he believes nonwhites are capable of republican self-government, as we see through the example of the peon prince Zumozin, whose status as an Indian and his alliance with Mexican Creoles and US northerners recall Benito Juárez. But Duganne also seems to fear the contamination of chattel slavery-like labor arrangements such as debt peonage on Mexican haciendas, which he compares to southern plantations. This may be another reason why his novels suggest that supporting a republican coalition comprised of Indians and creoles is a better idea than annexing all or part of Mexico.

In addition to stories of the recent US-Mexico War, readers of dime novels enjoyed historical romances about foreign lands, such as William Jared Hall's *The Slave Sculptor; or, The Prophetess of the Secret Chamber. A Tale of Mexico at the Period of the Conquest* (1860), which was reprinted three times in the decades that followed. Written by a judge from Ohio who also wrote short stories about Mexico and the South for the popular press, the novel capitalized on the popular interest in the Spanish conquest of Mexico inspired by W. H. Prescott's best-selling history, which was also issued in multiple editions over the course of the nineteenth century. As it does in many other dime novels of imperial adventure, however, the crisis over slavery erupts in *The Slave Sculptor* despite its faraway setting and distance in time. Hall takes great liberties with both popular and official histories as he focuses on the "slaves" of the Aztec empire and singles out for sympathy a former slave girl, Mazina, whose skin is "clear and white," exhibiting not "one tinge of the dusky, cinnamon hue, peculiar to the features of the aborigines" (ch. 1). Mazina is a key character in the novel, along with the former slave Maxtla, whose "dress was that usually worn by the laboring class, showing clearly the outlines of his muscular frame" (ch. 2). While Mazina's dress and body connect her to a white laboring class, Maxtla is also a great sculptor whose talent allows him to purchase his freedom. In the end, it is revealed that both Mazina and Maxtla are Spaniards who were sold into slavery in Mexico after a shipwreck. By offering two white slaves as points of identification, the romance rearticulates and transforms the white egalitarianism and Anglo-Saxon racism that had been popularized during the US-Mexico War years. Although Spaniards were ambiguously white in nineteenth-century US popular literature, this early dime novel emphasizes the whiteness of the slaves of European descent, and Mazina and Maxtla marry each other rather than persons of another race or another nation. At the novel's end, they live in a large palace near Mexico City, along with Meztli, a slave girl and "strange child of the Aztecs" whose "skin was much lighter than usual," who promises to be Maxtla's slave for life if he saves her from being offered as a human sacrifice. In the novel's last paragraph, Hall reveals that Meztli has remained "faithful to her pledge" and that "the kind-hearted Aztec was far from being a slave in a family of her friends"; the couple's children even call her "Aunt Mezzi" (ch. 20). Here, Hall imagines a household that includes a slave who is part of the family, thereby reproducing apologetic visions of happy slaves across space and time in a popular novel aimed at northern readers and published just before the US Civil War began—a time when many northerners were willing to compromise with the South over slavery to avoid secession and war.

Mexico is also an important setting in the first dime detective novel published by Beadle and Company: Victor's *The Dead Letter: An American Romance* (1866). Victor's novel reveals the indebtedness of detective fiction to the city mystery literature written by Lippard, Buntline, Poe, and others, for there are many connections between the two subgenres. The plot turns on the scandalous murder of one of what Lippard would call the upper ten: a New York banker who is supposed to marry a rich heiress. The detective who is sent to solve the crime ends up discovering the murderer is a poor relation who pays a criminal to kill the banker so he will inherit the family fortune. Ultimately, the detective disguises himself as a scientific explorer and tracks the murderer to Mexico. Both the Mexicans and the lower classes are objects of suspicion in Victor's novel: the Mexicans have a "code of right and wrong [that] is different from ours" (pt. 2, ch. 6), while the threat of the lower classes is embodied by the murderous poor relation and the abject Irish sewing girl who is connected to him. Although this detective novel is quite sentimental and upholds the values of respectable white middle-class womanhood, either Victor or her publishers decided to disguise her authorship, instead attributing the novel to the nonexistent Seeley Regester. The fact that Victor had actually written it was not revealed until four years later.

Here for perhaps the first time the author's gender seems to matter to readers of dime novels: the male pseudonym attached to the first dime-detective novel suggests that this new literary commodity might have less appeal if perceived as the work of a woman. Such gendered distinctions figured more prominently in the 1870s and especially in the 1880s. In 1882, the firm's flagship story-paper *Beadle's Weekly* began to run far fewer stories by women and disguised female authorship, as in the case of *The Dead Letter*, by using male pseudonyms or initials instead of female names. And by the late 1870s, almost all the novels published in Beadle's new half-dime library series were written by men and frequently had the word "boy" in the title. In the mid-1870s, Beadle launched gender-marked enterprises such as the *Boys' Books of Romance and Adventure* (1874), weekly story-papers like *Belles and Beaux* (1874), and *Girls of Today* (1875–76). These did not last very long, which suggests that for most of the 1870s, Beadle found it more profitable to target a large mass audience not explicitly marked by gender: the *Saturday Journal*, later known as *Beadle's Weekly* and *Banner Weekly*, which ran for almost three decades, appealed to just such an audience and included serialized novels by both male and female authors. But the 1882 move to disguise female authorship and reduce dependence on women writers as well as the success of new Beadle's series for young boys were huge changes with dramatic consequences for how the dime novel as a literary and cultural institution has been remembered.

Thus the 1877 debut of Beadle's half-dime library series, which was aimed at boys, made two kinds of important distinctions: between male and female, and younger and older readers. Although earlier dime novels had targeted a wide audience of readers across genders and generations, this new series focused on an audience of young boys. The first novel in the series, Edward Wheeler's hugely popular *Deadwood Dick, The Prince of the Road; or, The Black Rider of the Black Hills* (1877), was a sensational success that sold five million copies between 1860 and 1865 and inspired thirty-two successors. Even as it represented a break with older kinds of cheap literature in the explicit gender marking of the series that framed it, the novel also incorporated older character types and melodramatic conventions. The endangered and dangerous women of seduction narratives, stories of war and imperial adventure, and city mystery literature take on new forms in *Deadwood Dick*. Fearless Frank first encounters the beautiful Alice Terry, stripped to the waist and being whipped by the demonic Sitting Bull, while Calamity Jane, on the other hand, saves the hero from death at the hands of the white villains. Calamity Jane is a ruined woman who has lost her sexual virtue but retains others, in particular her courage and derring-do. Her many "boyish" traits are notable, and her prominence in the Deadwood Dick stories, along with the bowery girls, pirates' daughters, girl miners, female forgers, and detective queens in this series, suggest that gender is not completely fixed and binary in these novels, that some female readers were finding their way to them, and that the primary audience of boys could still enjoy reading about some female characters and might perhaps even identify with them.

During the 1880s and 1890s, such gendered distinctions would loom much larger. As new story-papers, dime novel series, and illustrated magazines appeared at the end of the century, love and romance were often considered subjects and genres particularly cherished by women and unappealing to boys, even though romance narratives were frequently incorporated into what were increasingly understood to be the "male" genres: westerns; detective fiction; and stories of science, war, and imperial adventure. In the 1880s and after, Street and Smith particularly targeted girls with working-girl fiction, such as Francis Smith's 1871 story *Bertha the Sewing Machine Girl; or, Death at the Wheel* as well as literature by women writers such as Laura Libbey. During the same years, they also published stories aimed at boys, such as the many Buffalo Bill novels that followed in the wake of Buntline's *Buffalo Bill, the King of Border Men* (1869–70), which was first serialized in Street and Smith's *New York Weekly.* And after Horatio Alger, Jr.'s influential *Ragged Dick; or, Street Life in New York with the Boot-Blacks* (1867) was serialized in the periodical *Student and Schoolmate,* publisher A. K. Loring signed him up to write several more uplift novels for boys that envisioned cross-class bonds between boys and men as the solution to poverty and class hierarchies. Dozens of Alger's pedagogical novels for boys with titles such as *Ben the Luggage Boy; or, Among the Wharves* (1870), *Tattered Tom; or, The Story of a Street Arab* (1871), *The Errand Boy; or, How Phil Brent Won Success* (1888), and *Mark Mason's Victory: The Trials and Triumphs of a Telegraph Boy* (1899) appeared in the decades that followed.

The Buffalo Bill novels, the Alger novels, and Beadle's half-dime library are all harbingers of the more dramatic shift that would take place in the 1880s. In the cheap novel before 1870, however, the familiar reclassification of dime novels as a boy's genre and as children's literature loomed on the horizon but had not yet transpired. Through the end of the 1860s, a strong distinction between adult and child readers, and between stories for boys and stories for girls remained to be precariously forged through the marketing categories to come, but even when these distinctions developed, women continued to write many more of these novels than we have remembered, while both boys' and girls' stories were often comprised of sensational adventure, romance, and sentimental instruction.

Part IV

LEADING NOVELISTS OF ANTEBELLUM AMERICA

14

JAMES FENIMORE COOPER: BEYOND LEATHER-STOCKING

WAYNE FRANKLIN

In 1850, near the end of his life, James Fenimore Cooper looked back over the crowded terrain of a long career. Since publishing his first novel, *Precaution* (1820), he had written a great deal: thirty-one other novels; five travelogues covering much of his European period (1826–33); histories of topics as diverse as his hometown and the United States Navy (in which he had served from 1808 to 1810); an array of periodical essays and reviews; and various controversial works, chief among them *The American Democrat* (1838). What would last? He had few doubts: "If anything from the pen of the writer . . . is at all to outlive himself, it is, unquestionably, the series of 'The Leather-Stocking Tales'" ("Preface to the Leather-Stocking Tales," 1850).

Many of his other books continue to be read today, in the United States and around the globe, but Cooper was right about the high claims of the five novels that, by the time he wrote the last of them in 1841, assured him continuing fame: *The Pioneers; or, The Sources of the Susquehanna* (1823), *The Last of the Mohicans: A Narrative of 1757* (1826), *The Prairie* (1827), *The Pathfinder; or, The Inland Sea* (1840), and *The Deerslayer; or, The First War-Path* (1841). From a later viewpoint, the novels perhaps acquire a kind of inevitability. But Cooper had hardly been programmatic about the series *as* a series. Far from it. Only after he had finished writing the last of them were they widely advertised and sold as a unified group. Furthermore, their central character, Leather-Stocking, also known as Natty Bumppo, seems not to have been an integral part of *The Pioneers*, at least when Cooper began work on it. At the time, Cooper was thinking not about Bumppo and his Indian companion Chingachgook—let alone the possible future installments of their joined lives—but rather about the lost world of Cooperstown, which the novelist's father had founded in the 1780s but which by 1821 was beyond the collapsed family's control. Set in the lightly fictionalized village of Templeton, the book evoked that lost world with poignant feeling: Cooper had written the book, he claimed in his original preface, "to please [him]self," and that comment rings true. Only later did he recognize that in creating Bumppo and his Mohican friend he had pleased American (and European) readers as well.

In part because of its personal meanings, *The Pioneers* had been difficult to finish. It sold very well, but in its wake Cooper did not immediately seize on Bumppo's frontier life as his inevitable subject. Instead, he returned to the subject of his previous book, *The Spy: A Tale of the Neutral Ground* (1821), a Revolutionary War story centered on a seemingly selfish peddler named Harvey Birch, who in fact is the secret agent of George Washington. With the fiftieth anniversary of the Revolution fast approaching, Cooper wrote two more war tales in quick succession: *The Pilot* (1824), a sea tale concerning a rebel raid on the English coast, and *Lionel Lincoln; or, The Leaguer of Boston* (1825), set in the Boston of Bunker Hill. Only then did he again think of Bumppo, and he did so in the least theoretical, almost leisurely, of ways. For *The Last of the Mohicans* did not begin as an overt resurrection of Natty. Cooper found the inspiration for it in a trip to Lake George, amid New York's Adirondack Mountains, undertaken in the summer of 1824 with a quartet of visiting young Englishmen. As they paused en route to admire the wonderfully chaotic plunge of the Hudson River through its rocky gorge at Glens Falls, one of the Englishmen, Edward Smith-Stanley (the future Earl of Derby), recalled that Cooper said he wanted to use that setting for a frontier romance. Later, as they toured the grounds of the ruined Fort William Henry on Lake George's shore, Cooper imagined that spot—site of an infamous massacre carried out by Indian allies of the French in 1757—as a second nodal point in what would become his sixth novel. Once he began writing it, he added Natty to the "Indian" tale Smith-Stanley remembered him envisioning.

There were gestures toward these Adirondack scenes in Natty's fugitive recollections in *The Pioneers* about "the old French war," and his service then under the legendary Sir William Johnson. But in no essential way had that novel pre-scripted, let alone necessitated, the new one. Once *The Last of the Mohicans* was published, however, Cooper's next step seemed clear. As he prepared to take his family to France in 1826, he began work on a third Leather-Stocking Tale, *The Prairie*, which would be finished and published in Paris the following year. In that novel, the death of Natty on the American grasslands carried out hints, at the end of *The Pioneers*, that Natty had no alternative, amid the wasteful squandering of the settled East, except to head west. But with the close of the old trapper's life in *The Prairie*, it seemed likely that Cooper was done with him.

Only after he had written another nine novels, his five travelogues, and a pile of controversial works did Cooper again return to Natty's story. He did so in a back-to-back pair of tales, *The Pathfinder* and *The Deerslayer*, in which he filled in two more periods of the character's earlier life. Because *The Deerslayer* is focused on Natty's early adulthood—its title refers to the fact that the eighteen-year-old hunter has yet to kill a man in warfare—the completed series eventually acquired a sort of mythic shape, prompting D. H. Lawrence to declare famously that Natty, like America, was born old and then grew young. Actually, the chronology of the series is more complicated; furthermore, by the time Cooper had finished the books he was beginning to think it best that readers approach them not in the sequence of their composition but rather in terms of Natty's life (hence his 1850 preface to the group of five, quoted at the head of this chapter, was placed in *The Deerslayer*, not *The Pioneers*). Moreover, Cooper clearly imagined, at various points in the 1840s, that he might write a sixth novel, rounding out the group with a tale depicting Natty's part in the Revolution.

The large-scale articulation of the Leather-Stocking Tales across the period from 1823 to 1841 was a remarkable accomplishment. Cooper wrote the books with a canny sense of the possibilities (and impossibilities) set up in the previous volumes. In the process, he followed a sophisticated line of improvisation. In each novel, Natty is recognizably separate. The books focus on different stages in his worldly career—hunter, scout, trapper—as well as different moments in his emotional life. He is the aged servitor of Elizabeth Temple in *The Pioneers*, the forest guide for Cora and Alice Munro in *The Last of the Mohicans*, the sage in *The Prairie*, the baffled lover in *The Pathfinder*, and the unbloodied innocent in *The Deerslayer*. In the original preface he wrote for *The Pathfinder*, Cooper remarked, "It is not an easy task . . . to introduce the same character in four separate works, and to maintain the peculiarities that are indispensable to identity, without incurring a risk of fatiguing the reader with sameness." Judged by this standard, he had succeeded splendidly in balancing the old and new.

Doing so took extraordinary flexibility and finesse, traits with which Cooper is not usually credited. Moreover, he learned a good deal in the long process. For one thing, he learned how to place his books in larger groupings. This was a key lesson, for in some ways Cooper was always a serial artist. He imagined large territories, and in various books he returned to them, narratively mapping fresh parts. One can appreciate the scope of this pattern by glancing for a moment beyond the Leather-Stocking Tales. When Cooper had just finished *The Pioneers*, his recent reading of Sir Walter Scott's *The Pirate* (1822) spurred him to think about how a real sailor (Cooper, as opposed to Scott) might write about the sea. That was a typically impulsive point of origin for a Cooper book: after the initial hesitations of his career, he usually did not think long and hard about a new book, or belabor its creation. But there was also something else going on with regard to *The Pilot*. The novel reworks some of the assumptions of *The Spy*—much as *The Pioneers*, in its portrait of Natty, had borrowed from the previous portrayal of Birch. (*The Pioneers* also borrowed two characters from *The Spy*: Betty Flanagan and her new husband, Sergeant Hollister, who, having survived the Revolution in Westchester County, now run The Bold Dragoon in Templeton.) In *The Pilot*, the mysterious "Mr. Gray" (acting as the book's Pilot, he is in actuality John Paul Jones) owes something to both Birch and Bumppo. Moreover, the plot of the sea story stems, in several instances (as in its use of a domestic microcosm to evoke the macrocosm of a world at war), from that of *The Spy*. In writing the new book, Cooper was aware that he was extending a mode he had established in the earlier one. In his next book, *Lionel Lincoln*, he became so taken with the potential for linking books that he ambitiously promised the public a grand series prematurely dubbed the "Legends of the Thirteen Republics." Following the unsatisfactory reception of *Lionel Lincoln*, however, Cooper largely abandoned that plan, another reason for his return to Bumppo in his next two books.

What certainly survived from the "Legends" idea was a network of looser connections among Cooper's books across the rest of his career. It is worth specifying at this point the various subsets into which his novels fall. The biggest group, initiated with *The Pilot*, includes his dozen or so sea stories, from *The Red Rover* (1828) and *The Water-Witch; or, The Skimmer of the Seas* (1830) to *The Two Admirals* (1842) and *The Sea Lions; or, The Lost Sealers* (1849). Although these books constitute the largest single group among Cooper's novels, they are nonetheless highly miscellaneous: the common maritime setting and themes do not preclude a great variety of other matter. For instance, *The Red Rover*, focused on coastal smuggling in colonial Rhode Island, devotes its first half to describing provincial life on shore in the decades before the Revolution. Thus, it is notably distinct from *The Sea Lions*, a nineteenth-century tale that uses the sealing trade in the South Atlantic to explore the moral contrast between the oddly paired masters of identically named ships. The earlier novel, whose hero is little short of a pirate, is full of romantic tropes; the second, in which the sealing ships are trapped by the ice of a fierce polar winter, is a mix of maritime realism and spiritual allegory.

The same point might be made in a more nuanced way about the five Leather-Stocking Tales, which are so strongly bonded to each other that we forget how varied they are, and how the individual books actually fit into other groupings as well. *The Pioneers* and *The Deerslayer* belong to a Templeton/Otsego set that also includes *Home as Found* (1838) and *Wyandotté; or, The Hutted Knoll* (1843), as well the nonfictional *Chronicles of Cooperstown* (1838). But *The Pioneers* also originated a series of settlement tales that would come to include *The Wept of Wish-ton-Wish* (1829) and *Wyandotté*, as well as *The Crater; or, Vulcan's Peak* (1847). *The Last of the Mohicans* and *The Pathfinder* belong with Cooper's other French and Indian War tale, *Satanstoe; or, The Littlepage Manuscripts* (1845), even though that book is more immediately tied to the other two Littlepage tales, *The Chainbearer* (1845) and *The Redskins; or, Indian and Injin* (1846). Seriality is as slippery a concept as it is a useful one when dealing with the sheer array and number of Cooper's works. In some ways, his unit of composition was the episode—and his skill at combining different kinds of episodes in different books helps account for the sheer number of his books.

There was no canon of American novels when Cooper began to write in 1820, and very few viable examples that he might imitate. He took his own inspiration from a combination of oral and print sources of a quite miscellaneous sort. Although we know that he read Charles Brockden Brown and was clearly indebted to him, his most important influence derived from Scott, whom Cooper read avidly and actively and met in Paris in 1826, when Scott graciously called on his American rival. Scott had demonstrated the peculiar interest historical fiction held for readers who had lived through the upheavals that began with the French Revolution in 1789 (coincidentally the year of Cooper's birth) and ended only with Napoleon's final defeat in 1815. Scott also provided countless separate examples of how to set up, exploit, and resolve various plot situations, as well as how to conceive, introduce, and develop various kinds of characters, both low and high. Perhaps less evident, but equally important, was the commercial inspiration that Scott's career provided for Cooper and other American writers of the time. Scott made a great deal of money through his novels, a virtually unexampled accomplishment at the time. Cooper, desperately short of cash following the collapse of his family's fortune, saw the author of *Waverley; or, 'Tis Sixty Years Since* (1814) as his model in this regard as well.

But the debt to Scott, though deep, did not blind Cooper to what he increasingly saw as Scott's shortcomings and biases. Almost from the start, republican Cooper drew important distinctions between his art and the more exclusive variety produced by the royalist Scott. To be sure, Scott also had his "low" characters. But when Cooper introduced seemingly similar figures in his books, Natty for example, he did so with a rather different intent. By the end of *The Pioneers*, Natty is, as it were, both outside society and above it: his worth is determined not by his social standing but rather his moral vision. Natty is a commoner, like Birch, but provides something more than the reassuring comic relief commoners usually offer in Scott: both of Cooper's characters represent one of the key innovations he wrought in his fiction, namely, opening up the novel to make it more fully reflect the demographic realities and ideological strivings of the American republic.

One may gain insight into the importance of this innovation by considering how Cooper makes room in his books for non-European characters. For all that can be said, from a modern perspective, against Cooper's portrayal of Native Americans, it needs to be recalled that, prior to *The Pioneers* and especially *The Last of the Mohicans*, Indians were few and far between in American fiction. When present at all, they usually were either murderous or dead, and there was little question of their having either cultural or moral significance. Cooper insisted on including Native Americans, and their culture, in his fictional portraits of the nation. In *The Pathfinder*, he puts into Natty's mouth his own credo, and it is a moving one: "A red-skin has his notions, and it is right that it should be so, and if they are not exactly the same as a Christian white man's, there is no harm in it" (ch. 2).

Cooper also included African Americans in his books, though less successfully, from the start of his career. The wonder is not that he failed to portray them as they soon were to portray themselves; it is that, at a time when he could have omitted them altogether, he chose instead to make room for them in the American novel. And even at the outset, he tentatively sought to include their own perspectives. When Birch in *The Spy* offhandedly uses a racial epithet, the Whartons' house slave, Caesar Thompson, interjects his own voice, twice correcting the American patriot. Thereafter, in deference to Caesar, Birch adopts a less objectionable term.

That little social drama was entirely unnecessary to Cooper's plot. He created it and inserted it in order to indicate the social and political consequences cast forward from the Revolution into the life of the new nation.

Cooper's attraction to his ordinary characters, be they red or white or black, was partly the reflex of his own social origins. Judge William Cooper, although a Federalist of prodigious ambition and hauteur, was in some ways a quite ordinary man who instilled in his children respect for the honest commoner's rights and voice. Some of that was probably a holdover not just from his modest economic origins as a Delaware Valley wheelwright but also from the Quaker heritage that he shared with his wife, Elizabeth Fenimore. More tellingly, the future novelist felt his own and his family's fall so acutely that he empathized with those who were humble in life or had been humbled by it. Aside from Natty and Birch, or Chingachgook and Uncas, the greatest beneficiaries of Cooper's empathy were the seamen who populated his fiction. Cooper knew sailors well, having berthed with them on the *Stirling* during his merchant voyage to Europe (1806–07) and having supervised—indeed, recruited—them during his stint in the US Navy. He understood the world of the sea from the perspective of command, but he also valued the rough dignity of the common sailor.

Cooper's empathy is traceable, too, in his openness to kinds of stories that rose up in the increasingly ebullient democratic society of the 1820s. Men like Natty he had met, in various semblances, amid the drifting population of the New York border, from Otsego to the shores of Lake Ontario, where he was posted during his naval years. What is remarkable about how he developed those few hints is the degree to which he gave his frontier hunter and fighter such unmistakable interiority. Although Natty belongs to his place and time, his essence is not defined by his historical circumstances. He is the democratic hero ripe for the coming of the Age of Jackson; a common man of uncommon skill and insight as well as deft action. Moreover, he is a man notable for the restraint he imposes on himself. He refuses to use force merely because he can, and he insists that one of the great powers in life is the power of leaving other things—and beings—alone. In *The Pathfinder*, Natty asserts, with his typically understated eloquence, "I do not seek blood without a cause. . . . I love no [Iroquois], as is just, seeing how much I have consorted with the Delawares, who are their mortal and natural enemies; but I never pull trigger on one of the miscreants, unless it be plain that his death will lead to some good end. The deer never leaped that fell by my hand wantonly" (ch. 5). One wonders whether Cooper heard such affirmations in the New York woods (or in Cooperstown during sessions of the court over which his father presided); one also wonders whether he learned there, too, about woodland adventures of the sort he gives Natty. Perhaps all he knew was that such a figure had to have a story, and his political optimism prodded him to believe that it would be a noble rather than an ignoble one. Fortunately for Cooper, such stories were acquiring great interest at the time among the reading public.

Birch provides a nice instance of that public interest. Cooper had heard the backstory for *The Spy* from statesman John Jay, probably in the summer of 1817, when Cooper moved his family back from Otsego to Westchester County. A few years later, as he sought to write his first decidedly American novel (*Precaution* was a knock-off of the British matrimonial romances he read alongside Scott), it occurred to him that Jay's espionage anecdotes were singularly suggestive. But it had not been mere chance that made those anecdotes available to Cooper or prompted him to use them. In all likelihood, Jay had told him the story because a modest hero of the Revolution, John Paulding, had been pilloried on the floor of the House of Representatives in 1817, when, old and sick, he had petitioned for a small increase in his pension. Paulding's claim on the nation's purse and memory stemmed from the fact that, with two other Westchester militiamen, he had chanced to stop Major John André when that disguised British spy was returning from his final meeting with the American arch-traitor Benedict Arnold in 1780. The attack on Paulding in Congress was carried out by the high-toned Yankee Federalist Benjamin Tallmadge of Connecticut; it spurred a bitter counteroffensive among New York writers and politicians. Among the incidents of the resulting war for public opinion was Jay's tale to Cooper and, a few years later, Cooper's story of the high-minded, though ill-educated spy, Birch.

Paulding's plight bespoke the profound shift in cultural politics taking place in the nation in the aftermath of the War of 1812. Cooper, fully the beneficiary of that shift, soon became a key proponent of it. Tallmadge's contempt for Paulding was contempt for the common man at large, and Cooper's enshrinement of first Birch and then Bumppo (and soon the besmirched John Paul Jones) marked his complete devotion to the ennoblement—indeed, the creation—of the democratic hero. Colloquial figures in American literature in earlier decades had hardly been absent. But it was Cooper's gift to sense that a nation proud of its republican institutions, however imperfect they might be, would soon welcome—even demand—a literature commensurate with its faith in the potentiality of ordinary men and women. Tallmadge represented the recessive values; Cooper the emergent and soon dominant ones. If he had given readers nothing more than Natty and his Mohican companions, or his array of seamen, he would have deserved the fame he soon garnered.

Cooper was also important in the history of the early American novel for two other reasons. First, the set of topics and forms that he improvised proved both useful and imitable for other writers. When Catharine Maria Sedgwick wrote her own Revolutionary novel, *The Linwoods; or, "Sixty Years Since" in America* (1835), she set it in New York rather than her native Massachusetts, employing Cooper's "Neutral Ground" and making use of the loathsome "Skinners" whom he had introduced. She also centered her story, as he had his own, on a family whose loyalties are deeply divided. However, even had Sedgwick written a Revolutionary War novel that explored entirely separate zones of national memory, the very act of choosing that topic would have marked the influential success of Cooper's example. In the thirty-eighth chapter of *The Linwoods*, Sedgwick deferred to Cooper's mastery of sea fiction, a sincere gesture but one that concealed her challenge to his equal dominance of the Revolutionary scene. She would not "attempt to describe" a boat chase in New York waters, Sedgwick explained, because "Heaven seems to have endowed a single genius of our land with a chartered right to all the *water privileges*" in American fiction.

His mastery of frontier themes was also obvious. He introduced the process of border settlement to American readers, especially in its newer, post-Revolutionary form. In this regard, *The Pioneers* was a surprisingly modern story: opening in the very year of the French Reign of Terror, it did not deal with settlement as a colonial topic from the first century of American experience (as Sedgwick soon would in *Hope Leslie; or, Early Times in the Massachusetts* [1827]), but rather as a matter of intense present interest to the post-Revolutionary nation. Moreover, the second and third of the Leather-Stocking Tales added to the theme of settlement two other aspects of the American experience of space: border warfare and continental expansion. In looking back to the French and Indian War in *The Last of the Mohicans*, Cooper established the mode of forest adventure as a staple of the American novelist's production. Herein lay the origins of the western as a popular form among dime novelists and, more recently, filmmakers as well. In *The Prairie*, he brought his hero down to the time of Lewis and Clark: this was not the West of the old French wars but rather of the present and future. The conflict over land was to become the core plot of American history as well as American literature, and it was Cooper who first fully developed its potential.

He was himself the initial beneficiary of these innovations: the repertoire of fictional types he established in his first decade guided his creativity in the 1830s and especially the 1840s. But more important was the service he provided other American novelists in the 1820s, when he produced nearly 10 percent of all American novels. And there was another side to that service. Badly in need of cash as he was, Cooper took to writing not only as a cultural experiment but also as a commercial endeavor. On the face of it, this was a Quixotic undertaking. There was no established market for fiction, or most other kinds of writing, in the country at the time. The typical early national novel was written by a one-time author who saw the book into print by a variety of expedients. Usually he or she paid for its publication and, if it did well enough, earned modest profits. Cooper self-published his first five novels, a lucrative enough procedure once *The Spy* went through two fresh editions within months of its appearance. New York bookseller Charles Wiley, acting as Cooper's agent, handled that novel as well as the next two: in return for a small commission, Wiley arranged for each book's printing, binding, and distribution, and out of friendship for Cooper even provided some literary and editorial advice. But Wiley invested little money in the books himself; Cooper guaranteed the costs and reaped the benefits. With his fifth book, *Lionel Lincoln*, Cooper initially reached similar terms with Wiley. But this was a particularly bad time for

Cooper as he still sought to settle old debts and deal with the ramifying effects of the collapse of his father's estate. He therefore offered Wiley a last-minute chance to acquire the novel, then in production, for a limited period of time, meaning that Wiley would receive all proceeds from the first printing (and, if need be, a second one)—but also would have to assume all costs.

As it happened, although *Lionel Lincoln* sold reasonably well, it was not as successful as the three books preceding it. When Cooper began *The Last of the Mohicans,* Wiley therefore had no incentive to acquire that new book. Only with Wiley's death in January 1826, just as production of the novel in New York was nearing its end, did Cooper manage to sell rights to it (for a term of four years) to a Philadelphia firm, Carey and Lea, that had been interested in acquiring his works for some time. Soon, Carey and Lea paid Cooper in advance for his next book, *The Prairie,* establishing the relationship of publisher to author that would become familiar in the later nineteenth and the twentieth centuries. In inventing the essential subject matter of the American novel, Cooper had done much. But at the same time, he invented a production system that made novel writing, at least potentially, a career for other writers. These two accomplishments were reciprocal: publishing as an economic practice required a predictable stream of new work, and Cooper's array of types—the sea story, the settlement tale, the frontier adventure novel, the Revolutionary romance—enabled just that.

On the other hand, once Cooper went abroad and encountered profoundly different political and social contexts, he found the forms to which he and his readers had become accustomed less and less satisfactory for treating what he now wished to write about. The first three novels he wrote in Europe, after having finished *The Prairie* there, reprised the modes he had pioneered in New York: *The Red Rover* and *The Water-Witch* were sea tales set largely in American waters, while *The Wept of Wish-ton-Wish* was a settlement tale concerned with Indian relations and imperial politics in seventeenth-century New England. With his next book, however, Cooper broke completely with his usual plots and his American settings. *The Bravo* (1831), set in Venice but intended as a critique of France in the wake of the July Revolution of 1830, is engaged with America only on the level of its political theme, for it holds that republicanism (especially of the American sort) is preferable to the corrupt institutions of contemporary Europe. Perhaps its title character, the oppressed commoner Jacopo, whom the elite rulers of Venice cloak with the blame for their tyrannical acts, carried forward some of the traits of Cooper's inwardly driven and solitary American characters of the previous decade—Birch, Bumppo, and Jones. But otherwise the book represented a sharp break with Cooper's old modes.

It also caused a break with his customary audience. Popular fiction—fiction as an item of trade, with the author and publisher partnering to supply an established commodity to the public—entails the regularization of production. It therefore follows that an author who departs from established modes without trying to bring his clientele along usually suffers the sort of decline Cooper encountered in the mid-1830s. Even without the political attacks that his radical republicanism engendered from conservative critics on both sides of the Atlantic, he was bound to lose market share. Herman Melville was to experience a similar loss when he turned from the adventure formulas he had borrowed from Cooper and Cooper's imitators and, in *Mardi: And a Voyage Thither* (1849) and then *Moby-Dick; or, The Whale* (1851), explored different zones of language and art.

Cooper at least learned how to come back. He might have retreated into bitterness. He promised to abandon fiction completely in his 1834 *Letter to His Countrymen* and for a time did so. Yet, even in that pamphlet, he singled out the individual attacks he found most galling and began paying them back in kind. He also threatened further action. When newspaper editors persisted in their attacks, tarring his art out of anger over his politics, he filed a series of libel suits against a half dozen of them and soon, arguing many himself, convinced judges and juries he was right. He liked the fray; it reinvigorated him, and that helped him return to his literary career, which he hardly could afford to abandon in any case. Soon he was writing fiction again and with a vengeance (in fact, he would publish more than half his novels in the third decade of his career). The resumption of fiction writing came about in two stages. Initially, he turned to satire, penning a fantastic voyage tale called *The Monikins* (1835), and then a pair of contemporary tales, *Homeward Bound; or, The Chase* and *Home as Found* (both 1838), in which he told, in a thinly veiled way, the story of his family's disillusioning return from Europe to Manhattan and eventually to Cooperstown in the mid 1830s. And soon Cooper managed a full return to the sorts of writing for which he had become famous in the previous decade. In 1840, he wrote the fourth Leather-Stocking Tale, setting it along Lake Ontario, where he had served at a naval outpost early in the century. The following year, he issued *The Deerslayer*, in which he returned again to the Otsego of a century before, this time without the overt political themes of *Home as Found*. Through *The Deerslayer* in particular he attracted an audience newly appreciative of his original talents. Even some of the editors he was still fighting in court found these new books a welcome rebirth of Cooper's art.

But change permeated Cooper's seeming return to old patterns. For one thing, he began experimenting with first-person narrative, which he had not yet employed in any of his novels. The origins of that experiment reached back to the later 1820s, when he wrote a fictional travelogue, *Notions of the Americans: Picked up by a Travelling Bachelor* (1828), in the epistolary form common in European accounts of the United States. He might have simply written a discursive answer to the many errors he had uncovered in such books, something his friend Robert Walsh had done in his *Appeal from the Judgments of Great Britain Respecting the United States of America* (1819). But, accustomed as Cooper was to storytelling, he instead chose to invent an ideal European traveler—intelligent, progressive, open-minded—and send him on an imaginary journey through contemporary America. Confining himself to that man's perspective across two hefty volumes taught Cooper a good deal about how viewpoint inflects narrative. He was learning something of the same lesson in these years as he wrote his own letters about Europe to his friends back home. Moreover, immediately after he saw *Notions of the Americans* through the press in London, it occurred to him that there might be a market for narratives based on his European experience, and in preparation for those books he, for the first time, began keeping journals. Work on the travel books was delayed until after he returned to the United States in 1834. At that time, Cooper made some use of the journals covering his travels in the Netherlands, Switzerland, Germany, and Italy. But in essence the five books, now known collectively as *Gleanings in Europe* (1836–38), were works of covert fiction rather than direct reportage. They are presented as collections of letters written on the spot to various real correspondents back home, but in fact all the letters were retrospectively fabricated by Cooper years later. In no case does he seem to have used actual letters from the period.

The experience of writing the *Gleanings* in this complicated manner was to have long-lasting effects on Cooper's exploration of limited first-person sensibilities in his fiction. There were also other sources for that exploration. When Cooper engaged in the series of controversies that began in France in 1831 and followed him back to the United States, he started writing extensively in his own voice for a variety of venues—in French and American newspapers and journals first but also in pamphlets and books. As he encountered a less receptive audience, and then a positively hostile one, he became more aware of his own position both politically and rhetorically. One can trace the evolution of this shifting conception of himself, and of human limitations at large, in the introductions he wrote for his three European novels. *The Bravo* has a preface like the ones Cooper had written for most of his earlier novels. But in *The Heidenmauer; or, The Benedictines* (1832) and then *The Headsman; or, The Abbaye des Vignerons* (1833), he inserted more personal introductions. For *The Heidenmauer*, in an unusual turn toward the first person, he narrated the means by which, during a chance afternoon stroll with his son in 1831, he had come across the ruined abbey that was to serve as his primary setting. The introduction to *The Headsman*, although it defaults to the third person, likewise concerns the origin of the ensuing tale in the author's experience, in this case in Switzerland in 1832.

One might say that Cooper was experimenting here, a bit before the fact, with the narrative mode he would employ in his *Gleanings*. He did the same in setting his next novel, *The Monikins*, in motion: for here, too—and in the most direct of first-person voices—Cooper established the context for that satire by telling of a personal journey through the Alps, in the midst of which the narrator (who we learn is "the Author of the Spy") encounters a party of English travelers. By the merest chance, he happens to save a woman of that party from slipping off the dangerous trail up the Furka Pass, which he has just descended. As a result, her husband promises to call on Cooper at a hotel in Geneva later that summer. The two never actually meet again. Instead, the man leaves at that hotel a package containing the manuscript of the ensuing fantastic voyage narrative. Of course, no such package was ever left for Cooper. In keeping with his experimental crossing of fiction and fact, Cooper based the narrative's frame on a real episode in his 1828 hike over the Furka, during which he indeed did encounter a party of English travelers. But Cooper the hiker never so much as spoke to those people, let alone saved one of them from death.

More interesting still is the fact that the novel to which this made-up narrative serves as an introduction was Cooper's first venture in first-person fiction. The novel's narrator, Sir John Goldencalf, is the same English traveler mentioned in the introduction. For an author who, while he punctuated his novels with occasional set speeches—the best are Natty's—tended to maintain aloof control of the narrative in his own offstage voice, this was a signal innovation. Experimenting with point of view, as he did here, allowed Cooper several advantages. For this fantastic tale, with its speaking monkeys and its monikin nations in the far Southern Hemisphere, stressing the distance between the book's "editor" (the role Cooper acknowledged on the title page) and Goldencalf was a useful dodge. And Cooper gained more. Maintaining the limits of his narrator's perspective through the two volumes naturalized for him the pose he would assume for his travel books, which he began writing immediately afterward.

First-person narrative came to assume an even more useful place in Cooper's fictional output in the 1840s. After finishing the travel books and returning to Natty's legend, Cooper wrote a pair of sea tales in the older narrative format—*The Two Admirals* and *The Wing-and-Wing; or, Le Feu-Follet* (1842). The next year, he wrote a third book, the frontier/Revolutionary War tale *Wyandotté*, also told from an omniscient point of view. But something was working itself to the surface of his mind at this time. Cooper wrote a series of naval biographies for *Graham's Magazine* from 1842 to 1845, which he later collected as *Lives of Distinguished American Naval Officers* (1846). This series set him thinking about history in a biographical, which is to say personal, mode. One of the sketches, in fact, was of his own commander on Lake Ontario, Melancthon T. Woolsey, so it was in this sense a piece of autobiography as well. Also for *Graham's* during the first four months of 1843, he wrote the curious "It Narrative," "The Autobiography of a Pocket Handkerchief," in which the title character, a finely crafted handkerchief that has survived the July Revolution in Paris, tells her own picaresque tale.

A similar, though longer, work emerged from a chance encounter in this same period: *Ned Myers; or, A Life Before the Mast* (1843). Edward Myers, a Canadian native (and rumored son of the Duke of Kent), had been Cooper's shipmate on the *Stirling* in 1806–1807. Thereafter, Myers had spent his life at sea—in both the merchant marine and the US Navy. Once at last retired to land, he had written the novelist on the off chance that he was the same "Jem Cooper" who had been on the *Stirling* four decades before. After the two men met and began swapping tales, Cooper became the amanuensis (and then some) for Myers, editing his foremast narrative as a sequel of sorts to Richard Henry Dana's recent *Two Years Before the Mast* (1840). Doing so provided Cooper with a rich narrative return to his own youth: we know as much as we do about his cruise on the *Stirling* precisely because Myers primed Cooper's memories while dictating his own.

Moreover, working with Myers suggested to Cooper the great appeal of first-person narrative as a means of probing the development of individual vision and values. This was in some ways the next logical step in his attempt to create fiction consistent with the republicanism to which, despite his diminished enthusiasm for the American experiment, he still remained attached. He therefore followed up *Ned Myers* with one of his most satisfying sea stories, the two-part *Afloat and Ashore* (1844), in which a sailor named Miles Wallingford, a Hudson Valley native, looks back across his long life. Wallingford, of a middling position in life, shares no obvious traits with Cooper's most famous low characters, Bumppo or Birch or Chingachgook. But he shares much with Cooper: autobiographical in form, the novel is also autobiographical in origin. This story imagines what might have been for Cooper had he not left the sea. Undoubtedly, one spur for writing *Afloat and Ashore* was the time Cooper had recently spent with Myers. Talking with Myers, a voice from far in his past, must naturally have set Cooper wondering what his own life would have amounted to had he, like Myers, remained afloat rather than returned ashore. This is true not only in general but also in specific terms. Details in Wallingford's life derive from the experience of his creator, at times with considerable fidelity.

The Wallingford double novel is one of Cooper's more charming tales. It was followed by a trio of other first-person novels, the Littlepage Manuscripts. These books, stimulated by Cooper's desire to counter the anti-rent activists of contemporary New York, begin with a portrait of life in the 1750s, *Satanstoe*, which is rich in its evocation of provincial customs and conditions. Among other things, Cooper created here his most suggestive portrait of African American life. His use of the Pinkster festival, based on his observations from his school days in Albany early in the century, remains useful as a firsthand source on a thinly documented aspect of Afro-Dutch culture. In the same novel, Cooper drew further portraits of early Albany that remain vivid and convincing today. Here, too, though in a more deflected manner, the narrative of Corny Littlepage is a kind of autobiographical outgrowth of the author's youth.

The novel also marks the deepening realism of Cooper's last period. For one thing, Corny, like the other narrators in the series—his son Mordaunt and great-grandson Hugh—is interestingly limited in his personal views and development. Even as Cooper wrote the series to evoke sympathy for the old landholding classes of New York, which he thought under attack by the Yankee interlopers who haunted his dreams, he did not make the Littlepages into figures of perfect judgment or deep intelligence. The family name itself suggests that they are heroes (and writers) in a minor chord. That he presents himself as the "editor" of the volumes suggests that he recognized, as he had with Goldencalf or Myers, the distance between his personal position and that of his narrators.

But this was as far as Cooper was prepared to push such formal innovations. They came precisely at the moment that Melville, returned from his oceanic wanderings, took up the mode of Dana—and *Ned Myers*—in *Typee: A Peep at Polynesian Life* (1846) and *Omoo: A Narrative of Adventures in the South Seas* (1847). Cooper was not deaf to what Melville promised. Indeed, in his own next novel, *The Crater*, he appears to have drawn on Melville's fresh portraits of the South Seas. In this novel, a pair of shipwrecked sailors who escape from the Pacific later return to an uninhabited island group there with a company of American colonizers. Before long, social and political uproar of the sort Cooper thought afflicted the contemporary United States breaks out in their would-be paradise. In the end, the towering volcanic crater that had provided the scene for their utopian experiment sinks, as if from divine displeasure, beneath the surface, wiping out the American proxy and providing America itself a lesson. Cooper's dystopian projection of American institutions and foibles into the heart of the Pacific is especially interesting for the social meanings he makes the novel bear. But the book also has other appeals. For one thing, Cooper, on whom the natural landscape always exerted a powerful pull, at last made it a full actor in one of his plots. It had been something like that in various earlier books. In the proto-ecological romance of *The Pioneers*, Cooper made the desiccated forest burst into flames, seemingly in protest over what Natty calls the settlers' "wasty ways" (ch. 30). In *The Last of the Mohicans*, the very first sentence—"It was a feature peculiar to the colonial wars of North America, that the toils and dangers of the wilderness were to be encountered, before the adverse hosts could meet in murderous contact" (ch. 1)—broaches an analogous theme, one that the setting throughout seems intent on reinforcing. In his other Leather-Stocking novels, a similar use of the environment for thematic and dramatic purposes can also be traced. And his other historical romances reveal similar patterns, from the "Neutral Ground" of *The Spy* and the dark, echo-filled forest of *The Wept of Wish-ton-Wish* to the haunted expanse enclosed within the "Heathen's Wall" in *The Heidenmauer.*

It is on the water, however, that the pattern achieves its most persuasive expression. For if Cooper's ships are animated, almost alive, as many readers have noticed, the element on which they make their way is always, as Joseph Conrad stressed with admiration, an embodiment of the force of nature over human life. That is true not just of the sea novels but also of the forest romances. Witness the importance of river and lake alike in *The Last of the Mohicans* and even of the gloomy spaces of a book like *The Bravo*, in which the canals of Venice, with their murky depths, pose mortal dangers to the characters while they suggest the fluid uncertainties of the Venetian state. Water provides freedom at times, as in Natty's escape down the Hudson River in *The Last of the Mohicans*. Similarly, in *The Water-Witch*, Tom Tiller can evade a pursuing ship by snaking masterfully through the perilous Hell Gate. But in one of Cooper's best novels, *Satanstoe*, the Hudson again proves the near master of human fate: the breaking up of the ice-bound stream at the heart of the book is a masterstroke, one that drives home Cooper's theme of human frailty in a world of force. If it were not such a powerful piece of natural description, one might almost take it to be a political allegory depicting the irresistible flood of change bearing down on the likes of Corny Littlepage as the devilish Yankees, eager to take over New York, cast envious eyes on the latter province's manorial grants.

The Crater is the penultimate expression of Cooper's enduring fascination with nature. The sea here is a world of force, from the shipwreck that strands Mark Woolston and Bob Betts on their extinct volcano to the sudden emergence of new lands when earthquakes and volcanic action become the dominant events in the plot. Moreover, as in *Satanstoe* (where the pride of the characters in their ability to control nature puts them at risk on the ice), the presumptions of the settlers whom Bob and Mark bring back to their enlarged paradise (they too are Yankees in fact or spirit) seem like the secondary cause of their doomed colony's subsidence when nature withdraws below the sea the temporary territory where the American community has sought to replicate its once promising homeland.

This brief discussion of *The Crater* ought to indicate the extraordinary range of Cooper's creative work. He has too often been understood as a rough precursor of what came after him rather than its real enabler—and he was a powerful figure in his own right. Of course he was no Henry James. But, Mark Twain to one side, he was no clumsy amateur either. His age was an age of energy rather than finish, and in literature and the other arts at that moment, accomplishment counted for more than thoroughness of design or idea. Indeed, craft was too wasteful of time in a transitional era when the mere achievement of American books was the main point. Furthermore, as the necessities of the 1820s were relieved by the stronger literary productiveness of the 1830s and 1840s, Cooper, like other writers, became more skilled at elaborating, not just roughing in, literary ideas. *The Bravo*, the first of his European trilogy, he seems to have completely rewritten—and it shows. Moreover, as in his experiments with first-person narrative, Cooper clearly became sensitive to the ways in which literature was a matter of technique, not just of invention. Shortly after Cooper's 1851 death, Melville, who had read Cooper's sea tales with particular delight, referred to Cooper in what remain the best terms: for Cooper was indeed "a great, robust-souled man, all whose merits are not seen," and, with Melville, one may hope that "a grateful posterity will take the best care of Fenimore Cooper" (*Memorial of James Fenimore Cooper* 1852, 30). Without him, much of what now seems inescapably obvious in the history of American fiction might well never have come to life.

15

CATHARINE MARIA SEDGWICK: DOMESTIC AND NATIONAL NARRATIVES

JAMES L. MACHOR

When Catharine Maria Sedgwick sat down to write her first novel, she actually had no intention of writing a novel at all. Rather, *A New-England Tale* (1822) began as a brief, quasi-fictional tract in the pamphlet war in New York City over the "scandal" of Unitarianism. Encouraged by her brothers, Sedgwick expanded that fledging document into a full-length but anonymously published volume as her initial venture into the novelistic world.

Modern Sedgwick scholars have disagreed over the significance of her decision to publish anonymously *A New-England Tale*, as well as the first editions of all her novels before 1850. Victoria Clements and Mary Kelley have pointed to that decision, along with her private remarks about her fiction, to argue that Sedgwick was a reluctant "private woman" on a "public stage," who ascribed little literary value to her novels (Kelley 1984, viii). Others have suggested, however, that such a view oversimplifies Sedgwick's relation to her art, for she was a woman who took substantial pride in her craft, pursued professional authorship with confidence and savvy, and even used anonymous publication as a marketing strategy to overcome public resistance to women writers.

There seems little doubt that at times Sedgwick did feel trepidation about the quality of her work and about public visibility. In a letter shortly after the publication of her first novel, she revealed how "anxious" she was "to remain unknown" (Dewey 1871, 154), and throughout her career, she expressed doubts about the literary merits of her novels. But in the former instance, Sedgwick was hardly alone, sharing anxieties about the new, faceless, nineteenth-century literary marketplace not only with other women writers but also with male authors such as James Fenimore Cooper and Nathaniel Hawthorne. Moreover, as her career progressed, she found considerable satisfaction in her public success as a fiction writer, recording in an 1834 journal entry: "I have as much pleasure in success & certainly as much in the consciousness of deserving it" (Oct. 1, 1834).

And successful she was. Although her novels were largely neglected for most of the twentieth century before her recovery by feminist critics in the 1980s, in the antebellum decades Sedgwick was the first woman novelist to achieve renown in the United States and one of the few before the Civil War to gain both critical and popular plaudits. Not only did her novels sell well; she was regularly grouped with Cooper and Washington Irving as leading figures in the developing American literary scene, to the point that Edgar Allan Poe called her "one of our most celebrated and most meritorious writers" (1846, 130). The *Ladies' Magazine and Literary Gazette* went so far as to "unhesitatingly place" Sedgwick "as the first and best American novelist" (July 1830, 320), a judgment echoed five years later by the *Museum of Foreign Literature*, which announced that "[b]y the more trained and fastidious of her countrymen, she is considered the first of American novelists" (Nov.–Dec. 1835, 540).

A New-England Tale launched that success, selling out its first two editions in only six months. Yet the novel was not the unqualified darling of readers. Some strong criticism was directed at its religious subject matter, particularly its representation of Calvinism through the character of Mrs. Wilson, a woman who professes an ardent devotion to Calvinist tenets, while leading a life of bigotry and religious hypocrisy devoid of Christian charity.

This depiction evolved from Sedgwick's own recent religious experiences. Born on December 28, 1789, to prominent western Massachusetts families on both her paternal and maternal sides, Sedgwick grew up in a household of staunch Calvinism, with its emphasis on human depravity and on God's saving grace as the sole path to salvation. But in 1821 she turned to the emerging Unitarian faith, with its more liberal view of potentially universal salvation through good works. Hence, Sedgwick conceived *A New-England Tale*, at least in part, as a fictionalized indictment of what she elsewhere referred to as "Calvin's gloomy interpretation of Scripture" (Dewey 1871, 193), which she demonstrated through a contrast between Mrs. Wilson and the novel's protagonist, Jane Elton, who evinces a commitment to good works and Christian virtue. The problem was that while the influence of Calvinism was waning in the United States in the early nineteenth century, some of Sedgwick's readers were taken aback by her depiction. Although we have little direct evidence of the way "common readers" responded to the novel, indirect evidence suggests something of her audience's ire. The *American Ladies' Magazine* summarized the overall reception of *A New-England Tale* by noting that "the portraiture of religious hypocrisy which that work contained . . . brought upon its author the charge of sectarianism" (Dec. 1835, 659). That popular note of dismay was also echoed by some reviewers.

Other readers, however, took a different view by praising the novel for its Americanness. In the wake of Sydney Smith's remark in the *Edinburgh Review* questioning whether anyone in the world read an American book, a rampant spirit of literary nationalism emerged in the 1820s, leading to calls for the development of a distinct US national literature. Accordingly, reviewers and critics in 1822 quickly seized on Sedgwick's novel as delivering exactly what was needed. Indeed, the novel's depiction of New England scenery and characters, often fleshed out through regional dialect, made *A New-England Tale*, as Carolyn Karcher has observed, one of the earliest manifestations of New England—and American—"women's regional fiction" (2003, 7). Transforming its New England focus into a synecdoche for American national and literary accomplishment, antebellum reviewers welcomed the novel for its depiction of the American character, played out in the domestic sphere.

Beyond its reception as a "domestic" novel, in both the familial and national senses of that word, *A New-England Tale* is important for being an early work of women's domestic fiction, which would become central to the shape of the US novel before the Civil War. Nina Baym has described this subgenre as the narrative of an older girl or adolescent, usually orphaned, who "is deprived of the supports she had . . . depended on . . . and is faced with the necessity of winning her own way in the world," usually with the help of other women, via an "overplot" that often ends with her marriage (1978, 11–12). *A New-England Tale* certainly displays that pattern. The novel opens shortly before the twelve-year-old Jane becomes orphaned and then taken in reluctantly by her bigoted aunt, Mrs. Wilson. Tormented by her guardian, Jane manages, with the help of a faithful serving woman, to carve out a life as an elementary schoolteacher. Along the way, Jane meets Robert Lloyd, a virtuous Quaker whom she eventually marries, enabling the novel to close with the promise of future domestic bliss.

Although this pattern would become a virtual formula for many women's novels, Sedgwick would not follow it slavishly. Her second novel, *Redwood* (1824), departs from the form of *A New-England Tale* in several ways. For one thing, *Redwood* is a more ambitious novel, with a two-volume format that made it more than twice the length of *A New-England Tale*. Additionally, while the novel's protagonist, Ellen Bruce, believes she is an orphan, the narrative eventually reveals that Ellen is actually the daughter of Henry Redwood, a wealthy southern planter. At the center of the story, Sedgwick also juxtaposes Ellen against the beautiful but spoiled Caroline, Redwood's daughter by his second wife. Around these characters, Sedgwick weaves a more complex narrative than in her first novel, stitching in several subplots, including the rescue of a young Shaker, Emily Allen, from the lecherous clutches of a Shaker elder named Reuben Harrington—a rescue effected by Ellen and Debby Lenox, the latter a strapping six-foot one, middle aged woman "imbued with the independent spirit of the times" (v. 1, ch. 1).

While *Redwood* avoids any forays into religious controversy, it does inject a new, politically roiling topic by making slavery a minor but suggestive component of its narrative in a chapter devoted to the story of the slave Africk. Although the novel renders that tale primarily to illustrate "the mercy of Heaven" (v. 1, ch. 3), Sedgwick does offer an oblique index to the text's view on slavery by having the haughty

Caroline assert that "labour . . . was made for slaves, and slaves for labour" and be appalled at the literacy of a free black farmworker (v. 1, ch. 7). Sedgwick's decision not to develop the subject more fully may have resulted from her mixed attitudes toward African Americans, slavery, and abolition. America's peculiar institution clearly troubled her, and she once said that "the emancipation of slaves" is our "great *best* cause" (Dewey 1871, 231). But Sedgwick was likewise uneasy with the abolitionist movement, fearing that its more radical wing threatened the union, and her prejudiced views of African Americans surfaced on several occasions, including a marginal note she added to an unfinished story, in which she expressed her decided belief that "the African is inferior to the Caucasian" (qtd. in Weierman 2003, 129).

Another new crease in *Redwood* comes in its depiction of both New England and Carolinian values, through which Sedgwick broadens the scope of her depiction of American life. So convincing did antebellum readers find the regional verisimilitude of *Redwood* that even the astute British observer of American life and letters, Harriet Martineau, called the novel "as nearly as possible, a transcript of actual life" (qtd. in Foster 1974, 59).

Redwood proved even more popular than *A New-England Tale*. Reviewers perceived Sedgwick's new novel as an advance over her first effort, with the *Atlantic Magazine* announcing: "The promise held forth by the 'New England Tale,' has been more than abundantly realised in 'Redwood'" (July 1824, 236). More fulsome was a review in the *Port Folio*. After grouping *Redwood* with Cooper's *The Spy: A Tale of the Neutral Ground* (1821) and *The Pioneers; or, The Sources of the Susquehanna* (1823) as "fill[ing]" a hitherto empty place in "the description of American manners," the *Port Folio* reviewer went on to call Sedgwick's novel "the first *American* novel, strictly speaking," that offers "a faithful delineation of our own fireside" (July 1824, 66, 69). The novel also appears to have sold well. Although no specific numbers survive, we do know that it was quickly reprinted in England and subsequently translated into French for continental publication, ostensibly extending Sedgwick's reputation across the Atlantic.

In the following year, Sedgwick published her third full-length work of fiction, *The Travellers: A Tale. Designed for Young People* (1825). Modern Sedgwick scholars have devoted virtually no attention to this work, tending to identify *Hope Leslie; or, Early Times in the Massachusetts* (1827) as her third novel. Yet despite the fact that it is considerably shorter than *Redwood* and about two-thirds the length of *A New-England Tale*, *The Travellers* clearly displays novelistic traits via a continuous narrative that focuses on a group of core characters—Mr. and Mrs. Sackville and their children, Edward and Julia—while tracing their journey through the Great Lakes to Montreal and Quebec. It also incorporates a subplot involving a Mrs. Barton, whom the Sackvilles aid in discovering her lost husband. The book, moreover, displays several features that characterized Sedgwick's previous two novels. Central again is her emphasis on virtuous action, embodied, in this case, by Edward and Julia's selfless kindness to Mrs. Barton. In depicting the variety of people the Sackvilles meet, from Native Americans and black laborers to Irish immigrants, the book offers a cross-sectional view of the nation's diverse population. Additionally, whatever appeal the novel had for its original audience no doubt stemmed in part from the repeated patriotic notes it strikes, from Mr. Sackville's panegyric to the country's "blooming gardens, and fruitful fields, associated . . . with innocent occupation and moral cultivation," to the praise of her Irish immigrants for the unmatched beauty of American scenery along Lake Ontario (48).

Following *The Travellers*, Sedgwick returned to the more ambitious two-volume format with *Hope Leslie*, but she did so in a new key by writing a historical novel set in seventeenth-century New England. Sedgwick's decision to turn to that subgenre probably resulted in part from the keen market sense she had developed by the mid-to-late 1820s. Viewing the massive successes of Walter Scott's novels as well as Cooper's *The Spy* and *The Last of the Mohicans: A Narrative of 1757* (1826), Sedgwick knew that historical fiction could offer an avenue to broad sales. But to speak of her marketplace savvy in this respect is not to imply that her decision was motivated purely by money. She was very concerned that her novels perform cultural work by reaching as many people as possible, and historical fiction was becoming a popular vehicle for doing so.

These goals came together in Sedgwick's decision to include for the first time in one of her novels Native Americans as major characters, along with the subject of Indian-white relations. For this was a time of substantial public interest in the issue of Indian removal east of the Mississippi River, which would soon be implemented under Andrew Jackson's administration and would embroil the country in virulent racism and genocidal atrocities.

Over the last forty years, *Hope Leslie* has received more critical attention than any of Sedgwick's other novels, partly because of its striking characters but also because of its ostensibly counter-hegemonic politics. For example, Judith Fetterley sees *Hope Leslie* as offering a radical argument against antebellum phallocentrism, which "reifie[d] the separation of public and private by gender" (1998, 495); Lucy Maddox calls the novel a "self-consciously feminist revision of male-transmitted history," citing its depiction of one of "the small rebellions of Puritan women against the domination of men" (1991, 103); and Elaine Showalter reads it as an exposé of the way "women are the victims of an exchange between men" (2009, 38). Parallel claims for the novel's subversiveness have been directed, almost as often, at its treatment of race. Mary Kelley calls *Hope Leslie* "a highly critical presentation of the Puritans' subjugation of the indigenous population" (1989, 47), while others have read the novel for its progressive views of Native Americans and its indictment of antebellum white racism.

It is not difficult to discern the basis for such readings. Sedgwick once again presents strong, active women protagonists who draw on personal integrity and independent ethical values grounded in heartfelt sympathy. But what is different in the novel's representation of autonomous female agency is Sedgwick's decision to mirror such traits in both the book's eponymous protagonist and the noble Indian maiden Magawisca. This signature atypicality of her text's heroines is most evident in Sedgwick's multiple uses of a motif she had first employed in *Redwood*: a young woman's heroic rescue of another woman. In *Hope Leslie*, however, this motif takes on a more radically gendered and racialized form. Not only does Magawisca save the life of Everell Fletcher, the novel's male protagonist. Hope succeeds, with Everell in a supporting role, in rescuing Nelema (an old Indian woman healer) and Magawisca, when both are unjustly jailed by the Puritan magistrates. Magawisca is doubly important in these developments. Not only does she demonstrate a disinterested altruism that contravenes dominant white historical representations of Native Americans as "'surly dogs,' who preferred to die . . . from no other motives than a stupid or malignant obstinacy" (pref.). Magawisca's account to Everell of the Puritan attack on her Pequot village also counters the dominant historical narratives of the event by revealing it as a bloodlust-driven slaughter of women and children.

There is, however, little evidence that Sedgwick's contemporary readers interpreted *Hope Leslie* as a critique of phallocentrism and racism. Although reviewers remarked upon Hope's admirable pluck, none read her as a challenge to patriarchal values. In contrast to modern critical claims that the novel presents a progressive defense of Native Americans and their culture, antebellum reviewers had little to say about Sedgwick's treatment of Native Americans as a people and seldom mentioned the text's other Indian characters: Mononotto and Monoca (Magawisca's father and mother), Oneco (her brother), and Nelema. Rather, nearly all attention, when directed at Sedgwick's Indians, focused on Magawisca. Reviewer comments about her character avoided the era's racial politics but instead involved debates over whether she was an idealized or believable Indian. In other words, reviewer response to Magawisca involved a technical question about novelistic verisimilitude.

Yet the gap between nineteenth- and twentieth-century interpretations of the novel is not quite as large as this difference would suggest. If antebellum readers saw no progressive politics in *Hope Leslie*, several modern Sedgwick scholars, including Fetterley, Maddox, and Dana Nelson, have also questioned its supposed counterhegemonic view of Native Americans, arguing instead that while the novel gestures in this direction, it ultimately reinscribes the dominant cultural ideology. Several pieces of evidence seem to support such a reading. Hope is appalled to learn that her sister, who is married to Oneco, has so completely gone native that she has virtually forgotten her white upbringing, and nothing in the narrative challenges Hope's reaction. Sedgwick also provides as the novel's epigraph a poem that articulates the ideology that the Indian is a vanishing American whose "sun has set." As if to emphasize this supposed inevitability, Sedgwick has Magawisca offer, in her speech before the Puritan court, the fatal reminder that "the sun-beam and the shadow cannot mingle. The white man cometh—the Indian vanisheth" (v. 2, ch. 9). Furthermore, the narrative's repeated invocations of the American landscape as a bountiful reclamation of "unused" Indian lands seem to promote the logic of white imperialism and native displacement as central to national progress.

Whatever interpretation might be constructed to explain the racial and gender politics of *Hope Leslie*, several factors probably contributed to its original popularity. The novel offers Sedgwick's first nod to the ideology of American exceptionalism through Hope's observation about the possibilities for women offered by the American scene, in contrast to the constrictions of Europe. The novel can also be said to employ an overtly nationalist motif that Sedgwick had used previously only in a modulated form. Although the link between imaginative literature and nation building has a long history in the nineteenth century, that connection became especially centralized in the relation between the novel and nationhood, both in Europe and in the United States. As Franco Moretti has demonstrated, one of the ways novelists participated in the construction of national identity was to employ a form of alterity. That is, novels sought to define and consolidate a particular sense of national selfhood by incorporating entities that hailed from another land or embodied traits at odds with those considered appropriate to a particular national identity. In *Redwood*, Sedgwick had included something along these lines in the contrast between Ellen, the virtuous New Englander who defines American values as disinterested virtue, and the spoiled Caroline, who, as Lucinda Damon-Bach has noted, plays the role of the "foreign misfit, not just from another part of the United States, but from another country," owing to what her father calls her "republican ignorance" (2003, 61). *Hope Leslie*, however, expands this technique, initially employing it in the opening chapter in the form of the English royalist and hard-line Anglican, Sir William Fletcher, who refuses to let his daughter marry his nephew, a Puritan dissenter. Such abrogation of individual rights and freedom of conscience quickly becomes the touchstone of foreignness against which Hope's and Everell's proto-American virtue is measured. However, the character of Sir Philip Gardiner, the duplicitous, Loyalist Catholic who serves as the novel's villain, becomes Sedgwick's most sustained means to define American identity via alterity. As a threat not only to Hope and Magawisca but also to the larger Puritan community in Boston, Gardiner is the foreign other whose death signals that aristocratic, Old World modes and manners have no place in American national identity. Quite likely, these additional dimensions of national formation, as part of the American imaginary of Sedgwick's era, were factors in the extensive praise *Hope Leslie* received in the US press.

In the wake of *Hope Leslie*, Sedgwick published half a dozen short stories over the next three years, and when she turned to another full-length project, she once again decided to produce a long, two-volume novel. *Clarence; or, A Tale of Our Own Times* (1830) marked a new turn in Sedgwick's craft in that it is her most full-fledged novel of manners, designed to both represent and satirize fashionable, upper-class New York society. Several Sedgwick scholars, in fact, have pointed to

Clarence as the seed of an American "homegrown novel of manners tradition" that would culminate in the fictions of Edith Wharton (Karcher 2003, 5).

As an early exposé of what Thorstein Veblen would late in the century call "conspicuous consumption," *Clarence* takes aim at the frivolities and superficialities of fashionable urban society in the United States, particularly among the nouveau riche. Not only does *Clarence* ridicule the irresponsibility and crudeness of new-moneyed Americans, but it also exposes the deleterious effects of ostentation on the families of such people and, by extension, on the well being of US society. Sedgwick juxtaposes against these people the Clarence family, and particularly the novel's protagonist, Gertrude, as embodiments of disinterestedness as the sine qua non of social behavior.

In that role, Gertrude not only parallels the traits and values of Sedgwick's previous female protagonists, but she also reprises, in a sense, Ellen Redwood and Hope Leslie in that her situation departs from the standard pattern for women's fiction. Although Gertrude has lost her mother, she has a close relationship to a caring, upright male. In this case, however, the relation is not with a father figure, as in *Hope Leslie,* nor does it evolve slowly over the course of the narrative, as in *Redwood.* In *Clarence,* Gertrude's nurturing connection is with her biological father, and it runs throughout the novel. Like her two previous long novels, *Clarence* also presents a woman protagonist who steps into roles conventionally reserved for male characters. Gertrude not only helps save the melancholy and emotionally unstable artist, Louis Seton, but also plays a major role in twice rescuing her friend, Emilie Layton, from peril: once from nearly drowning and later from the grasp of the unscrupulous "Spaniard" Pedrillo, to whom Emilie's father has forced her betrothal to avert blackmail. All the while, Gertrude, like Hope, follows her own internal compass, particularly her "inspiration of feeling," to determine the best way to proceed through difficulties (v. 2, ch. 5).

Pedrillo himself is a noteworthy character because, even more than Sir Philip Gardner in *Hope Leslie,* he fills the role of the corrupting foreign other against whom Sedgwick can define American national identity, here embodied by Gertrude; her father; and the intrepid, altruistic Gerald Roscoe, whom Gertrude eventually marries. In addressing the issue of national identity, *Clarence* also presents a new development within Sedgwick's corpus. Only part of the novel is set in the city; its pendulum of action actually swings between urban and rural locales. Within that alternating pattern, Sedgwick incorporates the country-versus-city dichotomy that had for decades become a standard motif in American thought and writing. Moreover, *Clarence* makes clear that Sedgwick's sympathies lie with a kind of Jeffersonian pastoralism, as the novel privileges rural life as the better choice for the country in its effort to develop a virtuous and healthy national character.

Over the next five years, Sedgwick went on to publish over a dozen short stories in periodicals, including youth-oriented magazines such as the *Juvenile Miscellany.* She also worked on two new full-length works of fiction, both of which were published in 1835: *Home* and the much longer *The Linwoods; or, "Sixty Years Since" in America.*

Interestingly, few modern Sedgwick scholars consider *Home* one of her full-fledged novels. Linking it with two of Sedgwick's works of fiction that would follow—*The Poor Rich Man, and the Rich Poor Man* (1836) and *Live and Let Live; or, Domestic Service Illustrated* (1837)—critics over the last thirty years have defined *Home* and its two companions, not as novels but as "domestic novellas" (Damon-Bach and Clements 2003, xxv); "collections of didactic essays and fiction" (Harris 2003, xix); "didactic tales" (Gates 2003, 174); "moral tracts" (Kelley 1989, 43); "conduct tales" (Avallone 2003, 199); a "didactic trilogy" (Foster 1974, 117); and as fictional domestic self-help manuals. In a sense, such claims have some credibility. *Home* did represent a departure from *A New-England Tale, Redwood, The Travellers, Hope Leslie,* and *Clarence* in that its genesis was quite different. In 1834, the Reverend Henry Ware, who was commissioning a group of novels that would exhibit "Scenes and Characters Illustrating Christian Truth," asked Sedgwick to write a new novel as part of that series. Sedgwick agreed and in the next year composed *Home.*

Yet Sedgwick's contemporary readers appear not to have read *Home* as a special case at all. Instead, reviewers linked it to Sedgwick's previous novels as another domestic tale performing valuable cultural work. A review of *Home* in the *New-York Mirror* pointed out that "the amiable authoress of 'Redwood' and 'Hope Leslie,' who has not disdained to devote her fine talents and elegant fancy to the illustration of the quiet walks of life" in those books, was doing the same with *Home* (May 30, 1835, 383). Likewise, a review in the *American Monthly Magazine* described *Home* as consonant with Sedgwick's fictions to date, since "we see in all her works . . . the marks of a true genius for commencing a literature for the mass of the American people." Identifying *Home* as a work that was both domestic and national, this reviewer interpreted the narrative as another representation of "the peculiar dignity of republicanism," manifested in "the simple temple of Family" (Jan. 1836, 21).

This ligature between Sedgwick's previous novels and *Home* extended to the marketplace success of the latter, which not only matched but outstripped the popularity of *Redwood* and *Hope Leslie.* In a little over two years, *Home* went through twelve editions, and within a decade it reached its twentieth edition. It is not hard to conjecture the reasons for this success. Like reviewers, readers probably saw *Home* as a book that gave them more of what they associated with and found attractive about Sedgwick's fictions: novels that were entertaining and informative, domestic and American in a way that met and reinforced their horizon of expectations. Sondra Smith Gates has suggested that part of that reinforcing appeal resulted from the economic message antebellum readers could take from the book, particularly in its story of William Barclay, the novel's male protagonist, who becomes a successful printer. For Sedgwick's readers, Barclay's story may have confirmed the triumphalist American exceptionalism of the time, which viewed penury as a "structural flaw" in English society but believed that "in America it is simply the ground floor upon which the industrious can build happy homes, given the tools of democracy" (Gates 2003, 178).

With her other novel of 1835, Sedgwick returned for a second—and last—time to the subgenre that had proved so successful with *Hope Leslie*: the historical novel. Sedgwick chose to set *The Linwoods*, however, during the American Revolution. This switch from the seventeenth-century ground of *Hope Leslie* seems to have resulted from several factors. In part, patriotic filiopiety encouraged her decision since, as Sedgwick explained in the preface, her goal was to give her "readers a true, if a slight, impression of the condition of their country at the most . . . suffering period of its existence" so as "to deepen their gratitude to their patriot-fathers." Then, too, historical novels set during the Revolution had become something of a vogue in the fourteen years since Cooper's *The Spy*. But Sedgwick was also writing *The Linwoods* at a time of substantial political and social turmoil in the United States. The lingering tensions of the nullification crisis, along with South Carolina's aborted threat of secession, continued to trouble the union; the survivors of the Revolutionary generation were almost all gone; and rampant market manipulation was fomenting the economy into a crisis that would explode in the Panic of 1837. By focusing on a time of unquestionable heroic suffering and triumph in America's past, Sedgwick could use that history to engage in cultural work for her own era.

In her actual treatment of the Revolution, Sedgwick departs from the precedent of *The Spy*. Seemingly taking a page from Anne Bradstreet's "Prologue" to *The Tenth Muse* (1650), published nearly 200 years earlier, Sedgwick dons the humble mask of the woman writer by eschewing any claim to treat battles, affairs of state, or empires begun. Instead, in a move characteristic of her novels, she focuses on families: the Linwoods of old New York and the Lees of Massachusetts.

Although Sedgwick previously had implied connections between family and nation, historical novels about the Revolution in the 1820s and 1830s, as Philip Gould notes, had repeatedly "employ[ed] family plots to symbolize political ones" (2005, 232). In *The Linwoods*, the family plots, accordingly, play out through a contrast between the Loyalist, Tory Linwoods and the Revolutionary Lees. Complicating the tension is the fact that Herbert Linwood, despite his family's politics, declares himself a Whig, which places him in the same political camp as young Eliot Lee. When the Revolution breaks out, both Eliot and Herbert join the Continental Army, and as fellow junior officers, they meet at West Point, where Eliot saves George Washington from a plot to kidnap him and end the war in one blow. Although Eliot and Herbert also take part in the assault on the British fort at Stony Point, much more narrative space goes to Eliot's commission by Washington to deliver dispatches to the British commander in New York—secretly attended by Herbert. But while there, Herbert is captured by the British. Amid these developments, Sedgwick weaves a subplot involving Eliot's sister, Bessie, and another Tory Loyalist, Jasper Meredith, who proves false to Bessie's love.

The novel's main narrative and subplots employ features that had played a role in several of Sedgwick's previous novels. Once again, *The Linwoods* works to define national identity through alterity, focusing on two characters. One is Mr. Linwood, whose royalist sensibilities cause him to denounce his son's patriotism and excoriate the rebels as mere traitors. But since father Linwood eventually comes to respect his son's integrity—and grudgingly, the rebels' victory—by the close of the novel, Sedgwick concentrates the function of the dangerous, foreign other in Jasper, whose Tory foppishness, "aristocratic and feudal" preferences, and position as Herbert's rival for Bessie reprise the role of Dimple in Royall Tyler's 1787 play *The Contrast* (v. 1, ch. 4). In a signature move, Sedgwick also makes central to the novel a strong woman protagonist, Isabella Linwood, whose loyalty to her father's Tory politics recedes through the course of the novel as she comes to respect and admire both her brother and the cause for which he fights. Isabella's intrepidity is evident especially in her successful effort, accompanied by her free African American servant, Rose, to rescue Herbert from prison. During the escape, the women overpower the despicable Tory jailer, Cunningham, whom Rose trusses up in her garters in a scene that suggests a symbolic unmanning of British power at the hands of a biracial cohort of newly forming American womanhood.

Like her previous novels, *The Linwoods* enjoyed popular and critical success. Of the 5,000 copies in its initial print run, 4,300 sold in the first year. Poe declared *The Linwoods* "superior to *Hope Leslie*, and superior to *Redwood*" (1835, 57), while the *North American Review* asserted, "We think this work the most agreeable that Miss Sedgwick has yet published" (Jan. 1836, 160). Several reviewers, however, questioned the novel's status as historical fiction. A review in the *Knickerbocker* decided that *The Linwoods* "cannot be judged as a historical romance" because the connection of "the action of the tale . . . with historical events" is "slight and casual" (Oct. 1835, 368). According to a review in the *Museum of Foreign Literature, The Linwoods* was not a "strictly historical novel. Washington, and General Putnam, and Governor Clinton, it is quite true, all figure in her pages, but merely as accessories to the true-hearted, noble Isabella Linwood, and the beautifully gentle and melancholy Bessie Lee" (Nov.–Dec. 1835, 540).

These critiques had some merit in terms of how Sedgwick handles her strictly historical materials. Unlike *Hope Leslie*, where events connect closely to historical occurrences, such as the burning of the Pequot village, the hostilities between natives and colonials, and the perfidy of Sir Philip toward the Puritans, *The Linwoods* seldom ties its events to the turmoil of the Revolutionary conflict. But this is only a half-truth. In this novel, Sedgwick is concerned with the way the Revolution, as a struggle between mother country and colony, strained and changed social relations, from the familial rancor embodied in the Linwood family, to the plot to capture Washington by using one of his old friends as bait. The specific upheavals caused by the Revolution, which produced rifts between fathers and sons, as well as between friends, disclose a psychological and emotional trauma in that struggle rarely presented by historians and other novelists of the time. In the process, Sedgwick provides a narrative that can be read as a cautionary tale for her contemporaries, dramatizing what could happen to both families and the nation should the embers of nullification be reignited into an internecine conflagration.

During the following two years, Sedgwick published the two other novels of her purported domestic trilogy: *The Poor Rich Man, and the Rich Poor Man* and *Live and Let Live.* Although antebellum reviewers responded to them as quintessential Sedgwickian domestic novels, *Poor Rich Man* and *Live and Let Live* differed in subtle but important ways. While both works can be seen as versions of the novel of manners, with each text Sedgwick succeeded in "modifying the form for laboring-class readers" (Avallone 2006, 119). In *Poor Rich Man*, Sedgwick engages in that effort by positioning at the center of her narrative working-class individuals Philip May and his daughters, Susan and Charlotte, and their family friend, Harry Aikin, an enterprising baker's boy. Their stories of suffering, frustration, and nose-to-the-grindstone dedication lead to Harry and Susan's marriage, which is marked by domestic happiness despite the meager means provided by Harry's work as an independent "carman." Juxtaposed against the Aikin family is that of Morris Finley, who, as the novel's rich poor man, seeks to marry money and seize the main chance. While the rich poor man's house is full of unruly children, familial bickering, and financial pressure to keep up with fashionable society, the Aikin children lead productive, salutary, and enlightened lives under the guidance of Susan and Harry.

Sedgwick's goals in this book seem multiple. One of the novel's themes can be distilled as the platitude that money can buy neither happiness nor a meaningful family life. But a specific political viewpoint also emerges, embodying both liberal-democratic and conservative strains in Sedgwick's thought. The novel's valorizing of the need for each working-class individual to follow one's own calling and to shape private and familial lives constitutes the Jacksonian egalitarianism to which Sedgwick was increasingly drawn. The conservative elements take several shapes. One is the text's insistence, despite the novel's title, that there is no "real poverty" in the United States that does not come from "vice or disease" (ch. 2). Indeed, the book is peppered with this and other expressions of American exceptionalism as articulated by its characters and narrator. Moreover, the text's representation of satisfied working-class poverty could well have been reassuring to Sedgwick's middle-class audience, who encounter in Harry a model, blue-collar American, who is industrious, virtuous, and eager to avoid the burdens of money.

Some of these same features reappear in *Live and Let Live.* Most overtly, the novel concerns the relation between middle-class families and their hired help, partly, as the preface explains, to "illustrate the failures of one party in the contract between employers and employed." To do so, Sedgwick focuses on the fortunes of the desperately poor Lee family, especially Lucy, "our humble heroine," who is placed into domestic service to help alleviate the family's financial sufferings (ch. 1). Tracing her jobs with various families, who cheat her out of her wages or otherwise exploit her, the novel offers a series of negative examples designed to encourage middle-class readers to appreciate, treat, and pay servants better. Despite the novel's cultural criticism being pitched at middle-class treatment of the working class, however, the text can be seen to possess a subtle undercurrent. At times it seems designed to encourage any domestics who might get hold of it to be happy in their labor. At other points, Sedgwick appears interested in assuaging at least part of the middle-class guilt the novel might induce by suggesting that the working poor are actually content in their poverty, provided that they can make a happy home somewhere.

Reviewers extensively praised both *Poor Rich Man* and *Live and Let Live*, and sales of both far outstripped anything Sedgwick had experienced with her previous novels, including *Home* and *Hope Leslie*. While the latter had quickly sold out its first edition of 2,000 copies, Harper and Brothers, who became her primary publisher in 1835, issued *Poor Rich Man* in a first edition of 9,000 copies, and all were sold within six months. By late 1839, the reading public had gobbled up nearly 20,000 copies of that novel. *Live and Let Live* enjoyed comparable success, with a two-year sales total of nearly 13,000 copies. Even in comparison to *Home*, these two novels performed extraordinarily. While *Home* had gone through fifteen editions in six years, *Poor Rich Man* took only three years to go through sixteen editions, and the sales of *Live and Let Live* exhausted twelve editions in less than two years.

Over the next eight years, Sedgwick went on to publish three collections of stories, a book of travel letters from abroad, and *Means and Ends; or, Self-Training* (1839), a self-help book employing quasi-fictional, didactic vignettes. Not until 1847 did she publish another full-length work of fiction with a continuous narrative line: *The Boy of Mount Rhigi*. Roughly the length of *A New-England Tale*, this new novel, like earlier Sedgwick fictions, focuses on young people, but with a difference. Its two protagonists, Clapham Dunn and Harry Davis, are males, and the narrative follows their disparate lives as played out in very different families. While Harry grows up nurtured by benevolent parents, Clap's family is headed by Norman Dunn, whose filth, violence, and exploitive behavior anticipate Mark Twain's Pap Finn by forty years. Indeed, *Boy of Mount Rhigi* seems a forerunner of *Adventures of Huckleberry Finn* (1884) in several ways. Like Tom Sawyer, Harry excels in reading and bookishness, while Clap's survival skills and colloquial speech patterns anticipate Huck's characteristics. Like Huck, Clap also "don't know much about Scripture stories" (ch. 1). Nonetheless, the novel is not quite a precursor of Twain's best-known narrative. Unlike Tom, Harry focuses on cultivating Clap's inherent goodness, as Sedgwick infuses heavy-handed didactic narrative comments, very contrary to Twain, but nonetheless in character with US fiction of the 1830s and 1840s.

During the next ten years, Sedgwick published several volumes of short stories, but her literary output dropped significantly over that period, in part because she was increasingly involved in other matters in the public sphere. She began working concertedly with the Women's Prison Association and teaching in her sister-in-law's school in Lenox, Massachusetts. Despite this work, Sedgwick nonetheless managed to complete one last novel, which she published in 1857 as *Married or Single?*

The title of the novel announces its main concern, one that Sedgwick had implicitly addressed from time to time in her fiction at least since *Hope Leslie*, whose narrator asserts at the novel's close, "marriage is not *essential* to the contentment, the dignity, or the happiness of woman" (v. 2, ch. 15). In *Married or Single?*, Sedgwick takes direct aim at the problems of gender and marriage.

Sedgwick's attitude toward marriage and single life seems marked by ambivalence. On the one hand, she never married nor appeared interested in pursuing marriage from her early thirties on. In an 1821 letter, she wrote, "Matrimony does certainly seem very meddling and impertinent" to single women like herself (Dewey 1871, 146), and in the late 1830s, she privately recorded, "I am inclined to think there is more individuality in single than in married women" (qtd. in Kelley 1984, 239). Yet Sedgwick also subscribed to the conventional belief that marriage was the superior, God-given destiny of women and described the "solitary condition" as "an unnatural state," adding, "from my own experience I would not advise any one to remain unmarried" (Dewey 1871, 198).

Apropos of this ambivalence, *Married or Single?* explores that question by splitting the protagonist role between two New York City sisters, Grace and Eleanor Herbert. Quite early in the novel, Sedgwick gives each sister's life a different trajectory. Approximately a third of the way into the first volume, Eleanor marries a young minister, Francis Esterly. Meanwhile, Grace is courted by a vain socialite, Horace Copley, whose position as a member of New York's fashionable, moneyed class attracts Grace. Meanwhile, secretly in love with her is a young lawyer and family friend, Archibald Lisle.

Around this main storyline, Sedgwick threads in several subplots and subjects echoing those of her previous novels. The issue of slavery—and the Fugitive Slave Law—surfaces in the story of Violet and her son, who are fugitive slaves being hunted by authorities and whom Grace aids in avoiding capture, in what is arguably the strongest abolitionist note in any Sedgwick novel. Through the manners and morals of several minor characters, *Married or Single?* also satirizes fashionable society, in a way reminiscent of *Clarence*. Additionally, American exceptionalism receives brief treatment, though in this novel Sedgwick strikes a note contrary to her usual unqualified trumpeting of this component of the American imaginary, in that she suggests a disturbing parallel between upper-class English society and the moneyed class that had developed in the United States.

All these elements, however, remain incidental as the main plot plays out via the juxtaposition of Eleanor's marital happiness and Grace's growing recognition that Copeland is a bounder, which leads her to break their engagement, and she decides to remain single for the rest of her life. But then something curious happens. The love Lisle feels for Grace and her long-suppressed admiration for him cannot be denied, and the two discover that their relationship can be, like Eleanor and Francis's, a union of kindred spirits. Of course, this turnabout raises a question: How does the title, which seems to promise an inquiry into the dominant culture's conception of the true life for women, fit Sedgwick's decision to have both Herbert women marry by the novel's end?

Several Sedgwick scholars have puzzled over this turn, and a number of antebellum reviewers evinced a similar consternation. A review in the *Ladies' Repository* observed, "The beginning of the volume gives one an idea that the authoress is about to insist upon the reality of female single blessedness. But the moral—was it accidental and inevitable, or done of a forethought?—is strongly in favor of married life" (Sept. 1857, 564). A review in *Harper's Weekly* agreed by asserting that "the moral can scarcely be said to be in favor of single life, since Grace, the heroine, around whom the whole interest of the story moves, like a true woman, loves and marries at last" (July 25, 1857, 470).

There is, however, another way to interpret the novel's conclusion vis-à-vis its title. The latter can be read as an abbreviation of a more specific question for women: Is a marriage, even a bad one, necessarily a superior condition to single life? The opening chapters suggest that this version of the query is the one posed by the novel. In those chapters, as Grace and Eleanor go through some family letters from previous generations, several disclose bad marriages in the family's past, providing a springboard for the assertion that "a want of true respect for women lies at the root . . . of many marriage wrecks" (v. 1, ch. 1). This idea emerges most overtly and forcefully in a discussion between Eleanor and Francis in volume two, in which Eleanor gently chides her husband, "[D]o not lend your voice to the general vulgar view of life, and say, 'A woman must be married.' Surely it is better she should be a lonely struggler . . . than to sacrifice her truth, to live in the closest and dearest relation of life, stripped of all that makes life dear." Though Eleanor, speaking here as Sedgwick's mouthpiece, regards marriage as a woman's "highest destiny," she adds that if a woman "can not fold her heart in the bands of conjugal affection . . . she can prepare her soul for its eternal destiny without marriage" as "sister, friend, and benefactor" (ch. 6). Sedgwick's point seems clear. Although marriage, in this logic, is superior to single life for women, that "truth" is accurate only if a woman can find someone who shares and respects her values and ideas. Otherwise, single life remains a preferable alternative through which women can find fulfillment in disinterested service and, possibly, "a healthy vigorous intellectual life" (v. 2, ch. 16).

Despite offering a position on women's marriage that was quite compatible with that of her previous novels, *Married or Single?* was not the success her novels of the 1820s and 1830s had been. Though no specific sales figures survive, apparently it sold only moderately, and reviews were mixed, with several critics deciding that the novel was either inconsistent in its ideas or troubled by Sedgwick's botched handling of her materials. Others concluded that *Married or Single?* was tedious, dismissing it, as a review in *Russell's Magazine* did, as "an ordinary domestic tale, meager in incident, and undramatic in action" (Sept. 1857, 572). A review in the New York *Albion* even found it shopworn and banal, since "the old subject of marriage and giving in marriage is the staple of this, as of ninety-nine out of a hundred kindred works" (Aug. 15, 1857, 393).

Although *Married or Single?* marked a decline in Sedgwick's antebellum reputation, her novels continued to be read and reissued throughout the next decade and after her death in 1867. While Sedgwick would largely be forgotten for much of the twentieth century, recent scholars have brought many of her novels to renewed attention and demonstrated the breadth of her achievements. A diverse writer, Sedgwick published in a variety of genres, including short stories, nonfiction essays, children's literature, travel narratives, biography, and advice manuals. Her greatest accomplishments lie, however, in her novels. Through them, she established herself as a pioneer of the US novel, helping turn a European form into a distinctively American version of the genre. In the process, she contributed to the shape and subsequent development of a number of novelistic subgenres, from the novel of manners and women's domestic fiction, to the historical novel, regionalist fiction, and the frontier romance. No doubt in the future, scholars, critics, and even general readers will continue to explore Sedgwick's fiction in ways that will enhance and solidify her status as one of the four or five most important US novelists before the Civil War.

16

HAWTHORNE AND THE HISTORICAL ROMANCE

LARRY J. REYNOLDS

In a journal entry of 1844, Nathaniel Hawthorne lamented, "Dead Men's opinions in all things control the living truth; we believe in Dead Men's religion; we laugh at Dead Men's jokes; we cry at Dead Men's pathos; everywhere and in all matters, Dead Men tyrannize inexorably over us" (1972, 252). He would develop this idea in *The House of the Seven Gables: A Romance* (1851), giving his character Holgrave similar sentiments to express, but the idea was planted like an oak in Hawthorne's own mind. Although *The Scarlet Letter: A Romance* (1850) is the only one of Hawthorne's novels set in the historical past, all of them reveal his acute sense of the baneful influence of the past on the present. He lived in hopeful times, but a spirit of pessimism, or the "great power of blackness" as Herman Melville called it (1987, 243), infused all four of Hawthorne's major novels, *The Scarlet Letter*, *The House of the Seven Gables*, *The Blithedale Romance* (1852), and *The Marble Faun: or, The Romance of Monte Beni* (1860).

Hawthorne began his career in the 1820s at the height of Sir Walter Scott's popularity and was influenced by Scott to turn to the American past to find historical materials to use in his own writings. From Scott, he learned to create dramatically lighted symbolic tableaux, which, as George Dekker has pointed out, are "modeled after the 'packed scenes' in historical paintings" (1987, 67). Hawthorne filled his painterly descriptions with emblematic details and used these scenes, rather than action, to advance his plots. He was familiar with James Fenimore Cooper's historical novels, of course, but as F. O. Matthiessen pointed out long ago, while Hawthorne professed "unwavering admiration" for Cooper's novels, "it is obvious that neither the form nor the content of Cooper's hastily improvised narratives bore any vital relation to his own" (1941, 201). Unlike Cooper, Hawthorne specialized not in exciting adventure but in symbolic explorations of the moral struggles of his characters. His major achievement was adding profound psychological depth to the history of the American novel. His best works, among his tales and romances, depend upon an acute and complex sense of the past, which would influence the work of later writers, most notably William Faulkner. This chapter will set out key features of Hawthorne's turn to history, show how it informed his theory of romance, and examine its innovative use in his novels.

Hawthorne's first novel, *Fanshawe* (1828), is an amateurish apprentice work. He began it during his years at Bowdoin College (1821–25), where he acquired a taste for gothic fiction, which he never completely lost. He was an avid reader of works by William Godwin, Charles Robert Maturin, and Matthew Gregory Lewis, as well as the American gothic novelist John Neal. A friend of Hawthorne's once reminded him of "the damned ranting stuff of John Neal, which you, while at Brunswick, relished so highly" (qtd. in Doubleday 1972, 35). He set *Fanshawe* in the Brunswick area several years in the past and borrowed heavily from Scott and the gothic tradition.

The protagonist Fanshawe is a young, detached scholar who would become a type in Hawthorne's later novels. He reluctantly becomes involved in thwarting a dark villain named Butler, who kidnaps and threatens to rape the lovely heroine, Ellen Langton. During a climactic struggle on a mountaintop, Fanshawe stands on the edge of a precipice, as Butler unsuccessfully climbs toward him: "[T]he adventurer grasped at a twig, too slenderly rooted to sustain his weight. It gave way in his hand, and he fell backward down the precipice. . . . With all the passions of hell alive in his heart, he had met the fate that he intended for Fanshawe" (ch. 9). Passages like this one indicate why Hawthorne soon became embarrassed by this work and tried to keep his authorship a secret. It would be some twenty years before he would write another novel.

The early part of Hawthorne's career (1830–37) was devoted to writing tales and sketches for gift books and annuals, and as he discovered his gift for writing psychological romance, he turned toward history and away from gothic sensationalism. In his explorations of his characters' psychic states, he anticipated many of the findings of modern psychology, not just Freudian theories of family dynamics, but the more recent discovery that certain mental aberrations—such as anxiety, paranoia, hysteria, delusion, and obsession—can be attributed to psycho-social causes. His works emphasize the role that religion and politics play in the construction of mental states deemed psychotic, and in this sense, they differ from those of Poe and other practitioners of the American gothic.

One of Hawthorne's early tales, "Alice Doane's Appeal" (1835), marks a transition in the type of fiction he sought to create. In the tale, he pairs an inner gothic story with an outer realistic account of accused witches being led to their executions. As the tale opens, the narrator and two pretty female companions visit Gallows Hill, and the narrator tries to impress the women by reading from a manuscript he has written. It features a young man named Leonard Doane, in love with his sister Alice, who is seduced by an unknown youth named Walter Brome, whom Leonard murders. These events, it turns out, result from the machinations of a wizard "who had cunningly devised that Walter Brome should tempt his unknown sister to guilt and shame, and himself perish by the hand of his twin-brother." The story climaxes in a crowded graveyard where a "company of devils and condemned souls come on a holiday, to revel in the discovery of a complicated crime; as foul a one as ever was imagined in their dreadful abode."

The young ladies find this story "grotesque and extravagant" and laugh at it. The narrator then detains them "a while longer on the hill" and makes "a trial whether truth were more powerful than fiction." He gives a moving account of an actual procession to Gallows Hill in 1692:

> Here tottered a woman in her dotage, knowing neither the crime imputed her, nor its punishment; there another, distracted by the universal madness, till feverish dreams were remembered as realities, and she almost believed her guilt. One, a proud man once, was so broken down by the intolerable hatred heaped upon him, that he seemed to hasten his steps, eager to hide himself in the grave hastily dug, at the foot of the gallows.

The narrator's listeners are profoundly affected by his account, and in this way, Hawthorne announces a change in the kind of fiction he would write. As Nina Baym has pointed out, Hawthorne's "work after 1830 shows one attempt after another to write more rational and conservative fiction" (1976, 39).

Hawthorne's turn to history was influenced not only by Scott but also by the numerous calls made during the decades following the War of 1812 for the creation of a distinctive national literature. The main topics usually suggested for literary treatment were frontier settlement, Indian wars, and the American Revolution. Hawthorne's initial response was two projected collections of tales, titled "Seven Tales of My Native Land" and "Provincial Tales," neither of which found a publisher. He apparently burned all the tales in the first collection, with the exception of "Alice Doane's Appeal," which he subsequently altered. He used New England colonial settings in a number of his most successful tales published separately, including "The Gentle Boy" (1832), "My Kinsman, Major Molineux" (1832), and "Young Goodman Brown" (1835). After he was recruited by John L. O'Sullivan as a contributor to the *Democratic Review*, he published in 1838–39 four tales, titled "Legends of the Province House," set in provincial Boston during the Revolutionary period. Despite the ardent nationalism of O'Sullivan's magazine, these "Legends" lightly satirize the patriotic treatments of the American past appearing in popular histories, including George Bancroft's monumental *History of the United States* (1834–74). Although Hawthorne supported the Revolution and critiqued British aristocratic pretensions, he also extended sympathy to those Loyalists victimized by American crowds and mobs.

During the twelve so-called "solitary years" Hawthorne spent at home in Salem following college, he developed a complex historical consciousness through assiduous study of such documents as local and regional histories, biographies, memoirs, tracts, sermons, annals, encyclopedias, old newspapers, and current periodicals. He took special interest in Thomas Bayly Howell's *State Trials* (1809–28), which reconstructed criminal cases. As he pointed out in his *Life of Franklin Pierce* (1852), "[W]hen the actual observation of public measures goes hand in hand with study, when the mind is capable of comparing the present with its analogies in the past, and of grasping the principle that belongs to both, this is to have history for a living tutor" (ch. 2). Past-present analogies would become a key feature of his major romances.

As a young man, Hawthorne had been a desultory student, and scholars have debated whether his later study of New England history was substantial. Neal Frank Doubleday has argued, "There is a tendency to overestimate the depth of Hawthorne's reading in history. . . . [F]or the most part the tales do not show, it seems to me, any great depth of knowledge of New England history or remarkable historical perceptiveness on Hawthorne's part" (1972, 40). On the other hand, Michael Colacurcio, in a well-known and highly regarded book, *The Province of Piety* (1995), argues that Hawthorne in his early tales went far beyond just writerly interest in what he could use from the past and actually had all the interests and skills of a moral historian. In Colacurcio's view, Hawthorne used "his extraordinary power critically to discern and dramatically to recreate the moral conditions under which earlier generations of Americans had lived and, in one way or another, sought salvation" (13). Colacurcio makes a persuasive case for Hawthorne's understanding of the life and thought of earlier generations; however, like all historical romance writers, Hawthorne was ultimately less concerned with the past than with the present, especially his career.

As Hawthorne studied historical documents and narratives, he formulated a theory of romance that privileged his own practice. His goal, he claimed in the preface to *The House of the Seven Gables,* was to reveal "the truth of the human heart" while connecting "a by-gone time with the very Present that is flitting away from us." In the early sketch "Sir William Phips" (1830), he asserted that the writings of biographers and historians offered knowledge like that of a "map,—minute, perhaps, and accurate, and available for all necessary purposes,—but cold and naked, and wholly destitute of the mimic charm produced by landscape painting." In deciding which persons to represent in his fiction, Hawthorne, like Cooper, preferred to elevate those without power or renown.

Hawthorne was a democrat and a pacifist, and even though he idealized Andrew Jackson, it was Jackson the friend of the common man, not Jackson the war hero, he admired. In the preface to a history book for school children, *Peter Parley's Universal History, on the Basis of Geography* (1837), Hawthorne told his young readers:

> As you lift the curtain of the past, mankind seem from age to age engaged in constant strife, battle, and bloodshed. The master spirits generally stand forth as guided only by ambition, and superior to other men in wickedness as in power. . . . [I]n telling of the vices and crimes that soil the pages of the past, I have taken advantage of every convenient occasion, to excite hatred of injustice, violence, and falsehood, and promote a love of truth, equity, and benevolence.

Similarly, some thirty years later, in the collection of essays *Our Old Home* (1863), he describes a visit to the great hall in Chelsea Hospital, London, filled with "trophies of battles fought and won in every quarter of the world," and declares in "Up the Thames": "In truth, the whole system of a people crowing over its military triumphs had far better be dispensed with, both on account of the ill-blood that it helps to keep fermenting among the nations, and because it operates as an accumulative inducement to future generations to aim at a kind of glory, the gain of which has generally proved more ruinous than its loss." Because of his pacifism, Hawthorne would eventually find himself accused of treasonous sympathies during the American Civil War.

Although Hawthorne presents himself in his prefaces as a modest and unassuming writer, he was convinced that his fictional treatments of the historical past offered his readers more insight into the workings of the human mind and heart than any so-called objective account. He often borrowed factual information from various historical records, but he combined these with imagined characters and scenes. In "The Custom-House" preface to *The Scarlet Letter*, he sets out his famous theory of romance. He begins by telling of his struggle to write in his deserted parlor, lit by glimmering coal-fire and moonlight, which casts a quality of strangeness and remoteness over everyday objects. This light, he says, is like romantic art. Both create "a neutral territory, somewhere between the real world and fairy-land, where the Actual and the Imaginary may meet, and each imbue itself with the nature of the other." As Richard Millington has pointed out, Hawthorne's practice of romance is unique in that it is less "a literary form than . . . the psychological and cultural place where his art happens, where writer and reader meet in a special sort of interchange" (1992, 43). The charm of Hawthorne's style is the way in which he establishes intimate relations with his readers, making them receptive to his sometimes marvelous scenes through genial humor and elegant prose.

"The Custom-House" provides a superb example of how Hawthorne worked to create the kind of romance that would earn him distinction as one of America's finest writers. In the preface, he takes his reader step-by-step into the past and, at the same time, into the realm of romance. He begins in the present (circa 1850), describing himself and an earlier generation of "aged men" who work in the Custom House. All represent real persons. In the "second story" of the actual Custom House, he discovers a manuscript (imaginary) compiled (circa 1750) by Jonathan Pue, an actual surveyor who worked there. Pue's manuscript is based on the oral testimony of an earlier generation of "aged persons" (imaginary) who in their youth (circa 1700) knew Hester Prynne (also imaginary) as an old woman. The fictional story about her takes place (circa 1650) when she's a vibrant young woman. As Hester steps forth from the Boston prison in the opening scene, the reader, thanks to "The Custom-House" preface, has been taken carefully and artfully into the past and into her world, where the actual and imaginary meet.

A number of scholars have studied the historical sources of "the faded incidents" upon which Hawthorne cast a "reviving light" in his writings ("Sir William Phips") and have found clues in his notebooks. An entry from 1844, for example, reads, "The life of a woman, who, by the old colony law, was condemned always to wear the letter *A*, sewed on her garment, in token of her having committed adultery" (Hawthorne 1972, 254). Despite his dependence upon early American histories, Hawthorne regarded them with skepticism. He drew heavily from Cotton Mather's *Magnalia Christi Americana* (1702); yet in Hawthorne's sketch "Main-street" (1849), he depicts Mather on horseback overseeing a pitiful group of accused witches being taken to the gallows. Hawthorne then asks:

> May not the Arch Fiend have been too subtle for the court and jury, and betrayed them—laughing in his sleeve the while—into the awful error of pouring out sanctified blood as an acceptable sacrifice upon God's altar? Ah! no; for listen to wise Cotton Mather, who . . . tells them that all has been religiously and justly done, and that Satan's power shall this day receive its death-blow in New England.

Obviously, Hawthorne's irony here delivers a heavy blow as well.

Hawthorne's interest in Puritan history was personal as well as professional, and his treatment of Mather, in fact, may have been informed by displaced hostility toward Hawthorne's great-great-grandfather John Hathorne. This ancestor served as a judge in the Salem witchcraft trials. He conducted the initial examination of the accused and sat on the bench during their trials. His prejudice against them and his belief in the lies of their accusers resulted in the imprisonment of more than 150 persons, the hanging of nineteen innocent persons, and the death by torture of another. In "The Custom-House," Hawthorne admits that this ancestor "inherited the persecuting spirit, and made himself so conspicuous in the martyrdom of the witches, that their blood may fairly be said to have left a stain upon him." Referring to him and another ancestor, John's father William, who had persecuted the Quakers, Hawthorne writes, "I, the present writer, as their representative, hereby take shame upon myself for their sakes, and pray that any curse incurred by them—as I have heard, and as the dreary and unprosperous condition of the race, for many a long year back, would argue to exist—may be now and henceforth removed."

Many years ago, Randall Stewart, a pioneer in modern Hawthorne studies, identified the four major themes in Hawthorne's fiction as "the isolation of the individual, the unpardonable sin, the influence of the past, and the elixir of life" (1932, lxxxviii). What the list leaves out are those political themes that emerged from the witchcraft hysteria in Salem. This historical tragedy was the single most important event shaping Hawthorne's art. It persuaded him that self-righteous attempts to rid a person, a village, or a nation of perceived evil could produce results just the opposite of those desired, especially if the means used were violent. For him, impassioned actions, however benevolent in intention, caused unanticipated pain and suffering, and this became a recurrent theme in practically all his writings. (His incorporation of it into his *Life of Franklin Pierce*, where he questions the wisdom of the immediate abolition of slavery, outraged antislavery New Englanders and became infamous in late twentieth-century scholarship.)

Hawthorne's tales and romances demonstrate how easily individuals can be led into a metaphorical hell, not just by their own base desires but also by exclusionary systems of values and beliefs. Today we would call these ideologies. Hawthorne and his wife Sophia called them "theories," and she bragged that her husband was "without theories of any kind" (Valenti 1996, 146). This was not possible, of course, but Hawthorne indeed was open-minded and tolerant, to a fault, some would say, and in his studies of the human psyche under duress, he shows his characters becoming deluded by various "isms," including Puritanism, Quakerism, nationalism, transcendentalism, and even utopianism. Hawthorne saw himself, especially during those years he lived in Concord among the Transcendentalists (1842–45), as a hard-headed realist resisting the dangerous appeals of what he described in "The Old Manse" (1846) as the "hobgoblins of flesh and blood" that fluttered around Ralph Waldo Emerson at the other end of town. His writings, during this stage of his career, shifted from the historical to the contemporary, and many pieces, especially "The Hall of Fantasy" (1843) and "The Celestial Rail-road" (1843), satirize various reform movements of the day.

Despite the appeal that the sensational exerted upon Hawthorne, he committed himself to moderation in his politics and his writing. He distrusted partisanship and enthusiasms of all kinds and believed they inevitably led to unintended consequences. His daughter Rose Hawthorne Lathrop captured his reserve in her excellent chapter "The Artist at Work" in *Memories of Hawthorne* (1897). She recalled "his perfect renunciation of artistic claptrap and artistic license": "He wrote with temperateness, and in pitying love of human nature, in the instinctive hope of helping it to know and redeem itself" (444). Even allowing for Rose's religious sensibilities (she became a Catholic nun), her observations are valid. A number of the supernatural features of his romances—specters, curses, bloody footsteps—which may appear to be mere gothic "claptrap," held personal resonance for him, as reminders of gloomy wrongs of the past.

The specters and ghosts that make their appearance in *The Scarlet Letter* and *The Marble Faun* had very real consequences in Salem in 1692 when Judge Hathorne accepted them as evidence against the accused. The curse, which figures so prominently in *The House of the Seven Gables*, echoes the real one uttered by Sarah Good shortly before her hanging in 1692. When one of the magistrates sitting beside Judge Hathorne told her she was a witch, she replied, "You are a lyer [*sic*]; I am no more a Witch than you are a Wizard, and if you take away my Life, God will give you Blood to drink" (Calef 1914, 358). The bloody footstep featured in the unfinished "American Claimant" romance also lay deep in Hawthorne's imagination. As he explains in "The Custom-House," his own Puritan ancestor had been "a bitter persecutor; as witness the Quakers, who have remembered him in their histories, and relate an incident of his hard severity towards a woman of their sect, which will last longer, it is to be feared, than any record of his better deeds, although these were many." The woman was the Quaker Ann Coleman who, by order of William Hathorne, was whipped through Salem, Boston, and Dedham, bleeding profusely.

In the process of drawing from New England history (which included his family history), Hawthorne altered what he found, shifting dates and places, and omitting key information, to support the themes he wished to develop. In "Roger Malvin's Burial" (1832), for example, he focuses on the relation between a young man, Reuben Bourne, and a mortally wounded older man, Roger Malvin, both survivors of "Lovell's Fight" in 1725. In his introduction to the tale, Hawthorne coyly suggests, "Imagination, by casting certain circumstances judiciously into the shade, may see much to admire in the heroism of a little band, who gave battle to twice their number in the heart of the enemy's country." These "certain circumstances," however, are that Captain Lovell's men were bounty hunters who began their scalp-hunting expedition by killing a party of Indians who were asleep. The tragic death of young Cyrus Bourne not only expiates Reuben's guilt about deserting Roger but also prophesies, as Colacurcio has pointed out, "some bloody purgation from national guilt" (1995, 121). Manifest Destiny was not a concept Hawthorne embraced, despite his friendship with O'Sullivan, who helped popularize the term. Hawthorne sympathized with Native Americans displaced by white settlers, as he did with Africans forced into slavery in the South.

In an 1846 review in the *Salem Advertiser*, Hawthorne criticized the southern novelist William Gilmore Simms for promoting historical romances advancing American nationalism: the "themes suggested by [Simms], viewed as he views them, would produce nothing but historical novels, cast in the same worn out mould that has been in use these thirty years, and which it is time to break up and fling away" (May 2, 1846). Five years later, with *The Scarlet Letter*, Hawthorne breathed new life into the genre of the historical romance by not only challenging the prevalent view of Puritans as defenders of liberty and fathers of the nation but also by revealing how tyranny can masquerade as radical righteousness.

Hawthorne's brilliant tale "Young Goodman Brown" anticipates *The Scarlet Letter* by showing how Puritanism generated delusions that caused permanent harm. The story tells of a young, good man's journey into the woods, where he apparently meets the devil and attends a witches' sabbath. He even believes he sees his wife, Faith, there as well. A dark figure resembling a Puritan divine stands atop an altar-like rock, surrounded by blazing pines, and tells the congregation that "[e]vil is the nature of mankind" and welcomes them to "the communion of [their] race." At the last moment, Brown resists his baptism, causing the scene to abruptly disappear, yet he becomes a deeply sad man as a result of what he has seen. Hawthorne asks, "Had Goodman Brown fallen asleep in the forest, and only dreamed a wild dream of a witch-meeting?" By answering the question with "Be it so, if you will," he challenges the superstitions of his readers. If they believe the witches' meeting real, they become like the villagers of Salem, willing to credit "spectral" evidence that has no basis in fact.

When Hawthorne started writing *The Scarlet Letter* after his firing from the Salem Custom House, he planned to make it into a short story that would complement his other fictionalized treatments of the New England past. According to his publisher, James T. Fields, the work was intended for a collection titled "Old-Time Legends: Together with Sketches, Experimental and Ideal." At Fields's urging, Hawthorne let the work stand alone as a historical romance. As *The Scarlet Letter* draws upon Puritan history, it subjects that history to critique, showing readers how religion and politics combined to inspire fear and hatred toward others. As Richard Brodhead once observed, "few American writers of the nineteenth century so consistently take the political as the scene for their life and work as Hawthorne does" (1984, 95). *The Scarlet Letter* teems with political energy, much of it hostile.

The "discourse on sin" offered by the Reverend John Wilson at the beginning of *The Scarlet Letter* provides a good example of the irony Hawthorne directs at the practice of fear mongering by those in positions of authority. During the "hour or more" Wilson addresses the people of Boston, he successfully demonizes Hester and her scarlet letter. When she is led back to prison, "it was whispered, by those who peered after her, that the scarlet letter threw a lurid gleam along the dark passage-way of the interior" (ch. 3). The actual John Wilson, a Puritan divine who lived from 1588 to 1667, engaged in similar treatment of the actual Anne Hutchinson, "the sainted Ann [*sic*] Hutchinson," as Hawthorne calls her (ch. 1), who was banished from Massachusetts in 1638 for questioning the doctrines of her ministers, including Wilson. When Wilson delivered her formal excommunication on behalf of the church, he asserted, "I doe not only pronounce you worthy to be cast out, but *I doe cast you out* and in the name of Christ *I doe deliver you up to Sathan* that you may learne no more to blaspheme to seduce and to lye" (Hall 1990, 388). As Colacurcio has shown, Hawthorne had the Hutchinson case in mind while writing about Hester Prynne. Both rebellious women, gifted with intelligence and courage, suffer at the hands of the patriarchy.

The abuse of Hester and other women in Hawthorne's works has led some critics to charge him with misogyny, but a strong case has been made, most notably by Baym and Monika Elbert, that Hawthorne actually admired and sympathized with strong women. He obviously identifies with Hester, who has become an icon of beauty, strength, and self-reliance. Her persecutors, on the other hand, show themselves to be "iron men," lacking in humanity (ch. 17). Hawthorne, it should go without saying, was no Puritan. Although he respected the Puritans' piety and fortitude, he detested their intolerance and cruelty, especially when, at the end of the seventeenth century, they proved themselves dangerous fanatics. In his sketch "Main-street," he observes, "The sons and grandchildren of the first settlers were a race of lower and narrower souls than their progenitors had been. The latter were stern, severe, intolerant, but not superstitious, not even fanatical." The witchcraft delusion marked the descent into fanaticism.

In *The Scarlet Letter*, as in his tales, Hawthorne altered and omitted factual information from the past in order to support the themes he wished to develop. None of the New England histories Hawthorne used as sources for *The Scarlet Letter* (including those by Mather, Joseph Felt, Caleb Snow, Thomas Hutchinson, and John Winthrop) mention a scaffold. Hawthorne used the scaffold as a dramatic setting and unifying structural device probably because he wished to critique political radicalism and violence. He hints at this in "The Custom-House" preface when he warns the reader that the book has a darkness "due to the period of hardly accomplished revolution and still seething turmoil, in which the story shaped itself." He thus alludes to his actual ouster from the Custom House, his decapitation, as he puts it, and the anxiety he now felt about how he would support his family. Other revolutions he had in mind include the Italian revolutions of 1848–1849 that his friend Margaret Fuller was reporting on for the New York *Tribune*; the English Revolution of 1642–1649; and the French Revolution of 1789, both of which he had recently read books about. These revolutions informed his account of Hester's rebellious spirit, embodied in Pearl. Arthur succumbs to Hester's plan for them in the forest and suffers "a revolution in the sphere of thought and feeling" on the way home, inciting him "to do some strange, wild, wicked thing or other" (ch. 20). His final confession and death dissipate this rebelliousness, contributing to the romance's conservative ending, which Sacvan Bercovitch and others have linked to the Compromise of 1850 and the politics of Hawthorne's friend Franklin Pierce.

For the most part, Hawthorne hid his politics in his fiction and advanced his argument for moderation through a transhistorical mist. He did the same with his religious views. Melville once claimed that Hawthorne's writings appeal to "that Calvinistic sense of Innate Depravity and Original Sin, from whose visitations, in some shape or other, no deeply thinking mind is always and wholly free" (1987, 243); yet the characterization describes Melville's writings more accurately than Hawthorne's. Unlike Melville, Hawthorne did not ponder his relationship with God. He was much more interested in moral issues than metaphysical ones. While at Bowdoin, he wrote his sister Elizabeth, "the worst of all is to be compelled to go to meeting every Sunday, and to hear a red hot Calvinist Sermon from the President, or some other dealer in fire and brimstone" (1984, 159). Unitarianism infused with Quakerism probably best describes Hawthorne's religion. He admired George Fox, the founder of the Quaker movement, and in "A Virtuoso's Collection" (1842) refers to him as "perhaps the truest apostle that has appeared on earth for these eighteen hundred years." As an adult, Hawthorne did not attend church.

His favorite books included Edmund Spenser's *The Faerie Queene* (1590; 1596), John Milton's *Paradise Lost* (1667), and John Bunyan's *The Pilgrim's Progress* (1678; 1684), yet religious dogma interested him only to the extent that it affected the lives of his characters. In *The Scarlet Letter*, Arthur Dimmesdale struggles to reestablish a proper relationship with the Puritan God and community, yet Hawthorne allows the reader to see that Arthur's deepest need is to acknowledge Pearl as his daughter. At his death, Hester asks Arthur if they will meet in heaven, but Arthur tells her to "hush," as if such matters were God's alone to decide. Hawthorne believed in divine Providence but thought anyone who tried to interpret God's will was a fool. He once told his sister-in-law Elizabeth Peabody, "Vengeance and beneficence are things that God claims for Himself. His instruments have no consciousness of His purpose; if they imagine they have, it is a pretty sure token that they are *not* His instruments" (1987b, 116). A sense of irony characterizes Hawthorne's religion, politics, and art, often leading to misunderstandings on the part of his critics.

Hawthorne's novels at their best evince a seductive charm that can be traced to the voice of his authorial persona, who is invariably modest, humorous, and ironic. This voice, especially in his prefaces, often casts a serene and apparently timeless haze over the scenes depicted, not unlike Washington Irving in "The Legend of Sleepy Hollow" (1820), except that Hawthorne's Edenic scenes often have a hidden danger lurking within them. In the delightful "Old Manse" preface to *Mosses from an Old Manse* (1846), the repose and sleep the author claims to offer his guests in his home is compared to "the Enchanted Ground, through which the pilgrim travelled on his way to the Celestial City," yet anyone who knows *The Pilgrim's Progress* knows that this enchantment was the work of the devil, an attempt to waylay the weary traveler as he approaches the Celestial City. Similarly, "The Custom-House" preface to *The Scarlet Letter*, which proclaims the political innocence of Surveyor Hawthorne, inflicts sly revenge on the Whigs who have driven him from office. When some Salemites saw through his pose and objected, Hawthorne declared in the preface to the second edition, "as to enmity, or ill-feeling of any kind, personal or political, he utterly disclaims such motives. . . . The author is constrained, therefore, to republish his introductory sketch without the change of a word." Hawthorne continued his revenge on Salem in his next novel, *The House of the Seven Gables*, by modeling the villainous Judge Pyncheon on the leader of the Salem Whigs, Reverend Charles Upham, and recalling the witchcraft delusion, the most shameful event in the town's past.

The disjunction between appearance and reality fascinated Hawthorne. One of its manifestations was the hypocrisy evinced by many of his characters, especially Judge Pyncheon. Another was the suggestion that historical truth is inaccessible, unknowable, and perhaps only fabulous. In other words, he saw the past covered by a veil, made of fictions. The multiple interpretations of what was on Arthur's exposed breast at the end of *The Scarlet Letter* provide a classic example, as do the multiple rumors about Donatello's ears and Miriam's past in *The Marble Faun*. In Hawthorne's fictional world, ambiguity and mystery suggest the epistemological challenge life presents to the visual observer.

For Hawthorne, the past could only be known through the present, and in his novels, he uses a layering technique to emphasize their simultaneity. He conceptualized history not in horizontal terms as an ongoing stream of time but in vertical terms as a circular spiral of sorts. In *The House of the Seven Gables*, he has Clifford declare:

> [A]ll human progress is in a circle; or, to use a more accurate and beautiful figure, in an ascending spiral curve. While we fancy ourselves going straight forward, and attaining, at every step, an entirely new position of affairs, we do actually return to something long ago tried and abandoned, but which we now find etherealized, refined, and perfected to its ideal. The past is but a coarse and sensual prophecy of the present and the future. (ch. 17)

Although Hawthorne did not share Clifford's simple-minded optimism about this spiral, he often uses time in this way, creating palimpsests that layer present experiences over those from the past, as for example, when the martyred Surveyor Hawthorne places the cloth letter "A" supposedly worn by Hester on his own breast and feels its heat.

Hawthorne's most subtle palimpsests appear in *The Scarlet Letter* and develop a critique of political radicalism. The action within the novel occurs during 1642–1649, the years of the English Revolution when Puritan "Roundheads" led by Oliver Cromwell defeated King Charles's Cavaliers. Charles was subsequently beheaded, at exactly the same moment that Arthur, victim of an overthrow of his thought and feeling, dies on the scaffold in Boston, surrounded by Puritans. Surveyor Hawthorne in the present, moreover, has been politically "decapitated" by Whigs acting upon "fierce and bitter spirit of malice and revenge" ("Custom-House"). Meanwhile, in Rome, Hawthorne's friend Fuller (one model for Hester and herself an unwed mother about to return to Boston), had applauded the revolutionary overthrow of Pope Pius IX and the assassination of his prime minister. These palimpsests serve to clarify the skepticism about political violence at the heart of the novel. Hawthorne sympathizes with Arthur and Hester in their roles as martyrs, and he critiques their behavior when they become subversive; however, he also "wishes us to discover that the most dangerous persons in the novel are not those characters who conjure up the specter of the devil by following their unruly passions . . . but those who perpetuate a society masking cruelty as righteousness, despotism as justice" (Reynolds 2008, 168). The positive conclusion of the novel thus goes beyond Pearl's shedding tears and pledging she would "nor for ever do battle with the world, but be a woman in it" (ch. 23) to the near certainty that she experiences happiness in another country, where beauty, love, and freedom are valued.

Soon after writing *The Scarlet Letter*, Hawthorne moved away from Salem to the Berkshire Mountains, where he met his new neighbor Melville and wrote *The House of the Seven Gables*. Responding to criticism of *The Scarlet Letter* as dark and gloomy, Hawthorne sought to fill this new romance with sunshine and humor. He achieved mixed success. The treatment of contemporary social changes and technological developments in the work has garnered positive critical attention, but the happy ending has been seen as forced and unfortunate. The explicit theme of the romance, set in the present but referring back to early Puritan times, is the struggle to overcome the influence of the past on the present. Hawthorne not only models his villain Judge Pyncheon on his main antagonist among the Salem Whigs, but also pairs the judge with his ancestor Colonel Pyncheon, guilty of falsely accusing Matthew Maule of witchcraft and causing his death by hanging, all in an attempt to secure his property. Judge Pyncheon continues this tradition in his persecution of Clifford.

Michael Davitt Bell has observed that "there are tokens of change in the romance as well as tokens of repetition" (1971, 216), and he points out how Holgrave (a Maule descendent) does not take advantage of the beautiful young Phoebe Pyncheon, but marries her, ending the cycle of Maule-Pyncheon mutual victimization. Yet Hawthorne calls Phoebe's mind "trim, orderly, and limit-loving" and shows her resistance to the insight that "judges, clergymen, and other characters of that eminent stamp and respectability, could really, in any single instance, be otherwise than just and upright men" (ch. 8). She thus becomes representative of a gullible public that allows hypocrites like Judge Pyncheon to acquire and maintain power.

At key moments in the work, Hawthorne suggests that political corruption and greed still hold sway over American society as they had in Colonel Pyncheon's day. After the judge's death, the "knot of subtle schemers" in Boston, who had planned to make him governor, are said to "steal from the people . . . the power of choosing its own rulers." The voice of the people, Hawthorne adds, "at the next gubernatorial election, though loud as thunder, will be really but an echo of what these gentlemen shall speak" (ch. 18). While Hawthorne was pleased that readers, including his wife, found the novel beautiful and lovely, he must have been secretly gratified that Melville, in a review letter he sent his new friend, perceived its darker side. Melville famously credited Hawthorne with saying "NO! in thunder," and possessing "the intense feeling of the visable truth," adding, "By visable truth, we mean the apprehension of the absolute condition of present things as they strike the eye of the man who fears them not, though they do their worst to him" (1993, 186).

After leaving the Berkshires and Melville, Hawthorne wrote *The Blithedale Romance*, in which he experimented for the first time with an unreliable first-person narrator named Miles Coverdale, a caricature of Hawthorne himself—shy, idealistic, and voyeuristic. His name, of course, refers to his habit of hiding and spying on others, especially Zenobia, the beautiful advocate of women's rights, and Hollingsworth, the charismatic and deceitful reformer with whom Zenobia falls in love. A fourth main character, Priscilla, Zenobia's pale and simple half-sister, also falls in love with Hollingsworth and cares for him in his despair at the end.

The Blithedale Romance has often been read as a fictionalized account of Hawthorne's experience at Brook Farm, the utopian community where he spent seven months in 1841, but it also addresses many issues and figures he contended with during his years in Concord, surrounded by idealistic writers and thinkers, including Emerson, Fuller, Henry David Thoreau, Ellery Channing, and Bronson Alcott. Zenobia and Fuller share a number of traits including intelligence, attractiveness, vitality, and a questionable past. Hawthorne began the novel, not coincidentally, in the wake of Fuller's sensational drowning in the summer of 1850, when she perished in a shipwreck along with her baby and the child's father.

Hollingsworth is a composite portrait of a reformer, with some traits Hawthorne attributed to Emerson. Hollingsworth's closest friend is "the cold, spectral monster which he had himself conjured up, . . . and of which, at last—as these men of a mighty purpose so invariably do—he had grown to be the bond-slave. It was his philanthropic theory!" (ch. 7). This theory allows him to act with coldness and cruelty toward others, especially Zenobia. When he learns that this beautiful feminist has no money to support his cause of prison reform, he rejects her, and Hawthorne's narrator observes, "I saw in Hollingsworth all that an artist could desire for the grim portrait of a Puritan magistrate, holding inquest of life and death in a case of witchcraft" (ch. 25). Within hours of this scene, Zenobia drowns herself, and only then does Hollingsworth abandon his spectral "theory," which he finally admits has transformed him into a murderer.

Another important context for Hawthorne's critique of Hollingsworth's "philanthropic theory" is the changing political climate in the United States following the Compromise of 1850, which provoked outrage throughout New England and presaged violent days ahead. Hawthorne was well aware that the issue of slavery was generating more and more political passion, and within several months of completing his romance, he defended his friend Pierce (soon to be president) from verbal attacks by "the fiercest, the least scrupulous, and the most consistent of those who battle against slavery" (*Life of Franklin Pierce*, ch. 6). Perhaps because Hawthorne addressed contemporary issues so directly and judgmentally in *The Blithedale Romance*, it contributed little to his reputation or to the development of the American novel. His characters tend to be mere types, their speeches wooden, and their behavior unsympathetic. Emerson called the novel "ghastly and untrue" (qtd. in Fields 1884, 459).

Because of his duties as American consul at Liverpool (a reward for his campaign biography of Pierce), Hawthorne did not publish his next novel, *The Marble Faun*, until eight years later. It was set in present-day Italy, 1858–1859, but its four main characters include two American artists (Kenyon and Hilda), one Anglo-Italian-Jewish artist (Miriam), and one Italian nobleman (Donatello). Hawthorne uses these characters to explore different perspectives on a mysterious crime, the murder of a shadowy figure who once posed as Miriam's model but later threatened her with harm. The novel is filled with descriptions of Italian art and scenery, many taken from Hawthorne's notebooks, but near and distant pasts endow the narrative with an atmosphere of danger and violence. It is one of the richest and most complex romances of its day, although its attention to art some readers find excessive.

The Italian Revolution of 1848 informs the work as seen in descriptions of the French infantry ready with muskets to protect the papacy if the Roman people try to revolt again. Robert Levine has speculated that Miriam, who resembles Fuller, can be viewed "as an anti-Catholic revolutionary, perhaps even an assassin, of 1848" (1990, 26). Miriam herself identifies with Beatrice Cenci, and her paintings link her to murderous women from the Biblical past, including Jael, who drove a tent stake through the skull of the sleeping Sisera; Judith, who killed Holofernes; and Salome, the daughter of Herodias, who asked for the head of John the Baptist. Donatello becomes her agent in the killing of the model, and Miriam ventures the "theory," as she calls it, that the two of them have gained depth of knowledge and character by this act of violence. Ultimately Hilda, Kenyon, and the author reject this rationalization.

In the preface to *The Marble Faun*, Hawthorne famously lamented, "No author, without a trial, can conceive of the difficulty of writing a Romance about a country where there is no shadow, no antiquity, no mystery, no picturesque and gloomy wrong, nor anything but a common-place prosperity, in broad and simple day-light, as is happily the case with my dear native land." This complaint has been used to support the notion that American authors lacked a usable past and that Hawthorne was blind to the evil of slavery. Henry James in his *Hawthorne* (1879) famously echoed Hawthorne's lament, declaring, "the coldness, the thinness, the blankness . . . present themselves so vividly that our foremost feeling is that of compassion for a romancer looking for subjects in such a field" (43). Yet Hawthorne was being disingenuous in this preface, as he was in previous ones. He was keenly aware of the "gloomy wrongs" in his "dear native land" that tyrannized over the present. He was not only a skilled artist but also a political animal, always aware of the dominant issues of his age and willing to address them through his art. The murder in *The Marble Faun* is a case in point, for it can be viewed as an act of political violence on behalf of an oppressed subject, not unlike 1850s reprisals in the United States on behalf of slaves. Hawthorne was well aware of the connection. He hints at it by suggesting that Miriam has African American blood in her veins, one of many rumors about her past.

A glance at the historical context of *The Marble Faun* indicates the political issues Hawthorne was indirectly addressing. Just before he began writing, he was visited in Italy by his old friend, ex-president Pierce, who expressed alarm about the growing violence between the North and the South caused by the slavery issue. A month later, as Hawthorne was collecting material for the romance, he discussed "Bleeding Kansas" with another engaged partisan, the poet and newspaper editor William Cullen Bryant, a leader in the national Republican Party. They discussed their mutual friend, the abolitionist Charles Sumner, who had been beaten senseless on the floor of the Senate for his "Crime Against Kansas" speech. Bryant told Hawthorne that Sumner had recovered from his physical wounds, but "the shock upon his nerves had extended to his intellect, and was irremediable." Hawthorne found this information "about as sad as anything can be," adding, "He was merely (though with excellent abilities) one of the best fellows in the world, and ought to have lived and died in good-fellowship with all the world" (1980, 223). As Hawthorne was completing his romance in the winter of 1859, John Brown was hanged for his attempt to incite a slave revolt at Harpers Ferry, Virginia. As the use of violence to destroy slavery was being debated in the United States Congress, Hawthorne was writing the preface to *The Marble Faun*, feigning disappointment at the bright past of his "dear native land."

After he returned to the United States and Concord in the summer of 1860, Hawthorne faced a multitude of difficulties writing his last two romances, which, had he been able to complete them, would again have been heavily historical and political. At this time, he suffered from poor health, troubled finances, a stalled career, and bellicose neighbors who thought Brown a saint. The first incomplete romance features a young American who travels to England in search of his ancestral home, and the second a young scholar living in Concord at the beginning of the American Revolution who devotes himself to the discovery of the elixir of life.

Fratricide is a theme in both, and because an actual civil war was breaking out as Hawthorne was trying to write, he found he lacked the distance and detachment needed to combine the actual with the imaginary. Living in wartime, he found it impossible to write romances about wartime. In an essay he wrote for the *Atlantic Monthly* in July 1862, titled "Chiefly About War-Matters, by a Peaceable Man," he declared, "[T]he general heart-quake of the country long ago knocked at my cottage-door, and compelled me, reluctantly, to suspend the contemplation of certain fantasies, to which, according to my harmless custom, I was endeavoring to give a sufficiently life-like aspect to admit of their figuring in a romance" (43). In many ways, the age of American romanticism was coming to an end as Hawthorne struggled unsuccessfully to revive his career as a romancer. He died in May 1864, a year before the war ended. Despite the multiple shifts in reading tastes and literary practices that have occurred since, including the so-called rise of realism, his reputation as a leading American author has remained strong, and his finest work, *The Scarlet Letter*, endures as a masterpiece of American literature.

17

HERMAN MELVILLE

JONATHAN ARAC

For almost a century now, Herman Melville (1819–91) has been famous as the author of *Moby-Dick; or, The Whale* (1851). This spectacular, multigeneric, polyphonic work now seems the prototype for the American "big, ambitious novel" (Wood 2004, 178) that has defined writers' horizons for the last half-century or more. Melville's *The Confidence-Man: His Masquerade* (1857) gained recognition yet more recently, as heralding aspects of postmodern fiction. Before his renown as a novelist, however, Melville was known as a writer of personal narratives, the "man who lived among the cannibals" (Melville 1993, 193). Melville's career shows extraordinary accomplishments in a variety of modes, and its struggles, tensions, and public failure have given it exemplary resonance for the vocation of literature in the United States.

The opening chapter of *Typee: A Peep at Polynesian Life* (1846), the pages by which Melville first became known to the reading public, show impressive power in evoking "Six months at sea!" Ordinary passengers, "state-room sailors," complain about a brief transatlantic voyage. Melville's more extreme experience contrasts the privileged leisure of tourists to sailors' exploited labor. The book takes its stand on the democratic, and the extraordinary, side. Against the sensory deprivation of maritime routine rise "strange visions," conjured by the very name of the Marquesas: "Naked houris—cannibal banquets—groves of cocoa-nut—coral reefs—tatooed chiefs— . . . *heathenish rites and human sacrifices*" (ch. 1). Conventional images come to life through the play of assonance and rhythm.

From its very beginning, *Typee* stood as an impressively, and suspiciously, powerful piece of writing; yet it was true enough. Melville had actually lived among the Typee. He got there just the way the book describes: he jumped ship with a companion, and they made their way through the difficult island terrain until they reached the wrong valley, for the Typee were believed to be fierce cannibals. Melville's sojourn lasted only four weeks, rather than the four months he claimed, and he required the aid of other books of travel and exploration to supplement his memories, but the force of his narrative rests on experience. The high cultural skills shown by a sailor, so unsettling to some early readers, have a simple explanation: the social mobility of the nineteenth century allowed Americans to fall in life as well as to rise.

Melville was born in 1819 into great financial comfort, and both his grandfathers were Revolutionary heroes. At first the family lived in New York. In 1830, when his father's business began to fail, they moved to Albany, his mother's base, and in 1832 the family's ruin was sealed by Melville's father's death. For the next years, Melville drifted, before his first experiment as a sailor, a voyage to Liverpool in 1839. In 1841, he sailed with the whaler *Acushnet* from New Bedford, Massachusetts. This was the ship he abandoned in the Marquesas. After fleeing from the Typee, he signed on with an Australian whaler, which he soon left in Tahiti under nearly mutinous circumstances. Another American whaler brought him to Hawaii, and after several months there, he returned home as a sailor on an American naval vessel, the *United States.*

Upon his return, Melville began writing the stories of his travels, and the success of *Typee* encouraged a sequel. *Omoo: A Narrative of Adventures in the South Seas* (1847) centers on Melville's time in Tahiti. *Omoo* (a Polynesian word for "wanderer") confirmed the reputation won by *Typee.* Already in *Typee,* Melville's commentary on missionaries caused so much discomfort that he removed nearly thirty pages from the second American edition, and even so, he had to change publishers for *Omoo,* moving to Harper & Brothers. In recounting the depopulation of Tahiti through European diseases, Melville cites an islander's cry to the missionaries, "Lies, lies! you tell us of salvation; and, behold, we are dying. We want no other salvation than to live in this world" (ch. 49).

What a reviewer called *Typee*'s paradisaical . . . . barbarism (Higgins and Parker 1995, 53) powerfully suggests, in the form of credible personal experience, that there might actually exist in the South Seas a heaven on earth. Melville drew on his time outside what was considered the normal life of the United States in order to challenge the values of that life. Yet he could not fully commit himself to this position, producing in *Typee* a novel at once fascinating and incoherent. Despite its biographical basis, no narrative identity can be firmly defined for Melville's pseudonymous "Tommo." The large narrative cycle of entry into and exit from the valley of the Typee contains an oscillation of feelings—from bliss to revulsion—that seems governed by no law beyond that of change. One may say as much of Ishmael, the narrator of *Moby-Dick.*

After *Omoo,* Melville married Elizabeth Shaw (daughter of the chief justice of the Massachusetts Supreme Court) and settled in Manhattan as a professional author. His next book, *Mardi: And a Voyage Thither* (1849), further complicated his relationship to his readers. It was an experiment that failed. His first two books had taken some liberties with literal truth and had relied on travel books to supplement gaps in his own knowledge or memory, but *Typee* and *Omoo* could still safely appear as nonfiction. In the months that he was working on *Mardi* and meditating a change of direction, Melville also changed the tenor of his reading. He moved away from travel narratives. His reading now included William Shakespeare's plays, Michel de Montaigne's essays, and Samuel Taylor Coleridge's *Biographia Literaria; or, Biographical Sketches of My Literary Life and Opinions* (1817), the most important critical book of English romanticism and a crucial text for the emergence of the modern idea of literature.

Melville had decided, as he wrote to his British publisher, to "change" his mode of writing to "Romance," "downright" and "out," "*real*" romance as opposed to the relative factuality of his earlier books. He explained that *Mardi* "opens like a true narrative," but from there "the romance and poetry" would "grow." By this departure from personal narrative, Melville hoped to gain a greater play of "freedom [and] invention" and to achieve a work that was "original." The result would be "better" and "so essentially different" from *Typee* and *Omoo* as a "literary ach[ie]vement" (1993, 106–7).

Readers hated *Mardi*, and Melville fled back to what he dismissed as the "*job*" of writing personal narrative (1993, 138). During five months in 1849, Melville wrote both *Redburn: His First Voyage* (1849) and *White-Jacket; or, The World in a Man-of-War* (1850). *Redburn* approaches the socially and personally explosive materials of Melville's own adolescence, the family's financial fall and the author's consequent voyage to Liverpool. It does so, however, in a more overtly fictionalized form than either *Typee* or *Omoo,* while *Redburn*'s subtitle, "Being the Sailor-Boy Confessions and Reminiscences of the Son-of-a-Gentleman, in the Merchant Service," works to neutralize the problems of credibility provoked by those earlier works.

By locating the book's experiences in a boy several years younger than he had been when he made the same voyage, Melville gains both intensity and distance, for, by convention, youthful perception and feeling are more acute and less reliable than those of adults. No matter how powerful, then, they need not be fully credited. Melville asserts this distance through the use of formal, third-person chapter titles, which show the control of the narrative persona (an older Redburn) over the youthful protagonist. The boy's perspective at once suggests, selects, and controls the topics that can emerge, and it makes possible Melville's first direct approach to the materials of contemporary American life, especially poverty and social conflict. Social animus marks life on shipboard. The insistent hard manliness of sailors means that no special concern is shown for a young newcomer, and Redburn, because he is also "a gentleman with white hands" (ch. 10), becomes a special butt, who feels himself an "Ishmael," "without a single friend or companion" (ch. 12).

The relatively limited focus of *Redburn* opens to far greater ambition in *White-Jacket,* subtitled "The World in a Man-of-War." In fictionalizing his service aboard the *United States*—and entrusting the narrative to a semifictional sailor known by his strange white jacket—Melville changes the name of the ship itself to the *Neversink.* The ship and its life microcosmically represents not the United States but the "world." American values still offer a new world that opposes the way of the world aboard the ship. The "world" of the *Neversink,* moreover, is that of men without women, of men at work; this world excludes the domestic life of home relations and feminine values, as if that sphere were wholly otherworldly. The world of *White-Jacket* is strenuously modern. The *Neversink* is not a knowable community but an endlessly subdivided society. Living on board ship "is like living in a market" (ch. 9), constantly crowded and lacking privacy. At the rare moments of leisure, when sailors can walk freely on deck, the effect is like that of promenaders on "Broadway" (ch. 13). And like a large city, the ship has street crime: when a "*gang*" (ch. 10) learns that a shipmate has three or four gold pieces, they lie in wait for him, knock him down, and carry off the cash. The result is a perverse, primitive communism as serial robberies establish a rough equality of poverty among all the sailors.

Thus in many respects the ship is highly disordered, despite the highly regimented atmosphere, "like life in a large manufactory": "the bell strikes to dinner, and hungry or not, you must dine" (ch. 9). The figure of speech by which a worker's hands stand for his whole person, so familiar in the dehumanizing industrial discourse of the nineteenth century, had already in the seventeenth century begun to dominate the way in which sailors were spoken of and to. Unlike the specialization of a factory worker, each sailor has so many different functions to perform, under various circumstances both regular and extraordinary, that the routines can only be known by numbers: "White-Jacket was given the *number of his mess;* then, his *ship's number,* or the number to which he must answer when the watch-roll is called; then the number of his hammock; then, the number of the gun to which he was assigned" (ch. 3). These numbers must be memorized by a sailor immediately upon coming on board, and severe penalties follow if they are forgotten. The minute, arithmetical detail that organizes the man-of-war annihilates all previous maritime experience a sailor may have accumulated. The modern social arrangements of this world contrast with its archaic politics. Life on board is a "despotism" (ch. 6).

Melville's portraits of modern society and archaic governance come sharply together when he considers flogging, an essential feature of military shipboard discipline. In a little over a year on the *United States,* Melville was required to witness the flogging of 163 shipmates, about one-third of the crew. Melville asks, "Is it lawful for you, my countrymen, to scourge a man that is an American?" (ch. 34). On the ships of some nations, flogging may "conform to the spirit of the political institutions of the country," but America is different, and, therefore, its navy "should not convert into slaves" any of its citizens. In the current state of affairs, for an American sailor, as for all those in 1850 still held in literal bondage, "our Revolution was in vain; to him our Declaration of Independence is a lie" (ch. 35).

As White-Jacket is about to be flogged, the narrative focuses on the way that he prepares his mind for the brutality. The book focuses on the mind of White-Jacket as he prepares for the flogging. Even though he feels his "man's manhood so bottomless" that nothing the captain could do would reach and degrade it, he yields to an "instinct diffused through all animated nature . . . that prompts even a worm to turn under the heel." He will seize the occasion to "rush" the captain and "pitch him headforemost into the ocean," even though he too would drown. Nature has given him "the privilege, inborn and inalienable, that every man has, of dying himself, and inflicting death upon another" (ch. 67). Here the social bond is reduced to its minimal elements of pure, conflicting individualities.

A powerful counterforce of imagination recalls White-Jacket to the world. The corporal of marines and the best of the sailors both vouch for White-Jacket's character, and he is spared by the captain. Both archaic political authority and modern, rationalized labor organization are overcome through the human respect that the captain suddenly feels for the calm judgment of his subordinates, and the sense of justice that moves them to speak out, at risk to themselves and with no individual interests to serve. Just when the "world" threatens to dissolve into warring, individual atoms, it is socially redeemed.

White-Jacket was widely and warmly reviewed, but one reviewer complained that the book had been discussed "in a literary light only." Readers had praised the "power and vividness of its descriptions, of its wit, its humor, its character-painting," as if it were simply another "new novel." This critic, however, judged that "the literary feature" of the book was trivial beside its "didactic" concerns. For the book was no "romance of fiction" but aimed instead at "great practical subjects," like the Articles of War and flogging. Here, however, the reviewer found the book severely flawed, for a successful literary writer, however gifted with "theories, fancies and enthusiasm," lacks the necessary "character, wisdom and experience" to discuss serious matters (Higgins and Parker 1995, 331).

The relation of Melville's work to the category of the "literary" proved crucial, and explosive, in his next two works, *Moby-Dick* and *Pierre; or, The Ambiguities* (1852). Melville dedicated *Moby-Dick* to Nathaniel Hawthorne, "in token of my admiration for his genius." This act signaled that after the failure of *Mardi* and the successes of *Redburn* and *White-Jacket*, Melville was again writing romance, the period's term for what I call literary narrative, prose fiction that had learned the lessons of Shakespeare taught by romantic criticism. As Melville had argued concerning *Mardi* and as Hawthorne elaborated it in his prefaces, romance allowed high inventiveness, unconstrained by everyday probability—what we now call creativity and originality. In *Moby-Dick*, this particular literary narrative displays its voracious capacity to swallow many other forms and kinds of writing, beginning with the learned "Etymology" and "Extracts" that launch the book from the library and place it in world history stretching back to the book of Genesis. The generic basis of *Moby-Dick* is first-person narrative, like his earlier work, but Melville pushed further. In a letter to his English publisher, he boasted untruthfully of "the author's own personal experience, of two years [and] more, as a harpooneer [*sic*]" (1993, 163). In *Moby-Dick,* Melville again supplemented his own experience with relevant books, both by natural historians and whale-hunters.

The narrative begins like local sketch writing, sharing the territory of "Down East" humor about Yankees and also of frontier tall tales of hunting prowess. The basic form *of Moby-Dick* follows that of T. B. Thorpe's "The Big Bear of Arkansas" (1841). Each frames a story about the most astonishing hunter of the most amazing animal. Yet the immensely greater size of *Moby-Dick* breaks the generic mold.

National narrative, like the fiction of James Fenimore Cooper, was the established large form of the time, and Melville, in *Moby-Dick,* as in *White-Jacket,* strikes key notes from the prevailing rhetoric of America. The claim for human equality helps justify treating the mates and harpooners of the whaler *Pequod* as characters capable of tragedy, even though they are workers, not nobles. The narrative calls upon the "great democratic God," who granted literary immortality to Cervantes the pauper and Bunyan the convict and who placed "Andrew Jackson . . . higher than a throne!" (ch. 26). National narrative, however shaded, was triumphal, but *Moby-Dick* is tragic.

Ahab's quest beyond the bounds of both creatural humility and economic reason makes *Moby-Dick* a literary narrative. Ahab hijacks national narrative by leading the *Pequod,* which in many ways represents America, into disaster, disrupting national triumphalism. As a tragic hero, modeled on Shakespeare's, Ahab fulfills the romantic program for the literary. Yet without Ishmael, Ahab could not achieve his tragic stature. The dramatically styled speeches of Ahab require the narrative contextualization and speculative interpretation provided by Ishmael as sensitive spectator. This suggests a combination of Shakespeare and Hawthorne, which Melville first sketched in his major critical essay "Hawthorne and His Mosses," written in early August 1850, just after he met Hawthorne. By importing the techniques of Shakespeare into a novel, Melville echoes the ambition and encounters the problems of Johann Wolfgang von Goethe's *Wilhelm Meister's Apprenticeship* (1795–96), which he borrowed while he was writing *Moby-Dick.* Goethe's novel inaugurated the tradition of the *Bildungsroman,* which focuses on the formation of a character and on the question of what this formed character can perform in the way of action. *Moby-Dick,* too, encounters problems concerning the status of action. Ishmael goes to sea to evade suicide by submitting himself to a regimen that frees him from the need for self-regulation. The activities that engross him throughout the book are therapy, not action. Ishmael is repeatedly healed or purged. Queequeg cures him of misanthropy; the "Mast-Head" chapter warns against his speculative excess; the "Try-Works" teaches him the danger of gloomy obsession; and in the "Epilogue," "tossed" overboard, "dropped astern," and "buoyed" by Queequeg's coffin, he is "picked . . . up." Only insofar as he acts as the book's writer, and insofar as the novel is being written, does Ishmael perform an action. This literary action, however, distinguishes itself from all other kinds of action available in the culture. Thomas Carlyle, whose pages on Shakespeare Melville echoes in "Hawthorne and His Mosses," had lamented in *On Heroes, Hero-Worship, and the Heroic in History* (1841) that the modern writer has "importance" only for the book trade. Otherwise, "He is an accident in society. He wanders like a wild Ishmaelite" (Carlyle 1969, 5:159).

In contrast to Ishmael, Ahab is modeled on tragic heroes, and the passionate power of his quest seems an obvious source of action, providing direction rather than wandering. Yet his revenge is only reaction. "I will dismember my dismemberer," Ahab proclaims (ch. 37). The overall movement of the book compromises the status of his action. The plot mocks human impotence: St. George confronts the dragon, and it does him in; there is no contest. Melville emphasizes this pattern throughout the climactic chase sequence. Ahab, the greatest of whale-hunters, actually finds the whale by "snuffing" like a dog, rather than using technical apparatus, such as the navigational quadrant that he has flung away and crushed. As the chase begins, Ahab is so eager to locate the whale that he cries out after it, "flattening his face to the sky." This image of intensity and eagerness is recast into humiliation after the whale, without even being harpooned, has caught Ahab's whaleboat by surprise and held it between his jaws, while Ahab, trying to get free, "fell flat-faced upon the sea" (ch. 133).

Melville's writing in *Moby-Dick* produces extraordinary entanglements for action, not only on the large scale of genre but also in particular passages. After Ahab first appears to the crew on "The Quarter-Deck" and exhorts them to join his mission of revenge, there follows a series of chapters that, in their formal variety and complexity, register Ahab's disruptive effect within the texture of the book. "Sunset" trumpets the model of Shakespeare. Its prose is metered to imitate blank verse, and it represents the speech of Ahab to himself alone, a soliloquy. This explodes the personal narrative. How could Ishmael report what Ahab says to himself? The next two chapters play off soliloquies by the mates, earnest Starbuck and jolly Stubb. "Midnight, Forecastle" is written as a stage scene involving all the crew in drunken talk and revelry. It looks back to the "Walpurgisnacht" of Goethe's *Faust: Part One* (1808) and forward to "nighttown" in James Joyce's *Ulysses* (1922). Following this chaos, Ishmael broods reflectively for two chapters, explaining to the reader what Moby Dick meant to Ahab and then what "The Whiteness of the Whale" meant to Ishmael as narrator.

Moby Dick, the whale itself, at every moment reminds readers that agency cannot be confined to human form or to human control. *Moby-Dick* explores the uncertain borders of agency. Things happen, but it remains a question how or why. To write a book that centered on the whale, rather than on its hunters, would go far beyond human powers of narrative, and yet even a narrative that merely includes Moby Dick shows that human individuality cannot account for the way the world works. In *Moby-Dick,* individuality is neither a goal nor a premise. At best, it represents a puzzling possibility.

Issues of action, agency, and responsibility first emerge in "The Quarter-Deck." Behind the "pasteboard masks" of all "visible objects," Ahab seeks a subject, "some unknown but still reasoning thing" that may be surmised through its effects "in each event—in the living act, the undoubted deed." This "inscrutable thing," hidden behind the "wall" of the "whale," yet, to Ahab's sight, "sinewing it" with "malice," he seeks to reach, but his only access is through the whale. Therefore, "be the white whale agent, or be the white whale principal, I will wreak that hate upon him." Ahab denies the possibility of blasphemy, which Starbuck has warned against, because he denies hierarchy: "Who's over me?" (ch. 36).

The emergence of the American literature that readers still recognize today, the novel or the romance as practiced by Hawthorne and Melville, is connected with the political crisis of the mid-nineteenth century. The impasse over slavery produced a situation that provoked Emerson to write in his journal, "Men live on the defensive, and go through life without an action, without one overt act, one initiated action" (Porte 1982, 400). New economic conditions multiplied the number of individuals who had no relations with each other beyond those of contractual equality. These newly emergent individuals had little scope for action, however; they were "free agents" in a restricted sense. The national consensus held that there was nothing to be done politically, and one's responsibility was silence; whatever was done economically was understood simply to have happened by the invisible hand.

Literary narrative offered a place to be heard separate from politics and only partially subordinated to the economy, but this privilege came at the cost of acknowledging literature as fiction, that is, as saying nothing that bore on the shared public world in the way that national, local, and personal narratives had done. To be thus outside partisan politics is to give ground in hope of finding a transcendent alternative. This is the effect of Ishmael's complex literary mediation. This compromise, a diminishment in the scope of the writer's action, may be seen also in the book itself as Ahab's failure to achieve individual agency. In this particular American form of the generic problem of action in the novel, what marks and mars Ahab is also what places *Moby-Dick* in its moment.

Moby-Dick approaches the transformative energies of the economy and therefore places action as a problem in the foreground. Ahab most strongly asserts his individuality at the moments when he is challenged by the impersonal structures of the economy. Rhetorically, he seizes that impersonality as freedom from hierarchy. When in "The Quarter-Deck" Starbuck challenges Ahab, "How many barrels will thy vengeance yield thee? . . . it will not fetch thee much in our Nantucket market," Ahab's response is to cut free from the question of "agent" or "principal," to proclaim that there is no power over himself, not even the invisible hand of the market: "But not my master, man, is even that fair play" (ch. 36). Ahab offers a heroic fantasy—both nostalgic and critical—of individuality. When Starbuck later challenges Ahab for the second time on economic grounds, he invokes the absent owners. Ahab rises to the challenge by applying an argument from John Locke that had once helped foment the American Revolution, "the only real owner of anything is its commander" (ch. 109). This individuality has often impressed readers as the book's accomplishment. Yet the complexity of *Moby-Dick* demonstrates, both in its overall shape and through the particular language of meditative moments, that such individuality cannot be sustained.

Writing to Hawthorne about *The House of the Seven Gables: A Romance* (1851), Melville strikingly imagines the autonomy both he and Hawthorne associated with literary narrative. Hawthorne has caught "a certain tragic phase of humanity," which may be found in "human thought in its own unbiased, native, and profounder workings." This "intense" exploration of the "mind" reveals what Melville calls "visible truth": "the apprehension of the absolute condition of present things as they strike the eye of the man who fears them not, though they do their worst to him." Such a man enjoys radical independence: "[L]ike Russia or the British Empire," he "declares himself a sovereign nature (in himself), amid the powers of heaven, hell, and earth." More solidly individual than anything Ahab achieved, this fearless, masculine vision makes possible "the grand truth about Nathaniel Hawthorne": "He says NO! in thunder; but the Devil himself cannot make him say *yes*." The brave truth tellers who say no are "unincumbered," traveling through life with only their "Ego," but "all men who say *yes*, lie" (Melville 1993, 186).

Even more than *Moby-Dick*, Melville's next novel experimented with radical negation. Published less than a year after *Moby-Dick, Pierre* is even less a personal narrative than *Mardi* or *Moby-Dick*. It is a third-person narrative primarily concerned with the moral and psychological development of the young man it is named after. It refers to and shapes itself in relation to Shakespeare's *Hamlet,* adapting the literary narrative mode opened by Goethe's *Wilhelm Meister.* Melville's first six published books had largely exhausted his direct maritime experience, and, unlike them, *Pierre* is set at home. It is doubly domestic, for, within its American locales, its action springs from and remains within the network of family relations. Its domestic, familial focus seems aimed to engage the wider "feminine" audience that had emerged since the middle 1840s, when Melville had begun his writing career, but it failed to satisfy this or any other audience.

Pierre lives in an idealized version of the Massachusetts countryside, where Melville had moved while writing *Moby-Dick.* Pierre's situation draws on elements of the wealthy, prominent families from which Melville was descended on both sides. A national framework is established by references to Indian land conveyances and Revolutionary heroism, but these concerns are eclipsed by Pierre's "interior development" (bk. 2, ch. 1). Pierre's inheritance is "patriarchal" (bk. 2, ch. 3), and, as in *Hamlet* or in Harriet Beecher Stowe's *Uncle Tom's Cabin; or, Life Among the Lowly* (1852), the book's action springs from a crisis in patriarchy. Pierre's deceased, revered father, it appears, had before he was married, fathered a daughter, Isabel, who is now living nearby, unacknowledged, in poverty.

Pierre must decide whether to acknowledge his "dark" sister (e.g., bk. 3, ch. 4), whose hand is "hard" with "lonely labor" (bk. 6, ch. 2). The color-coding evokes the narratives of slavery. The question for Pierre is posed in the language of sentiment.

Will he be "cold and selfish" (bk. 3, ch. 5) and yield to "the dreary heart-vacancies of the conventional life," or will he choose "God's anointed," "the heart" (bk. 2, ch. 1)? Despite her wild curls, Isabel is no "Gorgon" (bk. 3, ch. 2). The Gorgon turned people to stone, but Isabel's face could "turn white marble into mother's milk" (bk. 12, ch. 1), from conventionally masculine, cold hardness to conventionally feminine, flowing warmth. Pierre chooses the heart, and "thus, in the Enthusiast to Duty, the heaven-begotten Christ is born" (bk. 5, ch. 5).

Roughly the first third of the book brings things to this point. Then a different approach to psychology takes over, changing the book's emphasis from effusion to analysis. The further Pierre is subjected to individualizing scrutiny, the more ambiguous he becomes. Near the book's middle, a strange speculative pamphlet, no sooner read than lost, holds out a formula for resolving ambiguities—"by their very contradictions they are made to correspond"—but its purport remains obscure (bk. 14, ch. 3). Just like his father, Pierre hides a sexual secret. In order to grant his half-sister full familial honor and equality, Pierre presents her to the world as his wife, but this does not raise her; rather, it destroys his social position, and it devastates his mother and his pale blond fiancée, Lucy Tartan.

The first movement of *Pierre* criticizes the conventional social order, as had Stowe's radical sentimentality. In the second movement, Pierre's "enthusiasm," the gush of spirit that shatters convention, is criticized by the narrator, in the middle of the book, as "infatuated" (bk. 10, ch. 2). Without the institutions of family, church, or state to guide and support action, the heart proves weak and dangerous. Pierre acts "without being consciously" aware of the upshot of what he is doing; his actions are oriented by feelings that spring from sources of which he is "unconscious" (bk. 11, ch. 1).

By textualizing the unconscious, the book suggests literary narrative as the possible ground for bringing contradictions into correspondence. In the book's third and final movement, Pierre is revealed not only as a reader but also as a writer. He leaves his ancestral Saddle Meadows to start a new life with Isabel, as a writer in New York. Perhaps from Melville's bitterness at the reception of *Moby-Dick,* the novel severely satirizes the New York literary world as "Young America in Literature." After the narrator's attitude toward Pierre has shifted in the second movement, the book's relation to the audience also changes, with a declaration of independence: "I write precisely as I please" (bk. 17, ch. 1). In trying to follow the shifting "phases" of Pierre, readers must not hope for the guidance of any "canting showman" of a narrator: "Catch his phases as your insight may" (bk. 25, ch. 3). The reader too is granted freedom. Declaring himself sovereign in his intense, tragic exploration of mind, Melville breaks the bonds of the institutions of reading and writing in his time, just as Pierre breaks the institutional bonds of his home.

In trying to support himself as a writer, however, Pierre runs athwart of conventions that are just as firm as those at home had been, and even more crippling, because he is more vulnerable and needy. His publishers write, "Sir:—You are a swindler. Upon the pretense of writing a popular novel for us, you have been receiving cash advances from us, while passing through our press the sheets of a blasphemous rhapsody" (bk. 26, ch. 4). Something like this was also the situation of Melville, who considered Ahab's diabolic baptism the "motto," but the "secret one," of *Moby-Dick* (1993, 196). "Dollars damn me," he wrote to Hawthorne while composing *Moby-Dick*: "What I feel most moved to write, that is banned,—it will not pay. Yet, altogether, write the *other* way I cannot. So the product is a final hash, and all my books are botches" (1993, 191).

During this last phase of *Pierre,* the individuality on which nineteenth-century psychology is based proves unstable, for no thought or action "solely originates" in a single "defined identity" (bk. 10, ch. 1). This instability also challenges the "originality" on which the distinctive claims of literary narrative depend. The "creative mind" may promise a "latent infiniteness," but as surfaces are peeled away, influences foresworn, the final, central point may be "appallingly vacant" (bk. 21, ch. 1). It seems improbable that critics will ever achieve a satisfactory definition of the central meaning of *Pierre* because in its own time, and to modern readers, the book stands as a failure, though now an increasingly fascinating one. Its central vacancy, it seems, was produced through the interaction of conflicting impulses and intentions that exercised their effects at different stages in the largely undocumented process of composition. Nonetheless, the power of literary narrative makes form even out of such absences.

Reviewers hated *Pierre* so much that his publisher dropped Melville. Yet he needed income from his writing. By late 1853, Melville began a new phase of his existence as a writer, as a magazinist. By 1856, he had published fourteen tales and sketches plus a serialized novel in the pages of *Harper's New Monthly Magazine* and *Putnam's Monthly Magazine of American Literature, Science, and Art. Harper's* had been founded in 1850 and immediately achieved great popularity by reprinting the most interesting current works of English writers. In contrast, *Putnam's,* founded in 1853, aimed to bring American writers to the fore. Both magazines offered Melville a rate of five dollars per published page, the top rate they paid. Immediately after its serialization, *Israel Potter: His Fifty Years of Exile* (1855) was published by Putnam as a book, and in 1856, Dix and Edwards, successors to Putnam, published *The Piazza Tales,* which collected (with a new prefatory sketch) the five pieces that had appeared in the magazine to that point. Both *Israel Potter* and *The Piazza Tales* were well reviewed, recouping for Melville some of the esteem he had lost after *Pierre,* even if not restoring the prominence he had held after the completion of *White-Jacket.*

The Piazza Tales show off Melville's command of varied modes and locales. "Bartleby, the Scrivener" (1853), as first published in *Putnam's,* had been subtitled "A Story of Wall-Street." Part of the special force of the story, its narrator thinks, comes from its setting in a "solitary office," in a "building entirely unhallowed by humanizing domestic associations." The office building—a structure devoted exclusively to commerce with no residential units—was a relatively new development in urban life, and it added a third space to a world previously divided between "public street" and "private residence." This encounter of a narrator with the opacity of city misery plays a variation on earlier American stories, such as Hawthorne's "Wakefield" (1835)—concerned especially with private residence—and Edgar Allan Poe's "The Man of the Crowd" (1840)—concerned especially with the public street. Melville dramatizes the narrator, making him a character who speaks to the object of mystery rather than simply speculating, as in Hawthorne, or observing, as in Poe. This makes the story less metaphysical and more ethical: The narrator asks himself, "What shall I do?" Despite the narrator's character as a "*safe*," prudent lawyer, he is moved by Bartleby. The problem is that Bartleby is immovable. Among all the other things he "would prefer not to," Bartleby does not respond to the narrator's attempts to assist him. His passive aggression puts Stowe's sentimental structure in a new light. What if not the rich and powerful but the objects of sympathy, the poor and needy themselves, are like stone? This may be the self-serving fantasy of those who find it easier to do nothing, or it may be a powerful claim that the poor, too, have the privilege of stoicism.

Putnam's was based in New York, and much that it published, like "Bartleby," had a New York flavor, but its ambitions were national. *Israel Potter* began serialization with the subtitle "A Fourth of July Story." Potter was a New England farm boy who became a Revolutionary soldier, fought at Bunker Hill, served as a secret courier for Benjamin Franklin, and was stranded in London after the Revolution, only returning to the United States in advanced old age. In adapting Potter's story, Melville made a third-person account out of an existing personal narrative, which had evidently preoccupied him. As early as 1849, he had bought an old map of London "in case I serve up the Revolutionary narrative of the beggar" (1989, 43).

The middle chapters of *Israel Potter* extensively elaborate the earlier narrative. They nationalize the personal narrative by devoting several chapters to Franklin and some fifty pages to John Paul Jones, the great naval hero of the Revolution, absent from the original. Israel's adventures culminate in Jones's naval battle between the British *Serapis* and the revolutionary *Bon Homme Richard.* As the two ships grapple, the bloody horrors of this great victory become a figure of civil war: "It was a co-partnership and joint-stock combustion-company of both ships; yet divided, even in participation. The two vessels were as two houses, through whose party-wall doors have been cut" (ch. 19). Appalled witticism turns the language of commercial enterprise to destruction and turns cooperation to "combustion"; the door joining two houses opens only to let death enter. Jones had been earlier revealed as tattooed, like Queequeg in *Moby-Dick,* in a way "seen only on thorough-bred savages—deep blue, elaborate, labyrinthine, cabalistic" (ch. 11). After the battle, the narrator asks whether civilization is indeed "a thing distinct, or is it an advanced stage of barbarism?" (ch. 19)

After the election of Franklin Pierce as president in 1852, the problems of slavery, supposedly settled by the Compromise of 1850, reemerged over the organization of the Kansas and Nebraska territories, which soon escalated into guerrilla civil warfare, and elsewhere triggered "filibuster" activity by Americans determined to bring the Caribbean into American hands as slave territory. By drawing on popular traditions of personal narrative to gain a purchase on national narrative, *Israel Potter* succeeded in pleasing readers and provoking thought on important contemporary issues.

A similar strategy directs "Benito Cereno" (1855), which Melville had intended to be the title and lead piece of *Piazza Tales.* Without acknowledging his source, Melville takes his action from *A Narrative of Voyages and Travels, in the Northern and Southern Hemispheres* by Captain Amasa Delano (1817). Going on board a Spanish ship in trouble off the coast of South America, Delano is unaware that the ship is controlled not by its captain, Don Benito Cereno, but by the blacks on board, whom Delano believes to be slaves and who act the part, but who have previously mutinied and taken charge; he finally learns the truth, and his ship recaptures the blacks. Even the technical peculiarities in Melville's piece, what he calls "the nature of this narrative," the "intricacies" of materials "retrospectively" or "irregularly" ordered, have precedent in Delano's account. By removing the preliminary logbook record and shifting from Delano's retrospective first-person to a third-person narration closely tied to Delano's flawed perception and fluctuating thoughts, Melville gains the potential for both the suspense of a good magazine tale and the ironies of literary reflection.

In transforming the personal narrative into a tale, Melville uses gothic rhetoric, which combines the glamour of ruinous dilapidation with the danger arising from moral weakness. The ship is like a "strange house," perhaps "haunted." The "influence" of its atmosphere produces "heightened" impressions, "enchantments" such as might be felt by the "prisoner in some deserted château." The courtly reserve, the sudden coldnesses, and the agitated gnawing of his fingers by Cereno recall Poe's Roderick Usher. The climax of Poe's "The Fall of the House of Usher" (1839) figures here as a simile; the final revelation is like "a vault whose door has been flung back." Gothicism is not just decor. In "Benito Cereno," as in William Faulkner's *Absalom, Absalom!* (1936), gothicism is a technique for historical tragedy, representing the continuing power of the past in the present as the consequence of ancestral crime.

By changing the name of Cereno's ship from the *Tryal* to the *San Dominick,* Melville engaged a history living on into his present. The saint's name also names a place, first called Hispaniola, the Caribbean island where Columbus had landed; and Melville invents a figurehead for the ship, "the image of Christopher Colon, the discoverer of the New World." After the extermination of its native Indian population, this island received the first African slaves brought to the New World. This was also where the largest and most important uprising in the history of

African American slavery occurred, during the French Revolution, establishing the independent, black-governed state of Haiti as the second free nation in the Western Hemisphere. The ironic form of "Benito Cereno" means that Delano can feel every fear about his circumstances except the right one. He so underestimates the powers of blacks that even the ship's name does not recall to his mind "the horrors of St. Domingo," still felt (at the time Melville wrote the story) by Chief Justice Roger Taney of the US Supreme Court, responsible for the Dred Scott decision (qtd. in Fehrenbacher 1981, 284).

In *The Confidence-Man*, Melville draws on more recent popular narrative materials than he used in *Israel Potter* or "Benito Cereno." The term "confidence man" was coined in 1849, to describe a particular New York shyster. The key to his criminal technique was a direct appeal to a stranger to trust him. The term was immediately recognized as suggestive for thinking about many aspects of American life. Melville nationalizes his scene by removing the confidence man from the urban East to the American heartland, setting the action on a Mississippi steamer going south from St Louis.

The Confidence-Man focuses on a series of appeals to trust, made both to groups and in one-on-one conversations, by a variety of figures—among them a crippled black man, a mourning widower, an agent for Indian charities, an official of the "Black Rapids Coal Company," an herb doctor, and a "Cosmopolitan"—all of whom may be a "masquerade" by the single titular figure. The "Wall Street spirit" (ch. 7) pervading contemporary America is tested through the various traditional perspectives that the characters offer, such as "this ship of fools" (ch. 3) and "All the world's a stage" (ch. 41). Most notably, on this steamer named *Fidèle,* the first scene shows a deaf and mute man writing out St. Paul's words on "charity," including that "charity believeth all things" (ch. 1), and in the last chapter, characters discuss what belief should be granted the Apocrypha, "the uncanonical part" of the Bible (ch. 45). The book dwells on paradoxes, such as the "genial misanthrope" (ch. 30), and in the midst of this complexly satiric work, a character exclaims, "God defend me from Irony, and Satire" (ch. 24). This book's repeated staging of its incommensurability with itself is a virtuoso performance of literary narrative that reveals how marginal and improvisatory Melville's narrative remained.

The Confidence-Man was published by Dix and Edwards on April 1, 1857, and before the end of the month the publisher was bankrupt. By September, so were its successor firms, and the stereotype plates of their books were auctioned off. No one was willing to bid on Melville's works; he could not raise funds to purchase them himself; and he authorized their sale for scrap. Melville produced a good deal after 1857, but he wrote only poetry until the last years of his life, when he began a long story, "Billy Budd, Sailor" (1924), which remained incomplete at his death. By then, he inhabited a new nation. The prestige previously reserved for the "Union" and the "People" had passed to the state itself (in the sense of the sovereign power), which had been sanctified by virtue of the war and of Lincoln's death, understood as martyrdom. This new American reverence for earthly power undergirds "Billy Budd."

"Billy Budd" is the most fictional of Melville's works. It is not drawn from his life, nor does it rework historical documents. It is set in 1797 on a British warship, and Billy is not even American. America is no longer so unique that a major work by an American writer must treat an American subject. In the later 1800s, the United States was playing an increasingly large role in the world, and the empire of Britain, threatened by revolutionary France, might make a plausible analogy for the United States, which was soon to acquire an overseas empire of its own. After the Civil War, slavery ended, but other forms of social inequality increased, leading to farmers' populism and industrial workers' agitation, from the great railroad strike of 1877 onward.

Although "Billy Budd" is fiction, Melville's rhetoric is antifictional. Subtitled "An Inside Narrative," "Billy Budd" repeatedly appeals to the documentary expectations of narrative. Since this is "no romance" (ch. 2), it must, therefore, lack "the symmetry of form attainable in pure fiction" (ch. 28). Using a term not yet in the language when he began his career, Melville defends his procedures as "realism" (ch. 11). As an "inside" narrative, the work corrects the news account (itself part of the fiction) of the events it recounts.

"Billy Budd" performs an extraordinary historical reconstruction. It defines a limited fictional action within the "juncture" (ch. 21) of important public events. These events are not just the revolutionary wars, but, specifically, the mutinies of 1797 within the British Navy, and, yet more precisely, the constraints of commanding a ship detached from the fleet. Its "inside narrative" does not function to displace attention from history to psychology. Combined with the complex realism of its historical narrative, "Billy Budd" equally gains power through allegorical simplification. Billy, the natural child of an unknown lord, an illiterate "upright barbarian," is like "Adam" (ch. 2). Claggart, the master-at-arms, serves the ship as its corrupt "chief of police" (ch. 8); his eyes exercise "serpent fascination" (ch. 19), and he satanically lies in accusing Billy of treason. Tongue-tied by a natural speech-defect, Billy tries to speak in self-defense, but he "could only say it with a blow" (ch. 21), and he strikes Claggart dead. Captain Vere, a hero in action, yet a meditative reader of "unconventional" books (ch. 7), is "the troubled patriarch" (ch. 18) who must resolve the situation, which he summarizes: "Struck dead by an angel of God! Yet the angel must hang!" (ch. 19).

The "jugglery of circumstances" (ch. 21) means that Billy's righteousness counts as mutiny. In explaining the case to the drumhead court-martial he has summoned, Vere emphasizes the need to "strive against scruples that may tend to enervate decision" (ch. 21). At whatever pain, he avoids Hamletism. Vere shows that power may have conscience, and even moral beauty. Feeling still the "primeval in our formalized humanity," he takes Billy to his bosom like Abraham when he is about to sacrifice Isaac (ch. 22).

Melville in *Typee* first challenged his readers as "state-room sailors" on behalf of the crew. "Billy Budd," however, invokes "snug card players in the cabin" to set them against the lonely, agonized responsibility of "the sleepless man on the bridge" who guides the craft (ch. 21). Billy himself, condemned by Vere for his deed, cries out before being hanged, "God bless Captain Vere!" (ch. 25). The narrator concludes that "the condemned one suffered less" (ch. 22) than his judge did, for Billy's consciousness is like that of "children" (ch. 24), but Vere is a mature adult.

The Civil War, fought for the union and against slavery, had brought the state an imaginative moral legitimacy unavailable in the 1850s. In Melville's prewar "Benito Cereno," the Revolutionary slave Babo remains opaque to Cereno, to Delano, and to the reader. This is far different from the moral and intellectual comprehensiveness that allows Vere to sympathize with Billy and still judge him. Vere has incorporated the lesson of feeling, and his power to give himself pain by his own judgment enhances his authority. To the extent that readers accept Vere, "Billy Budd" reconciles force with principle. Yet this uncompleted work may also be read to quite different effect, far closer to the "unconditional democracy in all things" (Melville 1993, 191) that generated the radical innovation of *Moby-Dick*.

This capacity to sustain intensive reading to diverse effects defines Melville's currency as an American classic, which took a long time to achieve. After the critical failure of *Pierre* and the economic loss of Melville's property in his work, his reputation in the United States grew increasingly obscure, while in the British Isles his name was kept alive by a small but growing group of religious, sexual, and social radicals over several generations. In the early 1920s, things came together: the first biography of Melville was published, and a British publisher brought out the first collected edition of Melville's works, including the first publication of "Billy Budd," edited by the biographer Raymond Weaver. Meanwhile, D. H. Lawrence included extended discussion of Melville in his lyrical, speculative *Studies in Classic American Literature* (1923). Lawrence's work helped inspire F. O. Matthiessen, the Harvard scholar of Elizabethan literature and modernist poetry, to write *American Renaissance* (1941), which established the Melville we still know.

18

HARRIET BEECHER STOWE AND THE ANTISLAVERY CAUSE

JOHN ERNEST

Probably no novel is so firmly associated with the promotion of a cause as *Uncle Tom's Cabin; or, Life Among the Lowly*, and few authors have been so narrowly remembered and defined by a single book as Harriet Beecher Stowe. Published first in serial form from June 5, 1851 to April 1, 1852, in an antislavery newspaper, the *National Era*, *Uncle Tom's Cabin* appeared in book form on March 20, 1852, and was an immediate sensation. The first edition of 5,000 was sold out within two days; within a year, over 300,000 had been sold, and by the end of the decade over one million copies, in various editions and translated into more than fifteen languages, had been sold internationally, with actual readership extending far beyond sales. Such success was unprecedented. As Joy Jordan-Lake has observed, "few books have had more impact upon the history of the United States" than *Uncle Tom's Cabin*, and "few books have evoked such powerful emotional responses—and few continue, scores of years later, to do so" (2005, xv). Along the way, the novel became a centerpiece of the antislavery cause—not because Stowe had revealed anything new about the many injustices inherent in the US system of slavery, but because she had so forcefully brought established antislavery arguments to new life. *Uncle Tom's Cabin* revitalized antislavery sentiment both in Great Britain and in the United States, both by inspiring sympathizers and by provoking detractors—leading many in England to debate with new zeal questions of labor and class, and leading Abraham Lincoln to say, upon meeting her in 1862, "So you're the little woman who wrote the book that made this great war!" Few novels, indeed, have had such an observable, extended, and international impact.

Whether despite or because of that impact, Stowe has always held a difficult and tenuous position in American literary history. She was the author of the most successful and influential novel ever published in the United States, but, to many, an author of questionable ability. She was the author of many other novels, but few recognizable even by those who have read *Uncle Tom's Cabin*. In fact, though, the antislavery cause constituted only a phase of a long and prolific career. Stowe continued her commentary on slavery in *Dred: A Tale of the Great Dismal Swamp* (1856) and *The Minister's Wooing* (1859), though her attention in the latter novel was less on slavery than on the religious convictions that first led her to the antislavery movement (and that were her primary concerns when writing on its behalf). Following these novels, most of Stowe's writing was focused either on travel or on regional history and culture, and she was instrumental in popularizing local color fiction. Among the novels of religion, domesticity, and regional life that she published in the remainder of her career are *The Pearl of Orr's Island: A Story of the Coast of Maine* (1862), *Oldtown Folks* (1869), *My Wife and I; or, Harry Henderson's History* (1871), *Pink and White Tyranny: A Society Novel* (1871), *We and Our Neighbors; or, The Records of an Unfashionable Street* (1875), and *Poganuc People: Their Loves and Lives* (1878). In many ways, these novels—which often feature a narrator who speaks, in effect, from a pulpit to deliver a seemingly clear moral lesson—reveal Stowe's sense of what was most important about *Uncle Tom's Cabin*, as she returned from heated national debates to warm local climes in search of a solid moral guide for life.

As the title of this chapter, "Harriet Beecher Stowe and the Antislavery Cause," indicates, Stowe's achievements as an antislavery writer are an inevitable presence in the history of the American novel—but the nature of that achievement, and of Stowe's overall career as a writer, complicate this seemingly straightforward story. Certainly, there is reason to examine Stowe from the perspective afforded by her contributions to the antislavery cause, but there is also much to learn from the vision of the antislavery cause that emerges from both *Uncle Tom's Cabin* and its aftermath. This chapter offers an extensive consideration of *Uncle Tom's Cabin*, the tremendous response to that novel, and Stowe's own response to the culture she had inspired, in part to suggest that Stowe's position in the literary canon—be it as the author of the most influential antislavery novel or as an important writer of American regionalism—simplifies an important story in American literary history. The value of *Uncle Tom's Cabin* is that it offers such a compelling lens for viewing Stowe's peculiar genius for writing, and the value of the varied and spectacular response to that novel is that it reveals so much about the world peculiarly susceptible and open to Stowe's methods and voice. Ultimately, the story of Stowe's career is the story of how fiction emerged from and engaged a nation that was itself constituted of fundamental and unstable fictions—and since the world shaped by slavery was the most fundamental of those fictions, it is important to linger over *Uncle Tom's Cabin* if we are to understand this strangely undervalued but insistently prominent American novelist.

What characterizes all her work, one might say, is simply that Stowe wrote from a sense of moral conviction, and that she had a talent for doing so with some force. But many would add that this talent did not translate into the sort of literary sophistication one associates with a major writer, one capable of transcending her times to speak to the ages. Indeed, while *Uncle Tom's Cabin* has never left the cultural scene, scholarly appreciations of Stowe's work were, until at least the 1980s, hard to come by. In a time when scholars seemed determined to characterize the middle decades of the nineteenth century as an American literary renaissance, Stowe was prominent among the many women authors left out of the picture. Many critics over the years have come to the same conclusions that one of Stowe's most careful readers, E. Bruce Kirkham, reached in 1977: "The productions of her pen were not masterpieces. No one would claim that *Uncle Tom's Cabin* ranks as a literary work equal to *Moby-Dick* or *The Scarlet Letter*, although its social and historical impact has been far greater. Some writers have claimed that Mrs. Stowe's novel changed the course of history" (viii). These days, more and more readers would make more ambitious claims for the literary merits of *Uncle Tom's Cabin*, and for Stowe's achievements as a writer generally, but Stowe's reputation still rests largely on the "social and historical impact" of her most famous novel. Stowe's claims to prominence in American literary history remain, for many, suspect, even as scholars have begun to realize her importance in guiding the course of other currents in American cultural history, particularly the surging regionalism that became so prominent in the literary landscape during the second half of the nineteenth century.

Perhaps contributing to doubts about Stowe's talents as a writer is the nearly inexplicable response to her most famous novel, a response that seems disproportional to the seemingly conventional novel she produced. Ultimately, *Uncle Tom's Cabin* itself is best understood less for its contributions to the antislavery cause than as a study of the power of fiction to unleash various and contradictory forces simmering beneath the cultural surface. To say that a novel had some degree of "social and historical impact," after all, is to say very little—and while one can say that Stowe's novel influenced "the course of history," one would still be hard put to say what that course changed either from or to. As one critical assessment has it, Stowe "has had a complex mythic status in American consciousness: she is supposed to have single-handedly brought the abolitionist crusade against slavery to fruition yet also to have created our culture's most pernicious image of African Americans" (Kohn, Meer, and Todd 2006, xiii). Of course, Stowe did nothing single-handedly, nor did she create anything that wasn't there already, for various antislavery authors had recorded the abuses of slavery in great detail in other works, including the handful of antislavery novels that had previously been published. As Eric Sundquist has observed:

> By giving flesh-and-blood reality to the inhuman system for which the Fugitive Slave Law now required the North, as well as the South, to be responsible, it became a touchstone for antislavery sentiment. Stowe was hardly the first to call attention to slavery's destruction of both black and white families, but her novel perfectly combined the tradition of the sentimental novel and the rhetoric of antislavery polemic. (1986, 18)

Given her full-bodied immersion in concerns that had been reduced to rhetorical conventions, and given her reliance on those conventions, Stowe inevitably encouraged developing political and ethical differences and decidedly popularized pernicious images of African Americans—though, again, not single-handedly. If history is a river, then Stowe didn't redirect its course so much as contribute to its flooding, and when the floods subsided, her influence could be found in numerous and seemingly unrelated cultural pools. From resolutions against slavery to racist diatribes, from antislavery plays to blackface minstrel shows, from communities defined by a shared moral sentiment to communities shaped by a developing commercial culture, *Uncle Tom's Cabin* is everywhere in the nineteenth century and beyond, in the United States and around the world. The antislavery cause was simply the area most directly hit by the flood that followed the publication of this book, a flood that overwhelmed and reshaped Stowe's life and writing as much as it did the world around her.

A wife and mother of six children when she started writing the installments of *Uncle Tom's Cabin* for the *National Era*, Stowe was an unlikely candidate for a writer of international influence—but in fact her family background and her domestic responsibilities prepared her for her uniquely powerful approach to the system of slavery. Her father, Lyman Beecher, was a respected Protestant clergyman who moved the family from Connecticut to Cincinnati, Ohio, where he had been appointed president of the Lane Theological Seminary. As president, Beecher was confronted by a number of students who withdrew from the seminary in 1834, protesting Beecher's moderate position on slavery. Within a couple of years, Harriet's sister Catherine Beecher was also involved in a clash over antislavery reform, debating in print with Angelina Grimké of South Carolina over the proper role of women in the antislavery cause. Grimké argued for public activism by women in *Appeal to the Christian Women of the South* (1836) and *Letters to Catharine E. Beecher* (1838). The latter text was a response to Beecher's *An Essay on Slavery and Abolition, with Reference to the Duty of American Females* (1837), which argued that women should avoid public roles and exert influence through the home. While these debates were taking place, Harriet married Calvin Stowe, a professor of theology at Lane. When her husband accepted a position at Bowdoin College, Harriet, with three of their children, moved to Brunswick, Maine, to set up house and await Calvin's arrival. That same year, the federal government passed the Compromise of 1850, which included a tougher Fugitive Slave Law than that which had been in place from the nation's beginning. The new one required all US citizens to aid in the capture of fugitive slaves and established a legal process for such cases that put African Americans everywhere in jeopardy, making them likely to lose family members who had been enslaved or to be kidnapped and sold into slavery themselves. Agitated by her domestic responsibilities, provoked by this law, and inspired by her religious faith, Harriet devoted her time in Maine to writing against slavery, producing the serialized story that would develop into the century's best-selling novel.

The theological and domestic influence of her father, her sister, her husband, and her social environment shaped her approach to this unfolding story. While the novel's narrator addresses everything from disturbing shifts in social class—the process by which slave traders become gentlemen, for example, in the novel's opening paragraphs—to current politics, ultimately Stowe locates the force of the novel in her call for broad scale ethical rehabilitation, a process of "*feel[ing] right*," as she puts it in her concluding statement to the reader, through Christian observances that begin in the home (ch. 45). In this way, the novel is focused especially on the dynamics of gender, the ways in which women might influence the moral course of the nation, though her approach to women's power betrays the influence of Stowe's own regional, class, and racial position. The novel's title itself, focusing on Uncle Tom's *cabin* rather than on Uncle Tom himself, indicates what many readers have taken as Stowe's singular accomplishment in this novel: her success in locating antislavery political and sectional debates in the seemingly universal domestic spaces—the cabin, the kitchen, the parlor, the home—associated with women and especially with maternal love and authority. In a central scene in the novel, a fugitive mother and son seek shelter and protection from their pursuers at the home of Senator and Mrs. Bird. The senator and his wife have just had a disagreement about slavery, with the senator arguing for the "great public interests" that have led him to be a prominent legislative force for the protection of the system of slavery, and with Mrs. Bird arguing for Christian benevolence, what her husband characterizes as "private feeling." Although the senator had only recently, in Washington, "scouted all sentimental weakness of those who would put the welfare of a few miserable fugitives before great state interests," his wife soon has reason to tell him that she knows him better than he knows himself. His encounter with the fugitive mother Eliza changes his mind, and he quickly moves to help her escape (ch. 9). Such domestic encounters—the influence of wives over husbands, and the force of abstract political debates when they are given form and voice in the home—are central to Stowe's strategy throughout *Uncle Tom's Cabin*.

This is a strategy often either missed or dismissed by readers, even today. Many of Stowe's readers over the years have been uncannily like Senator Bird in rejecting the "sentimental weakness" of the most successful writers of the nineteenth century, the many women writers long left out of various understandings of the canon but central to the nineteenth-century literary landscape. Particularly since the 1980s, feminist scholars have challenged the standards of literary value behind such rejections, often by way of a deeply historicist approach to nineteenth-century American literary history. Jane Tompkins, for example, in her groundbreaking study *Sensational Designs: The Cultural Work of American Fiction, 1790–1860* (1985), simply turned the tables on traditional standards of literary merit by way of an "embrace of the conventional [that] led [her] to value everything that criticism had taught [her] to despise: the stereotyped character, the sensational plot, the trite expression" (xvi). In a study that did much to draw attention to the literary complexity of *Uncle Tom's Cabin*, Tompkins observes that "stereotypes are the instantly recognizable representatives of overlapping racial, sexual, national, ethnic, economic, social, political, and religious categories; they convey enormous amounts of cultural information in an extremely condensed form." Indeed, Tompkins argues, "as the telegraphic expression of complex clusters of value, stereotyped characters are *essential* to popularly successful narrative" (1985, xvi). No novel more fully exemplifies the force of the literary dynamics that Tompkins studies than *Uncle Tom's Cabin*, and no other novel manages to present characters and plot lines that so fully serve the "multilayered representative function" which for Tompkins and many others defines the nineteenth-century American literary landscape (xvi). Following such streams of thought, many readers similarly have found *Uncle Tom's Cabin*—and the protest tradition in literature that it was instrumental in fostering—to be a particularly revealing entrance into nineteenth-century American and European culture.

Indeed, Stowe's reliance on convention and stereotypes helped her place her novel at the center of the national stage. A good part of what distinguishes this novel is that Stowe represents struggles over slavery and the integrity of the white Christian republic by way of characters who represented the various cultural types that had come to inhabit the American social and literary landscape: earthy, inscrutable blacks; white southerners troubled by slavery; white southerners who aggressively defend both slavery and the South; white northerners who assume the moral superiority of the North; antislavery Quakers; and submissive, loyal, and pious slaves. Troubling these categories and driving both the novel's plot and its moral trajectory are various characters who do not quite fit into their assigned or assumed racial categories—a white southerner who is described as a "*non sequitur*" (ch. 19), light-complexioned African Americans who give voice to national ideals, and a US senator whose views on slavery are transformed by the very story that Stowe relates. The novel, in effect, explores a culture being changed by slavery—and as slave traders rise to the level of gentlemen and the most fully realized Christian characters die before the novel's conclusion, Stowe asks her readers, in effect, where they fit into this new world.

Feeling right, in short, involves managing a fit between the private and the public, the character of the individual and the character of the nation. The novel warns that the corrupted public sphere is invading the private sphere, compromising everyone who lives in the United States, regardless of whether they participate directly in the system of slavery. Indeed, Stowe has her narrator offer a running commentary on changes in the very language of morality and principle, pausing at times to ask her readers how to understand, in this world corrupted by slavery, such words as "humanity" (ch. 1) or "liberty" (ch. 37). The man who most fully embodies Christian belief, Uncle Tom, is killed by his owner, and the man who most fully gives voice to the principles of the American Revolution, George Harris, leaves the country for Liberia at the novel's end. The two ideological pillars of nineteenth-century American culture—Christianity and liberty—are, in short, forced out of the country, and those who remain face the challenge of a fundamental social reform that begins with individual redemption, a matter of learning to read all over again. When Senator Bird is moved to help the fugitive slave Eliza and her son, the narrator comments, "What a situation, now, for a patriotic senator," because Bird had supported legislation favorable to proslavery forces. "But then," the narrator adds, "his idea of a fugitive was only an idea of the letters that spell the word" (ch. 9). This is a recurring theme in a novel that ultimately argues that among the challenges of the antislavery cause is that of restoring meaning to language—of restoring stability to the language of Christianity, patriotism, and humanity by living the principles behind the words.

The great irony of *Uncle Tom's Cabin* is that instead of promoting a newly stable discursive community, it became the cornerstone for a great Tower of Babel, in part because the novel was so effective in its representation of slavery. That *Uncle Tom's Cabin* brought established debates to a newly feverish pitch is evident from the immediate, varied, and often vitriolic responses it provoked. Proslavery commentators "called it libelous and Stowe a liar," finding "dirty insinuations in the novel" and "the hoof of the beast" beneath Stowe's skirts (Ammons 2007, 3). As Elizabeth Ammons has noted, the favorable responses to Stowe's novel were equally as fervent: "The famous white poet and abolitionist John Greenleaf Whittier offered: 'Ten thousand thanks for this immortal book,' and Henry Wadsworth Longfellow called it 'one of the greatest triumphs in recorded literary history, to say nothing of the higher triumph of its moral effect'" (2007, 4). In England, *Uncle Tom's Cabin* proved even more popular than in the United States, revitalizing the British antislavery movement but also eventually serving the needs of English national chauvinism. But even those who praised the novel found ample reason to worry about its effect. "For many abolitionists," Ammons has observed, "*Uncle Tom's Cabin* from the beginning posed problems, especially on the subjects of race, gradualism as a strategy for ending slavery, colonization of Liberia by free blacks, and the whole issue of whites speaking for African Americans" (2007, 4). Both in spite of and because of such responses, Ammons adds, "the reading public in the United States and Britain, and then rapidly around the world, bought more copies of Stowe's novel than of any other book except the Bible, and its obscure author became an international celebrity virtually overnight" (2007, 5). Ultimately, *Uncle Tom's Cabin*, like the Bible itself, demonstrated the extent to which people can be divided by a common text.

Of course, the home ground for this Tower of Babel was the United States, where the various political tensions between the North and South increasingly found their focus in the issue of slavery, tensions that immediately centered on *Uncle Tom's Cabin*. In this climate, many readers saw in Stowe's novel an indictment against not just slavery but also the South itself, and the responses to the novel were accordingly sharp. As Jordan-Lake has observed, "most reviews of the book in Southern publications could best be classified as tirades" (2005, xvi). But the tirades were by no means limited to the printed page:

> [T]he South generally received the book with hostility. Angry townspeople in Mobile, Alabama, harassed a bookseller who dared to display *Uncle Tom's Cabin* in his window and chased him out of town. Students at the University of Virginia in Charlottesville held book burnings. A Maryland court sentenced a free black found with a copy of *Uncle Tom's Cabin* and abolition materials on his person to ten years in prison. (Jordan-Lake 2005, xvi)

At the very least, such responses testified to the power of fiction. Earlier generations had seen dramatic responses to novels of manners, sensibility, and sentiment, and many readers related so intimately to the title character of Susanna Rowson's *Charlotte Temple: A Tale of Truth* (1791) as to blur the line separating fact from fiction, but *Uncle Tom's Cabin* virtually destroyed that line. In response to those who claimed that her portraits of injustices of slavery were exaggerated, Stowe published in 1853 *A Key to Uncle Tom's Cabin; Presenting the Original Facts and Documents Upon Which the Story is Founded, Together with Corroborative Statements Verifying the Truth of the Work.* In the *Key*, Stowe drew from actual accounts of slavery—firsthand accounts by those who had been enslaved and accounts from southern newspapers—and from various commentators on slavery to verify the grounds upon which both her characters and her story were based. For many readers, though, the real-life accounts were instead, and more compellingly, verified by the fiction, as *Uncle Tom's Cabin* quickly populated the South with violent slave owners like Simon Legree; transformed living black men into walking representatives of Uncle Tom; made anyone's sweet daughter virtually a type of little Eva, the young white girl whose death became a centerpiece of staged versions of the novel; and reenvisioned all troublesome children as kin to Topsy, the imperviously mischievous and enslaved child who resists all efforts to train her in manners. In fact, Topsy-Turvy dolls would become quite popular. These white dolls that became black with a simple turn and adjustment of the skirt represent one of the many manifestations of how *Uncle Tom's Cabin* became for many the lens through which all ethical possibilities were viewed.

Fighting fire with fire, many who wished to challenge, subvert, or simply revise Stowe's portrait of both the system of slavery and the slaveholding South turned to fiction, generating significant contributions to the American novel. Donald E. Liedel has calculated that "approximately five dozen" antislavery novels were published in the United States between 1836 and 1861, with close to four times as many published after 1850 than before, of which over three dozen were written more or less directly in response to *Uncle Tom's Cabin* (1961, 2). While the number of antislavery novels itself might pale in comparison to the sentimental or other forms of popular fiction published during this time, it is still rare that any novel would inspire so many direct imitators and detractors. Stowe's novel, in short, sparked something of a cottage industry in novels about slavery. Indeed, as Sarah Meer observes, "In 1852 both Northern and Southern periodicals called for writers to answer Stowe in novel form: George Frederick Holmes argued in the *Southern Literary Messenger* for 'a native and domestic literature' to provide the most telling responses to *Uncle Tom*, while the *Pennsylvanian* asked 'friends of the Union' to 'array fiction against fiction'" (2005, 75). Such appeals were hardly necessary, for the response to *Uncle Tom's Cabin* was both swift and voluminous. W. L. G. Smith's *Life at the South; or, "Uncle Tom's Cabin" As It Is: Being Narratives, Scenes, and Incidents in the Real "Life of the Lowly"* was published in the same year, 1852, as Stowe's novel. Smith tells the story of a slave who escapes to the North only to experience unbearable hardships, and who, by the end of the novel, willingly returns to the plantation, having now recognized the value of the system and his "natural" place in it. Other novels were less direct in announcing their response to Stowe's novel, though they still were clear in positioning themselves in the field that Stowe had popularized, and they were regularly considered with *Uncle Tom's Cabin* in reviews and commentaries. Anti–*Uncle Tom* novels explored slavery from the perspective of various cabins—including Mary H. Eastman's *Aunt Phillis's Cabin; or, Southern Life As It Is* (1852) and John W. Page's *Uncle Robin, in His Cabin in Virginia, and Tom Without One in Boston* (1853)—and other plantation sites, as in T. B. Thorpe's *The Master's House: A Tale of Southern Life* (1854). Some, in effect, followed the trail of Stowe's closing gesture to attempts to colonize Liberia (established for this purpose) with former slaves, as in Sarah Josepha Hale's *Liberia; or, Mr. Peyton's Experiments* (1853). Others emphasized regional relations and tensions, as in Caroline Lee Hentz's *The Planter's Northern Bride* (1854) or Caroline E. Rush's *North and South; or, Slavery and Its Contrasts: A Tale of Real Life* (1852), and some picked up on Stowe's emphasis, in her subtitle, of "life among the lowly," as in Maria Jane McIntosh's *The Lofty and the Lowly; or, Good in All and None All-Good* (1853).

While these writers challenged Stowe's political views, they often echoed her sentiments on race, for a central aspect of Stowe's influence involved her blend of progressive reform and regressive representations of African Americans. While most of the racial types in *Uncle Tom's Cabin* were established long before Stowe set pen to paper, Stowe infused those stereotypes with new power. Although none of the characters in the novel can claim African birth, *Uncle Tom's Cabin* frequently ties its black characters to a condescending vision of Africa, and it is full of unselfconscious commentary on the essential nature of those of African origins. Readers are told that Africans are "naturally patient, timid and unenterprising" (ch. 10); that cooking is "an indigenous talent of the African race" (ch. 18); and that "the invariable 'Yes, Mas'r,'" has been "for ages the watchword of poor Africa" (ch. 12). Racial contrasts abound, particularly when the narrator pauses to explain a moment in the plot, as she does frequently. "The negro, it must be remembered," the narrator offers at one point, "is an exotic of the most gorgeous and superb countries of the world, and he has, deep in his heart, a passion for all that is splendid, rich, and fanciful; a passion which, rudely indulged by an untrained taste, draws on them the ridicule of the colder and more correct white race" (ch. 15). This story of the fortunes of a particular group of enslaved African Americans involves as well various reflections on the destiny of Africa. In this emphatically Christian novel, Africans are presented as naturally religious people who have discovered (through enslavement) the news of "a compassionate Redeemer and a heavenly home" (ch. 38). "The principle of reliance and unquestioning faith," the narrator adds, "is more a native element in this race than any other" (ch. 38). What this has to do with successful escapes from slavery, hopeless lives left in enslavement, and even the murder of Uncle Tom becomes clear only by way of Stowe's deeply racialized theological vision. While awaiting the great day of that vision, readers are left with what George M. Fredrickson has called the "romantic racialism" central to Stowe's novel—that is, the idealization of Africans (including all those of African heritage) as more spiritual, more emotional, and more submissive than Anglo-Saxons (1971, 97). Even the domestic revelations at the center of Stowe's vision for the novel are framed by the dynamics of race, for Eliza's entrance into the home is facilitated initially by the Birds' "colored domestic, old Aunt Dinah" and by "old Cudjoe, the black man-of-all-work" (ch. 9).

Beyond the vision Stowe brought to the antislavery cause, in other words, were the more powerful and pervasive visions for which she was a carrier. As Marcus Wood has observed, "*Uncle Tom's Cabin* is best approached as a cultural sample, as a culture in which the bacteria of nineteenth-century racism flourished" (2000, 186). Almost immediately following the publication of *Uncle Tom's Cabin*, an unprecedented popular culture began to develop, devoted to characters drawn from the novel. The novel's events were dramatized in various illustrations, printed on dishes, wallpaper, and jewelry; and the novel was used to sell a variety of products (for example, "Uncle Tom's pure unadulterated coffee") and was made the subject of jigsaw puzzles, board games, and card games. After the publication of Stowe's novel and the many others that quickly followed, references to "Cabin Literature," "Uncle Tomitudes," and the like began to appear regularly in the press. Such Tomitudes extended far beyond the abolitionist cause as the novel was adapted to the theater, beginning with a dramatization published the same year as Stowe's novel. Often borrowing from the most popular form of entertainment of the time, blackface minstrelsy, staged versions of *Uncle Tom's Cabin* proliferated, most of them selectively drawing from the novel and exaggerating still further the racial stereotypes that had influenced Stowe herself. Eric Lott has noted "the extent to which the great midcentury vogue of 'Tom shows' owed precisely to the blackface tradition. The stage conventions of such productions, which included minstrel tunes and blackface makeup, were clearly those of minstrelsy; dramatizations of *Uncle Tom* foregrounded not only sectional conflict but also the blackface forms that had shadowed it" (1993, 211). By 1859, such plays were so popular, and so well-established as a cultural staple, that four stage companies performed their versions of *Uncle Tom's Cabin* in New York City, offering as many as three shows each day. These productions often contended with Stowe's novel for cultural influence, as they were often the first or most memorable contact that many people had with Stowe's vision. When Louisa May Alcott has one of her characters in *Little Women* (1868) reference Stowe's character Aunt Chloe, for example, her memory seems influenced more by popular stagings of *Uncle Tom's Cabin* than by the novel itself.

Stowe participated in the response to *Uncle Tom's Cabin*, publishing in 1856 another antislavery novel, *Dred: A Tale of the Great Dismal Swamp*. As Robert S. Levine observes, *Dred* "was hardly an obscure footnote to her masterwork," for it "quickly emerged as one of the most popular novels of the time, selling upwards of 200,000 copies during the nineteenth century and earning the praise of many reviewers" (2000, ix). "Particularly attentive to what African American readers had to say about *Uncle Tom's Cabin*," Levine argues, "Stowe in *Dred* revises her racialist representations, attempts new strategies of point of view that would allow for a fuller development of black revolutionary perspectives, and implicitly rejects African colonization—endorsed in *Uncle Tom's Cabin*—as a solution to the nation's racial problems" (2000, x). Whereas Stowe decided in *Uncle Tom's Cabin* to send the most accomplished and rounded African American characters (all light-complexioned) to Liberia, *Dred*'s title character is a black revolutionary developing in the Dismal Swamp a band capable of striking out against slavery. Whether because or in spite of Stowe's edgy shift from the domestic cabin of *Uncle Tom's Cabin* to black political agency in the Dismal Swamp of *Dred*, the latter novel was still an international success, appearing in over a half-dozen different languages during the first two years of its publication. Within a decade, numerous stage adaptations of the novel were produced, some of which extended Stowe's vision by depicting the slave insurrection only implied in *Dred*'s pages.

In many ways, that shift exemplifies Stowe's own involvement in the cultural and political processes so dramatically affected by *Uncle Tom's Cabin*. As Levine has argued, Stowe's attention to the criticism of *Uncle Tom's Cabin*, particularly by African Americans, her increasing involvement in the international (and interracial) abolitionist movement, and her advocacy of African American artists and activists led to an even more dramatic and fundamental shift in vision in *Dred*, one exemplified by a passage that, Levine aptly suggests, "can be taken as a 'key' to Dred" (2000, xvii):

> There is no study in human nature more interesting than the aspects of the same subject seen in the points of view of different characters. One might almost imagine that there were no such thing as absolute truth, since a change of situation or temperament is capable of changing the whole force of an argument. We have been accustomed, even those of us who feel most, to look on the arguments for

> and against the system of slavery with the eyes of those who are at ease. We do not even know how fair is freedom, for we were always free. We shall never have all the materials for absolute truth on this subject, till we take into account, with our own views and reasonings, the views and reasonings of those who have bowed down to the yoke, and felt the iron enter into their souls. (ch. 21)

This vision of multiple perspectives and of the complacencies engendered by a comfortable distance from the realities of slavery was in many ways integral to *Uncle Tom's Cabin* as well. A central point of that novel is made through Stowe's handling of the abolitionist from Vermont, Miss Ophelia, as a woman who has firm antislavery views but little sense of the complex political and social world that had resulted from slavery's long and central presence in the United States. Among other things, Miss Ophelia is the recipient of a brief but revealing lecture from her slaveholding cousin Augustine St. Clare, who explains:

> Planters, who have money to make by it,—clergymen, who have planters to please,—politicians, who want to rule by it,—may warp and bend language and ethics to a degree that shall astonish the world at their ingenuity; they can press nature and the Bible, and nobody knows what else, into the service; but, after all, neither they nor the world believe in it one particle the more. It comes from the devil, that's the short of it;—and, to my mind, it's a pretty respectable specimen of what he can do in his own line. (ch. 19)

In *Uncle Tom's Cabin*, this vision is a threat viewed in contrast to the moral stability represented by the narrative perspective; in *Dred*, this vision *informs* the narrative perspective.

One could easily view much of Stowe's subsequent writing career as an attempt to retreat to more secure moral ground, to create a world defined by region, from which one might reassert moral and even cultural authority over the overwhelming and unstable worlds she both addressed and discovered in *Uncle Tom's Cabin* and *Dred*—an attempt, in effect, to restore Miss Ophelia's simple moral perspective. But Stowe's great talent, much like her eventual neighbor Mark Twain, is that she saw more and wrote better than she could have ever intended. In many ways, Stowe was like Twain—who drew from illustrations we would now consider racist for the images that adorned his acute statement on slavery and racist culture, *Adventures of Huckleberry Finn* (1884)—in that she was a thoroughly saturated product of her culture, alive with the contradictions that complicated and, at times, redeemed a culture hell-bent on feeding its ever-growing appetite for cultural chauvinism, racial domination, and self-justification. Just as Stowe's central example of moral independence and fortitude, Uncle Tom, became a symbol of obsequious submission, so much of her work deals in characters and stories that turn in on themselves, speaking of the sometimes startling differences between the world we think we inhabit and the worlds that inhabit us.

In her approach to a broad range of social issues, as with slavery, Stowe was less a social reformer than a strict moralist—and like many moralists, she found it easier to identify wrongs than to determine a course toward the right. Most of the problems she addressed in her work, after all, involved ideological assumptions and socioeconomic practices fundamental even to her sense of the social order, and how does one envision an entirely different social order? Stowe's primary theme in *Uncle Tom's Cabin* was not so much that slavery was wrong, but rather that slavery depended upon and encouraged a world of wrongs, ultimately destabilizing morality itself. Stowe could not transcend that world; she could only represent it in all its complexity, and she wrote from the inside of those complexities, a product of that culture. In *Uncle Tom's Cabin*, this cultural immersion is most evident in Stowe's problematic representation of her African American characters and her decision to end the novel by sending the most educated and articulate of those characters to Liberia, a colony established in Africa by white Americans anxious to rid the United States of free African Americans.

In many of her other works, Stowe wrote from the perspective of a woman in a deeply patriarchal culture, and again found her power in her ability not to resolve but simply to represent the ideological contradictions fundamental to that culture. Consider, for example, a novel that in many ways better represents Stowe's life work than *Uncle Tom's Cabin*, her 1871 novel *Pink and White Tyranny*. In this novel, the "tyrant" is a woman who simply fails to fulfill the domestic station expected of women, making this the story, as her Canadian publisher presented it in an advertisement for the book, of "the tyranny under which a loyal and chivalrous gentleman suffers" (qtd. in Martin 1988, vii). As Judith Martin puts it in an introduction to a 1988 reprinting of the book, "Uncle Tom's mother speaks out on domestic injustice—to condemn her own sex" (viii). But in this novel, as in *Uncle Tom's Cabin*, the value of Stowe's moral sternness is not in its message but in Stowe's unique ability to pull loose threads from her cultural environment that soon unravel the entire social tapestry. As Martin observes, *Pink and White Tyranny* is "not just an antique polemic about the nuisance of having a frivolous woman around the house. In her fairness, the author has delineated the pastel tyrant's own social grievances, as well as the husband-victim's disappointment, going beyond her stated intention of sympathizing with men who have pretty wives to explore the social forces that made them what they were" (1988, ix). One of Stowe's best critics, Judith Fetterley, similarly has argued that in another novel, *The Pearl of Orr's Island*, "Stowe describes a boy and a girl, Moses and Mara, growing up together in early nineteenth-century New England, and analyzes the social structures which lead the boy to view the girl as an inferior being and to treat her with contempt" (1994, 890). In most of her work, Stowe's ability to enter into such explorations of "social forces" and "social structures," her talent for representing the inconsistencies and philosophical contradictions of her world, is what makes her work particularly compelling. At the same time, Stowe brings a fervent moral certitude to an ambivalent vision of a possible social order, and in both her fervency and her ambivalence, in her clarity and in her blindness, Stowe was able to connect with her world in ways that few writers could.

In all her work, including *Uncle Tom's Cabin*, those social forces and structures were distinctively regional. *Uncle Tom's Cabin* is a study of people shaped by different regional environments, with the most absolute antislavery and proslavery positions represented by white individuals from New England (Miss Ophelia) and the Deep South (Simon Legree) respectively. The novel's plot is driven largely by its focus on slavery in the northern areas of the South, where various regional types meet—either through traveling slave traders, visiting relatives, or escaping slaves. In effect, the novel is a study of a national character forged through an uneasy mixture of stasis and mobility, of regional types who are secure in their views, in their sense of order and character, and within their regional borders, but who are destabilized when they inhabit other regions or encounter other regional types. The national character, the novel argues, is philosophically (even theologically) incoherent and dangerously unstable precisely because the nation's regions have been so firmly established.

In this way, *Uncle Tom's Cabin* is not a departure but a part of Stowe's primary authorial role as a leading (even pioneering) writer of literary regionalism. Stowe's career as a writer began with the 1834 publication, in the *Western Monthly Magazine*, of a story entitled "A New England Sketch," which Marjorie Pryse has called "one of the 'origin' texts of regionalism" (1993, 10). The story was later included, under a different title, in Stowe's first book, *The Mayflower; or, Sketches of Scenes and Characters Among the Descendants of the Pilgrims*, published in 1843, an expanded version of which (now titled "Uncle Lot") was published in 1855 under the title *The May Flower*. Before and after *Uncle Tom's Cabin*, in other words, Stowe presented herself as a writer of regional sketches. Indeed, as Joseph A. Conforti has observed, "Across the decades that stretched from 'A New England Sketch' to *Oldtown Folks*, Stowe dwelled on the 'smallness, isolation, cohesiveness, innocence, and unchangingness' of village-centered New England" (2001, 149). But as *Uncle Tom's Cabin* indicates, Stowe was always highly aware of the presence of the national (and even the global) in the regional, of the ways in which the world pressed on the borders of small New England villages, disrupting their cohesiveness, threatening their guarded innocence, and drawing them into the currents of inevitable change. In "A New England Sketch," Stowe announces that her story will not be set in Italy, Greece, France, or England, but rather in New England, "[T]he land of bright fires and strong hearts; the land of *deeds*, and not of words; the land of fruits, and not of flowers; the land often spoken against, yet always respected; 'the latchet of whose shoes the nations of the earth are not worthy to unloose.'" If this opening seems to speak for the cultural supremacy and philosophical security of a New England village, Stowe immediately opens the gates of those secure regional borders by commenting on her own "heroic apostrophe," calling it "merely a little introductory breeze of patriotism, such as occasionally brushes over every mind," and adding significantly that if this characterization of this secure village "should seem to be rodomontade to any people in other parts of the earth, let them only imagine it to be said about 'Old Kentuck,' old England, or any other corner of the world in which they happened to be born, and they will find it quite rational." In other words, Stowe quickly brings her readers not only to the complex history of "old England" but also to the regions that would later set Eliza running over the ice floes of the Ohio River in *Uncle Tom's Cabin*.

And so it is in virtually all her fiction. Stowe is a regionalist in a world that no longer allows for the security of regional character, a world in which one's regional home is both refuge and illusion. What is most significant about Stowe's relatively brief career as a writer of antislavery fiction, one might say, is that it amplified and sharpened her sense of the disquiet and confusion at the heart of isolated, peaceful, and seemingly coherent New England villages. Stowe, that is, is never far from the perspectival confusion that she placed at the heart of *Dred*, the study of "aspects of the same subject seen in the points of view of different characters," contesting perspectives that lead one to "almost imagine that there were no such thing as absolute truth, since a change of situation or temperament is capable of changing the whole force of an argument" (ch. 21). In her 1859 novel *The Minister's Wooing*, Stowe has her narrator observe, "when one has a story to tell, one is always puzzled which end of it to begin at. You have a whole corps of people to introduce that *you* know and your reader doesn't" (ch. 1). In all her fiction, Stowe draws her readers into stories that might begin, and might be told, a dozen different ways, depending on which character one favors. Ultimately, her stories are formed by the interaction of various characters who, as they get caught up in a web of mutual influences and contingent relations, represent not the security of but the fractures in the regional edifice.

The power of Stowe's work lies in her ability to translate such insecure foundations into literary voice and form, to approach the novel itself as a familiar home, and to work with the instabilities of that form. Again, her commentary in *Dred* is instructive here; her caution to her readers that "we have been accustomed, even those of us who feel most, to look on the arguments for and against the system of slavery with the eyes of those who are at ease" (ch. 21). As both a genre and a cultural pastime, the novel itself, Stowe realized, played to "the eyes of those who are at ease," and she worked both with and against such leisurely examinations of a troubled world. She did so in part by populating her fiction with characters who variously fulfill and fall out of conventions. Her main approach, however, involved engaging readers in the challenge of telling her story—be it the challenge of knowing where to start (or with whom), as in *The Minister's Wooing*, or the challenge of knowing what language to use, as in *Uncle Tom's Cabin*, in which Stowe cannot get past the first paragraph without pausing to comment on the inappropriateness of her own use of the word "gentlemen." In *Pink and White Tyranny*, Stowe begins her preface to her "Dear Reader" by announcing, "This story is not to be a novel, as the world understands the word," and she soon invokes the different settings (England, Italy, Switzerland, Japan, and Kamtschatka) that, as in "Uncle Lot," will not play a role in the story. But such notices are equivalent to holding up a sign that reads, "Pay no attention to this sign." The world in the regional and the novel in the story are, of course, central to Stowe's concerns, for she devoted herself to the global in the national, the national in the regional, the unfamiliar in the familiar—in short, to the incoherent world that was fundamental to the illusion of local coherence and stability.

Ultimately, it is difficult to identify the nature and extent of Stowe's influence in American (or global) literary and cultural history, beyond saying that she wrote one of the most influential novels ever published and that she encouraged the development of regionalism. Even focusing on Stowe's considerable contributions to the antislavery cause—including *Uncle Tom's Cabin*, *Dred*, and numerous essays and fictional sketches, not to mention the enormous body of literature published in response, both negative and positive, to her work—one would be hard pressed to establish a neat equation of cause and effect, of influence and consequences, that would account for the cultural phenomenon of which she was a part. In one of the better attempts to assess the international presence of *Uncle Tom's Cabin* and its aftermath, Henry James once wrote:

> Uncle Tom, instead of making even one of the cheap short cuts through the medium in which books breathe, even as fishes in water, went gaily roundabout it altogether, as if a fish, a wonderful "leaping" fish, had simply flown through the air. This feat accomplished, the surprising creature could naturally fly anywhere, and one of the first things it did was thus to flutter down on every stage, literally without exception, in America and Europe. If the amount of life represented in such a work is measurable by the ease with which representation is taken up and carried further, carried even violently furthest, the fate of Mrs. Stowe's picture was conclusive: it simply sat down wherever it lighted and made itself, so to speak, at home; thither multitudes flocked afresh and there, in each case, it rose to its height again and went, with all its vivacity and good faith, through all its motions. (1913, 159–60)

While *Uncle Tom's Cabin* is a much more accomplished novel than James allows here, this is still a fair attempt to account for Stowe's presence on the international cultural scene. A wonderful leaping fish that leaped over and beyond even the antislavery cause that was its raison d'être, leaving that cause, and much of Stowe's literary career, in the shadows. *Uncle Tom's Cabin* remains a statement of the power of the novel, a power that extends far beyond any author's intentions, beyond any identifiable cause, and far beyond any predictable outcome. Stowe's talent, one might say, was her ability to write her way into worlds where leaping fishes abound. Her career as a writer was defined in large part by her determination to understand such worlds, which, in many ways, involved locating the heart of her most famous novel not in the antislavery cause but in the social forces and structures that she explored in her extensive body of regional writing.

Part V

MAJOR NOVELS

19

THE LAST OF THE MOHICANS: RACE TO CITIZENSHIP

LELAND S. PERSON

> Would the people of New York permit each remnant of the Six Nations within her borders to declare itself an independent people under the protection of the United States?
>
> —Andrew Jackson, First Annual Message to Congress (December 1829)

Although Cooper adds the subtitle "A Narrative of 1757" to *The Last of the Mohicans* (1826), historical influences on the novel derive more from the 1820s than from the French and Indian War period. The 1820s featured numerous federal efforts to control Native American lands and define the conditions under which Native American peoples would live in the ever-expanding United States. That effort culminated in 1830 with the Indian Removal Act, paving the way for a series of forced evacuations, including the notorious Trail of Tears in 1838–1839. In his 1829 message to Congress, Andrew Jackson asserted, "Our conduct toward these [Native American] people is deeply interesting to our national character" (Prucha 2000, 48). Although set seventy-two years earlier, *The Last of the Mohicans* engages in an extended conversation about the future of Native American peoples, along with the effect their treatment will have on America's fifty-year-old democracy and the character of the nation.

Cooper explores both the character and the fate of Native Americans. Looking back in 1831 at his representation of Mohican culture, he notes in an introduction to the novel that "few men exhibit greater diversity" or "greater antithesis of character, than the native warrior of North America": "In war, he is daring, boastful, cunning, ruthless, self-denying, and self-devoted; in peace, just, generous, hospitable, revengeful, superstitious, modest, and commonly chaste." At the same time, Cooper recognizes that, regardless of their character or natural rights, their fate depends on policies such as those codified in the Removal Act:

> The Mohicans were the possessors of the country first occupied by the Europeans in this portion of the continent. They were, consequently, the first dispossessed; and the seemingly inevitable fate of all these people, who disappear before the advances, or it might be termed the inroads of civilization, as the verdure of their native forests falls before the nipping frost, is represented as having already befallen them.

Even as he assumes the virtual extinction of native peoples, Cooper uses them reflexively to assess the "national character" of their dispossessors. As Geoffrey Rans argues, the novel "consistently projects—and endorses—the Indian view of white European imperium: the conqueror, English or French, is as greedy a destroyer as any conquistador" (1991, 114). Forrest Robinson considers the novel's ethos more ambiguous. Although he also believes that this "story of violent racial conflict, dispossession, and annihilation" amounts to "an indictment . . . of the young republic that was rapidly spreading across the continent" (1991, 2), he notes that this indictment of the republic's Indian policies is contradicted by many other features of the novel. In fact, in Robinson's view, the novel's popularity derives from these contradictions: "[T]he novel anticipates in its readers an anguished sensitivity to the Indian's plight, and a countering impulse to diminish, if not to neutralize altogether, the painful sense of responsibility for the terrible injustice of the situation" (1991, 14).

In citing the "inevitable fate" (disappearance) of the Mohicans, Cooper was echoing the rationale of an 1823 Supreme Court decision (*Johnson and Graham's Lessee v. William M'Intosh*), which affirmed the principle of "title by conquest" and effectively granted the US government the right to all land east of the Mississippi River. That decision was rooted, moreover, in a profound prejudice against Indian tribal cultures and the familiar savage-versus-civilized dichotomy of racial and cultural difference. In Chief Justice John Marshall's condescending words, Indian tribes are "fierce savages," and "to leave them in possession of their country, was to leave the country a wilderness." What choice did Europeans have, Marshall reasoned, except enforcing their claims "by the sword, and by the adoption of principles adapted to the condition of a people with whom it was impossible to mix, and who could not be governed as a distinct society"? Otherwise, Marshall concluded, settlers faced the prospect "of remaining in their neighbourhood, and exposing themselves and their families to the perpetual hazard of being massacred" (Prucha 2000, 36). Whether or not Cooper had read this decision, Marshall's stereotypic terms and options establish a useful context for discussing *The Last of the Mohicans*, a novel about violence, competing land claims, differences between European and Indian values, and the possibility of racial and cultural "mixing."

These clashing forces combine in a narrative vision close to what we would now associate with an action film. At his best, Cooper staged thrilling episodes that he narrated, like a movie director, from multiple perspectives. *The Last of the Mohicans* features more of these action scenes than any other Leather-Stocking novel—from the violent attack on civilians that follows the siege at Fort William Henry, to the haunting scene behind the waterfall at Glen's Falls, to the canoe chase up Lake George, to the climactic fight atop the cliff in which Uncas, Cora Munro, and Magua meet their deaths. Cooper was less adept at plotting his novels. *The Last of the Mohicans* tells a cumbersome, repetitious story that derives from the popular Indian captivity tradition. Broadly considered, the novel features two difficult journeys sandwiched around the battle at Fort William Henry. In the first half of the novel, Natty Bumppo, Chingachgook, and Uncas escort Alice and Cora Munro, along with Duncan Heyward and others, to the fort. In the second half, after Magua and the Hurons kidnap the women, the three foresters track them to an Indian village. These two arduous journeys through the wilderness offer narrative cables for the scenes and episodes mentioned above.

The Last of the Mohicans is the most violent of the five Leather-Stocking Tales, and the sources of violence only sometimes reinforce the stereotypical distinction between Indian savages and civilized whites. In the most gruesome example of unchecked violence, Cooper restages a historical event—the August 1757 massacre of British soldiers, women, and children after the surrender and evacuation of Fort William Henry. Cooper's summary is particularly graphic:

> More than two thousand raging savages broke from the forest at the signal, and threw themselves across the fatal plain with instinctive alacrity. . . . Death was every where, and in his most terrific and disgusting aspects. Resistance only served to inflame the murderers, who inflicted their furious blows long after their victims were beyond the power of their resentment. The flow of blood might be likened to the outbreaking of a torrent; and as the natives became heated and maddened by the sight, many among them even kneeled to the earth, and drank freely, exultingly, hellishly, of the crimson tide. (ch. 17)

Cooper makes it clear, however, that a conjunction of political purpose and environment encourages such extreme violence. The allegedly civilized codes practiced by the French General Montcalm and the British Colonel Munro disguise their willingness to use violent means to achieve their political ends. As William Kelly puts it:

> The chivalric conventions of the French and British may disguise the horror of warfare more effectively than the codes of Indian combat, but the reality of their mission is the same. By scalping their victims and drinking their blood, the Indians unmask the violence at the core of human identity. Just as he defines Montcalm and Munro as parallel figures whose differences are inconsequential, Cooper links the white and red warriors at William Henry as characters driven by an identical will to power. (1983, 63)

Violence in *The Last of the Mohicans* serves another purpose in Cooper's examination of how wilderness conditions and white-Indian relations influence character. Natty Bumppo, as he says at the end of *The Pioneers; or, The Sources of the Susquehanna* (1823), has been "form'd for the wilderness" (ch. 41), and *The Last of the Mohicans* represents him at his wildest and most violent. "Whoever comes into the woods to deal with the natives," he instructs Heyward, "must use Indian fashions, if he would wish to prosper in his undertakings" (ch. 4). Usually pragmatic, Natty sometimes seems to relish violence for its own sake. For example, after he and the Mohicans attack the Hurons, who have captured Heyward, the singing teacher David Gamut, and the Munro sisters, they kill five Indians without suffering any serious injuries themselves. So eager are they for battle that in one case Heyward, Natty, and Uncas cooperate to kill a single Indian: "[T]he tomahawk of Heyward, and the rifle of Hawk-eye [Natty], descended on the skull of the Huron, at the same moment that the knife of Uncas reached his heart." The over-killing does not stop when five Indians lie on the ground. Chingachgook goes around "flaying the scalps," while Natty checks each body for any sign of life: "[T]he honest, but implacable scout, made the circuit of the dead, into whose senseless bosoms he thrust his long knife, with as much coolness, as though they had been so many brute carcasses" (ch. 12).

Such behavior is hard to reconcile with the stereotype of civilized whites and savage Indians or with Cooper's 1831 assessment of Natty as a "a man of native goodness, removed from the temptations of civilized life, though not entirely forgetful of its prejudices and lessons, exposed to the customs of barbarity, and yet perhaps more improved than injured by the association" (intro.). But Cooper clearly sees Natty as a hybrid character influenced by his adoption into the Delaware tribe as well as by his life in the woods. *The Last of the Mohicans* represents a study of race and character in this respect, with Natty as the first subject. In chapters 3 and 4, for example, Cooper focuses intently on Natty and his two companions, Chingachgook and Uncas, emphasizing their masculine and racialized—"native" and "white"—bodies: "While one of these loiterers showed the red skin and wild accoutrements of a native of the woods, the other exhibited, through the mask of his rude and nearly savage equipments, the brighter, though sunburnt and long-faded complexion of one who might claim descent from a European parentage" (ch. 3). Based on these descriptions, the two characters test the boundaries of racial categories. Barbara Alice Mann, in fact, has made a plausible case that Natty is part Indian. At the very least, environmental influences have all but erased racial difference.

Represented as a degraded "mixture of the civilized and savage states" in *The Pioneers*, Chingachgook keeps a "profusion of long, black, coarse hair" hung about his face as a "veil, to hide the shame of a noble soul, mourning for glory once known" (ch. 7). Cooper restores that "glory" in *The Last of the Mohicans*, set thirty-six years earlier. Chingachgook's "body, which was nearly naked, presented a terrific emblem of death, drawn in intermingled colours of white and black. His closely shaved head, on which no other hair than the well known and chivalrous scalping tuft was preserved, was without ornament of any kind, with the exception of a solitary eagle's plume, that crossed his crown, and depended over the left shoulder" (ch. 3). Natty, too, is obviously reinvigorated by the time travel to which Cooper subjects his character. Described in *The Pioneers* as "so meager as to make him seem above even the six feet that he actually stood," Natty has a "skinny" face that is "thin almost to emaciation," while "his scraggy neck was bare, and burnt to the same tint with his face" (ch. 1). The younger Natty of the 1826 novel is more vigorous: "His person, though muscular, was rather attenuated than full; but every nerve and muscle appeared strung and indurated, by unremitted exposure and toil" (ch. 3).

The pairing of Natty and Chingachgook has understandably elicited a lot of critical attention. This friendship between men of different races sponsors a tradition that continues to this day: Pym and Dirk Peters in Edgar Allan Poe's *The Narrative of Arthur Gordon Pym, of Nantucket* (1838), Ishmael and Queequeg in *Moby-Dick; or, The Whale* (1851), Huckleberry Finn and Jim. Leslie Fiedler famously called the pairing of Natty and Chingachgook "an archetypal relationship" that "haunts the American psyche: two lonely men, one dark-skinned, one white . . . they have forsaken all others for the sake of the austere, almost inarticulate, but unquestioned love which binds them to each other and to the world of nature which they have preferred to civilization" (1966, 192). More recently, Ivy Schweitzer shifts attention from the mythic to the social and political implications of the relationship. Noting the number of times white and Indian characters clasp hands in the novel, she argues that Cooper uses "interracial friendship . . . to explore the types of affective bonds linking people of different backgrounds in the new nation" (2006, 144).

On its face, the novel is ambiguous, even confused, in its representation of racial differences. Even though Cooper emphasizes that Natty is "genuine white," with "no cross in his blood," and describes Chingachgook as an "unmixed man" (ch. 3), in many places he implies a socially constructed or behavioral definition of race. For example, as Natty walks around stabbing the fallen Hurons, Uncas thinks first of the women and restores them to each other—a subtle way for Cooper to suggest some degree of amalgamation, as Uncas appears more civilized, Natty more savage. And Natty and Chingachgook seem assimilated to each other. They have protected and cared for each other for years (as the Leather-Stocking series illustrates). Uncas is "the child of [Natty's] adoption" (ch. 25). In this novel, Natty and Chingachgook effectively raise that son together and, finally, mourn his death.

As Cooper conceived him, Uncas has the attributes of a strong, tall, dark, and handsome leading man with a multicultural appeal. His "whole person thrown powerfully into view" by the light of a campfire, he reveals an "upright, flexible figure," "graceful and unrestrained in the attitudes and movements of nature":

> Though his person was more than usually screened by a green and fringed hunting shirt, like that of the white man, there was no concealment to his dark, glancing, fearless eye, alike terrible and calm; the bold outline of his high, haughty features, pure in their native red; or to the dignified elevation of his receding forehead, together with all the finest proportions of a noble head, bared to the generous scalping tuft. (ch. 6)

Cooper uses point of view like a movie director, and he deftly shifts to the other characters and their responses to this spectacle. First, he notes that everyone feels relieved because Uncas's appearance inspires confidence that he "could not be one who would willingly devote his rich natural gifts to the purposes of wanton treachery." In this respect, he is a character in transition, assimilating himself more than, say, his father into white culture. Uncas inspires other reactions as well—as a man: "The ingenuous Alice gazed at his free air and proud carriage, as she would have looked upon some precious relic of the Grecian chisel, to which life had been imparted, by the intervention of a miracle." A gendered inversion of the Pygmalion-Galatea myth, Uncas's appeal crosses gender boundaries. Heyward also seems transfixed and equally attracted to this "rare and brilliant instance of those natural qualities, in which these peculiar people are said to excel." Indeed, in Cooper's words, "Heyward, though accustomed to see the perfection of form which abounds among the uncorrupted natives, openly expressed his admiration at such an unblemished specimen of the noblest proportions of man" (ch. 6).

The energy created by the tension between the three expert foresters and the lost party from Fort Edwards (Heyward, the Munro sisters, and Gamut) drives the plot by providing Natty and the Mohicans plenty of opportunities to demonstrate their wilderness expertise. First—and improbably—they vow to escort the party to Fort William Henry; for as Uncas suggests, "it would not be the act of men, to leave such harmless things to their fate" (ch. 5). The French, of course, have laid siege to the fort and almost immediately force the British to surrender.

In this central episode—the massacre occurs in chapter 17 of 33—Cooper relegates his three heroes to the background, bringing them back just in time to save Heyward and Colonel Munro from the Indian attack. Cora and Alice, however, become prisoners. Heyward had worried earlier that "his unresisting companions would soon lie at the entire mercy of [their] barbarous enemies" (ch. 5). That nightmare comes true. The fort cannot protect its occupants. The French cannot restrain their native allies. A father cannot protect his children. A soldier cannot protect his fiancée. The massacre marks a sharp turning point in the narrative, as "the inroads of civilization," as Cooper calls them, prove to be dead ends. Cooper situates this novel within the Indian captivity tradition—the variant that derives from Mary Rowlandson's popular narrative, in which women face captivity and the threats entailed by being at the "entire mercy" of their captors. As Renée Bergland has noted, John Vanderlyn's well-known painting, *The Death of Jane McCrea* (1804), offers a visual touchstone: McCrea, one breast nearly exposed, torn between two very muscular Indian males, their violent connection triangulated by the tiny figure of her fiancé who rushes, too late, to her rescue.

Cooper exploits the energy his readers have invested in this triangle. Repeatedly, he places Cora and Alice at the mercy of their Indian captors. Both Alice and Cora are nearly scalped, and Magua, sexualizing the violence they face, proposes that Cora take the place of his lost wife and "live in his wigwam for ever." This proposal arouses a "powerful disgust" in Cora, but the prospect of amalgamation and possibly even rape lingers for the remainder of the novel. Only a few pages later, with torture and murder imminent, Magua offers Cora a deal: Alice's freedom in return for her agreement to "follow Magua to the great lakes, to carry his water, and feed him with corn." Instead of simply repeating her refusal, Cora presents the proposition to Alice and Heyward—a rather transparent device enabling Cooper to elicit additional opinions about amalgamation. Heyward's response is so spontaneous that it must have its roots in a deep-seated nightmare: "Name not the horrid alternative again; the thought itself is worse than a thousand deaths." Alice's response takes much longer, as she appears to shrink into a trancelike state, gathering a reply from deep within her imagination. Her arms fall before her, "the fingers moving in slight convulsions; her head dropped upon her bosom, and her whole person seemed suspended against the tree, looking like some beautiful emblem of the wounded delicacy of her sex, devoid of animation, and yet keenly conscious." "No, no, no," she exclaims, "better that we die, as we have lived, together!" (ch. 11). Why does Alice take so long to provide the standard-issue response? Is she tempted to let her sister sacrifice herself? Does Cooper want his readers to think seriously about the exchange being offered? Are we ready to sacrifice Cora (who feels no desire for Magua) so that Alice—and all she symbolizes—can survive? All these questions hang in the air as Natty and the Mohicans burst upon the scene and, after the violent fight described earlier, rescue the women.

Recent critics such as William Decker and Ian Dennis have paid increasing attention to Cora and the issues raised by her mixed-race character and her triangulated relationship to Uncas and Magua. Dennis cites "her superiority and strength of *character*, her freedom both to be desired, and to desire" (1997, 13), while Decker considers her "the novel's central character, partly because she exhibits a moral and physical courage to which women and men may equally aspire, but also because she reflects the mixed heritage that increasingly becomes the American norm" (2007, 202). Cora also has the most progressive attitudes toward race. She chides her sister and Heyward for distrusting Magua simply "because his manners are not our manners, and that his skin is dark!" (ch. 2). Shortly afterward, she praises Heyward when he expresses hope that Uncas will "prove, what his looks assert him to be, a brave and constant friend." "Now Major Heyward speaks, as Major Heyward should," Cora confirms, "who, that looks at this creature of nature, remembers the shades of his skin!" (ch. 6).

The Last of the Mohicans nevertheless sends mixed messages at best on the question of Native American character and the possibility of amalgamation. Magua's story is exemplary. He had been a Huron chief who succumbed to the temptations of alcohol and was "whipped like a dog" by Colonel Munro. He hides these marks on his back "like a squaw," even as he "may boast before his nation" about the "scars given by knives and bullets" (ch. 11). Given this history, he could be a sympathetic character, and John McWilliams rightly notes that Cooper never allows us to forget "why Magua acts as he does" (1995, 59). Instead, he plays the stereotypical role of merciless savage. Just a few pages after Cora spurns his proposal, for example, he threatens her with torture and decapitation. "Her head is too good to find a pillow in the wigwam of le Renard [Magua]," he snarls; "will she like it better when it rolls about this hill, a plaything for the wolves?" Cora's retort—"He is a savage, a barbarous and ignorant savage" (ch. 11)—does not indict a race or tribe but a particularly malignant individual. Cooper reinforces the point after Cora and Alice once again become prisoners. Magua gives a "yell of pleasure" when he discovers the two women, and the first words he utters repeat his proposal of cohabitation or marriage. As he places "his soiled hand on the dress of Cora," he says, "the wigwam of the Huron is still open. Is it not better than this place?" Magua taunts her, in fact, and even holds up his bloody hand to boast of the white people he has just killed: "It is red, but it comes from white veins!" (ch. 17).

The overall structure of *Last of the Mohicans*, with the massacre at Fort William Henry providing the pivot point for two extended plot movements—the first to a British outpost of civilization, the second into the wilderness to rescue Indian captives—resonated for several generations of Americanists interested in literary examples of American myth. Certainly the journeys that occupy the first and second halves of the novel point toward a mythic structure, a descent by arguably civilized and refined characters into an underworld where most of their assumptions about themselves and their place in the natural world will be challenged, perhaps even destroyed, and where they will encounter possibilities of change and rebirth.

Too often downplayed in mythic readings of the novel is the privileged inside look Cooper provides his readers into Native societies. In fact, sending his cast of characters and his readers to Fort William Henry at the moment of its failure to secure British imperial interests in the colonies provides an object lesson in British ineptitude, making the Revolutionary War of less than twenty years later seem appropriate. But it is not just the British who fail, for in the very process of taking possession of the fort, the French reveal a truly monstrous inability to preserve peace and protect the lives of those whose safety they have guaranteed. In contrast, the Indian camps to which characters and readers eventually make their way seem relatively civilized. As McWilliams notes, during the second half of the novel, "the supposed distinctions between French and English gradually blur and then drop away, while the conflict between the red and white cultures grows ever more important" (1995, 39).

The rhetorical question Jackson asked in his 1829 address to Congress suggests the possibility of separate tribal nations within the states. Jackson, of course, knew the "obvious answer" to his question, and he reports that he "informed the Indians inhabiting parts of Georgia and Alabama that their attempt to establish an independent government would not be countenanced by the Executive of the United States." He therefore "advised them to emigrate beyond the Mississippi or submit to the laws of those States" (Prucha 2000, 48). Although *The Last of the Mohicans* looks forward in many respects to the removal policy Jackson pronounces, Cooper's representation of Native culture at the end of the novel certainly belies the stark terms that undergird Jackson's rationalizations.

As he moves the narrative toward Native American villages, Cooper stages such a bewildering number of character disguises, impersonations, and cases of mistaken identity that readers might wonder if he had transported the forest of *A Midsummer Night's Dream* to upstate New York. Testing each character's potential to shift shape, even to change some fundamental facet of identity, Cooper plays with the possibility of a cultural transformation based on cross-cultural and racial assimilation and amalgamation. Heyward mistakes a beaver colony for an Indian village, and later Chingachgook actually disguises himself as a beaver. Although Heyward has repeatedly revealed a dangerous ignorance as a wilderness warrior, he helps rescue Alice, but only by disguising himself as an Indian playing a buffoon. To achieve this transformation, Chingachgook paints him to look like a Huron medicine man. Previously Heyward has been a fool disguised as a soldier; now he will be a warrior disguised as a fool. Even Alice, cynosure of pure, white womanhood, is disguised as a sick Indian woman so that she can be rescued from, among other things, the prospect of becoming an Indian woman. Most impressively, to free the captive Alice, Natty sneaks into the Huron camp disguised as a bear—actually, as an Indian disguised as a bear (figure 19.1)—and he fools Heyward, as well as Magua, into accepting his performance as the real thing. Natty subsequently exchanges costumes with Gamut, who takes Uncas's place in captivity, while Uncas dons Natty's bearskin. These exchanges enable Uncas to escape with Natty, although they leave Gamut a prisoner. Jane Tompkins considers this extended scene and the other examples of character disguise "the most ridiculous sequence of events in *The Last of the Mohicans*" (1986, 113), and even Cooper's narrator acknowledges that "there was a strange blending of the ridiculous, with that which was solemn, in this scene" (ch. 25). Along with Mitzi McFarland, Shirley Samuels, David Mazel, and others, I think these events at the Huron camp provide an appropriate climax to Cooper's efforts to explore questions of individual, racial, and national identity. Samuels says that "the disguises and substitutions of the novel indicate a more fundamental uneasiness about the constructedness of identity, or about whether the body is more than a theater for the performance of identity" (1992, 98). Mazel goes further in arguing that a "category crisis" looms at this point in the novel, "a breakdown in the very structures by means of which

Fig 19.1 N. C. Wyeth, *The Masquerader* (1919).

nature and culture have been demarcated in the first place" (2000, 108). And McFarland uses Mikhail Bakhtin's theories of dialogism and carnival to argue that "in this wildly sensational episode at the Huron camp, with its ludicrous repetitions of masquerade and deception, we see the primary values of the carnivalesque: the lines that distinguish races, nationalities, and even species are crossed and blurred" (2002, 262).

Are we suddenly in an imaginary world of performance and play in which identities become fluid? Do Cooper, his characters, and his readers have faith that, no matter what costumes or manners they put on, their core identities remain intact? When Natty enters Gamut's hut, still disguised as a bear, and tells him to stop playing his pitch-pipe, the startled Gamut demands, "What art thou?" "A man like yourself," Natty replies, "and one whose blood is as little tainted by the cross of a bear, or an Indian, as your own." To prove his point, Natty uncovers his face and declares, "you may see a skin, which, if it be not as white as one of the gentle ones, has no tinge of red to it, that the winds of the heaven and the sun have not bestowed" (ch. 26). Cooper does a brilliant job in this vignette of illustrating, even parodying, the instability of racial and other signifiers of identity. Here is Natty Bumppo pretending to be an Indian conjuror impersonating a bear who claims that his red skin proves his white identity because his color has an environmental cause.

Given the space Cooper devotes to this carnivalesque series of masquerades and impersonations, we might expect them to take the narrative in a new direction. Given the transformative potential of trans-species, transracial, and transcultural shape-shifting, we might expect the destabilization of categorical differences to last and to show the way forward, during the fiftieth anniversary celebration of the Declaration of Independence, to a new, more inclusive democratic republic. Possibilities for transformation are best represented in Natty and Chingachgook and in Cora and Uncas, the characters who have already gone furthest in assimilating across cultural boundaries. The endings they make, therefore, profoundly affect the cultural and political significance *The Last of the Mohicans* may finally have.

Nina Baym notes that Cora "could function as the possible progenitor of an American future in which the races were combined. Her already mixed blood, mixed again with an Indian's, would produce triracial children—the incarnate 'e pluribus unum' of the American national seal" (1992, 75). Decker echoes this view in arguing that, in Cora, the "narrative envisions even as it rejects a model of human merit transcendent of race and gender, a liberal interpretation of the principles of '76 that would not attain currency until well into the twentieth century" (2007, 214). Even some of Cooper's nineteenth-century readers regretted his decision to prevent Cora's marriage to Uncas, although their desire to witness such an interracial marriage resulted less from progressive notions of race relations than from a tendency to classify both Native and African Americans as dark, racial "others." An anonymous reviewer for the *United States Literary Gazette* asserted that "Uncas would have made a good match for Cora, particularly as she had a little of the blood of a darker race in her veins,—and still more, as this sort of arrangement is coming into fashion, in real life, as well as in fiction" (Dekker and McWilliams 1973, 100). We may blanch at the condescending racialism of this observation, but it does suggest an unexpected openness to interracial marriage. Lydia Maria Child's *Hobomok* (1824) and Catharine Maria Sedgwick's *Hope Leslie; or, Early Times in Massachusetts* (1827) reflect such openness—and condescension—in the interracial marriages they depict.

Since both Cora and Uncas die at the end of the novel, why does Cooper give them such heroic stature in these final scenes? Does he wish to illustrate the great loss to the new nation of two exemplary individuals and the possibilities they represent? Uncas certainly demonstrates leadership potential as he negotiates Natty's safety with Tamenund, the Huron patriarch and chief. Uncas responds by speaking across racial lines when Tamenund asks, "What name has [Natty] gained by his deeds?" "We call him Hawk-eye," Uncas replies, "for his sight never fails. The Mingoes know him better by the death he gives their warriors; with them he is the 'long rifle.'" Mention of Natty's French nickname (La Longue Carabine) angers Tamenund, who reproves Uncas: "My son has not done well to call him friend!" But Uncas rejects such categories. "I call him so who proves himself such," he instructs the old chief (ch. 30). Insofar as *The Last of the Mohicans* explores the terms of the democracy the colonists will declare in less than two decades, Uncas represents and espouses values of tolerance, cultural relativity, and equality.

Cora also acts heroically in these final scenes. Selflessly, in a scene spectacularly painted in two versions by the Hudson River School artist Thomas Cole (*Cora Kneeling at the Feet of Tamenund*, 1827), she pleads for Alice's life. She too makes a transcultural appeal. "For myself I ask nothing," she tells Tamenund. She appeals to his paternal feelings, which she compares to Munro's: "She is the daughter of an old and failing man, whose days are near their close." As a racial "other," she compares herself to Tamenund and his tribe: "Like thee and thine . . . the curse of my ancestors has fallen heavily on their child!" She exempts Alice, as a member of a seemingly chosen race, who she claims is "too good, much too precious, to become the victim of that villain." Tamenund takes up the racial angle of this plea in a way that suggests sympathy for Cora's assertion that she has been "cursed" by her racial heritage, but in the process he offers a strong critique of white racism and its obsession with racial purity:

> I know that the pale-faces are a proud and hungry race. I know that they claim, not only to have the earth, but that the meanest of their colour is better than the Sachems of the red man. The dogs and crows of their tribes . . . would bark and caw, before they would take a woman to their wigwams, whose blood was not of the colour of snow. (ch. 29)

This powerful insight into racial politics may drown out Natty's tedious claims to be "without a cross," and Tamenund's judicious handling of competing claims here at novel's end certainly makes him seem superior to Montcalm, Colonel Munro, or General Webb. He spares Alice, but not Cora because he considers her fairly Magua's prisoner. By encouraging Cora to go willingly with Magua, Tamenund also acts from a sense that interracial marriage is perfectly acceptable. When he tells her that by marrying Magua and having children with him her race will not end, he transcends the concept of racial difference he attributes to the "pale-faces."

In remanding Cora to Magua, Tamenund unwittingly condemns her to death, although as Magua leads her away, the three foresters follow with the intention of making one last attempt at rescue. Precipitating the violent climax, expertly staged in a natural amphitheater memorialized by Cole in *The Death of Cora* (1827), Uncas demands that Magua halt. Cora follows suit. "Kill me if thou wilt, detestable Huron," she cries, "I will go no farther!" In a climax surely inspired by Vanderlyn's painting of Jane McCrea's murder, as McWilliams suggests, Magua demands that Cora "choose; the wigwam or the knife of le Subtil!" (ch. 32). Cora resigns herself to death, with Uncas, like McCrea's fiancé, positioned just far enough away to be helpless to prevent her murder. With remarkable efficiency, Cooper dispatches his characters. Within the space of two paragraphs, Cora and Uncas both die. Uncas arrives just as one of Magua's assistants stabs Cora, and then, after killing her killer, he falls victim to Magua's own knife. Natty then shoots Magua, who falls off a cliff into oblivion. Cora and Uncas, in contrast, receive something on the order of a state funeral in the novel's final chapter.

Janet Dean calls this event a "bicultural ceremony that is at once funeral and wedding" (2003, 45), and the ceremony is remarkable in its assumption that the two characters should be memorialized together. Not only do the Delawares honor each character's individual life; the Delaware women, having discovered what Cooper calls the "truant disposition" of Uncas's desire, project a union into the afterlife. Giving with one hand and taking with the other, Cooper relates this vision—a version of *Liebestod*—through Natty's point of view. The scout "shook his head, like one who knew the error of their simple creed." Similarly, when Colonel Munro asks Natty to translate his words of thanks, assuring the Delawares "that the Being we all worship, under different names, will be mindful of their charity," and, remarkably, "that the time shall not be distant, when we may assemble around his throne, without distinction of sex, or rank, or colour," Natty refuses to convey such a transcultural message. "To tell them this," he says, "would be to tell them that the snows come not in the winter, or that the sun shines fiercest when the trees are stripped of their leaves!" (ch. 33).

Insofar as *The Last of the Mohicans* resembles the traditional novel of manners and possesses a courtship and marriage plot, character outcomes have larger implications for the social world of the novel. Who gets to marry whom and, presumably, produce children who ensure continuity by inheriting and creating the future? Chingachgook, we know from the end of *The Pioneers*, has fathered many sons and daughters, but all of them, he says, "left him for the land of spirits" (ch. 36). We know from *The Prairie* that the betrothal of Alice and Heyward results in marriage and children, because their grandson, Duncan Uncas Middleton, plays a key role in that novel and fills in the historical blanks through a narrative he relates to Natty. Duncan and Alice have at least two children, a son and a daughter. Middleton descends from their daughter, but like his uncle, he bears the name Uncas. Moreover, Middleton's brother and two of his cousins bear the name Nathaniel. Nominally, Cooper ensures that Natty and Uncas live on through at least two more generations. It would be fitting if Middleton's mother were named Cora, but he says nothing about her.

Promoting Duncan and Alice Heyward to such patriarchal and matriarchal positions might be considered a satiric comment on the American future—a cautionary note about the debilitating effects such anemic bloodlines will engender. Cooper focuses, after all, on the other four major characters in the novel's final scene, and the narrative ends with Natty vowing to stand by Chingachgook for the rest of their lives as they mourn Uncas's death. "The boy has left us for a time,"

Natty says, "but, Sagamore, you are not alone!" At which point, Cooper notes that "Chingachgook grasped the hand that, in the warmth of feeling, the scout had stretched across the fresh earth, and in that attitude of friendship, these two sturdy and intrepid woodsmen bowed their heads together, while scalding tears fell to their feet, watering the grave of Uncas, like drops of falling rain" (ch. 33). Jackson had asserted that US treatment of Native Americans is "deeply interesting to our national character." Surely this final vision, within the context of Indian removal, offers a remarkable alternative to official government policy as an example of what a multicultural "national character" can be. The tears Natty and Chingachgook shed represent a shared trail of tears, mourning the death of the son they have raised together and, symbolically, the absence of Native American citizens in the new republic.

20

THE SCARLET LETTER

MONIKA ELBERT

Of all US novels published before 1870, Nathaniel Hawthorne's *The Scarlet Letter: A Romance* (1850) is arguably the most popular and most frequently read among US high school and college students, assigned almost dutifully as a rite of passage. The book has never gone out of print. Not so Herman Melville's *Moby-Dick; or, The Whale* (1851), which might seem worthy to take its place beside *The Scarlet Letter*. Melville, who dedicated his opus to Hawthorne and lauded Hawthorne's American genius in his review, "Hawthorne and His Mosses" (1850), would fall into oblivion in the last decades of his life. The best-selling novel of the nineteenth century, Harriet Beecher Stowe's *Uncle Tom's Cabin; or, Life Among the Lowly* (1852), would lose its popularity as the century waned because of its limited topical appeal once the Civil War was over. *The Scarlet Letter* may be the great American novel, based on its longevity and ongoing appeal.

Although always reserved in his praise, Henry James deemed *The Scarlet Letter* Hawthorne's best novel: if, in his eyes, it lacked realism and made too much of "fanciful" elements and symbolism, it manifested the "beauty and harmony of all original and complete conceptions" (1879, 114, 120). He also praised it as the first major American masterpiece, worthy to compete with European literature: "Something might at last be sent to Europe as exquisite in quality as anything that had been received, and the best of it was that the thing was absolutely American; it belonged to the soil, to the air; it came out of the very heart of New England" (111). Willa Cather saw *The Scarlet Letter* as one of the three most significant works of American literature (along with *Adventures of Huckleberry Finn* [1884] and *The Country of the Pointed Firs* [1896]) and predicted its perennial appeal. This chapter explores the "American" qualities attached to the novel and the darkness associated with its appeal. Although the narrative lacks the optimistic outlook of the American experience perceived by Hawthorne's Transcendentalist friends, perhaps his understanding of the American scene is more profoundly true than that of his more idealistic contemporaries.

The dark tale moved many readers of *The Scarlet Letter*, from Hawthorne's wife Sophia, whose reading of it sent her to bed with "a grievous headache" (Hawthorne 1985, 311), to younger contemporary readers of Hawthorne, like Louisa May Alcott, who preferred the "lurid" style of *The Scarlet Letter* to more "wholesome" works. As Alcott put it so decisively, "I fancy 'lurid' things, if true and strong also" (1989, 63). Hawthorne himself admitted in a letter to his friend Horatio Bridge that his book lacked "sunshine": "it is positively a h—ll-fired story, into which I found it almost impossible to throw any cheering light" (1985, 311–12). James, though he does not consider Hawthorne either a pessimist or an optimist, finds in the novel little "gaiety" or "hopefulness," but he does predicate its success on this darkness: "It is densely dark, with a single spot of vivid colour in it; and it will probably long remain the most consistently gloomy of English novels of the first order" (1879, 109). D. H. Lawrence, who scoffed at Hawthorne's American naïveté, would also remark upon his "lurid" style but only to criticize it, accusing Hawthorne of being obsessed with sin and not passion: "He knows there's nothing deadly in the act itself. But if it is FORBIDDEN, immediately it looms lurid with interest. . . . Sin looms lurid and thrilling, when after all it is only just a normal sexual passion." But for Lawrence, this "lurid" quality was not praiseworthy—he declared that it "makes one feel like spitting" (1927, 225). Why then has *The Scarlet Letter*, a book about sinfulness, law, and unjust punishment, become the great American masterpiece, a text that teachers want to keep in the curriculum, perhaps as a cautionary tale about the price of nonconformity, and that the canon-makers of academe refuse to drop from their list of great books?

The romance has some of the conventions of a gothic thriller and all the trappings of a modern soap opera (as evidenced in the distorted 1995 Roland Joffé film)—with an illicit affair; a dangerous love triangle; and a wayward, illegitimate child. However, an adulterous relationship seems to be the pretext for the novel: in actuality, the secret suffering of each individual character informs the plot, which is more psychological than action-packed or plot-driven. As James astutely put it, "In spite of the relation between Hester Prynne and Arthur Dimmesdale, no story of love was surely ever less of a 'love-story.' To Hawthorne's imagination the fact that these two persons had loved each other too well was of an interest comparatively vulgar; what appealed to him was the idea of their moral situation in the long years that were to follow" (1879, 112). Edith Wharton might have erred when she labeled *The Scarlet Letter* one of the few exemplary novels of "pure situation" rather than a "novel of character" (1997, 90), even though it subjects three anguished souls to psychological examination. Like Alcott, Wharton, also a master of the gothic tale, felt that Hawthorne's niche was with Scott and Poe in "that peculiar category of the eerie which lies outside of the classic tradition" (28)—an eeriness which today we might read as the "uncanny."

Evert Duyckinck's 1850 *Literary World* review of the novel lauded Hawthorne's psychological acumen as a romancer, rather than as a novelist, a distinction that

Hawthorne forces upon the reader in his famous "moonlight" passage in "The Custom-House" introduction, where he envisions "the Actual and the Imaginary" converging in a "neutral territory," so that "each [might] imbue itself with the nature of the other." The nineteenth-century critic and novelist, William Dean Howells, proclaiming Charles Dickens the representative English author of his time and Hawthorne the representative American author, nonetheless distinguished between the romantic and realistic propensities of both authors: "Romance, as in Hawthorne, seeks the effect of reality in visionary conditions; romanticism, as in Dickens, tries for a visionary effect in actual conditions" (1901, 162).

Hawthorne, who already had served his apprenticeship writing tales of Puritan history, took on, in *The Scarlet Letter,* the challenge of writing a historical romance. Some critics have taken Hawthorne to task for fudging his historical details. James found that his Puritan characters were not speaking "the English of their period," but he conceded that the "book is full of the moral presence of the race that invented Hester's penance" and that Hawthorne is able to capture the tone of Puritanism objectively and subjectively (1879, 113). A contemporary of the author, Caleb Foote, complimented Hawthorne for evoking "personages and incidents" from the past and reproducing "their spirit—their very essence" (1850, 119). Charles Creighton Hazewell attacked those critics who would find fault with the historical accuracy of the novel and defended it, not as an historical novel but as an evocation of the Puritan age. Although Hawthorne writes ostensibly about seventeenth-century Puritan society in *The Scarlet Letter*, many of his concerns relate to the nineteenth-century political arena of women's rights, abolition, legal reform, economic upheaval, and shifting class constructs.

Early readings privileged psychology over history. Duyckinck asserts: "*The Scarlet Letter* is a psychological romance. . . . It is a tale of remorse, a study of character in which the human heart is anatomized, carefully, elaborately, and with striking poetic and dramatic power" (Idol and Jones 1994, 122). The self-torture of each character comes from pondering the meaning behind the letter of the law—a guilt so tinged by self-righteousness, fear, and indignation that it requires purges (such as Dimmesdale's self-scourging vigils) or results in public scapegoating (as in public humiliation upon the scaffold). It would be folly to pinpoint the evil or put the blame on one individual since all are implicated. Ironically, Chillingworth, with his overbearing intellect and amorality, understands that though Hester did "plant the germ of evil," she is not to blame, for "it has all been a dark necessity" (ch. 14), the legacy of Calvinist original sin. In Hawthorne's relativistic world, the badges of good or evil are not clearly distinct, and one necessitates the other. Chillingworth's exoneration of Hester and his self-portrayal as blameless seem strangely perceptive as he considers the nature of evil: "Ye that have wronged me are not sinful, save in a kind of typical illusion; neither am I fiend-like, who have snatched a fiend's office from his hands" (ch. 14).

Perhaps Hawthorne had the most visceral reader response when, upon completing the novel, he read the conclusion of *The Scarlet Letter* to his wife: "[I] tried to read it . . . for my voice swelled and heaved, as if I were tossed up and down on an ocean, as it subsided after a storm. But I was in a very nervous state . . . having gone through a great diversity and severity of emotion, for many months past" (Hawthorne 1997, 339–40). His turbulence relates to the personal trauma of losing his mother and the emasculation of losing his Custom House position. Hester's ennobling maternity (as a paradoxical "Divine Maternity" in the opening scene, in the many scenes with Pearl, and the final Pietà scene with the dying Dimmesdale) serves as a tribute to the author's recently deceased mother. Hawthorne recalls bursting into tears at his mother's deathbed: "I shook with sobs. For a long time, I knelt there, holding her hand; and surely it is the darkest hour I ever lived" (1972, 429). The "childlike" Dimmesdale shares this maternal longing and fantasizes about a distant mother when, after a session of self-scourging, he hallucinates, "Ghost of a mother,—thinnest fantasy of a mother,—methinks she might yet have thrown a pitying glance towards her son" (ch. 11). The phantasmagoric vision ends with a spectral Hester and Pearl gliding through his chamber, as if to suggest his present salvation depends upon the maternal Hester with child.

Dimmesdale's tormentor, Chillingworth, represents that part of Hawthorne's persona that demands revenge for his dismissal as the Custom House surveyor, with the election of the Whig party. However grateful we may be for Hawthorne's removal—and the subsequent creation of his masterpiece—he himself felt devastated and betrayed. His contempt for the Salemites is evident in his acerbic portrayal of torpid and lackluster bureaucrats in "The Custom-House" and in his final renunciation of Salem: "Henceforth, it ceases to be a reality of my life. I am a citizen of somewhere else." Though his proclamation insists upon his psychic removal from Salem, he, like his creation Hester, would never be able to be "a citizen of somewhere else." For all his vitriol against Salem, he would not forget it; the town inspired his next novel, *The House of the Seven Gables: A Romance* (1851), and when he abandoned the New England scene for European material in later years, he lost the creative drive that informed his trilogy of New England novels. Hester, too, cannot exorcise the past, as she returns, ghostlike, to her peninsula cottage in Boston: "[T]here was a more real life for Hester Prynne, here, in New England, than in that unknown region where Pearl had found a home" (ch. 24). Though it does not bode well for the American utopia that Hester's daughter should emigrate to Europe to start a family, it is telling that Hawthorne makes Hester's final home the place where she has experienced the most growth and suffering.

By writing Hester's story and by taking up her badge of infamy (which scorches him in the introduction), Hawthorne, as artist and outcast, identifies with her transgressive and proud artistry. In the narrative proper, we hear that the scarlet letter was "fantastically embroidered" and "had the effect of a spell, taking her out of the ordinary relations with humanity, and inclosing her in a sphere by herself" (ch. 2). Hawthorne feels similarly alienated, not only because of his rejection by Salemites, but also because of the ridicule he imagines from the ghostly forefathers who would have taunted him for his feminized vocation as a writer. But in "The Custom-House" Hawthorne admits his own guilt—on two counts: his proud affiliation with the persecuting Puritans of the past ("strong traits of their nature have intertwined themselves with mine") and his prior selling out to Uncle Sam for his livelihood ("Uncle Sam's gold . . . has . . . a quality of enchantment like that of the Devil's wages"). He admits that his "imagination was a tarnished mirror" and wonders "how much longer [he] could stay in the Custom-House, and yet go forth a man." Writing *The Scarlet Letter* was cathartic: for Hawthorne, it redeemed his soul.

Sophia Hawthorne considered the lesson of the novel to be "that the Law cannot be broken" (Hawthorne 1985, 313, n. 3). She was thinking narrowly of the biblical seventh commandment, the breaking of which would have consequences in the Puritan theocracy, as we hear that "religion and law were almost identical" (ch. 2). In this culture of surveillance where Hester is made a cautionary spectacle, the narrator is far more charitable to her in showing her superiority over the townspeople. Certainly, there are many types of laws described in the novel—religious, political, scientific, natural, and moral—and Hawthorne's vision of the law was not as narrow as his wife's. In the vacillating narrative voice, which seems more modernist than nineteenth-century, one sees various attitudes toward the religious and political law of the Puritan theocracy. Hester, who has a law of her own and hence unlimited freedom, is viewed as alternately positive and negative, liberated and misguided: "Her intellect and heart had their home, as it were, in desert places, where she roamed as freely as the wild Indian in his woods. . . . The tendency of her fate and fortunes had been to set her free. The scarlet letter was her passport into regions where other women dared not tread" (ch. 18). That all sounds positive, especially to modern-day feminist critics, but in the next instance, the moralizing voice of the narrator intervenes: "Shame, Despair, Solitude! These had been her teachers,—stern and wild ones,—and they had made her strong, but taught her much amiss." Nonetheless, her charitable nature and imaginative powers invest new meaning in the letter *A*, so that ultimately it comes to mean "Angel" and "Able," and the townspeople exhort her to remove the badge (which she, in defiance, does not). Pearl, the child of nature, the product and emblem of love and passion, represents "the freedom of a broken law" (ch. 10) and shares a similar latitude of experience, as she is more at home in the forest than with the intolerant Puritan children.

Dimmesdale, "a true priest, a true religionist, with the reverential sentiment largely developed" (ch. 9), lacks imagination and adheres to the religious law but for one moment, which might have been liberating but is not. The narrator seems to sympathize with him, however, for the accursed conventionality that has paralyzed him and forced him to dissemble to his congregation—a maddening compulsion that leads to his mental breakdown: "At the head of the social system, as the clergymen of that day stood, he was only the more trammelled by its regulations, its principle, and even its prejudices" (ch. 18). What modern readers find offensive are his sanctimonious behavior and his final exhortation to Hester's hopeful query about a meeting in the afterlife: "Hush, Hester, hush! . . . The law we broke!—the sin here so awfully revealed!—Let these alone be in thy thoughts" (ch. 23). What resounds in the modern reader's ears is Hester's earlier plaintive lament in the forest: "What we did had a consecration of its own" (ch. 17). Moreover, we know that Hawthorne hated above all the hypocrisy that typified Puritan culture, so we might rightfully assume that Dimmesdale is finally damned. Chillingworth, for his part, might also be considered one of the damned, as he lacks the human heart that Hawthorne felt more sacred than any wisdom, as witnessed in his stories about obsessed scientists (e.g., "The Birth-Mark" [1843] and "Rappaccini's Daughter" [1844]).

Almost an allegorical embodiment of vice, the misshapen Chillingworth knowingly forsakes his search for truth to pursue personal revenge, but the narrator does not allow us to see him in a monolithic fashion; rather, we must pity him: "The unfortunate physician . . . lifted his hands with a look of horror, as if he had beheld some frightful shape, which he could not recognize, usurping the place of his own image in a glass" (ch. 14). The townspeople, like a Greek chorus, recognize the transformation in Chillingworth from scholar to demon; they declare that he was "haunted either by Satan himself, or Satan's emissary" (ch. 9). The narrator suggests that the townspeople intuit rather than see the change, quite significant in a book which privileges heart over head: "When an uninstructed multitude attempts to see with its eyes, it is exceedingly apt to be deceived. When, however, it forms its judgments . . . on the intuitions of its great and warm heart, the conclusions thus attained are often so profound and so unerring, as to possess the character of truths supernaturally revealed" (ch. 9). Hawthorne obviously shared the Romantic predilection for intuition as well as belief in a higher, supernatural law, outside the realm of religion.

With recriminations and sympathy bestowed upon each character by the narrator, it is hard for the reader to take sides. But critics throughout the years have tried to do so, as they focus on favorite characters, especially in supporting an agenda or political bias, and dispense with the other characters—or let them recede into the backdrop. Stephen Railton has shown the disjunction between nineteenth- and twentieth-century reader responses, and though Hawthorne was trying to evoke some sympathy for Hester from his Victorian audience, the conclusion of the romance supports the conservatism of his times. Certainly, critics of Hawthorne's era would look more harshly at Hester than would critics now. Orestes Brownson, lapsed Transcendentalist and recent convert to Catholicism, damns Hester (and Hawthorne) in his 1850 review; he characterizes the story as written with "great naturalness, ease, grace, and delicacy" but considers it one "that should not have been told" (143). Tellingly, he introduces Hester merely as "an adulteress" and

Dimmesdale as "a meek and gifted and highly popular Puritan minister in our early colonial days" (143). Brownson tends to put the blame squarely on Hester and criticizes Hawthorne for trying to "excuse" her. The review ends with the condemnation of Hawthorne: "We should commend where the author condemns, and condemn where he commends. Their [the Puritans'] treatment of the adulteress was far more Christian than his ridicule of it" (146). In many early reviews, Chillingworth is written out of the text or seen as subhuman: Anne W. Abbott writes him off as "a gnome-like phantasm . . . an unnatural personification of an abstract idea" (1850, 127). Like Brownson, Abbott attacks Hester for her pride, but, surprisingly, sympathizes with Dimmesdale for "the anguish in his inmost soul" (130). She takes Hawthorne to task for labeling Pearl "elvish and imp-like," for her own maternal instincts see Pearl as a real child: "[A] capricious, roguish, untamed child, such as many a mother has looked upon with awe, and a feeling of helpless incapacity to rule" (130–31). The latter part of her portrait is quite accurate, as Hawthorne did take many of his *American Notebook* jottings about his impish and prescient daughter Una for his portrayal of Pearl. Religious critics, like Arthur Cleveland Coxe, saw Hawthorne's (and Hester's) feminist inclinations as blasphemous. Coxe notes the baneful influence of *The Scarlet Letter* on young female readers: "[S]chool-girls had, in fact, done injury to their young sense of delicacy by devouring such a dirty story" (1851, 151). One sole nineteenth-century voice resounds with approbation for Hester: Jane Swisshelm finds the "honorable characters of the book" utter bores but would readily travel to Boston "if there was such another woman as Hester Prynne" living there (1850, 274).

If nineteenth-century critics attacked Hawthorne's morality, twentieth- and twenty-first- century critics have found much to critique in Hawthorne's politics. Hawthorne was often seen as conservative because of his notorious laissez-faire statement in the campaign biography of Franklin Pierce that slavery would disappear through the intervention of "divine Providence" in "its own good time" (ch. 6). Equally problematic is the final passive assessment by the narrator of *The Scarlet Letter* that "*In Heaven's own time*, a new truth would be revealed" (ch. 24) to promote equality between the sexes (emphasis mine).

Yet recent critics have shown Hawthorne's political engagement and awareness as he grapples, in *The Scarlet Letter,* with pressing national issues related to class, race, and gender. Critics such as Gillian Brown and Ellen Weinauer explore the changing legal status of women through Hawthorne's depiction of Hester. Michael T. Gilmore, T. Walter Herbert, and Joel Pfister examine social mobility and the attendant anxiety wrought by changing roles in the middle-class family. Critics such as Jean Fagan Yellin, Sacvan Bercovitch, and Leland S. Person look at the slavery question and come to differing conclusions about Hawthorne's sympathies. Larry J. Reynolds's book on Hawthorne's "damned politics" offers the most tempered view of Hawthorne's relativistic politics leading up to the Civil War. Bercovitch and Reynolds (in his earlier work), see Hester's progressive thinking as akin to that of radical thinkers in the European socialist revolutions of Hawthorne's era (1848–49). From a transnational perspective, Laura Doyle and Teresa Goddu have recently focused on *The Scarlet Letter* to show how Hawthorne was perpetuating an Anglo-American or transatlantic colonialist position.

In the late nineteenth century, Henry James would participate unwittingly in the battle of the sexes, as he reconfigured the dynamics of the story to focus on the tight bond between Dimmesdale and Chillingworth: "The story indeed is in a secondary degree that of Hester Prynne; she becomes, really, after the first scene, an accessory figure. . . . The story goes on for the most part between the lover and the husband" (1879, 112). D. H. Lawrence also shifts the focus toward the male protagonists as he attacks Hester's sexuality and seductiveness: "Hester Prynne was a devil" (1978, 100). Lawrence's irreverent but provocative study of Hawthorne looks forward to gender studies in the late twentieth century, especially those (by critics such as Herbert, David Leverenz, and Karen Kilcup) dealing with concepts of manhood and homo-eroticism in *The Scarlet Letter*. For Lawrence, Chillingworth and Dimmesdale represent two negative and competing sides of patriarchy—rational and spiritual: "The two halves of manhood mutually destroying one another" (106). Hester recedes into the background, because the real jilted lover, in Lawrence's analysis, is Chillingworth, and that, twice over: "dodging into death," Dimmesdale leaves "Hester dished, and Roger, as it were, doubly cuckolded" (106).

The end of the twentieth century definitely brought Hester to the foreground, due in no small part to the influence of the feminist movement and to the progressive social movements of the 1960s—which recalled the feminist and abolitionist spirit of the 1840s and 1850s. Hester is a most remarkable character—perhaps the most skillfully wrought female character in nineteenth-century American literature and perhaps the only adulteress in nineteenth-century fiction who escapes a brutal death or suicide (cf. Kate Chopin's Edna Pontellier in *The Awakening* [1899], Flaubert's Madame Bovary [in the 1856 novel of the same name], or Tolstoy's Anna Karenina [in the 1877 novel]). Early and recent film versions of the novel have focused on Hester as the selling point by featuring a waiflike Lillian Gish (in the 1926 Victor Sjöström production), the flapper Colleen Moore (in the 1934 Robert G. Vignola production), the European beauty Senta Berger (in the 1972 German production by Wim Wenders), a reliable but maternal Meg Foster (in the 1979 mini-series), and a supersensual Demi Moore (in the 1995 Joffé production). Suzan-Lori Parks's *The Red Letter Plays* rewrite Hester's maternity so that it becomes monstrous; in *In the Blood* (1998), Hester is a downtrodden urban mother who beats her child to death; and in *Fucking A* (2000), Hester becomes an urban abortionist who is compelled to kill her adult son (escaped from a prison) to save him. Two recent novels have tried to resurrect Hester: a prequel, *Hester: A Novel about the Early Hester Prynne* by Christopher Bigsby (1994) and a sequel, *Hester: The Missing Years of* The Scarlet Letter*: A Novel* by Paula Reed (2010).

But Hester defies definition, despite the many (contradictory) badges that authors and critics have wanted to affix upon her. Contemporary scholars have viewed her as a gauge of Hawthorne's gender and race politics—equating her passivity or agency, her weakness or strength, with Hawthorne's conservative or liberal leanings. Hester is seen variously and contradictorily—as an emancipated woman who reflects Hawthorne's progressive view toward women; as a repressed or beleaguered woman who reflects Hawthorne's conventional attitudes toward women; as a compromising woman who reflects Hawthorne's softness on slavery; as a model citizen who represents Hawthorne's view of civic responsibility; as a slave mother whose situation shows Hawthorne's awareness of the horrors of slavery and sympathies toward abolition; as a silent treacherous woman who defies patriarchy by torturing her men with her silence; as a silenced, compliant woman who has no choice but to be quiet or whose love for Dimmesdale has hushed her; as a good mother; as a mother limited by repressive child-rearing practices; and as a bad mother, whose passions endanger the child. Hester has the passion—but not the helplessness—of the typical gothic heroine in Ann Radcliffe or Walter Scott. With her maternal qualities, she is the True Woman, to some extent, of sentimental novels whose authors Hawthorne decried as "a d—d mob of scribbling women" (1987a, 304). Ironically, Jane Tompkins has rendered Hawthorne, with his domestic themes, more like the scribbling women he ridicules than like Melville, with whom he was more often compared in the past. In my reading, Hester is stronger than the typical sentimental heroine: "[H]er temperament was not of the order that escapes from too intense suffering by a swoon" (ch. 3). Her status as an independent woman puts her in league with the eponymous hero of Fanny Fern's *Ruth Hall: A Domestic Tale of the Present Time* (1854), a widowed mother who makes good on her own and does not fall into the marriage trap so often the fate of well-behaved, sentimental heroines. It is little wonder that Hawthorne singled out Fern as the only "scribbling woman" he admired, for, as he put it, "The woman writes as if the devil was in her; and that is the only condition under which a woman ever writes anything worth reading" (1987a, 308). Prompted by a protective maternal instinct, Fern, her protagonist, and Hester do not simply survive, but triumph, and associations between the diabolic writer, Fern, and the demonic Hester abound. Yet Hester resists categorization, and we would be as guilty as the Puritans in assigning arbitrary meanings to the emblem she wears. With her many contradictory meanings, she is hard to pinpoint, and remains thus quintessentially American, to borrow the final definition of the litany of badges Lawrence affixes to the letter *A*.

The inspiration for Hawthorne's Hester might have come from his contact with many strong women, in his familial and intellectual circles: his distant but self-reliant mother, who survived (and triumphed) after the death of her husband, when Hawthorne was only three; his strong but eccentric sisters, Ebe and Louisa; his talented and multifaceted sister-in-law, Elizabeth Peabody, who mentored him; his artistic and sympathetic wife, Sophia; and his brilliant and radical Transcendentalist friend, Margaret Fuller. Hawthorne was also influenced by the nascent women's movement of his time: the Seneca Falls Convention (1848) marked the start of a serious national discussion on women's rights, and the married women's property acts of the 1840s challenged the notion of women as property of their husbands. Accordingly, Hester not only inhabits her own seaside cottage, albeit isolated from the community, but she thinks in radical and revolutionary ways that would have startled the Puritans: "The world's law was no law for her mind" (ch. 13). The narrator speculates that her liberated mind might have been more threatening to the community than her sexuality.

Hawthorne might have drawn his inspiration from a Puritan model of strong womanhood, Anne Hutchinson, whom he cites as being a forerunner to Hester (in "The Prison-Door" and "Another View of Hester"). Hester, like the Antinomian Hutchinson, derived her strength from inner wisdom and disregard for the Word as translated by Puritan patriarchs. However, the narrator, with his sometimes-Victorian (and concomitantly Puritan) sensibility asserts that Hester could never be such a prophetess of truth, as she was besmirched by sexual transgression: without Pearl, "she might have come down to us in history, hand in hand with Ann [*sic*] Hutchinson, as the foundress of a religious sect. She might, in one of her phases, have been a prophetess" (ch. 13). The mature Hester herself articulates the idea that, earlier, she had "vainly imagined" she could have been "the destined prophetess" but now realizes that such a mission could not be "confided to a woman stained with sin": "The angel and apostle of the coming revelation must be a woman, indeed, but lofty, pure, and beautiful; and wise . . . not through dusky grief, but the ethereal medium of joy" (ch. 24).

The prototype of such a savior woman who would establish gender equity might be found in Margaret Fuller's *Woman in the Nineteenth Century* (1845), which (along with its author) had a great impact on Hawthorne and his creation of strong female protagonists. Fuller describes her own vision for such a prophetess: "And will not she soon appear? The woman who shall vindicate their birthright for all women; who shall teach them what to claim, and how to use what they obtain?" (1994, 118). The ideal woman Fuller promotes, as embodied in the Virgin Mary goddess archetype, is a combination of self-reliant thinking ("virgin mind") and human compassion ("maternal wisdom and conjugal affections"). Hester fulfills her duties as an empathic mother to Pearl, though as a more liberal mother of the nineteenth century rather than as a stern Puritan mother, and she ends her life giving maternal counsel to lovelorn women. Hester's maternity, which saves her from going to the forest with Mistress Hibbins, also gives her redeeming value in Hawthorne's era, which promoted the cult of true womanhood—and it may have been one of the reasons why both Hawthorne and the Puritan community treat her adultery with some lenience.

Even though Hawthorne was not a Transcendentalist, Hester's self-reliance is especially compelling, as is her development from passion to wisdom; the narrator's equivocal relationship to Hester makes it unclear, however, whether her increasingly statue-like appearance—her "marble coldness" (ch. 13) and "marble quietude" (ch. 21)—and signs of her growing intellect are any more socially acceptable than her earlier passion. Fuller would have applauded her "self-dependence," and Hester can be viewed as a Transcendentalist heroine, in the terms Fuller establishes. Hester, the only independent thinker of the Puritan community, tries to instill this virtue of self-sufficiency into those she loves. Little Pearl, begging her mother to catch her some sunshine, is admonished: "Thou must gather thine own sunshine. I have none to give thee!" (ch. 7). Similarly, Chillingworth recognizes that his error is in seeking sustenance from Hester: "I drew thee into my heart, into its innermost chamber, and sought to warm thee by the warmth which thy presence made there!" (ch. 4). Dimmesdale, too, becomes dependent in his forest breakdown, as he implores Hester for advice: "Think for me, Hester! Thou art strong. Resolve for me" (ch. 17). Here Hester does commit a Transcendentalist gaffe—not allowing Dimmesdale to think for himself—by offering him the possibility of moving West or returning to England.

Dimmesdale's abortive first choice to return to England is as much an admission of the failed American experiment as is Pearl's emigration, at the end, to a home in Europe. This is part of a modern, almost existential dilemma—that the characters remain in a state of stasis or inertia, as if fearful of moving on. Their choice, or nonchoice (why do Dimmesdale and Chillingworth endure that hopeless living arrangement for seven years?), might be Hawthorne's tacit agreement with Thoreau's view in *Walden; or, Life in the Woods* (1854) that: "The mass of men lead lives of quiet desperation" (329). But that is where Hawthorne's agreement with the Transcendentalists might end; he knows too well, as articulated in "The Custom-House," that one cannot abandon the past. Hester, too, realizes she cannot abandon the past, though for one brief moment in the forest, she feels as if this is possible, when she flings off her scarlet letter and tells Dimmesdale, "Let us not look back. . . . The past is gone! . . . With this symbol, I undo it all, and make it as it had never been" (ch. 18). But another emblem of the past, Pearl, comes to point a scolding finger at Hester and to remind her that she cannot so easily let her hair down. And the ghostlike lovers who meet in the forest will never again consummate their love ("Each a ghost, and awe-stricken at the other ghost" [ch. 17]).

Unlike the optimistic Transcendentalists of Concord, Hawthorne realizes that one cannot escape the past: nothing new occurs in this "New" England utopian landscape. Hester has carried from England her free spirit and misguided ways: on trial in the first scaffold scene, she recalls her mother's "look of heedful and anxious love," which "had so often laid the impediment of a gentle remonstrance in her daughter's pathway" (ch. 2). Dimmesdale, though he "bring[s] all the learning of the age into our wild forest-land," carries with him the same cowardly demeanor and "nervous sensibility" that characterized his temperament in England, where he had already achieved some "high eminence" as a result of "eloquence and religious fervor" (ch. 3). And the deformed Chillingworth still retains the ruthless intellect and coldness that made him more at home in the libraries of Amsterdam than in the bedroom with his wife. He carries that intellect into the wilderness of New England, where he delights in discovering the secrets of potent medicinal herbs and where he uses his knowledge for ill purposes in the torture of his housemate, Dimmesdale. As Lawrence had articulated, "There was no change in belief, either in Hester or in Dimmesdale or in Hawthorne or in America" (98). The prejudices against Puritans in Anglican England turn into savagery against Indians, persecution of "witches," and intolerance of Quakers in Puritan New England. Not as optimistic as his fellow Concordians Thoreau and Emerson, and disappointed by his own failed utopian experience at Brook Farm (1841), Hawthorne realized that one cannot expunge one's national or personal past and begin anew in the Eden of one's imagination. The most damning indictment of the American experiment in democracy is Pearl's return to old Europe. With his Calvinist roots, Hawthorne also realized that sin and death were inevitable and inextricable: he presents the cemetery and prison as the first striking tableau at the threshold of the novel—and relieves us by offering us a wild rose-bush, or the rule of nature—which conveys a tacit offering of death, as he "pluck[s] one of its flowers" and "present[s] it to the reader" so that "some sweet moral blossom" may "relieve the darkening close of a tale of human frailty and sorrow" (ch. 1). Clearly, this is a death offering, which leads to the somber tombstone scene at the conclusion, where the light, "gloomier than the shadow," effaces any positive ending.

21

MOBY-DICK AND GLOBALIZATION

JOHN CARLOS ROWE

They were nearly all Islanders in the Pequod, *Isolatoes* too, I call such, not acknowledging the common continent of men, but each *Isolato* living on a separate continent of his own. Yet now, federated along one keel, what a set these Isolatoes were! An Anacharsis Clootz deputation from all the isles of the sea, and all the ends of the earth, accompanying Old Ahab in the Pequod to lay the world's grievances before that bar from which not very many of them ever come back.

—Herman Melville, *Moby-Dick; or, The Whale* (1851), ch. 27

Moby-Dick is widely recognized as the quintessential "American novel," despite its formal oddities and strong reliance on the devices of the romance. The critical judgment of the novel as characteristically American also seems odd, given *Moby-Dick*'s focus on the transnationalism of nineteenth-century commercial whaling. Of the novel's 135 chapters and its epilogue, 114 are set outside the geopolitical borders of the United States. The *Pequod*'s crew is drawn from the far corners of the earth, and the climactic, tragic action occurs northwest of New Guinea in the open waters of the Pacific. In its own time, *Moby-Dick* was neither a critical nor a commercial success, and it was certainly not greeted on publication in 1851 as the "great American novel."

Ishmael chooses to leave the United States, shipping out on a Nantucket whaler with a Polynesian harpooneer, Queequeg. Casting his lot unwittingly with the mad Captain Ahab, who intends to avenge himself on the whale who had torn away his leg in their last encounter, Ishmael is plunged into a strange world of Indian Parsee (Fedallah), Native American (Tashtego), African (Daggoo), and Polynesian (Queequeg), barely managed by Ahab's chief mate, Starbuck, second mate, Stubb, and third mate, Flask. Divided between obligations to the owners to fill the *Pequod*'s hold with whale oil and the mad pursuit of their captain for the white whale, the crew struggles to survive the many dangers of a two-year whaling voyage. Melville departs often from this wayward voyage, offering the reader an encyclopedic account of whales and maritime monsters in human history, as well as his own commentary on philosophy and religion. In the far reaches of the Pacific Ocean, Ahab finds Moby Dick, but in the three-day hunt the whale destroys the captain, two whaling boats, and the *Pequod* itself, drowning its crew and leaving Ishmael as the lone survivor to tell their tale.

In his introduction to the 1991 Vintage paperback of *Moby-Dick*, Edward Said first treats the novel in terms of its American exceptionalism, agreeing with Leon Howard, Newton Arvin, and Michael Paul Rogin that "the irreducibly American quality of [Melville's] life and work" distinguishes his reputation and confirms the scholarly cliché that *Moby-Dick* is "the greatest and most eccentric work of literary art produced in the United States" (2000, 358, 356). Having paid homage to the Americanists, Said stresses *Moby-Dick*'s "Euripidean" plot and "connections to Homer, Dante, Bunyan, Cervantes, Goethe, Smollett," proceeding to an extended comparison of Melville and Conrad (356, 358–359). Putting Melville in the comparative contexts of Europe and America, Said can then problematize the exceptionalist model of American literature by claiming: "I suppose it is true to say that only an American could have written *Moby-Dick*, if we mean by that only an author as prodigiously endowed as Melville was could also have been, as an American, so obsessed with the range of human possibility" (358). Said's rhetorical qualifications cause the reader to hesitate as well, so that the fiction of Melville's "Americanness" is effectively replaced by what Said concludes are the inherently transnational qualities of *Moby-Dick*: "The tremendous energies of this magnificent story of hunting the White Whale spill over national, aesthetic, and historical boundaries with massive force" (358).

The classic transnational interpretation of Melville's writings, especially *Moby-Dick*, is C. L. R. James's *Mariners, Renegades and Castaways: The Story of Herman Melville and the World We Live In* (1953). Writing eight years after the end of World War II, from a small detention cell on Ellis Island where he awaited deportation from the United States, James is rightly concerned with the rise of totalitarianism in the postwar United States. Captain Ahab exemplifies the fascist dictator whom James fears might be produced in the United States as a consequence of the internal contradictions of capitalism and democracy. For James, Ahab contrasts his command of the *Pequod* with the merchants who will profit without undertaking the voyage and its labor. But Ahab is no communist revolutionary; rather, he exemplifies a social character previously unrecognized and for that very reason even more dangerous as a phenotype of the fascist dictator:

> For generations people believed that the men opposed to rights of ownership, production for the market, domination of money, etc. were socialists, communists, radicals of some sort united by the fact that they all thought in terms of the reorganization of society by the workers, the great majority of the oppressed,

> the exploited, the disinherited. Some there were, of course, who believed that the experiment, if made, was bound to result in tyranny. Nobody, not a single soul, thought that in the managers, the superintendents, the executives, the administrators would arise such loathing and bitterness against the society of free enterprise, the market and democracy, that they would try to reorganize it to suit themselves and, if need be, destroy civilization in the process. . . . It is the unique and solitary greatness of Melville that he saw and understood the type to the last degree and the relation to it of all other social types. How he was able to do this a hundred years ago, we shall also show but the first point is to understand the totalitarian type itself. (James 2001, 9)

James's claim that *Moby-Dick* is centrally focused on the rise of totalitarianism in the figure of Ahab is by no means unique to Melville scholarship before or after 1953, but James's contention that such totalitarianism arises from within the ruling class of capitalism is original.

Melville's revival in the 1920s and 1930s was driven in part by communist and socialist interpretations of *Moby-Dick*, many of which focused on hints of a proletariat international in the "Anacharsis Clootz deputation" of the otherwise isolated men to whom Melville refers in the famous quotation that provides the epigraph for this chapter. Episodes such as Ishmael's night spent with Queequeg in the Spouter-Inn, Ishmael's fantasies of human brotherhood in the mutuality of workers in "Cutting In" and "A Squeeze of the Hand," and the negative example of the anarchy that breaks out on the *Town-Ho* when coordinated labor breaks down, have moved leftist scholars to interpret Melville's anticapitalism in terms of the proto-revolutionary brotherhood of labor composed primarily of working-class men responding to their oppression.

Yet in Melville's writings the instances of rebellion, whether successful or not, rarely demonstrate collective action. Although a contemporary of Karl Marx and Friedrich Engels, Melville does not hint at a proletariat awakened to class consciousness but instead offers primarily individuals like Ishmael who gradually acquire a complex self-consciousness through which to challenge authority.

Melville's reference to Anacharsis Clootz is generally understood as a comparison between Clootz's mad idealism and that of the cosmopolitan crew Melville assembles on the *Pequod*. Jean-Baptiste du Val-de-Grâce, Baron de Cloots was a Prussian nobleman whose financial and moral support of the French Revolution was inspired by his commitment to Enlightenment humanism. Baron de Cloots changed his given name to "Anacharsis" to identify with the eponymous hero of Jean-Jacques Barthélemy's novel, *The Travels of Anacharsis the Younger in Greece, During the Middle of the Fourth Century before the Christian Era* (1790–91), a book that powerfully influenced the Greek struggle for independence.

Anacharsis Cloots (spelled "Clootz" by Carlyle and Melville) modeled himself as an Enlightenment cosmopolitan who advocated universal rights and opposed monarchy and all organized religions. When the French Revolution broke out in 1789, Baron de Cloots traveled to Paris, where he hoped to establish his dream of a universal family of nations. On June 19, 1790, he appeared before the National Constituent Assembly with thirty-six foreigners, whom he had gathered from the streets of Paris, and declared himself head of a representative embassy of the "human race," which adhered to the Declaration of the Rights of Man and of the Citizen. In 1792, he donated a large sum to the new republic, assumed French citizenship, and declared his personal enmity to all organized religions. In September 1792, he was elected to the National Convention where he supported the execution of King Louis XVI in the name of the "human race."

In *The French Revolution* (1837), Thomas Carlyle mythologizes "Clootz" as spokesman for "the mute representatives of their tongue-tied, befettered, heavy-laden nations" (2002, bk. 8, ch. 10). Baron de Cloots's views are by no means unusual among Enlightenment philosophers, and his conception of a "federation of nations" anticipates by a few years Immanuel Kant's proposal in *Perpetual Peace: A Philosophical Sketch* (1795) of a global organization of constitutional republics that many modern commentators have considered a model for the League of Nations and more recently for the European Union. Carlyle's version of Clootz appears to be the most influential nineteenth-century legend, presenting Clootz as something of a foolish prophet, despite Carlyle's endorsement of his general principles.

Carlyle and Melville represent Anacharsis Cloots with some irony, because his enthusiastic endorsement of French revolutionary universalism ultimately met a tragic end. During the Reign of Terror, Maximilien Robespierre singled out not only Hébertist extremists but also falsely implicated Cloots in a purported "foreign conspiracy" supporting Robespierre's opposition. When he was guillotined on March 24, 1794, with the Hébertist leadership, Cloots became a martyr to his failed vision of transnational human rights and a scapegoat for "foreign" meddling in the new French republic.

But Anacharsis Cloots, especially as he was mythologized in the nineteenth century, represents a specific limitation to the eighteenth-century "representative man," who, in expressing his own views, thereby gave voice to the "mute," "multiform" humanity otherwise incapable of representing itself. The characteristic fear in nineteenth-century America was that without such leadership, the contrary desires of the great mass of men would turn into mob violence. Well-educated, usually independently wealthy (and thereby freed from undue influence), and cultivating the manners and bearing of high culture, the "representative man" from Alexander Pope to Ralph Waldo Emerson and Thomas Carlyle embodied civic virtues and exemplified classical liberalism. Yet Cloots's conflict with Robespierre, whose reputation as a tyrant dominates Victorian popular culture, suggests that advocacy of universal human rights was no match for a tyrant like Robespierre, who insisted on the subordination of human differences to his own will-to-power. In *Moby-Dick,* Melville allegorizes this problem of liberal individualism by pitting the Cloots-like Ishmael against an Ahab whose command of the *Pequod* compares favorably with Robespierre's French Reign of Terror.

Unlike Cloots, Ishmael survives alone, one of those "isolatoes" who must now internalize and represent in his own person or narrative the stories of the many culturally diverse whalers on board the *Pequod.* It is possible that Melville meant simply to distinguish between Ahab's Jacksonian, capitalist individualism and Ishmael's Transcendentalism, in which subjective individuality discovers its essential tie to all humanity. With the possible exception of Donald Pease, no scholar has seriously criticized Ishmael as the proper alternative to Ahab or even as an exemplary liberal individual. Melville was skeptical of the Transcendentalists' optimism, but his ironic versions of Transcendentalist ideas and values often identify him with the prevailing spirit of American Transcendentalism. Ishmael resembles the contradictory, metamorphic, and finally adaptable "self" of Emerson's *Nature* (1836) and Walt Whitman's *Song of Myself* (1855). Although little of Ishmael's personal history is given to the reader, Melville's few suggestive hints align him with Melville's own psychological profile and thus as the familiar authorial alter-ego of the nineteenth-century first-person narrative.

Nowhere is Ishmael's talent for skeptical identification more evident than in his relationship with Queequeg, arguably the most complexly represented non-European in the novel, if not in all of nineteenth-century US literature. From their first encounter in their shared bedroom at the Spouter-Inn to Ishmael's being "buoyed up . . . for almost one whole day and night" on the "soft and dirge-like main" by Queequeg's coffin, protected from the "unharming sharks" who "glid[e] by as if with padlocks on their mouths" (epil.), their relationship epitomizes that "Anacharsis Clootz deputation of all the isles of the sea" populating the *Pequod.* Learning from Queequeg not only the skills of harpooning and whaling in general but also moral lessons about human relations, Ishmael distances himself from Ahab's monomania in his friendship with Queequeg.

Yet Ishmael alone survives to tell the tale, despite Queequeg's greater experience as a whaler and knowledge of the world in general. Today it is commonplace to note how, in many popular narratives, a person of color is sacrificed for the salvation of his or her white friend. In the pattern of mythic heroism outlined by Joseph Campbell, the hero's helper, who often has magical powers, must somehow disappear for the hero to achieve his own apotheosis. It should not surprise us that in the modern West, defined as it has been by the "color-line," this mythic relationship is racialized. Melville understood the Hegelian master-servant paradigm for human self-consciousness and often represented it, as did his friend, Nathaniel Hawthorne, in terms of light and dark, frequently with explicit racial connotations. Ishmael gradually incorporates his dark other, Queequeg, in a process that culminates in the epilogue's explicit linkage of Queequeg's death—a death he himself prophetically anticipates—with Ishmael's survival by means of Queequeg's coffin and salvation by the cruising *Rachel.*

In the nineteenth-century liberal ideology of assimilation, Ishmael's incorporation of Queequeg might be understood as one of those "whitenings" of the dark, primitive other. From the colonial period to the late nineteenth century, pseudoscientists and ethnographers imagined that native and African Americans would literally "whiten" as they were assimilated into Euro-American society. Viewed from a perspective critical of Western imperialism, with its insatiable consumption of other people's labor and its systematic destruction of their cultures, Ishmael's internalization of his friend, Queequeg, appears cannibalistic, an ironic commentary on the common, usually imaginary, attribution of cannibalism to imperialism's victims.

For the Transcendentalists, "friendship" was a key concept, representing the foundational intersubjective relations through which different individuals ought to relate in broader social contexts. Emerson wrote two and Henry David Thoreau three essays on "Friendship." But their respective notions of philosophical friendship never encompassed a relationship between characters from radically disparate ethnic, cultural, or national backgrounds. In keeping with *Moby-Dick*'s consistently ironic treatment of Transcendentalist ideas, Melville uses the friendship between Queequeg and Ishmael to challenge the ethnocentric conception of Transcendentalist friendship. And yet Melville's irony also tends to expand and reinforce certain Transcendentalist notions, especially the crucial relationship between discrete individuals in the concept of "friendship."

Queequeg is introduced to us as a tattooed cannibal, as well as a primitive who trades "New Zealand" shrunken heads and worships a "Congo idol" (ch. 3). Smoking his tomahawk pipe in bed, shaving his face and spearing breakfast chops with his sharpened harpoon, he is a nineteenth-century caricature of the uncivilized Pacific Islander. Melville suggests that Queequeg's primitivism is a consequence of the ethnocentric prejudices of the Euro-Americans who attribute to him a wide range of premodern practices. Peter Coffin, the landlord, first reports Queequeg is selling "'balmed New Zealand heads" on the streets of New Bedford. Ishmael describes Queequeg's religious totem as a "Congo baby" and "idol" (ch. 3). Shortly after Ishmael has learned something of Queequeg's biography, he can dismiss "Peter Coffin's cock and bull stories about" Queequeg that "had previously so much alarmed [him] concerning the very person whom [he] now companied with" (ch. 13).

In *Whipscars and Tattoos: The Last of the Mohicans, Moby-Dick, and the Maori* (2011), Geoffrey Sanborn argues that Melville bases Queequeg on Maori models, drawing heavily on George Lillie Craik's *The New Zealanders* (1830), "a compendium of information about the Maori" (Sanborn 2011, 10). Sanborn's linking of Queequeg with Maori tattooing, anticolonialism, and spiritual *mana* suggests that Melville drew on Maori cultural backgrounds, but Melville himself plays with Queequeg's primitive identity, rendering ambiguous his precise origins in order to use him as a consumable figure of the "noble savage." In "Biographical," Ishmael tells us that "Queequeg was a native of Kokovoko, an island far away to the West and South.

It is not down in any map; true places never are" (ch. 12). Luther S. Mansfield and Howard P. Vincent speculate that "Kokovoko" sounds much like the "old capital of New Britain," which, before it was named "Rabaul, was Kokopo" (Mansfield and Vincent 1952, (624n.54.22)). William Dampier was the first western explorer to make landfall in 1700 on the island he named "Nova Britannia," the largest island of what is now the Bismarck Archipelago of Papua New Guinea. In "Wheelbarrow," Ishmael refers to the "people of his island of Rokovoko" (ch. 13), which Mansfield and Vincent conclude is an "inconsistency of Melville or the printer" (624n.54.22). It is likely that Melville intended to use this inconsistency to suggest Ishmael's unfamiliarity with Queequeg's hometown—yet another New Englander who finds in Queequeg the usual imperial fantasies of the Pacific Islander.

If Queequeg is from Kokopo, Papua New Guinea, then he is also a "New Englander" or at least a colonized resident of "New Britain," creating another bond with Ishmael, a direct descendant of New England colonists. If Queequeg's tribe does practice ritual cannibalism, then he is likely a member of the Tolai people, whose occasional cannibalism caused them problems with European missionaries well into the nineteenth century. Most populous in the region of Kokopo in East New Britain, the Tolai are best known for the secret society that revolved around the worship of the Duk-Duk, a totem in the shape of a leafy tree with a conical mask with large round eyes. But the Duk-Duk figure in no way resembles the "Congo idol" Ishmael describes Queequeg worshipping in their room at the Spouter Inn: "[A] curious little deformed image with a hunch on its back, and exactly the color of a three days' old Congo baby" (ch. 3).

The "Congo idol" identifies Queequeg with Africa and thus with the transatlantic slave trade. In "The Ship," Ishmael claims "Yojo" is "the name of his black little god" (ch. 16), prompting Mansfield and Vincent to speculate: "In the Koran and elsewhere the Mohammedan equivalents of Gog and Magog were Yâjooj and Majooj" (Mansfield and Vincent, 629n.67.5). If they are right, then Queequeg is also associated with Islam in the novel, although the term, "Yojo," if pronounced with a Spanish "h" for the "j," might also be a pun on the sailor's "yoho" or some play on the Spanish "Yo" ("I"). The tomahawk pipe he smokes identifies him with Native Americans but only after their contact with Europeans, because the tomahawk pipe was a European trade item. His "beaver hat" (ch. 3) associates him with the beaver trade conducted by Native Americans and frontiersmen in the Rockies and Northwest in the 1830s and 1840s. Although several tribes in Papua New Guinea and throughout Melanesia shrank the heads of their enemies in order to demonstrate their power over them, New Zealand Maoris did not practice such a ritual. Yet the popularity of "shrunken heads" in the West as tourist and collectors' items did produce a thriving trade in the commodity, inciting a substantial increase in the killing of victims for their heads. Such a practice may well have resulted in the specific market for shrunken heads in British New Zealand, with its several ports serving the global whaling industry. As a skilled harpooneer, Queequeg resembles those Maori, Hawaiians, Fijians, and Samoans who joined whaling ships and demonstrated special aptitudes for harpooning; Papuan New Guineans were not widely known to have been employed by whaling captains. Queequeg's tattoos are further evidence of his non-European origins, and Micronesians were known for their tattooing practices. Yet Melville certainly knew that Polynesian and Micronesian tattoos served very different social and religious purposes among the specific peoples employing them. It is also relevant to note the adoption of tattooing among seamen, which led to public fascination in the United States with the practice. In the 1840s and 1850s, James F. O'Connell was "the first tattooed man to exhibit himself in America" (Mifflin 2009, 164).

Sentimentalizing Queequeg's real origin by contending that "true places" never appear on maps (ch. 12), Melville creates a hybrid figure of the "noble savage," composed of African, African American, Middle Eastern, Native American, Papuan New Guinean, Maori, Hawaiian, Marquesan, Samoan, and Fijian qualities. Queequeg decides to leave his home, forcing his way on board a "Sag Harbor ship [that] visited his father's bay," "actuated by a profound desire to learn among the Christians, the arts whereby to make his people still happier than they were; and more than that, still better than they were" (ch. 12). Even before he meets Ishmael, then, Queequeg responds to the imperial mission of religious and moral enlightenment, although he becomes quickly disillusioned on his arrival in "old Sag Harbor" and "Nantucket," when he sees "what the sailors did there" and "how they spent their wages" (ch. 12). Fearing he has been corrupted while working as a whaler, Queequeg plans to return home to assume "the pure and undefiled throne of thirty pagan Kings before him," "as soon as he felt himself baptized again" (ch. 12).

Queequeg's pilgrimage to enlightenment parodies, of course, the ideology of Western imperialism, just as his disillusionment with Euro-American culture foreshadows its moral corruption and failure, rendering the allegory of Ahab's mad quest nearly unnecessary. Represented as one of those "multiform," "piebald" isolatoes accompanying Baron de Cloots to the National Assembly, Queequeg "speaks" for himself, albeit through Ishmael's narration, but very much in the manner of the colonial subaltern. Disillusioned by Western corruption and the propaganda of enlightenment, Queequeg nonetheless remains part of that political economy, honing his skills as an expert harpooneer and otherwise participating fully in a society in which he is distinctly racialized and thus marginalized. Like Olaudah Equiano, Queequeg is one of those colonial "hybrids," whose identity cannot be disconnected from Western imperialism.

Queequeg's composite identity, his *cosmopolitanism*, is not, however, his own but imposed upon him by the Westerners who find in him their own fantasies of the Pacific Islander, person of color, or uncivilized primitive. Queequeg is thus the central character in *Moby-Dick* to represent the consequences of nineteenth-century globalization, for better and for worse. Whereas other non-European characters can be discussed in terms of the stereotypes attributed to them by Ishmael, his shipmates, Ahab, or Melville, most of them are treated in terms of reductive, even tag-like identities. The three other harpooneers are: Fedallah, the "Parsee," identified almost exclusively with his Indian Zoroastrianism; Tashtego, the Gay-Head Native American (Wampanoag); and Daggoo, the tall, powerful African. Their names are nearly tag-names like those for the mates—Starbuck, Stubb, Flask—and the serving boys, Pip and Dough-boy. Only Queequeg carries with him the wide range of variant representations that render him a global cosmopolitan, despite his primitive origins.

Queequeg is the most subversive of the four subaltern harpooneers, threatening Western propriety by selling shrunken heads on the street, spurning Christianity and worshipping his "Congo idol," and responding to racial threats by drawing on his reputation as a primitive cannibal. To be sure, Queequeg will never individually overthrow the corrupt society he finds in the Christian West, and his tragic end as a subaltern is dictated from the beginning by his willing participation in the whaling industry and its imperial subtext. It is finally not Ahab who dooms Queequeg, however, but Ishmael, whose friendship lures Queequeg to the *Pequod* and thus to its tragic end in the middle of the Pacific.

Ishmael's motives in recruiting Queequeg are obvious enough. Although Ishmael has some experience in the merchant marine, he has none in whaling and fears he will not be accepted even as a common seaman. Accompanied by a skilled harpooneer, Ishmael is indeed taken on board the *Pequod*, even if his share of the voyage's profit is a fraction of Queequeg's. In addition, Queequeg acts as a big brother, protecting the more vulnerable Ishmael in the rough world of whaling, a security that stands Ishmael in good stead on several occasions during the voyage. Much as Ishmael insists that Queequeg is his "bosom friend" (ch. 10), the two could not be more different, suggesting either that Ishmael is deluded or that Melville uses their friendship to advocate an outlandish human universalism. In luring Queequeg on this particular voyage, Ishmael inadvertently quells Queequeg's subversive power. To be sure, Ishmael rationalizes his decision, claiming Queequeg's deference: "Yojo had told him two or three times over, and strongly insisted upon it everyway, that instead of our going together among the whaling-fleet in harbor, and in concert selecting our craft . . . that the selection of the ship should rest wholly with me" (ch. 16). Queequeg gives Ishmael a shrunken head as a token of their friendship, neutralizing its ghoulish aura. Joined by the other "pagan harpooneers" (ch. 96), Queequeg assumes the qualified authority of the subaltern—a skilled laborer whose colonial origins are never forgotten.

The new "baptism" Queequeg hopes will purify him of Western corruption and thus prepare him for his father's throne might well have been a revolution against Euro-American imperialism, but nothing of this sort of open rebellion surfaces among the non-Europeans on the voyage. The Quaker mate, Starbuck, is the only character to challenge Ahab's mad quest for the white whale, arguing not that Ahab is risking the lives of his crewmen but rather the owners' profits. "What will the owners say, sir?" is the substance of Starbuck's rebellion, prompting Ahab not only to insist upon his divine right to rule the ship but also to seize "a loaded musket from the rack" of his cabin and point it at Starbuck in recognition of incipient mutiny by his first mate (ch. 109). Given the unnecessary dangers faced by the crew in Ahab's quest of Moby Dick, it is remarkable that there is no concerted plan for mutiny. Indeed, only Ahab's rhetorical and psychological power over the crew allows him to keep their anger at bay.

The chapter immediately following "Ahab and Starbuck in the Cabin," in which Ahab violently quells Starbuck's challenge to his command, is "Queequeg in His Coffin," in which Queequeg's fever prompts him to ask the ship's carpenter to make him a burial "canoe" (ch. 110). When he suddenly recovers, Queequeg claims that he has "chosen" to live, much as he had earlier chosen to die, startling the crewmen with what appears another primitive superstition. But Queequeg's anticipation of his own death may suggest a symbolic recognition that his subaltern status has now become a version of what Orlando Patterson interprets as the "social death" of slavery (1982, 9–11). Anticipating as it does the climactic confrontation between Ahab and Moby Dick, Queequeg's decision to commission his own coffin marks the moment in which the revolutionary potential of exploited colonial people is sublimated by the dominant culture, in this case into the violence of the whale hunt. Suddenly recovering his health, Queequeg turns the coffin/canoe into his "sea-chest," carving the lid with "all manner of grotesque figures and drawings," which Ishmael compares to Queequeg's tattooed body (ch. 110). In New Bedford and Nantucket, the tattooed body of Queequeg poses a visible threat to Euro-American culture, but as we approach the climax of the novel's dramatic action, Queequeg's "mysteries" are those that "not even himself could read" (ch. 110). Thanks both to the totalitarian rule of Captain Ahab and to the friendship of Ishmael, Queequeg has been quelled, another "savage" turned to and consumed by the mad purposes of Western imperialism.

C. L. R. James concludes that Ahab's metaphysical rage actually expresses the internal contradictions of the capitalist-imperialist system of modern Western societies, explaining the rise of totalitarianism and predicting the eventual collapse of such a system. Yet what James misses is how dependent totalitarian rule is on the complicity of the colonized subaltern—Queequeg—and the working class—Ishmael. *Moby-Dick* addresses how exploited peoples delude each other in ways that collectively serve the rise of totalitarian power. The "white man's burden" we identify with Western imperialism is usually associated with the rulers, even though that "burden" was borne primarily by the soldiers, civil servants, and workers at home and abroad who variously demonized or patronized the colonized "savage."

How aware was Melville of this dilemma in his representation of class, social, and transnational relations in *Moby-Dick*? Does he intend us to understand the "friendship" between Queequeg and Ishmael as an insidious conspiracy of the imperial imaginary that would use the good-hearted and intelligent Ishmael to defuse the otherwise threatening rebel, Queequeg? I doubt Melville had anything like these conclusions in mind when he created the characters of Queequeg and Ishmael. Instead, he was puzzling over the fate of the liberal subject as Western imperialism brought such individuals into ever closer and sustained social, economic, and political relations with peoples and cultures in which "individualism" did not have its conventional Euro-American meanings. Melville had explored this philosophical conundrum in previous works, notably *Typee: A Peep at Polynesian Life* (1846), *Omoo: A Narrative of Adventures in the South Seas* (1847), and *Mardi: And a Voyage Thither* (1849), entertaining the idea that subjectivity was either an innate universal, a property of all human cognition, or that the "individual" was an invention of very specific Western social, economic, and political conditions.

In the twentieth century, the "American Century," *Moby-Dick* was invented as a canonical "American novel" and an exploration of American individualism, both its promise and its dangers. Ishmael's negative capability was understood as an antidote to the overreaching monomania of Ahab, and the drama enacted on the high seas allegorized the social and political situation at home in the United States. Scholars usually credit Raymond Weaver with the twentieth-century "Melville revival," both for his *Herman Melville: Man, Mariner and Mystic* (1921) and his publication of the unfinished *Billy Budd* manuscript in 1924. Both the subtitle of Weaver's biography and the tragic sacrifice of Billy Budd conformed to cultural ideals of liberal individualism, exemplified, for scholars like Carl Van Doren in *The American Novel* (1921) and D. H. Lawrence in *Studies in Classic American Literature* (1923), by Melville and his characters.

But F. O. Matthiessen consolidated the most enduring "myth" of Melville in *American Renaissance: Art and Expression in the Age of Emerson and Whitman* (1941). Melville is not named in the title, but he is pivotal, as is *Moby-Dick*, because Ishmael "symbolizes" the liberal individualism theorized by Emerson, lived by Thoreau, and canonized in Whitman's poetic Ego. Matthiessen's interpretation of romantic subjectivity was quickly transformed into a central symbol of the US nation.

In the 1950s and 1960s, scores of books and articles were published on *Moby-Dick* in which the ambiguous meanings of the whale and Ahab's Spanish doubloon emerged as secular versions of Puritan religious orthodoxy transformed into the "civil religion." The diverse interpretations of the whale, the doubloon, or the larger purposes of Ahab's quest put the crew of the *Pequod* (and tacitly the novel's readers) into social relations with each other and thus established a "commonweal." Charles Feidelson, Jr.'s *Symbolism and American Literature* (1953) exemplifies that odd chemistry in which formalist aesthetics combined with Cold War politics by bolstering the attenuated American self.

By the end of the 1980s, the Myth-and-Symbol school's reliance on liberal individualism as the central American myth had been challenged in countless new historicist, deconstructive, feminist, neo-Marxist, and queer reconsiderations of US literary culture. Wai Chee Dimock's *Empire for Liberty: Melville and the*

Poetics of Individualism (1989) makes one of the most powerful cases for considering Melville's writings as part of US imperialism and its reliance on liberal individualism. But scholarship does not often change popular attitudes, and the continuing success of Melville's work in the twenty-first century undoubtedly has much to do with the persistent myth of the self-reliant man exemplified in Ishmael.

Writing in the mid-nineteenth century, when Native Americans and African Americans were barred from US citizenship and women lacked basic human rights, Melville was working out problems of a social contract modeled on white liberal male identity. For most of the past century, his works have been interpreted positively and negatively in terms of liberal individualism, self-reliance, and ingenuity. The quest for the white whale was thus rarely understood as an imperialist project but rather as an allegory of American democracy in which the foreign peoples and settings should be read in terms of their US referents.

Would it be possible, in a future of transnational social relations foreseen by Melville (and in fact experienced by him at sea), for individualism to become the basis for a genuine "Anacharsis Clootz deputation," a new global order of social and human relations? Or was liberal individualism a fantasy produced from within the Western ideology that would cause Robespierre to suppress it by executing Baron de Cloots as a "foreign conspirator," a threat to his rule? Melville was sufficiently influenced by international romanticism—Kant and G. W. F. Hegel, in particular—and by his Transcendentalist neighbors to have hoped for the transnational utopia of a cosmopolitan individualism, sensitive to human differences and yet bound by common cognitive and affective faculties. Ironizing the Transcendentalist notion of "friendship" by representing it in the relation of Queequeg and Ishmael, he also tried to broaden it to encompass the radical strangeness of new global encounters. Although he overlaps historically with Marx, Melville was a liberal, not a socialist or proto-communist thinker. For Melville, the discrete, self-reliant, fundamentally isolated individual remains the locus of human agency and the paradoxical basis for social organization.

Ishmael is "saved" by "the devious-cruising Rachel, that in her retracing search after her missing children, only found another orphan" (epil.). Thousands of miles from home, in the open Pacific, buoyed by a Papuan New Guinean's coffin, Ishmael is saved by another New England whaling ship, *Rachel*, whose captain, Gardiner, has appealed desperately to the obdurate Ahab to help him look for his twelve-year-old son, lost in a missing whaleboat. The vast, remote Pacific becomes a modern Garden of Eden, where the Fall is reenacted in Ahab's refusal and Gardiner's loss of his son, but Ishmael's salvation turns the *Rachel*'s story as well as the *Pequod*'s into a fortunate fall. When Queequeg goes down with the ship, he is far closer to home than Ishmael, perhaps no more than 800 nautical miles from Kokopo, his home town on New Britain. Queequeg is not as fortunate as Ishmael, who is "saved" by the vast US maritime traffic in the otherwise desolate reaches of the Pacific. Queequeg, son of a king, cannot hope to be more than a "friend," never a "son" or "child" to the Westerners for whom he merely works. Buoyed by Queequeg's social death, Ishmael may return as a Biblical prodigal, celebrated on his return not only for what he has seen but also for what he has stolen.

Today the whaling stations across the Pacific have been replaced with military bases, and the Pacific islands Melville rendered in such fascinating, exotic terms are now populated with the US military, often in situations vigorously contested by indigenous populations. Ishmaels are everywhere across the Pacific, happily befriending the locals in the interests of US state security while offering them the promise of the "American Dream." In fact, the real lives of these US military personnel may differ little from the drunkenness, violence, and debauchery Queequeg condemned in Old Sag Harbor and Nantucket, but the bright promise of "individual freedom" and "universal human rights" still justifies our continuing military installations where they are no longer welcome (Rowe 2011, 15–20).

The liberal imagination from Emerson and Melville to Philip Roth has run its course as an equitable means of imagining social, economic, and political relations on this populous and complex planet. Born in the European Enlightenment, shaping and shaped by emergent European nationalisms, their imperialist projects, and their Creole counterparts in far-flung empires, liberal individualism cannot be universalized. Historically, economically, and geopolitically specific, it is now an archaic concept we should dispense with as we look toward postnational, "planetary," postcolonial, and other global forms of human socialization and governance. My conclusion does not mean that individuals will be inevitably woven into an indistinguishable "mass" or that human agency no longer matters, merely that the philosophical and psychological forms of subjectivity developed in Western modernity have limited applicability to the real conditions of globalization.

22

HARRIET BEECHER STOWE'S *UNCLE TOM'S CABIN*

DAVID S. REYNOLDS

Harriet Beecher Stowe's antislavery bestseller *Uncle Tom's Cabin; or, Life Among the Lowly* (1852) is one of the most influential books ever written by an American. As Henry James noted in his autobiographical *A Small Boy and Others*, Stowe's novel "had above all the extraordinary fortune of finding itself, for an immense number of people, much less a book than a state of vision, of feeling and of consciousness, in which they didn't sit and read and appraise and pass the time, but walked and talked and laughed and cried" (1913, 159).

James was right. The unprecedented popularity of *Uncle Tom's Cabin* came above all from its powerful appeal to the emotions. Sympathetic readers were thrilled when the fugitive slave Eliza Harris carried her child across the ice floes of the Ohio River and when her husband George fought off slave catchers in a rocky pass. They cried over the death of the angelic little Eva and the fatal lashing of the good Uncle Tom. They guffawed at the impish slave girl Topsy and shed thankful tears when she embraced Christianity. They loved to hate the selfish hypochondriac Marie St. Clare and the cruel slave owner Simon Legree. They were fascinated by the brooding, Byronic Augustine St. Clare. They were shocked by the stories of sexual exploitation surrounding enslaved women like Prue and Cassy.

Stowe's novel contained two main plots: a northern one, featuring escape from persecution (Eliza Harris) and active rebellion (George Harris), and a southern one, emphasizing tragic victimization (Uncle Tom, Cassy, and other slaves). The northern narrative traces the Harrises' flight to Canada with their child, Harry, aided by antislavery whites. The southern one follows the gentle, stoical Uncle Tom, who is torn from his family and sold to owners in the Deep South. Tom bonds with the kindly plantation owner Augustine St. Clare and his daughter, Eva, but after their deaths he is sold to cruel slave owner Simon Legree, who perversely hates the Christian Tom and commands his enslaved black overseers, Sambo and Quimbo, to whip him savagely. Tom's death becomes a symbol of Christlike sacrifice that is especially resonant because Stowe makes it clear that he will be meeting Eva and St. Clare in heaven.

These powerful plots proved irresistibly compelling to nineteenth-century readers. *Uncle Tom's Cabin* set sales records for American fiction. It gained many readers when it appeared in forty weekly installments in the Washington newspaper the *National Era* from June 1851 to April 1852. The novel created a sensation when the Boston publisher John P. Jewett published it as a book on March 18, 1852. It "has excited more attention than any book since the invention of printing," remarked the minister Theodore Parker Parker (1853, 1). Within a year, over two million copies had been sold internationally—310,000 in America and the remainder abroad. Within eight years, six million copies had been sold worldwide. Within a decade of its publication, *Uncle Tom's Cabin* had been translated into sixteen languages, a number that reached forty-two by the late nineteenth century. The book continued to enjoy strong sales. On May 24, 1903, the *New York Times* announced, "Next to the Bible, 'Uncle Tom's Cabin' is the book most read in our country to-day" (Connery 1903, 26).

The novel's broad appeal is explained largely by the fact that it absorbed images from virtually every aspect of culture and made them vehicles for a deeply human drama that articulated a crystal-clear social point: slavery was evil, and so were the political and economic institutions that supported it.

Born in Litchfield, Connecticut, in 1811, Harriet Beecher Stowe came from a prominent religious family that did more to undermine residual Puritan orthodoxy than any other in America. Her father, the prominent clergyman Lyman Beecher, preached a modified version of Calvinism in which human agency played an important role in salvation, a view that stood opposed to the predestinarian view of Jonathan Edwards, who had declared that God had foredoomed most people to hell. Orthodoxy was further challenged in the religion promoted by several of Lyman Beecher's offspring—notably Henry Ward Beecher, who became the nineteenth century's leading minister by preaching a gospel of love and good works, as well as several of Henry's clergyman brothers and his sister, the educator Catharine Beecher, who wrote anti-Calvinist tracts.

No one in the family had a greater influence on popular religious attitudes, however, than Harriet Beecher Stowe. While growing up, Harriet felt uneasy with the sternness and rigidity of orthodox Calvinism, and early she developed a notion that God was not cold and severe but intimate and loving. She experienced two religious conversions—one in 1825, when she was thirteen, and another two decades later, when she was a housewife and mother in Cincinnati—that gave her a sense of the closeness of the divine world. She once said that the source of *Uncle Tom's Cabin* was a vision she had in a Brunswick, Maine, church of an enslaved black man being whipped to death by the overseers of a brutal slave owner—a scene that became the climax of her novel and also impelled Stowe to write the long narrative leading up to this horrific moment. She said, "It all came before me in visions, one after another, and I put them down in words" (qtd. in Gossett 1985, 96).

Countless nineteenth-century readers were swayed by *Uncle Tom's Cabin*'s religious message. Not only did the novel spur the sale of Bibles throughout the world, but it was widely seen as a new Bible. It was the ideal expression of religion for the era. It offered a religion of love to all who truly believed—blacks and whites, the enslaved and the free, the poor and the rich, children as well as adults. It sped the decline of the old-time, grim Puritan view of God and the afterlife.

In the novel, Stowe took the unusual step of making a child and her enslaved black friend the centers of religious authority. Tom and Eva are Christlike figures whose deaths inspire others to become pious. The quintessential sinless child, Eva has "an undulating and aërial grace, such as one might dream of for some mythic and allegorical being" (ch. 14). When extending love to Topsy, she looks like "the picture of some bright angel stooping to reclaim a sinner" (ch. 25). She bonds with Tom through visionary ecstasy. As she reads the Bible with him at sunset near Lake Pontchartrain, she gazes into the distance and says that she sees the New Jerusalem. When Tom sings a Methodist hymn about "spirits bright . . . robed in spotless white," she tells him she has seen such spirits in dreams (ch. 22). Tom believes her. As she nears death, she talks about her forthcoming reunion with her loving Maker and assures Tom and others that she will meet them in heaven. Tom faithfully watches over her to the end, explaining that he wants to be present when Eva dies, for "when that ar blessed child goes into the kingdom, they'll open the door so wide, we'll all get a look in at the glory" (ch. 26). He indeed witnesses her joyful final moments, when she smiles and murmurs, "O! love,—joy,—peace" (ch. 26). After Eva dies, her aunt, Ophelia, tells Topsy, "Miss Eva is gone to heaven; she is an angel" (ch. 27).

Describing Eva gave Stowe the chance to indulge in the aestheticism she thought New England Protestantism lacked. Eva is surrounded by Catholic images. Tom looks at her "as the Italian sailor gazes on his image of the child Jesus" (ch. 22). Religious icons populate Eva's room. Over her bed is "a beautiful sculptured angel . . . with drooping wings, holding out a crown of myrtle leaves." On her fireplace mantel stands "a beautifully wrought statuette of Jesus receiving little children," flanked by vases filled with flowers (ch. 26). The novel also features a number of emblems—the coin given to Tom by the young George Shelby, Eva's widely distributed locks of hair, and the hair strand Legree receives from his pious mother as a keepsake—that prove to have religious significance, almost like Catholic rosary beads or icons.

Still, Stowe thought the Catholic Church stifled independent thought by putting priestly intermediaries between the individual and the Bible. *Uncle Tom's Cabin* transfers religious authority from churches and theology to an enslaved black man and a little girl. Tom is considered "a sort of patriarch in religious matters, in the neighborhood" and is "looked up to with great respect, as a sort of minister among them" (ch. 4).

Tom brings about the conversions of the bitter slave concubine Cassy and the brutish Sambo and Quimbo. Augustine St. Clare, a jaded agnostic who dismisses churches because of their hypocrisy, is won over to Christianity by Eva's unwavering faith. Topsy, so degraded by slavery that she mocks religion and flaunts her wickedness, eventually embraces religion when she receives love from Eva, who tells her that Jesus loves her too. Formerly wild, Topsy becomes a devout Christian who later serves as a missionary in Africa.

Besides featuring humble lay preachers, the novel brings the Bible to earth, making it accessible and relevant to contemporary life. Stowe imagines North America as a Biblical landscape that reflects the geography of slavery. Canada represents Canaan or heaven, the deep South Sodom or hell, and the Ohio River the Jordan River across which slaves flee. Stowe perceived that for enslaved blacks, Biblical images expressed yearnings for freedom.

Stowe's religious ideas dovetailed with her views on race. She was influenced by ethnologists such as Alexander Kinmont and Francis Lieber. Kinmont held that Caucasians tended to be aggressive, intellectual, scientific, and ambitious, as opposed to blacks, who were spiritual, imaginative, nonintellectual, and childlike. This romantic racialism assigned black people to what today seems like an inferior position but what in that era could be associated with Christian virtue. "The sweeter graces of the Christian religion," Kinmont wrote in *Twelve Lectures on the Natural History of Man* (1839), "appear almost too tropical, and tender plants, to grow in the soil of the Caucasian mind," whereas they "grow naturally and beautifully" among blacks (218). Kinmont prophesied a glorious epoch when blacks would establish a new Christian civilization in Africa that would "return the splendor of the divine attributes of mercy and benevolence in the practice and exhibition of all the milder and gentler virtues" (191).

For Stowe, too, black people had special religious gifts. She has St. Clare tell Ophelia that "the negro is naturally more impressible to religious sentiment than the white" (ch. 19). Her respect for childlike simplicity and humility in religious matters comes through in her comment that no race embraces Christianity "with such eager docility as the African," because "reliance and unquestioning faith . . . is more a native element in this race than any other" (ch. 38). Her longing for aestheticism was also answered by the exoticism and taste for beauty she connected with blacks.

Although Stowe absorbed some of the racial attitudes of her era—visible in passages about Anglo-Saxon intellectual superiority and about colonizing blacks abroad after educating and Christianizing them—her views were actually more progressive than those of many prominent Americans. By making marital fidelity between blacks the driving force of her novel's two main plots (the Harrises' escape to Canada and the tragic separation of Tom from his family), she challenged the then-prevalent view of blacks as subhuman beings indifferent to home and family. Thomas Jefferson had argued that black men were oversexed brutes who didn't mind being taken from their families because "love seems with them to be more an eager desire, than a tender delicate mixture of sentiment and sensation. Their griefs are transient" (qtd. in Finkelman 2003, 51). Another southerner, Louisa McCord, claimed that the typical enslaved man had no scruples about taking a new wife on each plantation, since "the negro, in fact, is proverbially a Lothario. He is seldom faithful to his vows. He loves to rove" (McCord 1853, 251). In the North, most whites had little sympathy either for the free blacks in their midst or for enslaved blacks in the South. Even an abolitionist like Theodore Parker could declare, "Lust is [black men's] strongest passion: and hence, rape is an offence of too frequent occurrence. Fidelity to the marriage relation they do not understand and do not expect, neither in their native country nor in a state of bondage" (qtd. in Finkelman 2003, 154). Abraham Lincoln, whose devotion to the cause of establishing a colony of free African Americans in Liberia was far deeper than Stowe's, declared, "I am not nor ever have been in favor of bringing about in any way, the social and political equality of the black and white races," because, he said, there was "a physical difference" between them that would forever prevent them from living equally in America (Holzer 2004, 189). Lincoln often used the then-common word "nigger," as did Walt Whitman, who, with all his devotion to democracy, once said, "The nigger, like the Injun, will be eliminated: it is the law of races. . . . [A] superior grade of rats comes and then all the minor rats are cleared out" (Traubel 1961, 2:283)—a mournfully ironic echo of nineteenth-century ethnographic theories that lay behind racial genocide.

Stowe did not accept such views. Instead, she directed her era's belief in racial difference toward what was then a radical idea: blacks had the ability to equal or even outshine whites in what counted most—true religion, domestic affection, and richly human expressiveness.

Religion in *Uncle Tom's Cabin* is emotional and simple but not mawkish or yielding. Critics who see Tom and Eva as symbols of a feeble faith reflecting a "feminized" mainstream Protestant liberalism neglect evidence to the contrary. Many nineteenth-century liberal Protestants emphasized not only feeling but grit. They believed that their own religion bred sturdiness, in contrast to orthodox Calvinism and Catholicism, which they saw as repressive systems that thwarted human effort and created languor and listlessness.

Stowe brought such ideas alive in a gallery of Christian characters who combine feeling with extraordinary strength. She arranged her narrative so that many of her Christian characters learn to mingle gentleness and toughness. The initially timorous Eliza learns to be brave during her daring escape north, while her hard, bitter husband George becomes milder when he settles in Canada with her and forms a Christian home. The Ohioans who help the Harrises escape—the motherly Mary Bird and the Quakers Ruth Stedman and Rachel and Simeon Halliday—are initially placid characters who toughen when they actively resist the Fugitive Slave Law. Several other characters—St. Clare, Topsy, Sambo, and Quimbo—at first are callously indifferent to religion but are humanized when they accept Christianity. Aunt Ophelia begins as a rigidly orthodox Christian who softens when she witnesses Topsy's conversion.

As for Eva, her illness and death show that optimistic, visionary faith can breed strength. Her death is affecting not because she is weak and lachrymose but because she is strong and confident. She remains cheerfully positive in spite of her debility. "I am not nervous,—I am not low-spirited," she assures her father. "I want to go,—I long to go!" (ch. 24).

Uncle Tom, whose name has become a byword for submissiveness, actually is not weak. True, he has the "impressible nature of his kindly race, ever yearning toward the simple and childlike" (ch. 14). This makes him the ideal Christian for Stowe, who put childlike innocence at the heart of religion. At the same time, he is self-reliant and strong. He is introduced as "a large, broad-chested, powerfully-made man," with "an expression of grave and steady good sense" and a "self-respecting and dignified" air (ch. 4). Often seen as sheepishly obsequious, he, in fact, has unusual strength because of his religious faith. He heroically saves Eva from drowning when she falls off the riverboat, and he remains tough in the face of Legree's atheistic taunts and sadistic cruelty. He could escape torture by telling Legree where Cassy and Emmeline are hiding, but he boldly refuses to do so, just as he had earlier refused to flee with Eliza because to do so would put Shelby's other slaves in jeopardy of being sold. We are told that Tom "felt strong in God to meet death, rather than betray the helpless." Legree regards Tom as a brash troublemaker who is despicable precisely because he is resilient: "Had not this man braved him,—steadily, powerfully, resistlessly,—ever since he bought him?" Through all, we are told, Tom's "brave, true heart was firm on the Eternal Rock" (ch. 40).

Besides religion, *Uncle Tom's Cabin* weaves into its antislavery argument images from temperance reform, domestic fiction, sensational novels, and minstrel shows. Before composing her antislavery epic, Stowe had written a number of stories promoting temperance. In *Uncle Tom's Cabin*, she advances this cause in scenes where evil schemes are hatched in an atmosphere of drinking. In the conversation that leads to the sale of Uncle Tom and little Harry, Arthur Shelby and the slave trader Dan Haley drink wine—an ominous sign for readers familiar with temperance writings. Later on, when Haley meets Loker and Marks in a tavern to plot the capture of the fleeing Eliza, the three are drinking heavily.

The temperance theme takes on an even darker tone when Augustine St. Clare is killed trying to break up a brawl between drunken men in a café. The enslaved woman Prue, after years of sexual exploitation, becomes a wretched alcoholic. The nefarious Simon Legree is surrounded by dark temperance imagery. His mother tried to guide him toward clean living, but he had rejected her: "He drank and swore,—was wilder and more brutal than ever" (ch. 35). Before she dies, she sends him an envelope containing a lock of her hair. He opens the envelope while "carousing among drunken companions" and burns the hair, after which he tries "to drink, and revel, and swear away the memory" of her, which proves impossible, for her ghost haunts him (ch. 35). Legree heads on a downward spiral that eventually produces murderous cruelty. Shortly before torturing Tom, Legree plies his lackeys Sambo and Quimbo with liquor and carouses with them.

The virtuous characters in the novel, in contrast, have no interest in alcohol. The northern people who help the fugitive slaves are portrayed as upright folk whose strongest drink is tea. The novel's main voice for temperance is Tom. When St. Clare warns Tom not to drink too often, Tom replies emphatically, "I never drink" (ch. 14). Marie St. Clare says of Tom, "I know he'll get drunk," but her husband assures her that Tom is "a pious and sober article" (ch. 15). Not only does Tom avoid liquor, but he convinces St. Clare to take a temperance pledge. Stowe thus created a black hero who brings about the regeneration of a dissipated white man.

Besides temperance, *Uncle Tom's Cabin* also drew images from contrasting kinds of popular literature: the sentimental-domestic novel and sensational fiction. Some of the longest reviews of *Uncle Tom's Cabin* argued that it was written by a radical reformer who had abandoned the domestic sphere and made a shocking entrance into the political arena. "Mrs. Stowe," wrote a reviewer for the *Southern Literary Messenger*, "belongs to the school of Woman's Rights," "one which would place woman on a foot of political equality with men, and causing her to look beyond the office for which she was created—the high and holy office of maternity" (Oct. 1852, 631). In June 1853, the same journal charged that Stowe "throws an ultra Christian hue over all her writing," but in fact reveled in "scenes of license and impurity, and ideas of loathsome depravity and habitual prostitution" (Holmes 1853, 328, 322). She owed her popularity to "the fashionable favour extended to the licentious novels of the French School, and the woman's rights' Conventions, which have rendered the late years infamous, have unsexed in great measure the female mind, and shattered the temple of feminine delicacy and moral graces" (Holmes 1853, 323).

Actually, Stowe supported many of the goals of women's rights but tried to present them in a way that accorded with middle-class values. *Uncle Tom's Cabin* packaged daring ideas about women in conventional wrapping. Like sentimental-domestic fiction, it is full of female moral exemplars devoted to home and religion. Family togetherness is the novel's most exalted value. Families shattered or disrupted by slavery are presented as tragic, while families that remain intact are idealized.

Within this conventional framework, Stowe assigns an unusually strong role to women. Domesticity, anchored in ethical instincts, challenges male-inflicted injustice. In the novel, several white and black women, along with the pious Uncle Tom (whom some describe as feminized), possess conscience and humanity in contrast to the amoral social institutions controlled by white males. Some women characters exercise real power over men and significantly influence events. Mrs. Shelby, though married to a slaveholder, is instinctively an abolitionist who defies him by facilitating Eliza Harris's flight from slavery. Mary Bird, whose senator husband supports the Fugitive Slave Law, induces him to adopt a new kind of politics by arousing his sympathy for the runaway Eliza. Cassy wields an uncanny power over Legree and eventually outwits him by saving the innocent Emmeline from him. Even little Eva, despite her physical frailty, holds great influence in the novel, since she provides an example of interracial togetherness and Christian faith that other characters espouse after her death.

In *Uncle Tom's Cabin*, Stowe mixes the values of piety and domesticity with the frank treatment of illicit sex, characteristic of sensational fiction. Many of the enslaved women in the novel are associated with the southern sex trade. The light-skinned Eliza Harris is ogled by Dan Haley, who calls her "a fine female article" and tells Shelby, "You might make your fortune on that ar gal in Orleans, any day. I've seen over a thousand, in my day, paid down for gals not a bit handsomer" (ch. 1). Haley later makes a deal with Loker and Marks that if they help him catch Eliza and Harry, he will take the boy and they can sell Eliza as a sex slave. Eliza avoids this fate, but George Harris's sister Emily does not. George, whose mother had been a slave breeder, reports gloomily of his sister, "I saw her chained with a trader's gang, to be sent to market in Orleans,—sent there for nothing else but that" (ch. 11). Prue, the pathetic drunkard and petty thief, is a used-up breeding machine. Emmeline, the fifteen-year-old quadroon girl sold at auction, is evidently headed for sexual slavery—her mother Susan realizes that "any man, however vile and brutal . . . may become owner of her daughter, body and soul" (ch. 30). Legree buys Emmeline with the apparent aim of taking advantage of her, though Cassy foils his design by protecting the girl. Cassy herself has an awful history of sexual exploitation. She has been passed between several men and is now the kept woman of the malevolent Legree.

In describing these women, Stowe sometimes uses a version of the voyeur style of sensational writing. Eliza, who has "a delicately formed hand and a trim foot and ankle," wears a "dress of the neatest possible fit" that "set off to advantage her finely moulded shape" (ch. 1). Emmeline has soft, dark eyes with long lashes; her mother asks her to comb back her beautiful curls so that she will not tempt lustful buyers—a plan that backfires when the auctioneer demands the curls, explaining that they "may make a hundred dollars difference in the sale of her" (ch. 30). But the erotic atmosphere of *Uncle Tom's Cabin* is light years distant from that era's most sensational literature. Women's charms are described with relative restraint and from a different vantage point than in sensational fiction. The male gaze is still there, but the men who gaze are proslavery types the reader loathes. The venal Haley, the money-grubbing slave auctioneer, Cassy's deceitful lovers, the brutal Legree—these are the ones who size up women's bodies for purposes of profit or pleasure. Illicit sex acts are always distanced by time or space. They occur in a threatened future (Eliza, Emmeline), in the past (Prue), or offstage (Cassy).

The enslaved women themselves are, in spirit, close to the chaste moral exemplars of sentimental-domestic bestsellers such as Susan Warner's *The Wide, Wide World* (1850) or Maria Cummins's *The Lamplighter* (1854). Eliza is a devoted wife and mother with a deep religious faith. Emily Harris had been "a pious, good girl,—a member of the Baptist church" before being sold in the Deep South, and at the end she reappears as the good Madame de Thoux (ch. 11). Susan and Emmeline are a loving, Christian mother-daughter pair. Cassy had once attended a convent school, and, after hellish experiences with slave owners, she regains a family on discovering that Eliza is her long-lost daughter.

Stowe's restrained treatment of eroticism, so different from sensational pulp fiction, was commended by a correspondent to the *New York Times* who argued that Stowe's novel did not "rank with that large class of fictitious works which pander to the lowest and worst passions of the heart; works which make vice attractive, decry virtuous principles, [and] inculcate the most pernicious moral lessons." Far from contributing to "the swarming issues of a filth-seeking press," Stowe dealt with controversial topics in a manner that was "decorous" and "widely wholesome" (Apr. 25, 1853, 2).

If Stowe transformed the treatment of sexual themes, she also deepened images from one of the era's most popular entertainment forms: minstrel shows. The first black character who appears in the novel, the young slave boy Harry, is surrounded by minstrel images. Harry's master, Shelby, greets him with "Hulloa, Jim Crow! . . . Come here, Jim Crow," and orders him to perform for the slave trader Haley (ch. 1). Harry sings a "wild, grotesque" song and makes "many comic evolutions of the hands, feet, and whole body." Haley is so pleased that he offers to buy the boy.

Behind the apparent fun of this minstrel episode are pathos and imminent tragedy. The minstrel performer here is not a white man in blackface but an enslaved child whose innocence makes his prospect of being sold truly alarming. His antics delight white spectators, as on the minstrel stage, but they are the prelude to a threatened separation of Harry from his mother Eliza, a hidden witness to the scene. Our sympathies flow spontaneously to Eliza as she prepares to save her son, and they blossom into cheering support as she uses wile and courage to elude pursuers and carry him toward freedom.

Minstrel techniques also appear in the scenes involving another Shelby slave, Black Sam. Like minstrel actors, Sam is comic and parodic. He spouts malapropisms, and he loves to "speechify" in nonsensical, inflated language. We laugh at him, but we also sympathize with him, since he acts cleverly to ensure that Eliza and Harry escape. The episode involving Sam's collaboration with Andy and with Mrs. Shelby to frustrate Haley's efforts to capture Eliza shows that outwardly conventional figures could function subversively. Sam and Andy, who seem like laughable minstrel "darkeys," team up with Mrs. Shelby to help Eliza violate the Fugitive Slave Law, thus undermining the authority of the white males who are trying to enforce the law.

Stowe also improves upon minstrelsy in her memorable portrait of the enslaved girl Topsy, with "her talent for every species of drollery, grimace, and mimicry,—for dancing, tumbling, climbing, singing, whistling, imitating every sound that hit her fancy" (ch. 20). Topsy's minstrel-like qualities have deeper dimensions. Like Sam, Topsy is a vehicle for attacks on social conventions. When she announces that she "never was born" but "just grow'd," we laugh, but on another level we feel pity for this enslaved child who is barred from knowing basic facts about her life. Our pity grows when Topsy courts punishment by stealing small household items. She expects to be whipped. She explains, "I's used to whippin'; I spects it's good for me." She jokes about Ophelia's feeble lashings, which she says "wouldn't kill a skeeter" and adds, "Oughter see how old Mas'r made the flesh fly; old Mas'r know'd how!" (ch. 20). This humorous—but at the same time appalling—repeated torture has inured this enslaved child to the horror of the slaveholder's whip.

It is a short step from Stowe's use of minstrel images in *Uncle Tom's Cabin* to the main theme of the novel: slavery. Stowe apparently visited a slave state only once, in 1833, when she made a short trip from her Cincinnati home across the Ohio River to nearby Kentucky, but she observed the ongoing battles between abolitionists and their opponents in Ohio, and she read a succession of slave narratives—by Frederick Douglass (1845), Lewis Garrard Clarke (1846), William Wells Brown (1847), Henry Bibb (1849), and Josiah Henson (1849)—which contained sources for some of her characters and graphic details of the horrors of slavery. For example, Josiah Henson, who took pride in being known as the "original Uncle Tom," had been brutalized as an enslaved young man in Maryland and then became a forgiving Christian who was so honorable that, like Tom, he passed up a chance to escape when he led a group of slaves through the free state of Ohio. (Only later, when he was betrayed by his master's brother, did Henson flee north.) Stowe's George Harris seems based on Lewis Clarke, an extremely light-skinned Kentucky quadroon with "European" facial features. Like George's sister, Clarke's pious sister was sold as a sex slave in New Orleans but escaped this fate when a wealthy Frenchman purchased, freed, and married her.

Both the northern and the southern plots dramatize what was then known as the higher law, a phrase popularized by Senator William Henry Seward, who, in a speech referring to the clause in the Constitution that demanded the return of fugitives from labor, had affirmed that there is "a higher law than the Constitution"—the law of justice and morality that was holier than society's laws which supported chattel slavery (Seward 1884, 74). *Uncle Tom's Cabin* was called a higher law novel. *Frederick Douglass' Paper* noted, "We doubt if abler arguments have ever been presented in favor of the *'Higher Law'* than may be found here [in] Mrs. Stowe's truly great work" (Apr. 8, 1852, 225). A reviewer for the *New Englander* described "the tears which [*Uncle Tom's Cabin*] has drawn from millions of eyes, the sense of a 'higher law,' which it has stamped upon a million hearts" (Nov. 1852, 591).

Stowe's northern plot directly flouts the Fugitive Slave Law. The heroes of this triumphant episode are the runaways and the kindly whites who assist them. The villains are those who enforce the law—the slave chasers Haley, Loker, and Marks. The short, frail Mary Bird becomes a powerhouse of subversive energy when she castigates her politician husband for having voted in the Senate for what she calls "a shameful, wicked, abominable law" (ch. 9). John Bird, in turn, willingly puts aside his legal obligation to uphold the law when he takes pity on the fugitives and conveys them to Van Trompe, who in turn forwards them to the Hallidays. Even as the Harrises make their way north, they remain in the malevolent grasp of the law. In the rocky pass scene, one of the slave chasers tells George, "We've got the law on our side, and the power," which prompts George's reply, "We don't own your laws; we don't own your country; . . . we'll fight for our liberty till we die" (ch. 17). This narrative stimulates the reader's enthusiastic approval of lawbreaking. The Harrises' flight appeals to the higher law of godly justice, morality, and patriotism, which glow like a halo around the fugitives and their abettors. Stowe evokes the American Revolution to valorize their revolt against slavery.

If the northern narrative exposes the injustice of the Fugitive Slave Law, the southern one highlights the cruelty of proslavery laws that made possible the sale of enslaved men and women. This domestic slave trade is condoned, Stowe tells us sarcastically, by "American legislators . . . our great men" who declaim loudly "against the *foreign* slave-trade" (ch. 12). Congress had abolished the international slave trade in 1808, leading to widespread complacency among southern politicians. As Stowe writes, "Trading negroes from Africa, dear reader, is so horrid! . . . But trading them in Kentucky,—that's quite another thing!" (ch. 12). Stowe wrote in *The Key to Uncle Tom's Cabin* (1853), her volume describing the factual bases of the novel, that the selling and buying of black men and women in the South was "the vital force of the institution of slavery" and "the great trade of the country" (ch. 4). And in *Uncle Tom's Cabin* she wrote that this business was "at this very moment, riving thousands of hearts, shattering thousands of families, and driving a helpless and sensitive race to frenzy and despair" (ch. 45).

She constructed her southern narrative strategically to accentuate the horrific aspects of the domestic slave trade. Tom's being sold three times was by no means beyond probability. His owners—Shelby, St. Clare, and Legree—typify a range of southern masters, from the kind to the sadistic. Economics and chance cause Tom's suffering, while law and proslavery religion sanction it. Tragedy also befalls several other slaves Tom encounters on his southern journey. In the chapter entitled "Select Incident of Lawful Trade," Tom witnesses the appalling spectacle of the enslaved Lucy committing suicide by leaping off the riverboat after hearing that her child has been sold and that she will not rejoin her husband. This scene yields the ironic observation by the narrator that the law and the church form a devilish league in support of slavery. Tom, we are told, sees Lucy's fate as "something unutterably horrible and cruel" because he is just a "poor, ignorant black soul" who doesn't take "enlarged views." Then comes this dart: "If he had only been instructed by certain ministers of Christianity, he might have thought better of it, and seen in it an every-day incident of a lawful trade; a trade which is the vital support of an institution which an American divine tells us has '*no evils but such as are inseparable from any other relations in social and domestic life*'" (ch. 12).

Also at work is a more basic form of persuasion—the appeal to human emotion. The novel begins by lamenting that proslavery law treats "human beings, with beating hearts and living affections" as "things" (ch. 1)—a notion underscored by the fact that Stowe's original working subtitle for the novel was the ironic *The Man That Was a Thing*. Stowe pointed out the outrageousness of the then-common view of blacks as subhuman. In virtually every scene of the novel, she showed that blacks were *not* things. They had human feelings and motivations—love, friendship, vindictiveness, desire for freedom, and so forth.

Stowe wrote *Uncle Tom's Cabin* at a time when abolitionism was highly unpopular and the antislavery movement in general was deeply divided, with factions that included radical Garrisonians, the evangelical Tappanites, the American Colonization Society, Free-Soil politicians, and Transcendentalists. Stowe surveyed the varied spectacle and decided that the institution of slavery could be gotten rid of only if the nation faced up to its sins. Politics, speeches, and sermons had failed to wipe out slavery.

What was needed was a novel that appealed to what a great leader would soon call "the better angels of our nature" (Lincoln 1989, 224). *Uncle Tom's Cabin* gave America iconic angels, in the form of a white girl and an enslaved black man who die for the redemption of others. It unsparingly exposed the toll that slavery took on blacks and whites who were bonded by a common humanity.

Uncle Tom's Cabin played a far larger role in the Civil War than is generally acknowledged. Lincoln declared in an 1858 debate with Stephen Douglas, "Public sentiment is everything. . . . —He who moulds public sentiment is greater than he who makes statutes" (qtd. in Holzer 2004, 26). No one molded public opinion more potently than Stowe. She wrote hopefully in *Uncle Tom's Cabin* that slavery might be abolished when individual Americans "see to it that *they feel right*" (ch. 45). Because she wanted the South to change its mind about slavery, she avoided the kind of wholesale demonization of slaveholders that she feared might alienate all southerners. She actually had three southern characters—Mrs. Shelby, St. Clare, and Eva—speak against slavery. By doing so, she challenged slavery from within by having southerners concede that it was evil.

But if she thought the South would in any way take her novel as a peace offering, she was sorely mistaken. In fact, her efforts to be compassionate made her seem far more dangerous than virulent abolitionists like William Lloyd Garrison, whose rancorous tone and calls for disunion made him easily dismissible in the South and unpopular even in the North. Besides, her concessions to the South were more apparent than real. She was not like Whitman, who, in an effort to keep the nation from falling apart, announced himself the poet of both slaves and their masters and who wrote lines about enslaved blacks working contentedly in the cotton fields. Nor was she like Nathaniel Hawthorne, who, in his indifference to slavery, penned a campaign biography of his dough-faced friend Franklin Pierce, who as president worked to appease the South.

Stowe's firm opposition to slavery comes through on every page of *Uncle Tom's Cabin*, and it is no surprise that the South rose up in fierce reaction to the novel. Many southern states banned its sale, and some criminalized it. In the 1850s, a whole new proslavery literature appeared in the South, much of it written in direct response to *Uncle Tom's Cabin*. Nearly thirty anti-Tom novels—proslavery fiction that often adopted Stowe's images but reversed their message—were written between 1852 and the Civil War. These works presented slavery as a God-ordained institution that provided inferior beings with shelter, food, and religious instruction, which was allegedly denied to them both in their barbaric native land and in the capitalist environment of northern cities. This argument was also made in proslavery poems, reviews, nonfiction volumes, and political speeches.

Conversely, Stowe's novel caused a remarkable upsurge of antislavery sentiment in the North, sparked not only by the novel's crescendoing popularity—amplified by its dissemination in popular merchandise and plays—but also by many new antislavery writings that followed in its wake. *Uncle Tom's Cabin* contributed to the rise of the antislavery Republican Party. Booker T. Washington noted that "the value of *Uncle Tom's Cabin* to the cause of Abolition can never be justly estimated"; he explained that it "so stirred the hearts of the northern people that a large part of them were ready either to vote or, in the last extremity, to fight for the suppression of slavery" (qtd. in Gossett 1985, 362).

And so Stowe's novel dramatically deepened national divisions over slavery. Lincoln's alleged remark that Stowe was "the little woman who made this great war" (Fields 1897, 269) may be apocryphal, but the sentiment was shared by many of the time, such as a southerner who claimed that the novel had "given birth to a horror against slavery in the Northern mind which all the politicians could never have created" and "did more than all else to array the North and South in compact masses against each other" (Hodgson 1876, 341).

Over time, the novel and its many emanations—plays, songs, games, figurines, food items, and many other products—influenced emancipation causes in Russia and elsewhere while having a strong impact on the entertainment industry, advertising, and racial stereotypes in America. In the twentieth century, it sparked a tremendous cultural war between progressives, such as W. E. B. Du Bois and the NAACP, and conservatives, represented by D. W. Griffith's film *The Birth of a Nation* (1915), the influential Dunning school of historians, and the New Critics. A host of Hollywood stars appeared early on in *Tom* roles, including Mary Pickford, Shirley Temple, Lillian Gish, Judy Garland, and Spencer Tracy. Christened "the Great American novel" by the author John W. De Forest in the *Nation*

(Jan. 9, 1868, 28) and praised highly by William Dean Howells and Leo Tolstoy, *Uncle Tom's Cabin* lost stature during the twentieth century, when its didacticism and political messages offended commentators, from the New Critics, who prized apolitical ambiguity, to African American writers such as James Baldwin, who found the novel demeaning to blacks. But since the 1970s, Stowe's novel has made a tremendous comeback, thanks largely to feminist criticism, new historicism, and cultural studies. *Uncle Tom's Cabin* is now considered compulsory reading for anyone seriously interested in the American past.

Part VI

CULTURAL INFLUENCES ON THE AMERICAN NOVEL, 1820–1870

23

TRANSATLANTIC CURRENTS AND POSTCOLONIAL ANXIETIES

PAUL GILES

The transatlantic dimension to American culture has a long and distinguished provenance, extending back to Spanish explorations of the sixteenth century, Puritan expeditions from England and Holland in the mid-seventeenth century, and the writings of French aristocrats such as Hector St. Jean de Crèvecoeur, and François-René de Chateaubriand, who traveled across the Atlantic in the years after the American War of Independence. Many of those credited with writing the first American novels also had strong links to countries outside the United States: for example, Peter Markoe, author of *The Algerine Spy in Pennsylvania* (1787), was born at St. Croix in the Caribbean and educated at Oxford University before emigrating to America and establishing himself as a lawyer in Pennsylvania in 1784. Similarly, Susanna Rowson, influentially categorized by Cathy N. Davidson as a "distinctive" American novelist for her appropriation of egalitarian female sentiment as a counterbalance to both the abstruse legal rhetoric of the founding fathers and the "demoralizing derision of Anglo-European arbiters of value and good taste" (2004, 3), was in fact born in 1762 in Portsmouth, England. It was there that Rowson wrote the first version of her best-known work *Charlotte Temple* (1794)—published in England in 1791 as *Charlotte: A Tale of Truth*—before moving to the United States with her husband in 1793.

In this sense, it is easy to see how a transatlantic imaginary has always been integral to the constitution of American literature. From a scholarly point of view, however, what is more remarkable and noteworthy is the extent to which such transatlanticism has systematically been marginalized in conventional academic accounts of the subject. There are, though, various compelling reasons for this kind of tunnel vision. In historical terms, the anxiety of Americans in the early years of the republic about the political status of their new nation induced an urgent compulsion to establish a corresponding republic of American letters, and this in turn led US public figures of the time often to repress, consciously or unconsciously, older colonial associations and legacies. Similarly, the nationalist temper of literary criticism in the middle years of the twentieth century led critical authorities to map out a discrete trajectory for the American literary heritage, one that effectively glossed over its complicated historical antecedents and variants. F. R. Leavis's assertion in *The Great Tradition* (1948) that the "great English novelists are Jane Austen, George Eliot, Henry James, and Joseph Conrad" (9)—despite the fact that James was brought up in the United States and Conrad in Poland—exemplifies a slippage in Leavis's critical viewpoint, where it is never quite clear whether "English" refers to language, nationality, or both; and Leavis's invocation here of what he calls "the central tradition of English fiction" (11) mirrors the earlier, similarly polemical approach of F. O. Matthiessen, who in the first paragraph of *American Renaissance* (1941) had set himself the task on behalf of American literary culture of "affirming its rightful heritage in the whole expanse of art and culture" (vii). It is true, of course, that Matthiessen's great work considers the idiosyncratic native genius of Nathaniel Hawthorne and Herman Melville alongside the Elizabethan world of Shakespeare and Francis Bacon; indeed, the burden of Matthiessen's argument involves tracing points of convergence as well as divergence between European and American cultural traditions. Nevertheless, both Leavis and Matthiessen were committed during the 1940s to an organicist model of development whereby the canonical consolidation of literary ideals could be seen to draw its strength from discrete, and sometimes competing, national paradigms. Such binary oppositions between rival intellectual models organized around national difference were subsequently sustained by influential critical works such as Richard Chase's *The American Novel and Its Tradition* (1957), which held that the "solid moral inclusiveness" of the English novel turned on issues of property and class, while the "freer, more daring" American novel concerned itself with questions of allegorical romance and metaphysical abstraction (viii). These kinds of nationalistic stereotypes, bolstered as always by the entrenched interests that came to be vested in textbook anthologies and curricula of higher education, have proved remarkably resilient and difficult to dislodge. Even though imaginary points of origin for national literary traditions have, in the wake of Jacques Derrida, long since been theoretically discredited, popular academic narratives that seek to read national character diachronically, through a contemplation of how works of fiction reflect the enduring idea of a nation, have continued to thrive. The idea of a "great tradition" of English fiction, like the concomitant notion of the "great American novel," is an unquiet corpse that many incisive critical stakes through the heart have been unable to inter.

One of the reasons for such conceptual incongruity lies in amnesia, the tendency simply to overlook the complicated social circumstances in which specific works of fiction were written and published. The first two generations after the establishment of political independence in the United States grew up in a time of widespread insecurity, with many in America doubting the ability of their experimental country to survive, in such an isolated state, the harsh social and economic conditions that prevailed at the turn of the nineteenth century. Charles Brockden

Brown's novels, published between 1798 and 1801, speak to the trauma of the bleak plague-ridden years in Philadelphia during the 1790s, while Washington Irving's burlesque *A History of New York* (1809) has been described by Robert A. Ferguson as "the first American book to question directly the civic vision of the Founding Fathers" (1984, 158). Ferguson argues that Irving's deflationary humor seeks deliberately to cast aspersions on the idealist designs of "William the Testy," a fictionalized version of Thomas Jefferson, with Irving consequently doubting that the etiolated designs of an idealistic Jeffersonian democracy could ever be grounded sufficiently in empirical common sense or social custom. But Irving's fears and concerns were not at all unusual in the first forty years of the nineteenth century, and the uncertainties about America's post-Revolutionary status expressed in his story "Rip Van Winkle" (1819)—in which the hero wakes up after twenty years asleep in the Catskill Mountains to find the "King George" inn renamed the "George Washington"—betray a more general sense of anxiety about the repercussions of decolonization across the new nation. Although such postcolonial anxieties were generally expurgated from conventional versions of American literary history, where Rip Van Winkle's discomfort was frequently written off as a pathological sign of his lacking the kind of full-blooded manliness that should typify a frontier spirit, the lingering sense of disquiet that afflicted Irving's fictional hero was something shared by many Americans at this time: "He doubted his own identity, and whether he was himself or another man." Such traumas are commensurate also with Irving's western narratives of the 1830s—*A Tour on the Prairies* (1835), *Astoria; or, Enterprise Beyond the Rocky Mountains* (1836), *The Adventures of Captain Bonneville* (1837)—where the author represents the Far West as a disputed space, a liminal territory, whose very lack of incorporation into the US political heartland betokens its openness to those double-edged qualities by which the author found himself aesthetically so attracted.

Irving's narratives, in other words, characteristically take place in a marginal or displaced geographical territory, whose instability connotes a quality of radical ambivalence. It is easy to forget that when Richard Henry Dana published his account of California in *Two Years Before the Mast: A Personal Narrative of Life at Sea* (1840), he was writing about a place that was still legally part of Mexico. Dana's characteristic comments on the shiftless Spaniards—"The Californians are an idle, thriftless people, and can make nothing for themselves"—derive in part from the author's deliberate counterpointing of Yankee industry with Catholic sloth, an opposition that emerges from Dana's distinct sense of Boston as "home" and the West Coast of America as "abroad" (ch. 13). Again, the outcome of the US war with Mexico that took place in the late 1840s and the consequences of the Civil War that reconstructed the nation after 1865 to its current geographic formation of "sea to shining sea" have tended historically to obscure the extent to which America in the mid-nineteenth century was a collection of disparate political territories rather than a unified national domain. When the English military explorer and spy George

Ruxton published his novel *Life in the Far West* in 1848, many American readers imagined that it had been written by an indigenous Rocky Mountain trapper, rather than an agent who was intent on reconnoitering the landscape and sending back reports to London about US designs on the Oregon Territory. Although the Young America movement that grew up in the 1840s tried to promote the idea that US national destiny was always designed to manifest itself in particular ways, this pressure group came into being at a time when many in America believed that the "natural" western boundary of the United States was, in fact, the Rocky Mountains rather than the Pacific Ocean. During the 1840s, the British consul to California, intent on preserving British imperial trade with China and the Far East, was sending back urgent messages to the Peel government in London about the strategic importance of making sure the United States did not obtain control of the port of San Francisco. In this sense, the self-consciously provisional feel of Irving's "rambling" narratives speaks eloquently to the structural indeterminacy that remained at this time a constituent part of the American body politic, and not until the gold rush of 1849 attracted large numbers of migrants to the Pacific region did the dynamics of the American West Coast change decisively.

One of the oddities of American literature as an academic field, as it has been constructed since the middle of the twentieth century, is that so much more attention has been given to fiction of the 1840s and 1850s than to that of the previous two decades. In many ways, of course, this is quite understandable, since the fiction of Nathaniel Hawthorne, Herman Melville, and others has been thought to exemplify an initial flowering of the American literary idiom; but one of the attendant effects of this particular temporal focus is seriously to underestimate the significance of writing from the 1820s and 1830s, when the idea of a national identity in American literature had not yet fully crystallized. Besides the hesitancies and ambiguities of Irving, the works of James Fenimore Cooper involve a comparative analysis of American culture that derives its power from a series of deliberate discursive juxtapositions with other domains. In *The Headsman; or, The Abbaye de Vignerons* (1833), set in eighteenth-century Switzerland, Cooper outlines the various cultural conflicts between different cantons in old Europe. He describes how romance and probity are undermined by the archaic Berne custom whereby the role of headsman, or public executioner, would descend automatically in a hereditary line. Christine, the daughter of headsman Balthazar, feels this ancient custom is a "curse" upon her family (ch. 18), one that impedes her marriage prospects. Cooper's novel contemplates issues such as fate and free will, social conservatism and progressive democracy. It is easy enough to see how this emphasis on local divisions within Europe comprises a cautionary tale for the new federal republic across the Atlantic. The author talks of how "the authority of Berne weighed . . . imperiously and heavily on its subsidiary countries, as is usual in such cases" (ch. 17), with "these contracted districts possessing nearly as many dialects as there are territorial divisions" (ch. 18); and in this sense, *The Headsman* might readily be construed as an allegory of confederation, an examination of the pitfalls involved in regional friction and dissension. Symptomatically, Cooper also talks at one point about the need for a nation to possess "unity commensurate to its means" to enable it to have "confidence in itself," since "small and divided states waste their strength in acts too insignificant for general interest" (ch. 20). Using a comparative poetics in this way, Cooper deploys Switzerland as a foil and counterexample to address by implication the political destiny of modern America.

It is, consequently, not difficult to see a continuum between fictional work such as *The Headsman* and the nonfictional commentaries on social and political affairs that Cooper published in the 1830s. His *Gleanings in Europe* series—two volumes on Switzerland in 1836, followed by others on France and England in 1837, and one on Italy in 1838—is mirrored in the unabashed national stereotypes of *The Headsman*, where Maso, for example, is said to have "the swarthy hue, bold lineaments, and glittering eye, of an Italian" (ch. 1). To put this another way, the 1830s was a decade when many travel writers were impelled to extrapolate an idea of national essence from their peregrinations, and much writing of this era seeks deliberately to compare and contrast different cultural formations in the interests of identifying and consolidating certain emergent forms of national identity. This is the basis of English travel writing from the likes of Captain Basil Hall, who generally categorizes Americans according to negative stereotypes and who, after an 1829 visit to America, said he had "often been so much out of humour with the people amongst whom I was wandering that I have most perversely derived pleasure from meeting things to find fault with" (Nevins 1948, 89). It is also the basis for Frances Trollope's negative account of the United States in *Domestic Manners of the Americans* (1832), where she observed that the "total and universal want of manners, both in males and females, is so remarkable that I was constantly endeavouring to account for it" (ch. 5). For Tories such as Hall and Trollope, the brave new world of America in the 1830s appeared to be an uncomfortable challenge to their familiar, established British state, and the publication of Trollope's book on the eve of the Great Reform Act in Britain suggests how both the author and her publishers conceived of *Domestic Manners* as a salutary warning of the direction Britain might take if, by misadventure, it were to fall on the slippery slope toward an American-style democracy.

Cooper explicitly takes issue with Basil Hall and Frances Trollope in his 1837 volume on England in the *Gleanings in Europe* series, saying that "Captain Hall" typifies the general "dislike" of the English for Americans (ltr. 6), while Mrs. Trollope's book displays "a malignant feeling, and calculations of profit" (ltr. 27). Based on visits to Britain that Cooper undertook in 1828 and 1833, the American author is particularly scathing about the class "ladder" that he sees as pervading every aspect of English society, where "every one is tugging at the skirts of the person above, while he puts his foot on the neck of him beneath" (ltr. 5). Describing the "hereditary principle" as "offensive to human pride, not to say natural justice" (ltr. 13), Cooper also complains that Walter Scott's "prejudice" in favor of "deference to hereditary rank" is an idea that "pervades his writings" (ltr. 11). Looking back in his preface to the spirit of 1776, Cooper argues that the events of this time involved "a declaration of political independence, only" and that there is also a need for "mental emancipation" to liberate Americans from an obsequious attachment to English customs and standards. At the same time, Cooper's own Leather-Stocking novels, from *The Pioneers; or, The Sources of the Susquehanna* (1823) to *The Deerslayer; or, The First War-Path* (1841), takes as its central concern the cultural conflict between an indigenous society and a colonizing power that seeks to marginalize or displace it. From this perspective, the comparative idiom of *The Headsman* and the travel writings is fundamentally commensurate with Cooper's broader artistic trajectory, whose scope involves interactions and power exchanges between different kinds of social formation. Edward Watts's observation about how American literature of the "early republic" suggests ways in which "one former colony could be both colonized and colonizer at once" (1998, 26) is thus played out in the landscapes of Cooper's postcolonial environment, where the American insurgency against British colonial authority is reflected in Native American resistance to US federal designs. Rather than simply portraying postcolonialism as the site of a self-fulfilling struggle for emancipation, Cooper's work represents it in a more circular way, where one form of structural domination and subjugation spawns another.

During roughly the first third of the nineteenth century, the political instability endemic to the new United States provided an extra rationale for exploratory travel narratives of the kind written by Hall and Trollope, where observers would annotate and interpret a country they took to be in an embryonic, inchoate state. The White House in Washington was actually burnt down by British forces during the War of 1812, and British officials had gone so far as to draw up detailed plans for moving into and administering the Louisiana Territory, before their schemes were halted by General Andrew Jackson at the Battle of New Orleans in 1815. By the 1830s, however, it was becoming clear that the United States was not going to collapse quickly and that nations on either side of the Atlantic were heading in fundamentally different political directions. It was this sense of irremediable divergence that helped generate a distinctive comparative consciousness in the work of Cooper, Alexis de Tocqueville, and others. Tocqueville's *Democracy in America*, written after a trip to the United States in 1830 and published in two volumes in 1835 and 1840, is another example of an extended travel narrative from the 1830s functioning as a form of comparative political analysis. Tocqueville's critique here of the relationship between church and state, and of ways in which civil religion in America works differently from religious establishment in Europe, has been particularly influential. But to make inferences about the inherent virtues of American democracy itself from the peculiarly slanted virtues of Tocqueville's analysis is a highly problematic strategy. Although *Democracy in America* was canonized by American studies scholars in the middle of the twentieth century as a template of the national character, their general mistake was to imagine Tocqueville as a neutral observer and thus to overlook his own ideological investments in a French aristocratic ethos, against which the idiosyncrasies of life in America could emerge only by way of intertextual dialogue. Just as Cooper contrasts US federal unity with Swiss regional fragmentation, so Tocqueville's version of democracy in America emerges through specific contrasts with his own privileged French heritage.

In this sense, America, in the first half of the nineteenth century, became a site where the aftershocks of the French Revolution were played out experientially, with Tocqueville's conservatism subsequently being balanced by more sympathetic representations of the French radical world. For example, in Melville's *Israel Potter: His Fifty Years of Exile* (1855), the protagonist encounters "the venerable Doctor Franklin" in Paris during the early 1780s (ch. 7), at the time of the Anglo-American conflict and shortly before France's own insurrectionary turbulence, in scenes that implicitly equate the French and American Revolutions as parallel challenges to established British authority. France is likewise the site for the reunion of George and Mary in William Wells Brown's *Clotel; or, The President's Daughter* (1853), a work of fiction that addresses cultural and economic circuits linking France to "the slave-market" of New Orleans, where Mary is purchased by a "French gentleman" who takes her away to Europe. "We can but blush for our country's shame," concludes the narrator, "when we recall to mind the fact, that while George and Mary Green, and numbers of other fugitives from American slavery, can receive protection from any of the governments of Europe, they cannot return to their native land without becoming slaves" (ch. 28). Whereas the French aristocrat Tocqueville in the mid-nineteenth century extolled a certain slanted version of American democracy, the African American radical Brown conversely looked to France as a guarantor of basic human liberties. As Bill Marshall has noted, New Orleans became a "haven" for diverse groups of French political exiles at various times in the post-Revolutionary era—royalists in the 1790s, anti-Bonapartists after 1799, Bonapartists after 1815, republicans after 1848 (2007, 40). This again suggests how the new United States not only located itself within transatlantic horizons but also responded in distinctively transnational ways to political events as they unfolded. Pioneering Swiss academic Auguste Viatte published in 1954 his *Histoire littéraire de l'Amérique française* (*Literary History of French America*) in which the literature of Louisiana plays a key role, while the more recent critical writings of Joseph Roach and others have accentuated these "circum-atlantic" dimensions in relation to theatrical performance as well as writing. From this perspective, the process of triangulation linking the new US republic during the nineteenth century to alternative systems of political representation in Europe can be seen as crucial to the emergence of American literary culture, which emerged in dialogue with both British traditionalism and French republicanism.

Similar comparative perspectives are embedded within Charles Dickens's writings about America, both in his nonfictional *American Notes for General Circulation* (1842) and his novel *The Life and Adventures of Martin Chuzzlewit* (1843–44);

indeed, Dickens's representation of America as a land of hypocrisy, where a loud commitment to high-sounding ideals serves to obscure both commercial greed and a widespread institutional complacency about slavery, might be understood as an extension of the author's own quarrels with the United States over the absence of an international copyright agreement, which was at this time costing him a fortune because of the mass reprinting of his novels in America. The larger political antagonisms between Britain and America during the late 1840s, particularly over unresolved US-Canadian boundaries in Oregon and in Maine, also contributed to this general sense of mutual hostility between the two nations. There is, concomitantly, a deeply conflicted attitude toward English cultural prototypes in writers of Matthiessen's *American Renaissance.* On the one hand, Ralph Waldo Emerson was scathing about what he called Victorian "novels of costume," suggesting "there is but one standard English novel, like the one orthodox sermon, which with slight variation is repeated every Sunday from so many pulpits" (1904, 376–7), and in his "American Scholar" address, he urged Americans to forsake the "courtly muses of Europe" in the interests of delineating authentic national prototypes (1971, 69). On the other hand, Emerson's own immersion in European cultural heritage—he wrote essays on Chaucer and Goethe, Michelangelo and Montaigne—ensured that he always positioned US culture self-consciously in relation to such antecedent models, so that American literary narratives emerge within a mode of refraction and reorientation rather than categorical independence. In "Hawthorne and His Mosses" (1850), Melville attributes Hawthorne's "mystical blackness" to a "Calvinistic sense of Innate Depravity and Original Sin" (2000, 916), thereby rescuing his compatriot from the accusation of being a merely "smooth" or sentimental writer, an "appendix" to Oliver Goldsmith (921); yet, even here, Melville seeks to validate Hawthorne by comparing his work to the "blackness" forming the "background, against which Shakespeare plays his grandest conceits" (916). This is of a piece with Melville's own fiction, which, through its extravagant range of intertextual references, aspires deliberately to rehouse the spirit of Shakespearian tragedy within the native confines of a New England whaling expedition in *Moby-Dick; or, The Whale* (1851), or amidst New York family life in *Pierre; or, The Ambiguities* (1852). Robert Weisbuch has suggested that Melville alone among American writers of this time was "essentially antagonistic toward the English romantic poets" (1986, 13). It is true that the naive sentimentality of the eponymous hero in *Pierre* is associated with textual echoes of William Wordsworth's poetry; but Melville, a devotee of Sir Thomas Browne and others, was also drawing upon a more extensive English literary heritage stretching back through Elizabethan times in order to align his work with what he took to be the darker, more enduring power of Renaissance writing.

It is arguable, then, that in their commitment to an American national idiom both Melville and Hawthorne see themselves paradoxically as the guardians of an older, tougher form of English literary art that had been glossed over by the commodifications of the nineteenth-century novel market on both sides of the

Atlantic. In his preface to *The House of the Seven Gables: A Romance* (1851), Hawthorne himself formulated an antithesis between "Romance" and "Novel"—the former claiming "a certain latitude, both as to its fashion and material"; the latter aiming "at a very minute fidelity, not merely to the possible, but to the probable and ordinary course of man's experience"—that came to be very influential in subsequent definitions of the American novel. Indeed, Chase's *The American Novel and Its Tradition*, in its argument that the focus on property and marriage markets in the novels of Anthony Trollope was counteracted by an emphasis on rarefied symbolism in the more abstruse romances of Hawthorne and Melville, follows Hawthorne's theoretical prescription almost exactly. It is, of course, not difficult to deconstruct such binary oppositions, to point out the multifarious ways in which Hawthorne evokes social contexts or, indeed, Trollope at times veers away from the more empirical and familiar. Nevertheless, this sense of working in parallel with, and sometimes in opposition to, the English cultural heritage was an important factor in the development of the nineteenth-century American novel, with the colonial legacy forming a matrix against which American writers chose to define themselves in refractory as much as compliant terms.

Hawthorne's compulsion toward comparative perspectives manifests itself clearly in his *English Notebooks*, written when he was serving as United States consul at Liverpool between 1853 and 1857. Commenting, for example, in 1854 on how a Welsh village near Rhyl is "squalid and ugly," he goes on to remark: "Just think of a New England rural village in comparison" (1997, 117). Similarly, *Our Old Home* (1863), Hawthorne's nonfictional account of English customs, is saturated in a comparative idiom, with the author contrasting what he takes to be an American "modern instinct . . . towards 'fresh woods and pastures new'" (1970, 60) with the "heavy air" of typical English attachment to "a spot where the forefathers and foremothers have grown up together, intermarried, and died . . . till family features and character are all run in the same inevitable mould" (59). Hawthorne also asks pointed questions in *Our Old Home* about what he perceives as the gross inequities of the British class system, contrasting an "aristocratic" wedding with a similar event amongst the "ragged people":

> Is, or is not, the system wrong that gives one married pair so immense a superfluity of luxurious home, and shuts out a million others from any home whatever? One day or another, safe as they deem themselves, and safe as the hereditary temper of the people really tends to make them, the gentlemen of England will be compelled to face this question. (309)

It is, however, the strength of Hawthorne's best writing that it seeks to "face" rather than to resolve such awkward questions. Hawthorne, like Irving, does not preach or dogmatize, but seeks rather to hold opposing potentialities in an unresolved tension. Hawthorne comments in *Our Old Home* on how he "grew better acquainted with many of our national characteristics" during his time in England,

and this is because his recognition of American identity emerged reflexively, or, in his own words, was "brought more strikingly out by the contrast with English manners" (10).

This comparative idiom is also interwoven systematically in *The Marble Faun; or, The Romance of Monte Beni* (1860), Hawthorne's last completed novel, which is set in Italy and plays the cultural values and belief systems of Rome and Boston, Catholicism and Puritanism, against each other. As Henry James observed in *Hawthorne* (1879), the "Puritan conscience" represented Hawthorne's "natural heritage," but the author's "relation to it was only, as one may say, intellectual; it was not moral and theological" (54). In its portrayal of idealistic New England protagonists trying to come to terms with the "labyrinth of darkness" embedded in Italian culture (ch. 3), *The Marble Faun* refuses closure in the way it establishes a sustained dialogue between cross-cultural perspectives. Indeed, Hawthorne's style of radical openness and ambiguity in this novel infuriated so many readers that the author was moved to add a postscript to the book's second edition, in response to what he called the general "demand for further elucidations respecting the mysteries of the story." The peculiar quality of *The Marble Faun* lies in the way it takes the more abstract aspects of New England Transcendentalism—Emerson's idealism, Thoreau's asceticism, Whitman's solipsism—and investigates how such qualities might intersect with a fully incarnated social and historical context. In this sense, it is not dissimilar thematically to Hawthorne's earlier novel *The Blithedale Romance* (1851), which also considers how the idea of a utopian community might operate within a more mundane, embodied world of ordinary human jealousy and passion. *The Blithedale Romance*, of course, confines itself to conflicts within the New England community, whereas *The Marble Faun* extends its geographic range much more widely, but by foregrounding questions of artistic form in the latter novel—Miriam is a painter, Kenyon a sculptor—Hawthorne's novel implicitly interrogates the extent to which aesthetic substance can incorporate the full range of human experience across time and space. Hawthorne's characters find themselves becoming enmeshed in statuesque legends, customs, and prototypes from all periods of Roman culture whose fate they cannot evade, so that *The Marble Faun* might almost be said to turn upon a discourse of archaeology, constantly uncovering the sediments of time to bring, as the novel puts it, "the remoteness of a thousand years ago into the sphere of yesterday." There is a detailed account of archaeological activities in the latter part of the novel, a description of grappling with "earth-mounds" and "heaped-up marble and granite," together with an acknowledgment of the opacities and obscurities endemic to this attempt to recover fragments of the past (ch. 45). In this sense, the valiant attempts by Hawthorne's American characters to infuse history with a distinct teleological spirit, to read it transcendentally, are traversed textually by a penumbra of archaeological indecipherability. If *Our Old Home* uses a comparative perspective to emphasize the idiosyncratic qualities of American national genius, *The Marble Faun* conversely embraces a transatlantic dimension to expose more subtly the epistemological limits of national consciousness of all kinds. Whereas in his journals, Hawthorne often plays the role of an American diplomatic politician intent on boosting national self-esteem, in his final novel, he more ambitiously examines ways in which the inherited cultural assumptions of America and Europe intersect with each other in an unresolved dialectical tension.

These kinds of transatlantic affiliation carry over from specific historical contexts into the more amorphous realms of literary form and genre. Transatlanticism does not just affect the particular scenes that fiction describes but also the ways in which they are artistically organized. When Frederick Douglass's first autobiographical narrative appeared in 1845, his account of what he calls his "escape from slavery"—with facts about the Underground Railroad ostentatiously suppressed so as not, said Douglass in his most tantalizing style, to "induce greater vigilance on the part of slaveholders"—was compared to Dickens's *Oliver Twist* and Eugène Sue's *Mysteries of Paris* as an example of how gothic writing could flourish in a real-life American setting. The racial milieu of the United States, as Richard Wright was to observe in his 1940 introduction to *Native Son*, provided a situation "dense and heavy enough to satisfy even the gloomy broodings of a Hawthorne" or a Poe (39), and some of the commercial success of these slave narratives among nineteenth-century readers was linked not so much to virtuous abolitionist sentiment but to the entertainment value typically associated with gothic representations of extreme horror. William Wells Brown also wrote and published *Clotel* during a series of antislavery lectures in England, with the author signing his preface to the novel from "22, Cecil Street, Strand, London," while in the book's introduction, Brown mentions how it "has been for years thought desirable and advantageous to the cause of Negro emancipation in America, to have some talented man of colour always in Great Britain, who should be a living refutation of the doctrine of the inferiority of the African race." In this way, the African American narratives of Brown and Douglass, no less than the canonical novels of Hawthorne and Melville, appropriate the English cultural landscape as a kind of mirror site, an alternative space in both a literal and a figurative sense, where social patterns are organized differently. The inverse dynamics of these British colonial scenes enable such American authors to highlight, by contrast, the specificity of their US cultural experience. The self-consciously intertextual aspects of these transatlantic parallelisms serve simultaneously to align American literature with long-established cultural models and also to illuminate particular junctures at which these models diverge rather than converge. Hawthorne's incomplete and unpublished final novel, which exists now as the ramshackle "American Claimant" manuscripts, thematizes these confusions of transatlantic family romance in the most explicit manner through the way it represents the threat of incest as a synecdoche of larger conceptual confusions, whereby the burdens of heritage and tradition turn families (and, by extension, nations) inward, thereby rendering them incapable of defining themselves according to any discrete form of identity. This incest theme, which manifests itself in Melville's *Pierre* as well as throughout Hawthorne's novels, might thus be understood as a metonymical version of postcolonial anxiety, where an absorbing entanglement in "family" life overshadows the prospect of full cultural independence.

Besides this intellectual rationale for what Melville in *Israel Potter* called "bewildering intertanglement" (ch. 19), the institutional contexts of publishing on either side of the Atlantic helped facilitate extensive transatlantic readerships throughout the nineteenth century. Just as the works of Dickens were reprinted cheaply in America because of the absence of an international copyright agreement, so Harriet Beecher Stowe's *Uncle Tom's Cabin; or, Life Among the Lowly* (1852) was an even bigger seller in Britain than in America, in part because the London publishers, owing no royalties to Stowe, could afford to offer it so cheaply. Indeed, when Stowe toured Britain in 1853, the suggestion surfaced that each reader should contribute one penny to the author to compensate her for these lack of earnings, a scheme that eventually enabled the author to return to America with more than $20,000 in her pocket. In Britain, the establishment of Mudie's circulating library in 1842 also helped bring American literature more to the attention of general readers, particularly since Charles Mudie himself—a radical in politics and a liberal in religion—was well disposed toward the culture of the United States and chose to keep many American volumes in his lists. William Gladstone in 1852 said that the "purchase of new publications is scarcely ever attempted by anybody" in Britain, except by "persons of extraordinary wealth," though he added that it was much more common to "find something from the circulating library" in the "houses of your friends" (qtd. in Gohdes 1942, 356). Mudie thus helped to popularize in Britain not only works by erudite Transcendentalists, such as Emerson, Theodore Parker, and Margaret Fuller, but also works of fiction by Irving, Cooper, Oliver Wendell Holmes, N. P. Willis, Fanny Fern, Susan Warner, and many others. Warner's novel *The Wide, Wide World* (1850), true to the global proclivities of its title, has scenes where the American heroine Ellen Montgomery visits Scotland, thereby allowing Warner to play the aristocratic Lady Keith's snobbish attitude toward "thick-headed and thicker-tongued Yankees" against the more democratic virtues of American fellow feeling. Warner thus contrasts European obfuscations of sentiment, epitomized in the novel by the "crooked ways" of the Edinburgh urban landscape, with American openness and transparency, as if to reinforce the virtues of American domestic security by contrasting it with the more sinister dimensions of global space (ch. 47).

Contrary to the kind of compartmentalized literary scholarship that has emphasized the establishment of separate national traditions, then, the cultural links between different sides of the Atlantic during the nineteenth century should be seen as amorphous and free-flowing. The farcical drama *Our American Cousin*, which was written by English dramatist Tom Taylor and features an American going to England to claim his family estate, was premiered in 1858 not in London but in New York, with the play subsequently achieving notoriety when Abraham Lincoln was assassinated in 1865 during a performance at Ford's Theatre in Washington DC. The broad popularity of this play's leading character, the dim-witted aristocrat Lord Dundreary, exemplifies the extent to which transatlantic cultural relations had become a fixed point of reference within US popular consciousness during this era. Victorian Americans often experienced a love-hate relationship with the apparatus and iconography of the British establishment, taking delight in mocking them but also bound up magnetically in their colonial (or postcolonial) orbit. Elisa Tamarkin has written of how many high-minded American abolitionists from the Boston area in the middle of the nineteenth century sought associations in England from motivations of pleasure as much as morality, traveling to the old country to combine "reforming zeal" with "having fun" (2008, 215). Indeed, on her trip to Britain in 1853, Stowe was entertained as a visiting dignitary at the Duchess of Sutherland's palatial country house, where the guests included all the great and the good from English society: Lord and Lady Palmerston, Lord John Russell, William Gladstone, and many others. Although she later wrote a famous indictment of Lord Byron's sexual misconduct, Stowe also admired the radical English poet—the reformist hero of her 1856 novel *Dred: A Tale of the Great Dismal Swamp*, Edward Clayton, is described there as "quite Byronic" (ch. 1)—and Stowe herself in many ways shared Byron's appetite for public fame and recognition.

During this 1853 London visit, Stowe was also guest of honor at a banquet hosted by the Lord Mayor of London, where she was seated opposite Charles Dickens. The two celebrated novelists were together toasted at the banquet as "having employed fiction as a means of awakening the attention of the respective countries to the condition of the oppressed and suffering classes" (qtd. in Hedrick 1994, 243). Though in an earlier 1843 essay Stowe had expressed some reservations about Dickens's tendency to make light of religion, the two authors shared a commitment to melodramatic forms of public address that garnered a wide readership, due in no small part to their skillful exploitation of commercial fictional forms. Particularly in *Dred*, where she delights in making fun of narrow-minded theologians who seek to justify the practices of slavery on philosophical grounds, Stowe internalizes a Dickensian property of burlesque whose aesthetic impulse is linked to the way it conjoins the commodified form of the serial novel—where, because of the structural discontinuities necessarily involved in the reading experience, the portrayal of characters has to be flattened to make them instantly recognizable—with a capacity for broad popular humor. This effectively differentiates Stowe from George Eliot, with whom the American author is more frequently compared, not only because of their shared gender but also because of their explicit mutual commitments to an ethics of social reform. However, Stowe and Eliot fundamentally disagreed about the pertinence of this comic principle in art, with the English author being notoriously hostile to the various fragmentations involved in the serialization process and preferring to emphasize instead what she called the inherent "organism" of a work of fiction (Benson 1975, 437). Unlike Charles Dickens and Anthony Trollope, who thrived commercially on the rapid production of their serial fiction, Eliot loathed writing her novels as they were simultaneously appearing in serial form, describing it as "scrambling on the slippery bank of a pool, just keeping my head above water" (Haight 1968, 443). She tried as far as possible to avoid these pressures by only allowing *Middlemarch* to be issued in eight lengthy parts at two-monthly intervals during 1872.

Stowe and Eliot never actually met, but they corresponded over many years, with Stowe, as she recalled in her autobiographical *Life of Harriet Beecher Stowe* (1889), trying as late as the 1870s to persuade Eliot to pay a visit to the "orange shades" of her home in Florida (ch. 20). But, although they both came from nonconformist backgrounds and were concerned to subject society to intense moral scrutiny, these two authors approached their material in very different ways, with Stowe advising the English author that what *Middlemarch: A Study of Provincial Life* (1871–72) fatally lacked was "jollitude," something the American writer claimed characteristic of "our tumble-down, jolly, improper, but joyous country." Stowe casts herself in this transatlantic correspondence as a proselytizer for American popular culture—"You write and live on so high a plane," she complains to Eliot—whereas Eliot herself holds to the cultural high ground by telling Stowe "that if a book which has any sort of exquisiteness happens also to be a popular, widely circulated book, the power over the social mind for any good is, after all, due to its reception by a few appreciative natures, and is the slow result of radiation from that narrow circle." The English author, then, was wedded to an unabashedly elitist conception of metropolitan influence filtering slowly into the wider community, while Stowe was far more immersed in, and committed to, a broader domain of market forces, whose circulation she understood in characteristically American terms as a power for good. As she recalled in her *Life*, Stowe also failed to convince Eliot in 1872 on the issue of "invisible spirits," which the American regarded as a natural phenomenon—citing Charles Darwin, she suggested to Eliot that "some day we shall find a law by which all these facts will fall into their places"—whereas Eliot herself responded by summarily dismissing "ideas of spirit intercourse and so on" as a "painful form of the lowest charlatanerie" (ch. 20). Nevertheless, the two writers always regarded each other with mutual respect, perhaps in part because they recognized the intractable nature of their intellectual disagreements. Eliot reviewed *Dred* very positively in the *Westminster Review* in 1856, calling it "a great novel" even while specifically declining to comment on its "political" pertinacity. What Eliot admired about *Dred* was not its position on what she called "the terribly difficult problems of Slavery and Abolition," but the fact that it retained a "keen sense of humour" and a strong "dramatic interest," something she found "all the more remarkable" given that the novel was clearly "animated by a vehement polemical purpose." In this sense, Stowe's "rare genius," in Eliot's eyes, lay in her capacity for encompassing "a national life in all its phases—popular and aristocratic, humorous and tragic, political and religious" (1967, 326–7). It was this multifaceted quality of *Dred*, rather than its narrowly evangelical spirit, that appealed to Eliot's artistic and critical imagination.

Eliot's recognition of Stowe's versatility as a novelist is commensurate with a key attribute of *Dred*, which is the way its author reconfigures the American South within a comparative context. The novel is set largely on a plantation in North Carolina, but Stowe is generally sympathetic toward her fictional slave-owning family, the Claytons, who are represented here as well-meaning reformers. Sympathy, indeed, was always an important aesthetic principle for Stowe: she saw it as the novelist's task not only to feel for and through her characters but also to achieve a state of empathy sufficient to endow her dramatis personae with a vital life of their own. Of course, such sympathy also goes along here with vituperative satire, with the vicious young white master, Tom Gordon, being treated by the author as harshly as he treats his slaves. But, as Eliot observed, it is the "genius" of Stowe to enter into the spirit of her various characters and to allow us as readers to see the world through their eyes. This is why a comparative aesthetic was entirely consistent with Stowe's overall moral design, which involves exposing enclosed minds and entrenched conventions to alternative points of view: the behavior of Tom Gordon, remarks the author, has suffered over the years from "the secluded nature of the plantation" on which he was born and bred (ch. 4). Consequently, one significant trajectory of *Dred* is linked to the novel's ever-expanding geographical range, starting from the "secluded" plantations of the South but subsequently bringing into play Canada, to where Edward Clayton eventually emigrates, and New York, to where he helps his former slaves escape. In *Uncle Tom's Cabin*, published four years earlier, Stowe had suggested a migration of African Americans to Liberia as a possible long-term solution to the nation's racial problems, whereas in the more legalistic and politicized world of *Dred*, no such general exodus or utopia is envisaged. Indeed, the outlaw Dred himself raises in this latter book a more overt prospect of insurrectionary violence, and in this sense, the novel projects a distinctly darker vision of American racial affairs on the eve of the Civil War. Conceptually, however, what is most noticeable about *Dred* is its receptiveness to the possibility of transformation of every kind, its acknowledgment of how the current history and geography of the United States comprise only contingent narratives. Edward Clayton's friend Frank Russel, for example, talks of the southern aristocracy's plan to extend their slaveholding empire by annexing Cuba and the Sandwich Islands, while he also describes the idea of American liberty as one of those "agreeable myths" that "will not bear any close looking into," since "Liberty has generally meant the Liberty of me and my nation and my class to do what we please" (ch. 32). Though *Dred* does not entirely endorse Russel's cynicism, it is, in its textual openness to displacement, generally hospitable to Russel's capacity for envisaging the encrusted state of the material world from radically different perspectives.

One of the key questions raised across an international axis by the US Civil War was the extent to which certain ideas—particularly those associated with liberty or freedom—might be construed as a universal right, or, conversely, the extent to which such concepts were bound by particular times and places. This, indeed, was in part what the Civil War was about: for Abraham Lincoln the right to freedom was indivisible, whereas for the Confederacy, it was a phenomenon that could be understood only in relative and localized terms. John Stuart Mill's *On Liberty* was published in 1859, and those in Britain who, like Mill, supported the Union cause tended to conceive of individual autonomy as a "sovereign" and "absolute" attribute. However, English writers of fiction (rather than of philosophy) characteristically balanced such etiolated designs with a more nuanced account of how these abstract ideas played out experientially, within the necessarily complicated conditions of social life. Elizabeth Gaskell, a friend and correspondent of Harvard professor Charles Eliot Norton, was a staunch supporter of the North during the Civil War, but she also recognized how the cotton famine in Manchester during the early 1860s was tied inextricably to events in the United States. Gaskell's writings about cultural divisions between the north and south of England, in *North and South* (1855) and her other novels, consequently reflect, as in an oblique mirror, those analogous tensions between north and south that she saw unfolding in a different guise across the Atlantic. In *North and South*, the northern industrialist John Thornton finds his business threatened by the development of international trade markets, and he complains of how "the Americans are getting their yarns so into the general market, that our only chance is producing them at a lower rate" (ch. 18). The social realism of the English Victorian novel, in other words, was not confined conceptually to the narrow circumference of domestic landscapes but took as its purview points of conjunction between national interests and the wider world.

In this sense, the transatlantic dimension in nineteenth-century fiction involves a paradoxical continuum that conjoins abstract and particular, global and local, in a single field. Fiction in both the United States and Europe during the nineteenth century swerved away from what Julia Kristeva has called the "mystical" notion of Volksgeist associated with Johann Gottfried von Herder's conception of a national state (1993, 33). Instead, it reformulated the idea of nation as what Kristeva called both a "*historical* identity" and "a *layering* of very concrete and very diverse causalities (climate, religions, past, laws, customs, manners, and so forth)" (55), thereby following Montesquieu's principle of *esprit général*, which acknowledges both local specificity and the possibilities of alterity. Such a "transnational" dimension, writes Kristeva, usefully deprives a nation of its supposedly "sacral aspects" (43) and allows access to the idea of "strangeness" (47) on both a psychological and a cultural level. Toward the end of the nineteenth century, the fiction of Henry James takes delight in cross-referencing national stereotypes, delineating in *Roderick Hudson* (1875) strait-laced Bostonians who become ensnared in the world of European art, and in *The Portrait of a Lady* (1881) an English aristocrat, Lord Warburton, who appears anomalously to lack conventional conservative assumptions. James's witting travesty of national forms of identity, something that becomes particularly prevalent in his later writing, represents a deliberate move away from the world of Cooper in the first half of the nineteenth century, when the spirit of nationalism was presented as being so deeply engrained in Cooper's fictional protagonists that they tended to allegorize a national idea within their own natural being. And whereas Stowe extrapolates an idea of race and nation from a sentimentalized conception of the family, James deliberately turns such nostalgic understandings of identity against prior understandings of themselves to undermine traditional assumptions of what might be meant by an "American" or a "European." The kind of comparative cross-referencing that lurks as a subliminal presence earlier in the nineteenth-century American novel becomes for James his most overt theme, and in his works of fiction, the teleological claims of national narrative come to enjoy only a spectral resonance.

24

THE TRANSAMERICAN NOVEL

ANNA BRICKHOUSE

To make a case for the "transamerican novel" as a useful category for literary historiography is to acknowledge the extent to which the concept of the "American novel," never particularly stable, has been rendered even more problematic by recent critical interventions. Neither part of the phrase—"American" or "novel"—can be called self-evident in a literary historical tradition that now routinely questions the following long-held assumptions: (1) that American writers are by definition born in the United States or, prior to 1776, in territory that falls within current national boundaries; (2) that American novels are written in English; (3) that the modification performed by the adjective "American" refers solely to the US nation and not the wider hemisphere; and (4) that the genre of the novel originated in Europe and eventually migrated to the so-called New World. The field known as "colonial American literature" or "early American literature" now routinely acknowledges the transatlantic mobility and mutuality of its object of study, both before and after the American Revolution, thus embracing as American novels works such as Daniel Defoe's *Moll Flanders* (1722) on the basis of its major, Virginia-set interlude; or British-born Susanna Rowson's *Charlotte Temple* (1791), first published in England but a bestseller in the United States. Similarly, the emergent field of multilingual American literature recognizes the vast body of literary works written in the United States (or what is now the United States) in languages other than English, including novels such as the anonymous *Jicoténcal*, published in Philadelphia in 1826, or Ludwig von Reizenstein's *Die Geheimnisse von New Orleans* (*The Mysteries of New Orleans*), published serially in Louisiana in 1854–1855.

At the same time, for scholars working in hemispheric, New World, or comparative American studies (to say nothing of the Latin Americanists with whom they seek to converse), the terrain of nineteenth-century American literature is a vast field of literary production across two continents, as Kirsten Silva Gruesz and Doris Sommer, among others, have shown: a field in which Gertrudis Gómez de Avellaneda's *Sab* (1841) or Juan León Mera Martínez's *Cumandá* (1879) claims as rightful a place in a volume on the American novel as Catharine Maria Sedgwick's *Hope Leslie; or, Early Times in the Massachusetts* (1827) or Nathaniel Hawthorne's *The House of the Seven Gables: A Romance* (1851). Finally, in light of Nancy Armstrong and Leonard Tennenhouse's suggestion that the novel might be reconceived not as a European innovation but as a fundamentally transatlantic one that "simultaneously recorded and recoded the colonial experience" (1994, 197), we have compelling reasons to consider many nonfictional texts, particularly captivity narratives, under the rubric of the American novel. *The Interesting Narrative of the Life of Olaudah Equiano, or Gustavus Vassa, the African. Written by Himself* (1789) provides a case in point, as a foundational slave narrative that also shares many literary features with eighteenth-century post-Revolutionary novels: indeed, the authenticity of its early African-set chapters has been disputed by Vincent Carretta and others. However problematic the terms of the debate surrounding the veracity of this text, the questions it raises do push us to recognize, as Cathy Davidson has argued, the literary and historical possibilities of construing Equiano, as much as William Hill Brown or Charles Brockden Brown, as the "Father of the American Novel."

All these arguments underlie the concept of the transamerican novel. For the purposes of this volume, organized as it is within a larger series on the history of the novel in English, I restrict my discussion in the following chapter to the *Anglo-American* genealogy of what I call transamerican novels: works produced within or in some way shaped by the ever-fluctuating borders between the mainland English colonies and the United States, on the one hand, and the wider American hemisphere, on the other. But "transamerican" also refers to a particular mode of critical delineation that depends specifically on close reading—though not toward the endpoint of formal singularity or unity. Rather, the transamerican interpretive mode must attend to the minute and varied textual details that muddy the ostensibly clear waters of national affiliation, the persistent discontinuities of history that trouble a national frame of reference, and the processes of social institutionalization that (often retroactively) generate assumptions about national identity and the nationality of meaning within a given work. In its mode of close reading, the transamerican interpretive impulse is necessarily *both* symptomatic, governed by the hermeneutics of suspicion, *and* open to the possibility that a text may embed its own theorization of how narratives generate meaning within, between, and across politically defined geographic spaces.

To this end, the bulk of this chapter considers in close detail two early novels that together suggest a prehistory of the transamerican novel whose full generic contours would emerge only later in the nineteenth century: Daniel Defoe's *Robinson Crusoe* (1719) and Leonora Sansay's *Secret History; or, The Horrors of St. Domingo* (1808). One is canonical, the other virtually unacknowledged until the last decade; one is written and published in England, the other written in Haiti and published in Philadelphia; one is cast as a tale of adventure, the other as a domestic novel of coquetry and marriage; one presents the singular history of an individual man, the other a history of multiple women whose lives intersect and define each other. Crucially, one appeared a half century before the political upheaval that would culminate in the American Revolution and the emergence of a national US imaginary; the other appeared within the half century following the Declaration of Independence. Both texts, however, articulate the conflicting structures of national feeling that define a later transamerican narrative genealogy, establishing the lineaments of a framework within which other novels may be meaningfully located: the narrative entanglement of domestic and foreign, the ambivalent plotlines of divided allegiances to statehood, and the ultimate impurity of narrators' desires and texts' national affiliations. Finally, both texts gesture toward a larger world system that exceeds the transamerican—a world system of novels in which the geographic axis of any given narrative is always in tension with other, less visible, axes that have been sliced away in the cartographic work performed by the text. Coupled together, *Robinson Crusoe* and *Secret History* thus illustrate the ways in which the transamerican novel might be defined by a performance of metageographical self-construction: a critical reflection upon both the transnational coordinates of the literary past and the charged political valences of literary place.

The Spanish Original of *Robinson Crusoe*

The literary origins of the quasi-American *Robinson Crusoe* are transatlantic, to judge from a number of influential studies, including that of Armstrong and Tennenhouse, who contend that the novel recasts the Anglo-American captivity narrative by "representing the English in the New World as an abducted body" (1994, 204). From a hemispheric perspective, however, Defoe's overt narrative of transatlantic English settlement is underwritten not only by Crusoe's sense of his own imprisonment ("my Reign, or my Captivity, which you please" [Defoe 2007, 117]) but also by his unacknowledged ambivalence about his own Englishness, and his repeated feelings of desire for and attachment to the southerly part of the American hemisphere, rather than England or its New World colonies.

Crusoe's latent Ibero-American fantasy shapes the novel almost from the beginning. Even during the period of his early African captivity, when Crusoe hopes for his freedom, he imagines that his eventual means of salvation will be not an English ship but a "*Spanish* or *Portugal* Man of War" (18). After his escape and settlement in Brazil, Crusoe finds himself easily translated from an Englishman into "Seignior Inglese" (32), a landowning man who "had not only learn'd the Language, but had contracted Acquaintance and Friendship among my Fellow-Planters" (34). Later in the novel, Crusoe will retroactively try to characterize his failure in Brazil as the failure of an English Protestant to relate to Catholic Brazilians—but it would be more accurate to say that Crusoe's failure lies in the impossibility, as he perceives it, of escaping the English destiny from which he is running—even while in Brazil.

Thus, measuring his middling income against that of the wealthy Portuguese and Brazilian owners of sugar plantations, Crusoe considers himself no better off than if he had taken his father's advice; he "might as well ha' staid at Home" in England (32). Moreover, the problem presented by this dreaded English fate turns out to be more specific than what his father calls "the very Middle Station, or upper Degree of low Life," for it hinges upon Crusoe's lack of "Help" on his new Brazilian land—a situation that causes him to regret selling his "Boy *Xury*," the African man who would otherwise now be his slave (31). The English outcome that Crusoe has failed to avoid—despite having "gone 5000 Miles off to do it among Strangers and Salvages in a Wilderness"—is thus a life without slaves: "no Work to be done, but by the Labour of my Hands" (32). Such a life is, in Crusoe's view, a life of extreme social privation: "I used to say, I liv'd just like a Man cast away upon some desolate Island" (32). Prophesying his own narrative trajectory, Crusoe thus avows that to be English is to be without slaves, which is in turn to be *islanded*—cut off from the hemispheric pleasures enjoyed by the Spanish and Portuguese.

When Crusoe does meet his islanded destiny, he appears at first to accept it and sets about guiding his conduct according to a newfound sense of Englishness, in particular by converting to Protestantism. Yet this English identity appears tenuous as soon as Crusoe considers the specific geography of his situation in what "must be Part of America"—and more specifically "must be near the *Spanish* Dominions," either on "the *Spanish* coast" or on a "*Savage* Coast between the *Spanish* Country and *Brasils*" (93). While this geographic realization prompts some initial anxiety about cannibals, it also reactivates Crusoe's desire for a fate other than his own Englishness by authorizing a particular fantasy of Spanishness. As Crusoe observes, "my Invention now run quite another Way; for Night and Day, I could think of nothing but how I might destroy some of these Monsters in their cruel bloody Entertainment" (142)—among other ways, by "putting twenty or thirty of them to the Sword" (143). The detail comes from Bartolomé de Las Casas's widely known *A Short Account of the Destruction of the Indies* (1552), as does Crusoe's rhetorical stance when he insists, "It would take up a larger Volume than this whole Work is intended to be, to set down all the Contrivances I hatch'd . . . for the destroying these Creatures" (142). Lest the reader miss the point that the protagonist's "Invention" is a Spanish one (as the Black Legend first inspired by Las Casas's work would have it), Crusoe spells out a high-toned disavowal of what are in fact his own professed desires by condemning "the Conduct of the *Spaniards* in all their Barbarities practis'd in *America*, and where they destroy'd Millions of these People, who however they were Idolaters and Barbarians, and had several bloody and barbarous Rites in their Customs, such as sacrificing human Bodies to their Idols, were yet, as to the *Spaniards*, very innocent People" (145). Characteristically, Crusoe undercuts the purported moral force of his outraged renunciation of Spanish-style bloodlust by acknowledging that violence is not a practical strategy for a single, stranded man who cannot, in any case, be "sure to kill every one" of the natives who might visit his island and then escape to tell others of his presence there. But neither "Principle" nor "Policy" can keep Crusoe off the Spanish fantasy, and within ten pages he finds himself again "in the murthering Humour," pursued "in the Night" by Black Legend dreams of "killing the Savages, and of the Reasons why I might justify the doing of it" (155–56).

Though the final third of the novel completes its transatlantic circuit by restoring Crusoe briefly to England, the narrative nevertheless relentlessly tracks the steady slide of its protagonist's inclination toward the hemispheric South. As if in response to Crusoe's Black Legend dreams, a wrecked Spanish ship appears off the island, materializing his fantasy, and inspiring in him desirous speculations unrelated to his actual situation on the island: "I had room to suppose, the Ship had a great deal of Wealth on board; and if I may guess by the Course she steer'd, she must have been bound from the *Buenos Ayres*, or the *Rio de la Plata*, in the South Part of *America*, beyond the *Brasils*, to the *Havana*, in the Gulph of *Mexico*, and so perhaps to *Spain*: She had no doubt a great Treasure in her" (162). In the scene that follows, Crusoe famously misrecognizes his own interest in the Spanish currency, lugging to shore the "fifty Pieces of Eight in Ryals" (*pieza de ocho reales*) despite claiming that he "had no manner of occasion for it: 'Twas to [him] as the Dirt under [his] Feet" (163). But the geographical specificity of his misrecognition also suggests a particular hemispheric fantasy—one located firmly in the "South Part of *America,*" far from England and its colonies. Even when Crusoe arrives at his famous conclusion that his early filial disobedience was a kind of "Original Sin," his momentary attention to the "excellent Advice of [his] Father" lapses immediately into thoughts of his life in "the *Brasils*, as a Planter" with "a settled Fortune, a well stock'd Plantation" (164). Indeed, though he casts his decision to leave Brazil as an error "of the same kind" as his initial "Opposition" to his father—the mistake "of not being satisfy'd with the Station wherein God and Nature has plac'd [him]"—Crusoe now retroactively fantasizes that this "Station" was not English at all but Brazilian. It was, as he now imagines it, hardly static: rather, it was a mere way-"Station" on his way to becoming "one of the most considerable Planters in the *Brasils* . . . worth an hundred thousand *Moydors,*" the original lack of slaves conveniently ameliorated through "Patience and Time" and the money to "have bought them at our own Door" (164). In this context, his current situation on the island takes on a new but still decidedly non-English, ironic resonance: with his hoarded *reales*, he now has "more Wealth indeed than . . . before" but "no more use for it, than the *Indians* of *Peru* had, before the *Spaniards* came there" (165).

When Friday finally arrives and offers a partial fulfillment of Crusoe's South American fantasy—for now there is simply no "wear[ing] off the edge of [his] Desire to the Thing," his "eager[ness] to be upon [the Savages] . . . so as to make them entirely Slaves to me" (169)—the novel grows significantly more specific about its ambiguous southerly setting somewhere "near the *Spanish* dominions." Crusoe now clarifies what he only "afterwards understood": that his island lies "in the Mouth, or the Gulph" of "the mighty River *Oroonooko*," while "to the *W.* and *N. W.* was the great Island *Trinidad*," land of "the *Caribbees*, which our Maps place on the Part of *America*, which reaches from the Mouth of the River *Oroonooko* to *Guiana*, and onwards to *St. Martha*" (181). The location of Crusoe's island, in other words, is the contested territory of Sir Walter Raleigh's two attempts to establish English access to a South American fortune in Indian gold that would rival the success of England's Spanish enemies. As if Crusoe has subliminally summoned his fantasy Spaniards merely by specifying the location of his island, the novel here introduces a mysterious group of "white bearded Men" who turn out to be living nearby (181–82). According to Friday, "they had kill'd *much Mans*, that was his Word; by all which I understood, he meant the *Spaniards*, whose Cruelties in *America* had been spread over the whole Countries, and was remember'd by all the Nations from Father to Son" (182). Crusoe draws directly from Raleigh's *The Discoverie of the Large, Rich and Bewtiful Empyre of Guiana* (1596), both in the Black Legend rhetoric and the claim, made via Friday, of an indigenous oral tradition recording Spanish atrocities. But his citation ultimately bears the mark of desire, even in its implied denunciation, as Crusoe's eager next question reveals: "I enquir'd if he could tell me how I might come from this Island, and get among those white Men; he told me yes, yes . . . [which] began to relish with me very well" (182). Within a few pages, Crusoe will explicitly admit what he has wanted all along: "From this time I confess I had a Mind to venture over, and see if I could possibly joyn with these Bearded-men, who I made no doubt were *Spaniards* or *Portuguese*" (190).

Fantasy is made flesh when a real Spaniard appears on the island, an arrival that allows Crusoe again to showcase his mastery of the "*Portuguese* Tongue"—but also to demonstrate, in a new act of linguistic affiliation, "as much *Spanish* as [he] could make up" (198). At first, Crusoe resolves the problem of Spanish-English translation with "Friday being my Interpreter . . . for the *Spaniard* spoke the Language of the *Savages* pretty well" (203). Soon, however, Crusoe and the Spaniard appear to converse fluently without Friday's interpretive services: "I had a serious Discourse with the *Spaniard*," Crusoe explains, "and when I understood that there were sixteen more of his Countrymen and *Portuguese* . . . I ask'd him all the Particulars of their Voyage, and found they [had been on] a *Spanish* ship bound from the *Rio de la Plata* to the *Havana*" (205). This communication, of course, uncannily matches Crusoe's own Spanish fantasy qua navigational hypothesis about the earlier ship, bound from the "South Part of America," from whose wreck he profited. Faced with his fantasy so close to coming true, Crusoe fears the obvious "Treachery and ill Usage" from the very countrymen he has been actively seeking to join (205): that "they should afterwards make me their Prisoner in New Spain, where an English Man was certain to be made a Sacrifice" to "the *Inquisition*" and "the merciless Claws of the Priests" (206). Here again, however, Crusoe quickly undercuts this Black Legend rhetoric with a return to what he clearly desires more than fears:

"I added, That otherwise I was perswaded." He again envisions his future in the southerly parts of the hemisphere: "if [the Spaniards] were all here, we might, with so many Hands, build a Bark large enough to carry us all away"—and not to England or the English colonies, but "either to the Brasils South-ward, or to the Islands or *Spanish* Coast Northward." Though Crusoe is adamant that he does not want to be carried "by Force among their own People," his desire to go voluntarily to the Spanish and Portuguese portions of America is clear enough (206).

The novel never tells us what language Crusoe and the Spaniard use after they begin communicating fluently. But the scale weighs toward Spanish, for Crusoe never mimics any halting attempts at English on the Spaniard's part, as he does with Friday. Moreover, when the English ship that eventually rescues him arrives on the island, Crusoe (knowing full well that the men he has been spying on are Englishmen) calls "aloud to them in *Spanish, What are ye gentlemen*?" (214). Neither the question nor the language makes much sense unless understood as an expression of the ambivalence about his own Englishness and the profound fantasy of Spanishness that he has struggled with since the opening pages of the novel (he is, after all, sired by "a Foreigner" and then named Crusoe "by the usual Corruption of Words in *England*" [5]). Crusoe's fantasy of Spanishness has been seriously thwarted by this twist in the novel that brings an English ship just as he is on the verge of joining with the Spaniards to build a boat and sail away for Brazil or Spanish America. He seems oddly backed into a corner when he switches languages and announces, "I am a Man, an *English-man,* and dispos'd to assist you" (214). One would go too far to suggest that he is lying by saying so—and certainly he does ask to be taken to England in making a deal with the captain—but by the time he has outmaneuvered the mutineers to restore the English captain to his rightful position, Crusoe has retranslated himself back into a Latin identity, referring to himself, somewhat pathetically, as "*Generalissimo*" (224).

As Crusoe still clings to his Spanish fantasy, his final, ambiguous gesture, before leaving the island for England, is to imagine *Robinson Crusoe* itself—its narrative, its authorship, its population of characters, its initial distribution and reception—as an indigenous production of his Ibero-American island, somewhere "between the *Spanish* Country and *Brasils*" (93). As there is no one left to receive his story in England—where he will arrive "as Perfect a Stranger to all the World, as if [he] had never been known there" and find "all [his] Family extinct" (234)—the narrative belongs in "the South Part of America":

> When [the English mutineers] had all declar'd their Willingness to stay, I then told them, I would let them into the Story of my living there, and put them into the Way of making it easy to them: Accordingly I gave them the whole History of the Place, and of my coming to it. . . . I told them the Story also of the sixteen *Spaniards* that were to be expected; for whom I left a Letter, and made them promise to treat them in common with themselves. I left them my Fire Arms . . .

> a Barrel and a half of Powder. . . . I gave them a Description of the Way I manag'd the Goats, and Directions to milk and fatten them. . . . In a Word, I gave them every Part of my own Story. (233)

If Crusoe endows the English mutineers with his weapons, supplies, and the material means of survival, he charges them with sharing it all with the "expected" Spaniards. At the same time, he is also contracting with these Englishmen—in exchange for their "Willingness" to stay on the island—to "let them into the Story" that is his novel. They will populate both his island and his text while simultaneously enacting the initial reception of his novelistic production, "the whole History of the Place" and "every Part of my own Story." Crucially, however, it is the "sixteen *Spaniards*"—whom Crusoe has never even met—who inherit, in the form of his "Letter," a written text rather than an oral narrative. These Spaniards constitute his initial *readership*, the ideal recipients of the missive that, it is implied, will become the novel itself. By the narrative's own logic of transmission, then, the original text of *Robinson Crusoe* arguably exists in *Spanish* before its translation into the first *English* novel.

If the text of Crusoe's novel is always already Spanish in its original state, its concluding section nevertheless stages the protagonist's internal struggle to maintain his Englishness despite his continual temptation toward "the South Part of *America*." In an odd but telling detail that has gone unmentioned during the narration of his Protestant conversion on the island, Crusoe casually announces that he was formerly a practicing Catholic in Brazil—"having profess'd [himself] a Papist" and "made no Scruple of being openly of the Religion of the Country" (241). Now, however, Crusoe finds that he has "some Doubts about the *Roman* Religion"—doubts that emerged "especially in [his] State of Solitude": to go to Brazil now, he argues, would mean choosing either to uphold his Protestantism and "die in the Inquisition," or to "embrace the *Roman* Catholick Religion, without any Reserve" (255). Crusoe presents his subsequent decision to sell his plantation and remain in England as a matter of "Principles"—though he has already admitted, quite recently in the narrative, that dying as a "Papist" is "not the main thing that kept [him] from going to the *Brasils*" (241). Indeed, just after declaring the opposition to Catholicism that ostensibly keeps him from returning to Brazil, Crusoe writes to "the Prior of St. Augustine" with "the Offer of the 872 Moidores . . . which I desir'd might be given 500 to the Monastery, and 372 to the Poor, as the Prior should direct, desiring the good *Padres* Prayers for me, and the like" (242). The money to the monastery will be used, as the narrative has earlier disclosed, "for the Conversion of the *Indians* to the Catholick Faith" (235). Crusoe may be temporarily cutting his economic ties to South America, but he is arguably strengthening his religious and ideological ones.

No wonder, then, that his terse narration of his life in England is so ambiguous and partial: "I in Part settled my self here," he hedges, adding as an afterthought that he has also married and had three children. It is abundantly clear that his heart is still "in the Spanish Dominions" or those of the Portuguese. "My Interest in the Brasils seemed to summon me thither," he explains, but even after he has sold his estate there, he concedes, "yet I could not keep the Country out of my Head." After his wife's abrupt death, Crusoe is only too happy to abandon his three English children to abscond with an already faintly Hispanicized nephew ("coming Home with good Success from a Voyage to *Spain*"). He can no longer resist "the strong Inclination" to return to his island. Significantly, he is not returning to learn if the English have survived but rather "if the poor *Spaniards* were in Being there" (256). Of the English "Rogues" he left behind, Crusoe wishes merely to know how they have treated the Spaniards, for they and not the Englishmen are his primary concern. It is the Spaniards and the "whole Story of their Lives"—and not the narrative of the English—that ultimately matter to Crusoe: how the Spaniards have been "insulted" by the English "Villains"; "how at last the *Spaniards* were oblig'd to use Violence with [the English]; how [the English] were subjected to the *Spaniards*; how honestly the *Spaniards* used them" (257). In perhaps his fullest gesture of novelistic affiliation, Crusoe terms the story of the Spaniards "a History, if it were entred into, as full of Variety and wonderful Accidents, as my own Part" (257).

In signaling these twinned narratives of adventure in the southern half of the hemisphere, Crusoe suggests that the origins of his own story are not just "American," as Armstrong and Tennenhouse have suggested, but are in fact defined by their differentiation from England and the English colonies under the sign of both "the Brasils" and Crusoe's "*Spaniards*" in the "South Part of *America*." To privilege the story of these Spaniards is to recast not just English belatedness in the New World colonial enterprise but, in fact, also the Anglo-Americanness of the very novel he narrates—and the original Spanish text from which it logically derives—by insisting on the novel's rightful (South) American inheritors: as Crusoe calls them, "my Successors the *Spaniards*" (257). The origins of this Anglo-American novel are not merely transatlantic, then, but hemispheric: in Crusoe's Spanish fantasy, in his disavowed desire for Ibero-America, and in the Spanish original subtending his anglophone narrative, we learn much about how to read the tradition of the transamerican novel in English.

The *Secret History* of Transamerican Desire

If Defoe's *Robinson Crusoe* presents an exemplary case for thinking through the transamerican underpinnings of the early "American" novel during the colonial period, a far less influential narrative from the early republican period usefully illuminates the complex literary and political intertwining of the post-Revolutionary United States with the wider hemisphere. Published anonymously in the revolutionary city that hosted the two Continental Congresses, *Secret History;*

or, The Horrors of St. Domingo was written by the still little-known Philadelphian author Leonora Sansay. Unwieldy and wayward in both its plotlines and its narrative voice, Sansay's epistolary novel is based loosely upon the author's own letters, written—as its title suggests—during her stay in revolutionary Saint Domingue from 1802 until her return to Philadelphia, via Cuba, in 1804. But the Caribbean-set novel is arguably just as much about the United States as it is about the titular "St. Domingo," as the remainder of its long title makes clear: *A Series of Letters, Written by a Lady at Cape Francois. To Colonel Burr, late Vice-President of the United States, Principally During the Command of General Rochambeau.* Withholding her authorial identity, Sansay specifies two contemporaneous figures as central characters within the ensuing novel, both of them veterans of the American Revolution: Vicomte de Rochambeau, the French general notorious for his massacres of rebellious slaves in Haiti; and Aaron Burr, the third vice president of the United States and Sansay's own erstwhile lover.

The roman à clef nature of *Secret History* might easily invite an oversimplified, quasi-travelogue reading of the novel were it not for a doubled authorial self-encoding in the text's two main female characters, the sisters Mary and Clara—each of whom represents a very different geographical trajectory for the novel's uncertain outcome. Both sisters share features with Sansay herself: "Mary," the primary epistolary narrator throughout most of the novel, was also the first name sometimes attributed to Sansay; "Clara" was the name that the married Sansay took up in order to write about herself in the third person in her quasi-love letters to Burr—a dissimulating gesture within her already illicit missives. The narratives proffered by the two sisters are ultimately in a kind of geopolitical competition for novelistic closure: while Clara is building an "empire" of devotion throughout the Caribbean, Mary longs for the United States and forms a plan to return both sisters to Philadelphia under the protection of Burr.

Within this transamerican frame, the novel hints at its own strategies of authorial self-concealment while also gesturing at the violent international history embedded in its ostensibly domestic problems. Alluding to the memoirs of Madame de Staël, whose essay on the passions she has been reading at the beginning of the novel, Mary remarks, "I have heard an anecdote of her which I admire; a friend, to whom she had communicated her intention of publishing her memoirs, asked what she intended doing with the gallant part,—Oh, she replied, je ne me peindrai qu'en buste" (ltr. 1). The quip—"I will paint myself but as a bust only"—was often attributed to de Staël in the early nineteenth century as a metaphor for autobiographical writing that concealed more than it revealed—painting only from the shoulders up, or *en buste,* thereby separating intellect from corporeal passions. But in the specific context of Mary's letter, the witticism suggests an image by then emblematic of the French Revolution, the ideals of which, by that moment, had arrived with violence in Saint Domingue: an authorial head severed from its body.

Secret History enacts a version of this splitting through its twinned, autobiographical protagonists, both of whom are in some sense partnered with Burr over the course of the novel—Mary, by virtue of her passionate letters to him, and Clara, by Mary's own implication in her last letter, plotting his union with her sister. Just after the letter that cites de Staël, the novel also makes a literal presentation *en buste*, when Mary tells the story of a jealous Creole wife who observes that a "beautiful negro girl" has captured the attention of her husband and then orders her to be decapitated: "I can give you something that will excite your appetite," she tells him over dinner and then—in another instance of the novel's mode of ironic twinning—promptly offers him "the head of Coomba" to make good on her promise (ltr. 2). The image of the murdered Haitian woman's head thus overlays the bust of the French de Staël, whose witticism foreshadows it, as well as the American bust of Mary herself, whose narration signals her own epistolary concealments. Beneath the colonial aggressions layered into the anecdote lies the event of writing as an act of sexually charged violence: like the Creole mistress's murderous work of art—Coomba *en buste*—Sansay's novel performs a political homicide of sorts by outing Burr on its title page as the narrator's correspondent and beloved.

Burr plays no role as a character in *Secret History*, though his presence is ubiquitous because the majority of Mary's letters are addressed to him; everything she narrates about herself, Clara, and the novel's other historical and minor characters must be contextualized by the political figure—the vice president of the United States within the novel's temporal frame—to whom its letters are primarily addressed. Significantly, however, Mary never interrogates Burr about his political work in the executive office—as Sansay did when she wrote to the historical Burr on May 6, 1803, to ask, "Have you raised an army to hinder the french taking possession of Louisiana?" (Drexler 2007, 230). By then the US government had completed the Louisiana Purchase, but Sansay could not have known this—and not only because she did not get the newspapers, as she tells Burr, but also because the treaty had not yet been made public. Thus while the historical letter suggests Sansay understands her experiences in revolutionary Saint Domingue through the lens of US military interests in national expansion—and her perception of Burr's vice presidential role in these matters—the novel on which the letters are based makes no reference to the historical context in which he is embedded. It is therefore useful to recall that the English genre of the secret history, to which Sansay's novel refers in its title, depends on the internalization of public concerns, as Michael McKeon has argued—and that *Secret History* domesticates some of the central international questions of the day, such as the one Sansay asks about Louisiana, through a narrative devoted to marriage and romantic intrigue in the Caribbean. Sansay's novel not only enacts this internalization, however, but also makes the internalizing process a self-conscious subject—which is why Mary, ostensibly reiterating Burr's criticism of her previous letters, writes, "You say, that in relating public affairs, or those of Clara, I forget my own, or conceal them under this appearance of neglect" (ltr. 8).

Mary's reference to this conflation of public affairs and Clara's affairs suggests one key to this roman-à-clef and to what I would identify as its secret history of transamerican desire. Consider, for example, Clara's observation at a dinner party early in the novel that "Washington should also have . . . a place" on the wall inscribed with the names of "Buonaparte . . . Frederic . . . Massena" in the colonial "Government house" where Rochambeau resides (ltr. 6). The implied request is a coy one, nonsensical because the wall is not just about prominent military leaders but about Napoleon specifically: Buonaparte appears alongside the military tactician he most admired and his most beloved commander in the French army. Yet Rochambeau responds to Clara's wishes at the next social event with a new inscription on the wall prominently facing the door—"Washington, Liberty, and Independence!" (ltr. 6)—a slogan that can only resound ironically in the home of a French general brought in to quell a revolution over "the blessing of liberty" that, as Mary observes, "the negroes have felt . . . and will not be easily deprived of" (ltr. 3). Mary's ironic distance from the *French* colonial project rings clear as a bell, but it is the *American* Clara's imperial sway that is "now considered assured" (ltr. 4): Rochambeau may have "preserv[ed] the Cape [François]" from the rebelling slaves, Clara tells him, but in doing so, he has merely "given her an opportunity of making the conquest" of his attentions (ltr. 4).

This imperial acquisition is not a matter of shared territory or mutual governance: "the heart of Clara acknowledge[s] not the empire of [the French] general," as Mary observes (ltr. 8). Even when Rochambeau has "laid an embargo" to prevent the American Clara from leaving the port (ltr. 8)—just as the French were then demanding an embargo of the lucrative American trade with Saint Domingue in order to help them starve out Toussaint L'Ouverture and the other revolutionaries—she eventually succeeds in escaping to Baracoa and on to St. Iago. The "contest for supremacy" fought against Clara's Creole husband, St. Louis, on the other hand, will be more difficult, and "will decide forever the empire of the party that conquers" (ltr. 6). Read through the backward lens of Sansay's question to Burr ("Have you raised an army . . . ?"), Mary's breathless, conspiratorial accounts of Clara's shifting romantic relations with her French suitor and Creole husband—and soon enough a new Cuban paramour—evoke the uncertain boundaries of the nascent US empire embodied by the two American sisters. Moreover, by the time *Secret History* appeared in print, the historical Burr had been accused, brought to trial, and acquitted precisely on the charges of "rais[ing] an army"—and with his own treasonous "contest for supremacy" in mind: a plan to establish an independent, transamerican empire out of Louisiana, the disputed western territories, and Spanish-held Mexico. Sansay herself appears to have collaborated in Burr's grand design—though the exact nature of the plan is still debated by historians.

That Sansay's novel interjects this political landscape into its disclosure of the secret history of Clara's adventures is clear enough. But it performs this act of narrative domestication with a telling degree of ambivalence, which emerges most clearly in the differentiation of its two narrative voices. From the novel's outset, Mary is determined to frame the story of Clara's Caribbean conquests within a very different geographical genre—the seduction narrative—by bemoaning the unfortunate "vein of coquetry" in a heroine otherwise "destined by nature to embellish the sphere of domestic felicity" (ltr. 4, 5). On one level, Mary intermittently defends Clara against the accusations introduced by her own narrative ("[Clara's husband] thinks [her] attached to the general. I know she is not! her vanity alone has been interested" [ltr. 8]). Yet Mary is always quick to return, in the guise of moralism, to the titillating sexual atmosphere surrounding Clara—"violent in her attachments, and precipitate in her movements"—and her seemingly inevitable slide into the seduction novel's central premise: "committing . . . an unpardonable act of folly" (ltr. 23). Yet there is a serious geographical impediment to the story Mary so clearly wants to tell: by her own definition, there are no "victims of seduction" on the depraved island of Saint Domingue: "In this country that unfortunate class of beings, so numerous in my own . . . devoted to public contempt and universal scorn, is unknown" (ltr. 10). It is this problem of location—perhaps more than her professed desire for "peaceful security"—that explains Mary's eagerness to bring Clara back to Philadelphia and the "happy country" where Burr resides (ltr. 9). Back on national terrain, Mary can resituate her sister's story within a legitimate narrative of seduction.

Indeed, when the sisters leave Saint Domingue and reach Cuba, Mary's determination to tell Clara's story as a seduction narrative increases with her proximity to her desired US destination. Once a new suitor, Don Alonzo de P—, has arrived on the scene, and Clara has gone missing, Mary is able to claim with certainty, "As for the world, its sentence is already pronounced" (ltr. 24). And though she laments that the judgment will be passed by "those who possess not a thousandth part of [her sister's] virtues," Mary insists darkly, nevertheless, that Clara "will be condemned" for her "elopement" (ltr. 24). Indeed, Mary almost anticipates that condemnation—"My heart [will] renounce her, and she will no longer have a sister," she threatens—though she suspends the renunciation until learning both "if she has sought the protection with another" and—more to the point—"if she will not accompany me" (ltr. 24). Given that her ultimate destination is "the continent"—where, by her own account, the "victims of seduction" are in plentiful supply and invariably punished with "universal scorn" (ltr. 10)—Mary's longing to bring Clara back to the northeastern United States seems suspiciously close to desiring for her sister the very fate that she rhetorically bemoans: "[S]hould I abandon this poor girl to misfortune? Should I leave her to perish among strangers?" (ltr. 26). The hypothetical fate she names is, of course, exactly what happens to the heroine of an early "American" seduction novel—most famously Rowson's *Charlotte Temple*, which became a bestseller in 1794 upon its first American publication in Sansay's hometown, Philadelphia.

But Clara thwarts the momentum of Mary's punitive narrative when she finally enters the novel as a narrator in her own right—and when, as Maria Windell notes, she writes back to her sister rejecting the transatlantic plot line of Anglo-American seduction. From her Caribbean locus of enunciation, Clara voices an alternative to the plot of the misguided Anglo girl corrupted by a French libertine or a Spanish Casanova: she discloses in her first letter that her Cuban "elopement" was not with Alonzo but with a female "protector" residing in El Cobre, homeland of the *cobrero* maroons and setting of a famous Cuban slave revolt (ltr. 28). Though she assures Mary that she gave Alonzo not even "a look of encouragement" in response to his attentions, and that she and her sister "will return to the continent together" promptly, Clara has moved closer to the revolutionary Haitian setting, and to the "empire" of suitors, in which the novel began (ltr. 28). Indeed, her next letter virtually teases Mary with its brazen announcement that Alonzo has arrived at her Cuban retreat with his "hints, in broken accents, [of] the passion he has felt" (ltr. 29). As for Mary's plan to return stateside, Clara straightforwardly delays this trajectory: "It will be impossible for me to leave [Cuba] in less than a month" (ltr. 29). By her final letter, when Clara announces her imminent departure on the trip to reunite with Mary, she describes a journey that "will be delightful," because, as she casually confesses, Don Alonzo will accompany her (ltr. 31). And though Clara avows her desire to see her sister, she also pronounces her reluctance to depart the Caribbean: "I feel something like regret at leaving this country" (ltr. 31). Perhaps she senses the literary fate that awaits her back in Philadelphia, for she has found another ill-fated female companion to bring home with her. Madame St. Clair is a woman of wasted "talents" who "has known nothing but misfortune" despite the fact that, or indeed because, "her beauty, the graceful sweetness of her manners, and her divine voice render it impossible to behold or listen to her with indifference" (ltr. 29). Preparing Mary to meet this potential, new victim of the passions—"You will love her, I am sure"—Clara takes up the language of assaulted virtue, announcing that the unfortunate Creole woman has been "seduced" by Clara's own descriptions of her northeastern homeland, a "peaceful country" that is, nevertheless, a nation of certain death for the coquette (ltr. 29).

Ultimately, then, *Secret History* is not precisely a seduction novel; rather, it is self-consciously *about* the nation-consolidating, domestication project of this early American genre, disciplining disobedient heroines and post-Revolutionary readers alike. Sansay's narrative intermittently reproduces and then distances itself from the trajectory of the seduction novel, performing a teasing dance that moves back and forth, shadowing its domestic counterpart with a transamerican critique of the genre voiced from the Caribbean margins. Thus when Mary's last letter announces her return to Burr with her wayward sister in tow and confirms Clara's status as a coquette—"It is true, [she] is said to be [one]"—it also reminds Burr and readers alike that this figure must be understood within a wider, international literary context: "[H]ave not ladies of superior talents and attractions, at all times and in all countries been subject to that censure?" (ltr. 32). Yet in its focus on her sister's future in Philadelphia, Mary's last letter continues to push Clara toward a specifically domestic American literary fate, virtually pledging to deliver the married Clara to the "late vice-president[ial]" arms of Burr. Assigning Burr the role of Clara's "protector"—and instantiating with this term a type of relationship for which Mary had earlier threatened to renounce her sister—the last letter makes clear the quasi-incestuous pandering that Mary has been performing all along in writing sensuously of Clara to Burr: now she advises the former vice president explicitly of her plan to "infuse into your bosom those sentiments for my sister which glow so warmly in my own" (ltr. 32). In some ways, then, Mary's apparent desire to dispossess Clara of her newfound Caribbean autonomy—by consolidating her relationship with Burr in letters of epistolary collusion—functions here as a romantic analogue for the famous political scandal surrounding "Burr's conspiracy," in which the historical Burr had by 1808 become embroiled. The secret history of Clara's coquetry is, in this sense, the political history of emergent US imperial desire. For Burr's dream of a transamerican empire—whatever the extent of his actual scheme—subtends the domestic, closeted history of Clara's intrigues and marital nightmares with the far-reaching public story of US imperial interests and its concomitant disavowal of hemispheric desire.

Secret History thus establishes in the early national period the defining feature of the genre of the transamerican novel as inaugurated by *Robinson Crusoe*: a conflicted structure of national feeling that we might call "hemispheric disavowal." Just as Crusoe simultaneously longs for the Iberian-American portion of the Americas while projecting onto it a morally suspect geography of "*Spaniards* in all their Barbarities" (145), so too does *Secret History* enact a tension between Clara's Caribbean empire of desire and the "happy country" (ltr. 9) that Mary imagines to be cordoned off from the rest of the hemisphere. Together the two novels anticipate in important ways what I have elsewhere called a "transamerican renaissance" that emerged during the rise of US literary nationalism in the 1820s, when the demise of a potential *inter*-American system of political relations gave way to a literary imaginary fraught with the anxieties and desires attending a nation whose geographic borders were expanding even as its imagined racial, ethnic, and linguistic borders were narrowing and calcifying (Brickhouse 2004, 2–7). In *The Last of the Mohicans: A Narrative of 1757* (1826), for example, James Fenimore Cooper—the first US author to write within the category of the "national narrative," in Jonathan Arac's estimation (2005, 5–6)—would consolidate the "American" identity of the British character Duncan Heyward precisely at the moment when Heyward becomes conscious of his antipathy for Cora, whose West Indian and racially mixed heritage has permeated the borders of the future US nation. Cora thus embodies the tangled history of disavowed US–West Indian relations as the novel's anxious diagnosis of Caribbean difference, necessarily excised from its narrative of future national emergence. But as Sansay's novel suggests, the history of the Haitian Revolution, and of Caribbean emancipation in other colonies, could not be so easily disentangled from the national US trajectory imagined by nineteenth-century novels. Thus, Edgar Allan Poe's self-conscious understanding of the "awful importance" of "recent events in the West Indies" (1836, 337) gives substance to the expansionist purview of his only completed novel, *The Narrative of Arthur Gordon Pym* (1838), a narrative that culminates in a vision of slave revolt in the "region of the south" (note). Harriet Beecher Stowe's *Uncle Tom's Cabin; or, Life Among the Lowly* (1852) similarly skirts the question of what might ensue in the antebellum United States "if ever the San Domingo hour comes" (ch. 23), while Herman Melville's novella "Benito Cereno" (1855) famously explores the answer to that question aboard a slave ship called the *San Dominick*. Frederick Douglass's only work of fiction, the novella titled "The Heroic Slave" (1853), conjoins the potentials of slave revolt to the proximity of US and Caribbean shores, while Martin Delany's *Blake; or, The Huts of America* (1859, 1861–62) deploys a vision of pan-American slave revolt to explore the hemispheric inextricability of race, colonialism, and slavery across the tangled genealogies of US and Cuban political and literary history.

At the same time, in a literary tradition that often casts only English as "the genuine tongue of a white-skin" (ch. 25), as Cooper's Natty Bumppo puts it in *The Last of the Mohicans*, the French are ever under suspicion of racial impurity—in part, as Cora's father says, for an aristocracy derived from Caribbean slavery, the "pretty degree of knighthood . . . which can be bought with sugar-hogsheads" (ch. 16). Throughout the nineteenth century, as anglophone US writers worked through the interrelations among Haiti, francophonie, and hidden interracial ancestry, a shadowy series of racially indeterminate francophone or French-identified figures proliferated across the national literary landscape, populating novels ranging from Walt Whitman's *Franklin Evans* (1842) to *Uncle Tom's Cabin*, to Melville's *Pierre; or, The Ambiguities* (1852). By 1867, anglophone novelistic representation of francophonie had become virtually synonymous with racial mixture. Lydia Maria Child, whose *Hobomok* (1824) is credited with inaugurating the tradition of miscegenation literature in the United States, created polyglot heroines in her post–Civil War novel *A Romance of the Republic* (1867), whose playful West Indian song in the narrative's opening pages—"Un petit blanc, que j'aime . . . " (ch. 1)—all but betrays the theme of interracial genealogy that becomes the novel's central problem. Perhaps not surprisingly then, the earliest novel of the African American literary tradition, William Wells Brown's *Clotel; or, The President's Daughter* (1853), plays on Franco-Africanism's uncanny twinnings, mutations of identity, and obscure revelations of hidden kinship as a provision of novelistic closure alternative to Stowe's controversial advocacy of colonization in Africa for her Franco-Africanist characters, Cassy, Eliza, Harry, and Madame de Thoux. In *Clotel*, France rather than

Liberia becomes the site of freedom from racial oppression, and the novel's Franco-Africanist ambiguity a source of cautious optimism rather than the anxious figuration of an encroaching Caribbean.

The hemispheric South did not always demand narrative removals and excisions, however; it could also generate a great deal of nineteenth-century novelistic desire. Like Defoe's Crusoe, the proslavery novelist William Gilmore Simms evinced a kind of Anglo-American hispanophilia, a scholarly obsession with sixteenth-century Spanish chronicles of New World conquest, in novels such as *Vasconcelos* (1853), even as he also, like Sansay's Burr, used his editorial position to advocate a southern US empire extending through the greater hemisphere. And even a novelist as seemingly disconnected from hemispheric concerns as Nathaniel Hawthorne found a means of addressing questions of imperial desire and transamerican racial ambiguity by simply moving his fictional universe to Italy where, as he acknowledged in the preface to *The Marble Faun* (1860), "actualities would not be so terribly insisted upon as they are, and must needs be, in America." Hawthorne's sister-in-law, Mary Peabody Mann, went on to publish *Juanita: A Romance of Real Life in Cuba Fifty Years Ago* (1887), the quintessential novel of imperial desire, late in the century. As its convoluted subtitle suggests, Mann's novel overlays genres (like *Secret History* it is loosely based on the author's letters describing real experiences in Cuba) as well as temporal and spatial dimensions. Told from a US and late-century narrative perspective, it revisits an 1830s Cuban scene to suggest a US annexation of the Spanish colony as the ultimate act of righteous home-making, of "manifest domesticity" (Kaplan 1998, 602)—an annexation that, by 1887, uncannily adumbrated the dawn of *explicit* US imperialism during the Spanish-American War of the next decade. Mann's novel thus returns the literary century full circle both to Crusoe's American "Husbandry" (193), his island "household . . . and Habitation" (60), and to Clara's Caribbean marital horrors, her Creole "husband . . . tyrant" (ltr. 32) and "[d]omestic [in]*felicity*" (ltr. 8). In the transamerican novel, then, the domestic and the hemispheric are forever interlocked in a repeating structure of desire and disavowal.

25

SLAVERY, ABOLITIONISM, AND THE AFRICAN AMERICAN NOVEL

IVY G. WILSON

In the decades before the end of the Civil War, the slave narrative dominated African American literary production. Over one hundred slave narratives appeared during these years, including Frederick Douglass's *Narrative of the Life of Frederick Douglass, An American Slave, Written By Himself* (1845), William Craft's *Running a Thousand Miles for Freedom; or, The Escape of William and Ellen Craft from Slavery* (1860), and Harriet Jacobs's *Incidents in the Life of a Slave Girl* (1861), among numerous others. These narratives were so important culturally and politically that they have been called the "locus classicus" of African American literature (Baker 1984, 31). In the critical debates of the late 1970s about relationships between literature, history, and what was then called "black studies," the historian John Blassingame battled with other scholars about the value of slave narratives as historical documents. At heart, Blassingame's opponents contended that slave narratives should not be used as primary sources because they intentionally obscured facts, blurred incidents, and sensationalized events. These narratives, in short, were less historical documents than they were literary objects. Although the slave narrative did in fact constitute one of the primary textual formats through which African Americans challenged the institution of slavery, fiction also formed a vital component of abolitionist discourse.

While antebellum African Americans engaged a number of concerns of the day, including religion, temperance, and women's rights, nearly every African American writer was preoccupied with slavery and indeed, for many of these writers, the slavery crisis offered the primary lens through which they assessed these other social issues. In this sense, almost all African American literature of the period had an antislavery theme. In using written expression as well as speeches and oratory to appeal to their audiences' consciences, African American writers tried to expose the horrors of slavery in a style that was as close as possible to documentary.

But if black antebellum writers were generally preoccupied with the question of slavery, they were also concerned with other issues such as northern racism, segregation, and class stratification. Indeed, of the handful of novels published by African Americans, two—William Wells Brown's *Clotel; or, The President's Daughter* (1853) and Martin Delany's *Blake; or, The Huts of America* (1859, 1861–62)—crucially concern slavery. (A third, Hannah Crafts's *The Bondwoman's Narrative*—written sometime between 1853 and 1860 but not published until 2002—also deals centrally with bondage.) Another two from the same period—Frank J. Webb's *The Garies and Their Friends* (1857) and Harriet E. Wilson's *Our Nig; or, Sketches from the Life of a Free Black* (1859)—primarily depict race and class stratification. Situated thematically between novels that focus on slavery and those that engage race and class stratification, Julia C. Collins's *The Curse of Caste; or, The Slave Bride* (1865) details the trials and tribulations of Claire Neville in the aftermath of emancipation, elaborating a complicated family history that includes her returning to the New Orleans plantation where her (white) father and (quadroon) mother met years earlier. Slavery so pervaded the African American experience that to write about northern racism might seem quaint, perhaps even injurious to the cause of emancipating the millions of enslaved blacks in the American South. In her novel *Our Nig*, Wilson shows an awareness of this, writing that she "would not from these motives even palliate slavery at the South, by disclosures of its appurtenances North" (pref.).

For African American writers of the 1850s, moving into the realm of fiction presented certain dangers. Apologists of slavery in both the North and South denounced slave narratives as exaggerated, fabricated, and untrue. They were essentially "stories," not authentic accounts. Even sympathetic antislavery and abolitionist audiences would occasionally demand that these authors expose their bodies as ocular proof that they were indeed the same persons portrayed in the narratives. With their mutual focus on the nominative self and modes of self-representation, the genre of the slave narrative shared conventions with autobiography. But they also often lacked some of the most basic personal facts common to autobiography, such as birthdates and parents' names. In addition to missing pertinent details, slave narratives often had an almost unbelievable quality that made certain aspects seem fictional. Detractors repeatedly complained that they exaggerated or falsified physical atrocities. But, if these narratives contained elements that seemed unbelievable, it was because, as Brown points out, the institution of slavery itself was a "truth stranger than fiction" (ch. 23).

Slavery was an important theme in many of the novels by white writers of the day as well, of which Harriet Beecher Stowe's *Uncle Tom's Cabin; or, Life Among the Lowly* (1852) presents only the most obvious example. Novels of the period included those that were decidedly proslavery, for example, William Gilmore Simms's *The Sword and the Distaff; or, "Fair, Fat, and Forty"* (1852) and Caroline Lee Hentz's *The Planter's Northern Bride* (1854) and those that were evidently antislavery including Richard Hildreth's *The Slave; or, Memoirs of Archy Moore* (1836) and Mattie Griffith's *Autobiography of a Female Slave* (1857), both of which masqueraded as authentic slave narratives. Other novels, such as Walt Whitman's *Franklin Evans; or, The Inebriate* (1842), took a much more ambiguous position on slavery.

As much as slavery was taken up as a theme by white novelists, fiction writing became a crucial complement to the slave narrative in the larger African American political campaign against chattel slavery and heralded the development of the African American novel in the twentieth century. The 1850s marked a groundbreaking moment in the genealogy of the African American novel with the publication of Brown's *Clotel*, Webb's *The Garies and Their Friends*, Wilson's *Our Nig*, and Delany's *Blake*. The novels by Webb and Wilson prefigure themes that would continue to resonate throughout African American literature for years, arguably even more so than *Clotel* or *Blake*. Compared to the two decades before and after the 1850s, the decade before the Civil War marked a notably fruitful moment for African Americans writers, who expanded the range of their writing to increasingly experiment with the genre of the novel.

This chapter traces the desire of African American writers to move beyond the documentary charge of the slave narrative and explore the genre of fiction as a means to depict different visions of freedom in the antebellum United States. Focusing on the tension between autobiography and fiction, realism and romance, this chapter explores the inception of the African American novel. In interrogating the forms of early African American novels, this chapter outlines the formal experiments with fiction that make these writings at once aesthetic and political.

One of the earliest African American attempts at fiction was Frederick Douglass's tale of Madison Washington, a slave who actually led a successful revolt in 1841 aboard the *Creole*, which had departed from Virginia bound for New Orleans. Published twelve years later, Douglass's "The Heroic Slave" (1853) mostly recounts Washington's life before the revolt. As the most commanding and visible African American public figure, Douglass campaigned against the "peculiar institution" with speeches on the antislavery lecture circuit, the publication of his *Narrative*, and his editorship of newspapers. "The Heroic Slave" marked his first and only foray into fiction.

Beyond its composition by the leading race man of the day, "The Heroic Slave" symbolizes a significant moment in African American fiction as a novella situated between the forms of the short story and the novel. Indeed, a few short tales predate "The Heroic Slave": Juan Victor Séjour Marcou et Ferrand published "Le Mulâtre" in 1837 and, as Frances Smith Foster has recently illustrated with the example of "Theresa—a Haytien Tale" (1828), early black periodicals often featured little known, sometimes anonymously authored, short stories. Initially serialized in Douglass's eponymous periodical, "The Heroic Slave" also figured in Julia Griffiths's *Autographs for Freedom* later that year in 1853. The gift book, produced on behalf of the Rochester Ladies' Anti-Slavery Society, raised funds for the organization.

Consisting of four parts, the novella uses different episodes to illustrate the six years of Washington's life before the revolt. Set in the Virginian woods, the first part introduces the reader to Washington and to Listwell, a white Ohioan who befriends Washington and becomes an abolitionist himself. The central scene stages Washington's eloquent soliloquy, overheard by the captivated Listwell, who thus dedicates himself to the abolitionist cause. The second part of the story leaps to a scene five years later where, sitting comfortably in their home, the Listwells hear a rap on the door. Incredibly, it is Washington, whom Listwell immediately recognizes; the fugitive recounts his desperate life in the swamps separated from his wife and his plans to escape to Canada. In the third part, Listwell finds himself on the outskirts of Richmond; there he sees a coffle of slaves being readied for auction, among whom is Washington, who relates the details of his capture. Listwell aids him by furnishing him metal files to cut through chains. The final section represents a coffee house tête-à-tête between two white patrons engrossed in a discussion about the *Creole* slave revolt.

Douglass's conspicuous staging of conversation as a mode of storytelling in "The Heroic Slave" illustrates the shifting dynamics of literary production among African American writers who were trying to negotiate the line between history and fiction. With the exception of part I, in which the soliloquy constitutes the primary action depicted in the present tense, the action scenes in the three other parts of the novella unfold in the past tense. Douglass's use of storytelling as a literary device splits the function of time in the novella, whereby the mutiny plot is recalled ex post facto, while the action of the story occurs in the present tense. The plot, in this sense, is conceptualized as history. By contrast, the present tense conversations between Washington and Listwell serve the didactic purpose of illustrating would-be or anticipated relations between black and white Americans and, as we see in part IV with Tom Grant and Jack Williams, between white Americans in dialog. In a sense, "The Heroic Slave" is less an account of the 1841 *Creole* affair than a proleptic imagining of future relations to come, engendered by Douglass's engagement with the genre of fiction more so than empirical history per se.

Perhaps the most noticeable method that Douglass uses to develop his character sketches is his stylization of speech. Washington first appears to the reader (and to Listwell) in the midst of the Virginian woods delivering a soliloquy. Equal parts existential philosophy and pragmatic politics, Washington's soliloquy is elegant, grand, and highly stylized, if not overwrought. But, as William L. Andrews notes, "[I]n an era when virtually all African Americans in popular literature spoke in gutturals or a laughable pidgen, Douglass's oratorical slave provided a needed cultural alternative" (1996, 131). Beyond using Washington's speech as a necessary corrective to the image of blacks commonly held in the wider social imagination, Douglass uses the soliloquy as a literary device to usher the reader into Washington's interior thoughts. As significant as the stylistics of the soliloquy were to Douglass's fashioning of the external presentation of

Washington, it also provided the reader an important and necessary window into Washington's psychology.

While Douglass's treatment of Washington's diction matters to the development of his protagonist's character, the speeches themselves make Douglass's experiments with the properties of fiction increasingly perceptible. "The Heroic Slave" shies away from first-person narration, but the story is often suspended by Douglass's narrative or authorial interjections, set off by parentheses. When Madison recounts his escape to the Listwells, Douglass makes unusual, if not unconventional, use of the parentheses:

> "And just there you were right," said Mr. Listwell; "I once had my doubts on this point myself, but a conversation with Gerrit Smith (a man, by the way, that I wish you could see, for he is a devoted friend of your race, and I know he would receive you gladly,) put an end to all my doubts on this point. But do not let me interrupt you." (pt. 2)

Douglass wants to use a relative clause to provide the reader with more information about Gerrit Smith, but his use of parentheses offsets the flow of Listwell's speech and renders conspicuous Douglass's presence as author. Rather than a strict relative clause, Listwell's parenthetical statement is more like an aside, a dramatic device in theater through which a character speaks directly to the audience, to produce the effect that Douglass is speaking both implicitly and explicitly to his readers. In a larger sense, the conversation between Washington and Listwell marks an important shift from the first-person mode of the slave narrative to the third-person omniscient mode of narration enabled by Douglass's entry into fiction, a mode that gives him more control over fashioning the plot, events, and, perhaps most importantly, the protagonist of his story.

One way to decode Douglass's strategy in fashioning Washington as the protagonist is to consider how he conceives the role that will mobilize his reader to join the abolitionist cause. Washington clearly represents the focal character, but there is also a sense in which Douglass intends Listwell to be recognized as a hero. If the genre of the slave narrative generically traces the conversion of the enslaved subject from bondage to freedom, Douglass's novella likewise emphasizes Listwell's conversion from apathetic citizen to committed abolitionist. In other words, the discourse of the text gains its political efficacy less at the moment when the reader sympathizes with (or even valorizes) Washington than when the reader empathizes with Listwell to the degree that she or he undergoes a similar conversion to a committed abolitionist politics. What Douglass needs, in short, are more Listwells—not necessarily more Washingtons.

Foregrounding the heroic slave, Douglass nevertheless crafts the character of Washington in a way that no other black figure had been fashioned in US fiction to counteract the degrading representations of black masculinity that were ubiquitous in much of US culture:

> Madison was of manly form. Tall, symmetrical, round, and strong. . . . His face was "black, but comely." . . . A child might play in his arms, or dance on his shoulders. . . . His broad mouth and nose spoke only of good nature and kindness. . . . He had the head to conceive, and the hand to execute. (pt. 1)

In the most immediate sense, Douglass portrays his protagonist as handsome, but the biblical reference to Song of Solomon 1:5 also has the residual effect of endowing Washington's exploits with the imperatives of Christian authority with which many of his contemporaneous readers would have sympathized.

Perhaps the closest literary antecedent to Douglass's Madison Washington in American fiction was George Harris of Harriet Beecher Stowe's *Uncle Tom's Cabin*. Stowe sets George in contradistinction to her titular character—where Tom is an older man, George is young; where Tom is pious, George is agnostic; and where Tom is seemingly passive, George is conspicuously militant. In one of the most important chapters of the novel, "In Which Property Gets Into an Improper State of Mind," George, who has facilitated his escape by disguising himself, confronts his former boss Mr. Wilson and condemns slavery as an institution that derives its power unjustly rather than through the consent of the governed (ch. 11). As a number of critics have noted, Stowe based George at least partially on Douglass because she was impressed by his oratorical sophistication. Douglass's Madison Washington, in this sense, represents a partial replica of himself via Stowe's George, a character inspired by what Robert S. Levine has called the literary conversation between Douglass and Stowe.

Of the noticeable inventions that identify "The Heroic Slave" as fiction, perhaps the most problematic is Douglass's fleeting portrait of Washington's wife. If little is known about Washington's life before the *Creole* affair, even less is known about his wife, whom Douglass names "Susan." The *Liberator* resuscitated her presence in its June 1842 edition by speculating whether she had been among the captured slaves aboard the *Creole*. Both of Douglass's contemporaries, Brown and Child, gave substance to speculation by furnishing fuller character sketches of Susan in an apparent appeal to the popular literary genre of sentimentalism. But whereas both Brown and Child portray the couple as reunited, she dies in Douglass's novella, the victim of an abortive escape. It is revealing that, while the *Liberator*, Brown, and Child all sensationalized the plot of a reunited family so fundamental to the ends of sentimental discourse, Douglass essentially reduces the wife's presence to accentuate the singularity of Washington's heroics. Given the reality that little was known of Washington's wife, one must ask why Douglass elected not to develop her as a character, not to envision her in fiction while she was disappearing from the realm of "fact."

Douglass's writing of "The Heroic Slave" was necessitated as much by his wanting to repair the holes in the historical archive concerning Washington as it was by his wanting to articulate his new political position on abolitionism. Douglass's reference to Gerrit Smith in the earlier quoted passage where Listwell speaks to Washington signals his shift away from the Garrisonians, as well as his former insistence upon moral suasion as the most suitable means to eradicate slavery. Douglass includes the reference to intimate his new position on the Constitution, violence, and the union. A radical abolitionist of a different vein, Smith was at various times associated with the Liberty Party, the Free-Soilers, and later the Republican Party; he was a social reformer from New York who contributed land and money to African Americans and financially supported John Brown's raid at Harpers Ferry in 1859. Douglass began to question the disuniting of North and South after his return from the United Kingdom in 1847 but did not formally break from the Garrisonians until a couple of years later.

Fiction thus furnished Douglass another avenue to express his ideas about the relationship between violent resistance and the abolition of slavery. As Robert B. Stepto notes, it also provided a different model of the black male hero in contrast to those illustrated in Stowe's *Uncle Tom's Cabin*. Douglass's willingness to accept that physical violence might be necessary to end slavery brought him closer to the political thought of a cadre of black male intellectuals, including David Walker, Charles Lenox Remond, and Henry Highland Garnet, who had all long foreseen, and indeed championed, the necessity of violence in their speeches and nonfiction writings. Rather than glorify black allegiance to the state as an illustration of the wrongs of slavery, as figures like William Cooper Nell had done with the legend of Crispus Attucks, these activists, and Douglass increasingly so in the 1850s, extolled figures like Madison Washington, Joseph Cinquez, Toussaint L'Ouverture, and Nat Turner as important examples of black resistance to slavery. Douglass's novella represents an important turn in the emergence of the African American novel as black writers began to experiment more freely and at greater length with the creative possibilities of fiction.

Whereas Douglass's novella focuses primarily on the exploits of one central protagonist and carries a residue of the slave narrative within its format, William Wells Brown's novel *Clotel* teems with multiple characters and multiple plots. Published in the same year as "The Heroic Slave," Brown's novel tells the story of two sisters, Clotel and Mary, the fictive daughters of Thomas Jefferson, and the vicissitudes of their living under slavery. Throughout the novel, other important characters emerge, including Georgiana Peck, a Christian woman who uses religious doctrine to emancipate her slaves; George Green, a mulatto who loves to hear his master read the Declaration of Independence and who later joins a slave rebellion; and Sam, a black slave who, although seemingly content, rejoices when his master dies. Unlike the conventional slave narrative, with its governing plot tracing the movement from enslavement to freedom, Brown's novel has no such punctuated conclusion. Mary and George are reunited in Europe in the end, but the title character Clotel dies. Like works such as Crafts's *The Bondwoman's Narrative* and Collins's *The Curse of Caste*, *Clotel* displays a fascination with the "tragic mulatto," a figure that would often recur in later African American fiction by Frances Ellen Watkins Harper, Charles Chesnutt, and Nella Larsen, among others.

Indeed, the different fates of Mary and Clotel signal a larger predicament with respect to how Brown uses fiction and primary documents in a novel inundated with embedded textual forms. Among these are excerpts from newspapers, letters from political figures, and the Declaration of Independence. Chapter 17, for example, consists largely of passages from Jefferson's *Notes on the State of Virginia* (1785) and his exchange with Jean Nicolas Démeunier (1786). But, as Andrews argues, while these documents are mobilized to strengthen the narrator's credibility, they also considerably undermine the fictive potential of the novel as a self-justifying genre. When "this new novelistic tradition regularly defers to the authority of extraliterary voices to shore up his or her pretensions to authority," Andrews asks, "then is there really a new voice in the early black novel?" (1990, 27). Furthermore, Andrews notes that the marshaling of these authenticating documents situates "the narrative in a distinctly liminal relation to the worlds of fictive and natural discourse" (31). In this sense, the significance of "The Heroic Slave" to the development of African American fiction, and to the novel in particular, is that Douglass by contrast feels no compulsion to authenticate his fictive discourse with the authority of primary documents.

Indeed, the very muddled textual arrangement of *Clotel* has prompted considerable criticism of the novel as too sentimental, too didactic, too contrived, too episodic, or too imitative, among other estimations. A number of critiques have noted that *Clotel* is overconstructed to the point that its formal elements are so obtusely rendered that the text's properties as a novel are compromised. Yet M. Giulia Fabi has argued that the unevenness of Brown's novel was a deliberate attempt by the author to make "the reader experience the powerlessness, the uncertainty, the absurdities that characterize slave life" (1993, 642). Similarly, John Ernest has contended that African Americans self-consciously flouted literary convention as an implicit commentary on the chaotic world produced by slavery itself—a contention that might well apply to Brown. While the debate about *Clotel*'s unevenness will most likely persist, it is clear that Brown intended to use the stories within the novel and the novel itself as forms of abolitionist discourse.

Well before the reader encounters the stories in *Clotel*, he or she discovers Brown's own *Narrative of the Life and Escape of William Wells Brown* (1853). The *Narrative* appended to *Clotel* differs from his earlier *Narrative of William W. Brown, a Fugitive Slave. Written by Himself* published in 1847 and a slightly different treatment that appeared in 1849. Importantly, with the version that precedes *Clotel*, Brown employs a narrative voice whereby he refers to himself in the third-person to fabricate a distance between the author and the narrator. In creating this distance, Brown attempts to establish himself simultaneously as the protagonist and a character, thereby pushing the conventions of the standard slave narrative closer to fiction.

With respect to their understanding of the relationship between history and literature, Douglass's "The Heroic Slave" and Brown's *Clotel* are inverted. Whereas Douglass seeks to fictionalize a historical account, Brown seeks to historicize a fictional account. *Clotel* is replete with traces of historical figures. The majority of these individuals only have a nominal presence in the novel; they appear less as characters than as the projections of specific political ideologies. Voltaire, Jean-Jacques Rousseau, and Thomas Paine signify Enlightenment thinking on the rights of man; the Kentucky Congressman Henry Clay figures as the supporter of the Compromise of 1850; while the South Carolinian John C. Calhoun represents the extension of slavery. Additionally, there is a second set of historical figures utilized by Brown as anecdotal evidence about the follies of racial formation, which include depictions of whites, such as Thomas Corwin and Daniel Webster, who are mistaken for black. But in neither of these instances do Brown's fictional characters interact with these historical figures in the same way that, for example, Herman Melville has the eponymous protagonist of *Israel Potter: His Fifty Years of Exile* (1855) interact with King George III, Benjamin Franklin, and John Paul Jones.

Clotel approximates historical romance, falling closer to romance than to historical fiction. One recurring difficulty in reading the novel is that Brown's characterization of Clotel and Althesa as Jefferson's daughters renders conspicuous his strategy of extending the plot chronologically so that he can situate his multiple stories in the context of the Fugitive Slave Act of 1850. Other anachronisms problematize *Clotel*'s status as a historical novel, such as the stagecoach ride where Clotel listens in on a debate about the Henry Clay-Martin Van Buren presidential contest of 1840—a discussion that could not have occurred in conjunction with Nat Turner's Rebellion some nine years earlier in 1831.

Perhaps the most noticeable element of the novel that pushes it toward romance is the concluding episode with its serendipitous reunion of George and Mary. After escaping from prison with Mary's help, George flees to Canada where he later learns that Mary has been sold further south to New Orleans. Disappointed that he is not able to rescue her, George decides to quit the American continent altogether and subsequently leaves for Liverpool, England. After a decade there he travels to France where he is at last reunited with Mary, now a widowed mother after her French husband's death. A fortnight after their reunion, the two are married "so that George and Mary, who had loved each other so ardently in their younger days, were now husband and wife" (ch. 28). Brown's work seems to obey many of the elements of fiction that Nathaniel Hawthorne outlines in distinguishing the "romance" from the "novel." In his preface to *The House of the Seven Gables: A Romance* (1851), Hawthorne writes that romance authors have the right to present "truth under circumstances, to a great extent, of the writer's own choosing or creation. If he think fit, also, he may so manage his atmospherical medium as to bring out or mellow the lights and deepen and enrich the shadows of the picture" (pref.). If there is one way of understanding Brown's treatment of the relationship between history and fiction, perhaps it is this recognition offered by Hawthorne; for Brown brings out the lights and illuminates the ugly truth of slavery. As unbelievable as the reunion of George and Mary may seem, Brown needs the episode for at least one important reason. Their reunion in France allows Brown to furnish an alternative geography of political freedom distinct from Canada or Liberia; having his characters transplanted to Europe also relocates them to the birthplace of the abolitionist movement.

If *Clotel* can be thought of as a romance, it is one noticeably marked by the conventions of sentimentalism. As a genre, sentimentality was not simply about emotion but the sensory alchemy produced by the unique relationship of affect, gender, and political sensibility. In *Clotel*, one particular scene where Brown deploys sentimentalism occurs in chapter 14, "A Free Woman Reduced to Slavery." Here, Althesa is found happily married to Henry Morton, a doctor originally from Vermont; they live in New Orleans with their two daughters. They also have a servant, Salome Miller, whose whiteness prompts Althesa to question whether she was born a slave. After learning Salome's history, which establishes her German ancestry, Althesa conveys the details to Henry, and they help pay for the trial by which Salome gains her freedom. Brown uses this chapter to illustrate how women can take political action and effect change through a strategic deployment of sentimentalism.

Brown's novel offers key responses to *Uncle Tom's Cabin*, the most popular nineteenth-century US novel. Stowe's work concludes by sending a group of African Americans to Liberia to establish a colony. When Georgiana rebukes Carlton for suggesting that her slaves might be sent to Africa in "The Liberator" chapter, Brown is ventriloquizing his own opposition to colonization. Later, however, in "The Christian's Death" chapter, Brown rescripts Eva's deathbed scene from *Uncle Tom's Cabin*. Brown's scene depends on his readers having the same emotional response as the characters who are gathered about Georgiana's bed. But more than making his readers feel for Georgiana's slaves, Brown needs his readers to identify with Georgiana as someone they should emulate. Whereas Eva's death does not prompt her father, St. Clare, to manumit his slaves, Brown has Georgiana materialize what only remains an impulse in Stowe's novel.

Like Douglass's "The Heroic Slave," Brown appeals to the religious attitudes of his intended audience to castigate slavery as a violation of Christian principles. While Brown wants to present George as a patriot or native son of sorts, his appeal to the founding fathers as justification for his participation in the insurrection would have been readily accepted only by the most sympathetic of audiences. By contrast, Georgiana figures as the embodiment of both patriotic and Christian sensibility, logic and affect. In order to portray Georgiana as such, Brown underlines her advocacy of Christian principles. Hence, when the reader is first introduced to Georgiana, she paraphrases the well-known maxim from Matthew 19:19 (that one should love one's neighbor as oneself) to condemn slavery well before Brown has her recapitulate Andrew Jackson's words about the loyalty of black soldiers in the War of 1812 as a sign of black allegiance to the country. George says few words about religion and, indeed, does not invoke Christianity to authorize his acts of insubordination; in this respect, Brown's George Green is a shadow of Stowe's George Harris, who has also forsaken religion.

The publication history of early African American fiction further illuminates the competing strategies of abolitionist politics within the wider arena of antislavery discourse. Brown's novel, which is commonly recognized as the first African American novel, was published in England while he was still a fugitive and had hopes that the novel would help galvanize abolitionist sentiment among the British. Brown mobilized an anglophile undercurrent in the novel to situate *Clotel* as a branch of a larger transatlantic movement against slavery. Published under the auspices of the Rochester Ladies' Anti-Slavery Society, however, Douglass could hardly afford to offend his target reading audience who purchased *Autographs for Freedom* at places like the Anti-Slavery Bazaar. In this regard, both "The Heroic Slave" and *Clotel* circumvent depictions of black male violence; Douglass and Brown both choose to summarize physical action rather than to display it explicitly within their respective stories.

By contrast, Martin Delany's *Blake*, which presents a West Indian hero trying to instantiate a hemispheric revolution throughout the Americas, first appeared in Thomas Hamilton's periodical, the *Anglo-African Magazine*, created for an African American readership. Delany's serialized novel shows black insurrection being incited among the masses in ways that both Douglass and Brown had refused to do in their fiction. One fundamental distinction between Delany, on the one hand, and Douglass and Brown, on the other, is that Delany seems more concerned with modeling forms of radical political agency that blacks themselves might emulate, rather than action a white reading audience might wish to mirror.

In the broadest outline, Delany's novel is evenly subdivided into two parts: the first concentrates on the protagonist's actions in the US South and Southwest as well as Canada; the second focuses on his actions in Cuba and excursions across the Atlantic as part of the African slave trade. *Blake* features commonplace episodes familiar to much antislavery fiction: inside views of black life on the plantation (in their own cabins or in temporarily "private" spaces like kitchens); philosophical discussions among white men of stature debating the efficacy of slavery and the notion of equality among the races; intimate conversations with white women who attempt to impress upon male family members the moral evil that slavery wreaks on the family model, black or otherwise; illustrations of fugitive life outside the plantation in swamps and forests; and an escape scene.

The primary action of part I centers on the actions Henry takes after his wife Maggie has been sold from Colonel Franks's plantation and Henry's increasing politicization as a black insurrectionary. In the first half of the novel, Delany crafts his hero as an expert rhetorician, one who inverts the dominant logic of America's slaveocracy in scene after scene. In chapter 9 "The Runaway," for example,

Henry justifies taking "from time to time, taken by littles," items from Franks as a reappropriating of payment for his labor, explaining to Mammy Judy that he has been exploited. Later when he, Andy, and Charles are planning their escape from Louisiana, Henry invokes scripture to compare their status to biblical slaves:

> God told the Egyptian slaves to "borrow from their neighbors"—meaning their oppressors—"all their jewels"; meaning to take their money and wealth wherever they could lay hands upon it, and depart from Egypt. (ch. 11)

Only a moment before this scene, Henry articulates the necessity of a large-scale movement to secure black freedom—and Delany thus intimates that individual or isolated examples of black freedom mean very little. To fashion Henry as a hero, Delany shows him taking on the task of crafting a subversive "organization in every slave state" (ch. 11). Among the locations to which Henry travels in this two-year period to create such an organization are Arkansas; the United Nation of Chickasaw and Choctaw Indians; New Orleans, Louisiana; Charleston, South Carolina; and Richmond, Virginia.

The protagonist's movements trace his development from a generic identity as a West Indian named Henrico Blacus to a US American renamed Henry Holland to an adopted Cuban identified as Henry Blake. Beyond these suggestive name changes, Delany's characterization of Henry importantly returns him to the Caribbean and broadens the novel's scope to the hemisphere of the Americas and the trans-Atlantic. Indeed, Henry's travels belie the putative value of a single, nation-based identity; as critics like Paul Gilroy have argued, readers can find in *Blake* the promise of transnational affinities. In Delany's novel, these affinities materialize in moments of coalitional politics between blacks and Native Americans (in part I) as well as the "mulatto" class and slaves (in part II). The radical impulse of Delany's political thought rests not only in his articulation of black insurrection but also in the representation of a coalitional insurrection that finds the novel's black characters joining forces with others, including artists like the poet Placido. But Delany's expression of this insurrection remains only an intimation—the last chapters of the novel (at least six of them) have never been recovered from lost issues of the *Weekly Anglo-African*; it remains unclear whether Delany had Henry and his compatriots succeed in inciting rebellion in Cuba or if it spread to the southern United States.

Delany's publication of *Blake* in the *Anglo-African* offers an important reminder of the vital role that periodicals served for abolitionist politics and for the larger field of African American culture. Like Charles Dickens and Stowe, Delany serialized his novel, first in the *Anglo-African Magazine* in 1859 and then in the *Weekly Anglo-African* in 1861 and 1862. (A book version of the novel would not appear for more than one hundred years when Floyd J. Miller collated the chapters and published them in 1971, a seminal moment in the institutionalization of African American Studies as an academic field of study.) In the first year of its existence, the

Anglo-African presented works by some of the most prominent African American figures of the day, including Frances Ellen Watkins (Harper), J. Sella Martin, James McCune Smith, and William J. Wilson. In the realm of fiction, the *Anglo-African* featured Watkins's (Harper's) important short story "The Two Offers" and Wilson's "Afric-American Picture Gallery" during the first year of its run. Later, the periodical would publish in serial form the second iteration of Brown's *Clotel* as *Miralda; or, The Beautiful Quadroon*, subtitled *A Romance of American Slavery* (1860–61). In a slightly different vein from the independent venture of the *Anglo-African*, Collins's *The Curse of Caste* indicates how institutions, like the black church, provided important support for African American writing through such venues as the *Christian Recorder* and *AME Church Review*.

Many antebellum African American writers gained access to publishing houses either through antislavery societies or by developing relationships with black periodicals, which makes Harriet E. Wilson's publication of *Our Nig* exceptional. Apparently without clear connections to either antislavery societies or the black press—indeed, without even taking slavery as her primary topic—Wilson's book in many respects prefigures the harsh realities of black life after slavery, addressing as it does northern racism.

The book relates the story of Frado, a young mulatto girl, who is abandoned by her mother and forced into servitude, indentured to the Bellmont family. Mrs. Bellmont and her daughter Mary are unusually cruel and constantly brutalize Frado; she is compelled to stay with them for over ten years until she is able to gain her freedom. Weak from years of abuse and trying to earn a living on her own, Frado eventually marries a slave named Samuel after being released from the Bellmonts. Samuel leaves her soon after she gives birth to their son, and Frado is once more forced to find a way to support herself. With its bleak if not realistic ending, *Our Nig* reveals how social inequality might circumscribe any African American attempt at writing a *Bildungsroman* or, at least, suggests that such inequality is intrinsic to the formative years of most African Americans. As much as *Our Nig* shares similar episodes with other African American novels of the period, it differs in significant ways from them. For example, whereas *Clotel* and *Blake* are primarily set in the South (and, in the latter case, also the Caribbean), *Our Nig* is set in the North. *Our Nig*'s most striking feature perhaps is its representation of a black indentured servant who is not quite a slave like those from Brown's novel nor one of Webb's upwardly mobile middle-class subjects from *The Garies and Their Friends.*

Rather than writing romance, Wilson exploits aspects of sentimentalism in her representations of femininity and domesticity. She uses the relationship between Frado, Mrs. Bellmont, and Mary to test the limits of sentimental fiction by accentuating sites of domesticity as arenas of feminist politics. Arguing that *Our Nig* is best understood as a gothic novel, Julia Stern notes that the domestic spaces of the book (the kitchen and dining room) are spaces of intense terror and violence. Wilson exemplifies this notion by continually comparing Mrs. Bellmont and Mary to maelstroms and tempests that wreak havoc on Frado. By contrast, Wilson represents the male members of the Bellmont family (and Aunt Abby) as compassionate.

In particular, the Bellmont men are what Mary Chapman and Glenn Hendler call "sentimental men." Of all the men in the story, James is the most sympathetic to Frado. His presence is usually enough to give Frado a reprieve from a beating by Mrs. Bellmont. Later, when James becomes ill, Frado is able to steal away to his room where she occasionally finds relief. Frado longs for James to take her back with him and his wife to their Baltimore home, away from the northern town in which the Bellmonts reside. This scene is significant because it reverses the geographic logic of most slave narratives and abolitionist novels that depict movement southward as a kind of descent and northern movement as a form of liberation. Perhaps the most conspicuously sensationalized episode of the novel, Wilson accentuates James's deathbed scene to illustrate the relationship between emotion and political sensibility:

> How poor you are, Frado! . . . You are old enough to remember my dying words and profit by them. I have been sick a long time; I shall die pretty soon. My Heavenly Father is calling me home. Had it been his will to let me live I should take you to live with me; but, as it is, I shall go and leave you. But, Frado, if you will be a good girl, and love and serve God, it will be but a short time before we are in a HEAVENLY home together. There will never be any sickness or sorrow there. (ch. 9)

While Wilson ostensibly uses the episode to tear at the reader's heart much like Stowe's Little Eva or Brown's Georgiana, James's deathbed scene fails to effect character conversions. *Our Nig*, then, parallels *Uncle Tom's Cabin* insofar as the deaths of two central characters do not become catalysts of transformations. Whereas Mr. Bellmont acknowledges that he has been remiss for not ensuring that Frado can attend religious services, Mrs. Bellmont continues her punitive ways.

While Frado is presented as being continuously under assault, Wilson also keenly depicts moments of resistance in maneuvers that stylize Frado as both the protagonist and the heroine of the novel. One such episode occurs in the chapter "Varieties," where James insists that the teenage Frado be allowed to eat in the dining room with the family rather than in the kitchen. Forced to concede, Mrs. Bellmont remains incensed that the social conventions between black and white, master and servant, have been compromised, and she seeks to reassert her authority:

> "Put that plate down; you shall not have a clean one; eat from mine," continued she [Mrs. Bellmont]. Nig hesitated. To eat after James, his wife or Jack, would have been pleasant; but to be commanded to do what was disagreeable by her mistress, because it was disagreeable, was trying. Quickly looking about, she took the plate, called Fido to wash it, which he did to the best of his ability; then, wiping her knife and fork on the cloth, she proceeded to eat her dinner. (ch. 6)

In this instance of quiet defiance and muted critique, Frado reverses the subordination of her social position—which has been depicted as being less than that of a dog—by using Fido to undercut Mrs. Bellmont's authority and, in a sense, to insinuate that Mrs. Bellmont is less than a dog. At a later moment, Frado defends herself yet again from a beating when she has not returned fast enough with firewood. When Mrs. Bellmont picks up a stick to beat the young girl, Frado insists that if she is struck, she will "never work a mite more for" Mrs. Bellmont and is overwhelmed with "the stirring of free and independent thoughts" (ch. 10).

As much as these scenes produce unexpected demonstrations of Frado's resistance, they signal the presence of the narrator and, in a larger sense, accentuate the strategies that Wilson employs to propel the narrative more toward fiction than history, more toward the novel than autobiography. Well beyond simply presenting a narrator who is sympathetic to the trials and tribulations of Frado, Wilson culminates the scene with a bit of irony—"Frado walked towards the house, her mistress following with the wood she herself was sent after. . . . Her triumph in seeing her enter the door with HER burden, repaid her for much of her former suffering" (ch. 10). This exceptional scene signals an important moment in the plot of the story as well as Wilson's own creative writing techniques that push *Our Nig* further into the genre of the novel; this is a heightened instance in her writing where Wilson puts a little spin on it, as it were.

These examples of Wilson's literariness put into high relief the question of whether *Our Nig* is closer to a novel or nonfiction (and specifically, autobiography). Henry Louis Gates maintains that *Our Nig* is a novel, while Andrews contends that it is closer to autobiography. The sense that one is reading nonfiction is conditioned from the very outset of the book, where Wilson depicts Frado in the third-person in contrast to chapter titles—such as "Mag Smith, My Mother," "My Father's Death," and "A New Home for Me"—that make it feel as if one is reading a first-person nonfiction narrative. Other works that vie with *Our Nig* as important first novels by African American women include Craft's *The Bondwoman's Narrative* and Collins's *The Curse of Caste*, recently republished after first appearing serially in the *Christian Recorder*.

The textual architecture of *Our Nig*, however, follows some of the conventions of the slave narrative with an appendix and letters of support. All three letters attest to her character and the truthfulness of her experiences, much the same way that many slave narratives are prefaced or concluded by what Stepto calls "authenticating documents" by white figures who attest to the veracity of the account (1991, 43). *Our Nig* is perplexing in this regard because if it were an unadulterated novel it would have no need for such authenticating documents. Two of the letters simply call *Our Nig* a book, with no indication that it is fiction. And the first letter, from one Allida, assumes that Wilson has produced nonfiction: "She availed herself of this great help, and has been quite successful; but her health is again falling, and she has felt herself obliged to resort to another method of procuring her bread—that of writing an Autobiography" (app.).

While the letters in the appendix ostensibly verify the episodes depicted in the story ex post facto, Wilson's own preface includes little about whether she intends the book to be read as fiction or nonfiction. Rather, it includes admissions of modesty and disclaimers against imperfections that were commonplace in nineteenth-century literature. Her declaration that "abler pens" could "minister to the refined and cultivated" (pref.) would be echoed by Jacobs who uses the same phrase in her *Incidents*. Yet, while Jacobs is resolute about assuring her reader that her narrative is no fiction, Wilson makes no such unequivocal statement. Without such a declaration from the author, should the reader accept the book as fiction? Would the reader be expected, in an antislavery context, to accept the book as nonfiction?

The documentary charge of antebellum African American writing—both embraced by black writers and leveled upon them—was largely mandated by the presence of slavery in the United States. While the slave narrative remained one of the most dominant literary forms of the period, African American writers did experiment with drama, poetry, and, as we have seen, fiction. As few as they remain, it is amazing that these early novels were written at all. Virginia Woolf's admonition that women needed a room of their own was especially true for free blacks, both men and women, most of whom had precious little space or time to pursue at leisure the demands of writing longer fiction like the novel. Furthermore, many free blacks may have felt a pragmatic obligation to use their faculties in other registers and genres. Poetry, for example, has a noticeable presence in the African American literary tradition starting with at least Phillis Wheatley at the end of the eighteenth century. The novel's presence is relatively scant through Reconstruction, when it emerges as one of the most dominant literary forms in the tradition, signaled by the publications of Harper's *Iola Leroy; or, Shadows Uplifted* in 1892 and Charles Chesnutt's *The House Behind the Cedars* in 1900, among others. If the novels by African Americans of the 1850s were simultaneously constitutive of and different from those identified with the American Renaissance, they might be thought of as seeds that would bloom into furious flowers cultivated by subsequent black writers decades later.

26

ETHNIC NOVELS AND THE CONSTRUCTION OF THE MULTICULTURAL NATION TO 1870

JOHN LOWE

Ethnic characters appeared often in nineteenth-century US literature, particularly after mid-century when increasing waves of immigrants arrived from Europe, fleeing pogroms, wars, famine, and poverty. All of them wanted to "make it" in the new country, and this often involved jettisoning their ethnic markers, particularly if they didn't speak English. Even the Irish, who did speak it, suffered persecution for their Catholicism and were often not considered white. Novels written by immigrants during this period reflect the diversity of their backgrounds and acculturation experiences, offering a telling survey of the opportunities, hardships, prejudices, and frequent disappointments they encountered after arriving in the United States.

In the literary marketplace, novels by immigrants competed with works published by native-born, Anglo-American authors, who often concentrated on ethnic characters and themes. For example, in Horatio Alger's fanciful stories of poor young boys who transform themselves into capitalist captains by hard work and enterprising hustling, figures such as "Ragged Dick" are defined by how they differ from immigrants. Alger contrasts this eponymous hero with the lazy and unambitious Johnny Nolan, an Irish youth who seems destined to follow the example of his wastrel drunkard father. Yet aspirant immigrant writers, if they were white, often endorsed views held by Anglos born in the United States, especially the idea of defining the quintessential "American" by his difference from the country's two most salient ethnic "others," African Americans and Native Americans. Because the preceding chapter addresses novels by African Americans and because representations of African and Native Americans by white writers such as James Fenimore Cooper and Harriet Beecher Stowe receive detailed treatment elsewhere in this volume, I will not consider those texts in this chapter, with the exception of the first Native American novel, John Rollin Ridge/Yellow Bird's 1854 *The Life and Adventures of Joaquín Murieta, the Celebrated California Bandit.*

African and Native Americans had of course been present from the very beginning of the settlement of the continent. Similarly, peoples of Spanish ancestry inhabited parts of Florida and what became the western United States well before the founding of colonies in New England and Virginia. These groups achieved a new degree of visibility after the first major US military excursion into Latin America, the US-Mexico War (1846–48), which constituted one of the nation's most important encounters with ethnic others. In the wake of the US victory, novels began appearing that involved the union of an American man—often a military figure—with a dark-skinned señorita, a plot that illustrated the imperialist notion of Mexico as an appropriate "bride" for the virile, expansionist United States. For instance, *Magdalena, the Beautiful Mexican Maid* (1847) by the prolific Ned Buntline (Edward Zane Carroll Judson) opens with General Zachary Taylor seeking a dark American spy among the ranks who can reconnoiter for him. He chooses for this mission Charley Brackett, a US soldier born from a Castilian mother, who desires revenge against the Mexicans for killing his mother and sister. The description of Brackett as "Castillian" rather than Mexican proves crucial, since Buntline consistently presents the latter ethnic group as people of color. Similarly, the heroine is the daughter of the wealthy Mexican landowner Don Ignacio Valdez, a "Castillian noble" (ch. 2). Analogous plot devices appear in *The Spanish Heroine* (1851), a novel written by William Faulkner's great-grandfather, William Clark Falkner, who served in the US-Mexico War, and, later, in the Civil War, when he rose to the rank of colonel, thus earning his family sobriquet, "the Old Colonel." Although this narrative often lapses into tired clichés and unbelievable plot contortions, it offers myriad insights into the culture and politics of the circum-Caribbean of the Old Colonel's time, which ultimately influenced his great-grandson's literary production. Unlike Buntline, Colonel Falkner had actually crossed the Gulf of Mexico to serve in the war and thus possessed a more accurate sense of cultural and geographical contrast, and perhaps a greater appreciation of the possibilities of transnational romance.

Aside from the invasion of Upper Canada during the War of 1812, the conflict with Mexico represented the "first foreign war" for the United States (Johannsen 1985, 12), and as such, it introduced thousands of soldiers—many of them from the US South, like Falkner—to the Caribbean. The widespread enthusiasm for the conflict, stoked originally by border conflicts in Texas, drew unprecedented numbers of volunteers and occasioned the construction and movement across great distances of the largest military apparatus in US history. Robert W. Johannsen notes that this was also the first US war covered by newspaper correspondents, and as the most important English-speaking circum-Caribbean city, New Orleans—with its nine newspapers—became the mouthpiece for disseminating war reportage throughout the nation, giving accounts of the conflict a strongly southern perspective. The stories in the press inspired novelettes and dime novels, and later still, hard-bound novels, plays, paintings, and military histories. Recent critical studies by Shelley Streeby and Jaime Javier Rodríguez analyze this body of literature in considerable detail, exploring how depictions of the war shaped ideologies of racial hierarchy, territorial expansion, and empire building.

A number of the earliest fictional treatments of the war feature women soldiers who disguise themselves as men, as in Buntline's *Magdalena*, Harry Halyard's *The Heroine of Tampico; or, Wildfire the Wanderer* (1847) and *The Warrior Queen; or, The Buccaneer of the Brazos* (1848), and George Lippard's *'Bel of Prairie Eden* (1848). Falkner may have read one or many of these novels, or while in Cincinnati, he may have seen a play based on the war. Like Falkner's tale, Buntline's *The Volunteer; or, The Maid of Monterrey* (1847) features the embattled town and a female warrior who falls in love with a Kentucky soldier, just as Falkner's Mexican Ellen adores her Appalachian lover Henry. Even earlier, however, Robert Montgomery Bird's first novel, *Calavar; or, The Knight of the Conquest* (1834), a tale ennobling the fallen Aztecs while condemning the Spanish conquistadores, included a cross-dressing Moorish woman named Leila who migrated to Mexico after the fall of Islamic Granada in 1492. In a bizarre intervention into history, Bird has Leila and her father instruct the Aztecs in modes of Western warfare, finding revenge against their enemy by helping another invaded people in the New World. They declare this a war of "tyranny against freedom" (v. 2, ch. 21)—a thematic later used by many American supporters of the war, who felt the troops carried the ark of liberty into a benighted country.

Streeby's *American Sensations: Class, Empire, and the Production of Popular Culture* (2002) provides an extensive account of the incredible popularity of sensational novels about the US-Mexico War, which developed in the wake of earlier urban exposé thrillers such as George Lippard's *The Quaker City; or, The Monks of Monk Hall* (1844) and Buntline's Bowery B'hoy series concerning lowlife adventure in New York City. Significantly, however, Buntline extended this genre of urban gothic thrillers to the South, in *The Mysteries and Miseries of New Orleans* (1851), which includes a striking segue that focuses on a filibuster incursion into Cuba, thus linking the urban South with imperialist missions in the Caribbean. Streeby's thesis asserts that sensational, populist fictions like Buntline's functioned as integral components of a political strategy aimed at consolidating white male voting blocs from what at the time was a fractured framework of whiteness created by questions and fears about recent immigrants, especially Catholics from Germany, France, Italy, and Ireland. As she notes, a majority of the troops fighting in the US-Mexico War for the United States were foreign born, the conflict produced more desertions than any other in US history, and many Irish soldiers fled to fight for Mexico, ostensibly because of religious loyalty.

The war's impact on novelists extended far beyond sensationalist fiction, providing storylines and settings for sentimental writers in both northern and southern literary circles. E. D. E. N. Southworth makes the war the nexus for several strands of her complicated plot in *The Hidden Hand* (1859), the story of the "madcap" Capitola. Southworth made little use of the real Mexico, and Christopher Looby suggests that she shifted her story there, rather late in the novel, so it would appeal to readers who had become interested in nostalgic fictions set during the war, which stimulated dreams of territorial expansion and national glory. While *The Hidden Hand* appeared serially in its pages, the *New York Ledger* also ran a number of shorter works set during the war, including "The Guerilla's Daughter; or, the Fandango Fight," "The Bandit Queen," and "The Escape: An Episode of the Mexican War" (Looby 2004, 205–6). Southworth, however, side-stepped the war's political aspects, which she well knew had sharply divided readers by prompting debates about the possibility of slavery spreading into new territories—and perhaps even newer territories yet to come.

Another novelist used her childhood in Texas as inspiration for a gothic potboiler. In *Inez: A Tale of the Alamo* (1855), the first novel by the teenaged Augusta Jane Evans—later one of the South's most widely read romance writers—young girls are menaced by an evil Catholic priest in San Antonio just before the fall of the Alamo. Evans devotes most of the novel's energy to a debate over Protestant and Catholic doctrine, neglecting the mostly maudlin romantic plots. In the end, these narrative strands register as far more important than the Texans' engagement with the Mexicans, although real-life figures such as General Santa Anna and Colonel James Fannin appear eventually. The titular heroine Inez, a "Spaniard," vainly loves a white Protestant doctor and abandons her Catholicism as she fights an evil Italian priest, whose "swarthy" face links him with "Indians" as an ethnic other (ch. 5). But unlike Falkner in *The Spanish Heroine*, Evans downplays the possibility of cross-ethnic/racial marriages, and her work appears less sympathetic toward its settings and their local customs, as well as more racially and religiously biased.

By contrast, the Latino culture of the new state of California found a knowledgeable observer in John Rollin Ridge, also known as Yellow Bird, a Cherokee Indian from Georgia whose family had been exiled to Oklahoma. Embroiled in tribal conflicts, Ridge fled to California with the intention of working as a miner, but he wound up writing the first Native American novel, *The Life and Adventures of Joaquín Murieta, the Celebrated California Bandit*, still the most popular and important of the myriad versions of this indelible myth. Ridge's novel exposes the broken pledges of the Treaty of Guadalupe Hidalgo (1848), which promised full US citizenship to Mexicans remaining in California and the other territories annexed at the end of the US-Mexico War. Murieta, a Mexican miner, has his claim stolen by Anglos, who rape his mistress in his presence. Swearing revenge, Murieta forms a group of banditti, who ravage the countryside in a series of daredevil raids and then retreat to their hidden mountain lair. Eventually, Texas Ranger Harry Love and his posse kill Murieta and his brutal sidekick, "Three-Fingered Jack," after which Murieta's head and Jack's hand are preserved in bottles and exhibited throughout the state. Native Americans appear briefly in several scenes, often in negative portraits, despite Ridge's background. The novel has inspired many other writers from the Americas, including the great Chilean Pablo Neruda, who transformed Murieta into his countryman in his play, *The Splendor and Death of Joaquín Murieta* (1967). The novel has proven especially influential in Mexico, where citizens welcome both a positive portrayal of their character and a quite negative reading of the US invasion and takeover. Recently, literary critics John Carlos Rowe and Timothy Powell have analyzed the novel's ideology, particularly its critique of imperialism, while Cheryl Walker has examined its submerged Native American aspects. My own reading considers the book's poetics of space as an arena for ethnic performance and power, its hybrid aesthetics, and its sense of a multicultural and dynamic West.

The Irish troops who fought for the United States and/or Mexico also suffered from damaging stereotypes, which hampered them and their relatives as they adjusted to living in the United States. While early Irish immigrants created little stir, the influx of refugees from the 1846–1850 potato famine in Ireland generated a negative portrait of poverty, excessively large families, drunkenness, and above all, degenerate "papacy." This stew of stereotypes developed partly from earlier fictional portraits; as Susan M. Griffin indicates, biased texts helped foment a tide of prejudice against Catholics, punctuated by the 1834 torching of the Ursuline Convent near Boston by a Protestant mob. Subsequently, Rebecca Theresa Reed's *Six Months in a Convent* (1835) and Maria Monk's *Awful Disclosures of the Hotel Dieu Nunnery of Montreal* (1836) fed the hysteria. Prejudice increased against Irish immigrants fleeing the potato famine and extended to the Civil War, fueled by the nativist propaganda of the Know-Nothing Party and works like Josephine Bunkley's *The Testimony of an Escaped Novice from the Sisterhood of St. Joseph* (1855), the tale of a Catholic convert whose romantic notion of the novitiate is shattered. After her escape, the young woman finds herself regarded by Protestant culture as "ruined," even though her virginity remains intact; she has, after all, been "seduced" by papacy.

The negative portrayals of the Irish were soon countered by Irish American writers, led by the prolific Mary Sadlier. Her many novels offered a positive image of Irish Catholicism, as well as the Irish family, and she drew lines of connection between immigrant aspirations and enduring American values. Born in Ireland in 1820, Mary Anne Madden sailed to Montreal after her father died. There she met and married James Sadlier, who moved his publishing company to New York in 1860, where it became the largest Catholic press in the United States and published most of her novels. She devoted the first part of her career to historical novels set in Ireland, but her focus shifted when she wrote *Willy Burke; or, The Irish Orphan in America* (1850) as an entry in a contest for Irish American writers organized by Orestes Brownson's *Quarterly Review*. The novel follows the diverging paths of two immigrant brothers; one stays true to familial and Catholic virtues, while the other embraces Protestantism and debauchery. Emboldened by the prize, Sadlier wrote seven other novels about the Irish in America, most memorably *The Blakes and Flanagans* (1855) and *Bessy Conway; or, The Irish Girl in America* (1861). In the preface to the former, Sadlier advises "all my writings are dedicated to the one grand object; the illustration of our holy faith, by means of tales or stories . . . taken from every day life." By tracing the divergent paths of three generations of the title families, Sadlier illustrates the pitfalls of American life, particularly those found in the public schools, where the Irish and Catholicism are scorned in equal measure. Harry Blake's son deserts his faith and ridicules his family, whereas the Flanagan children, profiting from proper parochial education, undertake "honest work" as leather tanners. Rather than benefiting from an Ivy League education, the corrupt Harry learns only snobbery, atheism, and dissolute ways from Columbia University aesthetes. In doing so, he forfeits the joys of Irish communal celebrations, from dances to traditional wakes. His children—the third generation—also wither morally at Columbia and join the Know-Nothing Party. Both families lose their daughters, but Susan Flanagan dies secure in her faith, while Eliza Blake, now a Protestant, dies in childbirth, vainly calling for a priest. Sadlier parallels the two title families with two others, the Dillons and the Reillys. The Dillon children, corrupted by American ways, drift into burglary and prostitution, while the Reilly son remains unmarried so he can care for his widowed mother, which Sadlier presents as an admirable act of renunciation, a kind of secular religious vocation.

Bessy Conway concentrates more narrowly on the dangers encountered by young Irish girls who go into domestic service in the United States, as well as on the urban pitfalls facing the Irish in "Babylons" like Boston and New York. The title character emigrates with a ship full of her townspeople, including the Protestant landlord's son, who loves her. Abandoning a job that requires her to pray with her Protestant employers, Bessy eventually acquires a tidy personal savings by faithfully serving prosperous Catholic families. Several friends from Ireland, however, lose their faith and succumb to materialism, alcohol, and loose morality. Although occasionally marred by a sermonizing tone, much of which comes from the observations of Father Daly, a saintly Catholic priest, the novel stands out among early works of immigrant fiction for its commentary on the Great Famine. In the end, a successful Bessy returns to redeem the old homestead with her savings, followed by the landlord's son, now a Catholic and a successful suitor for her hand. Bessy warns the younger girls against emigrating, despite the famine and the obvious success she has had abroad. This novel marked the first of several Sadlier wrote that concluded with a return to the "auld sod," a reminder that many immigrants from various countries did the same after becoming disillusioned with the realities of life in the United States, a fact that found only occasional representations in ethnic novels.

Sadlier's works became bestsellers in her time, but it seems unlikely that a modern-day press will bring them back into print. Although her use of detail contributed to literary realism, she encumbered her plots with pious characters and unlikely denouements. Her domestic concerns sometimes paralleled those found in books by Catharine Maria Sedgwick or Susan Warner, yet she avoided seriously questioning patriarchy. Nevertheless, her works did offer a vital corrective to the period's ugly anti-Catholic fictions and the machinations of the Know-Nothing nativists. Though often impoverished, her characters remain morally upright unless they lose their faith, which constitutes her way of diverting the charge that Irish culture possesses an inherent predisposition toward drunkenness, violence, huge and chaotic families, and overall squalor. By grouping the upright against the fallen, she not only rebuts the standard stereotype but also suggests how the corruption of the "fallen" stems from the rotten schemes of US capitalists. Thus her graphic depictions of the very real poverty and violence immigrants experienced shifts the blame from the Irish to their landlords and the prejudices and practices of urban oligarchies.

Polish Americans, however, needed no positive correction of their image, even though they were also overwhelmingly Catholic. Native US authors created a number of historical novels featuring Poles and/or set in Poland, including Oliver Cromwell's *Kosciuszko; or, The Fall of Warsaw* (1826), Samuel Lorenzo Knapp's *The Polish Chiefs* (1832), Susan Rigby Morgan's *The Swiss Heiress* (1836) and *The Polish Orphan* (1838), and Willie Triton's *The Fisher Boy* (1860). According to Thomas S. Gladsky, the sympathetic portrayals contained in these fictions stemmed from both the Polish uprising of 1830, which many US citizens felt echoed the American Revolution, and the memory of how Poles like Tadeusz Kościuszko had aided the American colonial forces in the fight for independence. Novels by actual Polish Americans would not appear until much later, but the era did feature notable accounts of travel and immigration to the United States, such as Julian Niemcewicz's *Under Their Vine and Fig Tree: Travels through America in 1797–1799* (1805) and August Jakubowski's *The Remembrances of a Polish Exile* (1835).

Works by ethnic writers frequently include casts of characters that represent two models of immigration: on the one hand, "preservationists" want to maintain the culture of the old country while adapting to the New World; on the other, "assimilationists" often jettison much of their heritage in a rush toward acculturation. This pattern appears particularly in the works of Irish and German American writers, and the largest numbers of immigrants from each group arrived in the United States at about the same time in the mid-nineteenth century, after the potato famine in Ireland and the revolutionary wars in Germany, which gave the immigrants the soubriquet "forty-eighters."

The French, however, had preceded both groups, particularly in Louisiana, where the rich and complicated Creole culture produced numerous writers, many of whom wrote for the lively French-language newspapers of New Orleans. The first Creole novelist, Charles Testut, described the Spanish heritage of New Mexico in *Calisto* (1849), although much of the tale focuses on a noble family that emigrates to New Orleans. Similarly, another Creole writer, Amédée Bouis, went far afield for his setting in *Le Whip-Poor-Will* (1847), which concerns interactions between white pioneers and Native peoples of Oregon. In 1849, Hypolite de Bautée published a southern variant of this plot, the serial novel *Soulier Rouge*, whose hero marries into the Choctaws after allying with their chief. This kind of liaison would later appear in George Washington Cable's classic tale, "Belle Demoiselles Plantation" (1874).

In terms of literary genres, the city mystery proved especially popular with immigrant novelists. As Scott Peeples notes in this volume, American imitations of Eugène Sue's sensational bestseller, *Les Mystères de Paris* (1842–43) began with George Lippard's lurid *The Quaker City*. That work's sensational representation of Philadelphia sparked comparable exposés of New York, New Orleans, and other cities, including Testut's *Les Mystères de la Nouvelle-Orléans* (1852–54), which focused on religious mysticism. The first German American version of the genre, the anonymous *Die Geheimnisse von Philadelphia*, appeared in 1850, followed quickly by Heinrich Börnstein's *Die Geheimnisse von St. Louis* (1851). This novel, like others written by German American Protestants, echoes Lippard's *Quaker City* with its anti-Catholic story of depraved Jesuits, a staple of US gothic thrillers. Susan M. Griffin notes how the possibility of Catholics "passing" as Protestants, allegedly so they could convert others to their faith, evoked the menacing aspects of immigration and imperialism, yet differed from those threats in that Catholicism could launch an internal attack. Further, as Robert S. Levine states, the supposedly "secret" and therefore conspiratorial nature of the church created the ingredients for exciting narratives, especially those that involved the "rescue" of Protestant women from convents. The shifting possibilities of religious affiliation and influence made it inevitable that Catholicism—both in positive and negative portrayals—would surface repeatedly in the popular domestic novels of the nineteenth century.

Börnstein's St. Louis "exposé" was succeeded by Emit Klauprecht's fascinating *Cincinnati, oder Geheimnisse des Westens* (1854–55), which catered to the large German population of the title city. Klauprecht, born in Mainz in 1815, sailed to the United States in 1832 and soon settled along the Ohio River, seen as a parallel to the Rhine by the Deutsch immigrants. Operating a lithographic shop and then embarking on a career in journalism, Klauprecht used his local knowledge as the basis for a number of historical novels, as well as many songs, about the region. As a progressive Republican, a skeptical anti-cleric, and an abolitionist, he followed the lead of Börnstein by populating the novel's plot with scheming Jesuits and sinister Irish immigrants. Klauprecht presents divisions within one family as characteristic of the schism within the German community between preservationists and assimilationists—here represented by Karl and Wilhelm Steigerwald. Another character, Washington Filson, occupies an intermediate position, since Klauprecht describes him as a protégé of the real-life figure, Senator Thomas Hart Benton, a politician favored by Germans because of his Free-Soil positions. The Jesuits wish to destroy Filson because his family claims title ownership of all the land in the city. The novel's overall portrait of Cincinnati, however, reveals a veritable Babel of immigrants, as well as a large African American population, whose popular culture teems with allusions to L'Ouverture, Ogé, Cinque, and other black revolutionaries of the hemisphere, revealing Klauprecht's opposition to slavery. But his main attack focuses on corrupt Anglo businessmen, whose ruthless maneuvers for profit include kidnapping and murder, along with a plot for blowing up a crowded steamboat, which evokes the actual explosion onboard the *Moselle* that killed 136 people in 1838. The demonic portrait of the Queen City's sordid underworld resembles the way city mysteries by authors such as Ned Buntline and the Baron Ludwig von Reizenstein depicted New Orleans, and indeed, Klauprecht includes several late scenes set in the Crescent City, where he shows the horrors of a slave auction. Alongside the romantic narratives involving the Steigerwalds, shady minor characters like Alligator prowl through the lower depths, mimicking the operations of the far more diabolical Devil-Bug in Lippard's *Quaker City*. Also, like Reizenstein, Klauprecht provides a graphic account of an epidemic—in this case cholera, rather than yellow fever. As Werner Sollors suggests, Klauprecht, though a politician and reformer, offers no detailed solutions for the problems depicted in his novel. Instead, he sends his now married major characters and their paterfamilias to new settlements in the West, echoing the fate of many German immigrants in both Cincinnati and New Orleans.

The virtual erasure of German American culture following the two World Wars has occluded the very substantial contributions made by German visitors and settlers to transnational portraits of the Americas. An early account of the new nation's varied cultures came from Charles Sealsfield, the pen name used by Karl Postl (1793–1864), a Catholic priest who left his vocation to seek a new career as a novelist in the New World. After writing travel narratives, in 1829 he published—in English—*Tokeah; or, The White Rose*, a fanciful story of Native Americans. He wrote most of his succeeding work, however, in German, including *Transatlantische Reisekizzen und Christophorus Bärenhäuter* (1834), the tale of a New Yorker who seeks a bride in frontier Louisiana, and *Der Virey and die Aristokraten oder Mexiko im Jahre 1812* (1835), a novel about Mexican history and politics. The year 1835 also saw the publication of his *Morton oder die grosse Tour*, an important forerunner of later German novels, in that it focused on varied business endeavors of German immigrants. Sealsfield followed it with other *Lebensbilder* ("life stories") told in first person, including *George Howard's Esq. Brautfahrt* and *Ralph Doughby's Esq. Brautfahrt* (1835), the latter of which features a backwoods Kentuckian who exemplifies Jacksonian principles. In 1836 Sealsfield brought out *Pflanzerleben* and *Die Farbigen*, episodic works that lack the cohesion of novels, although their composite portrait of Louisiana contains an overall unity. In these works, Sealsfield's heroes become part of the local aristocracy by marrying Creoles, forming intercultural unions that illustrate the transnational perspectives found in many ethnic novels.

With its representations of the diverse cultures entangled in a polyglot American city, *The Mysteries of New Orleans* [*Die Geheimnisse von New Orleans*], originally published in German by the Baron Ludwig von Reizenstein in 1854–1855, has become the most discussed German American novel of the nineteenth century, partially because of the recent publication of a complete English translation. First published serially in a German-language newspaper in New Orleans, this lurid thriller portrays a seductive but degenerate city, complete with a cast of sinning characters whose sexual combinations (including a lesbian pair) shift constantly. Reizenstein's urban gothic reflects the rogue image the Crescent City had acquired under French rule, a period admirably presented in Shannon Lee Dawdy's recent study, *Building the Devil's Empire: French Colonial New Orleans* (2008).

The lush tropical setting and the colorful, crowded streetscapes receive meticulous and inviting treatment, but the real interest lies in characterization. A variety of German immigrants, from differing levels of European society, interact with locals—both black and white—as well as with other new Americans. By the end of the novel, most of the key figures are dead, either killed through the machinations of the fiendish Hungarian villain, Lajos, or felled by yellow fever. The counterpoint to Lajos's pure evil comes from the mystic Hiram, who facilitates the union of Emil, the handsome, but already married, eldest son of the central German family, and Lucy, a lovely mulatto. Hiram proclaims that their child will become a new Toussaint, a black liberator of the hemisphere. Then, in a further prophecy about the region's future, Hiram attests that after the liberator's birth, yellow fever—the disease which had decimated New Orleans in 1853—will vanish from the earth.

Reizenstein's complicated gothic plot includes the machinations of the usual evil priest, in this case, Father Dubreuil, a rapist who preys on devout women and eventually leagues with Lajos. Emil's deserted wife, Jenny, lives with her sister Frida, who has also been abandoned by her husband, Lajos, although he eventually returns to her so he can complete his various schemes. Both women attract other suitors, and Jenny gives birth to an illegitimate child. Still, they and younger German girls in their circle form a rather patrician contrast to the exotic courtesans (many of them, like Lucy, black) who inhabit the novel, such as the sixteen-year-old but knowing "zambo negresse," Héloise Merlina Dufresne, the madam of the notorious brothel the Hamburg Mill, a center of intrigue for the novel's nefarious figures. The death of virtually all the characters at the novel's conclusion offers a negative verdict on New Orleans, as Hiram's mystical prophecies and projects indicate that slavery has doomed any enterprises here, whether by natives or immigrants.

Like Sealsfield and Reizenstein, the German writer Friedrich Wilhelm Christian Gerstäcker (1816–72) also provided an important early portrait of the Americas, using his own travels as the basis for evocative accounts of the Mississippi River Valley. Born in Hamburg to opera singers, Gerstäcker yearned to see North America after reading Cooper's novels. At age twenty-one, he set out for a six-year exploration of the United States, spending most of his time in Arkansas and

Louisiana. After returning to Germany, he began a career as a translator and fiction writer. His first novel, *The Regulators in Arkansas* (1846), was a detective story featuring a struggle between backwoodsmen and Indians (à la Cooper) against horse thieves and murderers. He followed it with another adventure novel set on the frontier, *The River Pirates of the Mississippi* (1848), before becoming involved in the revolutions of 1848 and then traveling to South America, California, Polynesia, and Australia for three years, thereby gaining material for subsequent travel accounts and novels. Later trips to the Americas and a journey to Africa bore similar results, most prominently his 1855 novel *To America! A Book for the People* and its sequel, *In America: A Picture of American Life in Recent Times* (1872), both of which concern German immigrants to the South and include scenes set in New Orleans. The latter novel features an interracial romance between a young couple—a German and a fair woman, Hebe, who can pass for white—but also details the brutal treatment of both former slaves and free people of color by whites. The representations of Louisiana in Gerstäcker's two novels about immigrants offered natural extensions of his early short stories, collected in *Pictures from the Mississippi: Light and Dark Sides of Transatlantic Life* (1847–48), which detailed life in Orleans, Pointe Coupée, and West Feliciana parishes.

A far less sympathetic commentary on American life came from the Austrian writer Ferdinand Kürnberger (1821–79). His *Der Amerika-Müde: Amerikanisches Kulturbild* (*The Man Who Was Weary of America: An American Cultural Portrait*, 1855) paints the horrified reaction of its German protagonist, Dr. Moorfeld, to the vulgar, xenophobic excesses of the American people, who appear incapable of cooking, raising children, or tolerating difference. While Africans and Native Americans fare worst in this scenario, German immigrants suffer persecution as well, and the finale features the torching of a German American neighborhood by Know-Nothing philistines, the kind of hooligans who burned the Ursuline convent near Boston. Since he had never set foot in the United States, Kürnberger based his diatribe on earlier accounts, such as Nikolaus Lenau's negative view of his visit to North America in 1832–1833.

Building on the audience established by Sealsfield, Reizenstein, Gerstäcker, and others, Reinhold Solger felt sure of attracting a large readership when he published *Anton in Amerika: Novelle aus dem deutsch-amerikanischen Leben* (*Anton in America: A Novel from German-American Life*, 1862). By the 1860s, German Americans formed the largest immigrant group in the United States, and over 250 German-language newspapers circulated in cities across the country. *Anton in America* appeared serially in the *New-Yorker Criminal-Zeitung und Belletristiches Journal* (the *New York Crime Reporter and Belletristic Journal*) after winning a competition the weekly newspaper sponsored for a new novel based on American life. Solger (1817–66) held a doctorate in history and had fled Germany following the revolution of 1848 because of his radical activities. Along with his work as a lecturer and writer, he taught history at a Concord preparatory school, where he met most of the

Transcendentalists, and became one of the models for Louisa May Alcott's Professor Bhaer in *Little Women* (1868–69).

Solger conceived *Anton in America* as a sequel to Gustav Freytag's popular novel *Soll und Haben* (*Debit and Credit*), published in Leipzig in 1855. Solger presents his immigrant hero as the son of Freytag's successful German merchant, Anton Wohlfart, whose rise to success from humble beginnings reads like a Prussian Horatio Alger tale. In this sequel, young Anton flees the German revolution and soon finds himself striving to become a successful businessman (like his father) in Chicago. His failure there parallels that of Anton's friend Wilhelmi and the US-born Wilhelm Dawson but contrasts with the success of the Irish businessman Paddy O'Shea. Solger's business-oriented novel dramatizes the transatlantic traumas of mid-century—the German revolution, the Italian unity movement, the Crimean War, and the rise of the anti-immigrant Know-Nothing Party that had already demonized the Irish immigrants immortalized by Sadlier. Eventually, Solger's probing of the anti-immigrant climate culminates with Anton's trial for murder. The jury convicts him, but he receives a pardon just before his scheduled execution, following the exposure of the real killer, a sequence of events which delineates the pitfalls of the US justice system.

Throughout *Anton in America*, Solger provides portraits of various ethnic groups, many of them stereotypical—especially regarding the Irish, whose poverty, huge families, and tendency to drunkenness he skewers—images offset by the warm-heartedness of the women and the spectacular rise from rags to riches of Paddy O'Shea, an early version of Alger's heroes. Anton realizes, however, that despite his education, he remains at a disadvantage compared to the jostling, street-wise Irish youths, like Paddy, who have quickly mastered American hustle. The Irish, particularly the beautiful but destitute Annie, whom Anton adopts as a "cause," further stand in contrast to the pompous rich characters like the Dawsons. Their fatuous daughter Mary, like many other New York damsels, becomes besotted with the French Count Roussillon, a false persona adopted by Grenier, a rake who earlier seduced, impregnated, and abandoned New England Annie. Solger presents the annoying arrogance of Roussillon as typically French, but also a magnet for status-hungry nouveau riche. Their desire for culture, however, creates an audience for Antonio's lectures on world art, through which he eclipses the fading aura of the fake count. Similarly, Antonio's encounters with American artists and intellectuals provide Solger with an opportunity for satirizing the shallow aesthetic pretensions of preening dilettantes, whose claims of originality prove hollow. These passages register as a send-up of Emerson's ringing call for an authentic American art; indeed, the "intellectual phrase mongerer" Reverend John Lovejoy seems based on Emerson (ch. 8). Yet the tycoon Dawson comes across as a shrewd, if ruthless businessman, and the Germans prove no match for this Yankee trader, as Solger emphasizes that "the dollar" qualifies as "the philosophers' stone, the truth of Yankee life" (ch. 9).

Like Baron Reizenstein's novel, *Anton in America*'s secondary source of interest lies in following the wily machinations of a villain. Following in the footsteps of the Baron's Lajos, Solger's malevolent Grenier, after abandoning Annie and their child, disguises himself as Count Roussillon with the intention of facilitating his bigamous marriage with Mary Dawson (conveniently, however, events keep the union from being consummated, and she at novel's end seems pledged to Antonio). Grenier plays havoc with the lives of virtually all the other major characters, most of whom die by the end of the novel after fatal entanglements in his web, alternately amorous and financial. As always, Solger alternates between narratives of business, both earnest and crooked, and love, both genuine and feigned.

This survey of several key ethnic novels published prior to 1870 suggests a number of trends. First, these works often foreground international connections with Europe, the Caribbean, and Africa, an indication that the rigid parameters of the nation had yet to emerge. Second, the novels stress that many immigrants, especially those from Ireland and Germany, possessed ambivalent feelings about the New World and eventually either returned home or moved further West for more opportunity and in hopes of escaping unexpected social strictures. Third, the novels also reveal the crucial importance of religion, as well as how religious difference impacted every aspect of the acculturation process, including the social, economic, and educational realms.

The years immediately following 1870 featured the publication of many more ethnic narratives, among them important works such as Drude Krog Janson's *A Saloonkeeper's Daughter* (originally published in Minneapolis in Norwegian in 1887) and the French Creole Alfred Mercier's novels *Le Fou de Palerme* (1873), *La Fille du Prêtre* (1877), and his masterwork *L'Habitation Saint-Ybars* (1881). The Yiddish novels of Sholem Aleichem and works in Yiddish and English by Abraham Cahan appeared later in the century. Building on the achievements and failures of their predecessors, they too struggled to find adequate expression for the wrenching but transformative dynamics of "coming to America."

When these works first appeared, they comprised integral components of a dynamic, jostling, and energetic literary marketplace, one that sought patronage from both ethnic insiders and members of the dominant culture. Similar narrative patterns and motifs emerged across the multiethnic literary scene as writers and readers found inspiration and novelty in works produced by other groups. Inevitably, however, virtually every ethnic community lost some of its particularity as the gradual but relentless process of acculturation occurred, particularly as intermarriage between groups became more common. Over the decades, many of these early texts disappeared from circulation as so-called American classics—in most cases, works by Anglo-descended white men—attracted formerly ethnic audiences now eager to assimilate by reading "American" books. The first literary histories followed this direction too, and early ethnic novels soon gathered dust on library shelves and in attics. This oblivion was also partly caused by the folding of ethnicity into the category of race; as the Irish, the Jews, the Italians, and others became "white," the mantle of other became increasingly racial, leading to "American literature" and "African American literature," with other texts falling between these stools. The ethnic revivals of the 1960s and 1970s, spearheaded in literary circles by the Society for the Study of the Multi-Ethnic Literature of the United States, *The Heath Anthology of American Literature*, and then by the American Studies Association, prompted the recovery of many ethnic writers, but mainly those of the late nineteenth and twentieth centuries. Our own age, overly fixated on modernism and postmodernism, must realize that without the recovery and interpretation of ethnic novels written before 1870, Americans will lack a full understanding of themselves as a people, and how they got here. Further, contemporary readers may better comprehend the origins of modernism by examining the protean creativity and experimentalism of many of these writers, who scrambled paradoxically to find new means of expression for conveying their unique experiences while clinging to their traditional forms of cultural identity. Their situations persist, as new groups have poured into the United States as a result of changing immigration laws. The ethnic story contains many new registers today; we can better understand them through the experiences of earlier sojourners, whose dreams and aspirations helped shape a common national destiny. As William Boelhower taught us two decades ago, ethnic writing *is* American writing.

27

WOMEN'S NOVELS AND THE GENDERING OF GENIUS

RENÉE BERGLAND

> The present century has from its beginning been remarkable for a forward stride in the individuality of women. From age to age, indeed, rare stars of feminine genius have risen upon the social horizon. In this age, illumination was promised from the start. Harriet Martineau, George Sand, George Eliot, Elizabeth Fry, Elizabeth Barrett Browning, in Europe, and in our own land, Miss Sedgwick, Margaret Fuller, Lydia Maria Child, the Grimké sisters, and the whole company of the suffragists, have taken a high place.
>
> —Julia Ward Howe, "What the Nineteenth Century Has Done for Woman" (1899)

In "What the Nineteenth Century Has Done for Woman" (1899), Julia Ward Howe described her own century as a remarkable age, illuminated by countless "stars of feminine genius" (1913, 178). Famous as the author of "The Battle Hymn of the Republic," Howe was a well-known woman of genius herself. She had published books of poetry, travel writings, and political and philosophical essays, as well as biographies of Margaret Fuller and Maria Mitchell, two hugely influential American women. Unbeknownst to her contemporaries, Howe had even tried her hand at a novel that was never published in her lifetime. Today, however, she is barely remembered, and many of the women she regarded as "stars of feminine genius" have been largely forgotten. In this context, it may come as a surprise that some fin-de-siècle Americans regarded the nineteenth century as a great era of female genius. Lecture manager J. B. Pond included Howe, along with many other women, in his reminiscences about American geniuses, remarking, "She is a person of great wit, as well as learning, being as a speaker essentially and intellectually womanly; but she can startle her audience even now by some unexpected and spirited outburst of opinion that justifies her high reputation as a poet and her noble record as a brave, clear thinker. Her intellectual activity is unremittent" (1900, 148). A century ago, this description would have seemed not effusive but self-evident to readers who saw Howe as representative of the remarkable women who transformed American letters in the nineteenth century.

For female novelists in the United States from 1790 to 1870, the issues of female genius, assertiveness, and "self-dependence" (as Fuller termed it) formed a nexus of inevitable concerns in a body of fiction produced against the grain of separate-spheres ideology and the conventions of female domesticity. In a culture still largely patriarchal and paternalistic, women who wrote novels about women not only defied warnings that novels were unsuitable for the "gentler sex," but also, by reaching out to a mostly female readership, worked to construct an audience that could admire independent action and resistance to male oppression. Female characters capable of courage, intelligence, and defiance thus became a hallmark of women's novels. As the early chapters of this volume have demonstrated, themes of female prowess emerged in some of the earliest novels published in the new nation. By the 1820s, however, as nation building inflected literary production, women writers became increasingly self-conscious about the cultural work of women in national history and the ongoing task of reforming a flawed, emerging republic. From Catharine M. Sedgwick, Lydia Maria Child, and Sarah Josepha Hale to later writers such as Fanny Fern, Harriet Beecher Stowe, E. D. E. N. Southworth, Augusta Jane Evans, and Louisa May Alcott, female novelists worked to redefine the role of women in US life and to explore women's educational and political rights. They often did so by featuring a female protagonist of uncommon intellect and self-possession, even a woman endowed with the genius long assumed to be a purely masculine attribute. Thwarted by convention or law, or wronged by powerful, domineering men, this plucky woman frequently (though not always) perseveres and prevails. An exploration of exemplary women's novels will help to illustrate the dynamic importance of such fictional figures in the formation of a national political consciousness and in clearing the way, later in the century, for the New Woman.

When feminist scholars and critics of the 1970s and 1980s began their efforts to recover nineteenth-century American women's writing, they defied the tradition in which they had been educated. Because they had been taught to scorn "the deplorable feminine taste in literature" (Baym 1993, 14), their interest in women's writing felt risky. Studying writing by women could mark them as less serious, less tasteful, perhaps even less intelligent than those who studied great works of American literature, all of which had been written either by men or by Emily Dickinson. As a result, they framed their challenges to the mid-century canon with great caution. Nina Baym prefaced *Woman's Fiction: A Guide to Novels by and about Women in America, 1820–1870* (1978) with a disclaimer: "A reexamination of this fiction may well show it to lack the esthetic, intellectual, and moral complexity and artistry that we demand of great literature. I confess frankly that although I found much to interest me in these books, I have not . . . hit upon even one novel that I would propose to set alongside *The Scarlet Letter*." Baym declared that she would not claim "literary greatness" for any of the novels she studied, but she also expressed her hope that later scholars might address the "bias in favor of things male" that shaped her contemporaries' criteria for greatness (1993, 14).

Just a few years after Baym, Jane Tompkins's *Sensational Designs* (1985) blasted literary historians for "struggl[ing] over the relative merits of literary geniuses" (201) and argued instead that literary history should concern itself with the "cultural work" performed by novels. Tompkins's arguments helped open up the canon and make literary study and literary history more inclusive, even though, like Baym, she accepted the premise that literary genius was inherently masculine.

Now, more than thirty years after Baym and her contemporaries embarked on their great work of recovery, the canon has definitely changed. Some readers prefer Sedgwick's novels to Hawthorne's, and few would now insist that this preference is a sign of "deplorable feminine taste." In some important senses, feminist critics have already won. In 1988, David S. Reynolds characterized the 1850s as "the American Women's Renaissance" (387), and in 1995 Michael Davitt Bell argued that "*the* crucial fact about American literature in the 1850s" was that by mid-century women had become the majority of fiction readers (76). In *A Jury of her Peers* (2009) Elaine Showalter invites readers today to imagine the mid-nineteenth century as the age of Julia Ward Howe and Harriet Beecher Stowe, rather than the age of Ralph Waldo Emerson and Walt Whitman (as F. O. Matthiessen had styled it). To do this, however, we need to take the ideas of Howe and Stowe on their own literary community seriously. Both women had read Emerson on genius ("A man should learn to detect and watch that gleam of light which flashes across his mind from within, more than the lustre of the firmament of bards and sages." ["Self-Reliance"]), but they also belonged to a vibrant female literary tradition that stretched from Mary Wollstonecraft and Madame de Staël through Fuller and Elizabeth Cady Stanton.

Although the French writer Germaine de Staël coined the word "Romanticism," she did not invent the literary movement singlehandedly and developed her ideas in conversation with a community of writers and thinkers. But Madame de Staël's influence on romantic thought was incalculable. Her novel, *Corinne* (1807), provided the central myth of the romantic genius that would structure artists' and authors' ambitions for at least one hundred years. The novel tells the story of the poetic triumph of the beautiful genius Corinne, who gains the world's praise for her poems about Italy, but loses her lover when he marries her more conventional sister. Madame de Staël's heroine exerted a profound influence on many of the nineteenth century's major female writers: Jane Austen loved Corinne; George Sand remembered her adolescence as her "days of Corinne." Sedgwick made a pilgrimage from Massachusetts to Coppêt, Switzerland, to visit Madame de Staël's grave; Child wrote a biography of the author; Stowe recalled feeling "intense sympathy" with

Corinne (qtd. in Moers 1976, 177); Fuller was known as "the Yankee Corinne." And when Jo March, the heroine of Alcott's *Little Women* (1868–69), retreated to her rat-infested attic to scribble, she wore a Corinne costume.

Throughout the nineteenth century, European and American women writers identified themselves with Corinne. Howe remembered Sedgwick, Child, Fuller, the Grimké sisters, and the suffragists as the American "stars of feminine genius." The novelists she mentions, Sedgwick and Child, were praised both by family members and by critics for their genius, and seem to have accepted the acclaim with relatively little anxiety. Perhaps their relatively uncomplicated relationship to genius stemmed from their status as authors of fiction, since at the time it was no longer shocking for women to read novels or to write them—though both authors (like some male contemporaries) published their earliest novels anonymously. Sedgwick indeed became the most popular female novelist in the United States through the first half of the century, creating bold, resourceful heroines in novels such as *Hope Leslie* (1827) and *The Linwoods* (1835). In the latter novel, set during the Revolution, no less a figure than the British commander-in-chief, Sir Henry Clinton, acknowledges the "superior mind" (ch. 25) of Isabella Linwood.

Although exact figures are hard to come by, thousands of novels were written and published by women in the nineteenth century. E. D. E. N. Southworth alone published more than sixty during a career that stretched from the mid-1840s to the end of the century. In this massive body of literature, the novelists treated hundreds of different themes, described a wide variety of settings, and peopled their works with all sorts of characters. The majority of novels by women (like the majority of novels by men) qualify as "domestic" in some sense because they focus on home environments and family relationships. Similarly, many of the texts register as "sentimental," since they emphasize emotions and seek to inspire emotional responses in readers. We must use these terms with care, however; as Judith Fetterley has pointed out, "domestic" and "sentimental" have often been used as derogatory synonyms for "female" (1985, 25). But we must also avoid the trap of dismissing domesticity and sentiment, both of which qualify as central components in the artistic strategies of many important novels written by both men and women. Neither should we assume that domesticity or sentimentality preclude literary merit, any more than femininity does.

Many women's novels ignored the question of female genius altogether or at least subordinated it within a familiar plot—a story, in Baym's well-known formulation, featuring a "young girl who is deprived of the supports she had rightly or wrongly depended on to sustain her throughout life and is faced with the necessity of winning her own way in the world" (1993, 11). Sometimes, to be sure, these young girls demonstrate their intellectual or artistic genius; sometimes that genius takes the form of ingenuity, or "street smarts." And sometimes, as in bestsellers such as Susan Warner's *The Wide, Wide World* (1850) and Maria Cummins's *The Lamplighter* (1854), female ingenuity expresses itself as self-control and masochistic self-sacrifice rather than intellectual achievement. The observation in chapter 1 of *The Wide, Wide World* that its young heroine's "passions were by nature very strong, and by education very imperfectly controlled" clearly signals the form that Ellen Montgomery's education will take over the course of the next 600-plus pages. Although some texts of this variety proved successful and important, they were not as revealing about the female tradition or community of women writers as the *Bildungsroman* novels that framed coming of age within the discourse of artistic genius. When women writers told stories about women writers or about other female artists, they offered important descriptions of how they saw themselves as authors within their own community of letters.

If the Age of Howe and Stowe began with the publication of *Uncle Tom's Cabin* in 1852, then Fanny Fern's *Ruth Hall: A Domestic Tale of the Present Time* (1855) probably qualifies as the first American novel of the period that focused on a woman of genius. Fern was the pen name used by Sarah Payson Willis, a journalist and critic who had reviewed *Uncle Tom's Cabin* glowingly, celebrating Stowe as a "genius" whose work showed that "a new order of women is arising" (qtd. in Showalter 2009, 106). Such praise indicates how Stowe evidently inspired Fern, who might have regarded herself as a member of this "new order of women." At any rate, her novel unabashedly affirms her heroine Ruth Hall's "genius and practical newspaperial talent" (ch. 68). John Walter, editor of the *Household Messenger*, immediately recognizes Ruth's genius when he reads one of her columns:

> "Who *can* she be? she is a genius, certainly, whoever she is," continued he, soliloquizingly; "a bitter life experience she has had too; she did not draw upon her imagination for this article. Like the very first production of her pen that I read, it is a wail from her inmost soul; so are many of her pieces. A few dozen of them taken consecutively, would form a whole history of wrong, and suffering, and bitter sorrow. What a singular being she must be. . . . What powers of endurance! What an elastic, strong, brave, loving, fiery, yet soft and winning nature! A bundle of contradictions! And how famously she has got on too!" (ch. 67)

Ruth Hall remains one of the strongest female characters in nineteenth-century American fiction in large part, as Joyce Warren argues, because Fanny Fern takes her "farther into independence than any other heroine of the period" (1986, xxiii). The novel begins where many others end—with its heroine married and enjoying her young children and a life at home. Even in this sunny domestic environment, however, Ruth stands out as a nineteenth-century super mom. An aspiring poet, she also rambles in the woods with her children (ch. 13). Ruth may be a genius, but she also works very hard at multiple tasks. Ruth's husband Harry dies shortly after the novel begins, for example, and the rest of the novel features Ruth's struggle to survive and then succeed as a single mother in the world of work—"to earn her living, like some other folks" (ch. 30). Gale Temple even calls her "Ragged Ruth" (2003, 150), anticipating the "rags to riches" plot Horatio Alger would inaugurate with *Ragged Dick* (1868). Effectively abandoned, Ruth and her children spiral downward socioeconomically. Ruth makes a gallant effort to find a job, the turning point coming when she determines to earn money by writing. Despite rejection by her editor brother, Hyacinth Ellet (modeled on Payson's brother, Nathaniel P. Willis), Ruth remains convinced that she has the creative talent to succeed. "I *can* do it, I *feel* it, I *will* do it," she vows, "but there will be a desperate struggle first" (ch. 56). Succeed she eventually does, writing under the pseudonym "Floy." Although aided by a sympathetic editor, John Walter, she quickly acquires a "market savvy that facilitates her ability to evaluate independently her own value" (Harris 2006, 349) and thus enables her to recognize her exploitation by previous editors. Another writer might have been tempted to create a romantic relationship between her heroine and such a benefactor, but Walter is safely married, and Fern aptly idealizes his relationship with Ruth as "*true* friendship" (ch. 90). Ruth's independence seems secured, in fact, when she acquires 100 shares of bank stock and continues to make "thousands" with her writing (ch. 87).

By the time *Ruth Hall* appeared in 1855, literature written by women had become so pervasive that Hawthorne wrote a now notorious letter to his publisher, William Ticknor, complaining about the "damned mob of scribbling women" whose books vastly outsold his own (1987a, 304). The past few decades of literary scholarship have transformed Hawthorne's bitter remark into a catchphrase summing up the vexed relationship between men and women in the literary marketplace. But after reading *Ruth Hall,* Hawthorne wrote to Ticknor a second time, with the intention of following up on his "scribbling women" letter, and correcting it:

> I enjoyed [*Ruth Hall*] a good deal. The woman writes as if the devil was in her; and that is the only condition under which a woman ever writes anything worth reading. Generally, women write like emasculated men, and are only to be distinguished from male authors by greater feebleness and folly; but when they throw off the restraints of decency and come before the public stark naked, as it were—then their books are sure to possess character and value. . . . I admire her. (1987a, 308)

In this passage, Hawthorne both praises and belittles Fern for "coming before the public stark naked." Her audacity amazes him, yet he openly admires it at the same moment that he condemns it.

Hawthorne was hardly so generous when, in 1857, he turned his pen toward Julia Ward Howe, writing, "She has no genius or talent, except for making public what she ought to keep to herself—viz. her passions, emotions, and womanly weaknesses. 'Passion Flowers' were delightful; but she ought to have been soundly whipt for publishing them" (1987b, 53). We can only imagine what Hawthorne might have written if he had encountered Howe's unfinished novel, *The Hermaphrodite*, and its protagonist, Laurence, an androgynous genius. Howe's novel in manuscript is narrated by this "beautiful monster," a talented and intelligent person whose strange anatomy gives him a choice between living as male and living as female (ch. 24). The novel, published for the first time in 2004, explores androgyny as a philosophical and emotional question, and positions Laurence as a strange being who scorns "the unworthy burthen of the flesh" and longs to escape the "abstract orphanhood" of androgyny (ch. 3). Gary Williams, the scholar who brought the manuscript to light, reads Laurence as a representation of Howe's husband Samuel Gridley Howe, who allegedly loved his friend Charles Sumner more than he loved his wife. Other critics read the androgynous Laurence as a representation of Howe herself, ill at ease in her difficult marriage and angry that her husband devalues her literary talents. Since Howe did not publish the book (she may not have finished it; only fragments remain), *The Hermaphrodite* had no impact on the literary world in which it had been created. It does, however, offer unique insights into Howe's view of the deep imbrication of gender, even genitalia, and genius. The manuscript shows that she was fascinated and horrified by the ways that anatomical particularities shape and limit human talents.

Another writer who meditated throughout her remarkable career on the plight of subjugated women—especially in her two volume *History of the Condition of Women* (1835)—was Lydia Maria Child, who explored in magazine tales of the 1840s and 1850s ideas of intellectual and sexual liberation. These themes were implicit in her daring early novel, *Hobomok* (1824), which features a strong-minded heroine who defies the Puritan patriarchy, bears a child by her Indian husband, and then (after Hobomok thoughtfully vanishes) marries her English beloved when he unexpectedly reappears in New England. Ever the reformer, she developed (as Carolyn Karcher remarks) a keen analysis of the male subjection of women and openly empathized in her *Letters from New York* (1843) with the "fallen woman." In 1857, when Child read Elizabeth Barrett Browning's *Aurora Leigh*, she crowed, "How glad I am that genius is under the *necessity* of being ever on the free and progressive side! How I delight in having old fogies tormented, always and everywhere!" (qtd. in Karcher 1994, 412). For Child, as for many of her contemporaries, genius was necessarily free and progressive, which made it a natural tool for challenging social conventions. Karcher explains that throughout her career, Child displayed a capacity for "recognizing and responding to a cultural need almost as soon as it had arisen" (1994, 146), an ability in keeping with her own description of the cultural roles mandated by genius.

Child's conception of genius as necessarily free and progressive helps illuminate Frances Harper's short story "The Two Offers," published in the *Anglo-African Magazine* in 1859. After her friend Laura chooses the wrong husband and fades away into death, Janette begins a literary career and dedicates her life to advocating on behalf of three unfortunate groups: little children, the poor, and, most significantly, slaves. She becomes a celebrated abolitionist, and the story ends in a delirium of public adoration for her genius: "Men hailed her as one of earth's strangely gifted children, and wreathed garlands of fame for her brow" (qtd. in Olwell 2011, 21). By avoiding marriage, Janette transcends the limitations of womanhood. She does not die like her deluded friend but dedicates herself to public activism. "The Two Offers" notably shows Janette fighting for abolition rather than for women's rights. Harper's abolitionist heroine indicates that by the late 1850s the relationship between women's genius and women's rights was seriously complicated by questions about race and slavery. And as the Civil War loomed on the horizon, women of genius disappeared suddenly from the discourse of progressives, reappearing—surprisingly—as advocates for slavery in the works of Augusta Jane Evans and Mary Virginia Hawes Terhune. This twist reflects bitter ruptures in the political community that would continue well into the twentieth century, as women and women's rights were set against African American men and their rights.

In this context, Evans and Stowe offer a fascinating contrast. Both were widely commended as women of genius, and both published best-selling novels during the Civil War. While Stowe, a northerner, distinguished herself as one of the nation's leading advocates for the abolition of slavery and the preservation of the union, Evans, a southerner, remained a staunch defender of slavery and secession. The writers also differed in their attitudes to women's rights: predictably, Stowe proved more supportive of women's political rights than Evans. But perhaps surprisingly, it was the southerner Evans whose novels focused on women's education and women's talents. Showalter describes Evans's 1859 novel *Beulah* as "the most *Jane Eyre*-ish book of the decade and the most original" (2009, 95). The novel charts the path of the title character, an orphan deemed a brilliant philosopher, through grave religious doubts and increasingly intense philosophical reflections that lead eventually to her publication of a treatise on faith. Celebrated for her genius, Beulah arrogantly determines never to marry, but eventually she learns the error of her ways and marries her wealthy guardian. Evans published *Beulah* before the Civil War, and although the novel did not condemn slavery, neither did it celebrate the institution. However, Evans's next book, *Macaria; or, Altars of Sacrifice* (1864), which appeared during the war, offers a much more explicit defense of bondage. The novel features two southern women of genius, the painter Electra and the astronomer Irene. *Macaria* became a great commercial and popular success, selling thousands of copies in both the North and South, despite the difficulties of publishing it from within the Confederacy.

Finally, the heroine of Evans's *St. Elmo* (1866), Edna Earl, is a writer of genius whose greatest work is a novel that argues against women's rights:

> The tendency of the age was to equality and communism, and this, she contended, was undermining the golden thrones shining in the blessed and hallowed light of the hearth, whence every true woman ruled the realm of her own family. Regarding every *pseudo* "reform" which struck down the social and political distinction of the sexes, as a blow that crushed one of the pillars of woman's throne,

> she earnestly warned the Crowned Heads of the danger to be apprehended from the unfortunate and deluded female malcontents, who, dethroned in their own realm, and despised by their quondam subjects, roamed as pitiable, royal exiles, threatening to usurp man's kingdom. (ch. 34)

Evans's novelist heroine criticizes the era's reform movements for disrupting the traditional divisions of labor between the sexes, commonly called the "separate spheres." By presenting any change in this relationship as an attack on the sanctity of the home, she reinforces notions of female domesticity, entreating women "if ambitious, to become sculptors, painters, writers, teachers in schools or families; or else to remain mantua-makers, milliners, spinners, dairy maids; but on the peril of all womanhood not to meddle with scalpel or red tape, and to shun rostra of all descriptions" (ch. 34).

Although Evans appears very explicit in her defense of true womanhood and separate spheres, her work contains a notable fascination with women's talents, intellects, and ambitions. She argues against women working in the public sphere (as surgeons, lawyers, politicians, or preachers), but she lavishes praise and attention on heroines working at the sorts of intellectual or artistic labor that can be performed at home or among children. In *Macaria*, the astronomer Irene (a character doubtless inspired by Maria Mitchell) manages to be an ambitious and important scientist without ever venturing away from home—her observatory is in her own house. Evans describes her as "queenly," a "miracle of statuesque beauty" (ch. 17), working through the night to calculate the orbits of unknown stars. But in a motif that offers a striking indication of Evans's proslavery politics, her novels imply that hard study makes the heroines whiter and whiter—Beulah, Irene, and Edna all signal their intense thought by the increasing pallor of their foreheads.

While Evans focused on heroic white women who supported the Confederacy and slavery, Stowe appeared much more interested in describing the effects of slavery on men and women, both black and white. When Stowe wrote about white women and girls in *Uncle Tom's Cabin*, they registered as much less goddess-like than Evans's women. The most heroic white woman in the novel, Mary Bird, is described as a "timid, blushing little woman, of about four feet in height" (ch. 9), but she defies her senator husband in aiding the fugitive Eliza and, in the process, convinces the senator to violate the Fugitive Slave Act for which he had recently voted. The best-known heroine of *Uncle Tom's Cabin*, and perhaps of nineteenth-century American fiction, was Little Eva, an innocent white girl whose dramatic (and prolonged) deathbed scene brought generations of readers to tears. But the novel featured a more diverse cast than just Little Eva: Stowe depicted a wide range of characters, young and old, proslavery and antislavery, with remarkable emotional depth and psychological dimensionality. She also managed to present a very complex plot with sure-handed grace and narrative urgency. The novel proved an immediate and outrageous bestseller, selling two million copies around the world in its first year of publication. Writers including Fanny Fern and George Sand praised it as a work of genius. But although Stowe presented many of its women characters, black and white, as intelligent, *Uncle Tom's Cabin* was not particularly concerned with either women's genius or their civic rights.

Later in her career, Stowe seemed more interested in depicting women of ambition and genius. Her three "society novels" (as she called them), *My Wife and I; or, Harry Henderson's History* (1871), *Pink and White Tyranny: A Society Novel* (1871), and *We and Our Neighbors; or, the Records of an Unfashionable Street* (1875) explicitly discuss women's social roles, women's labor, and women's genius. One such remarkable female, Caroline, gets to explain, in four or five pages early in *My Wife and I,* a woman's right to education and professional work. Her great talent enables her to write a bestseller and use the proceeds to fund her education at a medical school in France. Other peripheral characters in *My Wife and I* are more explicitly involved with women's rights, but Stowe presents them with broad comedy. Stella Cerulean is a beautiful spokeswoman for women's innate superiority, but Stowe satirizes her in a chapter suggestively titled "A Discussion of the Woman Question from All Points": "I never saw anybody that had such a perfectly happy opinion of herself, as she has. She always thinks she understands everything by intuition. I believe in my heart that she'd walk into the engine-room of the largest steamship that ever was navigated, and turn out the chief engineer and take his place, if he'd let her. She'd navigate by woman's God-given instincts, as she calls them" (ch. 25).

Stowe is even funnier concerning Audacia Dangyereyes, who shows up uninvited in a man's bedroom to declare: "I claim my right to smoke, if I please, and to drink if I please; and to come up into your room and make you a call, and have a good time with you, if I please, and tell you that I like your looks, as I do. Furthermore, to invite you to come and call on me at my room. . . . We're opening the way, sir, we're opening the way. The time will come when all women will be just as free to life, liberty and the pursuit of happiness, as men" (ch. 23). The hint of sexual impropriety in Audacia's behavior would have shocked nineteenth-century readers, reminding many of Victoria Woodhull, the political activist, Wall Street trader, and advocate for free love who would run for president of the United States in 1872. But they also would have laughed at her rather than despised her. Stowe's novel supports a gradual approach to women's rights; one character announces her own preference that women should be "educated *for* the ballot" rather than "*by* the ballot" (ch. 25). In sum, although Stowe's novel supports women's rights to education, it does not offer either strong support for or vitriolic criticism of women's political rights—Audacia Dangyereyes and Stella Cerulean are relatively harmless figures of fun, while the noble Caroline is exiled to France.

My Wife and I focuses instead on a girl named Eva—not the Little Eva of *Uncle Tom's Cabin,* but a similarly sweet and innocent, somewhat older Eva, whom the narrator calls his "child-wife" (ch. 2). The bright and pretty Eva eventually becomes a brilliant housekeeper. She explains to her husband, "That is what I call woman's genius. To make life beautiful; to keep down and out of sight the hard, dry, prosaic side, and keep up the poetry—that's my idea of our 'mission.' I think woman ought to be, what Hawthorne calls, 'The Artist of the Beautiful'" (ch. 44). With her sparkling eyes and her flair for upholstery, Eva manages to triumph over economic hardships and create a warm and welcoming home. The fireside features "a pair of elegantly carved book-racks enriched with the complete works of Longfellow, Whittier, Lowell, Holmes, and Hawthorne" (ch. 42), but no volumes of Browning, Brontë, Madame de Staël, or even Stowe. Since Stowe was widely celebrated, and much more financially successful as a writer than any of the men she lists (with the possible exception of Longfellow), it is notable that she does not include herself or any women writers on Eva's book rack. Apparently women's writing has no place at the hearth of Stowe's domestic angel—she's too busy reading Hawthorne!

It might surprise twenty-first-century readers that Stowe, whom Evans would have described as an advocate for "equality and communism," was so insistent on domesticity, while Evans, one of the Confederacy's best-known advocates for slavery, centered her novels on women's genius. Evans's strong belief in upholding social hierarchies may explain the seeming contradiction: aristocratic southern women whose slaves or servants manage the household and perform all domestic labor have more time for books and art than women in the more egalitarian North, who are more likely to be active participants in housekeeping. Evans focuses on astonishingly intelligent and regal women in part because they help her argue for a slavery-based social hierarchy that can support such figures of leisure and learning. Stowe, on the other hand, presents education as preparation for professional work, and consigns the noble Caroline to the hard fate of supporting herself as a doctor because the man she loves is afflicted with congenital madness. Women who marry well, she suggests, will not have to support themselves as lonely professionals. Nor will they be supported in lazy splendor, which she sees as even more pernicious. Instead, they will become middle-class housewives, whose genius and hard work will allow them to make their modest homes beautiful. Evidently, Frances Harper, the author of "The Two Offers," came to share Stowe's logic. Her 1892 novel, *Iola Leroy; or, Shadows Uplifted*, presented a talented and intelligent African American woman who also finally devoted herself to domesticity. Perhaps both writers had been swayed by Hawthorne: the fact that Stowe actually quotes Hawthorne when she describes the woman of genius as "The Artist of the Beautiful" shows that by 1871, only a few years after his death, Hawthorne had become a surprising arbiter of gender and genius.

In 1859, the same year that Evans published *Beulah*, E. D. E. N. (Emma Dorothy Eliza Nevitte) Southworth released her most popular and enduring work, *The Hidden Hand; or, Capitola the Madcap*. Southworth was a friend of Stowe and published many of her works as serials in the same abolitionist magazines that published Stowe's. Though her politics and her social attitudes resembled Stowe's, Southworth wrote novels more plot driven and less explicitly concerned with social issues. Like Stowe, Southworth remained cheerfully sympathetic to women's rights and profoundly uninterested in tragic women of genius. But rather than valorizing angelic housekeepers, *The Hidden Hand* offered her readers a charming tomboy who comically challenges gender conventions via the comic mode.

Joanne Dobson notes that Southworth's work "focuses almost exclusively on gender and gender relations," and thereby reveals "numerous irreconcilable elements packed within the complex and contradictory concept of gender" (1988, xxi). No single character better illustrates Southworth's remarkable achievements than Capitola Black, surely the feistiest female character in nineteenth-century American literature. Despite her forehead, "smooth as that of a girl," and her "little turned-up nose, and red, pouting lips," Cap enters the novel disguised as a "ragamuffin" newsboy on the streets of New York (ch. 4). In this wild adventure novel, Cap is discovered in New York by Major Ira Warfield, who makes her his ward and returns with her to his Virginia estate, where she is "metamorphosed again"—restored, as her guardian announces, "to her proper dress." Initially, she feels "transfigured" by this outward change (ch. 7), but she soon suffers an identity crisis as she recognizes the constraints such a role imposes: "Can this be really *I* myself, and not another? . . . Can this be *I*, Capitola, the little outcast of the city, now changed into Miss Black, the young lady" (ch. 15). Determined to have her gender dilemma both ways, Cap learns to act ladylike inside the house but also reserves time for exploring the "wild and picturesque country around" (ch. 15). The country includes the fascinating outlaw, Black Donald Bayne, a six-foot eight-inch master of disguise and leader of a gang of outlaws who terrorize the countryside.

Black Donald offers Cap a fitting antagonist for the rest of the novel, enabling her to demonstrate her crafty intelligence and her physical prowess in an ongoing battle of wits that parodies courtship and seduction rituals. Cap shocks the minister, for example, when she pretends she has a man hidden in her closet; the male, "Alfred Blenheim," turns out to be a poodle. Standing up to her guardian, she insists on her freedom, which she adamantly refuses to "exchange for any gilded slavery" (ch. 25). She later rescues a young woman, Clara Day, from imprisonment by the villainous Gabriel Le Noir by changing places with her. She even impersonates Clara at the altar, but when asked if she will have Craven Le Noir as her husband, she answers, "No! not if he were the last man and I the last woman on the face of the earth" (ch. 40). She even challenges Le Noir to a duel, shooting him six times in the face with split peas.

Despite the adventure and gender-bending that make *The Hidden Hand* an exciting read, Southworth resorts to a fairly traditional conclusion involving three simultaneous weddings, including Cap's to Herbert Greyson. Southworth does tease her readers with a final episode in which Cap confronts Black Donald, who hides in her bedroom and threatens to have his way with her. Cap wins the battle of wits, tricking him into standing on a trapdoor that she springs open, dropping him into an old cellar; he is consequently captured, imprisoned, convicted of several capital crimes, and sentenced to hang. In a neat turn of the gendered tables, Cap's marriage to a conventionally heroic male (a fair gentleman) collides with her obvious attraction to the dark male outlaw, so it is not surprising that she helps Black Donald break out of prison and light out for the western territories. Southworth hedges at the end of the novel, explicitly resisting what she calls the "lived happily ever after" ending. She knows "for a positive fact," for example, "that our Cap sometimes gives her 'dear, darling, sweet Herbert,' the benefit of the sharp edge of her tongue, which of course he deserves" (ch. 61). Despite the subversive energy that Capitola embodies, Southworth's narrative and the fictional conventions that she confronts seem too limiting. Southworth certainly hints that a wild life on the frontier with Black Donald—without benefit of matrimony and with all options open—would suit Cap's character.

The enduring popularity of *The Hidden Hand* may have provided part of the inspiration for characters created by Elizabeth Stoddard, Louisa May Alcott, and Elizabeth Stuart Phelps. In fact, Jo March, the tomboy heroine of *Little Women*, aspires to become a writer like Southworth, whom Alcott satirically refers to as "S.L.A.N.G. Northbury" (pt. 2, ch. 4). Stoddard's *The Morgesons* (1862), a "feminist *Bildungsroman*," as Sybil Weir has noted (1976, 427), features a heroine, Cassandra Morgeson, who differs "startlingly" from the "pious, selfless heroines typically found in domestic fiction" (Baumgartner 2001, 185). Stoddard uses first-person narration, enabling her to create a highly introspective character with a tongue and wit as sharp as Capitola Black's. The "one thing" Cassandra knows and prizes about herself, for example, illustrates her remarkable self-confidence: "I concealed nothing; the desires and emotions which are usually kept as a private fund I displayed and exhausted. My audacity shocked those who possessed this fund." As if she had read Emerson's advice to "write on the lintels of the door-post, *Whim*" ("Self-Reliance"), she acknowledges, "My whims were sneered at, and then followed. Of course I was driven from whim to whim, to keep them busy, and to preserve my originality, and at last I became eccentric for eccentricity's sake" (ch. 12).

Like *The Hidden Hand*, *The Morgesons* follows convention in representing the most significant tests of female character in romantic encounters with men. The novel divides neatly in half, as Cassandra first flirts with her married cousin Charles Morgeson and then with Desmond Somers. *The Morgesons*, however, represents women's bodies and sexuality in unusually forthright terms. Cassandra's attraction to her cousin threatens her integrity: "I was conscious of the ebb and flow of blood through my heart, felt it when it eddied up into my face, and touched my brain with its flame-colored wave" (ch. 15). Climactically, at a party, when Charles announces that he loves her and asks her to go away with him, the effect is violent. Cassandra chokes on a "convulsive sob" and bites her lip. She wipes "streaks of blood" away with her handkerchief, before telling Charles never to say "those frightful words again" (ch. 19). This potentially adulterous relationship ends abruptly and violently when both characters suffer injuries in a carriage accident.

Charles dies, while Cassandra ends up with a broken arm and scars on her face. Although the outcome of this relationship seems conventional—punishment for the adulterers—Stoddard breaks with convention in several ways. First, as Jennifer Putzi argues, Cassandra does not consider her scars, which she calls "tattoos," "as punishment for her sexual transgressions" (2000, 169). Second, Charles rather than Cassandra suffers the worse fate, and his death offers his not-so-grieving widow, Alice, a remarkable opportunity. Asked what she will do, Alice replies, "Take care of the children, and manage the mills." "I am changed," she adds, and then expresses her eagerness to begin life all over again (ch. 21).

Cassandra's feelings for Desmond Somers are equally powerful: "I was mad for the sight of him—mad to touch his hand once more" (ch. 32). Cassandra eventually marries him, although not before he endures two years of separation and rehabilitation for alcoholism, and critics disagree about whether Cassandra achieves a full-fledged feminist identity or settles for a more traditional, constricted life. The results seem mixed—"partial conformity, partial modification," as Sandra Zagarell puts it (1985, 50). If Cassandra started the novel energized by self-reliant, romantic idealism, she ends up a somewhat frustrated realist. "A woman of genius is but a heavenly lunatic," she tells Mr. Somers, "or an anomaly sphered between the sexes" (ch. 39). And as the novel ends, she finds herself in limbo. "I remain this year the same," she tells herself. "No change, no growth or development!" (ch. 40).

Alcott's Jo March, like Fanny Fern's Ruth Hall, achieves a much greater degree of fulfilling independence, in large part because, like her creator, she becomes a writer. Alcott describes her as an imitator of both Southworth and Madame de Staël. Jo's "scribblings" prove somewhat successful. She publishes them in newspapers in the manner of Fanny Fern or Southworth, until eventually a stern German professor teaches her the error of her ways. "I do not like to think that good young girls should see such things," he tells her, adding, "I would rather give my boys gunpowder to play with than this bad trash." Professor Bhaer acknowledges that writers of fiction earn money for their work, but he tells Jo that they are not "honest" because they "put poison in the sugar-plum, and let the small ones eat it. No; they should think a little, and sweep mud in the street before they do this thing!" (pt. 2, ch. 11). When Jo rereads her own work, "she seemed to have got on the Professor's mental or moral spectacles," and the stories "fill her with dismay." "They *are* trash," she remarks, "and will soon be worse than trash if I go on; for each is more sensational than the last" (pt. 2, ch. 11). She burns her manuscripts, gives up on her writing, and marries the professor in contrition. The tomboy, tamed, becomes a domestic angel in the sequels.

Alcott's own story was more sensational than Jo's; she did not marry or stop writing sensational stories. But *Little Women* became her best-known and most influential work. The story that *Little Women* tells about literary women is not wholly negative; readers treasure the book for Jo's cocky tomboy characteristics, and few find her renunciatory marriage completely convincing. But nonetheless, the era that had begun with the vivid figure of Corinne was clearly drawing to a close: Alcott presented Jo's genius as comical, stubborn, and ultimately childish, if not pernicious.

In the years that followed, Alcott published many more children's books, as well as a serious novel aimed at adults that discussed the possibilities open to intelligent women in the last decades of the nineteenth century. *Work: A Story of Experience* (1873) relates the travails of Christie Devon, a New England girl who declares independence in the first pages and heads to the big city of Boston to support herself. In the first volume, Christie tries her hand at most of the jobs available to women in the late 1850s: servant, actress, governess, companion, and seamstress. She manages to avoid prostitution, though her dearest friend does not; Alcott never mentions either the possibility of factory work, which she may have considered even less genteel than prostitution, or the possibility of Christie becoming a writer. But throughout the novel's first half, each job she tries brings her to grief.

The second volume finds her dependent on the hospitality of strangers, working as a helpful houseguest while she figures out how to reenact her own version of the *Jane Eyre* plot. After marrying, she almost immediately becomes a widow with a young child to care for and an inherited business to run. Since Christie marries her best friend's brother on the day that she and her husband both enlist in the Union army, she spends only a few pages as a married woman. Then, after her husband heroically sacrifices himself to help some escaping slaves, she sets up house with her dear friend (the reformed prostitute) and her (somewhat hastily conceived) daughter. All these experiences enable Christie to find her vocation, at the end of the novel, as a public speaker who preaches in favor of women's rights, acting as an "interpreter between the two classes" of genteel women and working women (ch. 20). With Christie's new role, Alcott indicates that the time for the emancipation of women comes after the abolition of slavery. Reflecting on the changes brought about by the conclusion of the Civil War, Christie acknowledges: "Others have finished the emancipation work and done it splendidly, even at the cost of all this blood and sorrow." She accepts the loss of her husband as a necessary sacrifice for the noble cause of ending slavery, but dismisses her own ministrations on behalf of the Union as coming "too late to do any thing" but enable her to "behold the glorious end" of the conflict. Instead, Christie dedicates herself to advocating women's rights, observing with humility that "This new task seems to offer me the chance of being among the pioneers, to do the hard work, share the persecution, and help lay the foundation of a new emancipation whose happy success I may never see" (ch. 20). She certainly does not call herself a genius, as Ruth Hall had done so blithely two decades before, but Victoria Olwell and Gustavus Stadler both read Christie as a genius figure anyway, in large part because her remarkable gift for public speaking makes her a clear daughter of Corinne, who possessed a great talent for improvising poetic speeches. Yet Alcott is careful to distance her heroine from Madame de Staël, as in the closing pages of the novel, when Christie explicitly cautions her young friend Bella: "I don't ask you to be a De Staël" (ch. 20). This statement suggests that in the decades following the Civil War, the idea of being a woman of genius had become deromanticized. And so, in *Little Women*, Jo renounces women's literature as "trash," while in *Work*, Christie closes with a fictional renunciation of genius, choosing a "loving league of sisters" over the less domestic world of ambitious thought (ch. 20). But both the renunciation and the denial appear somewhat suspect—readers may well find Jo and Christie much less domesticated than they claim to be.

Two years after the second volume of *Work* appeared, Elizabeth Stuart Phelps published *The Story of Avis* (1877), a *Bildungsroman* clearly in conversation with the works of her peers but decidedly sadder in tone. Her title character, Avis, is a genius painter who makes the fatal mistake of marrying. Domestic toil and sorrow gradually rob her of her talent, while her attempts to paint and her frustration with domesticity are partly to blame for the difficulties of her marriage and the eventual death of her husband and son. Left alone with a daughter to support (just like Christie Devon and Ruth Hall, who has two daughters), Avis returns to her studio to find that her talent has fled. She has damaged the muscles in her arms and hands carrying her sick child, so she is physically unable to paint. Her only hope is that life may someday be better for her daughter. "It would be easier for her daughter to be alive, and be a woman, than it had been for her: so much as this, she understood; more than this she felt herself too spent to question." Spent indeed. The final image likens Avis to "the country, wasted by civil war" (ch. 25), a comparison that parallels the toll exerted on her body through household labor with the larger devastation enacted on the nation by the bloody sectional conflict.

In just a few decades, genius had devolved from an attribute that made women more attractive to a psychic trauma comparable to shell shock. The actual Civil War may explain part of this transition, since during the war and in the years immediately following it, women had stepped in to fill men's places in many occupations. As the next generation of men grew to maturity, however, there was a broad push to remove women from the public sphere and return them to the home. But the world of novels was an odd place for this retreat from intellectual and social engagement to play out. Before the war, it had been more of a female realm than a male one, and this remained true after the war: more women wrote novels, and more women read them than men. But something had changed; women's writing was no longer a place for women of genius or even for pretensions to literary greatness. Perhaps as increasing numbers of women entered the literary marketplace, published novels, made money, and achieved prominence, the need to assert the existence of female genius lost its urgency. Then, too, the emergence of the New Woman in the 1880s and 1890s revealed not so much the brilliance of a few female minds as the willingness of progressive women to defy convention and claim new freedoms. Kate Chopin's *The Awakening* (1899) brilliantly captures in the demise of Edna Pontellier both the desire for a more liberated, independent life and the persistence of crushing cultural constraints.

The story does not end with Edna's suicide. After Phelps's *Avis*, many female authors would return to novels and tales about women of courage and genius. Constance Fenimore Woolson, Sarah Orne Jewett, Willa Cather, Edith Wharton, and Mary Austin are just a few of the novelists who would chronicle the obstacles and exploits of intelligent, ambitious women in the last decades of the nineteenth century and the early decades of the twentieth. But none would repeat the insouciant optimism that Fanny Fern conveyed with the heroine of *Ruth Hall*, the self-declared genius who had flourished at the beginning of the Age of Howe and Stowe.

28

MALE HYBRIDS IN CLASSIC AMERICAN FICTION

DAVID LEVERENZ

> I am a businessman. I am anything I need to be at any time.
>
> —Pascal (Ian Holm) in *Big Night* (1996)

During the decades when racialized capitalism took hold in the United States, writers often described compelling male characters as hybrids. Like the country, the men's disparate states seem uneasily united. Some are on the edge between white and black, white and Indian, civilized and savage, moral and immoral, even male and female. For others, mental power comes through doublings or self-abandonings, including the ability to inhabit an opponent's mind. These characterizations reflect and critique capitalism's abiding promise: you can remake yourself as whatever you want to be. Maneuvering among multiple selves manages risk by inward diversification, and the self-distancing inherent in role playing minimizes emotional buffeting. At the same time, multiple selves can mirror and seduce conflicting audiences.

From James Fenimore Cooper's Natty Bumppo to Edgar Allan Poe's Dirk Peters, from Poe's Hop-Frog to Nathaniel Hawthorne's Roger Chillingworth, hybridities enhance a character's force. In Harriet Beecher Stowe's *Uncle Tom's Cabin; or, Life Among the Lowly* (1852), George Harris's amalgamation of white and black makes him a bold, risk-taking slave. In *The Scarlet Letter: A Romance* (1850), both Chillingworth and Arthur Dimmesdale gain power when their desires make them seem possessed by Satan, or the "Black Man." A related line extends from Carwin, the ambiguously dangerous ventriloquist in Charles Brockden Brown's *Wieland; or, The Transformation* (1798), to Herman Melville's Ahab, who comes to think a malicious god is speaking his words and thinking his thoughts.

Much more benignly, the act of thinking makes Ralph Waldo Emerson feel ventriloquized by godlike spontaneities, and Henry David Thoreau's *Walden; or, Life in the Woods* (1854) represents the mind as intrinsically doubled. In his chapter on solitude, Thoreau relishes "a certain doubleness" that comes from seeing the "play" or "fiction" of himself, remarking, "With thinking we may be beside ourselves in a sane sense" (ch. 5). Later the pond becomes a naturally hybridized "Sky water," which purifies his "savage" impulses to eat a woodchuck raw (ch. 9). Poe's stories about C. Auguste Dupin celebrate what looks like the un-American opposite of self-reliance: a man whose mastery depends on becoming his opponent. His knack for self-doubling augments his control.

According to the *Oxford English Dictionary*, the word "hybrid" was used only rarely and dismissively before the nineteenth century. It meant either a mongrel cross-breed or something "composed of different or incongruous elements." Decades before Darwin, scientists became intrigued with creating hybrid plants, and most critics have focused on biological aspects of the term's cultural rise. I suggest that capitalist pressures were equally crucial.

In antebellum American literature, hybrid males emerged as extreme representations of opposing capitalist pressures to be gentlemanly or brutal, whichever helps a man's survival and status. Hybrid males emerged in tandem with doubled males and serial role players. Those three modes of amalgamated contraries variously displayed models for resourcefulness. How can a man be mobile and upwardly mobile among strangers? Try on some selves and see what works. Hybrids and doublings also displayed the tensions accompanying internalized opposites. Their strains expose the psychological cost of entrepreneurial capitalism before large corporations regularized men's work roles.

American fiction to 1870 registers the stresses and exuberances that men felt as European models of status and moral behavior confronted more heterogeneous possibilities for manly self-definition. Dandies, yeomen, artisans, suitors, soldiers, ministers, bachelors, sexual predators, plantation patriarchs, and explorers profusely persisted in many narratives. Yet the aristocratic ideal of the leisured gentleman conflicted with a more broadly accessible ideal of self-advancement through mental as well as physical work. Manual after manual proclaimed the benefits of manly industry and warned young men against idleness. More complexly, *The Young Man's Own Book* (1832) declared that developing intellectual as well as moral character produced respectability and success. The anonymous author advises his audience to read a great deal and to compose written arguments: "Thinking, not growth, makes manhood" (52). Be firm, "never take fire from an angry man" (165), and choose a wife who is a good manager, not a beauty. Be sure to "conform to the dress of others, and avoid the appearance of being tumbled" (197). The advice balances traditional gentry ideals with a new emphasis on building a calm and decisive mind.

Better writers played with those types and preachings. Thoreau and Walt Whitman celebrate laziness—Thoreau declares he worked only six weeks a year—and both writers taunt readers who define their worth by their possessions. From Aaron Burr to a great variety of con artists, many men soon realized that the mind's capacity for devious maneuvering dramatically improved chances for success. Ironically, the country's most mythic rags to riches hero displays his moral character by continually lying about his upscale connections. Horatio Alger's *Ragged Dick* (1868) presents the poor young bootblack as an endearing con man, whose "droll" fabrications about himself somehow make him respectable.

Another kind of narrative doubling reflects the strains in a narrator whose "we" struggles and usually fails to make sense of a loner who fascinates and appalls him. As Ishmael fades into an enslaved group of sailor spectators, he or they seem mesmerized by Ahab's solitary fixation on supernatural revenge. Short stories such as Hawthorne's "Wakefield" (1835), Poe's "The Man of the Crowd" (1840), and Melville's "Bartleby, the Scrivener" (1853) vividly dramatize what Poe's narrator calls an inability to "read" his subject. In all three stories, the anonymous narrator's baffled obsession with someone's idiosyncratic individuality partially exposes his fear that his pose of genteel belonging lacks a self. As Ahab does for Ishmael, the loner becomes his unacknowledged double. Together, and in their inability to be together, they become hybrids.

At least three basic cultural transformations shaped representations of manliness and unmanliness on the new continent. Most crucially, race became a defining dichotomy. What class has been to the English, race has been to Americans, in part because slavery defined unmanliness. The fear of being seen as slavish helped enable the other two transformations. As the provincial colony became an expanding nation, manliness became defined more through work than class status. Anglophile ideals persisted, of course. In the South, white workers could ally themselves with plantation gentry by claiming superiority over men of darker colors. In the North, pseudo-aristocracy persisted as white racism. Yet throughout the antebellum North, men idealized a new norm: self-reliant labor and inventiveness. Freedom brought the pursuit of upward mobility, which often required self-refashionings.

Early in *A Small Boy and Others* (1913), Henry James recalled that to his young eyes America seemed divided into "three classes, the busy, the tipsy, and Daniel Webster" (ch. 4). At the beginning of the nineteenth century, "business man" implied that a man was too busy; by the end of the century, "businessman" had become a one-word norm. In that century of hyperbolic speeches, Daniel Webster was more typical than anomalous. American men's relish for oratory and tall tales complemented their push for profit and adventure. A male slave was supposed to know his place, not talk back, and be a "boy." A white man was expected to put himself forward, verbally and physically, as far as he could dare. Frederick Douglass's "The Heroic Slave" (1853), a novella about the leader of a slave revolt, celebrates Madison Washington's oratory, the public role that had launched Douglass's own career.

As Benjamin Franklin wrote in "Information to Those Who Would Remove to America" (1784), "The almost general mediocrity of fortune" requires Americans "to follow some business for subsistence" without the usual vices arising from "idleness" or lordliness. It is "a general happy mediocrity that prevails." Whereas young men find trades closed to them in Europe, American artisans and entrepreneurs find wide-open markets. As a result, "people do not inquire concerning a stranger, *What is he?* But, *What can he do?*" The Indians' land seemed available for the taking. Resilient resourcefulness mattered more than lineage in determining a man's success, or at least that was the claim. Emerson celebrates that energy in "The Young American" (1844): "[T]he new and anti-feudal power of Commerce" combines with "heterogeneous" immigrants to make "a country of beginnings, of projects, of designs, of expectations."

Recent literary criticism has foregrounded "transnational" connections that transcend or undermine the nation-state. That intellectual movement has its own expansive capitalist dynamic, since it opened access to intellectual globalization when the market for studies of national literature seemed saturated. Scholars have found new worlds of textual juxtapositions to write about. But arguments for transnational literary fluidities tend to minimize political uses of power, which remain more national than international. They also discount the exceptional aspects of what Michael Kammen has called the "compound identities" encouraged by Americanization (1993, 30).

The male hybridities in American fiction grow from two such exceptions—one wholly negative, one relatively positive. First, the enduring presence of race-based chattel slavery and racial hierarchy has been far more intense and protracted in the United States than in any other country in the history of the world. No other country prohibited interracial marriage for so long. No other country enforced the "one-drop rule" so assiduously. More broadly, from the Know-Nothings of the 1850s to the formation of the Tea Party after the 2008 election, nativism has channeled white Americans' recoils against immigrants and "others," especially in hard times.

Second, the United States became the world's leading center for capitalist energies. In *The Relentless Revolution* (2010), Joyce Appleby defines early capitalism as a "Janus-like" culture of audacious innovation, ingenuity, and brutality (419). In America, the "slave-worked plantations and mechanical wizardry . . . must be recognized as twin responses to the capitalist genie" (122). After the Revolution, US capitalism's success depended partly on southern slavery, not only because slavery supplied raw materials for northern manufacturers as the colonies had done for Europe, but also because it became a contemptuous metaphor to goad men toward pluck and enterprise. Traditional class and institutional controls could not prevent the flux of plenty and panic. Kinships and genteel belonging became frail defenses in times of stress. As Melville opened his novel *Pierre; or, The Ambiguities* (1852), "In our cities families rise and burst like bubbles in a vat" (bk. 1, ch. 3). Almost a decade earlier, in *Lectures to Young Men* (1843–44), Henry Ward Beecher declared, "Every few years, Commerce has its earthquakes . . . it is disgraceful to lie down under [adversity] like a supple dog. Indeed, to stand composedly in the storm, amidst its rage and wildest devastations; to let it beat over you, and roar around you, and pass by you, and leave you undismayed,—this is to be a MAN" (qtd. in Derrick 1997, 10–11).

In 1832, Henry Clay invented the term "self-made man," and nine years later Emerson celebrated "Self-Reliance." A year earlier, in the second volume of *Democracy in America*, French aristocrat Alexis de Tocqueville wrote that individualism was one of the two great dangers to American democracy, since it threw every man back on "the solitude of his own heart" (ch. 2). Hawthorne would probe that dangerous solitude in story after story. Ironically, when Tocqueville popularized the new word, which conservative French Jesuits had only recently invented, Americans immediately turned individualism from a pejorative into a badge of identity. With compounded irony, the word's proud prescriptiveness became a collective ideology, of a piece with Tocqueville's second danger, "the tyranny of the majority" (v. 1, ch. 15). Business enterprise embraced and enhanced that contradictory state of mind.

In emphasizing capitalism rather than colonialism as the frame for representations of male hybrids, I'm amending the cultural theory of Homi Bhabha. During the 1990s, Bhabha's "hybridity," Judith Butler's "performativity," and Michael Warner's "heteronormativity" became the four, six, and eight syllable words to conjure with. Bhabha's *The Location of Culture* (1994) makes an elegant, if abstract, case for colonialism's production of "mimicry, hybridity, sly civility" as "a subversive strategy of subaltern agency" (185), reversing domination "through disavowal" (152), which is "at once a mode of appropriation and of resistance" (120). His argument is itself a hybrid, imitating and resisting new historicism's Foucauldian tendency to see power everywhere and agency nowhere. For Bhabha, hybridity resists the two "great connective narratives of capitalism and class [that] drive the engines of social reproduction" but don't allow the individuations arising from displacement (6). I argue that in a postcolonial country awash with mixed peoples and would-be capitalists, hybridity became a resource, not just a resistance.

Tocqueville was astonished at the contradiction between American men's affable democratic generosities and their ruthlessness toward Indians and slaves. In 1923, musing on Cooper's *The Deerslayer; or, The First War-Path* (1841), D. H. Lawrence concluded that despite Natty Bumppo's fraternity with Chingachgook, "The essential American soul is hard, isolate, stoic, and a killer" (73). Frederick Jackson Turner's immensely influential frontier thesis, first presented in 1893, argued that as "the meeting point between savagery and civilization," the frontier became a crucible for "rapid and effective Americanization" (1920, 3–4). By progressing from European gentility through often violent encounters with Indians, American men became hybrid fusions of savage and civilized. For Turner, Andrew Jackson's spluttering displays of rage on the Senate floor embodied that healthy transformation. In 1942, Joseph Schumpeter would define capitalism's energies as "creative destruction."

Many American novels tell stories of privileged white men who enter a "savage" environment and discover the savage in themselves. In Brown's *Edgar Huntly; or, Memoirs of a Sleep-Walker* (1799), the cultivated hero eats a panther, then kills someone with a tomahawk, while the still more murderous Clithero Edny, his double, becomes a starved, hairy brute. William Gilmore Simms's *The Yemassee* (1835) shows white men dispossessing Indians in old South Carolina. With considerably less violence, three autobiographical narratives show how effete easterners can become real men by heading west. Richard Henry Dana's *Two Years Before the Mast* (1840) recounts the story of a sickly Harvard lad who becomes a sailor, and Francis Parkman's *The Oregon Trail* (1849) recounts his journey from Harvard to the Wild West, where he regenerates himself through violence. Most complexly, Melville's first novel, *Typee: A Peep at Polynesian Life* (1846), tells of Tommo's intimacies with a South Seas cannibal tribe and passionate, brown-skinned Fayaway, until the prospect of being tattooed spurs him to terrified flight from full assimilation.

The most spectacular adventure novel along those lines has been almost wholly forgotten. Written by Robert Montgomery Bird and published anonymously, *Sheppard Lee: Written by Himself* (1836) purports to be the memoir of a desperate Philadelphia man's "transformations" into six dead men whose bodies he successively reanimates. Luckily for him, the last body is his own corpse. Until then, this nineteenth-century version of Woody Allen's Zelig had become a squire, a dandy, a miser, a philanthropist, and a surprisingly contented slave. The most powerful passages explore the strangeness of having two selves at once or of feeling oneself becoming someone else. Unfortunately, most of the novel tells a tedious tale of farcical abjections, spiced with conventional satire of political factions and social pretensions. Yet the serial hybridities undermine all of Sheppard Lee's stereotypical identities, including his own.

Lee's incarnation as Tom the happy slave reveals the conservative polemic under Bird's narrative playfulness. At first Lee recoils from his woolly hair, "smoked mahogany" skin, and "immense" red lips (v. 2, bk. 6, ch. 1). Soon he realizes his life is much better than any northern white laborer's. He can laze about, live for the present, work just a little, look in the mirror a lot, and play with the son of his gentle Virginia master. For the first time he is "satisfied even with *myself*" (v. 2, bk. 6, ch. 5). Yet when his fellow slaves discover an abolitionist pamphlet, Tom's hidden whiteness precipitously returns. Previously illiterate, he's suddenly the best reader in the group. When faced with the "evil" racial uprising that he has caused, he feels terrified for his master's two daughters, who die rather than be raped. Once restored to whiteness outwardly as well as inwardly, he writes a book proclaiming that books are bad for black people. It's fine for white people to refashion themselves in literature and life, but black people will remain "content" only if they can't read.

Arguably the four best-known antebellum novels feature male hybrids: *The Last of the Mohicans: A Narrative of 1757* (1826), *The Scarlet Letter*, *Moby-Dick; or, The Whale* (1851), and *Uncle Tom's Cabin*. Two of the novels make capitalist dynamics central to their plots, whether through whaling or slavery, though Ahab and Tom oppositely resist reducing the human spirit to a desire for profits. The other two novels offer the nostalgic pleasures and pains of imaginatively journeying to pre-capitalist worlds, whether with the Puritans or on the frontier. In all four of them, racialized hierarchy shapes male hybridity.

In Cooper's *The Last of the Mohicans*, Natty Bumppo proudly proclaims himself "a man without a cross" (ch. 7). Natty struts the phrase to disown any taint of racial mixing. Yet as Leslie Fiedler, Jane Tompkins, and Leland S. Person have variously pointed out, mixings constitute his identity. He lives Turner's frontier thesis, though without the rage. He's always on the edge between white man and Indian, gentleman and bumpkin, good manners and violence. Natty's buddyship with Chingachgook inaugurates what Fiedler memorably calls the chaste cross-racial marriage of wilderness males. Tompkins emphasizes the novel's "cultural miscegenation" and notes that Natty disguises himself as a bear (1985, 114). Person highlights the class mixture in "natty bumpkin" (1998, 89). Only gender hybridity seems absent. Natty is asexual, except when Cooper makes him a hapless suitor in *The Pathfinder; or, The Inland Sea* (1840), though he does love to fondle his long gun.

Lydia Maria Child's *Hobomok* (1824) has a racier plot, but without white hybridities, until the ending acknowledges and erases them. In newly founded Salem, a young white woman marries a brave Indian who reveres her. They even have a son, though Mary Conant's love for her husband seems mostly "gratitude" for freeing her from her rigid Puritan father. The novel's white people are stereotypical English colonials, including Charles Brown, the high-church Anglican lawyer who also loves Mary before her father bullies him back to England. Only Hobomok moves toward hybridity, though Mary privately can't shake the contrast between her husband's "uncultivated mind" (ch. 19) and Charles's "mental riches," even "genius" (ch. 11). In the climactic chapter, a friend muses that Hobomok "seems almost like an Englishman" (ch. 19). But when Charles (thought to have died at sea) unexpectedly returns, the Indian immediately reverts to Noble Savage by relinquishing his wife and son. After he wistfully disappears into the forest, Charles and Mary happily raise the hybrid child, named Charles Hobomok Conant. The son eventually graduates from Cambridge, and "by degrees his Indian appellation was silently omitted" (ch. 20).

In *The Scarlet Letter*, Roger Chillingworth appears as "a white man, clad in a strange disarray of civilized and savage costume" (ch. 3), and his successful doctoring depends on mixing traditional medicine with Indian herbs. More ominously, he looks like "a person who had so cultivated his mental part that it could not fail to mould the physical to itself," and his "heterogeneous garb" can't quite conceal that "one of this man's shoulders rose higher than the other" (ch. 3). His mind has grown the "slight deformity" that betrays him to Hester as her husband (ch. 3). Soon Hester asks him if he's "like the Black Man that haunts the forest" (ch. 4).

As doublings develop between Chillingworth and Arthur Dimmesdale, hybridities develop within them. After the cuckolded husband insinuates himself into sadomasochistic intimacy with the "tremulous" minister, the doctor sneaks up to his sleeping patient and discovers the scarlet *A* concealed on Dimmesdale's "bosom." Chillingworth responds orgiastically, with "extravagant gestures" as he "stamped his foot upon the floor!" (ch. 10). The doctor's "ecstasy" resembles "Satan's" when a human soul joins his kingdom. He has indeed become the "Black Man," the Puritans' term for the devil. His ecstasy differs only in having "the trait of wonder in it!" (ch. 10).

After agreeing to flee with Hester, Dimmesdale too becomes temporarily hybrid and satanic. His impulses shock him. He wants to blaspheme to a deacon, tell an elderly woman that the soul isn't immortal, inject impure thoughts into a young virgin's mind, and teach children some curse words. "What is it that haunts and tempts me thus?" he cries. "Am I mad? or am I given over utterly to the fiend?" (ch. 20). Chillingworth has gone to the devil long ago; now his prey seems on the verge of joining him. Earlier, as the minister approaches them in the forest, Pearl twice asks her mother, "Is it the Black Man?" (ch. 16).

On the scaffold at last, the dying minister exorcises his guilt by exposing the scarlet *A* on his skin under the "ministerial band" (ch. 23). Though the revelation proves that he was Hester's secret lover, the narrator's explanation preserves Dimmesdale's deeper bond with Chillingworth, now his double. Among the townspeople, "those best able to appreciate the minister's peculiar sensibility, and the wonderful operation of his spirit upon the body" whisper that the letter came from "the ever active tooth of remorse, gnawing from the inmost heart outwardly" (ch. 24). Both men's minds have deformed their bodies. Astonishingly, the narrator imagines Dimmesdale united not with Hester but with Chillingworth in heaven, "their earthly stock of hatred and antipathy transmuted into golden love" (ch. 24).

Perhaps that conclusion shows Hawthorne's own reluctance to "Be true!" beyond his genteel persona (ch. 24). His narrator is another anonymous "we" fascinated with a deviant individualist, this time a woman, whose private, passionate thoughts lure and appall him. His reiterated injunctions to be true to oneself betray some desperation, especially since they're so untrue. Chillingworth, and Holgrave in *The House of the Seven Gables* (1851), gain power and respect by sustaining false identities. Or perhaps that sententious moral shows Hawthorne's canniness about pleasing his readers. As several reviewers said, at least Hester remains satisfactorily miserable.

In *Moby-Dick*, Ahab begins as a hybrid who can't quite hold together. He's "a grand, ungodly, god-like man," Captain Peleg tells Ishmael (ch. 16). When Ahab appears at last, he "seemed made of solid bronze," traversed with "a slender rod-like mark, lividly whitish." Resembling a bronze sculpture, he also looks like "a great tree" hit by "lightning . . . still greenly alive, but branded." Ishmael uses "brand" three times in his first description (ch. 28). Something has seared the man, body and soul. The most flagrant hybridity, his ivory leg, embodies that branding. Later Ishmael compares Ahab to a bear, a moose, a sea-lion, a "black" man among "cannibals" (ch. 34), a locomotive, the contracting Hudson River or a captive "Caryatid" (ch. 41), and a Prometheus who creates his own vulture. Ahab's heart is a mortar shell in his "Egyptian chest" (ch. 41). His amalgamations enhance the "thousand fold more potency" gained through his crazed rage (ch. 41). Yet like Christ, he has "a crucifixion in his face" (ch. 28). Like Father Mapple, he knows God "chiefly . . . by [His] rod" (ch. 9).

Ishmael shares Ahab's amalgamation of contrary elements, though more intellectually. As his opening paragraph intimates, he too is on a suicide trip and he becomes Ahab's spectator double. His incessant shiftiness complements Ahab's fixed purpose. Nothing in this book can be pinned down to a stable meaning, not even Ahab's "monomania" for revenge. By the end, the captain starts to think that some supernatural force may be manipulating his rage for its own inscrutable ends. In the chapter "The Candles," he claims that "the queenly personality lives in me, and feels her royal rights" (ch. 119). Whatever that mysterious gender change may mean, it implies that he feels doubly possessed, by a bad king who hates him and a good queen who hates the king.

That audacious hybridity puts Emersonian transcendence in a paranoid mode. In Emerson's first essay, *Nature* (1836), he memorably describes his mind's ecstatic possession: "I become a transparent eyeball; I am nothing; I see all; the currents of the Universal Being circulate through me; I am part or parcel of God" (ch. 1). In other essays, he reaches for contradictory labels to describe the infinitude that flows into him when he's really thinking, such as "the aboriginal Self" or "Spontaneity or Instinct" in "Self-Reliance" (1841), and the titular phrase of "The Over-Soul" (1841). Those interchangeable terms imply a transcendent self there for each of us if we just let go of our "mean egotism" (*Nature*, ch. 1). In "Self-Reliance" Emerson declares, "We lie in the lap of immense intelligence, which makes us receivers of its truth and organs of its activity." Is that a cosmic mother or father, and if it's father, what "organ" in his lap have we become?

In still more unsettling modernist modes, Emerson pictures the "sturdy capitalist" as a "phantom" whose foundations are on a spinning sphere "floating in soft air, . . . a bit of bullet," a "wild balloon," all of which symbolize "his whole state and faculty" ("The Transcendentalist," 1842). In "Circles" (1841), thinking becomes an expanding circle experienced through "abandonment." In "History" (1841), as if echoing Poe's Dupin, an artist declares that to draw a tree or a sheep requires becoming the tree or sheep. To draw a child, "the painter enters into his nature" and paints from the inside out. Most joltingly, Emerson celebrates "the centrifugal tendency of a man, . . . his passage out into free space . . . to escape the custody of that body in which he is pent up, and of that jail-yard of individual relations in which he is enclosed" ("The Poet," 1844).

Emerson's delight in spontaneous thinking requires abandoning conformity, consistency, and the possessive ego as well as social relationships. Implicitly, he wants his mind to flee a hybridity that can't ultimately be escaped: the mind-body split, analogous for him to divinity's imprisonment in the human. Hawthorne and Melville saw physical and metaphysical dangers in the enticements of Emersonian mind-play. In *The Scarlet Letter*, Hawthorne suggests that the mind's control of the body can turn devilish rather than moral. In *Moby-Dick*'s "The Mast-Head," the threat of a plummeting body snaps Ishmael out of his Emersonian reverie: "Over Descartian vortices you hover" (ch. 35). The phrase suggests not only Descartes's theory of gravity but also a pun so bad that it's good: I sink, therefore I am. Worse, Ahab discovers the underside of Emerson's empowering God-self. As he senses that he will fail, he suspects that he's a conduit for supernatural malevolence. Like the sun, which he once vowed to strike, he may be only "an errand-boy in heaven" (ch. 132).

Earlier, with playful grandiosity, Ahab says, "I'll order a complete man . . . fifty feet high in his socks" and arms three feet thick, with "no heart at all" but a "sky-light on top of his head to illuminate inwards" (ch. 108). As Ishmael says in the first chapter, it's "that story of Narcissus, . . . and this is the key to it all." Then, as if mirroring Ishmael's swerve from Narcissus to Fate in "Loomings," Ahab muses to the carpenter, "How dost thou know that some entire, living, thinking thing may not be invisibly and uninterpenetratingly standing precisely where thou now standest; aye, and standing there in thy spite?" (ch. 108). Translation: every inch of you may be quivering with something that moves your body, thinks your thoughts, and is out to get you.

At the end of "The Symphony," that paranoid possibility has become a near certainty. Ahab despairingly asks, "[H]ow then can this one small heart beat; this one small brain think thoughts; unless God does that beating, does that thinking, . . . and not I." The lack of a question mark implies his answer. God even seems to be "beating" his heart, an ambiguous formulation. "Is Ahab, Ahab? Is it I, God, or who, that lifts this arm?" (ch. 132). In "The Cabin," when Pip begs Ahab to "use poor me for your one lost leg; only tread upon me, sir" (ch. 129), Ahab angrily flees from the sympathy that incorporating Pip into his hybridity would bring. Yet Ahab is already Pip's double, since he has demanded the same masochistic relation to his God. Like the differently crazed black boy, abandoned at sea and randomly rescued, Ahab has witnessed the dark side of American individualism. "The intense concentration of self in the middle of such a heartless immensity, my God! who can tell it?" (ch. 93).

Moby-Dick takes its readers from jaunty adventuring to sadomasochistic abjection. Melville's next novel, *Pierre*, wallows in abjection, and Poe's horror tales present men's self-abasements as spectacles. Melville's "Benito Cereno" (1855) presents a captain who seems flayed alive. Ahab vanishes from his narrative when he is "shot out of the boat," roped to the white whale (ch. 135). All these prostrations have a capitalist context. From Starbuck's point of view, *Moby-Dick* is a cautionary tale: don't mess with market forces. It's fitting that Starbucks coffee shops are named for him, though no reader feels sorry for the *Pequod*'s owners because they lose a ship. Instead, Ahab's monomania transcends the market. At first he seems a heroic champion in the Emersonian mode, abandoning himself to original thinking. By the end his thinking has enslaved him to the white whale. Now doubled with Pip's vision of God's heartlessness, Ahab's self-absorption turns out to be abandonment with no self at all, except in his awareness of being a pawn in someone else's game. As Pip says, looking at the doubloon Ahab has nailed to the mast to motivate his men, "I look, you look, he looks; we look, ye look, they look" (ch. 99). Everyone sees their orphaned selves in their dream of potential profits, and a few of them half know it. They plunge into an uncontrollable turmoil of desire, rage, powerlessness, and fatalistic narcissism.

That flux exemplifies the antebellum marketplace, where failures came thick and fast, and where resilience often seemed the only stay against desperation. David Anthony has argued that middle-class men had to turn abjection and humiliation into emotional virtues as well as new grounds for self-possession. Whiteness, too, became an available mode of self-stabilization. But Melville's narrative genius lies in his unsettlings. Like *Walden*, this book is an amalgam of contradictory genres, from travelogue and sermon to stage play and philosophical treatise. Ultimately, it's a tall tale about the biggest fish that ever got away. Even Ishmael's label of "fish" can't hold (ch. 32), since the white whale is a mammal that makes whiteness itself seem terrifyingly alien.

Melville's yearning subversions of Emerson are well known. In *The Confidence-Man: His Masquerade* (1857), Melville presents the mystical Mark Winsome and his disciple Egbert as satires of Emerson and Thoreau. They, too, are heartless individualists. Even the Cosmopolitan, the ultimate confidence man, rejects their "inhuman philosophy" (ch. 41). Disturbingly, the heroic alternative is Colonel Moredock, yet another loner, who has become an Indian-hater. The only survivor of a family killed by Indians, he becomes "a Leather-stocking Nemesis" bent on ethnic cleansing (ch. 26). Moredock's belief in the "diabolism" and "total depravity" of Indians gives him "self-possession" through rage. The rest of the novel recounts the protean manipulations of the confidence man. His devilish guises include Black Guinea, "a grotesque negro cripple" whose begging plays with the passengers' racism (ch. 3).

In effect, Melville dehybridizes the capitalist by splitting the devious profit-maker from the enraged killer. The hater seems more real than the confidence man, who succeeds as any good salesman does, by marketing himself as an illusion of what the buyer wants to see. Melville's continuing exaltation of Ahabian rage intimates his contempt for his readers as well as his increasing despair. Thereafter he published no more fiction.

The Scarlet Letter and *Moby-Dick* present hybrid white men whose devilish rage temporarily augments their power. In contrast, Harriet Beecher Stowe's *Uncle*

Tom's Cabin celebrates a gentle black man of simple and intensifying faith. Yet Tom's secular hybridity invites opposite readings of his character. When he talks to his wife, Uncle Tom sounds like an "Uncle Tom," the name African Americans give to black people who truckle to white people. Refusing to escape after Colonel Shelby sells him, Tom emphasizes his love for his master, though "it's natur" that Shelby doesn't "think so much of poor Tom" (ch. 10). Tom was eight when his one-year-old master was put into his care, and Shelby still calls him "boy" (ch. 7). As he proudly tells Chloe, "I never have broke trust" (ch. 5). Yet he's a man with backbone and tenacious intelligence as well as a "gentle, domestic heart" (ch. 10). Later he capably manages St. Clare's estate, and he stands up to St. Clare and Simon Legree when they disparage Christianity. In the end, Legree kills Tom for resisting orders to whip fellow slaves.

Another aspect of Tom's hybridity surfaces when he meets Eva. To win the favor of St. Clare's five- or six-year-old daughter, the slave gives her various toys, "and he was a very Pan in the manufacture of whistles" (ch. 14). Pan was a god of sex as well as nature, so Tom may be what Hortense Spillers suggests, a "potentially 'dirty old man,' 'under wraps'" (1989, 46). The possibility of interracial child molesting recedes into their chastely spiritual friendship, memorialized in innumerable nineteenth-century lithographs. The slave's "Uncle Tom" aspects also remain on display, since Tom had the toys in his pocket "for his master's children," not for his own (ch. 14).

The miscegenation denied in the main plot appears in several subplots. George Harris and his wife Eliza are light mulattoes who can pass for whites, and Legree's mistress Cassy—the novel's most complex characterization—is a quadroon. Stowe has a straightforwardly racist explanation of why George is so smart, entrepreneurial, and assertive. From his proud white father "he had inherited a set of fine European features, and a high, indomitable spirit. From his mother he had received only a slight mulatto tinge, amply compensated by its accompanying rich, dark eye" (ch. 11). "Inherited" lords over "received," and Stowe's "only" presumes that the darker color taints him, despite the "ample" compensation of his dark eyes.

Race is central to all these novels. Three prominent men of color are killed off: Tom, Queequeg, and Uncas, whose death leaves his aged father Chingachgook as "the last of the Mohicans," mourning his race as well as his son. Even the "Black Man" Chillingworth shrivels up and dies, once his vampiric sadism has nothing to feed on. Capitalist dynamics are more edgy. In the Leather-Stocking Tales, grasping men on the edge between civilization and savagery struggle and often fail, from Ishmael Bush in *The Prairie* (1827) to Hurry Harry in *The Deerslayer.* Cooper balances Natty's frontier adventures with a respect for estate-owning gentry like the author's own father, exemplified in Judge Temple of *The Pioneers; or, The Sources of the Susquehanna* (1823). *The Scarlet Letter* seems precapitalist, though it demonizes the cuckold's attempt to restore his honor. In *Moby-Dick* and *Uncle Tom's Cabin,* capitalism has triumphed, though the narratives differently advocate its overthrow. Each novel brings creative destruction in its wake.

Two exceptionally disturbing stories climax with moments of creative destruction. Unlike the four major novels, they leave readers torn between conflicting interpretations that can't be papered over with moral comfort, and they expose hybrids who don't even pretend to cohere. "My Kinsman, Major Molineux" (1831) was one of Hawthorne's first publications, and "Hop-Frog" (1849) was one of Poe's last. Both tales feature male hybrids and doublings, both unsettle hierarchies of white and black, and both ambiguously link tensions between aristocrats and plebeians to the rise of capitalism. Both tales also simmer with barely suppressed rage.

"My Kinsman, Major Molineux" tells the story of Robin, a rural lad coming to pre-Revolutionary Boston in search of his well-connected relative, who might help him advance in life. After many nightmarish bafflements, Robin sees his British kinsman being tarred and feathered by a mob. Robin at first experiences a catharsis of "pity and terror." Then the crowd's "contagion" catches him, and he "sent forth a shout of laughter . . . the loudest there." At the end, a seemingly benevolent bystander says, "perhaps, as you are a shrewd youth, you may rise in the world, without the help of your kinsman, Major Molineux."

As many psychological critics have pointed out, a two-faced man becomes Robin's emotional double. He's the leader of the insurrection, and his face reflects the inner divisions that the young man won't acknowledge in himself. When Robin first sees him in a tavern, the stranger seems to be a devil complete with horns: his "forehead bulged out into a double prominence," and his eyes glow "like fire in a cave." When Robin sees the stranger again, one side of his face "blazed of an intense red, while the other was black as midnight," with the lips reversing the colors. His "parti-colored features" suggest the emergence of party politics, or a Tea Party revolt, or a painted face on its way to a party. "Shrewd" Robin keeps his cool by refusing to think about these contradictory possibilities. Finally, on horseback, the man leads "a band of fearful wind-instruments" and "wild figures" dressed as Indians. He "appeared like war personified; the red of one cheek was an emblem of fire and sword; the blackness of the other betokened the mourning which attends them."

The narrator's simile rather patly explains the meaning of the man's hybrid face. But readers can't unite these states. Psychoanalytic critics focus on the mourning that accompanies quasi-Oedipal rebellion. That reading assumes readers sympathize with Robin. Political critics focus on the story's indictment of the American Revolution and the onset of what Tocqueville would call "the tyranny of the majority." That reading makes Robin the dim-witted butt of a satire. To take the political reading further, Robin has been possessed by an America that the narrator thinks is satanic. Not only does the two-faced man evoke the devil, but the "wind-instruments" allude to Dante's one dirty joke, when a devil summons other devils with a fart. Most subtly, the first seven meanings of "shrewd" in the *Oxford English Dictionary* concern demonic possession. Does upward mobility in a capitalist democracy require both modern shrewdness and ancient devilishness? As humorist Johnson J. Hooper has his confidence man say in *Some Adventures of Captain Simon Suggs* (1845), "It is good to be shifty in a new country" (ch. 1).

In Poe's "Hop-Frog," the devil has vanished, but white-black tensions are more prominent. Hop-Frog is a dwarf, a cripple, and the court jester of a fat and nameless king. The narrator, whose "we" defines him as a member of the court, recurrently links Hop-Frog to animals: a frog, a squirrel, a monkey, a parrot. The "fool" gives his master a hybrid pleasure: "both a jester to laugh *with*, and a dwarf to laugh *at*." Trippetta, another dwarf, "was universally admired and petted" for her beauty and graceful dancing. Her tri-petted nature complements Hop-Frog's role as "a triplicate treasure in one person."

Ostensibly the story satirizes master-slave relations in the South, where many masters saw black people as contemptible animals or useful creatures to exploit. More subtly, the story evokes sympathy for American writers, who are enslaved to capitalist readers. When the king insists that Hop-Frog provide some entertainment for an upcoming party, he shouts, "We want characters—*characters*, man—something novel—out of the way." After the king abuses Trippetta, the jester invents what he calls "a capital diversion" in which the king and his ministers will dress up as "the Eight Chained Ourang-Outangs." "'The beauty of the game,' continued Hop-Frog, 'lies in the fright it occasions among the women.'" "Capital!" shouts his audience, and the king adds, "Hop-Frog! I will make a man of you."

The ending becomes a horrific chiasmus, or reversal, a trope characteristic of slave narratives. The eight masters, now black beasts and chained slaves, get hooked by the chandelier, which Trippetta draws upward until the "ourang-outangs" dangle together in their "flaxen" coats. Then Hop-Frog sets them on fire. "The eight corpses swung in their chains, a fetid, blackened, hideous, and indistinguishable mass." It's a lynching, and all the white masters now look indistinguishably black, while Hop-Frog and Trippetta escape through the skylight. Like Robin, Hop-Frog rises in the world without the help of his patron.

The story was first published in an antislavery magazine, but its ending creates an impossible mix of admiration and shock. The leader of the slave revolt turns out to be more monstrous than the master. Several times a "*grating* sound" comes from his "fang-like teeth . . . as he foamed at the mouth" in "maniacal rage" at the king and ministers he has hoisted up to kill. The king's punishment for mistreating Trippetta seems grotesquely excessive. Yet whites regularly did that to black people. Whether the chiasmus consists of giving the slave power over his master, or giving the writer power over his readers, or turning readers' sympathies into terror, the story is even more unsettling than "My Kinsman." Both tales encourage hybrid interpretations that can't cohere. Both also expose racialized rage in the master-slave conflicts intrinsic to early capitalist transformations.

Over a decade earlier, Poe attempted a novel, *The Narrative of Arthur Gordon Pym, of Nantucket* (1838), which failed so badly that he never tried another. The jerry-built plot lurches through sensational extremes, from shipboard imprisonment to cannibalism to a black revolt in Antarctica. At first Pym and his friend Augustus seem conventionally genteel victims of the outlandish plot turns. But Pym's second friend, Dirk Peters, becomes Poe's most riveting version of a sensational hybrid. One of the "less blood-thirsty" men in the crew, he's the son of a white fur-trader and an Indian squaw. He's four-feet eight-inches tall and "enormously" strong. To conceal his "deformed" bald head, which is indented like "the head of most negroes," he wears various wigs made from "the skin of a Spanish dog or American grizzly bear." He has "exceedingly long and protruding" teeth never covered by his lips (ch. 4). In short, he's as amalgamated as any antebellum man can be, and Pym feels terrified.

Yet Peters preserves the lives of Augustus and Pym. Later, after Augustus dies at sea, the two men become another chaste cross-racial marriage of wilderness males. At the end, the voyagers land in Antarctica, where they warily encounter a seemingly friendly and civilized black tribe. When the tribe suddenly erupts in violence against them, every other crew member gets killed, and only Pym and Peters survive. At that point the hybrid becomes assimilated: "We were the only living white men upon the island" (ch. 21).

Most readers remember the chiasmus of Poe's ending, partly because the rest of the narrative often seems even more ridiculous than *Sheppard Lee*. As Pym and Peters escape by boat, they float toward the sudden opening of a "chasm" holding "a shrouded human figure" of gigantic proportions. The last sentence leaves readers with a rhythmically reverberating mystery: "And the hue of the skin of the figure was of the perfect whiteness of the snow" (ch. 25). Only Ishmael's meditation on "The Whiteness of the Whale" in *Moby-Dick* (ch. 42) comes close to giving that frisson. After Peters's hybridity disappears into whiteness, whiteness becomes a larger amalgamation, ominously human and inhuman, alive and dead, and more scary than a black revolt.

When Poe invented the detective story, he used unresolvable tensions between black and white to intensify the doubling. In "The Murders in the Rue Morgue" (1841), C. Auguste Dupin's last name connotes doubling, duping, and duplicity. His characterization is no doubt indebted to Brockden Brown's *Ormond* (1799), in which Ormond controls others through his talent for theatrical mimicry. Though Ormond dresses up as a black chimney sweep at one point, Poe's story more fully exploits white-black indeterminacies. The fictional Dupin loves thinking in the dark, and he is "enamored of the Night for her own sake." In the story's penultimate reversal, the detective deduces that a "fulvous" or "tawny" animal, sometimes an "Ourang-Outang" and sometimes an "ape," not a white Frenchman, has all but decapitated one woman and stuffed the other up a chimney. The horrific revelation plays with antebellum white fears of slave revolts and black beast rapists.

Extreme hybridity gives Dupin his extraordinary mental powers. Though he triumphs by thinking, he doesn't claim Emersonian access to an aboriginal self or abandonment to centripetal spontaneity. Instead, the fallen aristocrat fathoms other people's minds to gain control. When Dupin analyzes, "[H]is eyes were vacant in expression; while his voice, usually a rich tenor, rose into a treble." The narrator fancies that his friend is a "Bi-Part Soul, . . . a double Dupin—the creative and the resolvent." Keen observation gives Dupin access to the narrator's thoughts.

The grisly double murder reveals another set of doubled males: a sailor and his escaped "Ourang-Outang." The Bi-Part Soul returns as a beast who imitates his master shaving, then bolts when the master reaches for his whip. Intimations of slavery saturate this story, as critics have pointed out. Yet imitations and self-splittings are more basic. In the women's apartment, the beast's "probably pacific purposes" turn into "wrath" when Madame L'Espanaye screams because the beast is "flourishing the razor about her face, in imitation of the motions of a barber." Just after the murders, when the master finds his fugitive possession in the apartment, the beast thinks of "the dreaded whip," and its "fury . . . was instantly converted into fear." At that point, before the "Ourang-Outang" escapes again, the sensibilities of the Frenchman and his animal slave converge in "exclamations of horror and affright, commingled with the fiendish jabberings of the brute." Only Dupin keeps his cool control, by knowing what every other creature thinks. Readers feel torn between sympathy for the beast's motives and terror at its violence.

"The Purloined Letter" (1844) takes readers further into indeterminacies by turning hybrid and singular selves into language constructs. Once again Dupin and his friend love the dark as an aid to "reflection," and once again Dupin solves a problem—implicitly, a love letter stolen from the Queen's boudoir—by understanding the thoughts of an antagonist double, this time "the Minister D—." Dupin gets "even" with the minister by being what the prefect calls "odd." A schoolboy has told him the secret: to win the game of even and odd, you physically mirror your opponent's face, then wait to see what thoughts and feelings arise. The minds of Chillingworth and Dimmesdale shaped their bodies; Dupin reverses the process.

But Poe's emphasis on "letters" turns identities into language play. Dupin and "D—" converge; they are both mathematicians and poets. Replete with puns, or words whose meanings are hiding in plain sight, the tale makes fun of a prefect who becomes "a little discomposed" as he says, "*I* am *perfectly* willing to take advice." Dupin signals his triumph by substituting a letter "imitating the D— cipher, very readily, by means of a seal formed of bread." Though "Decipher" is the obvious pun, the more spectacular pun is bilingual: in French, "of bread" is "du pain." Once readers see Poe's play with letters and significations, responses can get quite vertiginous. In Poe's deconstruction of seemingly stable characters, purloined letters constitute their identities.

"The mind is its own place, and in itself / Can make a heaven of hell, a hell of heaven." That's how Milton's Lucifer tries to cheer himself up at the start of *Paradise Lost* (1667), after his vaulting ambition has led to the ultimate boom and bust. For those who see capitalist self-refashionings as seductive illusions, it's tempting to call them devilish, and Hawthorne did his best to blacken hybrid men wherever he could. Yet Lucifer's lines anticipate Emerson's ideal. Neither gentry nor theological controls could check men from bending their minds toward enterprise, and each man's mind became his most important resource. It's not just the things you can buy; it's the selves you can dream of. As Whitman proclaims near the end of the long word-flow that he later named "Song of Myself" (1855), "I contain multitudes." Like so many others, he learned to capitalize on his possibilities.

29

STUDYING NATURE IN THE ANTEBELLUM NOVEL

TIMOTHY SWEET

From the earliest days of colonization, explorers and settlers wondered how the New World's climate would affect European people, livestock, and crops. This question of environmental influence was bound up with an economic interest that equated nature with resources. In working through such questions, Europeans adapted pastoral and georgic literary modes to American circumstances. Human culture's economic relation to the nonhuman world was the purview of the georgic mode, broadly construed, which has traditionally focused on rural labor and production. When the georgic narrative of the cultivation or "improvement" of nature took an expansionist direction, a counter-narrative emerged in the veneration of wilderness, which drew on pastoral tropes of the countryside as a place of retreat from political and economic concerns. The literary construction of America as "nature's nation," in Perry Miller's phrase, thus involved a conflict between the narrative of improvement and wilderness veneration. The resulting nationalist-exceptionalist paradigm posed a dilemma, wherein uncultivated nature symbolized the promise of American newness, but nature had to be cultivated in order for the promise to be realized. The American pastoral mode captured such tensions at the interface of nature and culture, often, as Leo Marx argues in *The Machine in the Garden: Technology and the Pastoral Ideal in America* (1964), through an idyllic middle landscape between urban (or European) space and the wilderness. While pastoral dreams of the harmonious accommodation of culture to nature took many forms and genres, nonfiction prose would become the primary literary vehicle of environmental awareness from the mid-nineteenth century onward, as *Walden; or, Life in the Woods* (1854) and other writings by Henry David Thoreau gained cultural influence. Prior to Thoreau, however, the American novel addressed several themes bearing on the question of the human place in nature: environmental determinism and environmental risk; agricultural expansion and its counter-narrative of wilderness veneration; the mismatch between literary tradition and rural experience; the interpretation of landscape as moral register or political symbol; and even questions of the boundary between human and nonhuman nature.

By the late eighteenth century, the preoccupation with discovering universal laws governing natural processes had opened a broad intellectual debate over the question of environmental determinism. In *Notes on the State of Virginia* (1785), Thomas Jefferson responded to one of the more prominent determinists, George Leclerc, Comte de Buffon, who had claimed that the American environment was unfavorable to large, warm-blooded quadrupeds and favorable to cold-blooded animals. Buffon's followers extended this theory to human beings, arguing that Native Americans were less vigorous, socially "colder" than European peoples, and incapable of large-scale political organization. Recognizing the implications for the nascent United States in the post-Revolutionary era, Jefferson refuted Buffon by amassing statistics on American fauna and offering examples of Native Americans' genius, which he said wanted only education to bring it to the level of European civilization.

The debate over environmental influence on physiology and character, documented at length in Antonello Gerbi's *The Dispute of the New World: The History of a Polemic, 1750–1900* (1955), persisted into the next century. Setting aside value judgments of superiority and inferiority, one of the challenges to nationalism posed by the correlation of environments and inhabitants was the diversity of North American environments. What could unify a people whose local interests and commitments, and perhaps their very natures, varied so extensively, from New England to the subtropics, from coastal plains to mountains? This question troubles the narrator of Hector St. John de Crèvecoeur's quasi-epistolary novel, *Letters from an American Farmer* (1782). Crèvecoeur's protagonist, Farmer James, opens a series of letters to an English correspondent by describing an idyllic life on his Pennsylvania farm but becomes disillusioned as other locales reveal different answers to the motivating question posed explicitly in the third letter, "What is an American?" A disturbing view of slavery in South Carolina precedes two letters focusing specifically on natural history, all of which reveal a tension between local circumstance and universal natural law and investigate the problem of grounding the social order in the natural order. The last letter, in which Farmer James proposes to escape the violence of the American Revolution by going west to live with the Indians, continues this investigation. On the one hand admiring the Indians' supposed closeness to the natural order, while on the other hand wanting to bring them into a state of civilization, Crèvecoeur's Farmer James exhibits European Americans' ambivalence toward the idea of a state of nature. Subsequently, with increasing global economic expansion, this idea of a state of nature was projected onto other non-European peoples such as Pacific Islanders, as discussed later.

Where Crèvecoeur's *Letters* seemed to encompass all of North America, Charles Brockden Brown, in his novels *Ormond; or, The Secret Witness* (1799) and *Arthur*

Mervyn; or, Memoirs of the Year 1793 (1799–1800), focused the question of environmental influence on a local incident and setting—Philadelphia's devastating yellow fever epidemic of 1793. Brown's intellectual contemporaries generally followed eminent Philadelphia physician Benjamin Rush, who believed that the yellow fever was communicated by environmental factors such as noxious effluvia generated by urban filth, whereas others contended that the fever was communicated from person to person. Brown was interested in observing individuals' responses to the disease-ridden environment as well as in understanding causes. However much he favored an environmentalist account of the disease, he did not hold a deterministic view. Tracing continuities between mental and physical health, he suggested that environmental effects or influences, however malign, could be overcome or met with adaptation. In *Ormond*, the impoverished Dudley family all survive the epidemic by virtue of abstemious diet and strict moral hygiene while most of their neighbors die, the lethal power of the fever amplified by the victims' "force of imagination" (ch. 7). In *Arthur Mervyn*, characters predisposed to benevolence hold an environmentalist view of the disease, as in the cases of physicians Medlicote and Stevens as well as Mervyn himself, and this benevolence seems to protect them from contamination.

When novelists returned to the theme of urban environmental risk, beginning in the 1830s on the cusp of increasing urbanization, they often developed a strain of rural nostalgia that would have been foreign to Brown. Novels entered into the larger cultural debate over whether urban or rural life was more conducive to salutary domesticity. In Catharine Maria Sedgwick's short novel *Home* (1835), for example, the protagonist family, the Barclays, look for a long-delayed retirement to the country estate that was Mr. Barclay's childhood home but are kept in New York because of financial reversals; meanwhile, however, they live a frugal but pleasant domestic life. Eventually, through their son Harry's success in the printing business, they are able to fulfill their dream of country life, where "the occupations of . . . garden and farm . . . are far more agreeable" to Mr. Barclay than those of the "office," although Mrs. Barclay worries how well her urban manners will fit with her rustic neighbors (ch. 11). Rural nostalgia more forcefully directs the plot of Ann Sophia Stephens's best-selling novel *The Old Homestead* (1855), in which a poor orphan girl is adopted by a prominent New York judge and raised by his relatives on a farm upstate, thereby escaping the Children's Hospital and a life of urban poverty, misery, and crime. The urban environment seems unhealthy except for the financially well-off, whereas the rural environment is humble but wholesome. Numerous antebellum novels similarly divide the urban experience according to class. In Fanny Fern's *Ruth Hall: A Domestic Tale of the Present Time* (1855), for example, Ruth's blissful domestic life in a suburban cottage, where she decorates her table every day with fresh-picked flowers, rapidly descends to a life of urban poverty in a Boston tenement after the death of her husband Harry. Eventually successful in writing for the newspapers—a story that parallels Fern's own career—Ruth moves to suitable domestic quarters in a hotel, but even here a fire nearly kills her and her daughters. While Fern's own career took her from Boston to New York, Ruth's destination at the end of the novel remains unspecified. Rather than showing Ruth's arrival in New York, the novel ends on a pastoral scene in a cemetery, a visit to Harry's grave, while leaving open the possibility of urban domesticity.

Looking beyond the urban centers of the eastern seaboard, the novel engaged both agricultural expansion and the emerging counter-narrative of wilderness veneration. The earliest novel to address this tension was James Fenimore Cooper's *The Pioneers; or, The Sources of the Susquehanna* (1823), the first of the five Leather-Stocking Tales. Based on the founding of Cooperstown, *The Pioneers* thematizes various stances toward the natural environment through different characters, setting a complex georgic aesthetic against the veneration of wilderness. Judge Temple, a land developer modeled on Cooper's father, William, holds a proto-conservationist or wise-use position with regard to natural resources. Both the scientific improver Richard Jones and the laborer Billy Kirby thoughtlessly exploit nature. The judge's daughter Elizabeth has a genteel appreciation of landscape aesthetics shaped by her European education, but little understanding of the economic basis of culture. Natty Bumppo, whose adventures Cooper would go on to chronicle throughout the Leather-Stocking series, speaks for the wilderness, which provides his resources as a hunter. In his account of the region prior to white settlement, Natty describes Kaaterskill Falls—a site Washington Irving had mentioned in "Rip Van Winkle" (1819) and one that the founder of the Hudson River school, Thomas Cole, would soon make famous through paintings such as *Falls of the Kaaterskill* (1826)—as evidence of "the hand of God . . . in the wilderness" (*Pioneers*, ch. 26). Cooper dramatizes the tension between the expansionist narrative and wilderness veneration in episodes depicting the felling of maple trees, the seining of fish, and the shooting of passenger pigeons, while Natty criticizes the settlers' "wasty ways" (ch. 22). The conflict between Natty and the law, initiated when Natty kills a deer out of season, encapsulates the exceptionalist dilemma wherein the wilderness held America's promise but had to be transformed in order to realize that destiny. Cole would address this tension in his "Essay on American Scenery" (1836) and would register it forcefully in his painting *The Oxbow* (1836), with its diagonally divided composition: the left-hand foreground depicts a threatening sky looming over a cloud-covered mountain-top wilderness, from which the viewer surveys the sunny, peaceful agricultural valley below. In the ending of *The Pioneers*, Cooper suspends this tension by sending Natty west.

In *The Prairie* (1827), Cooper steps outside the narrative of agrarian settlement to depict the aged Natty working as a fur trapper on the Platte River. For information on the prairie environment, Cooper drew on narratives of western expeditions such as Lewis and Clark's and particularly Edwin James's *An Account of an Expedition from Pittsburgh to the Rocky Mountains* (1823). Cooper was one of many who were influenced by James's thesis that the western prairie was a great desert, inhospitable to civilization. Natty is at home in this desert nevertheless: his practical, intuitive approach to nature, though developed in the eastern forests, is easily adapted to his new environment. By contrast, the itinerant naturalist Dr. Obed Bat's pedantic, classificatory approach ironically turns the observing eye away from nature. Cooper's satire is rather broad here, as when Dr. Bat believes he has identified a new, monstrous creature, the "*Vespertilio horribilis*," and gives a full-blown taxonomic description; the beast turns out to be his own donkey, which he does not recognize in the dark (ch. 6).

In later novels, Cooper set aside Natty's complaints about the colonists' "wasty ways" (*Pioneers*, ch. 22) to follow wholeheartedly the progress of agrarian settlement. Novels on this theme, including *Wyandotté; or, The Hutted Knoll* (1843), the Littlepage trilogy (*Satanstoe*, 1845, *The Chainbearer*, 1845, *The Redskins*, 1846), and *The Crater; or, Vulcan's Peak* (1847), suggest the cyclical narrative of "the changes of time, and civilization, and decay" that Cooper says he found in "Cole's series of noble landscapes," *The Course of Empire* (1833–36) (*Crater*, ch. 30). The most interesting of these novels from an environmental perspective is *The Crater*, a variant on Daniel Defoe's *Robinson Crusoe* (1719), in which the shipwrecked merchant Mark Woolston and sailor Bob Betts rapidly transform a barren, rocky volcanic island into a fertile agricultural district. Cooper describes in extensive, quasi-scientific detail the process of manufacturing soil by composting available materials such as seaweed and bird guano, planting seeds salvaged from the ship, and sorting and cultivating crops to suit the peculiarities of climate. Woolston and Betts build a ship and import colonists and livestock to this new Eden, which flourishes until the population reaches carrying capacity. As Cooper pursues a pet theme of his later work—the evils of populism and the perils of demagoguery—the island society is destroyed by pirate attack and the whole landmass is later submerged by a volcanic earthquake.

Few antebellum novelists expressed the tension between agricultural expansion and wilderness veneration as deeply as the early work of Cooper and Cole. Rather, most novelists worked within the mediating cultural forms of the picturesque or pastoral modes. As improved roads and railroads began to link country to city in the 1840s, leading to the development of suburbs, the pastoral dream of harmony between nature and culture seemed within reach of the urban middle class. American architects, drawing on English traditions of landscape gardening and vernacular architecture, promoted the suburb as a refuge from the city and a space for the development of health, spirituality, and domesticity. Andrew Jackson Downing was especially influential with books such as *A Treatise on the Theory and Practice of Landscape Gardening* (1841), *Cottage Residences* (1842), and *The Architecture of Country Houses* (1850). While these were basically pattern books inclining to architectural homogeneity, promoters of the picturesque style anticipated modernist proponents of organic architecture such as Louis Sullivan and Frank Lloyd Wright in arguing that a house and garden ought to be designed to harmonize with the natural setting. Harmonious design would function, Downing proclaimed, as a "symbol" of the occupants' "intelligent and cultivated life" and their "social or domestic virtues" (*Architecture of Country Houses*, pt. 1, sec. 1). This taste for the rural was popularized through illustrated books such as Nathaniel Parker Willis's *American Scenery; or, Land, Lake, and River Illustrations of Transatlantic Nature* (1840) and G. P. Putnam's *The Home Book of the Picturesque; or, American Scenery, Art, and Literature* (1852) and travel pieces and rural essays in illustrated magazines such as *Harper's New Monthly Magazine* (which began publication in 1850).

Pastoral themes animated a range of prose genres, from seasonal nature journals such as Susan Fenimore Cooper's *Rural Hours* (1850) and Thoreau's *Walden*, to outdoor adventure stories such as Joel Tyler Headley's *The Adirondack; or, Life in the Woods* (1849), to the best-selling *Reveries of a Bachelor; or, A Book of the Heart* (1850) by Donald Grant Mitchell, who wrote under the pseudonym of Ik Marvel. Susan Cooper's proto-ecological *Rural Hours* exemplifies the antebellum fashion for amateur natural history. In *The Adirondack*, Headley grafts Transcendentalist spirituality onto accounts of wilderness camping, fishing, and hunting. *Walden*, largely ignored on first publication, later became a wellspring of American environmental literature. In Mitchell's sentimental *Reveries of a Bachelor*, the city-dwelling Marvel occasionally retreats to the farm where he grew up, now operated by a tenant, there to muse on life and love. Marvel's meditations from nature in *Reveries* and its sequel, *Dream-Life: A Fable of the Seasons* (1851), take a rather conventional form, as when spring is associated with youth and autumn with old age, and so on. However, Mitchell's *My Farm of Edgewood: A Country Book* (1863) more fully engages with the rural environment. Here the character of Marvel appears as a world-weary traveler who settles down to become a gentleman farmer in New England. Numerous practical details about soils, crops, orchards, livestock, and the management of laborers are woven together with aesthetic reflections whose standard of taste matches Downing's pastoral. While Marvel turns a modest profit, he measures success by "a constantly accumulating fertility" of soil "in connection with remunerative results" and landscape aesthetics (ch. 3). Thus he hopes that his example, an "economic demonstration of the laws of good taste," will "provoke emulation, and redeem the small farmer . . . from his slovenly barbarities and his grossness of life" (ch. 4). Mitchell followed *My Farm* with a series of essays (1863–64) for the *Atlantic Monthly* on ancient and modern agricultural literature, from Cato and Virgil to Jethro Tull and William Cobbett, which were collected and expanded in *Wet Days at Edgewood* (1865).

Pastoral thus provided the larger literary context for the antebellum novel's approach to the rural setting. The mismatch between aesthetic convention and the realities of rural life, as remarked by Mitchell, supplies much of the humor in Caroline Kirkland's autobiographical novel of the Michigan land boom, *A New Home—Who'll Follow?; or, Glimpses of Western Life* (1839). Narrator Mary Clavers, wife of a land speculator (as was Kirkland herself), complains that the "materials [of literary pastoral] are denied me; but yet I must try to describe something of Michigan cottage life, taking care to avail myself of such delicate periphrasis as may best veil the true homeliness of my subject" (ch. 30). At the outset, the distinctive park-like character of the oak savanna environment through which the Clavers family travels seems especially amenable to pastoral treatment (indeed, this is Cooper's approach to the same environment in *The Oak Openings; or, The Bee Hunters* [1848]), until the wagon sinks to the axles in a mud-hole and frontier reality intrudes. Like the setting, characterization runs up against the problem of literary convention. Historically, pastoral landscape imagery has functioned as a screen hiding the labor necessary to create and maintain its productivity and pleasing appearance. As Henry Nash Smith argues in his study of the literature of the American West, *Virgin Land: The American West as Symbol and Myth* (1950), literary pastoral, with its elite associations, has had difficulty accommodating working farmers as sympathetic central characters. Thus from Mrs. Clavers's perspective, rustic swains, those who actually work the Michigan farms, prove to be drunken louts or republicans with disturbingly egalitarian views about property and social authority. The plot of *A New Home* demonstrates the cultivation (in both senses of the term) of the frontier, as infusions of eastern capital reshape the landscape and establish a class hierarchy. By the end, the pastoral style that Mrs. Clavers had rejected at the outset can return in the romance of Cora and Everard, for the class structure and the landscape form can now accommodate it. Following Kirkland, novelists developed a domestic pastoral mode set in the West (the region we now call the Midwest). A few novels in this mode, such as Caroline Soule's *The Pet of the Settlement* (1860), depict first-generation settlement as Kirkland had done, thus bearing comparison to nonfiction accounts such as Eliza W. Farnham's memoir and emigrant's guide, *Life in Prairie Land* (1846). More popular were novels in which the heroine emigrates to an already cultivated western setting, such as E. D. E. N. Southworth's *India: The Pearl of Pearl River* (1856) or Maria Cummins's *Mabel Vaughan* (1857), both discussed later in this chapter. As in Kirkland's narratives, the point of view and stylistic register of these works align author and reader with the genteel Northeast, the source of economic and cultural capital. This cultural alignment with northeastern values was a key constituent of rural middle-class identity in the antebellum West.

Wilder spaces were accommodated to the pastoral dream of culture in harmony with nature through the picturesque mode. The picturesque found expression, for example, in the tourist itinerary that developed following the opening of the Erie Canal in 1825, as John Sears demonstrates in his history of American tourism, *Sacred Places: American Tourist Attractions in the Nineteenth Century* (1989). This itinerary featured locales that figured prominently in the works of Hudson River school artists: the Hudson River, the Catskill Mountains, and Niagara Falls. For novelists, accounts of picturesque tourism provided occasions to explore the use of the natural environment as a moral register. In Stephens's *The Old Homestead*, for example, the journey from New York City through the Catskills to place the two orphans Mary and Isabel in foster care, one on a farm upstate and another in a nearby town, invites reflections on Hudson River scenery. In her first excursion beyond urban limits, Mary gratefully receives a natural history lesson on the sunflower's heliotropism and shows herself naturally sensitive to rural landscape beauty. As she matures, she learns to view such scenes "with the eye of an artist and the spirit of a Christian" and hopes to become a landscape painter (ch. 33). The beautiful but less sensitive Isabel, who is raised by the fashionable, shallow Mrs. Farnham, sees but does not feel the landscape in the same way, despite having been exposed to the works of the great masters during a trip to Italy. However, Stephens does not extend this theme, as Mary's artistic aspirations are swept aside in a hasty denouement involving the discovery of long-lost heirs.

A character's interaction with the landscape not as artist but as sensitive spectator provided further occasion for moral reflection. In Cummins's female *Bildungsroman* entitled *The Lamplighter* (1854), for example, a picturesque tour from Boston to Saratoga is rendered especially poignant by the heroine Gertrude's position as traveling companion to the wealthy Emily Graham, who is blind. The pleasures of mountain scenery, which Gertrude communicates verbally to Emily, prove superior to those of the crowded Saratoga resort, as Cummins focuses on two sites familiar from landscape illustration: the Hudson River near West Point and the Catskill Mountain House, a prominent tourist hotel. At Catskill Mountain, Gertrude's naïve, aesthetically sensitive intuition of the divinity revealed in the luminist scene, light shining above the clouds, strikes a healing chord of sympathy in a melancholic stranger, Mr. Phillips (who will turn out to be Gertrude's long-lost father), evidently converting him from disaffected Transcendentalist to mainstream Protestant Christian. In Cummins's *Mabel Vaughan*, the extraordinary sublimity of Niagara Falls precipitates a more cathartic religious experience. The excursion to Niagara comes at the low point in the heroine's life, when her father has lost the family fortune through speculation and a suitor has betrayed her, and she must travel west to join her father on a pioneer farm. Like Mary in *The Old Homestead* and Gertrude in *The Lamplighter*, Mabel is intuitively sensitive to divinity in nature, experiencing "a fit of passionate and uncontrollable weeping" but requiring the tutelage of the wealthy and cultivated Madam Percival to perceive the lesson emblematized in the "glorious rainbow danc[ing]" above the thunderous falls: God's "raging torrent of affliction is spanned by the rainbow of His love" (ch. 30). Following the regenerative power of the Niagara episode, the plot takes Mabel on a course of upward socioeconomic mobility in which the family fortune is restored, and she eventually marries Madam Percival's son and returns to the East.

Contrasting with the pastoral aesthetic of rural leisure and contemplation was a georgic aesthetic of rural labor and production. Although primarily a nonfiction mode, georgic proved amenable to novelistic treatment, as for example in some of

Cooper's novels. In Mitchell's *My Farm of Edgewood,* as we have seen, Ik Marvel approaches georgic from the point of view of a gentleman farmer who manages others' labor. By contrast, Stephens's *The Old Homestead* depicts the daily lives of working owner-operators, the orphan Mary's foster parents Nathan and Hannah, who are specimens of the kind of "small farmer" that Marvel proposed to refine. Hannah's flower garden is somewhat neglected: why cultivate flowers where wild ones abound? However, the vegetable garden, viewed as sunlight plays on the neat rows of cabbages, ruby-tinged beet greens, and feathery parsnip tops, strikes the young protagonist Mary as "singularly beautiful" (ch. 29). The orchard is similarly well cultivated and one of Mary's chores is to glean the falls after a storm. The description of preparations for a corn-husking bee and dance evoke a sense of rural bounty, although the farm is encumbered by debt to finance the education of a nephew in New York. A similar accommodation of georgic to pastoral is evident in Susan Warner's *The Wide, Wide World* (1850). In this female *Bildungsroman,* the heroine Ellen's time at her aunt's farm in upstate New York teaches virtues such as patience and forbearance as well as domestic skills. A growing appreciation for picturesque landscapes helps Ellen adjust to rural life, as when she finds that a companionable neighbor girl has persuaded her brother and hired man to clear-cut a swath of hillside to open a view: "It was a very beautiful extent of woodland, meadow, and hill, that was seen picture-fashion through the gap cut in the forest;—the wall of trees on each side serving as a frame" (ch. 16). However, contrasting with this contemplative relation to the landscape is an experiential relation. For example, Warner gives a detailed account of hog butchering: "It was beautifully done. . . . The knife guided by strength and skill seemed to go with the greatest ease and certainty just where he wished it; the hams were beautifully trimmed out . . . and his quick-going knife disposed of carcass after carcass with admirable neatness and celerity" (ch. 22). Even so, as Ellen arrives at her destined, elite class position at the end of the novel, her relation to landscape reverts to the pastoral mode.

A pastoral frame surrounds the first extended fictional treatment of an urban industrial setting, Rebecca Harding Davis's novella *Life in the Iron Mills* (1861). Davis departs from the antebellum tradition of representing independent artisanal labor—as for example in John Neagle's painting *Pat Lyon at the Forge* (1829) or Henry Wadsworth Longfellow's poem "The Village Blacksmith" (1841)—to explore the plight of alienated factory hands, as glimpsed in Herman Melville's fictionalized account of a New England paper mill, "The Tartarus of Maids" (1855). Davis continues the investigation of environmental determinism that preoccupied Crèvecoeur and Jefferson and the investigation of environmental risk begun by Charles Brockden Brown. Opening on a panoramic view of Wheeling, Virginia, obscured by dense, clinging smoke, the narrative descends "into the thickest of the fog and mud and foul effluvia" to focus on the lives of Hugh, a Welsh iron puddler, and his cousin Deb, a textile worker. Hugh's natural artistic genius—he sculpts haunting figures from korl, a soft, stone-like waste from the smelting process—is thwarted by his class position. When Deb attempts to free the two from the bonds of the mill by stealing some money, the narrative, focalized through Hugh's "artist-eye," registers his desire for a better life by reenvisioning the opening panoramic view of Wheeling: "[T]he sun-touched smoke-clouds opened like a cleft ocean,—shifting, rolling seas of crimson mist, waves of billowy silver veined with blood-scarlet, inner depths unfathomable of lancing light." However, the two are convicted and Hugh commits suicide in prison. Deb does escape the urban environment after serving her sentence; she is adopted by Quakers whose farm "overlook[s] broad, wooded slopes and clover-crimsoned meadows," although the story closes before we see much of her life there.

This technique of coding moral symbolism in environmental description is especially evident in novels that address the increasing political sectionalism of the 1850s. Harriet Beecher Stowe's abolitionist novel *Uncle Tom's Cabin; or, Life Among the Lowly* (1852), for example, contrasts the pastoral setting of the Shelby farm in Kentucky, where slavery exists in its most benign form, with the sinister landscape of the villain Simon Legree's Red River plantation, which is surrounded by "dreary pine barrens" and "long cypress swamps, the doleful trees rising out of the slimy, spongy ground, hung with long wreaths of funereal black moss" (ch. 32). This is, as Stowe emphasizes with a chapter epigraph from Psalm 74, one of the "dark places of the earth . . . full of the habitations of cruelty." Southworth's *India* systematically contrasts three landscapes as it moves through a sectionalist political allegory: "Cashmere," a Mississippi cotton plantation on the Pearl River; a Shenandoah Valley mixed-culture plantation; and a western river-bluff town evidently modeled on Prairie du Chien, Wisconsin (where Southworth lived for four years). In the opening scenes of the novel, the Pearl River plantation is depicted as richly verdant and luxurious; the plantation heiress India is characterized as "an exotic, that can only bloom in a luxurious conservatory" (ch. 16). As the hero Mark moves west, disavowing the slave-owning culture that is his heritage, his wife Rosalie likens herself (in contrast to India) to a rugged flower that wilts in the hothouse but thrives in a western garden. On Mark's return to Mississippi, we see the South anew through his western eyes: no longer the verdant setting of the novel's opening, Cashmere now appears as a blighted landscape emblematizing the dissipation of the plantation's owner. However, despite the critique of slavery, the narrative does not contrast the plantation landscape to scenes of free-soil agrarianism in the west, for the hero is not a farmer but a lawyer. Rather, it grounds virtue in two domestic-pastoral settings inhabited by Mark and Rosalie: cozy Rose Cottage, with its neat kitchen, orchard, and garden, and later a lakeshore country estate.

In abolitionist novels such as Stowe's *Dred: A Tale of the Great Dismal Swamp* (1856) and Martin Delany's *Blake; or, The Huts of America* (serialized 1859, 1861–62) as well as in complacent plantation pastorals such as John Pendleton Kennedy's *Swallow Barn; or, A Sojourn in the Old Dominion* (1832, rev. 1851) and William

Gilmore Simms's *Woodcraft; or, The Hawks about the Dovecote* (1852), the swamp is a distinctive feature of the environment. The swamp has played a counterpart to the cultivated landscape in southern letters since William Byrd's *History of the Dividing Line* (1729). In *Swallow Barn*, set in Tidewater, Virginia, swamps provide topographic links to the Revolutionary era and thus function as implicit reminders of a dominant theme in antebellum southern culture, a sense of decline from the pinnacle of Revolutionary virtue. A small swamp, resulting from the natural filling in of a long abandoned mill-pond, is the object of a protracted lawsuit concerning the boundary between two plantations. The resolution of the suit sets the boundary "exactly *in statu quo ante bellum*," that is, as it was prior to the Revolutionary War and the building of the now disused mill (ch. 27). Nothing important, Kennedy humorously suggests, has happened in the South since then. Nearby, Goblin Swamp, a vast estuary below the plantations in which the main characters get lost, evokes another memory of the Revolution, being the haunt of an old Hessian who now ekes out a meager living as a trapper. Simms further explored the swamp's ambivalent associations with liberty suggested by these Revolutionary-era connections. Providing refuge for guerilla fighters such as Revolutionary commander Francis Marion (the "Swamp Fox") in *The Partisan: A Romance of the Revolution* (1835) and for Captain Porgy, the hero of *Woodcraft*, swamps also harbored ruffians such as the squatter Bostwick in *Woodcraft* or the villain Hell-fire Dick in Simms's *The Forayers; or, The Raid of the Dog Days* (1855). Simms does not, however, present the swamp as a site of liberty for slaves; on the contrary, Captain Porgy hides his slaves in a swamp to prevent them from being confiscated for debt repayment.

Stowe takes up this ambivalent association of the swamp with liberty in *Dred* as she shifts the site of antislavery action from the white benevolence envisioned in *Uncle Tom's Cabin* to black resistance. The title character, the son of frustrated rebel slave Denmark Vesey, has escaped to the Great Dismal Swamp at age fourteen and has lived there ever since, becoming the leader of a community of maroons (from the French *marron*, fugitive), runaway slaves who live independently of the plantation world. Stowe's use of swamp imagery interweaves two lines that resonate with the exceptionalist dilemma, one in which pure nature connotes liberty and another in which raw nature invites cultivation. As "an apt emblem . . . of that darkly struggling, wildly vegetating swamp of human souls, cut off, like it, from the usages and improvements of cultivated life," the swamp in its "savage exuberance" provides a "reflection" of Dred's "internal passions." His soul's natural inclination to liberty responds, in turn, to the "fearful pressure" of the environing swamp through the imagination of a violent antislavery insurrection (v. 2, ch. 27). Waiting for a sign from God that never comes, however, Dred dies shrouded in a more conventional visual aesthetic, a luminist cloudscape. Taking up Stowe's moral picturesque in *Blake*, Delany alludes to the Enlightenment discourse of natural law and natural rights when he has Blake explain the "organization" of the insurrection using imagery of both wild and cultivated nature: "[T]he trees of the forest or an orchard illustrate it; flocks of birds or domestic cattle, fields of corn, . . . and running of streams all keep it constantly before their eyes and in their memory" (ch. 11). While Delany focuses little on landscape imagery per se, settings are thematically important. When Blake first embarks on his journey across the South to organize a universal slave insurrection, the slaves on the home plantation pretend that Blake remains in a nearby swamp, thus diverting suspicion. The novel remains incomplete, however, breaking off as Blake becomes involved in the Creole rebellion in Cuba, and thus fails to illustrate the practical application, through universal slave insurrection, of the principle of liberty as nature.

Beyond the plantation South, other fiction writers reflected critically on the harmony of nature and culture projected by the pastoral mode. Notable among these are Alice Cary and Nathaniel Hawthorne. Hawthorne's critique of pastoral in *The Blithedale Romance* (1852) comes from the center of antebellum literary culture in the genteel Northeast. Loosely based on Hawthorne's six-month residence at the utopian community of Brook Farm, *Blithedale* takes the form of a pastoral interlude, a retreat to the green world of the countryside. Hawthorne reminds his readers of the literary history of the pastoral retreat through allusions to texts such as Shakespeare's *As You Like It* and Milton's *Comus*. The first-person narrator Miles Coverdale joins the Blithedale community as an aspiring young author, hoping to discover themes and experience fit for "true, strong, natural" poetry, perhaps in the manner envisioned in Ralph Waldo Emerson's 1844 manifesto "The Poet" (ch. 3). Yet Coverdale finds the encounter with nature to be both too artificial and too real, embodying a conflict between pastoral and georgic experiences of rural life. On the one hand, he complains, farm work impedes the intellect: "[W]e had pleased ourselves with delectable visions of the spiritualization of labor. . . . Our thoughts, on the contrary, were fast becoming cloddish. Our labor symbolized nothing, and left us mentally sluggish" (ch. 8). On the other hand, life at Blithedale feels like "a masquerade, a pastoral, a counterfeit Arcadia, in which we grown-up men and women were making a play-day of the years that were given us to live in" (ch. 3). This critique of pastoral's artificiality extends more broadly to elite culture's relation to the rural by means of novels, poems, paintings, tourist experiences, and utopian communities. The Blithedale utopians' play turns deadly serious with the costumed masque in chapter 24, after which the philanthropist Hollingsworth withdraws his affections from Zenobia (a character partly modeled on the Transcendentalist-feminist author Margaret Fuller), precipitating her suicide. In a curious turn on the conventional topos of death in Arcadia, Coverdale discerns "some tint of the Arcadian affectation" in the manner of Zenobia's suicide, which seemed to imitate "pictures . . . of drowned persons in lithe and graceful attitudes" (ch. 27). The imagery here evokes paintings in the vein of John Everett Millais's *Ophelia* (1852), a pastoral elegy that surrounds the drowned Ophelia (from *Hamlet*) with flowers.

Alice Cary's *Clovernook: Recollections of Our Neighborhood in the West* (1852–53) shifts the critical angle of vision from the genteel Northeast to the West. The first native westerner to publish significant fiction, Cary returns to the topic of agricultural settlement initially investigated in Cooper's *The Pioneers*, chronicling the transformation of the Ohio River Valley near Cincinnati from pioneer farming through urbanization and suburbanization. Cary narrates the transformation by means of flashbacks in various sketches, focalized through the experiences of various rural and suburban characters, enabling the reader to assemble an overall narrative of environmental history. By the end of the first volume, the "cottages and villas" of the "wealthy and fashionable" have "thickened" the rural landscape (v. 1). In these suburban landscapes, "green lawns . . . nicely trimmed groves, picturesque gardens, winding walks and shrubberies" have replaced the "blackened stumps and . . . patches of briers and thistles" of first-stage agricultural settlement, and Clovernook has become "the pleasantest summer retreat in the vicinity of any of the cities." Recollected through the eyes of the farm girl Ellie Hadly, the transformations indicate an increasingly stratified rural class system. Some formerly independent farmers now work as managers for gentlemen farmers, whom we can imagine as western versions of Mitchell's Ik Marvel. For Ellie, social events sponsored by the new rural elite, such as Mr. Harmstead, become scenes of humiliation. Even Ellie's prettier and more socially adept younger sister Zoe realizes that the likes of Mr. Harmstead will never marry the local farm girls. As Cary puts it in the second volume, "the lines which divide rusticity from the affluent life in country places, or the experience of the middle classes in towns, are very sharply defined." One of the longer sketches from the second volume, "Mrs. Wetherbe's Quilting Party," gives a panoramic view of diverse landscapes and their class associations as it moves from farms and rural cottages of varying prosperity, through suburban gardens, past noisy slaughterhouses and smoky soap and candle factories to two urban destinations, one a fashionable residential district and the other a tenement. Focalizing the perception of environment and its social correlatives through various characters, Cary can thus present the perspective of "the humbler classes" as a bid for sympathy or even as a subtle challenge to her middle-class readership (v. 2). This shift of perspective outside the bounds of the middle class, with its genteel northeastern identification, initiated a regionalist tradition that flourished later in the nineteenth century, fostering local community and opposing the artistic appropriation of "local color."

Novels of travel to exotic landscapes beyond the continental United States, such as Edgar Allan Poe's *The Narrative of Arthur Gordon Pym* (1838) and Herman Melville's *Typee: A Peep at Polynesian Life* (1846) and *Omoo: A Narrative of Adventures in the South Seas* (1847), complicated Americans' conceptions of the natural environment, human nature, and the relation between these two "natures." Fictional and nonfictional travel accounts alike were necessarily framed by a context of Euro-American imperialism, although they often disavowed any explicitly economic or political agenda. Poe's gothic picaresque, told in first-person narration by Pym, interweaves a racial allegory with an investigation of the human-animal boundary and speculation about the Antarctic environment so fantastic as to challenge any stable interpretation. These investigations begin when four survivors of a mutiny face imminent death from hunger and one proposes cannibalism, on the rationale that they "had now held out as long as human nature could be sustained" (ch. 12). If cannibalism activates humankind's animal nature, the next episode suggests a humanlike society and cooperation among animals, as Pym describes a vast island rookery of albatrosses and penguins, their nests alternately spaced with "mathematical accuracy" (ch. 14). Rescued by a merchant exploring ship voyaging southward, Pym summarizes the literature of previous Antarctic voyages, from Captain James Cook on, to present an air of credibility for the fantastic discoveries that follow. South of the farthest reaches of these voyages, Pym claims, the climate warms and the natural environment becomes increasingly organized in terms of strong color contrasts. On Tsalal island, nature presents a "vast chain of apparent miracles," including the water, which consists of laminar, internally cohesive veins in various hues of translucent purple (ch. 18). The island's human inhabitants have a morphology so unusual—jet black skin, hair, and even teeth concealed by "thick and clumsy" lips (ch. 19)—as to test the limits of the supposedly scientific race theory that began to emerge in the 1830s, exemplified in studies such as Samuel Morton's *Crania Americana* (1839). Pym's report that nothing on the island is light colored (the explanation, he imagines, for the islanders' fear of anything white) is especially curious, since he also identifies numerous familiar species of light-fleshed fish comprising the islanders' primary food source. Perceiving the natural environment in terms of resources, the Euro-Americans set the islanders to work preparing the abundant local sea cucumber for the Chinese market. The islanders pretend to acquiesce to this colonialist design but soon rebel, massacring the ship's crew. Pym and a companion survive by hiding in a cave, on the wall of which they discover curious marks of indeterminate origin. While Pym insists that the marks are natural and thus meaningless, a concluding note ascribed to "Poe," the ostensible editor of Pym's tale, decodes the markings as human, possibly Arabic script or Egyptian hieroglyphics, meaning "To be white" and "The region of the south." Pym's report on the Antarctic environment seems to verify "Poe's" interpretation of the curious marks: approaching the pole, the sea has a "milky hue" and a fine white ash perpetually falls. In a detail likely borrowed from John Cleves Symmes's expedition hoax *Symzonia: A Voyage of Discovery* (1820), the sea flows into a great cataract at the pole. Here, a humanlike giant whose skin color is "the perfect whiteness of the snow" looms in Pym's path as the narrative inexplicably breaks off (ch. 25).

Although *Pym* opens with a prefatory claim that it is truth published "under the garb of fiction," the outrageousness of the hoax subverts its pretensions to accuracy concerning the natural history of the South Seas. By contrast, *Typee* and *Omoo* purport to be factual accounts based on Melville's personal experience as a sailor who jumped ship in the Marquesas, was taken captive by the islanders, escaped, and later made his way to Tahiti. However, as the author complains in the preface to his third South Seas narrative, *Mardi: And a Voyage Thither* (1849), "in many quarters," *Typee* and *Omoo* "were received with incredulity." Indeed, sorting out fact from fiction in these tales and gauging Melville's reliance on sources such as William Ellis's *Polynesian Researches* (1833) have preoccupied readers ever since. Like Poe, Melville poses the question of nature most pointedly by way of two categories, human nature and nature as resource base, while providing (more reliably than Poe) natural history information on exotic environments. Melville cautions that nature counters our preconceptions. Even the most obvious landscape features are not as the reader imagines, "softly swelling plains, shaded over with delicious groves, and watered by purling brooks. . . . The reality is very different; bold rock-bound coasts, with the surf beating high against the lofty cliffs, and broken here and there into deep inlets" leading to "thickly wooded valleys" (*Typee*, ch. 2). As in *Pym*, the specter of cannibalism raises the question of human nature. Poe's account of cannibalism as a last resort for survival, rationally managed by means of a lottery and symbolically enacted as salvific sacrifice, reasserts the humanity of the participants. In *Typee*, Melville's account of cannibalism among the Marquesans explores a range of motivations fashioned by Europeans before apparently settling on a more sophisticated explanation than Poe's scenario offers. Any idea that cannibalism proceeds from hunger or appetite is easily dismissed in an environment where the stuff of life—breadfruit, coconuts, bananas, taro root, hogs—springs from the ground almost without labor. Whatever the truth of the practice (and it remains hidden from view), the threat of cannibalism functions to deter colonial intrusion. As a tactic of war, cannibalism thus pales by comparison to the cruelty and vindictiveness that Melville says "distinguish the white civilized man as the most ferocious animal on the face of the earth" (ch. 17). In any case, Melville spends more time on less scandalous aspects of the Polynesians' supposed state of nature. He comments ironically that the islanders are least industrious in areas where European economic and technological incursion has been greatest, to the point where they sometimes suffer hunger in the colonized areas. *Typee*, set primarily in the uncolonized valley of Nukuheva in which the narrator Tommo is held captive, contains some georgic passages—concerning the manufacture of the bark-cloth tappa and so on—within a primitivist-pastoral account of leisurely island life. Melville observes in *Omoo*, however, that in the colonized areas of the Society Islands, traditional native employments have disappeared as Europeans have shaped the environment, deliberately through plantation agriculture and less deliberately, though no less dramatically, through the introduction of invasive species such as cattle and mosquitoes. The narrator works on a sweet potato plantation managed by a Yankee to supply provisions for whaling ships; it is said that the islanders, apparently rendered naturally indolent by an environment that traditionally demanded so little labor for sustenance, refuse this colonial employment. Thus a primitivist-pastoral critique of "civilized" culture's relation to its resource bases—at times anticipating Thoreau's meditation on basic human needs in

Walden—undergirds the picaresque surface narrative of both *Typee* and *Omoo*. Yet Melville's first-person narrator returns, at the end of *Omoo*, to his earlier engagement with nature as resources, signing on board a whaling ship.

Although the whaling industry regards nature as an exploitable resource, Melville thinks more deeply into the question of nature in *Moby-Dick; or, The Whale* (1851), investigating the boundary between human and nonhuman nature. Melville surrounds the core narrative of the killing of a great beast—antecedents include traditional ballads such as "The Derby Ram" and hunting stories by southwestern humorists, such as Thomas Bangs Thorpe's "The Big Bear of Arkansas" (1841)—with numerous interpretive frames. The narrator Ishmael's insistence that "the whale is a fish" represents not biological ignorance, but rather a recognition that taxonomic biology (carried out here at almost satiric length) is but one approach among many, and not necessarily the most salient to one who makes his living hunting whales (ch. 32). Ishmael's concern for the extinction of the whale reorients traditional conceptions of the "oeconomy of nature," such as Thomas Jefferson's static account in *Notes on Virginia* (q. 6), to a dynamic view of human pressure on natural systems. Even so, Ishmael's belief in the persistence of the whale (like Jefferson's in the mammoth) may seem naively optimistic today. Our habit of anthropomorphizing animals, one source of our present-day concern over the extinction of megafauna such as whales and polar bears, resonates with the "The Prairie," "Grand Armada," and "Schools and Schoolmasters" chapters, suggesting a broader tendency toward empathy and community with the rest of nature. Ironically, Ishmael's animalization of human beings also suggests commonality, as when whalers are likened variously to cannibals, wolves, and sharks. Whales, according to Ishmael's account, are capable of a range of humanlike behaviors, yet also possess a distinctive, species-specific intelligence. For example, a curious behavioral trait, their occasional "perplexity" resulting from the dual perceptual field generated by nonbinocular vision, may partly explain Moby Dick's fatal approach to the *Pequod* on the third day of the chase (ch. 74).

Moby-Dick thus cycles through many of the American novel's environmental themes. The question of environmental determinism is revisited in details on the whale's natural adaptation to the marine environment and, differently, in details on the technological adaptations necessary for human beings to pursue whales. Pastoral passages, from Ishmael's opening flight from urban malaise through the late oceanic lure of "the seductive god . . . Pan" in the Pacific (ch. 111), suspend but cannot resolve the tension between the economic engagement with and veneration of nature. The particular form of Ahab's veneration—Moby Dick as "agent" or "principal" of the universe's "inscrutable malice" (ch. 36)—cautions against conceptualizing nature as moral register. Melville's delineation of the whale's distinctive, yet somewhat humanlike, physiology and psychology invites our identification with the nonhuman world even as the whale's manifest uniqueness defies identification. In this uncanny combination of similarity and difference, we may come to recognize the whale—and by extension, all of nature—as both other and self.

Pastoral narratives of the harmony of nature and culture, religious or Transcendentalist narratives of nature as moral correlative, georgic narratives of improvement and counter-narratives of wilderness veneration thus combined, often in conflicting ways, to present America as "nature's nation." These narratives assumed a conceptual separation of humankind from nonhuman nature. At the same time, however, they registered (albeit with varying degrees of self-reflection) the intertwining of human and nonhuman nature in the process of colonial expansion, as European literary forms met American environments. In this meeting, the georgic mode shaped the world to human need, while wilderness veneration imagined molding human behavior to nature's standard. The Transcendentalist sense of nature as moral register aligned human and natural existence with divine presence. The pastoral ideal imagined the resolution of a conflict between culture and nature that is as old as the story of the Fall of Eden, even as, in its more complex versions, it reflected on the invention of that story.

30

NOVELS OF FAITH AND DOUBT IN A CHANGING CULTURE

CAROLINE LEVANDER

"I have written twenty-five books, but I am not an author; I'm a parish minister" (Ward, *McClure's Magazine* Sept. 1893, 297). So says Edward Everett Hale, Unitarian minister and author of the famous story, "The Man Without a Country" (1863). Hale's immensely popular story "Ten Times One is Ten" (1870), with its motto "to look up and not down, look forward and not back, look out and not in, and lend a hand," as well as his "Lend a Hand" novels sparked immediate and widespread social reform when they first appeared. Nineteenth-century readers formed Lend-a-Hand Societies and Look-Up Legions to help those less fortunate, and the Lend a Hand Society continues today to further the Unitarian vision set out by Hale. When asked about his writing career, Hale declared that he turned to novel writing not because he cared "for the difference between Balzac and Daudet," but because he cared, as a Unitarian minister and humanist, about the people "who migrate to this country of mine" (Ward, *McClure's* Sept. 1893, 297).

We tend to think of the development of American religion and the emergence of an American literary tradition as two distinct features of the national landscape. And yet, as the example of Hale illustrates, religion and literature were interdependent, often mutually enforcing, phenomena in the early days of the United States. The two had much to say to each other and indeed are unintelligible when taken separately—religion, as we will see, depends on narrative and poetic form for its expression as much as literature has its origins in religious belief, crisis, and dissent.

In the early national period, conventional clergymen attacked the novel and fiction as deleterious to religious meaning. From their perspective storytelling violated the truth-value of religious doctrine. Puritan theology eschewed embellishment in the interest of preserving doctrinal purity. Prominent leaders like the Puritan Cotton Mather or the Methodist evangelist George Whitefield would declare that plays, romances, and imaginative writing precluded entrance into heaven because of their secularizing force. Even after the American Revolution this view remained largely unchanged among Calvinist ministers like Timothy Dwight who asserted that there was an impassable gulf between the Bible and novels or poetry.

Despite the fact that Puritan theology often dismissed literary expression as biblically inauthentic and therefore secularizing, some of the most famous Puritan sermons explicitly rely upon literary devices like metaphor, simile, metonymy, and imagery to powerfully move their listeners. John Winthrop's "A Model of Christian Charity" (1630), for example, challenges Puritan voyagers to understand themselves as undertaking a world-changing experiment in religious freedom and to imagine the new society they were preparing to build as "a city upon a hill" that would draw the eyes of all people throughout the world. On the one hand, Winthrop depends on the extensive use of imagery and simile to help his listeners visualize their future to be like a new city, the likes of which the world has never before seen. But he also invokes literary expression to warn them of the high risk of their undertaking, when he declares that, should they fail in their endeavor, they will be made a "story and a by-word through the world." This story, according to Winthrop, will empower enemies to shame God's servants and draw down curses upon rather than prayers for the Puritan project. Winthrop's sermon not only relied on literary devices but continues to be read as a founding piece of American literature as well as a founding document of national religion.

One hundred years later, preachers like Jonathan Edwards were using literary imagery with even more force to instill faith in congregations. Edwards's classic "fire and brimstone" sermon, "Sinners in the Hands of an Angry God" (1741), described the precariousness of human life and redemption through extended simile and the rich use of metaphor. Edwards paints a terrifying picture-story in which an angry God holds sinners over a pit of hell, burning with glowing flames that represent God's wrath. God holds each sinner "like a spider or some loathsome insect over the fire," dangling precariously and subject to the vicissitudes of an all-powerful and wrathful divine will. Edwards and Winthrop painted different visions of divine providence, but they transformed Americans' spiritual realities with their dramatic and highly effective imagery.

While early sermons employed literary figures of speech, from 1785 to 1850 many ministers and their congregations became increasingly frustrated with the nature of esoteric theological debate and so turned to narrative and, more particularly, to the novel to advance a simple code of morality and pious feeling. Indeed, the rise of religious tolerance throughout the nineteenth century was accompanied by the tendency to communicate religious lessons with narrative and stories rather than by sermonizing. Edwards's and Winthrop's impulse to turn to literary tools in order to awaken the interest and engage the moral conscience of congregants, in other words, became more developed and even ubiquitous as theological debate became increasingly dry and disconnected from the moral conundrums that Americans faced in daily life. By late in the nineteenth century, this trend had become so marked that Mark Twain would assert in 1871 that the Jesus story was disseminated to the American public through "the despised novel . . . and NOT from the drowsy pulpit!" (Twain 1973, 53). While literary expression was anathema to most seventeenth-century and much eighteenth-century theology, by the nineteenth century, literature and, more particularly, the novel became a powerful tool of the religious trade.

Why did American congregations turn away from the pulpit and to the novel for spiritual and religious guidance? And, more particularly, why and how did Americans come to see the novel as diverting and the pulpit as "drowsy"? First, many churchgoers found that conventional religious literature and sermons focused on orthodox dogma to the exclusion of all else. Ministers' entrenched resistance to casting moral lessons in the garb of lived experience caused resistance and incomprehension amongst congregations. As one church member put it, "the light, unthinking mind, that would revolt at a moral lesson from the pulpit, will seize, with avidity, the instruction offered under the similitude 'of a story'" (*The Gamesters; or, Ruins of Innocence* [1828], pref.). In order to meet their parishioners' increasing need to understand theological truth in relevant, everyday experience, popular ministers like William Ware, E. P. Roe, and Charles Sheldon became popular novelists, promulgating their religious messages through fiction. Ministers less successful at sermonizing likewise experimented with novel writing to see if their religious views could generate more interest in story form.

But ministers were not the only or even the primary literary agents of religiosity in the antebellum United States. Popular author Catharine Maria Sedgwick declared herself frustrated by "the splitting of . . . theological hairs" and "utterly useless polemical preaching" and turned to the novel to find rich opportunities to explore important religious and spiritual themes (1871, 59, 63). Not only did she become an avid novel reader, but she also authored numerous fictions that carried important religious messages to readers. Sedgwick began *A New England Tale* (1822) during a period of intense spiritual indecision. She disliked Calvinism's rigidity but was disappointed in Unitarianism, which she found cold and overly rational. Begun as a Unitarian tract, *A New England Tale* quickly became a novel about the follies of orthodoxy and the power of celestial imagery. Jane Elton, the novel's heroine, is an angel of goodness who confronts and conquers those characters who uphold the central precepts of Calvinist dogma. The novel does not include lengthy disquisition on religious doctrine but rather encourages readers to identify and sympathize with Jane because of her goodness.

Like *A New England Tale*, Sedgwick's most popular novel, *Hope Leslie; or, Early Times in Massachusetts* (1827), features female characters who take on angelic qualities in order to redeem their communities. Hope Leslie and the Native American protagonist Magawisca save a Puritan community that is compromised both from within and without. By setting her novel in Puritan times, Sedgwick framed her critique of contemporary religious practice at a historical remove from readers, but the message of the novel had great currency for its antebellum audience—spiritual redemption and religious faith are achieved through recognizing the potential divinity (rather than dwelling on the essential sinfulness) of each human being no matter how different. Magawisca is a spiritual exemplar whose self-sacrifice inspires Hope, and Hope, as her name suggests, models a virtue from which her stern Puritan town leaders eventually learn. Not only does Hope teach the Puritan community spiritual principles of liberality, free thinking, and inclusiveness, but she also has the power to root out the social threat of Catholicism. At one point mistaken for the Virgin Mary by a Italian sailor, Hope successfully uncovers a plot intended to establish Catholicism as the one true religion in the infant colonies. The novel's message is clear: spiritual vitality and democracy are jeopardized by dogma.

But it is in Harriet Beecher Stowe's writings that we find arguably the most politically impactful novel of faith and doubt of all time. When asked about the authorship of her internationally famous *Uncle Tom's Cabin; or, Life Among the Lowly* (1852), Stowe replied that she did not write it—God wrote it. In the book that, as Abraham Lincoln apocryphally declared, started the Civil War, Stowe features religious feeling as the cornerstone of her antislavery argument. "Feeling right" is more important than legal arguments that uphold slavery. Fictionalized religious leaders who condone slavery are lambasted in Stowe's novel. But most importantly, the promise of spiritual salvation and redemption guides characters and readers alike toward the promised land of freedom. Uncle Tom is a Christ figure who agrees to sacrifice himself for the greater good of his family, the other slaves, and the Shelby family who own him. His gradual descent into the hell of slavery culminates in his final and fatal confrontation with his third and most demonic slave owner, Simon Legree. Legree tries to force Uncle Tom to take up the whip against the other slaves, and when Tom refuses, he is beaten to death. But it is not only Tom's refusal to comply with his owner's demands that incites Legree. As Stowe writes, Legree "understood full well that it was GOD who was standing between him and his victim, and he blasphemed him" (ch. 38). Legree's violence toward Tom is violence toward God, and Tom's spiritual reliance on Jesus sustains him as he too becomes a Christlike martyr.

Many Americans described the reading of *Uncle Tom's Cabin* as a spiritual awakening that transformed them from passive bystanders in the anti- and proslavery debates into active participants in the abolitionist movement and finally into courageous soldiers on the battlefield. Many Union soldiers carried copies of *Uncle Tom's Cabin* in uniform pockets over their hearts, because they believed that it had talismanic power to protect them during battle. Conversely, popular southern proslavery novels like Caroline Lee Hentz's *The Planter's Northern Bride* (1854) and Augusta J. Evans's *Beulah* (1859) served the same spiritual purpose for Confederate soldiers. In such novels bourgeois northern women with preconceived notions about the evils of slavery move to the South only to learn that benign slave owners protect and guide their slaves in spiritual principles. Converting heathen to the one true faith, slave owners function as de facto missionaries and ministers for their easily misguided charges. *Uncle Tom's Cabin* recognizes southern slave owners' capacity to model Christian principles to unruly slaves and acknowledges the limitations of northern Calvinism in the project of assimilating African slaves into Protestant Christianity. Miss Ophelia, for example, is a northern spinster whose Calvinist worldview is insufficient to instruct the unruly child slave Topsy in Christian values. It takes the example of the truly spiritual, angelic child Little Eva to exert moral suasion successfully, so that Topsy wants to be good—to be just like Eva. When Eva's goodness and angelic nature confront the evils of slavery they "sink into [her] heart" (ch. 19) and prove too much for her, causing her to languish and finally die. Eva's untimely death crystallizes Topsy's desire for moral goodness and Miss Ophelia's recognition that her religious principles have not challenged her to overcome her unchristian prejudice against slaves. Unruly black slave and rigid Calvinist spinster form a genuine Christian bond, recognizing the power of love to overcome prejudice.

In her lesser-known novels, Stowe returns to these themes of the Christianizing influence of middle-class true womanhood. *The Minister's Wooing* (1859), for example, features a young girl through whom Stowe attempts to resolve the torments of New England Calvinism. Mary functions as a Protestant Madonna in the novel, bringing James, the middle-aged minister who is Mary's true love, a renewed spirituality and religious passion. This bundling of amorous and religious fervor is a pervasive feature of much woman-authored sentimental fiction in the antebellum era. Maria Cummins's popular novel *The Lamplighter* (1854) was second in sales only to *Uncle Tom's Cabin* during the 1850s, and its popularity was due in large part to the story of passionate religious awakening at its center. Gerty Flint, the young, indigent heroine of the story is a street urchin, abandoned by parents and evicted by a wicked caretaker when she tries to nurture a stray cat. She is informally adopted by a local lamplighter whose childlike religious faith, once coupled with the benevolent religious ministrations of a local gentlewoman, gradually transform the unruly and violent child. When the lamplighter brings her a Samuel—a figurine of a child praying—Gerty begins to learn in earnest about God, prayer, and the redemptive power of love. Much like Uncle Tom, Trueman Flint has a seemingly infinite capacity to love others, which is required to transform the juvenile delinquent into an icon of true womanhood. Gerty must go through many tests of her faith, but she learns the lesson of Christianity and is rewarded at the novel's end. Not only does her father reappear, but she also marries her one true love, has her fortune restored, and finds herself surrounded by loved ones as she creates a happy home of her own. Many antebellum novels would treat this theme of religious education through domestication. Indeed, the ties that bound middle-class domesticity with religious integrity were so profound that many began to criticize the ministry for becoming feminized. Once theologically rigorous and male dominated, American Protestantism was in danger, according to some social critics, of becoming overrun by zealously religious women who used novel writing as a pulpit from which to preach.

It was to this group of women writers that Nathaniel Hawthorne was referring when he railed against the "d—d mob of scribbling women" dominating the US literary scene (1987a, 304). This now notorious comment has been interpreted by scholars as a sign of Hawthorne's discomfort with literary competition from the ladies, but it also reflects his more particular discomfort with the competing religious visions distinguishing his less popular, dark romances from best-selling woman-authored domestic fiction. In his fiction, Hawthorne returns to the Puritan religious culture of his forebears rather than to the antebellum visions of benevolent, infinitely redemptive and theologically indeterminate domesticity with which his female contemporaries were concerned. In *The Scarlet Letter: A Romance* (1850), as well as in short stories like "The Minister's Black Veil" (1836) and "Young Goodman Brown" (1835), Hawthorne explores the Puritan origins of nineteenth-century American life and considers the legacy that this genealogy leaves for contemporaries who are facing unprecedented challenges to national unity. The scarlet *A* symbolizes the adulterous affair in which the novel's heroine Hester Prynne is involved. Though the Puritan community does not learn the fact until late in the story, readers discover that the Reverend Arthur Dimmesdale is not only the most prominent religious leader of the community but also the father of Hester's child. Dimmesdale is complicit in the affair as well as in the punishment meted out by religious leaders once the liaison becomes apparent in the person of Hester's illegitimate daughter Pearl. The scarlet *A* that Hester must wear as punishment brands her as an adulterer but it also symbolizes the hypocrisy and weak-mindedness of religious precepts that target one sinner but leave another at large. What happens when the unpunished sinner continues to be responsible for the spiritual well-being of a community? This is one of the questions that *The Scarlet Letter* asks. Scholars have long acknowledged Hawthorne's interest in Puritan religiosity and the damage that hypocritical and self-interested holiness has on innocent victims. Hawthorne's own family history was traceable to Puritan settlers, and his critique of Puritan practices upon which the United States was built reflects chagrin at the personal gain extracted from human pain and suffering.

In *The House of the Seven Gables: A Romance* (1851), for example, Hawthorne explores how religious leaders' acquisition of a homestead through the unfair manipulation of religious law continues to poison the happiness and opportunity of future generations of families who must live in the shadow of this traumatic religious legacy. In *The Scarlet Letter*, Dimmesdale internalizes his culpability—too weak to wear a scarlet *A* on his ministerial vest, he apparently stitches or brands one on his breast. The scarlet *A* that Dimmesdale feels on his breast is the cross he carries undetected through his daily religious duties. Is his own self-inflicted punishment greater or lesser than Hester's? Is it fair or right to punish two individuals for loving one another? Is it ethical to scapegoat one individual—demanding that she carry the burden of others' sins? These are the questions that *The Scarlet Letter* asks its readers to consider.

Because it is set in Puritan times, Hawthorne's novel may appear unconcerned with questions some Americans were wrestling with at mid-century, such as whether true religion sanctioned bondage, or whether the liberty of one part of the national community could be ensured only by the enslavement of another sector of the population. Americans were asking such questions with increasing frequency as Hawthorne was writing. But these are also questions that Hawthorne explores through his critique of the Puritan mores upon which the nation was founded. The scarlet *A* may stand not only for "adultery" but also possibly for "abolition," according to a few readers. The nineteenth-century abolitionists' challenge to an established order that refuses freedom to some community members is not unlike the Puritans' challenge to a national order that refused them freedom of worship. In such an interpretation of Hawthorne's writing, the religious history of the United States is integral to envisioning its future. The nation's Puritan roots are not irrelevant to contemporary political debate—far from it. The corrupt legacy of some religious practice is what the nation must contend with, and the fight to free slaves becomes nothing less than a fight to save the religious integrity of the country.

In Hawthorne's writing we begin to see how American literature not only engages but also dissents from American religious practice. Herman Melville's literary career presents a similar case in point. When we think of Melville's mariner stories we do not tend to think of religious commentary, and yet Melville's interest in religious practice and social welfare spanned his entire literary career. From the time he was a teenager in 1839 through the later poetry preceding his death in 1891, Melville engaged with—and sought alternatives to—the Protestant culture of the mid-nineteenth-century United States. In particular, Melville utilized Islamic rhetoric as a literary resource, as Timothy Marr has recently illustrated. In so doing, Melville was taking part not only in his own thought experiment in religious practice but also in a larger, sustained literary exploration of Islam. While Hawthorne, as Luther S. Luedtke has shown, embedded Oriental notions in his fiction, Melville developed a more transgressive literary vision of Islamic practice. Announcing the author's interest in a figure more widely known in the nineteenth century as the Abrahamic ancestor of the Arabs, the narrator of *Moby-Dick; or, The Whale* (1851) declares in the novel's famous opening line: "Call me Ishmael" (ch. 1). But it is in his late, long poem *Clarel: A Poem and Pilgrimage in the Holy Land* (1876) that we see the most developed portrayal of Muslims in early American literature. Through fictional figures that represent his poetic Islam, Melville expressed his continued search for spiritual fulfillment in an increasingly materialistic American culture. He visited Palestine in 1856 and over the following twenty years used literature to explore questions of faith, doubt, and God. Melville's writing asks why humans suffer and die, why God remains hidden and silent, and why spiritual comfort and certainty are so difficult to achieve.

Why might Melville turn to Islam to ask these religious questions? Not only did Islam offer him an alternative spiritual model in an increasingly secular American culture, but it also had long offered American writers a means of commenting on American religion. They invoked Islam because its precepts resembled the three major strands of American liberalism—Arianism, Unitarianism, and Arminianism. American writers used the Oriental motif to represent religious ideas that challenged the tenets of New England orthodoxy—the reward of virtue, perfectibility, toleration, and the universal benevolence of God. These ideas were still unpopular with late eighteenth-century Calvinist thinkers, and so Oriental fiction allowed American liberals to challenge Calvinist precepts while avoiding strict theological debate. Popular novels like Royall Tyler's *The Algerine Captive; or, The Life and Adventures of Doctor Updike Underhill* (1797) featured US sailors who, as onetime captives of Turks or Algerians, have the opportunity to report on Eastern religious practices. Conversely, novels like Peter Markoe's *The Algerine Spy in Pennsylvania* (1787) and Samuel L. Knapp's *Travels of Ali Bey* (1818) feature Oriental visitors to America who write home about doctrinal controversies in ways that implicitly weigh in on religious piety and make pleas for religious toleration.

While Islam continued to offer American writers rich opportunities to rethink prevailing tenets of American Protestantism, the spread of Catholicism provoked advocacy of Protestant Christianity as the one national religion. Anti-Catholic writing abounded throughout the late eighteenth and nineteenth centuries. The villain of Sedgwick's *Hope Leslie*, for example, is an English Catholic who infiltrates an American Protestant community with the secret goal of setting up a Vatican in the New World. In his popular tract *A Plea for the West* (1835), prominent preacher Lyman Beecher spread anti-Catholic sentiment by suggesting that the pope planned to take over the American West as an outpost of the Catholic empire. Anti-Catholicism or nativism flourished in the 1830s and 1840s because potato famines in Ireland brought unprecedented numbers of Irish Catholics to the United States and because the United States acquired vast territories from Mexico at the end of the US-Mexico War (through the Treaty of Guadalupe Hidalgo in 1848) that transformed a large number of Mexican (predominantly Catholic) citizens into US citizens. Anonymously written sensational novels of convent life fueled anti-Catholic sentiments. Maria Monk's *Awful Disclosures of the Hotel Dieu Nunnery of Montreal* (1836) created such a public outcry that the convent in question was searched by civic leaders to determine if the "first-hand" account of rape, infanticide, and torture was truthful. Southern and border fiction like Augusta J. Evans's *Inez: A Tale of the Alamo* (1855) likewise depicted priests propagating sinister plots to seduce young girls and the nation away from Protestant ideals. Catholic characters represent pervasive threats to religious integrity throughout much of American literature. If Islam offered authors alternatives and opportunities to challenge Protestant hegemony, the threat of Catholicism became a powerful device for upholding and encouraging that hegemony.

As we have seen, American evangelicalism and its democratizing, charismatic, and separatist energies were not simply important touchstones for much American literature; rather, there was a mutually interdependent dynamism at work between American literary and religious cultures that made the two integrally connected and arguably inseparable. African American communities, like their Anglo-American counterparts, developed effective literary strategies for engaging, contesting, and channeling American evangelical zeal.

Religious thought has been a central concern of African American writing since its origins in the early national period. We can begin to get a sense of the foundational importance of religious thought to such discourse by looking at early figures like John Marrant, Phyllis Wheatley, Absalom Jones, and Richard Allen. Of these four, only Phyllis Wheatley's name can be regularly found in anthologies of American literature and African American literature. However, the writing careers of these other, now lesser-known, authors illustrate the founding importance of religious belief to literary expression and the vital role that African Americans believed writing could have in their communities. As early as 1790, the evangelist John Marrant published his missionary *Journal* to describe his three-year mission to the largest all-black North American settlement in Birchtown, Nova Scotia. For Marrant, writing was an important way to disseminate religious belief to a larger audience than a single congregation. In his *Journal*, Marrant described in detail a covenant theology that reflected and was practiced by a particular community of exiled black Loyalists. The distinctive religious emphasis on exodus and Zionistic fulfillment that characterized the Birchtown settlement grew out of the particular needs of this African American community. Its defining features, in turn, became an important story that Marrant wanted to share with others. But if his primary goal in publishing the *Journal* was to describe a new religious community, he then also used his firsthand involvement with that settlement to credential himself as a writer.

Similarly, the religious training and firsthand religious experiences of Absalom Jones and Richard Allen became the starting point for their writing careers. Jones and Allen were religious leaders in late eighteenth-century Philadelphia, founders of the African Methodist Episcopal church, and authors of *A Narrative of the Proceedings of the Black People, During the Late Awful Calamity in Philadelphia* (1794)—a published story of their community's involvement in a yellow fever epidemic and its endurance as a spiritual community in the face of disaster. Allen was a former slave who had converted his owner and purchased his freedom. Jones was a fellow ex-slave and native Philadelphian who joined Allen in founding the Free African Society in 1787 and in organizing an African church in 1791. The leadership role that Allen and Jones played in developing the African American social and religious community in Philadelphia made them natural spokesmen against racial injustice when it erupted in 1793. Because African Americans were thought to be immune to yellow fever, the city of Philadelphia pressed them into hazardous service as nurses and gravediggers during the outbreak. This human rights abuse was exacerbated by accelerating racial panic as African Americans became identified with the fever, rather than acknowledged as heroic intercessors. The 1794 *Narrative* that Allen and Jones published was meant to set the record straight—to correct misrepresentations of African American responsibility for the epidemic, to impugn city leaders for their racist response to it, to correct accusations that blacks used the contagion as an opportunity for looting, and to reverse the mistaken idea that blacks were immune to the fever. Because of both authors' prominence in the religious community, the *Narrative* became an important and widely circulated document, constituting a watershed moment in black cultural history. The authors' religious careers and their literary activity were mutually supporting, even as they used religious metaphors and appeals to divine justice to argue their points.

Despite the importance of their writing to African American history, Allen, Jones, and Marrant have been largely forgotten. Such was not the case with all early African American writers, however. When we think about African American writing in the nineteenth century, we tend to think about early African American woman-authored and male-authored novels—Julia Collins's *Curse of Caste; or, The Slave Bride* (first published in the *Christian Recorder* [1865]) and William Wells Brown's *Clotel; or, The President's Daughter* (1853)—as well as the famous slave narratives of Harriet Jacobs, Frederick Douglass, Sojourner Truth, and Hannah Crafts. Key to all these texts are the critiques of ministers who use scripture to uphold slave owning and of religious communities that condone human injustice. *Clotel*, for example, ridicules the hypocrisy of plantation preachers and religious song. Harriet Jacobs's *Incidents in the Life of a Slave Girl* (1861) devotes a chapter to "The Church and Slavery" (ch. 13), which contains the narrative's most sustained commentary on the church's hypocritical position on slavery. According to Jacobs, slaveholders use religious instruction to keep slaves from murdering their masters. When confronted with the slave-owners' widespread fear that Nat Turner's slave insurrection was the first of many acts of slave violence, the clergy decide to hold separate Sunday services for slaves. Yet, as Episcopal, Methodist, and Baptist churches profess to include both slaves and free parishioners, these same churches use scripture to uphold slavery as divine law and to convince slaves to accept their servitude. The slaves are not so easily duped, and the black congregation of Rev. Mr. Pike's church laughs quietly at his gospel preaching. Yet slaves depend on religious instruction for strength, even as they resist coercive religious messages about their inferiority. They rely on scripture and on religious leaders who uphold the precept that God judges people by their hearts, not by the color of their skin. Learning how to negotiate a southern pulpit all too ready to tighten the bonds of slavery is the formidable task that every slave faces. Developing spiritual strength and fortitude in the face of such opposition is not impossible, however, and Jacobs describes slaves' heartfelt commitment to religious teachings and to the Bible. When her owner tells her that she should join the church, Jacobs's heroine responds that she would be glad to join if she could be allowed to live like a Christian woman. She quotes scripture to refute her owner's deployment of biblical passages that are intended to justify his attempts to seduce her; biblical knowledge, as Jacobs shows, can become a powerful weapon against abuse that cloaks itself in fallacious religious teachings. Thus, religion is a theme that takes on narrative complexity in *Incidents* and allows Jacobs to display her ironic wit. Because of her sophisticated engagement with religious thinking and institutions, *Incidents* exemplifies the characteristics that we tend to attribute to canonical literature.

Like Jacobs, Frederick Douglass was overtly critical of religious hypocrisy in his writing. In *Narrative of the Life of Frederick Douglass* (1845), slave songs as well as religious practices deriving from voodoo became pathways to slave resistance. One of the most famous passages of *Narrative* focuses on the unique spirituality of slave songs. Douglass describes in detail the long, deep, loud tones of the songs and how they "breathed the prayer and complaint of souls boiling over with the bitterest anguish" (ch. 2). Every note, according to Douglass, is "a testimony against slavery, and a prayer to God" powerful enough to depress his spirit and fill every listener with "ineffable sadness" (ch. 2). Douglass is most sorely tested when he is sold to the home of a slave owner who makes the greatest pretensions of piety and prays morning, noon, and night, but is cruel to his slaves. In the counsel of Sandy Jenkins, a slave with whom he becomes acquainted, Douglass agrees to seek alternative sources of strength to combat his oppression. One Sunday morning, Sandy gives him a root that he claims has the power to keep a slave from being whipped. Though initially skeptical, Douglass comes to think that the root might carry some spiritual power. The virtue of the root is tested when Douglass fights his overseer rather than submit to a whipping. In Douglass's *Narrative*, spiritual strength to combat slavery comes not from church sermons and Bible readings but from the songs and folklore of slaves who have the courage and the will to make use of spiritual strength. His appendix to the memoir offers a vehement critique of Christian hypocrisy in the slave South.

Like Jacobs and Douglass, the antebellum African American writer Martin Delany saw that religion could all too easily destroy the self-reliance and independence of blacks. Delany was born of a free mother and slave father in Virginia in 1812. Because of the law that offspring "followed the condition of the mother," Delany was born free rather than a slave. Nevertheless, he devoted his life and his writing to denouncing slavery not only in the United States but also throughout the Americas. At the time that Delany began his writing career, slavery was still pervasive in many parts of the Americas, for example in Cuba and Brazil. From 1843 to 1847 Delany edited a black newspaper called the *Mystery*, and from 1847 to 1849 he co-edited the *North Star* with Douglass. In addition to these important editorial positions, he delivered antislavery lectures and wrote long letters to the *North Star* about his work. However, it was in the early 1850s that his literary career took off. His novel *Blake; or, The Huts of America* (1859, 1861–62) was inspired by *Uncle*

Tom's Cabin. Delany wanted to refute the image of the docile slave at the center of Stowe's novel and to challenge her message that slaves must exhibit religious forbearance. Uncle Tom, as we have seen, sacrifices himself for the greater good of the slave community, and he repeatedly uses scripture and the example of Jesus to justify his self-sacrifice. Delany took issue with this image of black manhood by featuring an angry and rebellious black man as his protagonist. Refusing to accept Christian justifications for his suffering, Delany's protagonist Henry escapes to the dismal swamp to remake himself and society. Henry is literally transformed into Blake, a fugitive from slavery who travels throughout the US South and Cuba to proselytize for freedom. Blake is a messianic as well as disruptive presence throughout the Americas. His preaching is unorthodox but powerful among slaves, who protect him and the maroon community he forms. Blake does not wait for whites to emancipate him—he takes his freedom and assumes it as a condition of his humanity. In so doing, he becomes a trans-denominational religious leader for blacks throughout the Americas. When he visits Cuba and addresses a group of political leaders, he provides his listeners with a history of the religious training of his constituency: he was raised Catholic but became Baptist; his wife was raised Baptist; others in his congregations were pagan, Methodist, Episcopalian, and Swedenborgian. However, the community he forms has agreed to follow no sects or denominations—but only one religion that brings liberty. The ceremonies of this new religion have been originated by the community and adapted to its wants and needs. When Blake describes this religion and its practices to the Cuban community, his words become a prayer and sermon to which his listeners unanimously reply "amen" (pt. 2, ch. 61). Description of this new religion therefore becomes a religious act. His congregation is summoned into being throughout the Americas by his account of a resistant faith that knows no other truth than freedom.

The interconnections between religious practice and literary expression intensified, for Americans black and white, during and after the Civil War. Not only did the question of slavery generate writing that turned to religious precepts for guidance, but also religious figures increasingly relied on literary form and popular narrative techniques to affirm congregants' pro- or anti-slavery leanings. Lincoln asserted that a house divided could not stand, and this metaphor held true for the house of God as well as for the nation's domestic policy. Religious beliefs had helped to generate social justifications for the war. The idea that slavery was wrong gained widespread support through churches, and Union soldiers often described their reasons for engaging in the war as the result of religious conviction and a strong sense of right and wrong. The unprecedented carnage and protracted war, however, challenged religious institutions, faith networks, and spiritual communities in unprecedented ways. The sheer number of dead and severely wounded fractured communities. If religious conviction helped spur support for the war effort on both sides, then religious conviction was sorely challenged by the effect of the war on individuals, families, and local communities as well as on the national family. American writers grappled with the spiritual challenges posed by the war in various ways.

American writing not only faced its most difficult subject yet but also confronted a reading audience who brought new needs to the reading of literature. Elizabeth Stuart Phelps's writing career illustrates the postbellum literary milieu particularly well. Born in 1844, Phelps grew up in a Calvinist religious tradition because her father was a pastor and then a faculty member in a theological seminary. From childhood, Phelps was surrounded by sickness and loss—her mother died when Phelps was young and her father suffered a breakdown—but it was during the war that Phelps's faith and her writing were most severely tried. Though she had written children's stories before the war, it was her literary effort to envision the afterlife that made her a famous author. In writing *The Gates Ajar* (1868), she undertook to imagine life after death literally for readers suffering intense grief, loss, and spiritual crisis. The title refers to the gates of heaven, and the book explores daily life after death inside the pearly gates. Like her readers, Phelps imagined an afterlife that was not disconnected from earthly concerns but rather a natural extension of it. Instead of a heaven on earth, *The Gates Ajar* provides readers with an earthly heaven. Selling over 100,000 copies in the United States and England, this novel was translated into French, Italian, and German, and it was the only nineteenth-century novel to remotely rival *Uncle Tom's Cabin*. As Mary Louise Kete has argued, the three novels that Phelps wrote in the Gates series—the other two being *Beyond the Gates* (1883) and *The Gates Between* (1887)—helped readers contend with personal loss by constructing a community of grieving readers. Realizing that they were not completely abandoned by departed loved ones and that others were suffering similar feelings of bereavement, readers of Phelps's Gates series took part in a collective mourning process. Novels were key to this healing community. Instead of isolating individual readers within the pages of a book, Phelps's novels helped them join a group constituted through shared suffering. Crucial to the success of Phelps's fiction was her vision of salvation. Rather than providing readers with an abstract concept of life after death, Phelps sketched a picture of heaven that both shared familiar attributes with life on earth and reassured mourners that those who died remained connected to the families they left behind and thus retained a vital link to earthly life.

As Phelps's writing makes clear, Americans were searching for answers to spiritual dilemmas, and they brought renewed energy and urgency to this search in the postbellum period. We can see the development of this phenomenon by considering the writing of Ralph Waldo Emerson, Walt Whitman, and Louisa May Alcott. As early as 1832, Emerson preached a sermon on "The Lord's Supper" to the Second Church of Boston congregation in which he argued that the individual does not need a church, a priest, a doctrine, or any mediator between himself and God. Rather, the individual finds spirituality by turning to the self as the center of understanding. God was within human beings and extended beyond them to include the whole universe. The Transcendentalist thought that Emerson propounded therefore contended that individuals achieved unity by perceiving the soul to be at one with the cosmos. As had so many other religious thinkers, Emerson turned to literature to flesh out his ideas, and, with essays such as "Nature" (1836) and "The Divinity School Address" (1838), he became an outspoken advocate of individual freedom as opposed to an endorser of the authority of religion. Emerson's secular and religious writing broke down distinctions between the two forms, but it was in the writing of Whitman that Emerson and many Americans found a religion of the common man—a religion that celebrated every aspect of the self and contained all elements of humanity. In Whitman's estimation, even more than in Emerson's, churches stand in the way of real religion in the United States. God is everywhere if we could but know it, and the most sacred temple is not built with bricks and mortar but is human flesh and the human body. Whitman most fully and ambitiously innovated the American tradition of religious free-thinking with the six editions of *Leaves of Grass* that he published between 1855 and 1892. In the process, he became America's most prophetic poet and most poetic prophet. In Whitman, Americans found a poet, but they also found a spiritual leader—a successor to Jesus and the Buddha as much as a successor to Wordsworth, as Michael Robertson points out. One admirer suggested that future Americans would celebrate the birth of Whitman just as they currently celebrated the birth of Christ. Another described *Leaves* as the most religious book he had ever read. Whitman understood his writing to propound a radically democratic theology and to have a primarily religious purpose. In his cosmic consciousness, distinctions between priest and poet were nonexistent, and therefore he was as much prophet as poet.

While unprecedented, the Civil War was not the only test of faith that nineteenth-century Americans confronted. Scientific concepts of human evolution, natural selection, and survival of the fittest shook the religious faith of many Americans. Charles Darwin's *On the Origin of Species* (1859) and *The Descent of Man* (1871) created shock waves in religious communities when they arrived in the United States. They called into question the organizing principles of religious concepts such as divine selection, the creation of heaven and earth, and salvation, among many others. Was it possible that human beings were descended from monkeys and not made in the image of God? Was it possible that the earth had not been made in seven days but over the course of a much longer period? Finally, was it possible that "salvation" was less a matter of personal redemption and absolution from sin and more a matter of evolutionary principles that naturally selected certain traits as more useful than others? These questions rocked religious communities and created crises of faith among American believers. In the wake of the Civil War, Americans had questioned a God who could allow such human suffering and loss, but with scientific "proof" that discounted many religious precepts Americans found themselves forced to confront an entirely new and unprecedented set of challenges to their faith.

American writers responded to these questions in myriad, innovative ways. Sentimental literature of the antebellum era, as we have seen, emphasized religious growth and spiritual awakening as integral to social transformation and success. Extremely popular novels, such as Alcott's *Little Women* (1868), relied on sentimentality and on religious development as a key feature of their characters' growth. Reading *The Pilgrim's Progress* (1678), for example, gives shape and texture to the five March girls' lives as they develop into women. Alcott's novel was so successful that she quickly followed it with *Little Men* (1871). In this sequel, the March sisters are grown, with homes of their own, and Jo March has started a school called Plumfield for indigent boys. However, the most significant difference between the two novels can be found in the depiction of sin and redemption in *Little Men*. The school aims to turn at-risk boys into upstanding members of society, but the boys must first conquer their sinful natures. Sin in *Little Men* is explicitly imagined in Darwinian terms, and the seven deadly sins become evolutionary challenges that individual boys must overcome through internalizing adaptation techniques. Rather than being likened to religious pilgrims, the boys are repeatedly equated with animals—colts, owls, squirrels—and, like these animals in the natural world, they must adapt to their surroundings or become extinct. Through extensive literary metaphor, Alcott explores what it means for human beings to be incrementally, rather than essentially, different from animals. She provides examples of nature run amuck, as when she describes one of the boys' pets—a crab—eating its offspring. In the world of Plumfield, human beings must evolve beyond these savage, animalistic origins and natures if they want to succeed in life and in a world that is newly understood to be governed by scientific as well as scriptural principle.

The bonds between literary and religious imagination were, as we have seen, forged during the period of the early republic and the first half of the nineteenth century, when both literary form and religious life were dramatically changing shape and helping to construct a new nation—a nation that emerged out of Puritan ideals and an imagined separation between church and state. The novel became a dominant literary form in the first half of the nineteenth century, but its origins in the sermonic tradition, nonfiction prose, and oratory continued to shape the American novel long after it was established as the most popular form of writing. Indeed, the novel and religious thought worked hand in glove to make sense of the major conflicts defining the nineteenth century. The Civil War produced a crisis of faith as well as a crisis of literary expression among Americans, and the interconnections between faith and the novel would intensify after the war. American novels were integral to the religious life of many readers, connecting people to their preachers, challenging spiritual smugness, and conceptualizing ethical responsibility in a changing national landscape. Religious and literary innovators formed a loose but lasting collaboration that continues to shape how we read, listen, and pray.

Part VII

FICTIONAL SUBGENRES

31

TEMPERANCE NOVELS AND MORAL REFORM

DEBRA J. ROSENTHAL

To think about temperance and other moral reform movements in the nineteenth century is to think about the power of narrative to change society. Writers and activists involved in the antialcohol movement understood that effective storytelling could radically change both private drinking behavior and public policy toward drunkenness. Temperance advocates hoped that the right stories, told in the right way, could change the way society talked about itself and its values, how people saw themselves in relationship to alcohol, and what kind of citizens they hoped to be. Ironically, most reformers believed in the power of the pen to tell the truth, yet they commonly used fiction to convey that truth. In other words, reform efforts often blurred the line between fact and fancy, as novels and stories became the gateway to truth and change. Because alcohol affected so many strata of life, this chapter will focus on temperance fiction while also exploring the interconnectedness of several reform movements.

Law trials, news reports, and the often formulaic fictions that mirrored them, all promoted moral reform and tapped into the spirit of the times to nudge readers to amend their ways. But frequently, the exhortative work too enthusiastically embraced the very vice it was supposedly trying to correct. Many readers were thereby drawn to read "moral" antialcohol novels because of the ways such works so vividly provided wild and exciting examples of raucous drunkenness. Much writing of the nineteenth century thus drew its energy from both literary efforts to rectify social ills and the exciting, entertaining descriptions of such problems.

This tension over the function of alcohol—portrayed in literature both to condemn drunkenness and to celebrate revelry—was not new to the nineteenth century. Since the establishment of the thirteen colonies, the vigorous consumption of alcohol coexisted uneasily alongside what were at times equally forceful attempts to legislate against it. When towns were founded, the first structures built were a church and a tavern, suggesting residents' mutual appreciation of the Spirit and spirits.

According to estimates by scholars Mark Edward Lender and James Kirby Martin, the average US resident in 1830 drank an astounding seven gallons of pure alcohol per year; in comparison, Americans in 1985 drank only 2.6 gallons per person annually. Because of unsanitary water conditions, people in the eighteenth and nineteenth centuries drank alcohol on most occasions. It was also not uncommon for workers to drink beer or wine while on the job. For example, Benjamin Franklin writes in his *Autobiography* (1791) that his coworkers would pay an alehouse boy to bring them fresh beer several times a day in the belief that strong beer built strong bodies.

What accounted for such a dramatic reduction in the consumption of alcohol? Improvements in water purification certainly made water a safer option as the nineteenth century progressed, but this technological innovation alone cannot account for Americans switching their allegiance from the keg tap to the kitchen tap. In fact, the moral suasion techniques and increased legal action of the temperance movement played an enormous role in convincing people to put down the bottle. Inspired by a long history of national alcoholic overindulgence, the temperance crusade expanded in the early nineteenth century and swept through the country. Ultimately, the temperance movement, contemporaneous with the technological innovations of the railroad and telegraph, emerged as possibly the broadest, most durable social movement of the nineteenth century. The antiliquor effort culminated with Prohibition, legalized by the Eighteenth Amendment to the US Constitution in 1919, which made self-control and public virtue into issues of national interest. Supporters thus believed that morality could and should be legislated.

Those involved in the national movement to stop Americans from drinking had many concerns. They asserted that alcohol enslaved the drinker's body and will, just as African Americans who were legally enslaved did not hold control of their body or will. Temperance advocates argued that heavy drinking caused men to lose their jobs and thereby impoverish their families, that inebriation directly led to poor health, and that, furthermore, drunkenness indicated a sinful life. Advice manuals to young men coming of age were sure to address the topic of overindulgence. For example, William A. Alcott has a section called "On Forming Temperate Habits" in *The Young Man's Guide* (1833), in which he states that "*Drunkenness* and *Gluttony* . . . are vices so degrading that I deem any one capable of indulging in them to be hardly worthy of advice" (ch. 1, sec. 7). Much antidrink writing in the early nineteenth century was didactic and influenced either by Protestant clergymen such as Lyman Beecher, who theologically damned drunkards, or by rationalist medical and intellectual figures like Benjamin Rush, who based his opposition to drink on its injurious effects on the body.

Because both drunkenness and sobriety influenced so much of American politics, religion, and daily life, it was inevitable that these themes would seep into creative writing of the time. Authors used images of drink to structure plots, to signal character types, to embellish a theme, to teach a lesson, and to promote a cause. The American Temperance Union, an organization devoted to the dry cause, recognized the capability of temperance fiction to disseminate antialcohol propaganda to large numbers of readers. In 1836, members voted to endorse the use of such literature, especially didactic tracts, to spread its message. The National Temperance Society became a publisher of temperance fiction, which assured it a public voice in the fight against intoxication. Much fiction was aimed at a young audience, the purpose being "to teach children the ethos of self-denial," though the child often ended up serving as a sentimental figure abused by a drunken father (Sánchez-Eppler 1997, 72).

The nineteenth-century temperance tale enjoyed success by generally sticking to a formula: a young innocent boy, often from the country, moves to the city in search of work, has his first drink of alcohol, and rapidly degenerates into an unrepentant drunkard who impoverishes his family and dies inebriated. Although we now have a medical model of alcoholism as a disease, many people in the nineteenth century believed that inebriation was a sign of moral weakness, and the drinker was a morally defective sinner. Antidrink stories aimed to reveal to drunkards their unacceptable ways and show them how to lead a sober life blessed with economic security and familial love. Elaine Frantz Parsons identifies six key features of drunk narratives: (1) the young male protagonist "is a particularly promising young man"; (2) he "falls largely or entirely because of external influences"; (3) he is weak-willed and too eager to please his new friends; (4) his desire for drink overwhelms all else; (5) "he loses his control over his family, his economic life, and/or his own body"; and (6) "if [he] is redeemed, it is through a powerful external influence" (2003, 11).

The conventional or exhortatory writing typified by Rush or earlier by Benjamin Franklin eventually gave way, and temperance fiction became less didactic and increasingly sensational. David S. Reynolds calls this genre "dark-temperance," due to its tendency "to discard moralization altogether on behalf of bold explorations of psychopathic states" (1988, 69). With its antimoralistic leanings, such writing tended to lure and titillate readers with shock value: "The dark-temperance style illustrates well how the puritanical protest against vice, when carried to an extreme, could in fact turn into its opposite—a gloating over the grim details of vice" (Reynolds 1988, 68). Reynolds points to many temperance works that seem to celebrate the very sins they ostensibly protest. For example, he mentions sketches where inebriated husbands drag their wives by their hair and use an ax to chop up loved ones; in Maria Lamas's novel *The Glass; or, The Trials of Helen More* (1849), a boy locked in a closet by his drunken mother chews off his arm to sate his hunger.

Even earnest moral tracts employed a dark sensational style to enliven their didacticism. For example, Mason Locke Weems opens *The Drunkard's Looking Glass* (1812) with a depraved tale, supposedly the work of a Spanish monk, about a devil who offered great rewards to a preacher if he would commit one of the following sins: rape his sister, murder his father, or get drunk. The preacher recoiled at the mention of the first two but readily agreed to the last sin. The devil hoped the preacher would chose inebriation, because when the preacher got drunk, he raped his sister. When their father heard his daughter's cries and came to the rescue, the besotted preacher committed patricide. Weems summarizes the moral of this story: "There is no folly, no madness ever yet committed out of Bedlam, which a drunken man is not perfectly capable of" (60).

The alluring dark sensationalism of the antidrink movement also informed journalistic writing of the time. Even supposedly factual, reportorial venues like newspapers fell prey to the attractions of thrilling description and could not resist inserting a moral message. For example, in 1834 the *Salem Gazette* printed a "Horrid Case of Intemperance." The newspaper reports the discovery of a man's burnt body, with a nearby "whiskey bottle drained to the bottom. It appears that the miserable man was intoxicated and rolled from his board during the night and into the fire. How long he was there no one can tell, but the agony of his sufferings probably aroused him at last. . . . Early in the morning, he was found rolling about in the most excruciating agony and muttering curses against God and man." The *Gazette* ends its report of this incident with a lesson that echoes the didacticism of temperance novels: "[H]is face had changed color from white to black, and there he was prostrate with his mouth biting the ground, a terrible admonition to all who peril their lives by the excess of strong drink" (Jan. 3, 1834, 2).

Early dry activists were not drinkers themselves, but were "citizens concerned about the effects of alcoholism in the neighborhoods, particularly as regarded the presence of bars and saloons and the seeming prevalence of binge drinking" (Sánchez 2008, 181). Members of the Washingtonian movement, on the other hand, were actual working-class, heavy drinkers who wanted to reform their ways. This group, a major temperance organization of the nineteenth century, named themselves after the man who liberated the colonies from "King George," and they hoped that the weight of his memory could liberate themselves from "King Alcohol" (qtd. in Crowley 1997, 122). At Washingtonian meetings, drinkers shared aloud stories of their experiences, forming supportive and salvific bonds as they recognized familiar patterns of behavior in fellow members, not unlike what occurred at evangelical revivals. Often, drinkers' testaments became ever more dramatic. Full of graphic descriptions of nightmarish adventures and domestic violence, their titillating confessions drew ever-more people to the movement. Washingtonian discourse was often violent and lurid in its renderings of alcohol's ravages, and people were eager to read and hear about the degeneracy and wickedness they supposedly protested. The Washingtonian phase, which started in 1840 and extended in various forms until the early 1850s, had particular relevance to the development of American literature.

Timothy Shay Arthur gained popularity as a speaker and as a writer for his exciting and theatrical orations detailing his battles with "Demon Rum." According to María Carla Sánchez, "temperance as a movement became characterized by appeals to sympathetic, sentimental feeling" (2008, 182). Temperance writers tried to capture the immediacy of such a Washingtonian meeting "by putting listeners and readers in [the drunkard's] shoes, to heighten that listener or reader's sense of shared, common peril, emphasizing that next time it could be a brother, a son, a husband" (Sánchez 2008, 182). Arthur's *Ten Nights in a Bar-Room, And What I Saw There* (1854) is perhaps the antebellum period's most famous temperance novel, and it solidified his literary reputation, though he penned around 150 novels and short stories. The novel is divided into ten chapters, each one detailing a night over a ten-year period in the Cedarville Sickle and Sheaf tavern. The narrator is a traveling businessman who stays in an upstairs room at the tavern when in town on business and is able to observe the changes wrought on the tavern, the drinkers, and the community as time passes. The novel features much lengthy and preachy dialogue, but spices it up with scenes of melodrama and violence. For example, the town drunkard, Joe Morgan, is continually entreated to come home by his innocent daughter Mary, who must venture into the saloon to collect her father. One night the tavern owner, Simon Slade, becomes angry with Joe and throws a glass at him. The glass misses Joe and hits little Mary in the head, so that blood covers her face. Mary's deathbed scene is a crowning achievement of Victorian melodrama: florid rhetoric, soaring emotion, fluent tears, religious imagery, and gasping promises from Joe that he will never drink again. After having extracted such a temperance pledge from her father, angelic Mary serenely dies. The novel presents other degrading scenes and consequences of drinking but ends with a strong temperance message: the townspeople buy all the remaining alcohol in Cedarville and pass legislation to prevent any future sales.

John Gough was probably the best-known temperance lecturer and sensationalist of the second half of the nineteenth century. Gough himself had been an alcoholic, and he drew upon his theatrical training to shock his audiences with outlandish tales of his own nightmarish experiences. He drew large crowds with his riveting performances that gruesomely detailed the debauched excesses associated with drinking. For example, in his *Autobiography* (1845), Gough recalls his suffering a particular attack of the delirium tremens: "Hideous faces appeared on the walls, and on the ceiling, and on the floors; foul things crept along the bedclothes, and glaring eyes peered into mine. I was at one time surrounded by millions of monstrous spiders, that crawled slowly over every limb, whilst the beaded drops of perspiration would start to my brow, and my limbs would shiver until the bed rattled again" (103–4). His reputation was somewhat scarred when he was discovered inebriated in a whorehouse, yet he continued successfully as a Washingtonian lecturer.

Temperance themes also appeared in the works of prominent writers associated with the American Renaissance, the period of expansive creativity and publishing that scholars date from 1835 to 1860. Nathaniel Hawthorne wrote a popular temperance tale, "A Rill from the Town-Pump" (1835). Edgar Allan Poe sensationally portrayed the downward spiral of alcohol-induced depravity in "King Pest" (1835),

"The Black Cat" (1843), "The Angel of the Odd" (1844), and "The Cask of Amontillado" (1846). Poe's drunken habits became the object of ridicule in Thomas Dunn English's serialized novel *1844* (1844–46), which thinly disguised Poe as Marma-duke Hammerhead, the author of "The Black Crow" who likes to say "Nevermore." Moral antidrink messages found their way into other various major works of the period, including Frederick Douglass's *Narrative of the Life of Frederick Douglass* (1845), Herman Melville's *Moby-Dick; or, The Whale* (1851), Hawthorne's *The Blithedale Romance* (1852), Harriet Beecher Stowe's *Uncle Tom's Cabin; or, Life Among the Lowly* (1852), William Wells Brown's *Clotel; or, The President's Daughter* (1853), and Emily Dickinson's poetry. As well, numerous writers published temperance stories, poems, dramas, sketches, periodicals, and other novels. Those years also produced George Cheever's temperance bestseller *Deacon Giles's Distillery* (1835).

Few writers escaped the influence of Washingtonian temperance, which was egalitarian in spirit, imaginative in discourse, and riddled with contradictions and ambiguities that made it a fertile source of literary themes and images. For example, Walt Whitman wrote several temperance short stories: "Wild Frank's Return" (1841), "The Child and the Profligate" (1841), and "Reuben's Last Wish" (1842). Whitman wrote his only full-length novel, *Franklin Evans; or, The Inebriate* (1842), as a commissioned piece for the Washingtonians for seventy-five dollars. Although he later claimed that he wrote this temperance novel while drinking port and that the novel was "damned rot," it arguably stands as Whitman's best-selling work during his lifetime, selling some 20,000 copies.

The novel recounts the misadventures of the eponymous hero, a country bumpkin who moves to the city and becomes acquainted with wine, women, and song. He develops a taste for liquor and slides down the slippery slope toward licentiousness. The low point of Evans's adventures occurs when visiting the Virginia plantation of his friend Bourne. Evans finds himself attracted to a slave, Margaret, and his alcoholic haze lowers his inhibitions: "I could not help being struck with her beauty, and the influence of the liquor from the bottle by my side, by no means contributed to lessen my admiration" (ch. 16). Although Margaret shows a violent side when she attacks a lewd overseer with a farm instrument, Evans nonetheless decides to marry her. Bourne agrees to manumit Margaret, as well as her younger brother Louis, so that Evans would not have a slave for a relative. In his drunken stupor, Evans marries Margaret. Instead of spending the wedding night with his bride, Evans drinks even more with Bourne: "I signalized this crowning act of all my drunken vagaries, that night, by quaffing bottle after bottle with the planter" (ch. 16).

In the morning, Evans wakes up with hatred and disgust for both Margaret and himself: "I repented of my drunken rashness—for the marriage deserved no other name" (ch. 17). The novel reinforces prevailing racist views by seeming to argue that alcohol can confuse white men into marrying black women. According to the racial logic of *Franklin Evans*, sobriety could prevent miscegenation; alcoholic temperance would prevent racial intemperance. Of course, had Evans been sober, the default choice for interracial sexuality would have been rape.

To advance their cause of sobriety, temperance workers emphasized abstention, control, moderation, and restraint. Such emphasis on restriction and self-denial made the movement seem traditional and conservative. In contrast, the contemporaneous movements of suffrage and abolition stood as liberal and progressive because suffrage workers aimed to enfranchise women, and abolitionists tried to grant freedom to those enslaved. Thus, while temperance promoted the retraction of rights, suffrage and abolition championed the expansion of rights. Because antidrink literature dramatized how inebriates lost self-determination, "[T]he drunkard narrative had very real consequences. Americans from all walks of life contributed to a series of slow but massive cultural changes that would culminate, above all, in a generally weakened belief in individual volition and in the fuller participation of women in public life" (Parsons 2003, 4).

Although seeming opposites, the social movements drew energy from one another. The women's movement actually began with temperance workers: Susan B. Anthony, a foundational campaigner for women's suffrage, began her career as an antialcohol advocate and honed her organization skills in temperance meetings. Elizabeth Cady Stanton, another pivotal early suffragist, also worked for the antidrink cause and even published a temperance story, "Henry Neil and His Mother" (1850). Anthony, Stanton, and other suffragettes argued that women needed the ballot in order to defeat the bottle.

Although the female alcoholic remained largely invisible in temperance literature, alcoholism was very much a woman's concern: beholden to her husband, a woman's security depended on having a sober and responsible spouse. Drunken husbands held their wives in bondage in the way the bottle held drinkers in bondage with an addictive allure. Tavern culture coaxed intemperate husbands away from domesticity and emptied their pockets of the money their wives needed to run a home. Numerous temperance stories, many written by women, contrasted the ruin and loneliness of the drunkard's family with the bliss and strength of the temperate man's family.

Carol Mattingly argues that temperance fiction allowed women the socially sanctioned space to explore such sensitive women's issues as a husband's infidelity; physical abuse; victimization; and social, legal, and economic justice. As the moral arbiters of the home, women influenced their husbands and brothers, as well as the next generation of men, through their socio-moral instruction. By penning sentimental and morally righteous fiction, women writers established themselves as important bearers of ethical culture. The popularity of their titles also made them a force to be reckoned with in the literary marketplace. Gough strongly believed in women's power of moral suasion and wrote in his book *Platform Echoes* (1885) that "[m]any and many a man has been saved by waking to the consciousness that some tender-hearted, pure woman felt some sympathy for him and some interest in him, though he was debased and degraded" (ch. 27). Women's power accreted as the image of the dependent drunken man contradicted the basic American value of self-reliance. The dry cause allowed women to enter political life and the public sphere wearing a mantle of domesticity and propriety. Thus, "temperance women performed radical actions but explained them in traditional terms" (Parsons 2003, 10).

Metta Victoria Fuller Victor, for example, understood fiction's power to sway public sentiment. In 1853, she published a popular novel, *The Senator's Son; or, The Maine Law.* Victor writes in the preface, "Thousands are at this moment reeling towards a drunkard's grave. Experience has proved that in no way can the evils of the heart or of society be shown so plainly and effectively as under the garb of fiction. Here, casting aside the dull argument and dry statistics, the subject is mirrored in its natural beauty or deformity, unobscured by the mists of custom or familiarity. . . . Hence, in all reforms this kind of writing will be found most effective." *The Senator's Son* narrates the story of Parke Madison, an innocent boy introduced to wine at age four by his father. One night the elder Madison boasts, "Here, Parke, my boy, is a glass of wine; we are going to drink to the memory of George Washington." Parke drinks and whispers in his father's ear, "I like the wine very much indeed" (ch. 1). Parke's ensuing alcoholism during his adult years causes him to beat his wife, scald his young daughter with boiling water, and bring his mother so much grief that she dies. A ruined drunkard, Parke eventually commits suicide.

Similarly, Elizabeth Stoddard warned women against taking a drunken man as a husband in her novel *The Morgesons* (1862). The novel focuses on the development of the heroine, Cassandra Morgeson. She and her sister, Veronica, fall in love with a pair of alcoholic brothers, Desmond and Ben Somers. Whereas Veronica marries the unrepentant Ben, who dies as a result of his drinking habit, Cassandra marries Desmond only after he has become temperate.

While many nineteenth-century romance novels end with the heroine's future blissfully secured by a happy match, temperance fiction often begins with a poor match and details the downward spiral. Nina Baym thus claims a generic difference between woman's fiction and temperance fiction:

> In striking contrast to woman's fiction, which frequently uses the motif of the drunkard, the temperance novel stresses, as it must, the failure or inadequacy of feminine moral influence to solve this problem. Many women sacrifice themselves and exert influence to no avail. A temperance novel must show woman's power as insufficient because its purpose is to get temperance legislation passed. Were feminine power all that was needed, the "Maine laws" would not be required. (1993, 267)

Henrietta Rose shows drink to be very much a woman's issue but departs from the helpless female stereotype by imagining women having agency to effect social and legal opinion. In her 1858 novel *Nora Wilmot: A Tale of Temperance and Woman's*

Rights, Rose creates wife and mother Mary Price, who bemoans her drunken husband in a letter to Nora: "Oh! if there only was no more drink, no place where men could procure the means of self-destruction, no more temptation!" (ch. 11). Nora takes up her friend's cause by drawing up a petition, signed by more than forty ladies, asking the saloon owner, Amos Tradewell, to stop selling intoxicating beverages. Tradewell refuses, stating, "If men do not govern their appetites, it is their own fault, and not mine. I am not accountable for my customers, and do not wish to be so considered" (ch. 11). Rather than capitulating, the women decide to engage in civil disobedience: they hold a "knitting party" for several days in the saloon. A dozen women at a time occupy the saloon and cheerfully knit away. By introducing women and domestic activity into a heretofore masculine sphere, the saloon is no longer a sacrosanct space. The usual drinkers avoid the saloon and Tradewell loses money. Eventually the ladies convince Tradewell to sign a pledge that he will no longer sell alcohol. Although *Nora Wilmot* seems to show that women's suasion is enough to solve the alcohol problem, the novel nonetheless advocates for passage of antidrink legislation and still shows that the women's best bet is to convince Tradewell to sign a binding agreement.

Just as women gravitated to the antialcohol movement because they were legally bound to drunken husbands, temperance advocates in general drew analogies between drinkers and slaves. Gough claimed in his *Autobiography*, "Such a slave was I to the bottle, that I resorted to it continually, and in vain was every effort which I occasionally made, to conquer the debasing habit" (1870, 95). Alcoholics who quit drinking claimed they had been "redeemed," a word often used to refer to emancipation from slavery. However, many did not want to tether inebriation so closely to slavery; they wanted to make intemperance even more important, claiming that drunkards suffered more than slaves. The colonial triangle trade highlights the link between slavery and intoxication: Europeans sold Africans into Caribbean slavery to harvest sugar, which was then distilled into rum, and bartered for more slaves. Hence, because of the close association between antidrink and antislavery, the temperance movement did not gain a foothold in the slave-holding South.

Black Americans linked temperance to social acceptance, believing that sobriety and self-control could pave the way to economic opportunity. In her study *Philadelphia's Black Elite* (1988), Julie Winch explains:

> Temperance had long been a concern of the [black] elite, not only in Philadelphia but throughout the North. Since community leaders accepted the argument that they could secure civil rights if they proved to whites that they were capable of self-improvement, they advocated temperance in the belief that it would induce whites to look more favorably upon the black community. (148)

The northern white working class resented blacks who worked for lower wages. The black temperance movement in the North, which successfully organized, motivated, and elevated its members, threatened white economic dominance even further. According to Winch, in 1842 the dry movement motivated 1,047 blacks and 120 whites to sign the temperance pledge. Douglass espoused the importance of temperance to African Americans and in his autobiography writes that one way masters showed continued dominance over their slaves was to force them to drink until they became sick. Douglass writes that, during holidays, slave owners "disgust their slaves with freedom, by plunging them into the lowest depths of dissipation. . . . The most of us used to drink [alcohol] down, and the result was just what might be supposed: many of us were led to think that there was little to choose between liberty and slavery. We felt, and very properly too, that we had almost as well be slaves to man as to rum" (ch. 10).

Frances Ellen Watkins Harper published the first short story by an African American woman. Interestingly, this pioneering piece of literature is a temperance tale. Entitled "The Two Offers," the story appeared in 1859 in the *Anglo-African Magazine*, a publication of the African Methodist Episcopal Church that intended to inspire and instruct black readers. "The Two Offers" reflects Harper's lifelong devotion to the antialcohol movement: the plot revolves around Laura Lagrange, a wealthy young woman who receives two offers of marriage. Laura considers both to be good offers, but her poor cousin, Janette Alston, advises her to reject both men because it is better to remain an old maid than to marry someone just because he extends a tantalizing offer of marriage. Laura foolishly marries one of the men without realizing he is a drunkard. His wasteful ways and lack of affection cause Laura's premature death. Janette, on the other hand, remains happily single and devotes her life to literature and serving others. Heavily didactic, "The Two Offers" aims to instruct women on the importance of marrying a sober man and avoids the dark-temperance mode that relishes the horrifying details of inebriation.

"The Two Offers" is also notable because the characters are not marked as either black or white. At a time when African American intellectuals were concerned with abolition or black uplift, the deracialized discourse of this story works to facilitate Harper's dry agenda. A lifelong advocate of temperance, suffrage, and black elevation, Harper was not accepted by white temperance and suffrage organizations. For example, as Hazel Carby notes, Anthony and Stanton opposed voting rights for black women. Because of racism, blacks formed their own separate advocacy groups. For seven years, Harper served as chair of the Colored Chapter of the Philadelphia and Pennsylvania Women's Christian Temperance Union.

By publishing her story in a black church journal but making the race of her characters indistinct, Harper suggests that alcoholism is an equal opportunity disabler. The absence of race in the story implicitly normalizes black aspirations, class status, marital concerns, and options for women. This racial ambiguity elevates the status of the black characters in a progressive way that contrasts with the temperance movement's usual conservative rhetoric: "The dual narrative tensions between liberally resisting racial stereotypes while encouraging a conservative resistance to drink is paralleled in temperance literature's generic tension between its aim to unbind drunkards from the bottle and its method of achieving this aim through the binds of self-limiting reform" (Rosenthal 1997, 156). By keeping the characters' race in doubt, "The Two Offers" smoothes "the narrative tensions between coextensive progressive and conservative discourses by showing both to be a search for middle-class respectability" (Rosenthal 1997, 156). Harper thus participates in black elevation by showing that blacks and whites share the concern of promoting temperance.

To press the urgency of their cause, reform writers needed to bank on the truthfulness of their subject. They needed to convince empowered readers that such social ills did exist and needed immediate attention and action. If reformers were not believable, then their cause would lose traction. Hence reform writers' frequent interest in data, charts, reports, science, religious proclamations, and appeals to verifiable information. Yet although the truth stood as paramount, the novel gained a stronghold as a vehicle for conveying fact. Stowe understood this keenly. In the preface to her best-selling novel *Uncle Tom's Cabin*, Stowe wrote, "The object of these sketches is to awaken sympathy and feeling for the African race, as they exist among us; to show their wrongs and sorrows, under a system so necessarily cruel and unjust as to defeat and do away the good effects of all that can be attempted for them, by their best friends, under it." And in her novel *Dred: A Tale of the Great Dismal Swamp* (1856), Stowe claims that "a good historical romance is generally truer than a dull history; because it gives some sort of conception of the truth; whereas the dull history gives none" (ch. 11). Stowe thus wrote novels for the explicit reason that she knew fiction would be the best revealer of truth. And Stowe deliberately chose sentimental fiction because of the way that genre causes readers to feel for, to identify with, and to weep over disenfranchised characters. The intense ability of sentimental fiction to elicit readers' sympathetic identification and move them toward change blurred the line between truth and tale, so that literary license agitated for real-world improvement.

The temperance movement overlapped with other reform movements of the day, so that to talk about one was to talk about the other. For example, the antiprostitution and the male purity movements similarly blurred the lines between fact and fiction in order to press their causes. While the nineteenth-century use of fiction to convey truth had been the engine of the reform movement, in her critical study *Reforming the World: Social Activism and the Problem of Fiction in Nineteenth-Century America* (2008), Sánchez inverts the relationship between the two and asks:

> [H]ow might nonfiction borrow elements of fiction to paradoxically strengthen its claim to truth? . . . [F]ictional characters and stories are continuously appropriated in the representation of this reality. Thus moral reform writing broaches questions of the most basic genre distinctions, suggesting that reformers might *need* to blur the lines between fiction and nonfiction in order to represent the truth as they saw it. (25–26)

As an example, Sánchez points to William Sanger's *The History of Prostitution: Its Extent, Causes, and Effects Throughout the World* (1858), which was supposed to be a government report assessing the state and condition of prostitution around the world, along with recommendations for the authorities. The table of contents alone is impressive: Sanger starts with biblical and mythological courtesans, then addresses prostitution in Europe, Mexico, Central and South America, and such allegedly "semi-civilized nations" as Persia, Afghanistan, India, Japan, and others. However, the bulk of the study focuses on New York City.

The report derived its authority from its claim to truth about the lives and situations of prostitutes. On this point, Sánchez observes that Sanger's *History*

> blithely ignores distinctions of genre and style as it follows its fallen women from one scene of victimization to another, offering forgiveness, solidarity, sympathy, and asides about heroines and villains. . . . Sanger is not an author by profession. He is a medical doctor engaged in a project best understood as a combination of bureaucratic inquiry, social history, and early sociological research. He is not a novelist. But at times he sounds just like one, primarily because he utilizes sentimental narrative strategies of address, characterization, and theme in composing his governmental report. (2008, 92–93)

According to Sánchez, in Sanger's hands, "Moral reform writing reveals the centrality of sentimental narrative strategies to transforming fallen women's representation in dominant public discourse, and thus, beginning to transform her place in that public" (2008, 93). In other words, just as reform fiction tried to sound as close to the truth as possible, some factual documents borrowed from fiction's purview in order to sound more appealing to readers. Thus, nineteenth-century reform efforts deliberately blurred the lines between imagination and workaday reality to craft improved prospects for society and human behavior.

While lending a fictional touch to his statistics, Sanger also emphasizes the link between prostitution and alcohol; thus the admonitory discourses against promiscuity in sex and drink become one. Sanger writes, "It may be assumed as an almost invariable rule, that courtesans in all countries are in the habit of using alcoholic stimulants to a greater or less degree, in order to maintain that artificial state of excitement which is indispensably necessary to their calling." He cites an English prostitute as saying, "No girls COULD lead the life we do without gin" (1858, ch. 34). Sanger's sketch of the linked trajectories between prostitution and inebriation mirror the downward spiral familiar to temperance fiction, but with a medical veneer:

> The effects of this habit are well known. In the first instance the woman drinks but little, probably just enough to cause a slight artificial excitement, and bring a color to her cheeks. After a time the proportion must be increased as the effect upon the system is diminished, until the finale is a habit of confirmed and

> constant drinking. As a general rule, the horrible consequences then become apparent. The whole frame is relaxed, and every movement of the limbs is a motion of uncertainty; the brain is impaired; the reasoning faculties are destroyed; the powers of the stomach and digestive organs are weakened, and an attack of delirium tremens is the *ultimatum*, usually cured, if cured at all, at the public expense in a hospital or prison. (1858, ch. 34)

In a striking move, Sanger bolsters his report with, of all things, a novel. The paragraph just cited, which leans on the authority of Sanger's medical training and physician's expertise, somehow does not assay the truth sufficiently. Therefore, Sanger writes, "A work of fiction, published some ten years ago, gives the following truthful account of the effects of drunkenness on prostitutes, by one of whom the words are supposed to be used" (1858, ch. 34). Dr. Sanger then substantiates his medical studiousness with a scene from the British writer Elizabeth Gaskell's novel *Mary Barton* (1848):

> "I must have a drink. Such as live like me could not bear life without drink. It's the only thing to keep us from suicide. If we did not drink we could not stand the memory of what we have been, and the thought of what we are, for a day. If I go without food and without shelter, I must have my dram. Oh! what awful nights I have had in prison for want of it." She glared round with terrified eyes as if dreading to see some supernatural creature near her, and then continued: "It is dreadful to see them. There they go round and round my bed the whole night through. My mother carrying my baby, and sister Mary, and all looking at me with their sad stony eyes. Oh! it is terrible. They don't turn back either, but pass behind the head of the bed, and I feel their eyes on me every where. If I creep under the clothes I still see them, and, what is worse, they see me. *I must have drink. I can not pass to-night without a dram. I dare not.*" (qtd. in Sanger 1858, ch. 34)

Sanger recognizes that this scene is fictive, yet he has no qualms about using it to highlight a lived reality: "Although this is an imaginary picture[,] its counterpart can be seen at almost any time in the hospitals under the charge of the Governors of the Alms House on Blackwell's Island, New York City, where large numbers of such cases are constantly treated" (1858, ch. 34). Thus, through Sanger's medical expertise, the temperance movement received a bolster from a government report that relied on imaginative writing.

The male purity movement, like the temperance movement, tried to influence the throngs of unmarried men who gravitated to the cities in search of work. These young men usually lived in public boarding houses far from the watchful eyes of a mother and her domestic influence. Left to their own devices, young men inevitably felt the lure of such big-city attractions, both alcoholic and sexual, as bars, saloons, musical drinking establishments, and whorehouses. Drinking and masturbation became intertwined ills since both were considered nonproductive, wasteful, excessive, and indulgent behaviors. Antiliquor and antionanism campaigns functioned as prohibitionary discourses that warned against the pollution and destruction of masculinity by drunkenness and sexual indulgence. In Whitman's novel, as Vivian Pollak notes, Evans urged "his young male readers to marry as soon as possible to escape the loneliness of boarding house life. The rootlessness of boarding house life is presumed to precipitate alcoholism" (2000, 49–50). Whitman could thus discuss alcoholism and bodily pleasures at the same time by writing about boarding houses.

In his *A Lecture to Young Men on Chastity* (1834), Sylvester Graham discusses numerous topics, among them "self-pollution." He warns against excitement being "augmented in the organs of generation—increasing their influence on the condition and functions of the brain and alimentary canal" (154–55), and that such a "ruinous vice" (157) leads to bodily weakness: "The nerves of the genital organs partake, in common with those of the other organs, of this general debility and diseased excitability, and become exceedingly susceptible of irritation;—sympathizing powerfully with all the disturbances of the system, and especially of the brain and alimentary canal" (45). Most important, because "the sympathy and reciprocity of influence, between the mental and moral faculties and the genital organs become excessive and irresistible" (49), Graham opposes alcohol because it might stimulate young men's desires. He recommends boys "should always subsist on a plain, simple, unstimulating, vegetable and water diet" (156) and avoid "all kinds of stimulating and heating substances" (47), including alcohol. To help suppress what he considered unhealthy erotic urges, Graham developed and advocated the consumption of "Dr. Graham's Honey Biskets," also known as graham crackers. Eating such bland food for moral purposes was supported by John Kellogg, who invented corn flakes.

Drink, even at weddings, could be a dangerous way for a couple to start their married life. Some stories show the danger of toasting the bride on her wedding day, especially because abstinent guests were encouraged to drink "just this once" as a way to honor the bride. To provide wholesome reading options that normalized the dry life, such writers as Lydia Howard Huntley Sigourney in her collection *Water-Drops* (1848) and Louisa May Alcott in her *Silver Pitchers, and Independence* (1876) penned non-alcohol-related temperance novels and collections. These popular reform authors did not restrict their work to tales warning against drunken ravages or shattered homes. Instead, many antialcohol advocates, concerned that their men and boys might someday become drinkers, advocated sobriety and a vision of society in which all members engaged in productive, healthful activity. In his *Young Man's Guide*, William Alcott wrote, "*Water-drinkers* are universally *laughed at*: but, it has always seemed to me, that they are amongst the most welcome of guests. . . . The truth is, they give *no* trouble; they occasion *no anxiety* to please them" (ch. 1, sec. 7). In the first series of her *Letters from New York* (1843), Lydia Maria Child describes a Washingtonian procession in New York City:

"Troops of boys carried little wells and pumps; and on many of the banners were flowing fountains and running brooks. . . . As the bodies of men were becoming weaned from stimulating drinks, so were their souls beginning to approach those pure fountains of living water, which refresh and strengthen, but never intoxicate" (ltr. 2, Aug. 26, 1841).

Drinkers were not welcome in fictional worlds that imagined a range of useful opportunities and occupations available to all citizens. A glance through collections of temperance tales, similar to gift books in the 1840s and 1850s, reveals many positive and moralistic stories that do not treat the theme of alcohol. For example, in the preface to *Water-Drops*, Sigourney asks, "Is abstinence from the intoxicating cup, the *whole* of temperance? Is it wise to pamper all the appetites, and then expect the entire subjection of one? . . . Should not the whole of education teach the danger of self-indulgence, and the excellence of intellectual enjoyments?" Sigourney's collection of stories, poems, and essays demonstrates the value of being temperate in all appetites, as well as the moral benefits to society and the self that result from general sobriety.

Although sensational discourse persisted into the Civil War period and beyond, it lost dominance in the mid-1850s to the legalistic discourse associated with the prohibitionist movement, which produced a series of state laws banning the sale of alcohol, laws that presaged the advent of national prohibition in 1919 with the Eighteenth Amendment to the US Constitution. The prohibitory rhetoric of moral reform movements, with their emphasis on constraint and control, could be seen as opposing fundamental national mythology: the American Revolution was fought for the express purpose of securing individual liberty, and the Declaration of Independence assured freedom of choice.

Temperance reform has, nevertheless, been a major concern of Americans from colonial times to the present. Many modernist writers who wrote during Prohibition (1919–33) similarly addressed issues of drunkenness and attempts at sobriety. Many "Lost Generation" artists moved to Europe to write, paint, and compose because alcohol was widely available abroad, free of the restrictions and social censure that characterized the US Prohibition era. The nineteenth-century Washingtonian movement influenced today's Alcoholics Anonymous recovery narratives: alcoholics gather together to disclose personal accounts of their battles with the bottle to help each other achieve sobriety. Thus, reform movements, particularly regarding alcohol, suggest a link between identity, morals, and storytelling. The power of the pen endures, as writers hope that nudging the right words in the right direction can affect lasting social change.

32

NOVELS OF TRAVEL AND EXPLORATION

GRETCHEN MURPHY

Nineteenth-century Americans voraciously read and wrote travel narratives. Harold Smith's bibliography *American Travelers Abroad* lists over 900 nonfictional travelogues published prior to 1870, a list that does not include the numerous books written about travel to parts of what would become the forty-eight contiguous United States. A few Americans, such as Bayard Taylor and John Lloyd Stephens, achieved fame as professional travel writers, but American tourists, sailors, soldiers, settlers, missionaries, and diplomats also published accounts of their travels. Alongside these travelogues were official narratives of state-sponsored expeditions, usually written from notes at a later date by a professional writer hired as historian, such as Nicholas Biddle's *History of the Expedition under the Command of Captains Lewis and Clark* (1814) or Francis Lister Hawks's account of Commodore Matthew C. Perry's diplomatic voyage to Japan in *Narrative of the Expedition of an American Squadron to the China Seas and Japan* (1856). Professional writers also wrote about early US commercial expeditions, as Washington Irving did in *Astoria; or, Anecdotes of an Enterprise Beyond the Rocky Mountains* (1836), an account of John Jacob Astor's 1811 attempt to create a fur-trade post on the Oregon coast. Combining elements of the guidebook, the ethnography, and the memoir (and sometimes scientific observation, art criticism, history, or political analysis), the travel genre had a broad appeal for Americans exploring their place in the world.

Influential studies of colonial and nationalist discourse such as Mary Louise Pratt's *Imperial Eyes: Travel Writing and Transculturation* (1992) and David Spurr's *The Rhetoric of Empire* (1993) have brought new attention to travel narratives, as have approaches to autobiography that envision the genre as a highly constructed effort to place the self in a social context. In such studies, the line between "fact" and "fiction" is blurred, a division that becomes even murkier when we consider the influence of the travel genre on the American novel. From the earliest examples, novels in the United States have concerned travel. Washington Irving's *The Sketch Book* (1819–20) gains coherence as a composite novel through the satirical conceit that it comprises the musings of Crayon, an American gentleman traveling in Europe. Leonora Sansay's epistolary novel *Secret History; or, The Horrors of St. Domingo* (1808) used the device of Americans traveling through the Caribbean to structure a plot about the Haitian Revolution, as viewed by US women who remain more concerned with rebellion against the tyranny of marriage. Robert Montgomery Bird's historical romance *Calavar; or, The Knight of the Conquest* (1834) begins with a framing device in which a US tourist in Mexico is authorized to translate and publish a story about the Spanish conquest of Mexico because of his sensitivity to the country's sublime landscape and rich potential for national growth. As narrative expressions of postcolonial nationalism, hemispheric identification, or colonial desire, travel fictions often took on the form and ideological concerns of travel narratives.

If travel inspired novelists, novels also influenced how Americans viewed the act of travel and their various destinations. Nathaniel Hawthorne's *Italian Notebooks*, written during his 1858–1859 travels through Italy, provided details for *The Marble Faun* (1860), a romance that depicted major tourist sites so exhaustively that it was carried and read as a guidebook by Americans in Rome. Maria Cummins suggests the circuit of mutual influence linking fiction and travel writing in *El Fureidîs* (1860), a novel about an Englishman's visit to the Holy Land, in which the protagonist Meredith avoids the typical tourist routes glutted with annoying Europeans to find the hidden valley El Fureidîs (The Paradise), where he falls in love with Havilah, the half-Greek daughter of the owner of an American silk factory located there. The Holy Land (Palestine, Syria, and Egypt) was a popular destination for American travelers abroad, famously written about in Mark Twain's *The Innocents Abroad* (1869) and Herman Melville's *Clarel: A Poem and Pilgrimage to the Holy Land* (1876). But prior to those works, dozens of widely read Holy Land travel narratives appeared in print, such as Stephens's *Incidents of Travel in Egypt, Arabia Petraea, and the Holy Land* (1837), and these were the sources consulted by Cummins. As she states in her preface, well-known works such as William M. Thomson's *The Land and the Book; or, Biblical Illustrations Drawn from the Manners and Customs, the Scenes and Scenery of the Holy Land* (1858) guided her through the Holy Land, a place she never visited herself:

> I can but humbly follow [Thomson's and other travel writers'] example, and, as they have guided me through scenes of *actual* romance, pleasure, incident, and danger, invite those who may be so inclined to follow me in my imaginary experiences, trusting that there are some in whom I may be so fortunate as to awaken an interest in a land which has aroused my own enthusiasm, and that, pursuing with what patience they may the route that I have trod, they may come at last to feel, like me, at home in El Fureidîs.

For Cummins, her fictional novel can serve the same purpose as nonfictional travel narratives, to allow readers who have not visited the Holy Land to feel "at home" there, or rather, at home in the imaginary valley of El Fureidîs, a space for fantasizing about Christian tradition and US industrial progress coexisting in paradise.

Cummins draws a clear boundary between genres even while acknowledging their interconnection, but authors and publishers often deliberately blurred the line between fact and fiction by presenting novels as true stories with prefatory framing devices insisting on the truthfulness of even the most obvious fictions. Timothy Flint's *The Life and Adventures of Arthur Clenning* (1828) begins its fictional tale of romance on a desert isle with an assertion that the unquestionably true story was found by the narrator while seeking material similar to Captain James Riley's best-selling account of real-life shipwreck and captivity, *An Authentic Narrative of the Loss of the American Brig Commerce, Wrecked on the Western Coast of Africa, in the Month of August, 1815* (1817). Outrageous novels of sensation and fantasy such as Edgar Allan Poe's *The Narrative of Arthur Gordon Pym, of Nantucket* (1838) or Nathan Cook Meeker's *Life and Adventures of Capt. Jacob D. Armstrong* (1852) hid behind plain descriptive titles and realistic generic elements, such as the form of a daily travel journal or a ship's log listing cargo. Fact versus fiction was for many years the main topic of critical inquiry concerning Melville's *Typee: A Peep at Polynesian Life* (1846), originally published under another prosaic title, "A Narrative of a Four Months' Residence Among the Natives of a Valley of the Marquesas Islands." Melville states in his preface (and insisted to his publishers) that the work is "unvarnished truth" describing events "just as they occurred," but evidence showing that Melville resided among the Typee for only four weeks has encouraged new treatment of the text as a novel. Yet the importance of this classification diminishes when representation is perceived as an opaque lens for viewing the highly charged terrain of global travel and colonial encounter. Even the major British literary works that set generic conventions for US novels of travel (such as Thomas More's *Utopia* [1516], William Shakespeare's *The Tempest* [1611], Daniel Defoe's *Robinson Crusoe* [1719], and Jonathan Swift's *Gulliver's Travels* [1726]) took inspiration from the many stories of exploration and travel that accompanied British colonial expansion, making it difficult to chart literary influence through the murky sea of factual and fictional travels.

This generic interconnection informs the approach to novels of travel and adventure in this chapter, which will highlight the relationship of fictional works to their nonfictional and fictional sources and intertexts. It begins with a discussion of the concept of "adventure" as a genre by using Barbary captivity narratives as a test case, then moves on to describe novels about South Seas and Antarctic exploration inspired by the US Exploring Expedition of 1838–1842, as well as a series of American "Robinsonades," novels patterned after Defoe's *Robinson Crusoe*. Discussion of these works will highlight their use of fantasy and adventure to treat questions about territorial and overseas expansion, industrial capitalism and slavery, American exceptionalism, and US national identity. The conclusion links concerns expressed in fantasies of South Seas and Antarctic exploration to the ambivalence conveyed in fictional and nonfictional narratives about travel to California during the wave of Anglo migration that followed the US-Mexico War.

According to the *Oxford English Dictionary*, the word "adventure" entered into English describing "that which comes to us, or happens without design; [by] chance, hap, fortune, luck," but by 1700 the term had come to imply both intentionally taken risks (including pecuniary risks, a sense still captured by the term "venture") and exciting incidents. Indeed, during the nineteenth century, the term "enterprise" came to be synonymous with adventure as a voluntary and potentially rewarding act of initiative and daring. The growing importance of individual intention in modern conceptions of adventure is highlighted by considering forms of travel writing that are now typically excluded from the genre: slave and captivity narratives. Both genres are largely autobiographical or "as told to" accounts, usually featuring descriptions of movement through a country, including its local customs, and comprising incidents of danger and violence. But neither genre is mentioned in Martin Green's *Seven Types of Adventure Tale: An Etiology of a Major Genre* (1991). (Green does include "the Hunted Man story" as one of his types, but his conception of the subgenre involves only white fugitives who evade captors.) When in 1842 Charles Ellms patched together an anthology of first-person narratives under the title *Robinson Crusoe's Own Book; or, The Voice of Adventure, from the Civilized Man Cut Off from His Fellows, by Force, Accident, or Inclination, and from the Wanderer in Strange Seas and Lands*, he excerpted stories of Barbary captivity, such as *The Narrative of Robert Adams, a Sailor Who Was Wrecked on the Western Coast of Africa, in the Year 1810* (1816), clearly seeing them as real-life adventures. But since then, the relative passivity of these figures makes them hard to reconcile with a genre that likens adventure to enterprise. Royall Tyler's novel *The Algerine Captive; or, The Life and Adventures of Doctor Updike Underhill* (1797) takes the form of a picaresque throughout the first volume, describing a young man's travels through the United States as he attempts to make his fortune as a schoolteacher and doctor, observing local customs along the way. However, when he goes to sea and ends up being taken captive by Algerian pirates, his "adventures" begin to represent him as a victim of circumstance whose loss of self-determination, he anticipates, might lead "my dear countrymen [to] censure my want of due spirit" (v. 2, ch. 2). My goal here is not to correct this exclusion, especially since slave and captivity narratives are treated elsewhere in this volume (chapters 1, 8, and 25), but to point out an important linkage between the genre of adventure and the rise of the liberal subject of industrial capitalism and modernity—a subject who is viewed as having responsibility for his self-possession, who is more often white than black, free than enslaved, male than female, and who thus has all these freedoms to venture—to put at risk—in the adventurous enterprise. This discussion excludes the historical romance, the American frontier romance, and the US-Mexico War melodrama, both because these are discussed elsewhere in this volume and because those fictions often portray complex forms of social conflict (such as war), while "adventure" has come to imply more individualist endeavors, as indicated by Ellms's subtitle, "*the Civilized Man Cut Off from His Fellows.*"

This focus leads me to begin with maritime narratives that highlight both the dangers and potential gains of capitalist enterprises, since, as Melville wrote in the preface to *Typee*, "sailors are the only class of men who now-a-days see anything like stirring adventure." A major inspiration for sea-going novels was the US Exploring Expedition, which departed in 1838 to chart the waters of the South Seas and to surpass the *ne plus ultra* set by British Captain James Cook in the Antarctic waters. Led by Charles Wilkes (and known to history as the Wilkes Expedition), it was the first federally sponsored naval mission for the purpose of exploration, and thus a source of both nationalist pride and debate. Many of the era's major writers commented on the Wilkes Expedition: Henry David Thoreau took a swipe at its extravagant expense and effort in *Walden; or, Life in the Woods* (1854); Poe's proleptic *The Narrative of Arthur Gordon Pym* ends with a facetious note suggesting that the Exploring Expedition might confirm the outrageous phenomena the novel describes in the Antarctic Sea; Hawthorne, still on the lookout for a government sinecure, sought a position on board as the Expedition's naval historian. Wilkes himself decided to compile the massive, five-volume *Narrative of the United States Exploring Expedition* (1845), which provided descriptions of the geography and ethnology of South America, the South Pacific islands, Australia, Hawaii, and the western coast of North America, as well as evidence of the Antarctic landmass whose existence Wilkes confirmed. Once it was published, the *Narrative* served as an authoritative source for writers on the South Seas, including Melville, who drew upon Wilkes's *Narrative* in *Typee* and cited it in his next novel, *Omoo: A Narrative of Adventures in the South Seas* (1847).

Fiction inspired by the Wilkes Expedition ranges in tone from satire to sensation to didactic moralism, but a common theme arises from oceanic exploration's potential to disrupt key notions of nineteenth-century national identity. One such notion was the idea of a clean break from history, a fresh start in the new world, reinvigorated by the ever-receding frontier. For example, in the essay "The Great Nation of Futurity" (1839) from the *Democratic Review*, John L. O'Sullivan proclaims: "We have no interest in the scenes of antiquity, only as lessons of avoidance of nearly all their examples. The expansive future is our arena, and for our history. We are entering on its untrodden space, with the truths of God in our minds, beneficent objects in our hearts, and with a clear conscience unsullied by the past" (427). O'Sullivan's periodical, which would later popularize the concept of manifest destiny, here renders the future as an "untrodden" territory to be colonized, evincing a brand of nationalism that begs the question of what would and would not be new about America. For some agrarian philosophers, including Thomas Jefferson, the United States had broken not only with European monarchy but also with industrial capitalism and all its inequalities. According to this view, the nation should shift its economic interests to western lands and to independent subsistence farming, thus moving away from the sea. But the motives behind the Wilkes Expedition deliberately contested agrarianism and in doing so provoked uncertainty about US national identity and American exceptionalism.

One of the expedition's most vocal supporters was Jeremiah N. Reynolds, whose *Address on the Subject of a Surveying and Exploring Expedition to the Pacific Ocean and South Seas* (1836) was delivered before Congress and subsequently published in a widely reviewed pamphlet. Attacking what he calls "the sylvan nursery philosophy" of American development, Reynolds criticizes those political economists who think that Americans should seek seclusion on the frontier as farmers and promotes instead commercial, military, and scientific ambition (14). His *Address* pits a mobile will-to-progress against a preindustrial submission to European imperial superiority, leaving no room for Edenic isolation in an American garden. "[W]ith an impetuous rush," he claims, Americans "trod this Arcadian theory underfoot":

> [N]either Fauns nor Dryads can protect the grove when it is wanted for the saw or axe. . . . If any there be who mourn over these changes, we are not among them. The great branches of our national industry will constantly go on, destroying and recombining the elements of productiveness, till every atom is made to bear its greatest amount of value, and the wildest speculations of the theorist are more than equalled by the reality. (14–15)

The conflict here is not only between Democrat and Federalist, land and sea, but between an imagined escape on the frontier and the ways in which sea travel could complicate that vision. In fictional narratives of voyages, Americans sail around the globe seeking trade routes, island possessions, and returns on maritime investments; their heroes consort and compete with European traders and whalers, reckoning with the forces of capitalism that have propelled them to the ends of the earth. As meditations on US identity, they offer not just more distant, watery frontiers, but also commentaries on westward expansion and American exceptionalism that raise (and sometimes ward off) the suggestion that colonizing the West actually extended, not evaded, European circuits of trade. Implying that California was not a terminus but a way station to the China trade, they invoked not just expansive optimism but doubtful ambivalence. If Reynolds's boyhood stories of voyages and travels inspired him to see historical continuity between westward and overseas expansion, this fictional genre produced by US writers in the early nineteenth century expressed both enthusiasm and skepticism for visions of commercial, military, and scientific competition with European powers.

The anonymously authored novel *Symzonia: A Voyage of Discovery* (1820) describes a journey to the Antarctic inspired by Reynolds's partner in promoting federally funded exploration, John Cleves Symmes. Symmes began petitioning Congress in 1818, suggesting that the South Pole offered not only an abundant land source with a temperate climate, but also contained a passageway into the inhabitable interior of the earth. (Reynolds initially helped Symmes with his widely publicized campaign, but after Symmes's death in 1829, Reynolds stressed less outlandish arguments for naval exploration.) *Symzonia* satirizes the imperial motivation behind Symmes's bizarre theory of holes in the poles. The novel describes Captain Adam Seaborn's voyage to an internal continent, which he names in Symmes's honor, and which appears to be a utopia of agrarian simplicity. Symzonians eat simple foods raised by each household, trade among themselves only for convenience, never pursue any kind of personal profit, and keep their national borders closed to commerce from the outside. They maintain this local economy by choice and in spite of their advanced technological knowledge, eschewing their neighbors the Belzubians who are unhealthily addicted to trade. Seaborn initially associates the Symzonians with his own country and the Belzubians with Great Britain, but eventually the Symzonians learn the falsity of this claim and cast him out of their utopia. Indeed, Seaborn's very presence belies his claim to agrarian simplicity. He begins his narrative by explaining that his adventure is motivated by enterprise and a search for wealth and novelty, and early scenes parody his taste for intemperate expansion.

This unfortunate difference between Symzonia and the United States is curiously underscored by their people's racial characterizations. The Symzonians are exceedingly white, so when Seaborn rolls up his sleeve to show a man portions of his skin not exposed to the sun, he admits that "I was not a white man, compared with him" (ch. 7). Symzonian whiteness is a product of their isolated and abstemious economy, and Seaborn's comparative darkness results from his culture's debasing greed, a symbolic version of the era's rhetorical condemnation of "wage slavery" and new forms of consumption curtailing the freedom of white men. Were the United States more perfectly isolated, Americans might be able to maintain such a singular whiteness in their Edenic New World, but because of the nation's expansion by sea, they—like Seaborn—cannot.

In *The Narrative of Arthur Gordon Pym*, Poe sought in anticipation to sensationalize rather than satirize the Wilkes Expedition, postulating another fantastic land near the South Pole. After endorsing the general idea of South Seas exploration in an August 1836 review, Poe enthusiastically supported Reynolds's arguments for such an expedition in the January 1837 *Southern Literary Messenger*, appealing to the national glory and commercial benefits associated with planting the flag "on the axis of the earth itself!" (72). But the novel's gruesome violence belies these rewards, taking the southern latitudes instead as a space to explore irrational states of mind. Indeed, Pym is attracted to scenes of "adventure" that threaten his self-possession as a rational liberal subject. He begins his journey with "melancholy" fantasies "of shipwreck and famine; of death or captivity among barbarian hordes; of a lifetime dragged out in sorrow and tears, upon some gray and desolate rock, in an ocean unapproachable and unknown" (ch. 2). Even when misfortune befalls him on his journey—in the form of near suffocation in a ship's hold, a violent mutiny, shipwreck, and turning to cannibalism to survive being lost at sea—Pym has no second thoughts. Just pages after being rescued from a drifting boat where he was driven to eat a fellow survivor and then toss overboard the rotting body of his childhood friend, reduced to a "mass of putrefaction," Pym again experiences a blind desire for adventure, this time to sail past Captain Cook's *ne plus ultra* to the Antarctic (ch. 13). He disparages the British captain who rescues him for lacking the enterprise to disregard profit and safety in the single-minded push toward exploration, but the seemingly nationalist distinction this sets between British commercialism and American knowledge-seeking is utterly undermined by Pym's character flaws and his inability to interpret clues about the mystery he faces in the southern latitudes. Despite the novel's racist portrayals of treacherous, ignorant savages and Poe's apparently sincere support for Reynolds, *The Narrative of Arthur Gordon Pym* is highly ambivalent about the power of rationality as the basis for an imperial project. Pym's failure as a rational subject empowered to uncover truth prevents any simple conclusions about colonial progress by land or sea. If the sea in Poe's novel is a space for racialized violence, depravity, and irrational states of mind, the American frontier accompanies it in the form of Dirk Peters, Pym's Upsaroka Indian sidekick, and his interest in Biddle's *History* of the Lewis and Clark Expedition, which he reads while stowed away in the ship's hold on the way to his own adventures.

James Fenimore Cooper's *The Sea Lions; or, The Lost Sealers* (1849) also takes inspiration from the Wilkes Expedition but draws a clearer moral from the topic of Antarctic exploration. In this novel, two sealing ships barely survive being stranded on a frozen island in the high southern latitudes over the harsh winter. The ships pass Cook's *ne plus ultra* in order to exploit a particularly rich sealing island, a dangerous scheme financed by the miserly Deacon Pratt of Long Island and led by Roswell Gardiner, the hopeful fiancé of the Deacon's niece Mary. Awaiting his return, the pious Mary asks the deacon, in a line that echoes *Symzonia*'s appeal to subsistence agriculture, "Ah! why cannot men be content with the blessings that Providence places within our immediate reach, that they must make distant voyages to accumulate others!" (v. 2, ch. 5). The deacon readily answers that Mary does like her tea, sugar, and silks, but the novel ultimately supports her when, after Roswell's return from the Antarctic, the young couple moves "to the great west," where he works as a miller (v. 2, ch. 15). Set in 1820, the story ends with an indignant regret that the Long Island township they left behind, Oyster Pond, has since that time gained a railroad terminus and changed its name to "Orient," a suggestion that only by heading west can Americans evade the expanding China trade. Cooper's frontier leads to agrarian isolation, not to Pacific trade.

Of course, trade was one of the practical goals behind the US Exploring Expedition. The South Pacific was seen to offer both island way stations on the route to Asia and sources of commodities like sandalwood for the China market. Behind even the dreamy nationalism of Antarctic exploration was the land's proximity to the dangerous passage around Cape Horn regularly braved by US traders entering the Pacific. Trade, not exploration, is the motivation behind the voyage taken in Meeker's Swiftian satire *Life and Adventures of Capt. Jacob D. Armstrong*, the farcical story of a stern Presbyterian sea captain shipwrecked on the island of Nede, where he discovers a peaceful and contented society (compared at several points to that of the Ancient Peruvians) that he seeks to transform by introducing all the unnecessary and detrimental aspects of industrial capitalism and modernity. (Meeker was a *New York Tribune* newspaper man who would later, along with Horace Greeley, found a utopian colony in Colorado.) The novel amusingly sets Armstrong against another castaway, Horatio Young. This radical freethinker manages to organize a revolutionary group called the "Communitists" and depose Armstrong after the captain introduces factories, banks, insurance companies, fashion, a completely unnecessary railroad, and an unwieldy representative government replete with ministers and lawyers. The islanders, called Nedeans, are a neuter gendered, asexually reproducing amphibious species with human form. After living with Armstrong's improvements for a time, they begin to transform spontaneously into anatomical men and women, a bizarre symbol perhaps of the notion that civilization promotes sexual divergence or of American utopianism's challenge to gender roles.

Despite the sharp anticolonialism in Meeker's obvious satire of "civilized" pretentions to cultural superiority, his portrayal of Nedeans as passive and easily manipulated (the revolution that liberates them from Armstrong is led by other castaways, not the Nedeans themselves) reinforces the absence of political agency ascribed to real South Sea islanders and Native Americans alike. The contradiction takes on sad significance in light of what Meeker is primarily known for in American history, which is not his farcical novel or his utopian commune, but the violence that erupted from his poor decision-making during his subsequent appointment as the Indian Bureau Agent at the White River Ute Indian Reservation. In 1879, Meeker and eleven others were killed in what became known as the "Meeker Massacre," a conflict that escalated from his narrowly conceived attempts to transform the Utes through his ideas of religious and agricultural reform. Because he could not view the Utes (or the Nedeans) as political agents, Meeker replicated Armstrong's mistakes. In fact, this sort of mixed message is common throughout these works of fiction. Cooper's moralistic *Sea Lions* highlights the appeal of enterprise and Christian introspection that occurs on the voyage of discovery, while still criticizing its threatening mercantile motivations. *Symzonia* celebrates the secluded utopia but also predicts its demise due to the unstoppable forces of trade and colonization. And *Pym*'s Tsalalian treachery seems to support the opinion that Poe expressed in his review of Reynolds, namely that the South Sea islanders' "murderous hostility" required intimidation by the United States government (1837, 68). None of these works can be called simply "anti-imperialist." Rather, they express uncertainties about the mode, direction, motivation, and results of expansion.

A similar ambivalence can be found in Melville's *Typee*, which takes place immediately after France claimed possession of the Marquesas Islands in 1842 and includes numerous asides criticizing the corruption of savage simplicity by European missionaries and traders. This criticism aims at European conquest, but references to an earlier US occupation of the islands (in 1813 by Captain David Porter) and the novel's criticism of the wants and cares associated with so-called civilized life implicate the United States in the spread of European colonialism. This primitivist vision of an exotic people who are simple, childlike, and natural reflected and challenged discourses on civilization, portraying the South Pacific as a space for pleasure removed from parochial notions of sin and propriety, an appeal that Charles Warren Stoddard makes more strongly through the homoeroticism of his Tahitian travel sketches in *South-Sea Idyls* (1873). Yet, the US sailor Tommo's ultimate determination to escape the valley of the Typee complicates his Rousseauian celebration of their idyllic way of life. He comes to fear being engulfed by the tribe, by either being marked as one of their own with facial tattoos or, more horribly, being literally ingested in a cannibal ritual. If primitive simplicity is idealized, it is also associated with a limited scope that Tommo seeks to escape by returning to the hierarchies and commercial investments of life aboard a whaler. Whether Tommo is leaving behind libidinal temptation, agrarian isolation, or the confining bonds of community, his escape reaffirms his identification with civilized life.

Read as autobiographical narratives, *Typee* and its sequel *Omoo* resemble in some aspects Richard Henry Dana's *Two Years Before the Mast* (1840), depicting the author's voyage around Cape Horn to the California coastline. Dana, like Melville, left a genteel upbringing to labor temporarily as a sailor. Before becoming an influential lawyer, Dana left Harvard to sail in 1834 on a ship engaged in the California hide and tallow trade for Bryant, Sturgis, and Co. Unlike Irving in *A Tour on the Prairies* (1835) and Francis Parkman in *The Oregon Trail* (1849), however, Dana and Melville did not travel as gentlemen led by hired guides or military escorts, but as common sailors whose uncommon education allowed them to speak to bourgeois readers as equals and share with readers a glimpse of not only Pacific others (in Dana, Californios and Hawaiians working on the California coast) but also the white working class. Both *Omoo* and *Two Years Before the Mast* criticized strenuously the condition of sailors on long voyages facing mismanagement and tyrannical abuse by captains. Dana describes his initial satisfaction that he, a landlubber and gentleman's son, can learn the ways of the sea, but his pleasure dissolves when he recounts both the captain's violent misuse of authority and the fear that the dwindling supply of furs on the California coast will extend his voyage more than the agreed upon two years. He fears this extension of service will put him far behind in his studies and that laboring with coarse sailors and Californios for so long will ruin his mind and morals. This fear belies the notion that the sea could provide a frontier for nurturing independence. Instead, the ship undermines white male labor even more explicitly than metaphorical wage slavery in industrial capitalism, as Dana illustrates in a scene where the captain mercilessly flogs an innocent sailor, shouting, "[Y]ou've got a driver over you! Yes, a *slave-driver—a negro-driver!* I'll see who'll tell me he isn't a negro slave!" (ch. 15). But in his final reflections on what could help American sailors, Dana here stops short of calling for legal measures addressing workers' rights (as he had in his *Seaman's Friend* [1838]). Rather than questioning the corporate interests that motivate the voyage, Dana instead sees American business enterprise as exactly what California needs. Idle and shiftless, Spanish Californios appear to Dana to be wasting a potentially productive land.

A crucial influence on American adventure narratives was Defoe's *Robinson Crusoe.* Even Bayard Taylor, accompanying gold rush forty-niners to California in *Eldorado; or, Adventures in the Path of Empire* (1850), compared their situation to Crusoe's. Hearing the stories of more experienced emigrants, Taylor facetiously comments that their time in California "sounded more marvellous than anything I had heard or read since my boyish acquaintance with Robinson Crusoe, Captain Cook and John Ledyard" (v. 1, ch. 5). The unlikely parallel of California—already colonized for 300 years by the Spanish—with Crusoe's desert island makes sense only insofar as the story had come to stand for more than survival after a shipwreck. Reprinted in the United States in dozens of juvenile and adult editions, *Robinson Crusoe* was enormously popular, perhaps aided by Rousseau's recommendation that the book, itself a lesson in experiential education, be the only one given to young pupils. Accordingly, Defoe's novel frequently functions within the diegetic frame of adventure fiction as a pedagogical influence on the genre's enterprising heroes. The eponymous New England protagonist of Flint's *Francis Berrian; or, The Mexican Patriot* (1826) confesses that as a young man, he "became extravagantly fond of books of voyages and travels. . . . I fancied myself on a floating island, and wafted into the depths of unknown oceans. I delighted in the position of Robinson Crusoe and his Friday in their lonely isle" (v. 1, ch. 1). While his subsequent adventures (rescuing a Spanish maiden first from the Comanches and then from tyrannical nobles and priests in the Mexican War of Independence) have as little to do with shipwrecks and islands as do Taylor's Californian travels, Crusoe's narrative represents in both texts a blending of exciting incident with capitalist enterprise, moral self-improvement, and colonial mastery.

And yet, as cited and adapted as a generic template in US fiction of the early nineteenth century, *Robinson Crusoe* provides not a confident allegory of colonial accomplishment, but a dialogic field for nineteenth-century debates about expansion. Jay Fliegelman has argued that American abridgements of the novel highlighted the problem of rebellion from patriarchal authority in the Revolutionary era, but nineteenth-century adaptations of the story seem less caught up in rebellion from paternal authority and more concerned with distinguishing US expansion. Disobedience to a father is seldom an issue in the hero's decision to leave home. Instead, these rural youths are more often prompted to depart by economic factors, seeking not an escape from overbearing parental authority but an equivocal space for rearticulating class boundaries and evading the flaws of modern capitalism and democracy—a place that improves upon the mythic western frontier's fantasy of virgin land. But if the islands they find are spaces for redressing the contradiction of US expansion on even more fantastically imagined natural grounds, they are in some versions also fragile utopias that recall the continuing disappearance of "unsettled" land in the United States and the extensive reach of Euro-American colonization and trade.

Flint's *The Life and Adventures of Arthur Clenning* treats the island on which his castaways find themselves as a pastoral paradise for luxuriating in some of the most romantic myths of frontier life. Flint, known primarily as a western writer, began his writing career with the memoir, *Recollections of the Last Ten Years in the Valley of the Mississippi* (1826), about his years as a missionary in the Mississippi River Valley. He had no sense of the South Seas setting he employed in *Arthur Clenning* (the island's kangaroos, which the heroes easily domesticate, wail plaintively through the night), but the lack of geographical realism matters little when the island stands as a symbolic Eden that his heroes, once they find their way back to the United States via Sydney and London, can only recreate on the Indiana frontier. A New York farmer's son who has gone to sea, Clenning finds himself shipwrecked with Augusta Wellman, the haughty and spoiled daughter of an aristocratic British landowner. At first, Arthur, who takes a sort of temperance pledge to remain humble, respectable, and restrained around Augusta, tries to respect her superior class status and sexual purity, but the two eventually declare themselves married, inspired by the island's beauty to see themselves as "Adam and Eve" (ch. 3). The leveling of class status is a frequent theme in such domestic frontier narratives as Caroline Kirkland's *A New Home—Who'll Follow?; or, Glimpses of Western Life* (1839), but *Arthur Clenning* draws also on the sentimental tradition of restrained respectability leading to self-improvement and class mobility. For all the novel's appeals to nature, the couple's single-minded pursuit of Victorian ideals of leisure and aesthetics (they spend most of their time domesticating animals as pets, enjoying views, and decorating their grotto) reads less as a romantic retreat into noble savagery than a proving ground for the bourgeois sensibilities of the rural hero and aristocratic heroine. Indeed, their attempt to recreate their island paradise on the frontier in Indiana seems mainly a quest for truly genteel living, away from urban crowds and competition. If class is thus equivocally leveled on Flint's frontier, racial divisions remain firm. The couple rescues from cannibals a native woman (as a nod to Crusoe's incidentally named Friday, they name her Rescue), who voluntarily becomes their lifelong servant, allowing Augusta to resume only appropriately bourgeois female activities. Rescue accompanies the family to Indiana, where her impending marriage to a Pottawatomie chief underscores the moral equivalence of the island pastoral and the frontier retreat from modernity.

Published before the peaking of interest in Pacific trade that accompanied the US-Mexico War, the annexation of the California and Oregon territories, and the Wilkes Expedition, *Arthur Clenning* treats its South Sea island as a symbol for the potential of the American frontier, which in Flint's depiction registers as remarkably free of conflict. For instance, once Rescue is rescued, the invading cannibals are easily scared away. But in the 1840s and 1850s, novels with similar plots cast their islands not merely as metaphoric frontiers but also as potentially lucrative colonies and outposts for Pacific trade. In Cooper's *The Crater; or, Vulcan's Peak* (1847), the hero, Mark Woolston, enjoys none of the pastoral leisure of Flint's castaways. Instead, he works tirelessly to make his South Sea island productive, and he is so satisfied with the fruits of his labor that after being rescued he chooses to remain there, inviting his wife and eventually hundreds of other colonists (calling themselves "Craterinos") to create a more perfect society with its own government. They enter into the sandalwood trade with China and make a fortune, but eventually their utopia begins to crumble under the weight of its own progress, as Cooper turns the colony's fate into a commentary on Jacksonian democracy. Like *Symzonia*'s conflict between the ideal of isolated American origins and the corrupting forces of American modernity, *The Crater* warns what could happen when a society grows too large and complex for simple, temperate forms of production and economy.

This ambivalence toward colonization resembles Cooper's Leather-Stocking Tales, which both champion and mourn the process of European settlement. But in contrast to the frontier romance, the castaway story typically emphasizes the emptiness and availability of the island territory. Rather than a scene of violence and threatened racial mixture to be ordered, as in *The Last of the Mohicans: A Narrative of 1757* (1826), the desert islands in these American Robinson Crusoe tales are initially empty. If natives appear at all, they are represented as belated intruders into the virgin land that the colonizer has already improved through his labor. Irving describes the Mississippi River Valley in *A Tour on the Prairies* as filled with "half-breeds, creoles, [and] negroes of every hue . . . that keep about the frontiers, between civilized and savage life" (ch. 3). Cooper's crater, however, is not only totally uninhabited, but also a reef of bare rock with neither water nor vegetation to support life. In a literal enactment of the Lockean idea that a man's improvements justify his title to a piece of land, Mark composts soil from seaweed, sand, and guano, using his reason and the tools he salvages from his wreck to turn the inhospitable rock into a nourishing garden. Later, an underwater earthquake naturally expands his fully entitled territory, raising from the ocean floor a series of island "possessions," as his wife calls them, free from any other claim (v. 1, ch. 14). When a tribe of South Sea islanders "discovers" the Crater, the Craterinos have to use their ingenuity and diplomatic skill to keep their island's riches to themselves, just as they hide from passing European ships to ward off colonizing powers.

A similar erasure of conflict, mixture, and native presence from the colonial scene occurs in George Payson's *The New Age of Gold; or, The Life and Adventures of Robert Dexter Romaine* (1856). Robert is a New England youth who, like Clenning, ships out to make his fortune but is ultimately cast away on a South Sea island with a rich merchant's daughter, Alice. Robert at several points reports seeing signs of natives. Each time the sight instills in him the same dread that the sight of a footprint instills in Crusoe, but each time he finds he is mistaken, recognizing instead in one case an orangutan or in another a cluster of large gourds that he originally mistook for "negro huts" (ch. 6). In fact, after Robert defeats another shipwrecked sailor's claim of ownership, he asserts that "the island was as exclusively our own as if it had been surrounded by a wall a hundred miles in height" (ch. 7). This total seclusion allows the hero to engage in a pastoral fantasy similar to the one described by Flint in *Arthur Clenning*, but like Cooper, Payson emphasizes the social weaknesses that cast his characters out of their Eden. Robert and Alice declare themselves married and raise children, but Robert's discovery of gold on the island transforms domestic contentment into avarice and ambition. Following this plot development, the book's title, *The New Age of Gold*, takes on a dual meaning. While at first Robert and his family "fleet the time carelessly, as they did in the golden age" (ch. 29), the final chapters comment on how commercial ambition and the California gold rush are changing the frontier from an imagined agrarian retreat to a restless, self-destructive scene of capitalist desire. This parallel is made explicit when Robert returns to the United States in 1854 via San Francisco, a city he has never heard of because he has been absent from the United States for fifteen years, to find his story of quick riches a common one among the miners. Stifled by civilization, Alice and the children pine for their lost paradise, so following their deaths, Robert forsakes his fortune and sets sail to rediscover his island. Payson darkens the optimism of Flint by imagining a secluded paradise that contrasts with the realities of the American frontier, which through the annexation of California becomes associated not with agrarian simplicity but restless greed and corrupting wealth. Unlike Flint's blissful Indiana, California cannot re-create the Edenic conditions of the island before the fall. The idea echoes Cooper insofar as the story describes two "modes" of westernization: first, the imagined pastoral retreat of agrarianism and total isolation in nature; and second, the loss of that ideal due to an expansion of systems of commercial exchange.

Many accounts of the gold rush era echoed Payson's theme of temptation and ruin. His novel, *Golden Dreams and Leaden Realities* (1853), more directly described greed and disappointment in the California gold fields, as did William Shaw's travel narrative, *Golden Dreams and Waking Realities* (1851). Mrs. D. B. Bates, a merchant's wife who told her story of travel in *Incidents on Land and Water; or, Four Years on the Pacific Coast* (1857), described the hopeful argonauts she met in terms that could apply to Payson's shipwrecked characters in *The Golden Age*: "Alas! Many of the number never reached the goal they so ardently desired, and for which they had sacrificed their own happiness, and that of those dearer to them than aught else except gold, the yellow dust of temptation" (ch. 10). Her words also applied to herself. Forced to move to California in 1850 because of her husband's business ventures, Bates endured a series of mishaps en route worthy of Arthur

Gordon Pym: the burning of three successive ships, storms, and a shipwreck off the South American coast. She had little of the enthusiasm for California that Eliza Farnham expressed in another domestic travelogue, *California, In-Doors and Out* (1856). Farnham, author of the earlier *Life in Prairie Land* (1846) about her stay on the Illinois frontier in the 1830s, maintained that American women would properly domesticate the new territories, and she even sought to charter a benevolent mission in which white women would lend their civilizing presence by simply moving to California. In the domestic serenity that Bates longed for and Farnham hoped to transplant, women enjoy the opposite of adventurous risk-taking.

California came to symbolize American expansion gone awry for several reasons: as land taken from Mexico, it suggested a new form of national conquest beyond the defeat of "uncivilized" Native American tribes; it stoked fantasies of trans-Pacific trade; and the discovery of gold in 1848 complicated the idea that the frontier would foster natural morality and independence. In *Eldorado*, Bayard Taylor expressed reservations about drunkenness, gambling, and changing social norms among the miners, as "weather-beaten tars, wiry, delving Irishman, and stalwart foresters from the wilds of Missouri" gratified impulses with rapidly gained fortunes (v. 2, ch. 1). In general, however, he optimistically viewed California as a place for the leveling of social class through a new respectability for labor (especially in light of California's abrupt entrance into the union in 1850 as a free state, where slaves would never work side by side with whites in the minefields). More ambivalence about reconciling travel to California with national narratives of frontier life can be found in Fanny Foley's fictional *Romance of the Ocean: A Narrative of the Voyage of the Wildfire to California* (1850), a light comedy told in the briskly modern voice of an army officer's daughter writing in her travel diary. The events of the voyage are less adventure than marriage plot. The narrator embarks as a mischievous tomboy, but ends in California with plans to marry an earnest young minister. Despite travel being the scene of the narrator's maturation, *Romance of the Ocean* also portrays California as the destination of mistaken impulses for its working-class characters, similar to the California subplot of Fanny Fern's *Ruth Hall* (1855), in which Ruth's lazy, henpecked neighbor, Mr. Skiddy, abandons his family to search for gold.

While Taylor fantasized about California as a setting for a new Crusoe's colonizing adventures, some fiction of the era acknowledged the perspective of Mexicans. John Rollin Ridge's *The Life and Adventures of Joaquín Murieta, the Celebrated California Bandit* (1854) is notable for its sympathetic portrayal of Mexicans being displaced and cheated by Anglo settlers, and also for its focus on violence and revenge rather than romance and rescue, the latter being characteristic of the conventional marriage plots between US soldiers and Mexican daughters found in much US-Mexico War literature. Ridge tells what he presents as the true story of a famed Mexican bandit driven by Anglo injustice to kill and steal from white miners. A real bandit (or bandits) who called himself Joaquín did exist, but whether Ridge's tale is mostly fictional, with elements drawn from Robin Hood and popular melodramas, or mostly biographical, with elements drawn from local historical sources, remains a controversy, especially because the legend of Joaquín as a symbol of Chicano rebellion lives on through numerous retellings in fiction, poetry, film, and song. Whether Ridge extensively researched or largely invented the events of Murieta's life, he invested it with meanings drawn from his own personal history as the son of a Cherokee tribal leader who signed the treaty leading to the Trail of Tears and removal to western reservation land. Ridge's family was caught up in the intertribal violence that stemmed from the decision. Both his grandfather and his cousin, the Cherokee writer Elias Boudinot, were murdered by factions blaming them for the tribe's loss of land, and before heading west to California, Ridge himself killed a man suspected of supporting his grandfather's murderer. This intertribal violence was prompted by Ridge's resentment toward the injustice of the United States in using law to displace his people, which he saw as paralleling his hero's motivation to fight the Anglos taking away his rights in California. Interestingly, *Joaquín Murieta* follows not Ellms's formula for adventure, so notable in Anglo representations of frontier and sea adventure, the *Civilized Man Cut Off from His Fellows, by Force, Accident, or Inclination, and . . . the Wanderer in Strange Seas and Lands,* but a story of revenge and group-identity formation. Joaquín attracts a group of male and female Californio outlaws who together use violence to rectify an unjust political system.

Both land and sea exploration nourished an emerging sense of American empire, but as suggested here, novels about overseas exploration have tended to raise the specter of commercial expansion and European competition, highlighting rather than concealing the problem of an ever-disappearing frontier. Stories of fanciful desert islands brought home the conflicts raised by territorial expansion, making California seem like both a space to relive the fantasy of Robinson Crusoe and a problematic new possession where the fantasy of American exceptionalism threatens to slip away. The genres of travel and adventure allowed Americans to locate themselves globally, to stake claims about the difference of the New World from the Old, and to explore the possibilities of cultural, political, or economic expansion. More than fictive fantasies of expansion and influence, these works allowed US Americans to express doubt and uncertainty about the growth of their own capitalist democracy.

33

THE CITY MYSTERY NOVEL

SCOTT PEEPLES

In February 1842, Charles Dickens, already famous for his evocations of London's urban squalor, visited New York's Five Points district during his tour of the United States; he published his description of the seedy, overcrowded neighborhood in *American Notes for General Circulation* (1842):

> What place is this, to which the squalid street conducts us? A kind of square of leprous houses, some of which are attainable only by crazy wooden stairs without. What lies beyond this tottering flight of steps, that creak beneath our tread?—a miserable room, lighted by one dim candle, and destitute of all comfort, save that which may be hidden in a wretched bed. (ch. 6)

Dickens conveys a sense of mystery and danger as he moves through the Five Points—"What place is this," "what lies beyond," what source of comfort is hidden in the bed?—and, as Hans Bergmann observes, "Through him we will learn how we might make meaning of what seems at first not to fit into our explanatory schemes at all" (1995, 119). It would be only a slight exaggeration to say that Dickens put the Five Points district and the urban "underworld" it represented on the map; Almack's, the interracial saloon he visits there, became known as "Dickens' Place" or "Dickens' Hole" soon after the publication of *American Notes*. Dickens anticipated—with his early novels as well as his visit to Five Points—a wave of American fiction that would attempt to interpret the modern city, to shape readers' perception of a mysterious new environment.

The "city mystery" genre encompasses a wide range of texts, but most often the term refers to novels set in large cities and driven by complex, overlapping plots highlighting vice and crime, particularly prostitution and extramarital sex, as well as various types of theft, gambling, and drunkenness. They are not "mysteries" in the whodunit sense but rather in their insistence on exposing activities and locations usually "hidden" from the view of casual visitors and genteel readers. In this respect, they are essentially gothic—the word "mystery" harkens back to Ann Radcliffe's *The Mysteries of Udolpho* (1794)—in their preoccupation with invisible, irrational, and often subterranean worlds that threaten the seemingly rational visible world. The genre might also be labeled, as it sometimes was in its heyday, "mysteries and miseries" fiction, as its authors sought to expose not only crime and corruption but also the poverty generative of and generated by vices such as prostitution and drunkenness. In the process, they sensationalized city life and helped shape the way both urbanites and nonurbanites comprehended the new environment. Rev. Peter Stryker, visiting New York tenements in 1866, recounted being mocked by children who sarcastically called out to him, "The miseries of New York!" aware of their having been made into a cliché of popular literature (qtd. in Homberger 1994, 3).

Along with Dickens, Eugène Sue's *Les Mystères de Paris* (1842–43), a scandalous adventure/reform novel populated by killers, thieves, and vigilantes, and G. W. M. Reynolds's *The Mysteries of London* (serialized from 1844 to 1856) are frequently cited as inspirations for American city mysteries. But homegrown sources were probably equally influential. In the early 1840s, American newspapers and magazines frequently featured regular correspondence from New York, typically offering an insider's guide to various parts of the city. The most famous example is Lydia Maria Child's *Letters from New York* (serialized from 1841 to 1844, published in book form in 1843 and 1845), which combined descriptions of New York attractions and street life with personal reflections and appeals for social reform. Meanwhile, New Yorkers had been reading sensationalized coverage of vice and crime in penny newspapers since the *Sun* began publishing in 1833; and, by the mid-1840s, the short-lived weekly papers known collectively as the "flash press" simultaneously exposed and celebrated the excesses of masculine "sporting life," with a special interest in prostitution. By the mid-1840s, then, a new urban literature had emerged, not only in New York but also in other rapidly growing cities such as Philadelphia and Boston.

Indeed, these new, sensational ways of writing about the city crossed genres to such an extent that the term "city mysteries" could denote a trend extending well beyond the novel. George Foster's *New York by Gas-Light* (1850) contains fictional elements but presents itself as a nonfictional guidebook. A 20-page pamphlet titled "The Mysteries and Miseries of Philadelphia" (1853) includes a grand jury report on prisons and institutions for the poor, followed by a brief, informal report on the city's most squalid neighborhoods. Another pamphlet, "The Mysteries of Charleston" (1846), by "Eugene Sue, Jr.," consists of a verse satire on local political corruption. At the other end of the spectrum, Ned Buntline's *The Mysteries and Miseries of New York: A Story of Real Life* (1848) and Baron Ludwig von Reizenstein's German-language *The Mysteries of New Orleans* (1854–55) are five-volume serialized novels with lengthy casts of colorful lowlife characters. As for the most frequently cited example, George Lippard publicly objected to an advertisement for a reprint edition of *The Quaker City; or, The Monks of Monk Hall* (1844) with "Mysteries and Miseries" in the title; and indeed, Lippard's use of symbolism, psychology, and the occult distinguishes it from most other works associated with city mysteries fiction. As Paul Erickson points out, for various reasons, most of them having to do with its literary sophistication, *The Quaker City* is a misleading example of what was in fact a highly flexible "genre."

The difficulty of defining the "city mystery" novel illuminates the fluidity of nineteenth-century literary genres generally but also argues for the relevance of "mysteries and miseries" to other nineteenth-century narrative forms. City mysteries overlap in obvious ways with reform novels and sentimental fiction. For example, it was virtually impossible for city mystery writers to avoid editorializing against the vices they described or against what they saw as the root causes of those vices. And neither the reform novel nor the city mystery novel would be possible without the lexicon of sentimentalism, no matter how vociferously writers like Lippard opposed themselves to domestic fiction. In the opening chapter of *Hot Corn: Life Scenes in New York Illustrated* (1854), a series of sometimes lurid temperance tales, Solon Robinson forecasts the effect he wants his book to have: "Your heart, if it has not grown callous, will be pained as mine has been at the sights of misery you will meet with, and you will then exclaim, 'What does it mean that I see these things in the very heart of this great commercial city, where wealth, luxury, extravagance, all abound in such profusion?'" Most city mystery writers seem less sincere than the authors of sentimental novels about changing readers' hearts, yet they frequently profess the goal of raising consciousness through emotional appeal. They have a great deal in common with adventure novels as well: while Five Points was not literally as distant as the South Pole, fictional works like *Hot Corn* and *Mysteries and Miseries of New York* took readers to an exotic, foreign territory; and often the way there was through a kind of rabbit hole, typically a trapdoor leading to the bowels of the city, the hollow earth just below our feet. Like earlier frontier novels and even more like the western dime novels they prefigured, city mysteries promised and generally delivered suspense and violence, along with sometimes shocking descriptions of "alien" cultures within the United States. Less predictably, perhaps, the city mystery form resembled slave narratives in seeking to shock readers by depicting the tyranny of brute force as well as the dehumanization and depravity that accompany it. Like other popular nineteenth-century literary genres, the city mystery novel insists on its truthfulness and acquires its cultural power from readers' belief in that truthfulness. Like reform novels and slave narratives, city mysteries describe events that (the author claims) not only *can* happen, not only *have* happened, but *are* happening now and *will* happen again tomorrow.

Three of the most significant novels associated with the city mystery genre deserve more intensive examination. *The Quaker City* and *Mysteries and Miseries of New York* both sold over 100,000 copies, the former topped only by Harriet Beecher Stowe's *Uncle Tom's Cabin; or, Life Among the Lowly* (1852) among pre–Civil War novels. Sales figures for George Thompson's *City Crimes; or, Life in New York and Boston* (1849) are not available, but Thompson was certainly one of the most prolific and popular sensational novelists of the period. Each writer has a particular distinction in the evolution of the city mystery: Lippard's success motivated other fiction writers to take up urban crime and vice, yet he was clearly a more ambitious novelist than his successors; Thompson took the form as far as the law and popular taste would allow in his depiction of sex and sadism; and Buntline tested the limits of a novel's engagement with current events, bantering with city officials and insisting more emphatically than his contemporaries on the truth of his narrative. Although *The Quaker City* is the earliest of the three, I discuss Buntline's *Mysteries and Miseries of New York* first because it best establishes the genre's conventions and contradictions. By highlighting the elements these novels share, I hope to convey a sense of how city mysteries generally "worked"; by contrasting them, I hope to demonstrate something of the genre's stylistic range.

Buntline's *Mysteries and Miseries of New York* goes well beyond the usual claims of truthfulness familiar to readers of the early novel. Predictably, the title page announces "A Story of Real Life," and the preface insists, "Not one scene of vice or horror is given in the following pages which has not been enacted over and over again in this city, nor is there one character which has not its counterpart in our very midst." But Buntline presses on: "Accompanied by several kind and efficient police officers, whom, were it proper, I would gratefully name, I have visited every den of vice which is hereinafter described, and have chosen each character for this work during these visits. Therefore, though this book bears the title of a *novel*, it is written with the ink of truth and deserves the name of a *history* more than that of a *romance*." Every scene, every location, every character: not only do they have actual counterparts, according to Buntline, but he also claims to know them firsthand. It seems unlikely that Buntline's early readers took these claims at face value, yet his insistence that he is writing a present-day history rather than a romance invokes a tension that certainly fueled the book's popularity and the appeal of city mysteries generally. This "tension" is not a guessing game over which specific details are true and which are fabricated. Rather, it is a tension between the entire narrative—which is an artificial construction by its very nature and, in the case of *Mysteries and Miseries of New York*, a rather contrived one—and the lived experience of most New Yorkers in the 1840s.

"I have an aim in this work," Buntline piously declares in the preface to the first part: "it is to do good." He uses the prefaces to future volumes to advertise the "good" his narrative is accomplishing and the hackles it is raising. In "Prefatorial to the Second Part," he boasts about "threats, anonymous letters, &c." received from "the very villains whom he had *commenced* to lash." To those readers who have suspected that "some of its scenes are over-wrought and untrue," he offers to provide a reality tour, "to show you an original, or counterpart for every scene." The boasting and bantering continue, as he takes credit for recent missionary and Sons of Temperance activity in Five Points in the preface to part III and uses the preface to part IV as an open letter to city officials:

> In our last number, as a *trial*, we named the locations of *four* "hells" [gambling houses] kept open every night. We sent marked copies of that work gratis to several Aldermen; a copy was sent to the Mayor, twenty-five copies were sent gratis to the Police. And yet not one of these gambling houses has been disturbed—not one of these law-breakers has been even frowned at by the law-protectors.

In a footnote to that passage, Buntline comments hopefully on the election of William Havemeyer as mayor and the establishment of a new city council. Whether *Mysteries and Miseries of New York* had the kind of impact the hucksterish Buntline advertised or not, he clearly promoted the novel as a means of agitating directly for reform and used its serial publication to enhance this effect, so much so that local conditions would come to affect the direction of his fiction.

Throughout the novel proper, Buntline inserts details and asides to maintain that sense of fluidity between real life and his "story of real life." More than most city mystery writers, Buntline has characters speak in "flash" slang, which he highlights by appending a glossary to the first volume, as if to authenticate his use of phrases like "cracking a crib" (housebreaking) and being "jugged" (imprisoned) and to demonstrate a fluency that goes well beyond the terms used in the novel. Elsewhere he simply declares that his characters are based on specific individuals. Describing the tenderhearted thief Big Lize, he remarks, "No doubt many of my readers have seen her as she has passed to and fro on the Broadway-tide: if so, they will recognise this description" (bk. 1, ch. 1). After an early scene between a brother and sister, he pays tribute to his own sister, calling her by name. He repeats a description of the conniving Sam Selden to help readers identify (and presumably avoid) "the original of him" (bk. 3, ch. 15). Another character, Mary Sheffield, is clearly based on Mary Rogers, the "Beautiful Cigar Girl" whose mysterious death created a sensation and inspired Edgar Allan Poe's detective story "The Mystery of Marie Rogêt" (1842–43). Six years after the actual incident, Buntline advances the popular theory that Rogers only appeared to have been murdered by a gang of ruffians but actually died during an abortion procedure. He alters the name of Madame Restell (Caroline Lohman), a well-known abortionist suspected but never charged in the Rogers case, to "Madame Sitstill" and devotes the greater part of a chapter to shaming her: "There were marks of violence upon [Mary], not inflicted by a 'gang of rowdies,' but by a hag, a she-devil, an abortion of her own sex, one whom it would be blasphemy to call a *woman*, Caroline L. Sitstill" (bk. 5, ch. 11).

In the final 40-page appendix to the 500-plus-page novel, Buntline piles on statistics (over 1,000 brothels to 225 churches in New York!), testimonial letters, and newspaper clippings to bolster his editorial claims, some of which are anti-immigrant but most of which call for more aggressive law enforcement by magistrates and city officials, particularly in regard to gambling and prostitution. Finally, he attacks one Harrison Gray Buchanan, a rival city mystery novelist who had publicly criticized him, reproducing two letters (with permission of "the city authorities") by Buchanan in which he blackmails women, essentially threatening to write them into his novel if they refuse to deliver large sums of money. The incident advertises the cut-throat nature of Buntline's trade, as the crusading author exposes his corrupt counterpart who employs tactics characteristic of city mystery villains. But, as in the novels themselves, appearances are likely deceptive: Buntline's biographer, Jay Monaghan, conjectures that Buntline invented Buchanan, writing the city mystery novel *Asmodeus; or, Legends of New York* (1848) under that name and attacking "Ned Buntline" therein; moreover, he reports that Buntline practiced the very sort of blackmail for which he condemns "Buchanan."

Thus, if Monaghan is correct, Buntline pretends to be reporting on a scandal that he is actually fabricating, and the same is true of the plot of *Mysteries and Miseries of New York*. While Buntline the narrator and the plot itself present an urban world out of control, at every turn readers can detect the machinery manufacturing suspense, coincidence, and outrage. As in a television serial drama, individual chapters or scenes skip from one plot to another, but the plots intersect and characters cross paths at pivotal moments. One thread follows Angelina, a poor, pious sewing girl pursued by the libertine Gus Livingston. Befriended by the "panel thief" Big Lize, who on three occasions fights off Livingston or his partner-in-crime Harry Whitmore, Angelina escapes sexual ruin but not poverty nor the physical ailments that accompany it. A second thread involves another protracted seduction, as Whitmore relentlessly pursues the beautiful, innocent Isabella Meadows. When his sham marriage attempt—straight out of Susanna Rowson's *Charlotte Temple* (1791)—fails, he resorts to brute force and imprisonment. Isabella's brother Charley Meadows, a clerk who in the early chapters becomes a gambling and drinking companion of Gus and Harry, drives the third plot, as he embezzles money from his employer to support his gambling habit. Henry Carlton, a gambling-house owner, provides Charley with enough cash to replace what he stole but blackmails him, forcing him to sign a confession in exchange for the money. Using the threat of exposure, Carlton convinces Charley to kill a man who has had an affair with Carlton's wife. Three additional subplots spin off from the semi-organized crime network presided over by an English immigrant named Jack Circle.

As in many nineteenth-century novels, coincidences abound, from the repeated rescues of Angelina by Lize, who turns out to be her cousin, to an equally chance meeting of Lize and her estranged father (now a pauper who dies before she can help him), to a moment when two carriages cross paths, one of them delivering Isabella to her sham wedding and the other carrying Mary Sheffield to Madame Sitstill, the abortionist (one woman unwittingly following the other's path). But ultimately these coincidences do not add up to a providential plot in which virtue is rewarded. Instead, the teleological thrust of the novel is that the mysterious activities of the city lead only to misery, particularly for those who are innocent, well-intentioned, and female. After a series of narrow escapes spanning the novel, Isabella is raped by

Whitmore and is last seen as his unhappy but emotionally dependent mistress. The other major female characters—Lize and Angelina—are dead.

Within this controlled universe of tragedy, the quest for control—through manipulation, imprisonment, threats, and blackmail—forms a central motif. The libertines want to own their mistresses, as Whitmore proves when he arranges to have Isabella locked in a room at a brothel for several days in an attempt to break her spirit. Lize has freedom of movement and apparent self-possession until she defies the underworld network; to keep her quiet, the crime boss Circle locks her in a dark cellar. A charlatan sorcerer goes to great lengths to mystify the mother of a kidnapped boy—keeping her in his power is preferable to a quick ransom. When Carlton's wife is abandoned by her lover and her infidelity discovered by her husband, she agrees to aid in the lover's murder. "Speak on," she tells her husband, "I am henceforth your slave, Henry" (bk. 4, ch. 8). Similarly, Charley, the triggerman, repeatedly bemoans the fact that he is Carlton's "slave." Rather than depict chaos lurking just below the surface of an orderly city, Buntline presents a superficially chaotic city in which ruthless men (and a few women, specifically brothel owners and abortionists) seize and maintain control.

Yet the novel, written hurriedly in installments, appears improvised and open-ended. Most obviously, this is because its closing chapter conspicuously sets up a sequel, *The B'hoys of New York* (1848), rather than tying up loose ends or, in the manner of *Mysteries of Paris* and Thompson's *City Crimes*, briefly reporting the major characters' fates in a postscript. Other characters (and plot lines) prove expendable and are jettisoned, such as Lize's father, who is alluded to several times before his appearance but disappears after one meeting with her. Buntline seems to have included the Mary Sheffield story, which is completely detachable from the rest of the plot, strictly to attack Madame Restell, who was serving a prison term during the novel's publication for performing an abortion.

As other characters disappear, a new one—Mose the Bowery B'hoy—arrives in book four. Inspired by Benjamin Baker's popular musical, *A Glance at New York* (1848), which featured Frank S. Chanfrau as the quintessential b'hoy, Buntline wrote Mose into the fourth and fifth books of *Mysteries and Miseries of New York*. The first three books contain no references to b'hoys, but in book four a gang led by Mose temporarily takes over the brothel where Whitmore has imprisoned Isabella. The b'hoys stroll in, order the "she boss" around, drink champagne, spit on the floor, kiss and "cuff" the prostitutes, then take their leave. But by the time of Mose's next appearance, the obnoxious thug has been transformed, as he gallantly fights off a member of a rival gang who assaults Lize. He later attempts to rescue Isabella from her brothel prison when she drops a note—written in blood—into the street below. "But into no better hands could her note have fallen," explains the narrator, "than into those of the red-headed Mose, the Bowery butcher-boy, one who with some faults possessed some of the most sterling virtues that ever warmed the human heart" (bk. 5, ch. 1). Buntline adds a footnote advertising Chanfrau's performance as Mose in *A Glance at New York* and its spin-off, *New York As It Is*, which were running simultaneously at the Olympic and Chatham Theatres (bk. 5, ch. 1). The rather clumsy introduction of Mose says more about Buntline's opportunism than it does about any conscious authorial vision, yet it epitomizes a fluidity and open-endedness at odds with the novel's small urban world in which thieves, gamblers, and prostitutes, along with honest, respectable businessmen and seamstresses, are all mysteriously connected.

Thompson makes the same claims of adherence to truth and reform impulses that pervade Buntline's *Mysteries and Miseries of New York*, but in *City Crimes*, as in Thompson's fiction generally, these claims are not just dubious but ridiculous, given the brazen sensationalism of his plots. In chapter 4, we meet the "majestic, voluptuous" Julia Fairfield, who is engaged to the novel's hero, Frank Sydney. Having become pregnant through an affair with her African American servant, Julia gives birth in secret and has the infant strangled and disposed of, then marries Sydney with no intention of breaking off her sexual relationship with Nero, whom she calls her "superb African" (ch. 8). In the middle of an earlier chapter, Thompson pauses to defend himself against anticipated charges of making all this up:

> Those who are disposed to be skeptical with reference to such scenes as the foregoing had better throw this volume aside; for crimes of a much deeper dye, than any yet described, will be brought forward in this tale: crimes that are daily perpetrated, but which are seldom discovered or suspected. We have undertaken a difficult and painful task, and we shall accomplish it; unrestrained by a false delicacy, we shall drag forth from the dark and mysterious labyrinths of great cities, the hidden iniquities which taint the moral atmosphere, and assimilate human nature to the brute creation. (ch. 4)

According to Thompson, then, the reason these "crimes" seem too depraved to be real is that this sort of degenerate activity has never been exposed before.

Like other city mysteries, *City Crimes* features a large cast of mostly dishonest and deviant characters, but here all the subplots spin off the central hero/villain relationship between the crusading philanthropist Sydney and the superhuman ruler of New York's underworld, known as the Dead Man. Much like Prince Rodolphe from Sue's *Mysteries of Paris*, Sydney devotes himself to alleviating suffering in the city, but quickly learns that to venture into the seamy side of New York is to court extreme danger. On his first night out, he encounters a would-be robber and a prostitute: he gives fifty dollars to the former and sleeps with the latter, after she has told him the story of her enslavement at the hands of her abusive husband. Several chapters later, when Sydney arrives at her apartment with money for her relocation, he is forced to hide behind the bed curtains when the husband shows up and then witnesses her murder. As the husband, Fred Archer, escapes, Sydney picks up the bloody knife and immediately finds himself arrested for the crime (he is cleared when Archer, trapped in a bank vault, scrawls his confession before dying).

When Sydney's wife Julia visits him in jail, she taunts him, her hatred fueled by his discovery of her affair with the servant Nero, after which Sydney casts her off. Julia tells Sydney she believes he is innocent, "[Y]et I rejoice none the less in your fate. Your death will free me from all restraint. . . . And now in the hour of your disgrace and death, I spit upon and despise you!" (ch. 11).

These incidents, in themselves only a fraction of a complex plot, offer a clue to the multiple links from Sydney to the Dead Man and the overlapping relationships in the novel. Archer and the Dead Man turn out to be partners in crime, whom Sydney entraps by luring them to break into his house; Archer escapes from the crime scene, and when the Dead Man escapes prison, he vows revenge. Julia becomes ensnared by the Dead Man as well; he blackmails her when she changes her name and remarries. And the robber to whom Sydney gives fifty dollars in the opening chapter reappears—as "the Doctor"—to rescue him and eventually wreak vengeance upon the Dead Man.

David S. Reynolds and Kimberly R. Gladman have observed that *City Crimes* "contains no panoramic vistas or broad cityscapes, but instead abounds in visions of small or enclosed spaces: 'the Dark Vaults,' the 'Infernal Regions,' a 'subterranean village,' small hovels, the forty-foot cave. The Dead Man spends one chapter nailed inside a box; Fred Archer suffocates in a vault; Frank is imprisoned in the Manhattan jail called the Tombs" (2002, li). These cells and enclosed spaces are part of a recurring emphasis on interpersonal control, the enslavement and dehumanization of enemies and victims, which is even more pronounced in *City Crimes* than in *Mysteries and Miseries of New York*. For instance, when the Dead Man captures Sydney, he tortures him first by placing him in a dark, underground cell with his deformed, blood-sucking offspring (referred to as "the Image"), and then by forcing him into an "iron maiden" device made even more painful by the use of hot coals.

Not surprisingly, the means by which one human being controls another in *City Crimes* are sex, violence, and blackmail. Julia marries a kind old man for his money then kills him to pursue a younger man (who turns out to be Sydney in disguise). Similarly, a lascivious mother-and-daughter team, Lucretia and Josephine Franklin, have their husband/father killed to free them for uninhibited sexual adventures (including one with a minister who becomes sexually "enslaved" to Josephine). In each case, the means to sexual freedom is a wealthy, dead husband. Even Archer's wife, before meeting him, "tortured" (her word) a lecherous minister by enticing him and then withholding sex. In short, Thompson's women control the men who lust after them until some man finds a way to control them.

Armed with both brute force and the knowledge that Julia, still legally the wife of Sydney, is about to marry again, the Dead Man literally enslaves her. After raping her, he humiliates her before her servant and recently discarded lover Nero: "Mark how she will obey me in what I order her to do: Julia, love, my shoes are muddy; take them off my feet, and clean them." The narrator reports that despite her extreme pride, the now helpless Julia "took off the vile ruffian's dirty shoes, with her delicate hands; then with an elegant pearl handled pen-knife, she scraped off the filth, and afterwards, at the order of her *master*, washed them with rose-water in a china ewer, and wiped them with a cambric handkerchief—and all in the presence of her negro footman" (ch. 19). Thompson's narrator has already expressed his disgust with Julia's "vile intimacy with a negro menial" (ch. 4), so this scene seems calculated to punish her for that sin. The emphasis on the inappropriately fine materials she uses to clean the Dead Man's boots underscores the complete reversal of fortune she has suffered, while offering male readers a scenario whose pornographic appeal is anchored in class resentment. The Dead Man comes for the Franklin women as well, prepared to ruin them by revealing the murder of Mr. Franklin. Though he does not make them clean his boots, he extorts $1,000 from them, forces them to move to Boston to escape him, burns down their New York mansion, follows them to Boston, and finally disfigures Josephine by throwing vitriol in her face when she resists his sexual advances. Reynolds and Gladman argue that the Dead Man "embodies many of the social oxymorons that, in Thompson's texts, make virtue and vice empty signifiers" (2002, liii). Virtue and vice are replaced by a ruthless struggle for control: given the amoral economy of the novel, it is unsurprising that neither Julia nor the Franklin women change their ways after the Dead Man strips them of luxury and security. Julia goes on to commit another murder before killing herself; Josephine attempts to trick a suitor into marrying her without seeing her scarred face (and it works until, after the ceremony, he recoils from the sight of her and throws her out in the street).

Needless to say, *City Crimes* offers a dim view of human nature. After pursuing each other for the entire novel, Sydney and the Dead Man meet for a final showdown, which, thanks to Sydney's reformed criminal ally The Doctor (who, it turns out, really was a doctor before being reduced to poverty and crime), ends with the Dead Man tied up at Sydney's mercy. The Doctor thanks Sydney again for helping him turn his life around and vows to become a legitimate doctor again. But first, he wants to torture the Dead Man before killing him. Sydney, the novel's dark knight, walks away, leaving the Doctor to inject pain-inducing drugs into his victim, keeping the Dead Man alive and in agony until he cuts open his abdomen, loads it with explosives, and blows him to pieces. The combination of the ridiculous and the sadistic in *City Crimes* might put twenty-first century readers in mind of superhero comic books and the films they inspire. But the relationship between Sydney and the Dead Man also suggests postmodern gothic literature and film, particularly David Lynch's *Blue Velvet* (1986), in which the privileged, innocent Jeffrey Beaumont (played by Kyle MacLachlan) goes on an extralegal manhunt, falls into a surreal, nightmarish criminal underworld, and confronts his bestial alter-ego, Frank Booth (played by Dennis Hopper). Like Jeffrey, who has sex with the woman he seeks to protect from Booth minutes after Booth has raped her, Sydney quickly becomes implicated in the deviant behavior and crime that he encounters, sleeping with the prostitute Mrs. Archer the first night he meets her and (much later) unwittingly causing the death of his wife's new husband. And just as *Blue Velvet* concludes, after Booth is killed, with an ironically stylized return to "normalcy" and romance, *City Crimes* ends with a letter from Sydney's new wife, the "good" Franklin sister Sophia, extolling the pleasures of life in the country: "I am happy . . . very, very happy; and oh! may no care or trouble ever o'ershadow our tranquil home" (ch. 30). But this wish, along with the life of peace and healthy marriage, is undercut by the previous chapter's image of Sydney leaving the Dead Man in the hands of a torturer.

I invoke *Blue Velvet* not to itemize coincidences (of which there are more, by the way), nor to claim direct influence, but to legitimize the study of *City Crimes* and other novels in the genre and to better understand this novel's mixture of gritty realism, surrealism, sadistic violence, stylized romance, and irony. That effect is both exhilarating and disturbing. In particular, it is difficult (as it is with *Blue Velvet*) to know how to respond to the pornographic presentation of not just "sex and violence" but also transgressive and often sadistic behavior. It is even harder, of course, to know how readers of the 1850s responded.

For that matter, it is also difficult to know how seriously nineteenth-century readers took the threat implied by the constant nearness of the criminal underworld to the ostensibly civilized city where the Dead Man was only a bad dream or a fictional monster. Along with the enclosed spaces and generally claustrophobic atmosphere of *City Crimes*, Thompson, like Lynch, emphasizes the close proximity of the two worlds, and the ease with which criminals can intrude on the property and lives of "respectable" people. Sydney ventures in and out of the "Dark Vaults," a network of sewers and tunnels emanating from "a large open space," literally constituting a city beneath the city:

> Myriads of men and women dwelt in this awful place, where the sun never shone; here they festered with corruption, and died of starvation and wretchedness—those who were poor; and here also the fugitive murderer, the branded outlaw, the hunted thief, and the successful robber, laden with his booty, found a safe asylum, where justice *dare not* follow them[.] (ch. 6)

When Sydney tells a magistrate what he has seen, the magistrate replies that he knows about the Vaults but that the secret entrances and passageways make it impenetrable to police. As for the suffering poor beneath the city, the official explains, "[I]f we took them from that hole, what in the world should we do with them? Put them in the prisons and almshouse, you say. That would soon breed contagion throughout the establishments where they might be placed, and thus many lives would be sacrificed thro' a misdirected philanthropy" (ch. 7).

Poverty and disease may stay underground, but the criminal inhabitants of the Dark Vaults move freely from one realm to the other. Passages to the underworld connect to houses throughout the city, not just the slums. One of the Dead Man's

accomplices works as a servant, first in Sydney's house and then in the house of Julia's second husband. And when the Dead Man and Archer show up at a fancy masquerade ball, we are told that party crashing is common among criminals, and that "[i]n the bustle and confusion of receiving such a large company, they found but little difficulty in slipping in, unnoticed and unsuspected" (ch. 9). Of course, crimes are perpetrated by inhabitants of both worlds, and, as Reynolds and Gladman argue, the hypocritical parents, ministers, merchants, wives, and husbands are as deplorable spectacles of depravity as Archer or the Dead Man. When, near the end of the novel, the Dead Man throws vitriol into Josephine's face, he is inflicting on her a disfigurement he earlier endured himself, having altered his appearance with chemicals to escape detection. Though the pontificating narrator lets this opportunity pass, he might have pointed out that Josephine is finally forced to appear as monstrous as her behavior has made her. The underworld that the Dead Man embodies both threatens and reflects the corrupt society above ground.

The same dynamic of a "hidden" underworld that, when exposed, reflects the corruption of respectable society is built into Lippard's *The Quaker City*: Monk Hall, the central location of the novel's action, is divided into three above-ground stories and "three stories of spacious chambers below the level of the earth" (bk. 1, ch. 6). Above ground, prominent male citizens carry on sexual escapades or drink themselves into a stupor; but trapdoors and secret passageways lead to below-ground vaults where bodies are disposed of and an army of desperate criminals hides out during the day. Despite Lippard's objections to the "mysteries and miseries" label, his best-known novel clearly inspired Buntline and Thompson, as well as Robinson, Foster, and many others. Like his successors, Lippard constructs his plots around seduction, adultery, and abduction; every character is either deeply corrupt, vengeful, or both; the novel depicts and editorializes on social injustices; and the city setting is crucial: not only are specific landmarks and street names evoked repeatedly, but Philadelphia's status as a symbol of American ideals underscores Lippard's irony as he reveals its true character. As Samuel Otter observes, "In the symbol of Monk Hall, the famous grid is pivoted, skewed, excavated, and undermined, as Lippard uses architectural space to impart urban devolution" (2010, 173). "To Monk Hall!" various characters call out when their plans are in place, and, indeed, the novel insists that Monk Hall, a den of depravity presided over by a scheming, misshapen caretaker named Devil-Bug, is where all Philadelphia, and perhaps the entire nation, is heading. The men who hold power in the city—merchants, ministers, editors, and lawyers—are already there.

The plot that frames the novel is fairly simple: three nights before Christmas, Gus Lorrimer, the consummate libertine, bets his skeptical new friend Byrnewood Arlington that he will "marry" a girl from one of the city's first families that very night. On their way to Monk Hall, they visit an astrologer, who foretells that one of them will kill the other at sundown on Christmas Eve. At Monk Hall, when Byrnewood discovers that the victim of Lorrimer's sham-wedding is his own sister

Mary, he breaks up the ceremony but is taken prisoner by Lorrimer and Devil-Bug; meanwhile, Lorrimer rapes Mary. Byrnewood barely escapes death at Devil-Bug's hands and suffers partial amnesia from being drugged during his captivity, but ultimately he fulfills the prophecy, shooting Lorrimer in a boat on the Delaware River. Two other main plots unfold alongside this one. A cold-blooded social climber, Dora Livingstone, plans to kill her husband and marry one Algernon Fitz-Cowles, a con man whom she believes is an English nobleman. She is thwarted by her former lover Luke Harvey and by her husband, who is guided by Luke first to discover his wife's infidelity and then to inflict a merciless, fatal revenge on her. Meanwhile, in the third main plot, a beautiful young woman, at various times known as Mabel, Ellen, Nell, and Izolé, is abducted, nearly raped by a man pretending to be her father, sold by him to Fitz-Cowles, stolen by a sorcerer named Ravoni, then rescued by Luke and Devil-Bug, who, it turns out, is her real father.

Yet as these sensational plots unfold, Lippard thickens and complicates his novel in ways that his successors either were incapable of or deliberately avoided. Take, for example, the first page of book four, which reads, in various typefaces:

BOOK THE FOURTH
THE SECOND DAY
Ravoni the Sorcerer
CHAPTER FIRST
GOD IS JUST

And then the chapter begins: "The night drew near its close. From the dark azure of the sky, the cold winter stars shone down over the streets of the silent city."

This piling on of mile markers, including both book and chapter titles, along with the portentous opening sentences, assure us, four hundred pages into a novel that still has three books to go, that we are in the midst of a literary epic. In contrast to the breakneck pace of *City Crimes*, for instance, scenes unfold slowly in *The Quaker City*. The novel encompasses an eventful three days, but it presents them in great detail and layers simultaneous scenes in successive chapters—occasionally even moving backward in time—slowing temporal progress to a crawl. For instance, when the narrator describes the physical beauty of the femme fatale Dora, he lingers over every visible feature, devoting an entire paragraph to her feet: "And then, the feet! Ha, ha, we have come down to the feet, and these, let me tell you, are not the most contemptible of Dora's beauties! The high instep—do smile at our minuteness—the long and narrow form, the shape of the toes, the nails, like the fingers, tinged, each of them, with a deep circlet of red!" (bk. 3, ch. 2). At two points in the story we are admonished not to skip the important sections that follow, implicitly acknowledging readers' impatience. Indeed, those sections *are* important: one of them, describing the history and architecture of Monk Hall, establishes the central symbol of the novel. As a result of the thick description, symbolism, and character development, *The Quaker City* in some ways as much

recalls traditional gothic novels (Horace Walpole's *The Castle of Otranto* [1764], for instance, or the works of fellow Philadelphian Charles Brockden Brown, to whom Lippard dedicated his book) as it does the city mysteries of the late 1840s.

As with Brown's novels, much of what Lippard describes are scenarios in which characters are lost, and readers are likely to get lost along with them. For example, when in an early scene, Byrnewood, a novice to Monk Hall, is trying to find Lorrimer, the following excerpt comes midway through a lengthy passage describing his progress:

> Up the winding staircase he again resumed his way, and in a moment stood upon the landing or hall of the third floor. This was an oblong space, with the doors of many rooms fashioned in its walls. Another stairway led upward from the floor, but the attention of Byrnewood was arrested by a single ray of light, that for a moment flickered along the thick darkness of the southern end of the hall. Stepping forward hastily, Byrnewood found all progress arrested by the opposing front of a solid wall. He gazed toward his left—it was so dark, that he could not see his hand before his eyes. Turning his glance to the right, as his vision became more accustomed to the darkness, he beheld the dim walls of a long corridor, at whose entrance he stood, and whose farther extreme was illumined by a light, that to all appearance, flashed from an open door. (bk. 1, ch. 7)

Most readers are presumably as mystified as Byrnewood is at this point. Eventually he will discover that his sister is Lorrimer's victim, but the path to that discovery follows winding staircases, multiple doorways, and dark corridors. In passages like the one above, Lippard is not simply exposing the underside of the city—guiding the reader through the Old Brewery at Five Points or an oyster saloon that fronts for a brothel—he is sowing confusion, getting Byrnewood, the reader's surrogate at this point in the novel, lost in the distorting surfaces of a reality he cannot yet discern. Much later in the novel, the narrator boldly proclaims, "We like to look at nature and at the world, not only as they appear, but as they are!" (bk. 3, ch. 8). Captain Ahab would say something similar about the "pasteboard masks" of appearances in a novel published seven years later (Melville, *Moby-Dick*, ch. 36). In *The Quaker City*, Lippard allies himself aesthetically with "dark Romanticists" and the gothic tradition of privileging symbolic truths regarding human motivations and fears over journalistic realism.

"To us," writes Lippard, in the sentence following the one just quoted, "the study of a character like Devil-Bug's is full of interest, replete with the grotesque-sublime" (bk. 3, ch. 8). On one level, Lippard is defending—against an imagined dandified author/critic, "penner of paragraphs so daintily perfumed with quaint phrases and stilted nonsense"—his choice of gritty subject matter, but on another he is asserting the importance of character study itself, as Devil-Bug emerges as the novel's central and most complex figure. The phrase "grotesque-sublime," as Otter points out, suggests how "the modern arts were distinguished by mixtures of the high and the low" (2010, 168), and indeed, Devil-Bug is simultaneously driven by base impulses of childish sadism (his catchphrase, usually applied to mayhem, is "I vonders how *that'* ill vork!") and absolute devotion to his estranged daughter and the memory of her mother. "Could you have seen Devil-Bug's soul at the moment it was agitated by this memory, you would have started at the contrast, which it presented in comparison with his deformed body," the narrator tells us. "For a moment the soul of Devil-Bug was *beautiful*" (bk. 3, ch. 12). Devil-Bug delights in abetting Lorrimer's seduction and rape of Mary; is gleeful at the prospect of burying Byrnewood alive; demands sex from Dora as payment for a murder; and kills the unarmed sorcerer Ravoni, attacking him from behind. And yet Lippard repeatedly evokes sympathy for him. Born in a brothel, physically deformed, unloved, Devil-Bug even lacks a legal name: the name he sometimes insists on, Abijah K. Jones, belonged to a previous caretaker and was left on the door of Monk Hall. The narrator upbraids privileged readers who would judge him harshly:

> Oh, tell us, ye who with all these gifts and mercies, flung around you by the hand of God, have, after all, spurned his laws, and rotted in your very lives, with the foul pollution of libertinism and lust; tell us, who shall find most mercy at the bar of Avenging Justice—you, with your prostituted talents . . . or Devil-Bug, the doorkeeper of Monk-Hall, in all his monstrous deformity of body and intellect, yet with *one* redeeming memory, gleaming like a star, from the chaos of his sins? (bk. 2, ch. 9)

Unlike other city mystery villains, Devil-Bug primarily serves others—the mind-controlling Ravoni treats him as his slave, and to Lorrimer he is both servant and hit-man—and he kills himself only when he is satisfied that his daughter will receive Livingstone's inheritance and be "a lady all her life" (bk. 6, ch. 3). Devil-Bug gets his wish: Mabel inherits a fortune and marries Luke, the closest thing to a conventional hero in the book.

But Devil-Bug is the novel's true hero, embodying its contradictions; its fatalism; its righteous anger; and even, through his daughter Mabel, its glimmers of hope. "Hur-ray for Monk Hall," says Devil-Bug at one point. "It's the body, I'm its soul!" (bk. 3, ch. 8). Moreover, he is the soul of *The Quaker City*, which, as Reynolds points out, "is like Monk Hall, a labyrinthine structure riddled with trap doors that are always opening beneath the reader's feet and leading to another dimension" (1995, xxi). The last chapter of book three, "Devil-Bug's Dream," transforms the novel's outrage at the corruption of republican ideals into an apocalyptic vision of a 1950 Philadelphia in which Independence Hall has become a royal mansion and "Liberty [has] long since fled from the Quaker City." Consequently the city itself is doomed to destruction: corpses walk its streets, and a message in the sky proclaims "Wo Unto Sodom." Devil-Bug's spirit guide tells him, "To-morrow will be the last day of the Quaker City. The judgment comes, and they know it not" (bk. 3, ch. 14).

Lippard based his novel on the recent (1843) murder of Mahlon Heberton by Singleton Mercer, who, like Byrnewood, was acquitted because Heberton had seduced Mercer's sister. "Would to God that the evils recorded in these pages, were not based upon facts," writes Lippard in the preface to an 1849 edition. Specifically, he tells us, his narrative is based on the notes left to him by a lawyer who challenged him to "lift the cover from the Whited Sepulchre, and while the world is crying honor to its outward purity, to show the festering corruption that rankles in its depths." Lippard, then, employs a conventional authenticating device without insisting, as Buntline and Thompson do repeatedly, on his strict adherence to fact. And yet there seems to have been no uncertainty as to the identity of the "real" Byrnewood: Mercer, displeased by Lippard's fictionalization of his case, threatened to lead a riot when a theatrical version of *The Quaker City* was scheduled to open; the play was never performed.

All three novels, then, and dozens of others more or less like them, attempt to transform the relationship between the textual world and the real world. Buntline insisted that his book was history, not romance, while Thompson referred to his fiction as a "romance of the real," yoking terms that his contemporaries recognized as antithetical. But the description is apt: these novels are stylized, cartoonish, or, to use Lippard's word, "grotesque," and yet they seek not to carry readers away from grim realities but to force them to confront poverty, corruption, and crime. Lippard, like many reform novelists, was deeply committed to social change, founding a weekly paper devoted to "social reform through the medium of popular literature," as well as a labor organization, the Brotherhood of the Union. Foster, the author of *New York by Gas-Light*, promoted Fourierism, while Buntline and Thompson appear to have been more opportunistic than idealistic or revolutionary. But regardless of the intentions of individual authors, city mystery novelists shared with writers of reform literature a belief in the novel's status as a social text, which is why it was necessary to insist on the "reality" of their fiction and on their fiction's potential to change that reality. Equal parts gothic, sentimental, reformist, and journalistic, their novels both reflected the literary values of their own time and looked forward to a period in history more associated with social realism. They also looked forward, with some excitement but considerable fear, to an increasingly urban American culture.

34

SURVIVING NATIONAL DISUNION: CIVIL WAR NOVELS OF THE 1860s

PAUL CHRISTIAN JONES

Published in 1868, Elizabeth Stuart Phelps's first novel, *The Gates Ajar*, details how a young woman, Mary Cabot, mourns the death of her brother Roy, a Union soldier in the Civil War. Appearing just three years after the end of that devastating conflict, Phelps's narrative consoled a large readership, many of whom had lost spouses, parents, children, or siblings in the war and desperately wanted to be reassured of the inevitability of reunion with those loved ones, if not in this life, in the afterlife. The novel's grieving narrator Mary is comforted by her visiting aunt Winifred, who offers her a description of heaven, one based on emerging spiritualist beliefs, wherein dead souls, like her brother's, retain their individual identities, their physical bodies, their memories, and familial affections, thus making it possible for suffering survivors to expect to be reunited with the dead at some point in the future. This comforting potential of reunion is, for Mary, infinitely preferable to the version of heaven articulated by the voices of the established church in the novel. The minister Dr. Bland and Deacon Quirk condemn Winifred's notions and offer instead church-approved characterizations of the afterlife as a completely spiritualized state, where disembodied souls spend eternity glorifying God, that give Mary little hope of a restored relationship with her beloved brother. In Phelps's novel, these two narratives are evaluated by the central character and also by readers. Each narrative addresses how those who have suffered the trauma of loss and separation can and should think about the potential for reconnection with lost loved ones. For Phelps, her character Mary, and the multitude of readers who read this best-selling novel, the narrative that promises a reunion becomes more appealing, and the traditional narrative that cannot guarantee such a reunion, at least as living human beings can conceive of it, is exposed as woefully insufficient.

The widespread appeal of *The Gates Ajar* suggests that it also addressed broader desires for reunion beyond the spiritual. That is, American readers suffered through the heightened sectional division of the late 1850s and early 1860s, the bloody conflicts in Kansas, John Brown's raid at Harpers Ferry and his subsequent execution, the secession of eleven southern states following the election of Abraham Lincoln, the brutal and costly conflicts of the years of the Civil War, and the assassination of Lincoln. Then they confronted the extraordinary challenges of restoring the Union and bringing together its disparate elements—North and South, black and white, rural and urban. The unflappable confidence in reunion conveyed by Phelps's novel spoke to a larger need in her readership, a need to be reassured that the fractured Union itself could indeed be put back together from the ruins of the war. If living people could be reunited with the dead (as they are in Phelps's fiction), then perhaps there was hope for the United States. Of course, *The Gates Ajar* was not alone in offering this glimmer of hope. Many of the novels published in this tumultuous decade were similarly engaged in responding to the current state of the Union and shaping their readers' attitudes about it. In the early years of the 1860s, novels reflected anxiety about the welfare of the Union and expressed both doubt about whether the Union should or could any longer exist and assurance that it would withstand these unprecedented challenges. In the years of the war, novels strengthened the resolve of both sides—the Blue and the Gray—and reassured them of the rightness of their actions. And, most importantly, after the war, novels took on a vital role in healing the nation's wounds and allowing it to move on and reframe its narratives in order to make reunion a feasible and credible outcome.

Literary histories of American writing have typically given the novels produced in the 1860s minimal attention, either completely ignoring them or, if acknowledging these narratives at all, dismissing them as markedly inferior to the more acclaimed fiction of preceding and subsequent decades. For example, Edmund Wilson famously begins *Patriotic Gore* (1962), his seminal study of the literature of these years, with the assertion that "the period of the American Civil War was not one in which belles lettres flourished," and he suggested that scholars turn to "speeches and pamphlets, private letters and diaries, personal memoirs and journalistic reports" for the "remarkable literature" of this time (ix). Similarly, Daniel Aaron, in *The Unwritten War* (1987), proposes that "national convulsions do not provide the best conditions for artistic creativeness" as a way of explaining "the paucity of 'epics' and 'masterpieces'" during and immediately after the war (xxii–xxiii). While these scholars give little attention to the fiction produced in this period, other literary historians have more explicitly acknowledged the existence of novels in the 1860s only to reject them as unworthy of serious consideration. In *The American Novel* (1921), for example, Carl Van Doren argued that the Civil War "contributed little to the mode of fiction except new materials for the incessant popular romancers who turned their pens from the past to the present. . . . What the wicked Tory or the fierce Indian had been, the crafty Confederate or the cruel Federal . . . now became" (125). This dismissive view of the decade's fiction served to justify its critical neglect for much of the twentieth century. The single novel from this era that has almost universally avoided critical dismissal has been John W. De Forest's *Miss Ravenel's Conversion from Secession to Loyalty* (1867), which one critic has called "the one novel of the decade that is still readable" (Leisy 1950, 157). De Forest's work is often praised as the beginning of American realism and thus presented as the sole treasure amidst the inferior trash of these years. Because critics have focused so much on De Forest's book, they have missed a number of fascinating texts that, like *Miss Ravenel's Conversion*, were engaged in important ways in responding to the crisis of national disunion.

In many respects, this critically dismissive opinion is quite understandable, as few of the celebrated male writers who have become landmarks in the history of the American novel published novels in this decade. Of the antebellum giants, James Fenimore Cooper died in 1851, Herman Melville spent the 1860s working on poetry rather than fiction, and Nathaniel Hawthorne published his final novel, *The Marble Faun*, in 1860, unable to finish another novel-length work before his death in 1864. Similarly, none of the major postbellum novelists, including William Dean Howells, Mark Twain, and Henry James, published book-length fiction in the 1860s, as they spent these years writing short fiction, newspaper pieces, and travel narratives. Their full-length works of fiction would not emerge until the 1870s. While scholars like Alice Fahs, Susan V. Donaldson, Frank Mott, and Herbert Smith have drawn readers' attention to the wealth of fiction published in these years, the majority of that work was written—as it is in every decade—by popular writers, like Ned Buntline, E. P. Roe, J. T. Trowbridge, Oliver Optic, and Horatio Alger, rather than those canonized figures mentioned earlier. Harriet Beecher Stowe, the one female author almost always permitted into the ranks of Hawthorne, Melville, James, and Twain by twentieth-century histories, did—unlike her celebrated male peers—continue to publish novels regularly throughout the 1860s, including *Agnes of Sorrento* (1862), *The Pearl of Orr's Island* (1862), and *Oldtown Folks* (1869). And, she had much company among female novelists. Louisa May Alcott, for example, published, in this decade, the fictionalized version of her wartime nursing experiences, *Hospital Sketches* (1863), the adult novel *Moods* (1864), and her most famous book for children, *Little Women* (1868); Rebecca Harding Davis published *Margaret Howth* (1862), *Waiting for the Verdict* (1868), and *Dallas Galbraith* (1868); and Elizabeth Stoddard published all of her novels—*The Morgesons* (1862), *Two Men* (1865), and *Temple House* (1867)—in this decade. Best-selling popular writers, like E. D. E. N. Southworth, Augusta Jane Evans, Ann S. Stephens, Mary Jane Holmes, A. D. T. Whitney, and Susan Warner, produced novels on an almost annual basis throughout these years. Well-established names from the antebellum period, like Lydia Maria Child, Maria Cummins, Elizabeth Oakes Smith, and Maria McIntosh published their final works of fiction in this decade. And writers like Phelps and Frances E. W. Harper, who would produce a number of works in subsequent decades, produced their first novels at the end of this period.

The literary establishment in the nineteenth century, as well as the academy in much of the twentieth and twenty-first centuries, has been eager to write off much of this literature as subliterary (as work with no claim to Wilson's definition of "belles lettres") and thus unworthy of serious consideration. As early as the 1860s, critics like Howells and James were diminishing this writing as inartistic and unimportant. For example, in his lionizing 1867 review of De Forest's *Miss Ravenel's Conversion*, Howells sets up a contrast between the merit of De Forest's realistic work and the bulk of female-written popular literature: "The heroes of young-lady writers in the magazines have been everywhere fighting the late campaigns over again, as young ladies would have fought them. We do not say that this is not well, but we suspect that Mr. De Forrest [*sic*] is the first to treat the war really and artistically" (121). The implication that these female-authored works are less than artful led to dismissive assertions like those of Wilson and Aaron cited above.

Fortunately, a number of revisionary projects have attempted to remedy this perception of the literature of the Civil War and Reconstruction years by determinedly turning their focus to the large body of fiction written by women in these years. For example, Elizabeth Young in *Disarming the Nation* (1999), her important study of women's writing during and about the war, argues that traditional literary history—like that of Wilson and Aaron—has found "no male canon of great American Civil War novels as such but, rather, a hole precisely where one ought to be" (2). Young argues that in their attempts to focus only on the male experience and perspective of war, these scholars have "displace[d] the female author and reader from their foundational positions within the making of Civil War fiction" (1999, 10). Studies by Fahs, Lyde Cullen Sizer, and Kathleen Diffley have recovered much of this fiction by women, and this shift of focus to women's fiction has proven important to understanding the role that novels—especially those that consumers were buying and reading—played in the culture during this tumultuous period. Women's fiction clearly began to dominate the market in these years. For example, "in 1872, nearly three-fourths of the American novels [published] in that year were written by women" (Tebbel 1975, 170). Because of the increasing dominance of female authors in this decade, this chapter will emphasize works written by women, even though these books have often been excluded from standard literary histories of the past.

Even before the war, American fiction was often engaged in repairing the damage done to the Union by the strident sectionalist rhetoric that threatened popular support for the national government throughout the 1850s' debates over slavery. Resistance reached its peak following the 1860 election of Lincoln, leading to the quick secession of South Carolina and other southern states. As Karen Keely has noted, many antebellum authors wrote novels structured around courtship plots that imagined "national harmony brought about by love and marriage between a Northerner and a Southerner." While this subgenre of fiction—often called the "romance of reunion" or the "romance of reconciliation"—became even more prominent in the postbellum period, novelists of the 1850s, like Caroline Hentz in *The Planter's Northern Bride* (1854) and McIntosh in *The Lofty and the Lowly; or, Good in All and None All-Good* (1853), depicted "North-South lovers successfully find[ing] personal happiness and thus, symbolically, bring[ing] about national peace" (1998, 622). In Gregory Jackson's description of the political work of these popular novels, he notes that these writers "sought to bridge increasingly political and regional tensions through love plots . . . between Northerners and Southerners and their hybrid 'national' children born of the intersectional union." They "held out the hope of reconciliation in the allegory of young lovers whose passion for each other overcame regional prejudice and averted a war" (2003, 281–82).

In the fiction of the early 1860s, this optimistic use of marriage plots attesting to national unity becomes less frequent. Instead, the anxiety of the war years seems to have led American authors, even if they were not explicitly writing about sectional conflict, to express serious concern about whether a Union made up of participants with such different characters, backgrounds, and values could indeed survive. And the sectional divisiveness in the nation made fictional plots about marital intrigue resonate with larger political implications. For example, when Southworth serialized her novel *Love's Labor Won* in the heat of the 1860 presidential election and had her heroine Marguerite wonder, "Is not the cloudiest union more endurable than dreary severance?" (ch. 5), her readers could not but help hearing one of the questions many Americans, especially perhaps those in the slaveholding states, were asking themselves as they anticipated the election's results.

While Southworth's text implies that her readers should continue to support the Union rather than risk an uncertain disunion, other writers used their novels' marriage plots to express pessimism about the future of a union between sections. For example, in Stowe's *Pearl of Orr's Island*, which began its serialization in early 1861, her central romance is rich with national implications. Though set in a coastal Maine village in the early nineteenth century, it reveals Stowe's skepticism about the current state of affairs. The heroine, Mara Lincoln, is orphaned at the beginning of the book and left to be raised by her grandparents; she is soon joined by another orphan, Moses, a young boy who is taken into the same household after he washes up on shore alongside his mother's corpse after surviving a shipwreck. The novel follows the orphans' childhood and eventual young adulthood. Mara is bookish and devoted to Moses; he is adventurous, narcissistic, and blind to (and even disrespectful of) her feelings toward him. Late in the novel, Stowe provides Moses's backstory as a means of explaining his character, revealing him to be the descendant of a Florida family possessing the "stormy natures" of "the Southern climates" (ch. 26). Though the novel builds up its readers' expectation that Mara and Moses will someday wed, we watch her years of constancy, while he is gone to sea for long stretches of time, only to see Mara die before they can be married. Unlike the antebellum "romances of union," Stowe's conclusion suggests serious doubt about whether a union between such strikingly different partners could succeed or should be pursued at all.

Stoddard's novel *Two Men*, begun in 1863 and not published until after the war's end, reveals similar anxiety about the state of the Union. The novel follows two generations of a family in the village of Crest, Maine, beginning with the working-class Jason Auster's arrival in town and his unlikely courtship and eventual marriage to aristocratic Sarah Parke. The couple soon has a son, Parke, and takes in Sarah's brother's daughter, Philippa, whose quirks are attributed to her "Southern constitution" (ch. 12). The novel depicts a couple of decades in the family's history. It portrays a difficult cohesion as the Auster house is forced to contain very different characters and personalities, not only this "cousin from the South" (ch. 18) living among her northern kin, but also those with aristocratic pretensions living with those with working-class values, as well as those with various prejudices—about region, class, and race—forced to share space with people they despise, and provincial types coexisting with would-be citizens of the world. The household—clearly a metaphor for the nation—seems far from affectionate and loving. Instead, many family interactions betray hostility and antagonism, constantly threatening dissolution of the family, with little common ground to justify their staying together. And, what does hold the family together seems more habit and tradition than affinity or healthy bonds. In a plot device that will become more frequent in novels after the Civil War, Stoddard has Parke become sexually involved with Charlotte, the daughter of a free black family who has moved to Crest. She soon becomes pregnant with his child and dies from complications during the pregnancy, after which Parke flees the village and the household. Perhaps in a gesture toward the end of the Civil War, Stoddard does conclude the novel with a marriage, uniting the now-widowed Auster and his ward Philippa, who has long loved her cousin Parke. For readers, this union hardly seems one to celebrate, as it appears the product of compromise and even desperation. Jennifer Putzi has suggested that this ambiguous conclusion forces readers to wonder, "What would the nation look like as it made its way toward reunion and reconstruction?" (2008, xlvii).

While Stowe's and Stoddard's works reflect northerners' anxiety about the future of the United States during the years of the war, some authors—usually those living in the Confederate states—more explicitly voice outright hostility to the idea of union and aggressively justify the secession of the southern states. Augusta Jane Evans's *Macaria; or, Altars of Sacrifice* (1864), which is often referred to as a Confederate bestseller, might be the best example as it is unapologetic about its support of secession as the South's only option. The novel follows the lives of two southern heroines, Irene Huntingdon and Electra Grey, one representing the aristocracy and one the poor, through the heated sectional debates of the 1850s and the early part of the Civil War. While Evans has her characters make strong arguments in favor of secession and the war against the North, her novel makes many of its points through the romantic plots involving Irene and Electra. Irene's story shows her resistance to her father's pressure to marry her cousin Hugh, whom she does not love. She makes the case that a marriage made up of such different partners can only be "an unholy union": "We are utterly unlike in thought, taste, feeling, habits of life, and aspirations; I have no sympathy with your pursuits, you are invariably afflicted with *ennui* at the bare suggestion of mine. Nature stamped us with relentless antagonisms of character; I bow to her decree." She declares that this feeling stands as "an everlasting barrier to our union" (ch. 19). Her rejection of a forced union is repeated throughout the remainder of the novel: "I can not endure to live, and bring upon myself the curse of a loveless marriage; and, God is my witness, I never will!" (ch. 22). An aspiring painter, Electra similarly declines the marriage proposal of Clifton, her older painting teacher. These plots parallel and usefully reinforce the political plot as the South rejects the "Union" that has become "everywhere the synonyme of political duplicity, despotism, and the utter abrogation of all that had once constituted American freedom" (ch. 28). The novel ends with the Civil War still raging, and, atypical of a sentimental narrative, its two heroines proudly flaunting their resistance to loveless marriages. To prove that good ends could come from an unmarried state, the women start an academy for young girls, anticipating a future outside of union, both marital and national.

After the conclusion of the war, defiant anti-unionism disappears from American fiction and even the anxiety about the Union's ability to contain diverse sections is more or less muted. In novels by northern authors, readers find encouragement to put the war behind them, forgive the South and its citizens, and begin the healing work of reintegrating the Confederate states back into the Union. For example, in the celebrated minister Henry Ward Beecher's *Norwood; or, Village Life in New England* (1867), a novel that follows the impact of the war on the denizens of a western Massachusetts village, he characterizes the appropriate view of the rebels:

> In every generous bosom rose the thought—"These are not of another nation, but our citizens." Their mistakes, their evil cause, belonged to the system under which they were reared, but their military skill and heroic bravery belong to the nation, that will never cease to mourn that such valor had not been expended in a better cause, and that the iron pen must write: "The utmost valor misdirected and wasted." (ch. 57)

Beecher sets the tone for northern authors who will write in these days following the war; "iron pens" must honor the valor of the Confederacy, while regretting its cause, and must welcome its members back into the Union as citizens.

Many postbellum novelists took up this restorative work by utilizing romance plots, similar to those in antebellum novels, that, as Nina Silber has explained, lead to "marriage between northern men and southern women" (1993, 6) and suggest "the North . . . had tamed and subdued and would now control the South in much the same way that husbands were assumed to take control in marriage" (1993, 116). In scholarly studies of this reconciliation fiction, De Forest's *Miss*

Ravenel's Conversion has come to be the representative template of this formula. De Forest's southern heroine, Lillie Ravenel of New Orleans, begins the novel residing in Connecticut (called "Barataria" in the novel) with her father, a doctor who is sympathetic to the causes of abolition and Union. By contrast, Lillie is "a rebel": "She was colored by the soil in which she had germinated and been nurtured; and during that year no flower could be red, white and blue in Louisiana" (ch. 1). Two very different men compete for her affection, the New Englander Edward Colburne, a recent college graduate and lawyer, and the older Virginia-born Colonel Carter. Even though both men become Union officers upon the outbreak of war, De Forest uses them to represent the opposing regions of their birth. Colburne is upright, disciplined, reliable, responsible, and completely devoted to Lillie, though he lacks the age and manly carriage of his rival; Carter is experienced, worldly, and virile, but also hard-drinking, reckless, and financially unethical. Lillie is won over by Carter's southern charms and marries him, but she soon discovers that her husband has been unfaithful to her by having an affair with Madame Larue, Lillie's Creole aunt. The contrast between the loyalty of Colburne and the infidelity of Carter becomes a contrast between the two regions. Following Carter's death in battle, Lillie eventually accepts Colburne's marriage proposal, but insists that they live in the North: "Always at the North! I like it so much better!" (ch. 36). Though in subsequent decades, De Forest's novel was most praised for its realistic battle scenes—which critics argue anticipate those in Stephen Crane's *The Red Badge of Courage* (1895)—and its cynical depiction of the military bureaucracy (both based on the author's experience), in the 1860s, the marriage plot proved most crucial to the work of reconciling and healing the divide in the postwar nation.

Miss Ravenel's Conversion's place as the representative example of this romance formula is to some extent problematic. The basic dynamic of this marriage plot was replicated in dozens of novels in the second half of the 1860s, some written before De Forest's work. And, this formula appears not only in novels by northern authors like De Forest but also by those written by southern writers, including Marion Harland's *Sunnybank* (1866), a work depicting the effects of the war on the residents of a Virginia plantation and concluding with an unsurprising marriage between its southern heroine Elinor Lacy and her northern suitor Harry Wilton, a Union lieutenant. While many of these novels strictly follow the formula described by Silber and illustrated in De Forest's text, with a feminized South submitting to northern governance through marriage, some of the most popular romances of reunion mark exceptions to this rule. For example, Southworth's novels *Fair Play; or, The Test of the Lone Isle* (1868) and *How He Won Her* (1869), first serialized in the *New York Ledger* in 1865 and 1866 as *Britomarte, the Man-Hater*, featured a number of pairings between lovers whose sympathies were on opposite sides of the war. Yet, it is her heroines—Britomarte Conyers, Elfie Fielding, and Erminie Rosenthal—who are most connected to the Union, though they are all southerners. The one character in the novel to parallel Miss Ravenel is the Confederate loyalist, Alberta Goldsborough, daughter of a wealthy Richmond merchant, who ends up married to a rebel guerilla and dies by a Union bullet. On the other hand, the adventurous Elfie, a farmer's daughter, attempts to get drafted into the Union army and protests when they will not accept a woman. Britomarte, an ardent feminist, named for the virgin knight of chastity in Edmund Spenser's *The Faerie Queene* (1590, 1596), goes even further, cross-dressing and entering the army under the name "Wing." She fights alongside the male soldiers, is awarded with a promotion to captain, and is eventually captured and incarcerated in a Confederate prison. Though a strong advocate of women's rights, who refuses to marry until laws are passed to protect women's property and freedoms within marriage, Britomarte does, after over a thousand pages since his original proposal to her, finally accept the hand of her beloved Justin Rosenthal, affirming the Union, even if theirs is not quite a marriage of equals. The subplots featuring Erminie and Elfie have each heroine marrying a Confederate officer in an act that represents northern forgiveness of southern transgressions. For example, Erminie, a minister's daughter, postpones her marriage to the much older Colonel Eastworth when she learns of his Confederate loyalties. After the war, the two are reunited in a hospital, where he convalesces from his injuries, including a lost arm. When he admits his "remorse" and confesses to having supported a "bad cause," she greets him with love and forgiveness. They are soon married, and *How He Won Her* does not hide the larger implications: "So these two were reconciled, and this was but the forerunner of a deeper and broader reconciliation yet to come" (ch. 44).

The emphasis on De Forest's romantic plot has led readers to assume that all of fiction's reconciliatory work happens through depictions of intersectional marriage plots. A good example of a text that strays from this expectation is the decade's most popular novel for children, Alcott's *Little Women*. Like much of the adult fiction written about the war, Alcott's book casts it as a threat to union, in this case the familial union of the March family. The first half of the novel depicts the March women, Mrs. March and her four daughters, Meg, Jo, Beth, and Amy, living on their own and worrying about the well-being of Mr. March as he fights in the war. When Mr. March returns, wounded but alive, the threat to the family union passes. And, the novel's first volume ends with a celebration of union in the marriage of the oldest March daughter, Meg, to her beloved John Brooke. In the second volume, Alcott made the controversial choice to have her beloved and independent heroine Jo reject the proposal of Laurie, her childhood friend and kindred spirit. Jo tells him, "I don't believe I shall ever marry; I'm happy as I am, and love my liberty too well to be in any hurry to give it up for any mortal man" (pt. 2, ch. 12). However, contradicting this declaration of independence, Jo soon consents to marry the aging German, Professor Friedrich Bhaer, whose seriousness seems so at odds with her adventurousness. While many critics have offered explanations for this abrupt shift in Jo's perspective, we might read this union between Jo and

Bhaer, who have such different characters, in the context of reuniting a divided nation, as reassurance that the necessary marriage between the disparate regions following the war could indeed lead to a long and happy union, which readers witness in the novel's sequels, *Little Men* (1871) and *Jo's Boys* (1886).

While the reconciliation romances just discussed are ultimately quite optimistic about the restoration of the Union, it is striking that they focus primarily on imagining the reunion of white citizens from the North and South and give little or sometimes no attention to black citizens, who are no longer slaves following the war (yet another drawback of using a single text, *Miss Ravenel's Conversion*, to illustrate the cultural work done by fiction in this period). As writers considered the future of the nation, in the wake of the congressional debates in the late 1860s about the Fourteenth and Fifteenth Amendments to the US Constitution, which would, among other things, grant black men full and equal status as citizens, the challenge of incorporating the nation's black population harmoniously into white-dominated society certainly evoked great anxiety for some. In the novels of the 1860s that do address the racial dynamics of reunion, especially those by white writers, there is very little optimism displayed about this transition being an easy one. Indeed, Child's *A Romance of the Republic* (1867) is the rare example that takes a positive view of this racially unified future. Child's story centers on the Royal sisters, Rosa and Flora, who discover upon their father's death that their deceased mother had been their father's slave and that because he had never manumitted them they were now considered property to be used to settle his debts. The bulk of the novel depicts the two young women's struggle with the very different treatment that they now receive from antebellum American society when viewed as black females. As in the examples of reunion fiction discussed previously, Child's text uses marriage to depict the possibility of a Union containing very distinct differences, and the latter part of the novel finds both Rosa and Flora, despite taking individual journeys over the course of the narrative, married to white northern men, Alfred King and Franz Blumenthal, in a vision of racial unity. While Child has been praised by some critics for her vision of racial intermarriage as a solution to the racial divide in the United States, others have noted that the sisters are easily assimilated into white culture (of course, they were raised to view themselves as white) and seem to pose little threat to the dominant white culture. As Sizer notes, the implication of Child's conclusion is that "for blacks to enter white society as equals, they must become white" (2000, 234). Whether or not this criticism is valid, Child's text attempts to reassure its readers that it is possible for free blacks and whites to coexist happily as part of the Union.

Unlike Child, other novelists, noting the fierceness of white racism, were less sanguine about intermarriage (whether literal or figurative) as a solution to racial division. For example, in her novel of the Civil War, *Waiting for the Verdict*, Davis features the traditional reconciliation romance between a northerner and a southerner in a plot that depicts the successful marriage of Rosslyn Burley, a

Philadelphia abolitionist, to Garrick Randolph, an aristocratic slave owner. However, the plot's interracial romance does not end as felicitously. John Broderip is a former slave, who has been able to pass as white, acquire an education, and become a prominent doctor in Philadelphia. When he reveals his racial identity to his beloved Margaret Conrad, the daughter of a rural Methodist minister, she breaks off their relationship, unable to consider marriage to a black man. Her rejection drives Broderip to abandon his medical practice and enlist in an African American regiment; he eventually is shot in battle and dies from his wounds in Andersonville Prison. Unlike the novel's intersectional romance, which depicts the regions moving past their differences to create a healthy Union, the interracial one ends tragically because of the intense racism on the part of its white half. Even as the government was embarking on the process of granting equality to black men, the novel seriously questions whether the nation's white citizenry will ever allow real equality to happen. Late in the novel, Anny, a former slave, expresses this uncertainty to Rosslyn as she discusses her son's future: "Dar's four millions of his people like him; waitin' for de whites to say which dey shall be—men or beasts. Waitin' for the verdict, madam" (ch. 43).

Similar concern about the threat that intense white racism poses to a union of black and white citizens is demonstrated in *What Answer?* (1868), the only novel by activist Anna Elizabeth Dickinson. Her narrative traces the romance of her white hero Willie Surrey and black heroine Francesca Ercildoune, who has been passing as white (like the characters in Child's and Davis's books) and is well educated by her wealthy father. When Francesca's racial identity is revealed to Willie, upon his return from the war, where he lost an arm, he is undeterred from his desire to marry her, even when he faces rejection by his family and friends. The romance ends tragically when the couple find themselves in the middle of the New York Draft Riots of July 1863, when a working-class mob (most of them Irish immigrants) turns its anger about the war on the black population of the city. Both Willie and Francesca are killed in the ensuing violence, suggesting that the reconciliation of the races might be long in coming. This notion is reinforced in the novel's closing chapter, which takes place two years later, following the conclusion of the war. Robert, Francesca's brother, who has served heroically as part of a black regiment, is encouraged by a white friend to go to the polls to vote on election day, but, when he hands over his ballot, it is not accepted. He asks, "1860 or 1865?—is the war ended?" His friend responds, "That is for the loyal people of America to decide" (ch. 22). Dickinson's novel encourages white readers to view their own biases as a serious impediment to the healthy recovery of the Union.

The novels written by African American novelists in the years following the war are less doubtful, and some might even be read as optimistic, about the potential for black integration into white society. For example, in Julia C. Collins's unfinished serialized novel *The Curse of Caste; or, The Slave Bride* (1865), the heroine Claire Neville is an orphaned young woman in Connecticut who accepts a position as a governess for the Tracy family in Louisiana. Once there, she begins to unravel her own obscure history to discover that she is the daughter of Richard Tracy, who was estranged from his family because of his relationship with Lina, a family slave. Claire's return thus is a homecoming, with the potential for heartbreak, especially as we are uncertain how Colonel Tracy, her white supremacist, proslavery grandfather, will react to the arrival of his black granddaughter. Even though the conclusion of the novel was never published (and perhaps not even written since Collins died in November 1865), the last serialized chapter held open the possibility that Claire was going to be accepted into her white southern family and implied that she might be married to a white man, the Frenchman Count Sayvord.

Unlike the unfinished *The Curse of Caste*, the 1853 novel *Clotel; or, The President's Daughter* continued to get new endings as author William Wells Brown revised it throughout the 1860s. The 1867 version, *Clotelle; or, The Colored Heroine*, his final revision of the novel, might be read as a hopeful take on the place of African Americans in the postwar United States. This version concludes by having Clotelle and her husband, Jerome, return from Europe to New Orleans in 1862 to participate in the war on the Union side. The previous revisions of Brown's novel—in 1860 and 1864—had ended with the black protagonists fleeing the racial oppression of America for the tolerance of Europe. That this final version returned his characters to the United States and has them invested in a Union victory suggests Brown's confidence that there would be a place in the restored nation for African Americans. In the new chapters, Jerome joins "the Native Guard," a black regiment and is killed in battle at Port Hudson, Louisiana (ch. 36). Now a widow, Clotelle devotes her life to nursing wounded soldiers and earns the nickname "The Angel of Mercy." She eventually travels to Andersonville Prison to nurse captured Union soldiers and even participates in a foiled plot to help hundreds of them escape the infamous detention camp. After the close of the war, she returns to Mississippi to buy the land where she was once a slave and opens a school for freedmen. While Brown does not depict a marital relationship between black and white characters in the new chapters of the novel, he does imply that black loyalty to the Union will be justly rewarded by a place in the reintegrated society.

Written a couple of years later, as the failure of Reconstruction had become apparent, Harper's *Minnie's Sacrifice* (1869) is less hopeful than the novels of Collins and Brown. The novel's black protagonists, Minnie and Louis, are each the product of a white father and a slave mother and each has been raised as white (Minnie by abolitionist Quakers in the North, and Louis in the South by strong supporters of slavery). At the beginning of the Civil War, they each discover the truth about their race, decide to proudly claim black identity (though both are capable of passing for white) and realign their loyalties. For Louis, this means he must leave the Confederate army and join the Union forces: "I can never raise my hand against my mother's race" (ch. 13). As Louis's loyalties shift to the Union, the narrative reinforces the rightness of this allegiance by also paralleling it with the marital union of Louis and Minnie. Committed to the uplift of their race, the couple decides to move south at the end of the war to open a school for freedmen. Tragically, because of these efforts, Minnie is lynched by the Ku Klux Klan. Dispirited by the circumstances he sees, Louis begins to lose hope in government efforts toward Reconstruction, which he views as corrupt and uninterested in the lives of freed blacks: "Here was outrage upon outrage committed upon these people, and to tell them to hope and wait for better times, but seemed like speaking hollow words" (ch. 19). While Harper's novel does not display confidence in the union between black and white, it is ultimately more interested in the uniting of extremes in the nation's black population, those who have found success and prosperity in the North and those who have been left in poverty and blight in the postwar South. The "lesson of Minnie's sacrifice," Harper explains in the conclusion, is "that it is braver to suffer with one's own branch of the human race,—to feel, that the weaker and more despised they are, the closer we will cling to them, for the sake of helping them, than to attempt to creep out of all identity with them in their feebleness, for the sake of mere personal advantages." Like so many of the novels written in this decade, Harper's work seeks to repair a rift in order for the nation to move toward progress.

Despite the valuable cultural work going on in many of the novels discussed earlier and others like them, the critical elite began to pronounce the "decline of the novel" by the end of the decade. For example, in May 1868, a writer for the *Nation* explored the loss of the novel's "predominance and supremacy" and attributed it to a kind of generic exhaustion as well as to its poor handling by "inferior" authors who had become the producers of most of the published work: "all possible methods of working up the novelist's materials are familiar to the point of weariness" as "the literary insufficiency of the vast majority of mechanical people who set themselves to producing what has long been the most popular of literary products has had the effect of indisposing really able, ambitious workmen to range themselves as fellow workmen in the decaying fraternity" ("Decline of the Novel" 389–90). De Forest expressed similar concerns in his essay "The Great American Novel" (1868), wherein he lamented the dearth of fiction that provides "the picture of the ordinary emotions and manners of American existence" and "paint[s] the American soul within the framework of a novel" (27). He yearns for "a single tale which paints American life so broadly, truly, and sympathetically that every American of feeling and culture is forced to acknowledge the picture as a likeness of something which he knows" (28). He notes the failure of antebellum American novelists—he specifically names Cooper, James Kirke Paulding, Charles Brockden Brown, John Pendleton Kennedy, William Gilmore Simms, and Hawthorne—to produce a "tableau of American society" that would match the ones William Makepeace Thackeray and Anthony Trollope produced in England or Honoré de Balzac and George Sand produced in France. He praises Stowe's *Uncle Tom's Cabin* (1852) for being "the nearest approach to the desired phenomenon" because of its "national breadth," its "truthful outlining of character," and its "picture of American life, drawn with a few strong and passionate strokes" (28).

De Forest finds little written since *Uncle Tom's Cabin* to approach its accomplishment as a national portrait. The specific novels from the 1860s that he mentions include Oliver Wendell Holmes's *Elsie Venner* (1861) and *The Guardian Angel* (1867) and Stowe's *The Pearl of Orr's Island* (of which De Forest writes: "an exquisite little story, . . . but how small!" [28]). He calls these works "localisms," asserting that they are "not American novels; they are only New England novels" (28). He similarly characterizes the work of Donald Grant Mitchell, Bayard Taylor, and Henry Ward Beecher. The one novel that De Forest views as approaching *Uncle Tom's Cabin* in its breadth is Davis's *Waiting for the Verdict*. However, he expresses an "abhorrence of the execution" of that novel, noting that "bad taste in the selection of minor features and a rushing of adjectives to the head spoil a book which, in its table of contents, gives grand promise of an American novel" (28). In the end, De Forest voices pessimism about the capability of novels to offer the desired national portraits. He believes that "a society which is changing so rapidly" as the United States might only "be painted . . . in the daily newspaper" (29). Additionally, because he finds the country to be essentially "a nation of provinces," he proposes that no novel may be able to offer a depiction of every American: "When you have made your picture of petrified New England village life, . . . does the Mississippian or the Minnesotian [*sic*] or the Pennsylvanian recognize it as American society?" (29).

In the latter years of the 1860s, with this growing sense of the potential failure of broad narratives that could serve the entire nation, writers responded in different ways. Some chose to resurrect earlier national narratives. Think, for example, of Alger's rags-to-riches tales, like *Ragged Dick* (1868) and *Struggling Upward* (1890), which once again offer the Franklinian promise that hard work and honest character will lead to prosperity in American life. Other writers turn to the American-European contrast in an attempt to define a universal American character demonstrated in stark relief to European manners and culture. Marian Reeves's *Ingemisco* (1867), a novel that sends a southern family on the Grand Tour, is one of the earliest postbellum works to adopt this scenario. The American-European contrast would soon become essential to the period's major authors, including Twain in his nonfiction masterpiece, *The Innocents Abroad* (1869), and James in many of his books, including his novels of the next decade, *Roderick Hudson* (1875), *The American* (1877), and *Daisy Miller* (1878). These efforts illustrate how American writers turned to past narratives in search of those that would appeal to and serve the newly reunited nation.

Many American novelists seemed content with the "nation of provinces" approach and simply wrote about their own "province" rather than aspiring to works meeting De Forest's grander idea. While much of this work took the form of short stories, many novel-length works, like Beecher's *Norwood*, Taylor's *The Story of Kennett* (1866), and Trowbridge's *Lucy Arlyn* (1866), clearly reflect this preference for regional focus over national breadth. Stowe is usually discussed as the first major author to make this shift in direction in her 1860s work. For example, her *Oldtown Folks* follows orphaned siblings, Harry and Tina Percival, in Oldtown, Massachusetts, as they are raised by various guardians, educated, and grow to adulthood. In her preface, Stowe foregrounds her regionalist agenda and her goal "to interpret to the world the New England life and character in that particular time of its history which may be called the seminal period." However, Stowe maintains that there are national implications in her "interpretation" of this region. As she explains, New England "has always been a capital country to emigrate from, and North, South, East, and West have been populated largely from New England, so that the seed-bed of New England was the seed-bed of this great American Republic, and of all that is likely to come of it" (pref.). Stowe's turn toward the regional anticipated the direction subsequent American fiction writers from every region—Bret Harte, Sarah Orne Jewett, George Washington Cable, Edward Eggleston, Hamlin Garland, Rose Terry Cooke, Grace King, Mary Wilkins Freeman, and Charles Chesnutt, to name only a handful—would follow. Importantly, Marjorie Pryse has argued that this regionalist work more broadly had a reconciliation agenda similar to the romances discussed earlier. She explains that this fiction, especially in what came to be known as the "local color" vein, "could seem to reduce the fear of sectional and regional differences by making 'colorful' characters humorous to readers outside the region" (2004, 132–33). Thus, contrary to De Forest's fears, provincial writing too would serve the efforts of reunion.

In Phelps's *The Gates Ajar*, the text with which this chapter began, readers found differing narratives about spiritual reunion in competition. In the end, the narrative that provided the most assurance that there would indeed be reunion in the future won Phelps's heroine's and likely her readers' embrace. Like the competing narratives about heaven in that novel, multiple narratives about national reunion were offered to American readers of novels in the years following the Civil War. Many of these provided comforting conclusions that reassured the reader that the divided nation was now a unified one. And, while others voiced anxiety about whether such distinct sections, races, and characters could ever easily unite, they still suggested that a strong union should be the ultimate end. While novelists and their readers considered which vision of the nation's future they could embrace with confidence, the United States in the 1860s appears as a nation still in search of a national literary narrative that could take it into the later decades of the nineteenth century as its population grew more diverse and its place on the world stage became more prominent.

COMPOSITE BIBLIOGRAPHY

AARON, DANIEL (1987). *The Unwritten War: American Writers and the Civil War.* Madison: University of Wisconsin Press.

ABBOTT, ANNE W. (1850). "*The Scarlet Letter.*" *North American Review* 71, 135–48.

ACHOLONU-OLUMBA, CATHERINE (2007). *The Igbo Roots of Olaudah Equiano: A Linguistic and Anthropological Search.* Rev. ed. Abuja: Afa.

ACHOLONU-OLUMBA, CATHERINE (2009). "The Igbo Roots of Olaudah Equiano," in Korieh, Chima J. (ed.), *Olaudah Equiano and the Igbo World: History, Society, and Atlantic Diaspora Connections.* Trenton: Africa World Press, 49–66.

ALCOTT, LOUISA MAY (1989). *The Journals of Louisa May Alcott.* Joel Myerson and Daniel Shealy (eds.). Boston: Little, Brown.

ALCOTT, WILLIAM (1833). *The Young Man's Guide.* 4th ed. Boston: Samuel Colman.

ALLEN, RICHARD, and ABSALOM JONES (1794). *A Narrative of the Proceedings of the Black People, During the Late Awful Calamity in Philadelphia, in the Year 1793; and a Refutation of Some Censures, Thrown upon Them in Some Late Publication.* Philadelphia: William W. Woodward.

AMMONS, ELIZABETH (2007). "Introduction," in Ammons, Elizabeth (ed.), *Harriet Beecher Stowe's* Uncle Tom's Cabin: *A Casebook.* Oxford: Oxford University Press.

AMORY, HUGH (1993). "Proprietary Illustration: The Case of Cooke's Tom Jones," in Harvey, D. R., Wallace Kirsop, and B. J. McMullin (eds.), *An Index of Civilisation: Studies of Printing and Publishing History in Honour of Keith Maslen.* Clayton: Centre for Bibliographical and Textual Studies, Monash University, 137–47.

ANDERSON, BENEDICT (1983). *Imagined Communities: Reflections on the Origin and Spread of Nationalism.* London: Verso.

ANDREWS, WILLIAM L. (1981). "The 1850s: The First Afro-American Literary Renaissance," in Andrews, William L. (ed.), *Literary Romanticism in America.* Baton Rouge: Louisiana State University Press, 38–60.

ANDREWS, WILLIAM L. (1990). "The Novelization of Voice in Early African American Narrative." *PMLA* 105.1, 23–34.

ANDREWS, WILLIAM L. (ed.) (1996). *The Oxford Frederick Douglass Reader.* New York: Oxford University Press.

ANON (1800). "Thoughts on the Probable Termination of Negro Slavery in the United States of America." *The Monthly Magazine, and American Review* 2.2, 81–4.

ANON (1817). *The Irish Emigrant.* Winchester: VA: John T. Sharrocks.

ANON (1832). *The Young Man's Own Book.* Philadelphia: Key, Mielke and Biddle.

ANON (1834). "Horrid Case of Intemperance." *Salem Gazette* 3, 2.

ANON (1846). "Literary Phenomena." *American Review* 4, 405–8.

ANON (1852a). "Literary Notices." *Frederick Douglass' Paper* 5, 225.

ANON (1852b). "Literature of Slavery." *The New Englander* 10.40, 588–613.

ANON (1852c). "Notices of New Works." *Southern Literary Messenger* 8.10, 630–8.

ANON (1853). "To the Editor of the *New-York Daily Times*." *New York Times* 25 April, 2.

ANON (1855). "Ruth Hall." *Southern Quarterly Review* 11, 438–50.

ANON (1868). "Decline of the Novel." *Nation* 6, 389–90.

ANTELYES, PETER (1990). *Tales of Adventurous Enterprise: Washington Irving and the Poetics of Western Expansion*. New York: Columbia University Press.

ANTHONY, DAVID (2009). *Paper Money Men: Commerce, Manhood, and the Sensational Public Sphere in Antebellum America*. Columbus: Ohio State University Press.

APESS, WILLIAM (1992). *On Our Own Ground: The Complete Writings of William Apess, a Pequot*. Barry O'Connell (ed.). Amherst: University of Massachusetts Press.

APPLEBY, JOYCE (2010). *The Relentless Revolution: A History of Capitalism*. New York: Norton.

ARAC, JONATHAN (2005). *The Emergence of American Literary Narrative, 1820–1860*. Cambridge, MA: Harvard University Press.

ARMSTRONG, NANCY (1994). "Why Daughters Die: The Racial Logic of American Sentimentalism." *Yale Journal of Criticism* 7, 1–24.

ARMSTRONG, NANCY, and LEONARD TENNENHOUSE (1994). *The Imaginary Puritan: Literature, Intellectual Labor, and the Origins of Personal Life*. Berkeley: University of California Press.

ARMSTRONG, NANCY, and LEONARD TENNENHOUSE (2008). "The Problem of Population and the Form of the American Novel." *American Literary History* 20.4, 667–85.

AVALLONE, CHARLENE (2006). "Catharine Sedgwick and the Circles of New York." *Legacy* 23, 115–31.

BAKER, ERNEST A. (1924–39). *The History of the English Novel*. 10 vols. London: H. F. and G. Witherby.

BAKER, HOUSTON A. (1984). *Blues, Ideology, and Afro-American Literature: A Vernacular Theory*. Chicago: University of Chicago Press.

BARKER-BENFIELD, G. J. (1992). *The Culture of Sensibility: Sex and Society in Eighteenth-Century Britain*. Chicago: University of Chicago Press.

BARLOWE, JAMIE (2000). *The Scarlet Mob of Scribbling Women: Rereading Hester Prynne*. Carbondale: Southern Illinois University Press.

BARNARD, PHILIP, AND STEPHEN SHAPIRO (2009). "Introduction," in Barnard, Philip and Stephen Shapiro (eds.), *Ormond; or the Secret Witness, with Related Texts*. Indianapolis: Hackett, ix–lii.

BARNES, ELIZABETH (1997). *States of Sympathy: Seduction and Democracy in the American Novel.* New York: Columbia University Press.

BARNES, ELIZABETH (2010). "Novels," in Gross, Robert A., and Mary Kelley (eds.), *An Extensive Republic: Print, Culture, and Society in the New Nation, 1790–1840.* Vol. 2 of *A History of the Book in America.* Chapel Hill: University of North Carolina Press, 440–9.

BARNES, JAMES J. (1974). *Authors, Publishers and Politicians: The Quest for an Anglo-American Copyright Agreement, 1815–1854.* Columbus: Ohio State University Press.

BARTHÉLEMY, JEAN-JACQUES (1923). *The Travels of Anacharsis the Younger in Greece, During the Middle of the Fourth Century before the Christian Era.* 5 vols. Jean Denis Barbie du Bocage (trans.). New York: Nabu Press.

BAUER, RALPH (2003). *The Cultural Geography of Colonial American Literatures: Empire, Travel, Modernity.* Cambridge: Cambridge University Press.

BAUMGARTNER, BARBARA (2001). "Intimate Reflections: Body, Voice, and Identity in Stoddard's *Morgesons.*" *ESQ: A Journal of the American Renaissance* 47.3, 185–211.

BAYM, NINA (1976). *The Shape of Hawthorne's Career.* Ithaca: Cornell University Press.

BAYM, NINA (1978). *Woman's Fiction: A Guide to Novels by and about Women in America, 1820–1870.* Ithaca: Cornell University Press.

BAYM, NINA (1982). "Nathaniel Hawthorne and His Mother: A Biographical Speculation." *American Literature* 54.1, 1–27.

BAYM, NINA (1984). *Novels, Readers, and Reviewers: Responses to Fiction in Antebellum America.* Ithaca: Cornell University Press.

BAYM, NINA (1992). "How Men and Women Wrote Indian Stories," in Peck, Daniel (ed.), *New Essays on The Last of the Mohicans.* New York: Cambridge University Press, 67–86.

BAYM, NINA (1993). *Woman's Fiction: A Guide to Novels by and about Women in America, 1820–1870.* 2nd ed. Urbana: University of Illinois Press.

BAYM, NINA (2004). "Revisiting Hawthorne's Feminism." *Nathaniel Hawthorne Review* 30, 32–55.

BEECHER, LYMAN (1835). *A Plea for the West.* Cincinnati: Truman and Smith.

BELL, MICHAEL DAVITT (1971). *Hawthorne and the Historical Romance of New England.* Princeton: Princeton University Press.

BELL, MICHAEL DAVITT (1980). *The Development of American Romance: The Sacrifice of Relation.* Chicago: University of Chicago Press.

BELL, MICHAEL DAVITT (1995). "Conditions of Literary Vocation," in Bercovitch, Sacvan (ed.), *The Cambridge History of American Literature, Volume Two: Prose Writing, 1820–1865.* Cambridge: Cambridge University Press, 9–123.

BENJAMIN, WALTER (1998). *The Origins of German Tragic Drama.* John Osbourne (trans.). London: Verso.

BENSON, JAMES D. (1975). "'Sympathetic' Criticism: George Eliot's Response to Contemporary Reviewing." *Nineteenth-Century Fiction* 29.4, 428–40.

BERCAW, MARY K. (1987). *Melville's Sources.* Evanston: Northwestern University Press.

BERCOVITCH, SACVAN (1975). *The Puritan Origins of the American Self.* New Haven: Yale University Press.

BERCOVITCH, SACVAN (1988a). "The A-Politics of Ambiguity in *The Scarlet Letter.*" *New Literary History* 19.3, 629–54.

BERCOVITCH, SACVAN (1988b). "Hawthorne's A-Morality of Compromise." *Representations* 24, 1–27.

BERCOVITCH, SACVAN (1993). *The Rites of Assent: Transformations in the Symbolic Construction of America.* New York: Routledge.

BERGLAND, RENÉE L. (2000). *The National Uncanny: Indian Ghosts and American Subjects.* Hanover, NH: University Press of New England.

BERGMANN, HANS (1995). *God in the Street: New York Writing from the Penny Press to Melville.* Philadelphia: Temple University Press.

BERKHOFER, ROBERT F., JR. (1978). *The White Man's Indian: Images of the American Indian from Columbus to the Present.* New York: Vintage.

BHABHA, HOMI K. (1990). "Dissemi Nation," in Bhabha, Homi K. (ed.), *Nation and Narration.* London: Routledge, 291–321.

BHABHA, HOMI (1994). *The Location of Culture.* New York: Routledge.

BLACK HAWK (2008). *Life of Black Hawk, or Mà-ka-tai-me-she-kià-kiàk, Dictated by Himself.* J. Gerald Kennedy (ed.). New York: Penguin.

BLASSINGAME, JOHN ET AL. (eds.) (1979). *The Frederick Douglass Papers, Series One.* New Haven: Yale University Press.

BOELHOWER, WILLIAM (1987). *Through a Glass Darkly: Ethnic Semiosis in American Literature.* New York: Oxford University Press.

BREITWIESER, MITCHELL (1990). *American Puritanism and the Defense of Mourning: Religion, Grief, and Ethnology in Mary Rowlandson's Captivity Narrative.* Madison: University of Wisconsin Press.

BRICKHOUSE, ANNA (2004). *Transamerican Literary Relations and the Nineteenth-Century Public Sphere.* New York: Cambridge University Press.

BRIGHAM, CLARENCE SAUNDERS (1958). *Bibliography of American Editions of Robinson Crusoe to 1830.* Worcester: American Antiquarian Society.

BRISSENDEN, R. F. (1974). *Virtue in Distress: Studies in the Novel of Sentiment from Richardson to Sade.* London: Macmillan.

BRODHEAD, RICHARD (1984). "Hawthorne and the Fate of Politics." *Essays in Literature* 11, 95–103.

BROOKS, JOANNA (2004). "Held Captive by the Irish: Quaker Captivity Narratives in Frontier Pennsylvania." *New Hibernia Review* 8.3, 31–46.

BROOKS, LISA (2008). *The Common Pot: The Recovery of Native Space in the Northeast.* Minneapolis: University of Minnesota Press.

Brooks, Peter (1985). *Reading for the Plot: Design and Intention in Narrative.* New York: Vintage.

Brown, Bill (1997). "Reading the West: Cultural and Historical Background," in *Reading the West: An Anthology of Dime Westerns.* Boston: Bedford/St. Martin's, 1–40.

Brown, Gillian (1991). "Hawthorne, Inheritance, and Women's Property." *Studies in the Novel* 23.1, 107–18.

Brownson, Orestes Augustus (1850). "*The Scarlet Letter.*" *Brownson's Quarterly Review* 4, 528–32.

Buell, Frederick (1994). *National Culture and the New Global System.* Baltimore: Johns Hopkins University Press.

Buell, Lawrence (1995). *The Environmental Imagination: Thoreau, Nature Writing, and the Formation of American Culture.* Cambridge, MA: Harvard University Press.

Burnham, Michelle (2001). "Introduction," in Winkfield, Unca Eliza, *The Female American; or, The Adventures of Unca Eliza Winkfield.* Michelle Burnham (ed.). Peterborough, ON: Broadview, 9–28.

Burstein, Andrew (2007). *The Original Knickerbocker: The Life of Washington Irving.* New York: Basic Books.

Busick, Sean R. (2005). *A Sober Desire for History: William Gilmore Simms as Historian.* Columbia: University of South Carolina Press.

Byrd, Max (1974). "The Detective Detected: From Sophocles to Ross MacDonald." *Yale Review* 64, 72–83.

Calef, Robert (1914). *More Wonders of the Invisible World,* in Burr, George Lincoln (ed.), *Narratives of the Witchcraft Cases, 1648–1706.* New York: Scribner's, 288–393.

Calloway, Colin (1995). *The American Revolution in Indian Country: Crisis and Diversity in Native American Communities.* New York: Cambridge University Press.

Campbell, Maria (1848). *Revolutionary Services and Civil Life of General William Hull.* New York: D. Appleton.

Carby, Hazel (1987). *Reconstructing Womanhood: The Emergence of the Afro-American Woman Novelist.* New York: Oxford University Press.

Carlyle, Thomas (1969). *Complete Works of Thomas Carlyle in Thirty Volumes: Centenary Edition* (1896–99). New York: AMS Press.

Carlyle, Thomas (2002). *The French Revolution: A History.* New York: Modern Library/Random House.

Carrere, Marissa (2013). "'Let Them Sink Into Oblivion': Genealogical Form and Familial Forgetting in Susanna Rowson's *Reuben and Rachel.*" *Eighteenth-Century Studies* 46, 183–95.

Carretta, Vincent (2005). *Equiano, the African: Biography of a Self-Made Man.* Athens: University of Georgia Press.

Casper, Scott E., et al. (eds.) (2007). *The Industrial Book, 1840–1880.* Vol. 3 of *A History of the Book in America.* Chapel Hill: University of North Carolina Press.

Cather, Willa (1988). "The Best Short Stories of Sarah Orne Jewett" (1925), in *Willa Cather on Writing.* Lincoln: University of Nebraska Press, 47–59.

Catlin, George (1989). *North American Indians.* Peter Matthiessen (ed.). New York: Penguin.

Chapman, Mary, and Glenn Hendler (eds.) (1999). *Sentimental Men: Masculinity and the Politics of Affect in American Culture.* Berkeley: University of California Press.

Charvat, William (1968). *The Profession of Authorship in America, 1800–1870: The Papers of William Charvat.* Columbus: Ohio State University Press.

Chase, Richard (1957). *The American Novel and Its Tradition.* Garden City: Doubleday-Anchor.

Chielens, Edward E. (ed.) (1986). *American Literary Magazines: The Eighteenth and Nineteenth Centuries.* New York: Greenwood Press.

Child, Lydia Maria (1998). "Letter II. August 26, 1841," in Mills, Bruce (ed.), *Letters from New-York.* Athens: University of Georgia Press, 12–15.

Chiles, Katy (2008). "Within and Without Raced Nations: Intratextuality, Martin Delany, and *Blake; or, The Huts of America,*" *American Literature* 80, 323–52.

Cho, Yu-Fang (2007). "A Romance of (Miscege)Nations: Ann Sophia Stephens' *Malaeska: The Indian Wife of the White Hunter* (1839, 1860)." *Arizona Quarterly* 63.1, 1–25.

Clark, Robert (1984). *History, Ideology and Myth in American Fiction, 1823–1852.* London: Macmillan.

Clements, Victoria (1995). "Introduction," in Sedgwick, Catharine Maria, *A New-England Tale.* Victoria Clements (ed.). New York: Oxford University Press, vii–xxvii.

Cohen, Lara Langer (2011). *The Fabrication of American Literature: Fraudulence and Antebellum Print Culture.* Philadelphia: University of Pennsylvania Press.

Colacurcio, Michael J. (1972). "Footsteps of Ann Hutchinson: The Context of *The Scarlet Letter.*" *ELH* 39, 459–94.

Colacurcio, Michael J. (1984). *The Province of Piety: Moral History in Hawthorne's Early Tales.* Cambridge, MA: Harvard University Press.

Conforti, Joseph A. (2001). *Imagining New England: Explorations of Regional Identity from the Pilgrims to the Mid-Twentieth Century.* Chapel Hill: University of North Carolina Press.

Connery, Thomas B. (1903). "Paul Jones in School Libraries." *New York Times,* 24 May, 26.

Corson, James C. (1963). "Some American Books at Abbotsford." *Bibliotheck* 4.2, 44–65.

Coultrap-McQuin, Susan Margaret (1990). *Doing Literary Business: American Women Writers in the Nineteenth Century.* Chapel Hill: University of North Carolina Press.

Coxe, Arthur Cleveland (1851). "The Writings of Hawthorne."*Church Review and Ecclesiastical Register* 4, 489–511.

Cowie, Alexander (1948). *The Rise of the American Novel.* New York: American Book Company.

Crowley, John W. (1997). "Slaves to the Bottle: Gough's *Autobiography* and Douglass's *Narrative*," in Reynolds, David S. and Debra J. Rosenthal (eds.), *The Serpent in the Cup: Temperance in American Literature.* Amherst: University of Massachusetts Press, 115–35.

Dalke, Anne (1988). "Original Vice: The Political Implications of Incest in the Early America Novel." *Early American Literature* 23.3, 188–201.

Daly, Robert (1973). "William Bradford's Vision of History." *American Literature* 44.4, 557–69.

Damon-Bach, Lucinda L. (2003). "To 'Act' and 'Transact': *Redwood*'s Revisionary Heroines," in Damon-Bach, Lucinda L. and Victoria Clements (eds.), *Catharine Maria Sedgwick: Critical Perspectives.* Boston: Northeastern University Press, 56–73.

Damon-Bach, Lucinda L., and Victoria Clements (2003). "Introduction," in Damon-Bach, Lucinda L. and Victoria Clements (eds.), *Catharine Maria Sedgwick: Critical Perspectives.* Boston: Northeastern University Press, xxi–xxxi.

Darwin, Charles (1859). *On the Origin of Species.* London: John Murray.

Darwin, Charles (1871). *The Descent of Man.* London: John Murray.

Davidson, Cathy N. (1986). *Revolution and the Word: The Rise of the Novel in America.* New York: Oxford University Press.

Davidson, Cathy N. (1989). "The Life and Times of *Charlotte Temple*: The Biography of a Book," in Davidson, Cathy N. (ed.), *Reading in America: Literature and Social History.* Baltimore: Johns Hopkins University Press, 157–79.

Davidson, Cathy N. (2004). *Revolution and the Word: The Rise of the Novel in America.* Expanded ed. New York: Oxford University Press.

Davidson, Cathy (2006). "Olaudah Equiano, Written By Himself." *Novel* 40.1–2, 18–51.

Davis, Leith, Ian Duncan, and Janet Sorensen (eds.) (2004). *Scotland and the Borders of Romanticism.* Cambridge: Cambridge University Press.

Dawdy, Shannon Lee (2008). *Building the Devil's Empire: French Colonial New Orleans.* Chicago: University of Chicago Press.

Dayan, Joan (1991). "Romance and Race," in Elliott, Emory (ed.), *The Columbia History of the American Novel.* New York: Columbia University Press, 89–109.

Dean, Janet. (2003). "Stopping Traffic: Spectacles of Romance and Race in *The Last of the Mohicans*," in Strehle, Susan and Mary Patricia Carden (eds.), *Doubled Plots: Romance and History.* Jackson: University Press of Mississippi, 45–66.

DECKER, WILLIAM MERRILL (2007). "'Surely Cora Was Not Forgotten': Remembering Africa in the Leather-Stocking Tales," in Walker, Jeffrey (ed.), *Reading Cooper, Teaching Cooper*. New York: AMS Press, 201–21.

DEFOE, DANIEL (2007). *Robinson Crusoe* (1719). Tom Keymer (ed.). New York: Oxford University Press.

DE FOREST, JOHN W. (1868). "The Great American Novel." *Nation* 6, 28.

DEKKER, GEORGE, and JOHN P. MCWILLIAMS (eds.) (1973). *Fenimore Cooper: The Critical Heritage*. London: Routledge and Kegan Paul.

DEKKER, GEORGE (1987). *The American Historical Romance*. Cambridge: Cambridge University Press.

DEKKER, GEORGE (1997). "Border and Frontier: Tourism in Scott's *Guy Mannering* and Cooper's *The Pioneers*." *James Fenimore Cooper Society Miscellaneous Papers* 9, 1–6.

DELBANCO, ANDREW (1991). *The Puritan Ordeal*. Cambridge, MA: Harvard University Press.

DELORIA, PHILIP J. (1999). *Playing Indian*. New Haven: Yale University Press.

DENNING, MICHAEL (1987). *Mechanic Accents: Dime Novels and Working-Class Culture in America*. London: Verso.

DENNIS, IAN (1997). "The Worthlessness of Duncan Heyward: A Waverley Hero in America." *Studies in the Novel* 29.1, 1–16.

DEROUNIAN, KATHRYN ZABELLE (1988). "The Publication, Promotion, and Distribution of Mary Rowlandson's Captivity Narrative in the Seventeenth Century." *Early American Literature* 23.3, 239–61.

DEROUNIAN-STODOLA, KATHRYN ZABELLE (ed.) (1998). *Women's Indian Captivity Narratives*. New York: Penguin.

DERRICK, SCOTT S. (1997). *Monumental Anxieties: Homoerotic Desire and Feminine Influence in 19th-Century U.S. Literature*. New Brunswick: Rutgers University Press.

DESALVO, LOUISE (1987). *Nathaniel Hawthorne*. Atlantic Highlands: Humanities Press.

DEWEY, MARY E. (ed.) (1871). *Life and Letters of Catharine M. Sedgwick*. New York: Harper.

DIFFLEY, KATHLEEN (1992). *Where My Heart Is Turning Ever: Civil War Stories and Constitutional Reform, 1861–1876*. Athens: University of Georgia Press.

DI MAIO, IRENE (ed. and trans.) (2006). *Gerstäcker's Louisiana: Fiction and Travel Sketches from Antebellum Times Through Reconstruction*. Baton Rouge: Louisiana State University Press.

DIMOCK, WAI CHEE (1989). *Empire for Liberty: Melville and the Poetics of Individualism*. Princeton: Princeton University Press.

DINIUS, MARCY (2004). "Poe's Moon Shot: 'Hans Phaall' and the Art and Science of Antebellum Print Culture." *Poe Studies* 37, 1–10.

DOBSON, JOANNE (1988). "Introduction," in Southworth, E. D. E. N., *The Hidden Hand; or, Capitola the Madcap*. Joanne Dobson (ed.). New Brunswick: Rutgers University Press, xi–xli.

DODDRIDGE, JOSEPH (1868). *Logan, The Last of the Race of Shikellemus, Chief of the Cayuga Nation* (1823). Cincinnati: Robert Clark.

DONALDSON, SUSAN (1998). *Competing Voices: The American Novel, 1865–1914*. New York: Twayne.

DOODY, MARGARET ANNE (1996). *The True Story of the Novel*. New Brunswick: Rutgers University Press.

DOOLEN, ANDY (2005). *Fugitive Empire: Locating Early American Imperialism*. Minneapolis: University of Minnesota Press.

DOUBLEDAY, NEAL FRANK (1972). *Hawthorne's Early Tales: A Critical Study*. Durham: Duke University Press.

DOUGLAS, ANN (1977). *The Feminization of American Culture*. New York: Knopf.

DOUGLASS, FREDERICK (1997). *Narrative of the Life of Frederick Douglass, An American Slave, Written By Himself* (1845). William L. Andrews and William S. McFeely (eds.). New York: Norton.

DOWNES, PAUL (1996). "Sleep–Walking out of the Revolution: Brown's *Edgar Huntly*." *Eighteenth-Century Studies* 29.4, 413–31.

DOWNING, ANDREW JACKSON (1850). *The Architecture of Country Houses*. New York: D. Appleton.

DOYLE, LAURA (2007). "'A' for Atlantic: The Colonizing Force of Hawthorne's *The Scarlet Letter*." *American Literature* 79.2, 243–73.

DRINNON, RICHARD (1980). *Facing West: The Metaphysics of Indian-Hating and Empire Building*. Minneapolis: University of Minnesota Press.

DREXLER, MICHAEL J. (2007). "Appendix A: Biographical Documents," in Sansay, Leonora, *Secret History; or, The Horrors of St. Domingo and Laura*. Michael J. Drexler (ed.). Peterborough, ON: Broadview, 223–42.

DUNCAN, IAN (1992). *Modern Romance and Transformations of the Novel: The Gothic, Scott, Dickens*. Cambridge: Cambridge University Press.

DUYCKINCK, EVERT A. (1850). "*The Scarlet Letter*." *Literary World* 6, 323–5.

EDWARDS, JONATHAN (2003). "Sinners in the Hands of an Angry God," in Stout, Harry S., Nathan O. Hatch, and Kyle P. Farley (eds.), *The Works of Jonathan Edwards: Sermons and Discourses, 1739–1742*. New Haven: Yale University Press, 400–35.

EDWARDS, JUSTIN (2001). *Exotic Journeys: Exploring the Erotics of US Travel Literature 1840–1930*. Hanover, NH: University Press of New England.

EDWARDS, PAUL (1967). "Introduction" to Equiano, Olaudah, *Equiano's Travels: His Autobiography*. London: Heinemann, ix–xviii.

EKE, MAUREEN N. (2009). "(Re)Imagining Community: Olaudah Equiano and the (Re)Construction of Igbo (African) Identity," in Korieh, Chima J. (ed.), *Olaudah*

Equiano and the Igbo World: History, Society, and Atlantic Diaspora Connections. Trenton: Africa World Press, 23–47.

ELBERT, MONIKA (1989). "Hester on the Scaffold, Dimmesdale in the Closet: Hawthorne's Seven-Year Itch." *Essays in Literature* 16.2, 234–55.

ELBERT, MONIKA (1990). "Hester's Maternity: Stigma or Weapon?" *ESQ: A Journal of the American Renaissance* 36, 175–207.

ELIOT, GEORGE (1967). *Essays of George Eliot*. Thomas Pinney (ed.). New York: Columbia University Press.

EMERSON, RALPH WALDO (1883). "Nature" (1844) in *The Complete Works of Ralph Waldo Emerson*. Vol. 3. Boston: Houghton Mifflin, 167–96.

EMERSON, RALPH WALDO (1903). "An Address Delivered before the Senior Class in Divinity College, Cambridge, July 15, 1838," in *The Complete Works of Ralph Waldo Emerson*. Vol. 1. Boston: Houghton Mifflin, 117–51.

EMERSON, RALPH WALDO (1904). "Europe and European Books" (1870) in *The Complete Works of Ralph Waldo Emerson*. Vol. 12. London: Archibald Constable, 365–78.

EMERSON, RALPH WALDO (1971). "The American Scholar" (1837) in Spiller, Robert E. and Alfred R. Ferguson (eds.), *The Collected Works of Ralph Waldo Emerson, I: Nature, Addresses, and Lectures*. Cambridge, MA: Harvard University Press, 49–70.

EMERSON, RALPH WALDO (1983). *Essays and Lectures*. Joel Porte (ed.). New York: Library of America.

EQUIANO, OLAUDAH (2003). *The Interesting Narrative and Other Writings*. Vincent Carretta (ed.). New York: Penguin.

ERICKSON, PAUL (2003). "New Books, New Men: City Mysteries Fiction, Authorship, and the Literary Market." *Early American Studies* 1.1, 273–312.

ERICKSON, PAUL (2005). *Welcome to Sodom: The Cultural Work of City-Mysteries Fiction in Antebellum America*. Ph.D. diss., University of Texas.

ERNEST, JOHN (2009). *Chaotic Justice: Rethinking African American Literary History*. Chapel Hill: University of North Carolina Press.

ERSKINE, JOHN (1910). *Leading American Novelists*. New York: H. Holt.

EXMAN, EUGENE (1965). *The Brothers Harper: A Unique Publishing Partnership and Its Impact Upon the Cultural Life of America from 1817 to 1853*. New York: Harper.

FABI, M. GIULIA (1993). "The 'Unguarded Expressions of the Feelings of the Negroes': Gender, Slave Resistance, and William Wells Brown's Revisions of *Clotel*." *African American Review* 27.4, 639–54.

FAHS, ALICE (2001). *The Imagined Civil War: Popular Literature of the North, 1861–1865*. Chapel Hill: University of North Carolina Press.

FANON, FRANTZ (1967). *Black Skin, White Masks* (1952). Charles Lam Markmann (trans.). New York: Grove.

FEHRENBACHER, DON E. (1981). *Slavery, Law, and Politics*. New York: Oxford University Press.

FEIDELSON, CHARLES (1953). *Symbolism and American Literature.* Chicago: University of Chicago Press.

FERGUSON, ROBERT A. (1984). *Law and Letters in American Culture.* Cambridge, MA: Harvard University Press.

FERN, FANNY (1852). "To Jack Plane." *Olive Branch,* 13 March, n.p.

FERN, FANNY (1868). "A Word to Editors." *New York Ledger,* 5 May, n.p.

FETTERLEY, JUDITH (ed.) (1985). *Provisions: A Reader from 19th-Century American Women.* Bloomington: Indiana University Press.

FETTERLEY, JUDITH (1994). "'Not in the Least American': Nineteenth-Century Literary Regionalism." *College English* 56.8, 877–97.

FETTERLEY, JUDITH (1998). "'My Sister, My Sister!': The Rhetoric of Catharine Sedgwick's *Hope Leslie.*" *American Literature* 70, 491–516.

FETTERLEY, JUDITH, and MARJORIE PRYSE (2003). *Writing Out of Place: Regionalism, Women, and American Literary Culture.* Urbana: University of Illinois Press.

FICHTELBERG, JOSEPH (2003). *Critical Fictions: Sentiment and the American Market, 1780–1870.* Athens: University of Georgia Press.

FIEDLER, LESLIE A. (1966). *Love and Death in the American Novel* (1960). 2nd ed. New York: Stein and Day.

FIELDS, ANNIE (1884). "Glimpses of Emerson." *Harper's New Monthly Magazine,* 457–68.

FIELDS, ANNIE (1897). *Life and Letters of Harriet Beecher Stowe.* Boston: Houghton Mifflin.

FINKELMAN, PAUL (2003). *Defending Slavery: Proslavery Thought in the Old South: A Brief History with Documents.* Boston: Bedford/St. Martin's.

FITZPATRICK, TARA (1991). "The Figure of Captivity: The Cultural Work of the Puritan Captivity Narrative." *American Literary History* 3.1, 1–26.

FLEIGELMAN, JAY (1982). *Prodigals and Pilgrims: The American Revolution Against Patriarchal Authority.* New York: Cambridge University Press.

FOOTE, CALEB (1850). "*The Scarlet Letter.*" *Salem Gazette* 19 March, 2.

FOSTER, EDWARD HALSEY (1974). *Catharine Maria Sedgwick.* New York: Twayne.

FOSTER, FRANCES SMITH (1990). "Introduction," in *A Brighter Coming Day: A Frances Ellen Watkins Harper Reader.* New York: Feminist Press, 3–40.

FOWLER GEORGE (1813). *A Flight to the Moon; or, The Vision of Randalthus.* Baltimore: A. Miltenberger.

FRANCIS, RICHARD (1997). *Transcendental Utopias: Individual and Community at Brook Farm, Fruitlands, and Walden.* Ithaca: Cornell University Press.

FRANKLIN, BENJAMIN (1987). *Writings.* Leo J. A. Lemay (ed.). New York: Library of America.

FRANKLIN, WAYNE (2007). "Financing America's First Literary Boom." *Proceedings of the American Antiquarian Society* 117, 351–78.

FREDRICKSON, GEORGE M. (1971). *The Black Image in the White Mind: The Debate on Afro-American Character and Destiny, 1817–1914.* New York: Harper.

FREIBERT, LUCY M., and BARBARA A. WHITE (eds.) (1985). *Hidden Hands: An Anthology of American Women Writers, 1790–1870*. New Brunswick: Rutgers University Press.

FULLER, MARGARET (1994). *Woman in the Nineteenth Century and Other Writings* (1845). Donna Dickenson (ed.). New York: Oxford University Press.

FULLER, THOMAS (1952). *The Worthies of England* (1662). John Freeman (ed.). London: George Allen and Unwin.

GARDNER, ERIC (2009). *Unexpected Places: Relocating Nineteenth-Century African American Literature*. Jackson: University Press of Mississippi.

GATES, HENRY LOUIS (ed.) (1987). *Classic Slave Narratives*. New York: Penguin.

GATES, HENRY LOUIS (1988). "The Trope of the Talking Book," in *The Signifying Monkey: A Theory of African American Literary Criticism*. New York: Oxford University Press, 127–69.

GATES, SONDRA SMITH (2003). "Sedgwick's American Poor," in Damon-Bach, Lucinda L. and Victoria Clements (eds.), *Catharine Maria Sedgwick: Critical Perspectives*. Boston: Northeastern University Press, 174–87.

GATTA, JOHN (2004). *Making Nature Sacred: Literature, Religion, and Environment in America from the Puritans to the Present*. Oxford: Oxford University Press.

GERBI, ANTONELLO (1973). *The Dispute of the New World: The History of a Polemic, 1750–1900*. Jeremy Moyle (trans.). Pittsburgh: University of Pittsburgh Press.

GILMORE, MICHAEL T. (1994). "Hawthorne and the Making of the Middle Class," in Dimock, Wai Chee and Michael T. Gilmore (eds.), *Rethinking Class: Literary Studies and Social Formations*. New York: Columbia University Press, 215–38.

GILROY, PAUL (1993). *The Black Atlantic: Modernity and Double Consciousness*. Cambridge, MA: Harvard University Press.

GINSBERG, LESLEY (2001). "The ABCs of *The Scarlet Letter*." *Studies in American Fiction* 29.1, 13–31.

GLADSKY, THOMAS S. (1992). *Princes, Peasants, and Other Polish Selves: Ethnicity in American Literature*. Amherst: University of Massachusetts Press.

GLEACH, FREDERIC W. (2003). "Controlled Speculation: Interpreting the Saga of Pocahontas and Captain John Smith," in Brown, Jennifer, S. H. Brown and Elizabeth Vibert (eds.), *Reading Beyond Words: Contexts for Native History*. Peterborough, ON: Broadview, 39–74.

GODDU, TERESA A. (2001). "Letters Turned to Gold: Hawthorne, Authorship, and Slavery." *Studies in American Fiction* 29.1, 49–76.

GOHDES, CLARENCE (1942). "British Interest in American Literature during the Latter Part of the Nineteenth Century as Reflected by Mudie's Select Library." *American Literature* 13.4, 356–62.

GORING, PAUL (2005). *The Rhetoric of Sensibility in Eighteenth-Century Culture*. Cambridge: Cambridge University Press.

Gossett, Thomas F. (1985). *"Uncle Tom's Cabin" and American Culture,* Dallas: Southern Methodist University Press.

Gough, John B. (1870). *Autobiography and Personal Reflections of John B. Gough.* Springfield: Bill, Nichols.

Gough, John B. (1885). *Platform Echoes.* Hartford: A.D. Worthington.

Gould, Philip (1996). *Covenant and Republic: Historical Romance and the Politics of Puritanism.* Cambridge: Cambridge University Press.

Gould, Philip (2005). "Catharine Sedgwick's Cosmopolitan Nation." *New England Quarterly* 78, 232–58.

Gould, Stephen Jay (1981). *The Mismeasure of Man.* New York: Norton.

Grabo, Norman S. (1981). *The Coincidental Art of Charles Brockden Brown.* Chapel Hill: University of North Carolina Press.

Graham, Sylvester (1838). *A Lecture to Young Men, on Chastity, Intended Also for the Serious Consideration of Parents and Guardians.* 4th ed. Boston: George W. Light.

Gray, John Chipman (1826). "Art VII.—*The Rebels, or Boston before the Revolution.*" *North American Review* 22.51, 400–8.

Green, James N. (1995). "Ivanhoe in America," in *Annual Report of the Library Company of Philadelphia for the Year 1994.* Philadelphia: Library Company of Philadelphia.

Green, James N. (2000). "English Books and Printing in the Age of Franklin," in Amory, Hugh and David D. Hall (eds.), *The Colonial Book in the Atlantic World.* Cambridge: Cambridge University Press.

Green, James N. (2010). "The Rise of Book Publishing," in Gross, Robert A. and Mary Kelley (eds.), *An Extensive Republic: Print, Culture, and Society in the New Nation, 1790–1840.* Vol. 2 of *A History of the Book in America.* Chapel Hill: University of North Carolina Press, 75–127.

Green, James N., and Peter Stallybrass (2006). *Benjamin Franklin: Writer and Printer.* New Castle, DE: Oak Knoll.

Green, Martin (1991). *Seven Types of Adventure Tale: An Etiology of a Major Genre.* University Park: Pennsylvania State University Press.

Greenberg, Amy S. (2005). *Manifest Manhood and the Antebellum American Empire.* New York: Cambridge University Press.

Greenspan, Ezra (2000). *George Palmer Putnam: Representative American Publisher.* University Park: Pennsylvania State University Press.

Griffin, Susan M. (2004). *Anti-Catholicism and Nineteenth-Century Fiction.* Cambridge: Cambridge University Press.

Griswold, Rufus W. (1847). *The Prose Writers of America: With a Survey of the History, Condition, and Prospects of American Literature.* Philadelphia: Carey and Hart.

Gross, Robert, and Mary Kelley (eds.) (2010). *An Extensive Republic: Print, Culture, and Society in the New Nation, 1790–1840.* Vol. 2 of *A History of the Book in America.* Chapel Hill: University of North Carolina Press.

Groves, Jeffrey D. (2007a). "Courtesy of the Trade," in Casper, Scott E. et al. (eds.), *The Industrial Book, 1840–1880.* Vol. 3 of *A History of the Book in America.* Chapel Hill: University of North Carolina Press, 139–47.

Groves, Jeffrey D. (2007b). "Trade Communication," in Casper, Scott E. et al. (eds.), *The Industrial Book, 1840–1880.* Vol. 3 of *A History of the Book in America.* Chapel Hill: University of North Carolina Press, 130–8.

Gruesz, Kirsten Silva (2002). *Ambassadors of Culture: The Transamerican Origins of Latino Writing.* Princeton: Princeton University Press.

Habermas, Jürgen (1998). *The Structural Transformation of the Public Sphere: An Inquiry Into a Category of Bourgeois Society* (1962). Thomas Burger (trans.). Cambridge, MA: MIT Press.

Haight, Gordon S. (1968). *George Eliot: A Biography.* Oxford: Oxford University Press.

Hale, Edward Everett (1886). "The Man Without a Country," in *The Man Without a Country and Other Tales.* Boston: Roberts Brothers, 5–47.

Hale, Edward Everett (1910). "Ten Times One Is Ten," in *The Works of Edward Everett Hale: Ten Times One Is Ten, and Other Stories.* Boston: Little, Brown, 3–110.

Hall, David D. (1990). *The Antinomian Controversy, 1636–1638: A Documentary History.* Durham: Duke University Press.

Hamilton, Gail (1870). *A Battle of the Books, Recorded by an Unknown Writer for the Use of Authors and Publishers.* Cambridge, MA: Riverside.

Hardt, Michael, and Antonio Negri (2004). *Multitude: War and Democracy in the Age of Empire.* New York: Penguin.

Harris, Jennifer (2006). "Marketplace Transactions and Sentimental Currencies in Fanny Fern's *Ruth Hall,*" *American Transcendental Quarterly* 20.1, 343–59.

Harris, Sharon M. (1991). *Rebecca Harding Davis and American Realism.* Philadelphia: University of Pennsylvania Press.

Harris, Sharon M. (1995). "Hannah Webster Foster's *The Coquette*: Critiquing Franklin's America," in Harris, Sharon M. (ed.), *Redefining the Political Novel: American Women Writers, 1797–1901.* Knoxville: University of Tennessee Press, 1–22.

Harris, Sharon M. (2005). *Executing Race: Early American Women's Narratives of Race, Society, and the Law.* Columbus: Ohio State University Press.

Harris, Susan K. (1990). *Nineteenth-Century American Women's Novels: Interpretive Strategies.* New York: Cambridge University Press.

Harris, Susan K. (2003). "Introduction," in Sedgwick, Catharine Maria, *A New England Tale.* New York: Penguin, vii–xx.

Hart, James D. (1950). *The Popular Book: A History of America's Literary Taste.* New York: Oxford University Press.

Hawthorne, Nathaniel (1853). "International Copyright." *United States Review* 1, 352–5.

Hawthorne, Nathaniel (1862). "Chiefly About War–Matters." *Atlantic Monthly* 10, 43–62.

Hawthorne, Nathaniel (1970). *Our Old Home: A Series of English Sketches* (1863). Fredson Bowers and L. Neal Smith (eds.). Vol. 5 of *The Centenary Edition of the Works of Nathaniel Hawthorne*. Columbus: Ohio State University Press.

Hawthorne, Nathaniel (1972). *The American Notebooks*. Claude M. Simpson (ed.). Vol. 8 of *The Centenary Edition of the Works of Nathaniel Hawthorne*. Columbus: Ohio State University Press.

Hawthorne, Nathaniel (1980). *The French and Italian Notebooks*. Thomas Woodson (ed.). Vol. 14 of *The Centenary Edition of the Works of Nathaniel Hawthorne*. Columbus: Ohio State University Press.

Hawthorne, Nathaniel (1984). *The Letters, 1813–1843*. Thomas Woodson et al. (eds.). Vol. 15 of *The Centenary Edition of the Works of Nathaniel Hawthorne*. Columbus: Ohio State University Press.

Hawthorne, Nathaniel (1985). *The Letters, 1843–1853*. Thomas Woodson et al. (eds.). Vol. 16 of *The Centenary Edition of the Works of Nathaniel Hawthorne*. Columbus: Ohio State University Press.

Hawthorne, Nathaniel (1987a). *The Letters, 1853–1856*. Thomas Woodson et al. (eds.). Vol. 17 of *The Centenary Edition of the Works of Nathaniel Hawthorne*. Columbus: Ohio State University Press.

Hawthorne, Nathaniel (1987b). *The Letters, 1857–1864*. Thomas Woodson et al. (eds.). Vol. 18 of *The Centenary Edition of the Works of Nathaniel Hawthorne*. Columbus: Ohio State University Press.

Hawthorne, Nathaniel (1997). *The English Notebooks, 1853–1856*. Thomas Woodson and Bill Ellis (eds.). Vol. 21 of *The Centenary Edition of the Works of Nathaniel Hawthorne*. Columbus: Ohio State University Press.

Hayes, Kevin J. (2000). *Poe and the Printed Word*. Cambridge: Cambridge University Press.

Hayford, Harrison, and Merton M. Sealts, Jr. (eds.) (1962). *Billy Budd Sailor: (An Inside Narrative)*, by Herman Melville. Chicago: University of Chicago Press.

Hazewell, Charles Creighton (1851). "Review." *Boston Daily Times*, 2.

Hedges, William L. (1965). *Washington Irving: An American Study, 1802–1832*. Baltimore: Johns Hopkins Press.

Hedrick, Joan D. (1994). *Harriet Beecher Stowe: A Life*. New York: Oxford University Press.

Henderson, Harry (1974). *Versions of the Past: The Historical Imagination in American Fiction*. New York: Oxford University Press.

Henson, Josiah (1878). *An Autobiography of the Rev. Josiah Henson (Mrs. Harriet Beecher Stowe's "Uncle Tom")*. John Lobb (ed.). London: Christian Age.

Herbert, T. Walter (2001). "Pornographic Manhood and *The Scarlet Letter*." *Studies in American Fiction* 29.1, 113–20.

Higgins, Brian, and Hershel Parker (eds.) (1995). *Herman Melville: The Contemporary Reviews*. New York: Cambridge University Press.

H. L. (1800). "Thoughts on the Probable Termination of Negro Slavery in the United States of America." *Monthly Magazine, and American Review* 2.2, 81–4.

Hobsbawm, Eric (1983). "Inventing Traditions," in Hobsbawm, Eric and Terence Ranger (eds.), *The Invention of Tradition*. New York: Cambridge University Press, 1–14.

Hochman, Barbara (2004). "*Uncle Tom's Cabin* in the *National Era*: An Essay in Generic Norms and the Contexts of Reading." *Book History* 7, 143–69.

Hodgson, Joseph (1876). *The Cradle of the Confederacy; or, The Times of Troupe, Quitman, and Yancey*. Mobile: Register Publishing Office.

Hoffman, Charles Fenno (1990). *Greyslaer: A Romance of the Mohawks* (1840). Daniel A. Wells (ed.). Albany: New College and University Press.

Hoffman, Daniel (1961). *Form and Fable in American Fiction*. New York: Oxford University Press.

Holman, C. Hugh (1962). "Introduction," in Simms, William Gilmore, *Views and Reviews of American Literature, History, and Fiction: First Series* (1845). C. Hugh Holman (ed.). Cambridge, MA: Harvard University Press, vii–xxxvii.

Holman, C. Hugh (1972). *The Roots of Southern Writing: Essays on the Literature of the American South*. Athens: University of Georgia Press.

Holmes, George Frederick (1853). "A Key to *Uncle Tom's Cabin*." *Southern Literary Messenger* 19.6, 321–9.

Holzer, Harold (ed.) (2004). *The Lincoln-Douglas Debates: The First Complete, Unexpurgated Text*. New York: Fordham University Press.

Homberger, Eric (1994). *Scenes from the Life of a City: Corruption and Conscience in Old New York*. New Haven: Yale University Press.

Homestead, Melissa J. (2008). "The Beginnings of the American Novel," in Hayes, Kevin J. (ed.), *The Oxford Handbook of Early American Literature*. New York: Oxford University Press, 527–46.

Homestead, Melissa J., and Camryn Hansen (2010). "Susanna Rowson's Transatlantic Career." *Early American Literature* 45, 619–54.

Hook, Andrew (1975). *Scotland and America: A Study of Cultural Relations, 1750–1835*. Glasgow: Blackie.

Hook, Andrew (1999). *From Goosecreek to Gandercleugh: Studies in Scottish-American Literary and Cultural History*. East Linton, UK: Tuckwell Press.

Horsman, Reginald (1981). *Race and Manifest Destiny: The Origins of American Racial Anglo-Saxonism*. Cambridge, MA: Harvard University Press.

House Document no. 12, Legislature (1844). Ottawa Petition. *Documents of the Senate and of the House of Representatives at the Annual Session of the Legislature of 1844*. Detroit: Ragg and Harmon, 1944.

Howe, Julia Ward (1913). *Julia Ward Howe and the Woman Suffrage Movement: A Selection from Her Speeches and Essays*. Florence Howe Hall (ed.). Boston: Dana Estes.

Howells, William Dean (1867). Review of *Miss Ravenel's Conversion from Secession to Loyalty*, by John De Forest. *Atlantic Monthly* 20, 120–2.

Howells, William Dean (1901). "Hawthorne's Hester Prynne," in *Heroines of Fiction*. New York: Harper, 161–74.

Hubbell, Jay (1957). "The Smith-Pocahontas Story in Literature." *The Virginia Magazine of History and Biography* 65.3, 275–300.

Idol, John J., Jr., and Buford Jones (eds.) (1994). *Nathaniel Hawthorne: The Contemporary Reviews*. New York: Cambridge University Press.

Irving, Washington (1978). *Letters*. Ralph M. Aderman, Herbert L. Kleinfeld, and Jennifer S. Banks (eds.). 4 vols. *The Complete Works of Washington Irving*, Richard D. Rust (ed.). Boston: Twayne.

Irwin, John T. (1983). *American Hieroglyphics: The Symbol of the Egyptian Hieroglyphics in the American Renaissance*. Baltimore: Johns Hopkins University Press.

Jackson, Andrew (2000). "First Annual Message to Congress (December 1829)," in Prucha, Francis Paul (ed.), *Documents of United States Indian Policy*. 3rd ed. Lincoln: University of Nebraska Press, 47–8.

Jackson, Gregory S. (2003). "'A Dowry of Suffering': Consent, Contract, and Political Coverture in John W. De Forest's Reconstruction Romance." *American Literary History* 15.2, 276–310.

Jacobs, Harriet A. (1861). *Incidents in the Life of a Slave Girl*. Lydia Maria Child (ed.). Boston.

Jacobs, Harriet A. (1987). *Incidents in the Life of a Slave Girl* (1861). Jean Fagan Yellin (ed.). Cambridge, MA: Harvard University Press.

Jacobs, Robert D. (1969). *Poe: Journalist & Critic*. Baton Rouge: Louisiana State University Press.

James, C. L. R. (2001). *Mariners, Renegades and Castaways: The Story of Herman Melville and the World We Live In*. Hanover, NH: University Press of New England.

James, Henry (1879). *Hawthorne*. London: Macmillan.

James, Henry (1888). *The Aspern Papers; Louisa Pallant; The Modern Warning*. London: Macmillan.

James, Henry (1913). *A Small Boy and Others*. New York: Charles Scribner's Sons.

Jefferson, Thomas (1954). *Notes on the State of Virginia*. William Peden (ed.). New York: Norton.

Jennings, Francis (1975). *The Invasion of America: Indians, Colonialism, and the Cant of Conquest*. Chapel Hill: University of North Carolina Press.

Johannsen, Robert W. (1985). *To the Halls of the Montezumas: The Mexican War in the American Imagination*. New York: Oxford University Press.

Johnson, Susan Lee (2000). *Roaring Camp: The Social World of the California Gold Rush*. New York: Norton.

JONES, CATHERINE (2003). *Literary Memory: Scott's Waverley Novels and the Psychology of Narrative.* Lewisburg, PA: Bucknell University Press.

JORDAN-LAKE, JOY (2005). *Whitewashing "Uncle Tom's Cabin": Nineteenth-Century Women Novelists Respond to Stowe.* Nashville: Vanderbilt University Press.

KAMMEN, MICHAEL (1978). *A Season of Youth: The American Revolution and the Historical Imagination.* Ithaca: Cornell University Press.

KAMMEN, MICHAEL (1993). "The Problem of American Exceptionalism: A Reconsideration." *American Quarterly* 45, 1–43.

KANT, IMMANUEL (1948). *Perpetual Peace, a Philosophical Essay.* M. Campbell Smith (trans.), A. Robert Caponigri (ed.). New York: Liberal Arts Press.

KAPLAN, AMY (1998). "Manifest Domesticity." *American Literature* 70.3, 581–606.

KARCHER, CAROLYN L. (ed.) (1986). *"Hobomok" and Other Writings on Indians,* by Lydia Maria Child. New Brunswick: Rutgers University Press.

KARCHER, CAROLYN L. (1994). *The First Woman in the Republic: A Cultural Biography of Lydia Maria Child.* Durham: Duke University Press.

KARCHER, CAROLYN L. (2003). "Catharine Maria Sedgwick in Literary History," in Damon-Bach, Lucinda L and Victoria Clements (eds.), *Catharine Maria Sedgwick: Critical Perspectives.* Boston: Northeastern University Press, 5–15.

KEELY, KAREN (1998). "Marriage Plots and National Reunion: The Trope of Romantic Reconciliation in Postbellum Literature." *Mississippi Quarterly* 51, 621–48.

KELLEY, MARY (1984). *Private Woman, Public Stage: Literary Domesticity in Nineteenth-Century America.* New York: Oxford University Press.

KELLEY, MARY (1989). "Legacy Profile: Catharine Maria Sedgwick." *Legacy* 6, 43–50.

KELLY, WILLIAM P. (1983). *Plotting America's Past: Fenimore Cooper and the Leatherstocking Tales.* Carbondale: Southern Illinois University Press.

KILCUP, KAREN (1996). "'Ourself behind Ourself, Concealed—': The Homoerotics of Reading in *The Scarlet Letter.*" *ESQ: A Journal of the American Renaissance* 42.1, 1–28.

KINMONT, ALEXANDER (1839). *Twelve Lectures on the Natural History of Man.* Cincinnati: U.P. James.

KIRKHAM, E. BRUCE (1977). *The Building of "Uncle Tom's Cabin".* Knoxville: University of Tennessee Press.

KLAUPRECHT, EMIL (1996). *Cincinnati, or The Mysteries of the West.* Don Heinrich-Tolzmann (ed.), Steven Rowan (trans.). New York: Peter Lang.

KNAPP, SAMUEL L. (1818). *Extracts from a Journal of Travels in North America: Consisting of an Account of Boston and Its Vicinity.* Boston: Thomas Badger.

KOHN, DENISE, SARAH MEER, and EMILY B. TODD (2006). "Reading Stowe as a Transatlantic Writer," in *Transatlantic Stowe: Harriet Beecher Stowe and European Culture.* Iowa City: University of Iowa Press, xi–xxxi.

KOLODNY, ANNETTE (1975). *The Lay of the Land: Metaphor as Experience and History in American Life and Letters.* Chapel Hill: University of North Carolina Press.

KOLODNY, ANNETTE (1984). *The Land Before Her: Fantasy and Experience of the American Frontiers, 1630–1860.* Chapel Hill: University of North Carolina Press.

KOLODNY, ANNETTE (1992). "Letting Go Our Grand Obsessions: Toward a New Literary History of the American Frontiers." *American Literature* 64.1, 1–18.

KOPLEY, RICHARD (1987). "The 'Very Profound Under-Current' of *Arthur Gordon Pym*," in Myerson, Joel (ed.), *Studies in the American Renaissance 1987.* Charlottesville: University Press of Virginia, 143–75.

KORIEH, CHIMA J. (ed.) (2009). *Olaudah Equiano and the Igbo World: History, Society, and Atlantic Diaspora Connections.* Trenton: Africa World Press.

KRISTEVA, JULIA (1993). *Nations Without Nationalism.* Leon S. Roudiez (trans.). New York: Columbia University Press.

LARKIN, ED. (2006–2007). "The Cosmopolitan Revolution: Loyalism and the Fiction of an American Nation." *Novel* 40.1–2, 52–76.

LATHROP, ROSE HAWTHONE (1923). *Memories of Hawthorne.* Boston: Houghton Mifflin.

LAUTER, PAUL (1991). *Canons and Contexts.* New York: Oxford University Press.

LAWRENCE, D. H. (1923). *Studies in Classic American Literature.* New York: T. Seltzer.

LAWRENCE, D. H. (1927). "Review of *Americans,* by Stuart P. Sherman," in Reeve, N. H. and John Worthen (eds.), *Introductions and Reviews.* New York: Cambridge University Press, 221–8.

LAWRENCE, D. H. (1978). *Studies in Classic American Literature* (1923). New York: Penguin.

LEARY, LEWIS (1972). "Review of Rees, Robert A. and Earl N. Harbert (eds.), *Fifteen American Authors before 1900.*" *Nineteenth-Century Fiction* 27, 235–38.

LEAVIS, F. R. (1948). *The Great Tradition: George Eliot, Henry James, Joseph Conrad.* London: Chatto and Windus.

LEE, MAURICE (2009). "Probably Poe." *American Literature* 81, 225–52.

LEISY, ERNEST (1950). *The American Historical Novel.* Norman: University of Oklahoma Press.

LEMAY, J. A. LEO (1992). *Did Pocahontas Save Captain John Smith?* Athens: University of Georgia Press.

LENDER, MARK EDWARD, and JAMES KIRBY MARTIN (1987). *Drinking in America: A History.* New York: Free Press.

LEPORE, JILL (1998). *The Name of War: King Philip's War and the Origins of American Identity.* New York: Vintage.

LEVERENZ, DAVID (1983). "Mrs. Hawthorne's Headache: Reading *The Scarlet Letter.*" *Nineteenth-Century Fiction* 37, 552–73.

LEVIN, HARRY (1958). *The Power of Blackness: Hawthorne, Poe, Melville.* New York: Knopf.

LEVINE, ROBERT S. (1989). *Conspiracy and Romance: Studies in Brockden Brown, Cooper, Hawthorne, and Melville.* Cambridge: Cambridge University Press.

Levine, Robert S. (1990). "'Antebellum Rome' in *The Marble Faun*." *American Literary History* 2.1, 19–38.

Levine, Robert S. (1992). "*Uncle Tom's Cabin* in Frederick Douglass' Paper: An Analysis of Reception." *American Literature* 64.1, 71–93.

Levine, Robert S. (2000). "Introduction," in Stowe, Harriet Beecher, *Dred: A Tale of the Great Dismal Swamp*. Chapel Hill: University of North Carolina Press, ix–xxxii.

Lewis, R. W. B. (1955). *The American Adam: Innocence, Tragedy, and Tradition in the Nineteenth Century*. Chicago: University of Chicago Press.

Liedel, Donald Edward (1961). "The Antislavery Novel, 1836–1861." Ph.D. diss., University of Michigan.

Limerick, Patricia Nelson (1987). *The Legacy of Conquest: The Unbroken Past of the American West*. New York: Norton.

Lincoln, Abraham (1989). "First Inaugural Address," in *Speeches and Writings 1859–1865*. New York: Library of America, 215–24.

Looby, Christopher (1993). "George Thompson's 'Romance of the Real': Transgression and Taboo in American Sensation Fiction." *American Literature* 65.4, 651–72.

Looby, Christopher (2004). "Southworth and Seriality: *The Hidden Hand* in the *New York Ledger*." *Nineteenth-Century Literature* 59.2, 179–211.

Loring, George Bailey (1850). "Hawthorne's *Scarlet Letter*." *Massachusetts Quarterly Review* 3.12, 484–500.

Loshe, Lillie Deming (1907). *The Early American Novel*. New York: Columbia University Press.

Lott, Eric (1993). *Love & Theft: Blackface Minstrelsy and the American Working Class*. New York: Oxford University Press.

Lowe, John (1996). "'I am Joaquin!': Space and Freedom in Yellow Bird's *The Life and Adventures of Joaquin Murieta, the Celebrated California Bandit*," in Jaskoski, Helen (ed.), *Early American Native Writing: New Critical Essays*. Cambridge: Cambridge University Press, 104–21.

Lowell, James Russell (1843). "Introduction." *The Pioneer* 1, 1–3.

Lowell, James Russell (1845). "Our Contributors, No. XVII: Edgar Allan Poe." *Graham's Magazine* 27, 49–53.

Lowell, James Russell (1848). *A Fable for Critics; or Better, A Glance at a Few of Our Literary Progenies from the Tub of Diogenes; That Is, a Series of Jokes, by a Wonderful Quiz*. New York: Putnam.

Luedtke, Luther S. (1989). *Nathaniel Hawthorne and the Romance of the Orient*. Bloomington: Indiana University Press.

Lukes, Steven (1971). "The Meanings of 'Individualism'." *Journal of the History of Ideas* 32, 45–66.

Lund, Michael (1993). *America's Continuing Story: An Introduction to Serial Fiction 1850–1900*. Detroit: Wayne State University Press.

Machor, James L. (2011). "Response as (Re)Construction: The Reception of Catharine Sedgwick's Novels," in *Reading Fiction in Antebellum America: Informed Response and Reception Histories, 1820–1865*. Baltimore: Johns Hopkins University Press, 201–55.

Maddox, Lucy (1991). *Removals: Nineteenth-Century American Literature and the Politics of Indian Affairs*. New York: Oxford University Press.

Mahoney, Timothy R. (1999). *Provincial Lives: Middle-Class Experience in the Antebellum Middle West*. Cambridge: Cambridge University Press.

Mann, Barbara Alice (2007). "Race Traitor: Cooper, His Critics, and Nineteenth-Century Literary Politics," in Person, Leland S. (ed.), *A Historical Guide to James Fenimore Cooper*. New York: Oxford University Press, 155–85.

Manning, Susan (1990). *The Puritan-Provincial Vision: Scottish and American Literature in the Nineteenth Century*. Cambridge: Cambridge University Press.

Manning, Susan (2002). *Fragments of Union: Making Connections in Scottish and American Writing*. Basingstoke and New York: Palgrave.

Mansfield, Luther S., and Howard P. Vincent (1952). "Explanatory Notes," in Melville, Herman, *Moby-Dick; or, The Whale (1851)*. Luther S. Mansfield and Howard P. Vincent (eds.). New York: Hendricks House, 569–832.

Marsh, Margaret (1990). *Suburban Lives*. New Brunswick: Rutgers University Press.

Marshall, Bill (2007). "New Orleans, Nodal Point of the French Atlantic." *International Journal of Francophone Studies* 10.1–2, 35–50.

Martin, Judith (1988). "Introduction," in Stowe, Harriet Beecher, *Pink and White Tyranny: A Society Novel*. Judith Martin (ed.). New York: Plume, vii–xiv.

Matthiessen, F. O. (1941). *American Renaissance: Art and Expression in the Age of Emerson and Whitman*. New York: Oxford University Press.

Mattingly, Carol (1998). *Well-Tempered Women: Nineteenth-Century Temperance Rhetoric*. Carbondale and Edwardsville: Southern Illinois University Press.

Marx, Leo (1964). *The Machine in the Garden: Technology and the Pastoral Ideal in America*. New York: Oxford University Press.

Mazel, David. (2000). "Performing 'Wilderness' in *The Last of the Mohicans*," in Tallmadge, John and Henry Harrington (eds.), *Reading under the Sign of Nature: New Essays in Ecocriticism*. Salt Lake City: University of Utah Press, 101–14.

McCord, Louisa S. (1853). "Stowe's *Key to Uncle Tom's Cabin*," *Southern Quarterly Review* 8.15, 214–54.

McFarland, Mitzi (2002). "'Without a Cross': The Carnivalization of Sex, Race, and Culture in Cooper's *Last of the Mohicans*." *ESQ: A Journal of the American Renaissance* 48.4, 247–73.

McGill, Meredith L. (2003). *American Literature and the Culture of Reprinting, 1834–1853*. Philadelphia: University of Pennsylvania Press.

McKeon, Michael (2002). *The Origins of the English Novel, 1600–1740* (1987). Baltimore: Johns Hopkins University Press.

McKeon, Michael (2005). *The Secret History of Domesticity: Public, Private, and the Division of Knowledge.* Baltimore: Johns Hopkins University Press.

McNeil, Kenneth (2007). *Scotland, Britain, Empire: Writing the Highlands, 1760–1860.* Columbus: Ohio State University Press.

McWilliams, John (1995). *"The Last of the Mohicans": Civil Savagery and Savage Civility.* New York: Twayne.

Meer, Sarah (2005). *Uncle Tom Mania: Slavery, Minstrelsy and Transatlantic Culture in the 1850s.* Athens: University of Georgia Press.

Melville, Herman (1852). Letter to the Committee, in Putnam, George P. (eds.), *Memorial of James Fenimore Cooper.* New York: G. P. Putnam, 30.

Melville, Herman (1987). "Hawthorne and His Mosses," in Harrison Hayford et al. (eds.), *The Piazza Tales and Other Prose Pieces, 1839–1860.* Vol. 9 of *The Writings of Herman Melville.* Evanston and Chicago: Northwestern University Press and the Newberry Library, 239–53.

Melville, Herman (1989). *Journals.* Howard C. Horsford and Lynn Horth (eds.). Vol. 15 of *The Writings of Herman Melville.* Evanston and Chicago: Northwestern University Press and the Newberry Library.

Melville, Herman (1991). *Clarel: A Poem and Pilgrimage in the Holy Land.* Walter E. Bezanson and Harrison Hayford (eds.). Vol. 12 of *The Writings of Herman Melville.* Evanston and Chicago: Northwestern University Press and the Newberry Library.

Melville, Herman (1993). *Correspondence.* Lynn Horth (ed.). Vol. 14 of *The Writings of Herman Melville.* Evanston and Chicago: Northwestern University Press and the Newberry Library.

Melville, Herman (2000). "Hawthorne and His Mosses" (1850), in Tanselle, G. Thomas (ed.), *Moby Dick, Billy Budd and Other Writings.* New York: Library of America, 909–28.

Memorial of James Fenimore Cooper (1852). New York: G. P. Putnam.

Merchant, Carolyn (1989). *Ecological Revolutions: Nature, Gender and Science in New England.* Chapel Hill: University of North Carolina Press.

Merritt (2003). *At the Crossroads: Indians and Empire on a Mid-Atlantic Frontier, 1700–1763.* Chapel Hill: University of North Carolina Press.

Mifflin, Margot (2009). *The Blue Tattoo: The Life of Olive Oatman.* Lincoln: University of Nebraska Press.

Mihesuah, Devon (1996). *American Indians: Stereotypes and Realities.* Atlanta: Clarity Press .

Mihm, Stephen (2007). *A Nation of Counterfeiters: Capitalists, Con Men, and the Making of the United States.* Cambridge, MA: Harvard University Press.

Miller, David C. (1989). *Dark Eden: The Swamp in Nineteenth-Century American Culture.* Cambridge: Cambridge University Press.

Miller, Perry (1956). *Errand into the Wilderness.* Cambridge, MA: Harvard University Press.

Miller, Perry (1967). *Nature's Nation.* Cambridge, MA: Harvard University Press.

MILLINGTON, RICHARD H. (1992). *Practicing Romance: Narrative Form and Cultural Engagement in Hawthorne's Fiction*. Princeton: Princeton University Press.

MINTER, DAVID (1973). "By Dens of Lions: Notes on Stylization in Early Puritan Captivity Narratives." *American Literature* 45, 335–47.

MOERS, ELLEN (1976). *Literary Women*. Garden City: Doubleday.

MONAGHAN, JAY (1952). *The Great Rascal: The Life and Adventures of Ned Buntline*. Boston: Little, Brown.

MOORE, STEVEN (2010). *The Novel: An Alternative History: Beginnings to 1600*. New York: Continuum.

MORETTI, FRANCO (1998). *Atlas of the European Novel, 1800–1900*. London: Verso.

MORETTI, FRANCO (2005). *Graphs, Maps, Trees: Abstract Models for Literary History*. London: Verso.

MOTT, FRANK LUTHER (1938–68). *A History of American Magazines*. 5 vols. Cambridge, MA: Harvard University Press.

MOTT, FRANK LUTHER (1947). *Golden Multitudes: The Story of Best Sellers in the United States*. New York: Macmillan.

MULFORD, CARLA (1996). "Introduction," in Brown, William Hill and Hannah Webster Foster, *The Power of Sympathy and The Coquette*. Carla Mulford (ed.). New York: Penguin, ix–li.

MULLAN, JOHN (1988). *Sentiment and Sociability: The Language of Feeling in the Eighteenth Century*. New York: Clarendon.

MULVEY, CHRISTOPHER (2006). *Clotel* by William Wells Brown: An Electronic Scholarly Edition. University of Virginia Press. http://rotunda.upress.virginia.edu:8080/clotel/.

NASH, GARY B. (2005). *The Unknown American Revolution: The Unruly Birth of Democracy and the Struggle to Create America*. New York: Viking.

NELSON, DANA (1992). "Sympathy as Strategy in Sedgwick's *Hope Leslie*," in Samuels, Shirley (ed.), *The Culture of Sentiment: Race, Gender, and Sentimentality in Nineteenth-Century America*. New York: Oxford University Press, 191–202.

NELSON, DANA D. (1993). *The Word in Black and White: Reading "Race" in American Literature, 1638–1867*. New York: Oxford University Press.

NELSON, DANA D. (1998). *National Manhood: Capitalist Citizenship and the Imagined Fraternity of White Men*. Durham: Duke University Press.

NEUBERG, VICTOR (1989). "Chapbooks in America: Reconstructing the Popular Reading of Early America," in Davidson, Cathy N. (ed.), *Reading in America: Literature & Social History*. Baltimore: Johns Hopkins University Press.

NEVINS, ALLAN (ed.) (1948). *America Through British Eyes*. New York: Oxford University Press.

NEWTON, SARAH EMILY (1994). *Learning to Behave: A Guide to American Conduct Books Before 1800*. Westport: Greenwood.

NOVAK, BARBARA (1980). *Nature and Culture: American Landscape and Painting, 1825–1875*. New York: Oxford University Press.

NUDELMAN, FRANNY (1997). "'Emblem and Product of Sin': The Poisoned Child in *The Scarlet Letter* and Domestic Advice Literature." *Yale Journal of Criticism* 10.1, 193–213.

O'BRIEN, JEAN M. (1997). *Dispossession by Degrees: Indian Land and Identity in Natick, Massachusetts, 1650–1790.* New York: Cambridge University Press.

OELSCHLAEGER, MAX (1991). *The Idea of Wilderness: From Prehistory to the Age of Ecology.* New Haven: Yale University Press.

OKKER, PATRICIA (2003). *Social Stories: The Magazine Novel in Nineteenth-Century America.* Charlottesville: University of Virginia Press.

OKKER, PATRICIA (ed.) (2012). *Transnationalism and American Serial Fiction.* New York: Routledge.

OLWELL, VICTORIA (2011). *The Genius of Democracy: Fictions of Gender and Citizenship in the United States, 1860–1945.* Philadelphia: University of Pennsylvania Press.

O'SULLIVAN, JOHN L. (1839). "The Great Nation of Futurity." *United States Magazine and Democratic Review* 6.23, 426–30.

OTTER, SAMUEL (2010). *Philadelphia Stories: America's Literature of Race and Freedom.* New York: Oxford University Press.

PARFAIT, CLAIRE (2007). *The Publishing History of "Uncle Tom's Cabin," 1852–2002.* Aldershot, UK: Ashgate.

PARKER, THEODORE (1853). "Speech of Theodore Parker at the Annual Meeting of the Massachusetts A. S. Society, Friday Evening, Jan. 28, 1853." *Liberator* 8, 1.

PARKMAN, FRANCIS, JR. (1996). *The Oregon Trail.* Bernard Rosenthal (ed.). New York: Oxford University Press.

PARRINDER, PATRICK (2006). *Nation and Novel: The English Novel from Its Origins to the Present Day.* New York: Oxford University Press.

PARSONS, ELAINE FRANTZ (2003). *Manhood Lost: Fallen Drunkards and Redeeming Women in the Nineteenth-Century United States.* Baltimore: Johns Hopkins University Press.

PATTEE, FRED LEWIS (1935). *The First Century of American Literature, 1770–1870.* New York: Appleton-Century.

PATTERSON, ORLANDO (1982). *Slavery and Social Death: A Comparative Study.* Cambridge, MA: Harvard University Press.

PEARCE, ROY HARVEY (1953). *Savagism and Civilization: A Study of the Indian and the American Mind.* Baltimore: Johns Hopkins University Press.

PEASE, DONALD E. (2001). "Introduction," in James, C. L. R., *Mariners, Renegades and Castaways: The Story of Herman Melville and the World We Live In.* Hanover: University Press of New England, vii–xxxiii.

PERSON, LELAND S. (1989). "The Power of Silence in *The Scarlet Letter.*" *Nineteenth-Century Literature* 43, 465–83.

PERSON, LELAND S. (1998). "The Historical Paradoxes of Manhood in Cooper's *The Deerslayer.*" *Novel* 32, 76–98.

Person, Leland S. (2001). "The Dark Labyrinth of Mind: Hawthorne, Hester, and the Ironies of Racial Mothering." *Studies in American Fiction* 29.1, 33–48.

Pfister, Joel (1991). *The Production of Personal Life: Class, Gender, and the Psychological in Hawthorne's Fiction*. Stanford: Stanford University Press.

Poe, Edgar Allan (1835). "Review of *The Linwoods*." *Southern Literary Messenger* 2, 57–9.

Poe, Edgar Allan (1836). "Slavery." *Southern Literary Messenger* 2.5, 336–9.

Poe, Edgar Allan (1837). "South Sea Expedition." *Southern Literary Messenger* 3.1, 68–72.

Poe, Edgar Allan (1845). "Some Secrets of the Magazine Prison-House." *Broadway Journal* 15, 103–4.

Poe, Edgar Allan (1846). "Catharine M. Sedgwick." *Godey's Magazine and Ladies Book* 33, 130–2.

Poe, Edgar Allan (1984a). *Essays and Reviews*. G. R. Thompson (ed.). New York: Library of America.

Poe, Edgar Allan (1984b). *Poetry and Tales*. Patrick F. Quinn (ed.). New York: Library of America.

Poe, Edgar Allan (1994). *The Imaginary Voyages*. Burton R. Pollin (ed.). Vol. 1 of *The Collected Writings of Edgar Allan Poe*. New York: Gordian Press.

Poe, Edgar Allan (1997). *The Southern Literary Messenger: Nonfictional Prose*. Burton R. Pollin and Joseph V. Ridgely (eds.). Vol. 5 of *The Collected Writings of Edgar Allan Poe*. New York: Gordian Press.

Poe, Edgar Allan (2008). *The Collected Letters of Edgar Allan Poe*. John Ward Ostrom, Burton R. Pollin, and Jeffrey A. Savoye (eds.). 2 vols. New York: Gordian Press.

Pollak, Vivian (2000). *The Erotic Whitman*. Berkeley: University of California Press.

Pond, J. B. (1900). *Eccentricities of Genius: Memories of Famous Men and Women of the Platform and Stage*. New York: G. W. Dillingham.

Porte, Joel (1969). *The Romance in America: Studies in Cooper, Poe, Hawthorne, Melville, and James*. Middletown: Wesleyan University Press.

Porte, Joel (ed.) (1982). *Emerson in His Journals*. Cambridge, MA: Harvard University Press.

Post-Lauria, Sheila (1996). *Correspondent Colorings: Melville in the Marketplace*. Amherst: University of Massachusetts Press.

Powell, Timothy (2000). *Ruthless Democracy: A Multicultural Interpretation of the American Renaissance*. Princeton: Princeton University Press.

Pratt, Mary Louise (1992). *Imperial Eyes: Travel Writing and Transculturation*. London: Routledge.

Prucha, Francis Paul (ed.) (2000). *Johnson and Graham's Lessee v. William McIntosh*, in *Documents of United States Indian Policy*. 3rd ed. Lincoln: University of Nebraska Press, 35–7.

PRYSE, MARJORIE (1993). "'Distilling Essences': Regionalism and 'Women's Culture.'" *American Literary Realism* 25.2, 1–15.

PRYSE, MARJORIE (2004). "Stowe and Regionalism," in Weinstein, Cindy (ed.), *The Cambridge Companion to Harriet Beecher Stowe*. Cambridge: Cambridge University Press, 131–53.

PUTZI, JENNIFER (2000). "'Tattooed Still': The Inscription of Female Agency in Elizabeth Stoddard's *The Morgesons*." *Legacy: A Journal of American Women Writers* 17.2, 165–73.

PUTZI, JENNIFER (2008). "Introduction," in Stoddard, Elizabeth, *Two Men*. Lincoln: University of Nebraska Press, xi–lviii.

QUINN, ARTHUR HOBSON (1936). *American Fiction: An Historical and Critical Survey*. New York: D. Appleton-Century.

QUIRK, TOM (1982). *Melville's Confidence Man: From Knave to Knight*. Columbia: University of Missouri Press.

RAABE, WESLEY NEIL (2006). "Harriet Beecher Stowe's *Uncle Tom's Cabin*: An Electronic Edition of the *National Era* Version." Ph.D. diss., University of Virginia. http://www3.iath.virginia.edu/wnr4c/index.htm.

RAGUSSIS, MICHAEL (1982). "Family Discourse and Fiction in *The Scarlet Letter*." *ELH* 49.4, 863–88.

RAILTON, STEPHEN (1993). "The Address of *The Scarlet Letter*," in Machor, James L. (ed.), *Readers in History: Nineteenth-Century Literature and the Contexts of Response*. Baltimore: Johns Hopkins University Press, 138–64.

RANDALL, DAVID A. (1935). "*Waverley* in America." *Colophon* 1, 39–55.

RANS, GEOFFREY (1991). *Cooper's Leather-Stocking Novels: A Secular Reading*. Chapel Hill: University of North Carolina Press.

READ, MARTHA MEREDITH (1807). *Margaretta; or, The Intricacies of the Heart*. Charleston: Edmund Morford.

REES, ROBERT A., and EARL N. HARBERT (eds.) (1984). *Fifteen American Authors before 1900: Bibliographic Essays on Research and Criticism* (1971). Madison: University of Wisconsin Press.

REID, MARGARET (2004). *Cultural Secrets as Narrative Form: Storytelling in Nineteenth-Century America*. Columbus: Ohio State University Press.

REILLY, ELIZABETH CARROLL, and DAVID D. HALL (2000). "Customers and the Market for Books," in Amory, Hugh and David D. Hall (eds.), *The Colonial Book in the Atlantic World*. Vol.1 of *The History of the Book in America*. Cambridge: Cambridge University Press, 387–99.

REISING, RUSSELL J. (1986). *The Unusable Past: Theory and the Study of American Literature*. New York: Methuen.

REIZENSTEIN, LUDWIG VON (2002). *The Mysteries of New Orleans*. Steven Rowan (trans. and ed.). Baltimore: Johns Hopkins University Press.

REMER, ROSALIND (1996). *Printers and Men of Capital: Philadelphia Book Publishers in the New Republic*. Philadelphia: University of Pennsylvania Press.

Reynolds, David S. (1986). *George Lippard, Prophet of Protest: Writings of an American Radical, 1822–1854*. New York: Peter Lang.

Reynolds, David S. (1988). *Beneath the American Renaissance: The Subversive Imagination in the Age of Emerson and Whitman*. Cambridge, MA: Harvard University Press.

Reynolds, David S. (1995). "Introduction," in Lippard, George, *The Quaker City; or, The Monks of Monk Hall*. David S. Reynolds (ed.). Amherst: University of Massachusetts Press, vii–xli.

Reynolds, David S., and Kimberly R. Gladman (2002). "Introduction," in Thompson, George, *Venus in Boston and Other Tales of Nineteenth-Century Life*. David S. Reynolds and Kimberly R. Gladman (eds.). Amherst: University of Massachusetts Press, ix–liv.

Reynolds, Larry J. (1985). "*The Scarlet Letter* and Revolutions Abroad." *American Literature* 57.1, 44–67.

Reynolds, Larry J. (2008). *Devils and Rebels: The Making of Hawthorne's Damned Politics*. Ann Arbor: University of Michigan Press.

Rice, Grantland S. (1993). "Crèvecoeur and the Politics of Authorship in Republican America." *Early American Literature* 28, 91–119.

Richardson, Charles Francis (1878). *A Primer of American Literature*. Boston: Houghton, Osgood.

Richter, Daniel K. (2001). *Facing East from Indian Country: A Native History of Early America*. Cambridge, MA: Harvard University Press.

Ridgely, Joseph V. (1974). "George Lippard's *The Quaker City*: The World of the American Porno-Gothic." *Studies in the Literary Imagination* 7, 77–94.

Ridgely, Joseph V. (1994). "The Growth of the Text," in Pollin, Burton R. (ed.), *The Imaginary Voyages*. Vol. 1 of *The Collected Writings of Edgar Allan Poe*. New York: Gordian Press, 29–36.

Rifkin, Mark (2009a). "John Rollin Ridge's *Joaquín Murieta*." *Arizona Quarterly* 65.2, 27–56.

Rifkin, Mark (2009b). *Manifesting America: The Imperial Construction of U.S. National Space*. New York: Oxford University Press.

Rigney, Ann (2001). *Imperfect Histories: The Elusive Past and the Legacies of Romantic Historicism*. Ithaca: Cornell University Press.

Rigney, Ann (2012). *The Afterlives of Walter Scott: Memory on the Move*. Oxford: Oxford University Press.

Ringe, Donald (1966). *Charles Brockden Brown*. New York: Twayne.

Roach, Joseph (1996). *Cities of the Dead: Circum-Atlantic Performance*. New York: Columbia University Press.

Robertson, Fiona (1994). *Legitimate Histories: Scott, Gothic, and the Authorities of Fiction*. Oxford: Clarendon Press.

Robertson, Fiona (2013). *The United States in British Romanticism*. Oxford: Oxford University Press.

Robertson, Michael (2008). *Worshipping Walt: The Whitman Disciples*. Princeton: Princeton University Press.

Robinson, Forrest G. (1991). "Uncertain Borders: Race, Sex, and Civilization in *The Last of the Mohicans*." *Arizona Quarterly* 47.1, 1–28.

Rodgers, Esther (1701). "The Declaration and Confession of Esther Rodgers," in Rogers, John, *Death the Certain Wages of Sin to the Impenitent*. Boston: B. Green and J. Allen, 121–53.

Rodríguez, Jaime Javier (2010). *The Literatures of the U.S.-Mexican War: Narrative, Time,and Identity*. Austin: University of Texas Press.

Rogin, Michael Paul (1991). *Fathers and Children: Andrew Jackson and the Subjugation of the American Indian*. New York: Transaction.

Rorty, Amélie Oksenberg (1976). "A Literary Postscript: Characters, Persons, Selves, Individuals," in Rorty, Amélie Oksenberg (ed.), *The Identities of Persons*. Berkeley: University of California Press, 301–23.

Rosenthal, Bernard (ed.) (1981). *Critical Essays on Charles Brockden Brown*. Boston: G. K. Hall.

Rosenthal, Debra J. (1997). "Deracialized Discourse: Temperance and Racial Ambiguity in Harper's 'The Two Offers' and *Sowing and Reaping*," in Reynolds, David S. and Debra J. Rosenthal (eds.), *The Serpent in the Cup: Temperance in American Literature*. Amherst: University of Massachusetts Press, 153–64.

Rosenthal, Debra J. (2004). *Race Mixture in Nineteenth-Century U.S. and Spanish American Fictions: Gender, Culture, and Nation Building*. Chapel Hill: University of North Carolina Press.

Rosenthal, Debra J., and David S. Reynolds (1997). "Introduction," in Reynolds, David S. and Debra J. Rosenthal (eds.), *The Serpent in the Cup: Temperance in American Literature*. Amherst: University of Massachusetts Press, 1–9.

Rowe, John Carlos (1992). "Poe, Slavery, and Modern Criticism," in Kopley, Richard (ed.), *Poe's* Pym: *Critical Explorations*. Durham: Duke University Press, 117–38.

Rowe, John Carlos (1997). *At Emerson's Tomb: The Politics of Classic American Literature*. New York: Columbia University Press.

Rowe, John Carlos (2000). *Literary Culture and U.S. Imperialism: From the Revolution to World War II*. New York: Oxford University Press.

Rowe, John Carlos (2011). "Transpacific Studies and the Cultures of U.S. Imperialism," in Hoskins, Janet and Viet Nguyen (eds.), *Transpacific Studies*. Durham: Duke University Press.

Rowlandson, Mary (1997). *The Sovereignty and Goodness of God, with Related Documents*. Neal Salisbury (ed.). Boston: Bedford.

Rowson, Susanna (1794a). "[America, Commerce and Freedom.] New Song, Sung by Mr. Darley, Jun. in the Pantomimical Dance, Called the Sailor's Landlady. Words by Mrs. Rowson: Music by Mr. Reinagle." Philadelphia: n.p.

Rowson, Susanna (1794b). "I'm in Haste. A New Song." London: n.p.

Rowson, Susanna (1794c). *Slaves in Algiers: or, A Struggle for Freedom*. Philadelphia: Wrigley and Berriman.

Rowson, Susanna (1804). "Ode, on the Birthday of *John Adams*, Esquire, President of the United States of America, 1799," in Rowson, Susanna, *Miscellaneous Poems*. Boston: Gilbert and Dean.

Rowson, Susanna (1811). *A Present for Young Ladies; Containing Poems, Dialogues, Addresses, &c. &c. &c. As Recited by the Pupils of Mrs. Rowson's Academy, at the Annual Exhibitions*. Boston: John West.

Rubin-Dorsky, Jeffrey (1988). *Adrift in the Old World: The Psychological Pilgrimage of Washington Irving*. Chicago: University of Chicago Press.

Rust, Marion (2008). *Prodigal Daughters: Susanna Rowson's Early American Women*. Chapel Hill: University of North Carolina Press.

Said, Edward W. (1978). *Orientalism*. New York: Random House.

Said, Edward (2000). *Reflections on Exile and Other Essays*. Cambridge, MA: Harvard University Press.

Salisbury, Neal (1984). *Manitou and Providence: Indians, Europeans, and the Making of New England, 1500–1643*. New York: Oxford University Press.

Samuels, Shirley (1992). "Generation Through Violence: Cooper and the Making of Americans," in Peck, Daniel (ed.), *New Essays on "The Last of the Mohicans."* New York: Cambridge University Press, 87–114.

Samuels, Shirley (1996). *Romances of the Republic: Women, the Family, and Violence in the Literature of the Early American Nation*. New York: Oxford University Press.

Sanborn, Geoffrey (1998). *The Sign of the Cannibal: Melville and the Making of a Postcolonial Reader*. Durham: Duke University Press.

Sanborn, Geoffrey (2011). *Whipscars and Tattoos: "The Last of the Mohicans," "Moby Dick," and the Maori*. New York: Oxford University Press.

Sánchez, María Carla (2008). *Reforming the World: Social Activism and the Problem of Fiction in Nineteenth-Century America*. Iowa City: University of Iowa Press.

Sánchez-Eppler, Karen (1997). "Temperance in the Bed of a Child: Incest and Social Order in Nineteenth–Century America," in Reynolds, David S. and Debra J. Rosenthal (eds.), *The Serpent in the Cup: Temperance in American Literature*. Amherst: University of Massachusetts Press, 60–92.

Saxton, Alexander (1990). *The Rise and Fall of the White Republic: Class Politics and Mass Culture in Nineteenth-Century America*. London and New York: Verso.

Schachterle, Lance (2009). "The American Novel before 1820: A Bibliographical Essay," in *Literature in the Early American Republic: Annual Studies on Cooper and His Contemporaries*. Vol. 2. New York: AMS Press, 229–70.

Schulz, Max F., William D. Templeman, and Charles Reid Metzger (1967). *Essays in American and English Literature Presented to Bruce Robert McElderry, Jr.* Athens: Ohio University Press.

SCHUMPETER, JOSEPH (1975). *Capitalism, Socialism, and Democracy* (1942). New York: Harper.

SCHWEITZER, IVY (2006). *Perfecting Friendship: Politics and Affiliation in Early American Literature.* Chapel Hill: University of North Carolina Press.

SEARS, JOHN F. (1989). *Sacred Places: American Tourist Attractions in the Nineteenth Century.* New York: Oxford University Press.

SEDGWICK, CATHARINE MARIA (1834–35). Journal. Catharine Maria Sedgwick papers I. Massachusetts Historical Society.

SEDGWICK, CATHARINE MARIA (1871). *The Life and Letters of Catharine M. Sedgwick.* Mary E. Dewey (ed.) New York: Harper.

SEDGWICK, CATHARINE MARIA (n.d.). Informal accounting sheet. Catharine Maria Sedgwick papers I. Massachusetts Historical Society.

SELLERS, CHARLES (1991). *The Market Revolution: Jacksonian America, 1815–1846.* New York: Oxford University Press.

SEWARD, WILLIAM H. (1884). "Freedom in the New Territories," in Baker, George E. (ed.), *The Works of William H. Seward.* Vol. 1. Boston: Houghton Mifflin, 51–93.

SHAPIRO, STEPHEN (2008). *The Culture and Commerce of the Early American Novel: Reading the Atlantic World-System.* University Park: Pennsylvania State University Press.

SHAW, HARRY E. (1983). *The Forms of Historical Fiction: Sir Walter Scott and His Successors.* Ithaca: Cornell University Press.

SHOEMAKER, NANCY (2004). *A Strange Likeness: Becoming Red and White in Eighteenth-Century North America.* New York: Oxford University Press.

SHOWALTER, ELAINE (2009). *A Jury of Her Peers: American Women Writers from Anne Bradstreet to Annie Proulx.* New York: Knopf.

SHUFFELTON, FRANK (1986). "Mrs. Foster's Coquette and the Decline of the Brotherly Watch." *Studies in Eighteenth-Century Culture* 16, 211–24.

SIEMINSKI, GREG (1990). "The Puritan Captivity Narrative and the Politics of the American Revolution." *American Quarterly* 42.1, 35–56.

SILBER, NINA (1993). *The Romance of Reunion: Northerners and the South, 1865–1900.* Chapel Hill: University of North Carolina Press.

SILKO, LESLIE MARMON (1977). *Ceremony.* New York: Penguin.

SIMMONS, CLARE A. (2004). "*Hope Leslie, Marmion*, and the Displacement of Romance." *ANQ* 17.1, 20–5.

SIMMS, WILLIAM GILMORE (1962). *Views and Reviews in American Literature, History, and Fiction: First Series* (1845). C. Hugh Holman (ed.). Cambridge, MA: Harvard University Press

SIZER, LYDE CULLEN (2000). *The Political Work of Northern Women Writers and the Civil War, 1850–1872.* Chapel Hill: University of North Carolina.

SLOTKIN, RICHARD (1973). *Regeneration Through Violence: The Mythology of the American Frontier.* Middletown: Wesleyan University Press.

SLOTKIN, RICHARD (1985). *The Fatal Environment: The Myth of the Frontier in the Age of Industrialization, 1800–1890*. Norman: University of Oklahoma Press.

SMITH, ADAM (1984). *The Theory of Moral Sentiments* (1759). D. D. Raphael and A. L. Macfie (eds.). Indianapolis: Liberty Fund.

SMITH, ADAM (2002). *The Theory of Moral Sentiments* (1759). Knud Haakonssen (ed.). Cambridge: Cambridge University Press.

SMITH, HENRY NASH (1950). *Virgin Land: The American West as Symbol and Myth*. Cambridge, MA: Harvard University Press.

SMITH, HERBERT F. (1980). *The Popular American Novel, 1865–1920*. New York: Twayne.

SMITH, JAMES (1996). *Scoowa: James Smith's Indian Captivity Narrative* (1799). Columbus: Ohio Historical Society.

SMITH, SUSAN BELASCO (1995). "Serialization and the Nature of *Uncle Tom's Cabin*," in Price, Kenneth M. and Susan Belasco Smith (eds.), *Periodical Literature in Nineteenth-Century America*. Charlottesville: University Press of Virginia, 69–89.

SOLGER, REINHOLD (2006). *Anton in America: A Novel from German-American Life*. Lorie A. Vanchena (trans.). New York: Peter Lang.

SOLLORS, WERNER (1986a). *Beyond Ethnicity: Consent and Descent in American Culture*. New York: Oxford University Press.

SOLLORS, WERNER (1986b). "Emil Klauprecht's Cincinnati, *oder der Geheimnisse des Westens* and the Beginnings of Urban Realism in America." *In Their Own Words* 3.2, 161–86.

SOLLORS, WERNER (ed.) (1998). *Multilingual America: Transnationalism, Ethnicity, and the Languages of American Literature*. New York: New York University Press.

SOLLORS, WERNER (2002). "Ferdinand Kürnberger's *Der Amerika–Müde* (1855): German-Language Literature about the United States, and German-American Writing," in Shell, Marc (ed.), *American Babel: Literatures of the United States from Abnaki to Zuni*. Cambridge, MA: Harvard University Press, 117–29.

SOMMER, DORIS (1999). *Proceed with Caution, When Engaged by Minority Writing in the Americas*. Cambridge, MA: Harvard University Press.

SPENGEMANN, WILLIAM C. (1977). *The Adventurous Muse: The Poetics of American Fiction, 1789–1900*. New Haven: Yale University Press.

SPENGEMANN, WILLIAM C. (1989). *A Mirror for Americanists: Reflections on the Idea of American Literature*. Hanover: Dartmouth University Press.

SPENGEMANN, WILLIAM C. (1994). *A New World of Words: Redefining Early American Literature*. New Haven: Yale University Press.

SPILLERS, HORTENSE (1989). "Changing the Letter: The Yokes, the Jokes of Discourse, or, Mrs. Stowe, Mr. Reed," in McDowell, Deborah and Arnold Rampersad (eds.), *Slavery and the Literary Imagination*. Baltimore: Johns Hopkins University Press, 25–61.

SPURR, DAVID (1993). *The Rhetoric of Empire: Colonial Discourse in Journalism, Travel Writing and Imperial Administration*. Durham: Duke University Press.

STADLER, GUSTAVUS (2006). *Troubling Minds: The Cultural Politics of Genius in the United States, 1840–1890*. Minneapolis: University of Minnesota Press.

STAVANS, ILAN (2001). *Imagining Columbus: The Literary Voyage*. New York: Palgrave.

STAVANS, ILAN (ed.) (2011). *The Norton Anthology of Latino Literature*. New York: Norton.

ST. CLAIR, WILLIAM (2004). *The Reading Nation in the Romantic Period*. Cambridge: Cambridge University Press.

STEPTO, ROBERT B. (1986). "Sharing the Thunder: The Literary Exchanges of Harriet Beecher Stowe, Henry Bibb, and Frederick Douglass," in Sundquist, Eric J. (ed.), *New Essays on "Uncle Tom's Cabin."* Cambridge University Press, 135–53.

STEPTO, ROBERT B. (1991). *From Behind the Veil: A Study of Afro-American Narrative*. 2nd ed. Urbana: University of Illinois Press.

STERN, JULIA (1995). "Excavating Genre in *Our Nig*." *American Literature* 67.3, 439–66.

STERN, JULIA (1997). *The Plight of Feeling: Sympathy and Dissent in the Early American Novel*. Chicago: University of Chicago Press.

STERN, MADELEINE B. (ed.) (1980). *Publishers for Mass Entertainment in Nineteenth Century America*. Boston: G. K. Hall.

STERN, MADELEINE B. (1991). "The No Name Series." *Studies in the American Renaissance*, 375–402.

STEWART, DAVID M. (1998). "Cultural Work, City Crime, Reading, Pleasure." *American Literary History* 9.4, 676–701.

STEWART, RANDALL (1932). "Introduction," in Hawthorne, Nathaniel, *The American Notebooks*. New Haven: Yale University Press, xiii–lxxxix.

STILGOE, JOHN R. (1990). *Borderland: Origins of the American Suburb, 1820–1939*. New Haven: Yale University Press.

STONE, JOHN AUGUSTUS (1996). *Metamora: Or, the Last of the Wampanoags* (1829). New York: Feedback Theatrebooks and Prospero Press.

STOVALL, FLOYD (ed.) (1956, 1963). *Eight American Authors: A Review of Research and Criticism*. New York: Modern Language Association.

STOWE, HARRIET BEECHER (1853). *The Key to "Uncle Tom's Cabin."* London: Clarke, Beeton.

STREEBY, SHELLEY (2002). *American Sensations: Class, Empire and the Production of Popular Culture*. Berkeley: University of California Press.

SUNDQUIST, ERIC J. (ed.) (1986). *New Essays on "Uncle Tom's Cabin."* New York: Cambridge University Press.

SWANN, CHARLES (1991). *Nathaniel Hawthorne: Tradition and Revolution*. Cambridge: Cambridge University Press.

Sweet, Timothy (2002). *American Georgics: Economy and Environment in Early American Literature.* Philadelphia: University of Pennsylvania Press.

Swisshelm, Jane (1850). "From *The Saturday Visiter,*" in Person, Leland S. (ed.), *"The Scarlet Letter" and Other Writings* (2005). New York: Norton, 271–4.

Tamarkin, Elisa (2008). *Anglophilia: Deference, Devotion, and Antebellum America.* Chicago: University of Chicago Press.

Tebbel, John (1975). *A History of Book Publishing in the United States*: Vol. 2, *The Expansion of an Industry, 1865–1919.* New York: Bowker.

Temple, Gale (2003). "A Purchase of Goodness: Fanny Fern, *Ruth Hall,* and Fraught Individualism." *Studies in American Fiction* 31.2, 131–63.

Tennenhouse, Leonard (2006). "Is There an Early American Novel?" *Novel* 40, 5–17.

Tennenhouse, Leonard (2007). *The Importance of Feeling English: American Literature and the British Diaspora, 1750–1850.* Princeton: Princeton University Press.

Thomas, Brook (2001). "Citizen Hester: *The Scarlet Letter* as Civic Myth." *American Literary History* 13, 181–211.

Thomas, Dwight, and David K. Jackson (1987). *The Poe Log: A Documentary Life of Edgar Allan Poe 1809–1849.* Boston: G. K. Hall.

Thompson-Gillis, Heather Joy (2007). *"Maddened By Wine and By Passion": The Construction of Gender and Race in Nineteenth-Century American Temperance Literature.* M.A. thesis, Oxford, OH: Miami University.

Todd, Emily B. (1999). "Walter Scott and the Nineteenth-Century American Literary Marketplace: Antebellum Richmond Readers and the Collected Editions of the Waverley Novels." *Papers of the Bibliographical Society of America* 93.4, 495–517.

Todd, Emily B. (2009). "Establishing Routes for Fiction in the United States: Walter Scott's Novels and the Early Nineteenth-Century American Publishing Industry." *Book History* 12, 100–28.

Todd, William B., and Ann Bowden (1998). *Sir Walter Scott: A Bibliographical History, 1796–1832.* New Castle, DE: Oak Knoll.

Todorov, Tzvetan (1984). *The Conquest of America: The Question of the Other.* Richard Howard (trans.). New York: Harper.

Tompkins, Jane (1985). *Sensational Designs: The Cultural Work of American Fiction, 1790–1860.* New York: Oxford University Press.

Traister, Bryce (2000). "Libertinism and Authorship in America's Early Republic." *American Literature* 72.1, 1–30.

Traubel, Horace (1961). *With Walt Whitman in Camden* (1907). Vol. 2. New York: Rowman and Littlefield.

Tresch, John (2002). "Extra! Extra! Poe Invents Science Fiction" in Hayes, Kevin J. (ed.), *The Cambridge Companion to Edgar Allan Poe.* Cambridge: Cambridge University Press, 113–32.

TURNER, FREDERICK JACKSON (2008). *The Significance of the Frontier in American History* (1893). New York: Penguin.

TWAIN, MARK (1973). "The Indignity Put Upon the Remains of George Holland by the Rev. Mr. Sabine" (1871), in Baender, Paul (ed.), *What Is Man? and Other Philosophical Writings*. Berkeley: University of California Press, 51–5.

USNER, DANIEL (1992). *Indians, Settlers, and Slaves in a Frontier Exchange Economy: The Lower Mississippi Valley Before 1783*. Chapel Hill: University of North Carolina Press.

VAIL, R. W. G (1932). "Susanna Haswell Rowson, the Author of *Charlotte Temple*: A Bibliographical Study." *Proceedings of the American Antiquarian Society* 42, 47–160.

VALENTI, PATRICIA DUNLAVY (ed.) (1996). "Sophia Peabody Hawthorne's *American Notebooks*," in Myerson, Joel (ed.), *Studies in the American Renaissance*. Charlottesville: University Press of Virginia.

VANDERWERTH, W.C. (ed.) (1971). *Indian Oratory: Famous Speeches by Noted Indian Chieftains*. Norman: University of Oklahoma Press.

VAN DOREN, CARL (1921). *The American Novel*. New York: Macmillan.

VIATTE, AUGUSTE (1954). *Histoire littéraire de l'Amérique française: des origins à 1950*. Paris: Presses Universitaires de France.

WALD, PRISCILLA (1995). *Constituting Americans: Cultural Anxiety and Narrative Form*. Durham: Duke University Press.

WALKER, CHERYL (1997). *Indian Nation: Native American Literature and Nineteenth-Century Nationalisms*. Durham: Duke University Press.

WARD, HERBERT D. (1893). "The Man with a Country." *McClure's Magazine* 1.4, 291–300.

WARREN, CAROLINE MATILDA (1828). "Preface," in *The Gamesters; or Ruins of Innocence*. Boston: J. Shaw, ii–iv.

WARREN, JOYCE (1986). "Introduction," in Fern, Fanny, *"Ruth Hall" and Other Writings*. New Brunswick: Rutgers University Press, ix–xxxix.

WATERMAN, BRYAN (2007). *Republic of Intellect: The Friendly Club of New York City and the Making of American Literature*. Baltimore: Johns Hopkins University Press.

WATERMAN, BRYAN (2009). "Introduction: Reading Early America with Charles Brockden Brown." *Early American Literature* 44.2, 235–42.

WATT, IAN (1957). *The Rise of the Novel*. Berkeley: University of California Press.

WATTS, EDWARD (1998). *Writing and Postcolonialism in the Early Republic*. Charlottesville: University Press of Virginia.

WATTS, STEVEN (1994). *The Romance of Real Life: Charles Brockden Brown and the Origins of American Culture*. Baltimore: Johns Hopkins University Press.

WEAVER, RAYMOND (1921). *Herman Melville: Man, Mariner, and Mystic*. New York: George H. Doran.

WEBSTER, DANIEL (1825). *Address Delivered at the Laying of the Corner Stone of the Bunker Hill Monument*. Boston: Cummings, Hilliard.

WEEMS, MASON LOCKE (1929). *The Drunkard's Looking Glass* in *Three Discourses: Hymen's Recruiting Sergeant, The Drunkard's Looking Glass, God's Revenge Against Adultery*. New York: Random House.

WEIERMAN, KAREN WOODS (2003). "'A Slave Story I Began and Abandoned': Sedgwick's Antislavery Manuscript," in Damon-Bach, Lucinda L. and Victoria Clements (eds.), *Catharine Maria Sedgwick: Critical Perspectives*. Boston: Northeastern University Press, 122–38.

WEINAUER, ELLEN (2001). "Considering Possession in *The Scarlet Letter*." *Studies in American Fiction* 29.1, 93–112.

WEIR, SYBIL (1976). "*The Morgesons*: A Neglected Feminist Bildungsroman." *New England Quarterly* 49.3, 427–39.

WEISBUCH, ROBERT (1986). *Atlantic Double-Cross: American Literature and British Influence in the Age of Emerson*. Chicago: University of Chicago Press.

WEST, ELLIOTT (1998). *The Contested Plains: Indians, Goldseekers and the Rush to Colorado*. Lawrence: University of Kansas Press.

WEYLER, KAREN A. (2004). *Intricate Relations: Sexual and Economic Desire in American Fiction, 1789–1814*. Iowa City: University of Iowa Press.

WHARTON, EDITH (1997). *The Writing of Fiction* (1924). New York: Simon and Schuster.

WHITE, ED (2010). "The Ends of Republicanism." *Journal of the Early Republic* 30.2, 179–99.

WHITE, RICHARD (1991). *The Middle Ground: Indians, Empires and the Republics in the Great Lakes Region, 1650–1815*. New York: Cambridge University Press.

WHITMAN, WALT (1996). *Poetry and Prose*. New York: Library of America.

WHITMAN, WALT (2005). *Leaves of Grass*. David S. Reynolds (ed.). Oxford: Oxford University Press.

WILLIAMS, GARY (2004). "Speaking with the Voices of Others: Julia Ward Howe's Laurence" in Howe, Julia Ward, *The Hermaphrodite*. Gary Williams (ed.). Lincoln: University of Nebraska Press, ix–xliv.

WILLIAMS, RAYMOND (1975). *The Country and the City*. New York: Oxford University Press.

WILLIAMS, SUSAN S. (1997). *Confounding Images: Photography and Portraiture in Antebellum American Fiction*. Philadelphia: University of Pennsylvania Press.

WILLIAMS, SUSAN S. (2007). "Authors and Literary Authorship" in Casper, Scott E. et al. (eds.), *The Industrial Book, 1840–1880*. Vol. 3 of *A History of the Book in America*. Chapel Hill: University of North Carolina Press, 90–116.

WILSON, EDMUND (1962). *Patriotic Gore: Studies in the Literature of the American Civil War*. New York: Oxford University Press.

Winans, Robert B. (1975). "The Growth of a Novel-Reading Public in Late-Eighteenth-Century America." *Early American Literature* 9, 267–75.

Winans, Robert B. (1983). "Bibliography and the Cultural Historian: Notes on the Eighteenth-Century Novel" in Joyce, William L. et al. (eds.), *Printing and Society in Early America*. Worcester: American Antiquarian Society.

Winch, Julie (1988). *Philadelphia's Black Elite: Activism, Accommodation, and the Struggle for Autonomy, 1787–1848*. Philadelphia: Temple University Press.

Windell, Maria (2009). *The Diplomacy of Affect: Transamerican Sentimentalism in Nineteenth-Century US Literary History*. Ph.D. diss., University of Virginia.

Winship, Michael (1983). "Printing from Plates in the Nineteenth Century United States." *Printing History* 5.2, 15–26.

Winship, Michael (1987). "Getting the Books Out: Trade Sales, Parcel Sales, and Book Fairs in the Nineteenth–Century United States," in Hackenberg, Michael (ed.), *Getting the Books Out*. Washington, DC: Center for the Book, Library of Congress, 4–25.

Winship, Michael (1995). *American Literary Publishing in the Mid-Nineteenth Century: The Business of Ticknor and Fields*. Cambridge: Cambridge University Press.

Winship, Michael (2007). "Distribution and the Trade" in Casper, Scott E. et al. (eds.), *The Industrial Book, 1840–1880*. Vol. 3 of *A History of the Book in America*. Chapel Hill: University of North Carolina Press, 117–30.

Witherington, Paul (1981). "'Not My Tongue Only': Form and Language in Brown's *Edgar Huntly*" in Rosenthal, Bernard (ed.), *Critical Essays on Charles Brockden Brown*. Boston: G. K. Hall, 164–83.

Whipple, Edwin Percy (1850). "Review of New Books." *Graham's Magazine* 36.5, 345–6.

Wood, James (2004). *The Irresponsible Self: On Laughter and the Novel*. New York: Farrar, Straus and Giroux.

Wood, Marcus (2000). *Blind Memory: Visual Representations of Slavery in England and America, 1780–1865*. New York: Routledge.

Wright, Lyle H. (1939). "A Statistical Survey of American Fiction, 1774–1850." *Huntington Library Quarterly* 2.3, 309–18.

Wright, Richard (1972). *Native Son* (1940). London: Penguin.

Yarborough, Richard (1990). "Race, Violence, and Manhood: The Masculine Ideal in Frederick Douglass's 'The Heroic Slave.'" in Sundquist, Eric J. (ed.), *Frederick Douglass: New Literary and Historical Essays*. New York: Cambridge University Press, 166–88.

Yellin, Jean Fagan (1989). *Women and Sisters: The Antislavery Feminists in American Culture*. New Haven: Yale University Press.

Young, Elizabeth (1999). *Disarming the Nation: Women's Writing and the American Civil War*. Chicago: University of Chicago Press.

Zagarell, Sandra A. (1985). "The Repossession of a Heritage: Elizabeth Stoddard's *The Morgesons.*" *Studies in American Fiction* 13, 45–56.

Zboray, Ronald J. (1993). *A Fictive People: Antebellum Economic Development and the American Reading Public.* New York: Oxford University Press.

Zoellner, Robert (1973). *The Salt-Sea Mastodon: A Reading of* Moby-Dick. Berkeley: University of California Press.

INDEX OF AMERICAN NOVELISTS TO 1870

GENERAL INDEX